A lone wolf. An apt description.

What else do you call Yeshin's child as she sits in silence in her own domain, seven days undisturbed, unattended save for a handful of servants who ensured she was kept fed and clean like a kennelled dog? Seven days home, and no one who could've called themselves family or friend had spoken to me. I heard of comings and goings of various officials and royals over the last few days, but they presented themselves either to Ozo or to my husband, Rayyel.

I struggled to remember I was once queen.

To be seen, but not heard; to know that they uttered your name between hissed breaths and gritted teeth, and if you disappeared into thin air they would carry on as if your substance could be sustained by their falsehoods. Perhaps you are prepared to take such things from your enemies, but from your own? From the people who claimed to care for you, even love you, who once assured you they would never turn on you come hell or high water? They had lives to live, and for that they were willing to bury me at first light.

Praise for K. S. Villoso and the

CHRONICLES OF THE BITCH QUEEN

"*The Wolf of Oren-Yaro* is intricate, intimate, and intensely plotted. Full of subtle poignancy and remarkably genuine characters—even the rotten ones. I loved this book." —Nicholas Eames, author of *Kings of the Wyld*

"Intimate and epic. It compels you to read on, because it's a story about people not characters, civilizations not settings, and deadly power plays not sanitized throne-room politics." —Evan Winter, author of *The Rage of Dragons*

"A powerful new voice in epic fantasy. Villoso deftly creates an intricate and compelling world of high fantasy intrigue and adventure dominated by a crafty, whip-smart heroine determined to unite her kingdom at any cost." —Kameron Hurley, author of *The Light Brigade*

"Deeply compelling and wonderfully entertaining, *The Wolf of Oren-Yaro* feels at once timely and timeless. K. S. Villoso's lush and finely crafted world envelops readers from the first page, as she takes us on an adventure full of heartache, hope, and triumph. It's a fabulous read!" —Josiah Bancroft, author of *Senlin Ascends*

"A tale balanced on the blade's-edge between intrigue and action—and then Villoso twists the knife." —Gareth Hanrahan, author of *The Gutter Prayer*

"Delivers complex and intriguing characters, and an action-packed plot full of surprising twists and deep, vivid worldbuilding." —Melissa Caruso, author of *The Tethered Mage*

BY K. S. VILLOSO

CHRONICLES OF THE BITCH QUEEN

The Wolf of Oren-Yaro

The Ikessar Falcon

The Dragon of Jin-Sayeng

THE DRAGON OF Jin-Sayeng

CHRONICLES OF THE BITCH QUEEN: BOOK THREE

K. S. VILLOSO

orbitbooks.net

Copyright © 2021 by K. S. Villoso
Excerpt from *The Jasmine Throne* copyright © 2021 by Natasha Suri

Cover design by Lauren Panepinto
Cover illustration by Simon Goinard
Cover copyright © 2021 by Hachette Book Group, Inc.
Map by Tim Paul
Author photograph by Mikhail Villoso

Orbit
Hachette Book Group
1290 Avenue of the Americas
New York, NY 10104
orbitbooks.net

First Edition: May 2021
Simultaneously published in Great Britain by Orbit

Orbit is an imprint of Hachette Book Group.
The Orbit name and logo are trademarks of Little, Brown Book Group Limited.

The publisher is not responsible for websites (or their content) that are not owned by the publisher.

The Hachette Speakers Bureau provides a wide range of authors for speaking events. To find out more, go to www.hachettespeakersbureau.com or call (866) 376-6591.

Library of Congress Cataloging-in-Publication Data
Names: Villoso, K. S., 1986– author.
Title: The dragon of Jin-Sayeng / K.S. Villoso.
Description: First edition. | New York, NY : Orbit, 2021. | Series: Chronicles of the bitch queen ; book 3
Identifiers: LCCN 2020034293 | ISBN 9780316532723 (trade paperback) | ISBN 9780316532747 (ebook)
Subjects: GSAFD: Fantasy fiction.
Classification: LCC PR9199.4.V555 D73 2021 | DDC 813/.6—dc23
LC record available at https://lccn.loc.gov/2020034293

ISBNs: 978-0-316-53272-3 (trade paperback), 978-0-316-53273-0 (ebook)

Printed in the United States of America

LSC-C

Printing 1, 2021

To Mikhail

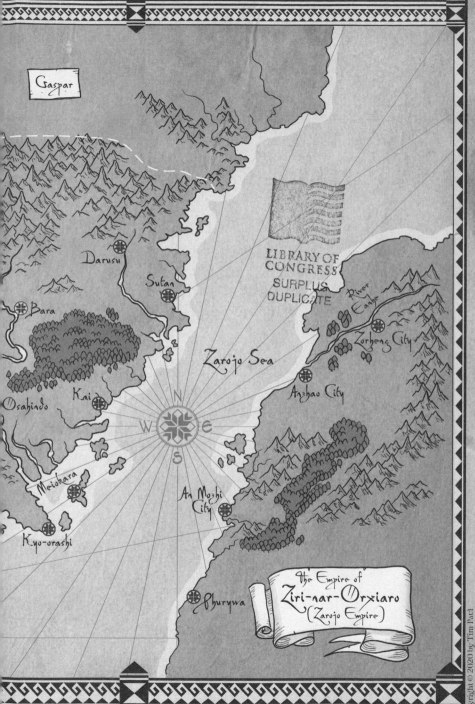

Gaspar

Darusu

Sutan

Bara

Osahindo

Kai

Meiokara

Kyo-orashi

An Mozhi City

Phurywa

LIBRARY OF
CONGRESS
SURPLUS
DUPLICATE

River Eahe

Zorheng City

Zarojo Sea

Anzhao City

The Empire of
Ziri-nar-Orxiaro
(Zarojo Empire)

THE STORY SO FAR...

The chosen lie on a bed of nails.

Trapped across the sea, a long way from home, the queen of Jin-Sayeng finds herself not-quite a prisoner of the slumlord Han Lo Bahn. Everyone is wrestling with the aftermath of the ill-fated visit to the Anzhao government office, which ended in the deaths of both the Anzhao governor Zheshan and the emperor's Fifth Son, Prince Yuebek.

Or so Talyien is convinced. In the political upheaval that follows, she is captured by the acting governor, Qun, who seems to want to find Talyien's husband, Rayyel, as much as she does. Qun is an ambitious, opportunistic rat, but she senses other forces at work. She is broken out of prison by a woman claiming to be from the Shadows, a group of assassins once employed by the Ikessars. Now led by a rich merchant, Dai alon gar Kaggawa, they have come to bring Queen Talyien home.

Talyien distrusts them, knowing this aid will come with a hefty price. She refuses. Ditching her guards Nor and Agos, she heads on to her husband's last known location with only the con artist Khine Lamang at her side. Their journey is fraught not just with danger, but also with Talyien's feelings of dread over meeting her husband yet again. She is reminded all too often that she would rather be free than chasing after the very shackles that had imprisoned her all her life. Yet to turn her back on her duties would be to turn her back on her son, whose life is at increasing risk the longer she stays away.

They venture to the Ruby Grove, an area known for its vast quantities of featherstone, a volatile substance that enhances magic spells and is used to strengthen spell runes on structures, even when the raw material is deadly to those who live among it. Talyien meets up with Nor and Agos again, and is gravely injured during an encounter with white dragons when she falls into a patch of the toxic featherstone. She wakes up in a crumbling village in Phurywa, where she is nurtured back to health by Khine and his mother, Mei. Here, she learns that the elders have been freely giving blood to the local priests under the guise of helping find a cure for the ailments that plague them from living in the area. Talyien's husband has been seeking these same priests. He and Talyien agree on an uneasy truce after he reveals that his desire to kill their son if he's a bastard stems from fear of what his mother will do to the boy if she finds out. Because he is a bastard himself, it positions the boy even further as a proper successor. The meeting leaves Tali feeling more hollow and raw than ever before.

They travel to the temple up the mountain to meet with the priests, only to realize they've walked into a trap orchestrated by none other than Prince Yuebek, who is very much alive despite looking less so. Held together by magic, he reiterates his offer of marriage to Queen Talyien while pointing out that her father would have never wanted a bastard to be her husband.

They are attacked by walking effigies and mages. The effigies, for some reason, all fall to the ground, and Tali and her companions barely escape the temple with their lives. Rai is gravely injured. Tali learns from Agos that the Shadows have extended the same offer to him back in Anzhao and that he has led Lahei to her. The agent reiterates her offer.

While Talyien processes the events, she finds out the reason why the effigies stopped working—the elders, whose blood had provided a connection that gave the effigies life, all committed suicide, sacrificing their lives to free themselves from the taint of blood magic.

In the wake of Khine's devastation over his mother's death, Tali agrees to accept the Shadows' assistance. They scheme their way out of the embargo from the city of An Mozhi. The Shadows take Tali straight to the Kag, instead of Jin-Sayeng, where she meets Dai Kaggawa himself.

Dai's term is simple—her son's hand in marriage to his daughter. Tali wants to refuse, but Dai won't give her that opportunity yet, and instead takes her straight into the Sougen that she might see Jin-Sayeng's troubles with her own eyes: The people are turning into foul, bloodthirsty monsters. The same phenomenon that occurs in the dragons in the area is now affecting the locals, and if an answer isn't found soon, Jin-Sayeng will be overrun. But the threat of civil war prevents Dai from doing anything. The region's warlord and his sons seem adamant in embracing the mad dragons, consequences be damned—instead of finding a cure, they want to *tame* the beasts instead.

Talyien visits the Anyus in their city of Yu-yan, and is attacked by a mad dragon. During the fight, Eikaro Anyu is taken, and she chases after him into the mountains. She manages to find him, alive but gravely injured. With no choice left for survival, Eikaro Anyu decides to trade places with the mad dragon, allowing its corrupted soul to go into his body while his own rides the dragon instead. His body falls from the sky and dies; Eikaro lives on as a dragon.

The tensions in the region escalate as Dai Kaggawa blames the Anyus for his daughter, who was injured in the dragon fight. A proclamation from the east declares Talyien Orenar's claim on the throne as void until she can clear her name and prove she hasn't planted a false heir. When Talyien explains to the Anyus that she thinks it is a foil created by the Zarojo prince, they decide to retaliate against the Kaggawas.

The timing of a civil war, right at the mention of the Zarojos' arrival, strikes Talyien as odd. But Huan, Eikaro's brother, claims he knows nothing. She returns to save her companions from Kaggawa's growing fury; during the process, her cousin and Captain of the Guard, Nor, defects, claiming that Talyien's mismanagement of her affairs has jeopardized the nation and her own daughter's life. Dai Kaggawa reveals his secret: that he is two souls in one man. One is the son of a merchant, the other the son of a would-be king—despite his words assuring Talyien otherwise, his lust for power is suddenly evident. Tali wants nothing to do with it.

Down to three companions, Talyien escapes Kaggawa's clutches, only to land in Qun's. She is taken to Kyo-orashi, where the warlord San sends her to battle a dragon in his arena to prove her might to the people. He is working with Qun, who still wants her to be queen—Yuebek still needs to claim his prize. Tali fights the dragon and realizes it is Eikaro, who seems to have grown mad and no longer responds to her voice. Before she is fatally injured, Khine arrives, provoking the dragon as part of Warlord San's show—if he sacrifices his life for the queen, the people will see her as truly worthy.

Tali manages to set the dragon free before he kills anyone; she faces the crowd in defiance, killing a smaller, weaker dragon from the dungeons to end Warlord San's show. Qun's plans to use the Zarojo soldiers to save her in front of the crowd is foiled, and he leaves in a huff.

Khine almost dies from his injuries. Furious over his antics and fearful over what else he might do to protect her, she decides to set him, and his feelings, free by sleeping with Agos.

Her actions, once enough to drive Rayyel away, don't work on Khine. He insists on following her anyway. They journey to Oren-yaro, hampered by Qun's attacks that are meant to slow them down so he can arrive in Oren-yaro first, where he claims he will kill Talyien's son if she doesn't submit to his prince. They are also attacked by assassins.

During their escape, Tali—in a moment of weakness—admits to Khine she thinks she is growing mad. Her vision from Yuebek's dungeons felt all too real, and her own exhaustion is pulling her from both ends. They share a kiss, one that is over quickly. Khine takes off with an assassin after him; Tali takes care of the rest. She reunites with her husband, Rai, once more, and finds out that Kaggawa must have sent the assassins. At the same time, they sort out their feelings over their marriage and Tali's son, whom Rai is still not sure is his. It is revealed that he was crushed by the revelation that he might not be his simply because he loved the boy.

They reach Oren-yaro and reunite with Khine, who finds a way to Tali's castle from the tunnels underneath Old Oren-yaro, where her brothers had died after dealing with the last Dragonlord's mad dragon. While dealing with the last assassin, she has visions of what happened to her brothers, and finds the truth lying at the bottom of a staircase: Her father was, indeed, responsible for bringing the dragon to Oren-yaro. His hands are drenched with the blood of his own sons.

Her son is missing when she arrives in the castle. She encounters Qun, who claims to know where he is if she would just follow him. This is revealed to be a plan to get Tali to sacrifice herself. Qun wants her to jump and break her body, so Yuebek could stitch it back together and she would stop running away and become dependent on him. Not knowing what else to do to save her son, and echoing Mei Lamang's sacrifice, she jumps.

But a woman like her doesn't break easily; she catches Qun off guard when he jumps down to check on her, and kills him with a rock. She returns to Rai, and they find their son in the great hall. Before they can have a proper reunion, the Shadows arrive, and Tali learns that Agos was working with them and had let them into the castle. He says he had worked out a deal with Kaggawa where he would spare Tali's life. The only price he wants now is Rayyel.

Agos and Rai fight in the throne room. Tali knows that Agos can kill Rai, who isn't a fighter, but he refuses to listen to her order to stop. Just before Agos can deal Rai a fatal blow, the Ikessars arrive and shoot him with arrows. Agos falls to the ground and dies.

The story ends with Tali being taken as prisoner in her own castle, awaiting a trial while the fires of civil war begin. With no one to save Jin-Sayeng, the whole nation hovers at the precipice of destruction...

ACT ONE

THE APPROACH

CHAPTER ONE

WHERE THE ASHES LIE

ᛏ◌

C ourage is overrated, or so cowards like me say.
        Courage implies choice.

Magister Arro used to lecture me about the nature of things: how a tree must remain a tree, for instance—straight and stalwart, branches spreading to the sky, roots reaching down below. Build a fence around a sapling and the tree will break it as it grows—swallow it, even, wire and wood sinking into the trunk like it was quicksand. "And so," my father said once, interrupting such a lecture with a sweep of his arm, "a wolf must remain a wolf, no matter what. Never forget this, Talyien."

Presumptuous, pious, arrogant Oren-yaro. No wonder we were hated and feared. Hated more than feared, if you learned to read between the empty smiles and polite gestures. I once took pride in the fear I wielded, cloaking myself in my father's rhetoric like a child wrapping herself in a blanket to ward away the cold. But if I remained a wolf, I was now a lone wolf, one yearning to break free as hunters tore after her with spears and arrows. No pack to be part of, no cave to hide in, no moon to howl at . . . it wasn't courage that kept me running. They had branded my son a fugitive, and a trial was hanging over my head like an executioner's axe; to stop would be to entertain a fate worse than death.

It made me wonder what my father thought of me, holding me as an infant. Did he see a girl-child, no more than a babe that carried his eyes and his smile? Did he count my small, delicate fingers one by one, or stroke my hair with his thumb while a part of him swore to change his ways? The servants used to say that the old man doted on me. Without a mother in the picture, I was irrevocably Yeshin's, and they said he guarded me with the same ferocity he murdered his enemies with. He didn't like the nursemaids leaving me alone in my crib—I was a bad sleeper, and he insisted they carry me in a sling at all times. And if I woke up in the middle of the night, he would tear down from his quarters to snatch me from my wet nurse's arms and sing me back to sleep himself.

Tall tales, people say. This could not be the same Warlord Yeshin of the War of the Wolves, the same man who once drove his horse into an unguarded Ikessar hamlet, fifty men behind him, and cleared the way to the village square with his spear. By the time he was done, his horse was red from the neck down. But I could believe it. I could remember his smooth voice, the way his chest rumbled as he pulled my blankets up to my chin and sang me to sleep. On summer nights, he would use a paper fan to chase the warm breeze away, long and furious enough that his arm must've stung from the effort. I was his, and nothing in the world could change that. I never doubted what he would do to protect me.

A girl's naivety. Even before I learned of my father's dealings with Yuebek, a part of me always knew that the truth could be as complex as a shaft of light through a cut gem. Turn it, view it from another angle, and it shifts. Sometimes it is telling, a burst of clarity on a dark streak, brightness to chase away shadows. Sometimes it is blinding.

———

A wolf must remain a wolf.

You are courage, my father used to tell me. *You are strength.* I carried his words deep within my bones, seeds that would sprout into the person I would become. Would I have survived the circumstances of my son's birth had I not been Yeshin's daughter? For the entirety of my labour, all I wanted to do was close my eyes between the tremors and blood, and die. Instead, my father's voice—the one that seemed to echo inside my head years after his death—told me not to be ridiculous. Women dealt with this pain all the time. Would his daughter be defeated so easily?

But it wasn't really a choice, you understand. And so it couldn't have been courage.

You can't argue with a voice like that without looking like a madwoman. Reasons were excuses to Yeshin. Did it matter that I had been unattended in a damp, dark cave while my remaining guardsmen fought rebels on the road below? The Ikessars had insisted that it would be a good omen if I gave birth in the Dragon Palace; for some irritating reason, the council agreed. I was forced to pack up late in my term and waddle on the road after my husband, who had been living there for a few months to attend to his duties as Minister of Agriculture.

Screaming into a piece of cloth stuffed into my mouth, my hands clasping the wet dirt under me, I counted the dripping of water from the walls between my groans. The pain that spread from my spine down to my thighs and around my belly did its fair job of drowning out my fears. I didn't really have time to wonder if my guards were winning. If they were, it wasn't as if they could help at all. The bastards couldn't even keep my handmaids and the midwife alive during the ambush. If they lost—well, perhaps the rebels could hurry up and put me out of my misery.

"There's still a dozen up in the woods!" Agos called as he came stomping into the cave. He was covered in more blood than I was and yet at the sight of me, terror flared in his eyes. His face paled. "Gods, Princess, is it time yet?"

I spat the cloth out. "No, I just like to pull my undergarments down and lie on my back for no reason."

He stared at me for a heartbeat.

"Of course it's time, you son of a—" A tremor seized me. I bit back into the cloth before it passed and screamed into it until my ears rang. I'd never had a mining pick jammed into my tailbone before, but I imagined that this might be exactly what it felt like. Agos took a step forward and I threw the damp cloth at his face.

Perhaps I looked worse than I felt, because he didn't even protest. "Is there anything I can do?"

"What the hell *can* you do?" I hissed. Another tremor sent my fingers digging into the ground so deep, I could feel the soil under my fingernails. The contractions were coming in faster, each one tightening my insides more than the last with a force that left me breathless. "—back out there and *finish* those bastards!" I managed to cry out as I felt the child inside of me turn. "Now!"

He shuffled his feet. "I'll...I think...I'm sure the men have it covered. I have to stay here and protect you. Are you...do you know how to...did the midwife tell you anything?"

"Gods, Agos, just stop talking!"

Something clenched inside of me and I found myself sitting up. The sounds that clawed their way up my throat felt different, sharper, more urgent. Sweat pooled around my throat and dripped down my chest with each tremor, which now ended with a pressure that threatened to rip me apart.

"I think," Agos said, not realizing how dangerously close I was to stabbing him in the gut, "that you have to start pushing."

I responded with a groan.

You are a wolf of Oren-yaro, I thought. *This is nothing to you.* Or so I contended, even as all of my parts felt like they were being pulled at the seams. The contractions were no longer giving me time to breathe or think—the entire bottom half of my body burned as if it was on fire. I began to push in an attempt to stall the pain and instead found the pressure barrelling its way out of me, wet and sharp and tearing. For a moment, maybe more, I was convinced it was my guts sliding their way out of my body. The stink of slime, blood, and rancid sweat filled the air.

I couldn't really see what was happening between the darkness of the cave and the haze of pain, but I caught sight of Agos breaking from his stupor and stepping forward. I didn't have the energy to push him away—my only focus was on the child that slipped out of me so fast that I almost didn't realize it at first. Agos caught the child. "It's a boy," he managed, before handing him over to me. There was an odd expression on his face.

My attention drifted to the child in my arms and then that was it—nothing else mattered, not Agos or the screaming outside or the pain of my ripped parts. Even the contractions that followed as I laboured to push the afterbirth felt weightless. My shaking fingers traced a line across the infant's forehead and down to his smooth cheeks. The blinking, wrinkled face was the most beautiful thing I had ever seen in my life. The smell of my son's damp hair and the sound of his soft breathing restored me to my senses. I felt the fog recede from my thoughts. I remembered there were still bandits outside and reached down to wrench the dagger out of my belt.

My son had yet to cry. I always thought that infants came out bawling—instead, he just stared back at me, as if wondering if the dishevelled woman before him could really be his mother. I noticed his eyes looked like mine. Like my father's. My heart tightened. I didn't know how I was supposed to feel about that.

"Someone's coming up the path," Agos said. He drew his sword.

My hand tightened around both the dagger and my son. I wasn't going to let them take us without a fight.

Agos's stance relaxed as the shadows of my guardsmen appeared at the entrance. They bowed. "We've cleared the road, Beloved Princess."

I allowed myself to breathe. "Are they all dead?"

"Some," one continued. "The rest ran off. We'll have to send a party after them."

"Not until the princess is in Shirrokaru," Agos broke in. "Our priority is getting them back to safety."

"Them—" The guard swallowed, noticing the infant for the first time. Wordlessly, he fell to his knees. The others followed suit, leaving only Agos standing. "The blood of the Oren-yaro is strong," the guards said in unison. "Warlord Yeshin will be pleased."

I grew nauseated at their words. I always knew the child I carried was Yeshin's grandchild. That he was heir to the Dragonthrone, the first Dragonlord that would ever carry the blood of two royal clans—the Ikessar and the Orenar. But now that I was looking at this child in my arms, he was only my son, only my boy with those eyes and dear gods, that mouth, that smile...

It filled me with terror. The word *heir* was damned, a word that doomed him to a life of servitude and chains. I felt an urge to get up and run off with him, to scream at them to find someone else. I didn't want the burden of Warlord Yeshin to loom over my child like storm clouds, threatening to burst with enough floodwater to wash him away. I closed my eyes and willed away the urge to shelter him, to protect him from the worst of my father's legacy. What was there to protect? Didn't Yeshin have the largest army in all of Jin-Sayeng?

Yet I had the sense that for me, it was already too late. I was made in Yeshin's image, the nature of things careening down with me like a shadow—ever-present, impossible to deny. With or without the mold, my funeral bells had begun.

A lone wolf. An apt description. What else do you call Yeshin's child as she sits in silence in her own domain, seven days undisturbed, unattended save for a handful of servants who ensured she was kept fed and clean like a kennelled dog? Seven days home, and no one who could've called themselves family or friend had spoken to me. I heard of comings and goings of various officials and royals over the last few days, but they presented themselves either to Ozo or to my husband, Rayyel.

I struggled to remember I was once queen.

Because you couldn't see it even if you tried. Since my return, the servants handed me my meals, replaced my sheets, laid out fresh clothes, and accompanied me to the bathhouse without ever once looking me in the eye. An almost impressive feat, had I been in the mood to be impressed. But I wasn't. These were people who had known me my whole life, who had served my father when I was little and once seemed to have cared for me in their own way.

I found it hard to believe that they respected Ozo enough for them to forget the way things used to be. He must've made threats on their lives, their families. I could see it in their empty faces and dead eyes. Polite, but walled in, unreachable. I tried to speak to them honestly, to call those I knew by name. I was met with abject silence. As the days wore on, I started to see less of them. Lately, my meals were left on a tray outside the door, and the servants stopped coming.

To be seen, but not heard; to know that they uttered your name between hissed breaths and gritted teeth, and if you disappeared into thin air they would carry on as if your substance could be sustained by their falsehoods. Perhaps you are prepared to take such things from your enemies, but from your own? From the people who claimed to care for you, even love you, who once assured you they would never turn on you come hell or high water? They had lives to live, and for that they were willing to bury me at first light.

I couldn't even muster anger. All of that left with Agos the night he turned on Rayyel—my husband's life in exchange for mine and my son's, an equation so simple for him he didn't even see he was being used like the rest of us. It was difficult to become angry with a dead man, especially one whose insolence had saved your son. Agos had handed Thanh over to Kaggawa as a hostage just before the Zarojo soldiers could kill him. A treachery deflecting other treacheries—there was an irony in that somewhere. Be damned if I could be bothered to look, though. The double-headed spear of grief and fear had rendered me incapable of much else. Certainly not the rage that would've once vaulted me over the window and straight to wherever Ozo had cloistered himself, to demand he hand back everything.

What had he taken, anyway, that I hadn't thrown away myself?

I stared at the walls of my chambers, trying to silence my thoughts, to remind myself I'd made it this far. There was still a chance for me to regain my crown and sit on the throne as was once promised. I was no longer that young, naive queen who left this castle a year ago. Beaten gold is still gold. Thinned, it remains unyielding. So fashion it into a chain. Strangle your enemies. I was Yeshin's daughter. Tainted as I was by the weight of those words, I could take everything that was good about that and show the land that despite all the cracks, despite all the mistakes I've made, despite that my own father didn't think me worthy, I had what it took to be a capable ruler. If I could be queen again, I would show them. I could rise from these ashes and be the leader they had yearned for all these years.

The knocking from the window broke my thoughts. I pretended to ignore it, but the sound persisted. With a sigh, I made my way to the end of the room and undid the latch. Khine stepped in, his hair damp from the drizzle. Water dripped from his boots.

A correction—no one I would consider family or friend had come to talk to me. Lamang was neither. After everything that had happened the past few days, I wasn't sure how to examine my feelings for him under this new light. His presence continued to give me an odd mixture of anticipation and repulsion.

"Go away, Lamang," I muttered, walking towards my bed.

"You're the one who opened the window," Khine pointed out.

"Do I have to throw a bucket of cold water on you?"

"I happen to know that you don't have one handy."

"I have a chamber pot. It's full."

"Now, now. Let's not be hasty."

"They could arrest you for this, you know," I pointed out. "The bastards should just kill me and be done with it."

"They wouldn't do that."

"Who's *they*, Khine? Because between Ozo, Ryia, and Yuebek, I can think of about a thousand reasons."

"They wouldn't do it now, with the whole nation's eyes on you. They'd make it look like an accident, at least. Poison in your food, maybe throw scorpions on your face while you slept..."

"What are you doing?"

"Trying to scare you into coming with me," Khine said, holding out his elbow and patting it. He gave a sheepish grin. "Come on. They won't miss you for an evening."

"You tell me that *every* night. We're not in the empire anymore, Khine."

"I know we're not." Khine's face grew sombre as he reached for my shoulder. Carefully, he turned me around so that I could face him. "I'm sorry. I know this may be one thing too many, but this... this is the last night of the vigil. They're lighting the pyre at dawn."

"They won't let me see him," I said. "I already asked."

"They don't have to know."

"What will they do if they find you here? They did worse to Agos, and he—"
I swallowed back the rush of tears and allowed my eyes to linger on his shoulder. His wounds had healed weeks ago, but the ones I could see near his neck
were still pink. "You're still recovering from your injuries, too."

"That? It's nothing a brush with the assassin didn't fix."

"You never even told me what happened with her."

"I survived. That's all that matters, Tali." Khine squeezed my shoulder, and
a rush of warmth surrounded me. "You'll regret it if you don't come," he whispered, his voice as soothing as it had ever been. He tucked a strand of hair over
my ear. "You owe it to him. The man loved you. He died for you."

My insides knotted at his words. I'd refused to see it that way before, a stubborn denial that I could cause harm with something so simple. Whatever I had
with Agos was...a mistake. I glanced down, my eyes on the cracks of the floor
as I tried to will away the image of Agos's corpse on his funeral bed, the once
strong body covered in arrow wounds. Did I need a better reminder of what
my choices brought to the world? Everything I touched turned to ashes. But he
was right. As much as I wanted to turn back time, to have Agos untainted by
the shadows that followed me, it was already done. Like a river, time could only
flow one way. The least I could do was honour it.

I turned to change into warmer clothes before following Khine through the
window.

It had been years since I last scrambled on the rooftops of Oka Shto. What
had been one of my favourite childhood pastimes did not seem becoming for
the wife of a future king. Arro often told me that it wasn't becoming for the
wife of *anyone*, period. "And I'm supposed to turn you into a queen..." he'd
often mumble under his breath after catching me chasing cats with Agos.

Without Agos and Arro, Oka Shto Castle felt empty. I fought back another
incoming sob and focused on the grey horizon, where the first rays of sunlight
crept on the city of Oren-yaro below. We reached the edge of the rooftops,
which pressed right up against the mountain cliffs on the northern side.

"Why *haven't* you been arrested yet?" I found myself wondering out loud.

Khine gave one of his characteristic smiles. "You've so little faith in me. Do
I look like a criminal?"

I stared at him.

"If you really must know," he continued, before I could open my mouth, "it's your husband. He's vouched for me and Inzali. We assisted him in the empire, which means Jin-Sayeng should consider us friends. No one argued with him, so I assume they agree."

"So suddenly you think you're allowed to sneak around the castle."

"No one said I couldn't."

"Your idiocy knows no bounds."

"You and Inzali should catch up."

I gave a thin smile as I ventured towards the narrow ledge along the cliff, right where it met the rooftops. I motioned for him to be careful. The ground was always a little crumbly here, especially in the summer. It was late autumn now, at the cusp of winter, and the rain had done its fair job of tearing the trail apart. I couldn't recall it being so cramped. Dusty roots burst through the soil, brushing the top of my head.

"Agos and I made this path," I said as we turned a corner, past caked, sandy soil that collapsed with every step. "His idea. They kept a close eye on us in the castle. Made it hard even to breathe sometimes. He thought we needed to escape once in a while." I paused, one foot in front of the other. It was a steep drop to the left. We had once been small enough that the thrill of freedom eclipsed the danger—small, and young, and fearless.

The ledge led to a small crag that dropped straight down to the main path. I managed a quick landing without making an embarrassment of myself and waited as Khine clambered down behind me. I supposed he didn't want to miss a footing in the dark—the sort of man who needed to be sure of his next step, even as he hurtled after my recklessness.

"I didn't realize you and Agos were so close," Khine said as he came up to join me. "I knew you grew up together, but..."

"There were no other children in the castle. He must have found me an annoyance most of the time. I thought of him as an older brother. And then he left for the army, and I became busy with my studies...and with Rayyel."

We fell silent as I wrestled with the memories. I could hear our laughter echoing between the trees, imagined shades of me and Agos as children running up the steps from the city. I swallowed. Tears burned in my chest like water swallowed too fast. I continued to walk, the mountain's looming shadow behind us. Ahead, Oren-yaro sprawled like a rough blanket draped over the hills. Small pockets of mist drifted between the crevices and down to the valleys to the east. My fingers shook.

"I should've never taken things this far," I whispered. "If I had...found a way to push him away, perhaps he wouldn't have taken it upon himself to try to protect us the way he did. His death is on me. I gave him hope when I shouldn't have."

Khine gave a soft sigh of resignation. "You gave him precious memories that he took to the grave." He cleared his throat. "Tali, you know what I feel about...about you and him."

"Do I, really?"

He smirked. "If you don't, then I won't burden you with my problems. But as a man of two minds about this whole situation, I can at least tell you that he wouldn't have regretted a thing. He loved you. He was only doing what he thought was right. And you? You believed that, too. You cared for him, you found comfort with him. It's enough. There are no right or wrong answers. We make choices and then we simply...live with the cost."

I fell silent again. We reached the city square, and he gestured to me to begin climbing the butchers' warehouse near the market. Traversing the rooftops like cats, we made our way towards one of the poorer districts of Oren-yaro. I could see the River Agos gleaming behind the grey light in the distance, and the slums continuing along the southern banks. The buildings were almost on top of each other here, a crisscross of shadows and dilapidated wood: roofs of rusted shingles instead of clay tiles, and stone fences imbued with broken glass on top, to keep people out. Not that they worked, if our presence there was any indication. Khine once said that if you wanted to steal something and get out alive, you didn't break down the front door.

"Down there," Khine started when we reached an alley. I struggled to keep my composure again as I recognized the district from when we had arrived, swimming our way from the river. Khine watched me as I sucked in a lungful of muggy air. "We can stop here if you want," he ventured.

"I'm all right."

He said nothing, waiting. Knowing I had more to say.

"It's just that...Agos was a captain, a decorated soldier of the Oren-yaro army. His pyre should be in the city square, where he could be honoured by his men and fellow soldiers, not on some dirty street corner. I did that. I tarnished his name. I ruined him." I gazed down at the small square where a group of people were gathered around a still form lying atop a pile of stacked logs. I suddenly found it very hard to breathe.

"They're about to light it now," Khine said. "It's your last chance to see the body."

The bells tolled. Torchlight filled the streets. Through the blur of my tears, I saw the people walk towards the pyre. The first was unmistakably his wife; two little boys toddled in solemn silence behind her. I recognized the other faces as off-duty soldiers and castle staff. Some threw objects into the fire—small tokens, prayer beads, sealed letters containing their final goodbyes. I almost wished I'd had the foresight to write one myself. Not that I would've known what to say. Even now, my own thoughts seemed difficult to gather, drifting between memories of our time together and my revulsion over what my actions had caused.

Agos's mother threw herself at the foot of the pyre and began to weep hysterically. His wife bent down to pick her up, murmuring something into her hair.

"You're wrong, you know," Khine continued. "Honour could be found here, too. Look at all those people. What better than to be remembered? To be missed? As far as they're concerned, he's a hero. And maybe they're not wrong."

I steeled myself and climbed down the roof. Khine followed a step behind. I pressed a handkerchief above my nose as we joined the back of the line, hoping it was enough of a disguise. We had barely shuffled in place when we heard a commotion from one of the alleys. The crowd parted, revealing guards in full Oren-yaro armour. They marched forward. I stiffened, heart pounding. Khine drew me towards him, his hand cradling the back of my head in an attempt to hide my face even further.

The guards stopped several paces away, ignoring me as they assumed a formation around the pyre. There was a moment of silence as they bowed, faces solemn with respect. Another figure emerged. This one was in Oren-yaro armour, too, but in the green and yellow colours of the Tasho clan, with a warlord's helmet that towered over the rest of his men.

"Ozo," I hissed under my breath. I was torn between wanting to flee and lingering out of curiosity. Khine's arm blocked me from deciding on the former. I peered past his shoulder at the sight unfolding, my breath gathering on the folds of his sleeve.

The general's movements were slow and deliberate as he made his way to the pyre. He stopped about a foot away, close enough that the heat must've been uncomfortable. He removed his helmet and cradled it under his arm. Agos's mother, Hessa, gave another cry. He made a sharp gesture without even looking at her. One of the guards pulled her aside.

I wondered if this was an elaborate ploy to draw sympathy from the crowd, but Ozo gave no speeches—not a single word fell from his lips. He stood in silence, head slightly bent, eyes downcast. The flames cast dancing shadows on his face, deepening the lines. Eventually, he turned on his heel and, after one quick glance at Agos's sons, began walking away. The guards followed him out of the square in single file, the cracked cobblestones quaking under their boots.

"Agos was always his favourite," I said in Zirano. "He never quite forgave me when I sent him away. Now I don't think he ever will. It must have grated to learn where his best man's loyalties lay, let alone what he would die for."

I turned my head as several people came up to console Hessa. "Ignore him," they whispered. "You raised a good son. The gods have welcomed him to their domain." They crowded around the old woman until I couldn't see her anymore.

We finally reached the blaze. By now, the body was shapeless, no more than a lump of charred meat and bones in a sea of fire. It was no longer Agos. Guard, friend, lover . . . whatever he had been was long gone. I remembered that I hadn't brought anything for the pyre and felt the pang of grief again. I never could really give him anything, could I? Not my heart. I tried, but you cannot will a heart to love any more than you can ask it to stop. The worst part is that he knew. He always knew.

Khine slid a sheathed sword into the flames, his brows knotted together. I recognized the sword Agos had lent him days ago, when we were cornered by the assassin in Old Oren-yaro. Like Ozo, he uttered no words. Eventually, he stepped to the side and gestured. My thoughts drifted back to the pyre, to what lay within it.

Agos. I wanted to say his name out loud. I felt like if I heard it with my own ears, I could convince myself that a part of him lingered on. That I could call and he would bolt down to be by my side like the dog I treated him no better than. Not wanting to stir the crowd, I took my handkerchief instead, allowing it to touch my lips before I threw it into the flames.

"It's the queen!" somebody cried.

I froze. Khine drew his arm over me again. He was too slow. Recognition stirred on their faces. It felt like the moment before a thunderstorm—no rain yet, but a humming in the air, thick enough to make your skin crawl.

Agos's wife reached me first. Her hand struck me with a sound that resonated through the square.

CHAPTER TWO

OLD WOUNDS

ꗳꙮꝥ

I stood there, stunned. If I had been attacked for any other reason, I would have stabbed her before she got close. But this was different. I barely felt the sting on my skin. It was the look in her eyes that reached deep, a dagger through my soul. The devastation of betrayal gleamed from them. She knew about me and Agos.

It never even occurred to me to deny it, to pretend that she had gone mad with grief and that I was merely paying my loyal guardsman a visit. I was in the exact same place nine years ago. Nine years ago now, nine years too long, but still so clear in my mind it felt only like yesterday. I leaned forward, dropping my head. "I'm sorry," I began. "I—"

She struck me a second time, sending jolts coursing from my head and down to my fingertips, and then again and again until stars exploded in my sight. I could feel the blood dropping down my jaw where my skin had split open, could feel it pounding through my skull with every blow, but I didn't move.

"Sayu!" Hessa barked.

She fell to the ground, weeping. Her sons—Agos's sons—were staring at us. A boy with hair that spilled along his shoulders, and then a smaller one with balled fists, his cheeks still bulging with folds of fat. They were dark of skin like their mother, with Agos's thick hair and stocky build. Before I could start looking for any resemblances to Thanh, I felt Khine return his grip on my arm. "It's time we head back," he whispered.

I got up and we left the square. My thoughts were a blur. I didn't even notice when it began raining. Cold water dripped down my face, washing the blood away. It felt like nothing.

Khine brushed his thumb over the cut. "You're just human, Tali," he said in a low voice. "Queen or not, you have to forgive yourself for it."

"Have *you*?" I asked.

I wasn't sure if I meant it as a genuine question or a joke. The side of his mouth quirked up as he gazed at me thoughtfully.

"Answer me," I found myself saying, my hands crawling up to his chest. I could feel his heartbeat against my fingertips.

"Why does it matter what I think?" Khine whispered. "I'm just a con artist from Shang Azi." But even as he said this, he lifted his arms to envelop me into an embrace, as if he wanted to shield me from the whole world.

I was glad for the rain and how it cloaked my tears. *Only human.* After a lifetime of wolves and falcons and whatever foolish words I've hid behind all this time, to hear it put that way was a balm to my senses. I wanted to tell him what it meant to me that he did—how I didn't think I would still be here if not for him. That I would be dead, or dead inside, or somehow gone from the world if he had not found me on the streets of Anzhao the day we met. I didn't think I could do it without becoming incoherent.

But I kept myself there. In all the times I had found myself in his arms, I could always pretend to be someone else, and it was easier to do that now more than ever. The only discomfort I felt was the dreaded knowledge that it would soon end, as it had all those other times.

And yet...

I took another breath and in a wave of courage, reached up to kiss him. I didn't know if he had been expecting it, because his only response was to kiss me back. Truly a liar, this man—he had said he would never let it happen again. Instead, he dared to deepen it, dared to let his hands wander where he had once visibly restrained himself from touching me. Gone was the desperation of the first. The warmth of his lips was a stark contrast with the cold, pelting rain. Hard to control, this human part of us; I wanted him to belong to me as much as I wanted to belong to him. I wanted to run my fingers through his hair, wanted him to make me forget everything there was in my wretched life. What was the Dragonthrone to this? To someone who accepted the truth of what I was and still found a way to be there? I didn't know what to do with this newfound knowledge of him, of what he was in my life. It was like being handed a chest from another kingdom's treasury—you didn't know what was inside or what it was worth, you just had the sense it was valuable.

"Are you there, Talyien?"

Straight from the dark, my husband's voice slid through the air like a loosed arrow.

I pulled away from Khine, suddenly self-conscious, and allowed my hands to drop to my sides. "Rai," I called, attempting my most sardonic tone to chase away the heat that remained on my cheeks.

He sauntered up from the end of the street. I didn't think he had seen anything—he would've said something if he did.

"I'm surprised your nursemaids allowed you out of the castle," I commented dryly.

Rai never did get my jokes. He glowered at me from behind the strands of his wet hair, as if he had been running through the city all morning. "You're supposed to be in your room."

"Blessed Akaterru, Rai, do you realize you sounded just like Magister Arro right now?"

"I don't—"

"Yes, yes. You don't understand, you don't look anything like Arro. Let's just go." I began to walk down the street. My heartbeat pounded against my ears. I needed to be more careful. Whatever it was I *wanted*, however that made me feel, I was still Rayyel Ikessar's wife.

Rai threw Khine an irritated glance—at least, as close to irritated as Rai could manage—before hurrying after me. "This sort of behaviour is ill-advised at this time," he said. "The rest of the council—Ikessars, and representatives from your own lords—will be arriving any moment. I sent you transcripts from the last council meeting to prepare yourself on the off chance that—"

"That Thanh's father truly is Agos? You can say it for what it is, Rai. We've spent too many years tiptoeing around the truth. Your son could be another man's, and while we worried over it like dogs snarling over a bone, Jin-Sayeng has fallen into shambles. The farmers in the west have rebelled against their unwanted warlord, led by a merchant with more resources than we could have ever dreamed possible. The same magical aberrations that caused mad dragons these past few decades are starting to affect people. A mad, foreign prince is coming for us under my own father's orders, *and we're more concerned about whether a boy is a fucking bastard or not.*"

He glanced away. I couldn't tell if it was the swearing or my tone he found the most discomfort in. "When the council calls for you, you need to be ready. The less fault they find with you—"

"Ah," I said. "With me. Always, it comes down to me. What about you? What about the things *you've* done?"

His jaw remained taut. "Once this trial is over, we can proceed with dealing with the war out west and the Zarojo and whatever mess your father's brought us to," he said, deflecting my argument with the same ease he always did. "The less opposition we have in court, the better."

"I don't see the point."

He regarded me with silence.

"How do I put this so I don't confuse you..." I rubbed my temples. "The trial only concerns the legitimacy of our son. I don't know what the hell kind of show you or the council have planned, and I'm not sure I care. Maybe I'm glad he's with Kaggawa, even if he *is* a power-hungry commoner with more money than sense. He's safer there than around you vile snakes. Gods, I should've—"

Rai's eyes narrowed. "Why are you wounded?" he asked, changing the conversation.

"You're seeing things."

"There's blood on your face."

"I ran into a wall."

He glanced at Khine, who crossed his arms and quickly pretended something else in the distance was more interesting. Rai sighed. "You went to your lover's funeral, I suppose."

"You knew that was today."

"Why else did you think I sent you the transcripts? I thought it would occupy you for a few hours, long enough for this to be over before you realized it."

"How thoughtful of you, dear husband. Too bad I burned them in the fireplace."

"You burned the... you're impossible. Lamang, does she listen to you? Ever?" Khine's eyes widened.

"Don't answer that if you know what's good for you," I hissed. I turned back to Rai. "How did you think I would react to all of this? To the secrecy? As far as your council is concerned, I'm already guilty. Going through those transcripts wouldn't have done a damn thing, and if I wanted to know what happened there word for word, I could just as easily ask you. I'm sure you have it all memorized."

"Don't be overly dramatic. There is every intention of judging you fairly."

"So say you, the Ikessar, talking to the *other* Ikessars."

"You know the Oren-yaro lords aren't allowed to have their say. They would be biased—"

"—like hell they will! Have you seen the way Ozo looks at me? If you could stab with a stare—"

"Why are you angry with me? Do you blame me for your lover's death?"

I swallowed. Guilt, again, spreading now. Agos had seen the way I looked at Khine, but Rai had never been good at reading me. If I pretended it didn't exist, maybe he would never know. Maybe I could protect Khine that way.

Khine coughed. "Not to interrupt this merry argument, but I believe I heard guards down the street. We need to go."

I felt the exhaustion weighing me down as I nodded. Rai stiffened his jaw, ever the proud man.

Khine strode ahead, leaving me to walk beside my husband. A strange arrangement, not even considering the circumstances that brought us there in the first place. Tangled like roots, muddier than a rice paddy during monsoon. I thought about Agos's wife back at the square and the people around her, the ones who hadn't stopped her from lashing out. If we had been back in the castle, she wouldn't have been able to lay a hand on me. And yet out there amongst other common folk, it was as if we had been stripped bare of everything: two women, one who wronged the other, and nothing more.

We reached the winding steps leading up to the mountain. "We should get you back to your quarters," Khine said. "Does anyone else know she's missing?"

"I did alert my guards," Rai replied with an almost embarrassed look on his face.

I sighed. "Of course you did."

"I thought it was Kaggawa. I was not about to take any chances after what happened last time. That man...One could almost admire the audacity in thinking he could overturn the monarchy overnight."

"The audacity is backed with full coffers, a far cry from our bankrupt throne. The Anyu clan took the Sougen province for themselves when the rest of Jin-Sayeng was busy. If ambitious, landless royals could succeed, why shouldn't a rich farmer try the same thing?"

"He has your son."

"*Our* son, Rai."

His eyes skipped past me. "I do worry," he said under his breath. "I worry about what Kaggawa would do to the boy in his attempt to grab power for himself. There is too much chaos out in the west, the sort of thing we are ill-equipped to deal with. Jin-Sayeng has been kept in the dark about the *agan* for far too long. What do we know about magic?"

"You seemed confident they would agree to a trial that involves a mage."

"This Jin-Sayeng isn't the Jin-Sayeng of the past. Rysaran's dragon ensured that. It may not be something we speak about openly, but it is steeped in our history. The council accepted it readily."

"Did they, truly? Or is some other foul thing afoot? You heard your mother's creature the night Agos died. They don't care. *It is enough that he is my son.*"

He fell silent, a shadow over his face.

We came up to the gates, where the guards saluted at the sight of us. Ikessar soldiers—the falcon crest was clear even in the dark. The bastards had invaded the castle from the ground up. They allowed us through and followed us down the path and into the great hall before they dispersed.

I lingered at the entrance. The doors still showed signs of last week's assault—bent rails, splintered wood, shattered glass laced with black soot. The blood had been scrubbed clean from the floor, but the cuts from Agos's sword as he tried to kill Rai were still there. Even without closing my eyes I could still see them both, phantoms in that dreaded dance. My heart clenched yet again over the outcome. If I had stopped it before the Ikessars arrived...

I heard Khine curse under his breath. Ozo stood in the middle of the throne room like a statue.

"Wondering if you could steal *that*, too?" I called to the old man. I nodded towards the throne. "You're welcome to try."

Ozo placed his hand on the hilt of his sword before he turned to face me. For a moment, I caught a glimpse of the general he had been. He was one of the youngest during the War of the Wolves—celebrated, feared, admired by men and women alike. They said that he cut quite a stunning figure: tall, long-haired, strong enough to wield a war club with one hand and crush his opponent's face with one blow, helmet and all. He still stood straight and tall, and the withered muscles of his tattooed arms remained formidable, but he looked exhausted now, an old man who seemed just about done with life even before it was done with him.

He took one long breath, considering my words like they were genuine. "I wouldn't want it," he said at last. "The Oren-yaro never needed it, as far as I was concerned. The squabble for the damn thing cost us more than we gained."

"I find that hard to believe."

He gave a quick burst of laughter. "You would, pup. You never did understand our people. You carried the name, but the *very* essence of the Oren-yaro...childish scribbles on the wall, as far as you were concerned. Perhaps we were all to blame. Maybe we neglected you. We should've never let you grow up under Magister Arro's care. What did a half-Xiaran know about our ways?" He sniffed. "I knew something was up when I heard the Ikessar guards out and about. Did you try to escape?"

"I accompanied Lady Talyien to the gardens," Rai said. "She needed the exercise."

Ozo looked like he wanted to take a fist to Rayyel's head. "At this hour? What is she, a hound to let loose and piddle on the leaves? You Ikessars go too far."

"*You* could do with some exercise, you bloated eel," I said. "If the Ikessars bother you so much, why don't you do a damn thing? I suppose you're too busy trying to enjoy your privileges as warlord now. If my father was alive, he'd have had your head mounted on a spike already."

"He would have!" Ozo's face grew dark. "But he's dead, Lady Talyien. And if you had lived up to his name and not allowed yourself to become distracted with your ridiculous whims, we wouldn't be here today."

"If you're saying what I think you're saying—" I snarled.

"You snap at enemies where there are none. I have served your family all my life. The least you can do is give me the benefit of the doubt."

"You refused to grant your queen assistance and then took control of her lands. Are these good enough reasons for me to think maybe—just maybe—you don't have my best interests at heart?"

"You were gone for a year, and then returned at the heels of disgrace," Ozo replied evenly. "*Someone* had to rule." He cocked his head to the side. "I asked you not to go to the empire, if you recall. I advised you to stay in Oren-yaro and stake your claim on the throne as Yeshin's daughter, *not* as Rayyel Ikessar's wife."

"And you may well recall what I told you: I have no desire for civil war. Remind me again how I have ruined your plans, Ozo. You wanted me to ride against the Ikessars. I have the bigger army, after all, and the Ikessars are pathetic. You've told me that for the better part of five years. And you know if I had done it, the rest of the land would have come roaring to their defense. Was that when Prince Yuebek was supposed to sweep in to save me? I was never supposed to meet him in the empire, but amidst the blood and fire of my own lands. And you thought—what? That I would somehow be so grateful I would both marry him and somehow gift you Oren-yaro along the way?" I smiled. "I'm close to the truth, aren't I?"

"You know nothing of the truth," Ozo said, eyes blazing.

I gazed back at him, unflinching. Nothing the old man did had ever intimidated me, and the gods know he had tried all these years. Less so, when my father was alive; when Yeshin still stalked the halls of Oka Shto, Ozo was nothing but a scowling, skulking shadow in the background, a general who would only show his face to receive orders before riding off to disappear for the rest of the year. After my father's funeral, I had expected to see even less of him. His lands were along the river to the south, with some of Oren-yaro's most prosperous towns—he had no reason to grace the city itself with his presence.

Instead, he was in Oka Shto Castle nearly every week, poking his nose into the guardsmen's affairs and arguing with Arro over every little thing. And for long stretches at a time, he would live in the Oren-yaro barracks at the base of the mountain, becoming as much of a fixture in the city's politics as Magister Arro. I didn't mind his presence back then—my soldiers were always more disciplined when he was around, and he seemed to have taken a personal interest in making sure I knew how to fight properly. But now I had to wonder if he had been slowly poisoning my people with his influence instead. I was just about done with old men and their ambitions.

He crossed the room with his arms crossed as he considered the tapestries and banners on the wall. *My* wall, his colours.

"They wanted you dead," Ozo remarked.

I smiled. "Who, exactly? There's a long list."

He snorted. "I must confess, you've done an impressive job making enemies and adding to it yourself. No—after your father died, many of the warlords wanted you gone. *We don't want a trace of Yeshin in this land*, they told me."

"They told you," I repeated. "Ah. They asked you to sell me out."

"Their terms were very good," Ozo laughed. "At least one offered to have you lured away in exchange for fifty rice fields. *Your conscience will be clear. You'll never know what really happened.* But even if I had been tempted—"

"Were you?"

"You know the answer to that."

"I'm so very grateful you decided not to sell me out *then*, Ozo, it really gladdens my heart," I drawled.

Beside me, I heard Rai sigh. But he had always been intelligent enough not to butt in to Oren-yaro affairs and seemed, at the very least, glad he wasn't on the receiving end this time.

"I had no desire to be indebted to those bastards," Ozo said. "They wouldn't even sign their letters—too afraid to be found out, the damn cowards. I don't deal with men playing it safe." He turned to me, pulling down his sleeve to bare his arm. There was a scar down to his elbow, a gash concealed beneath the mass of curly hair and tattoos.

I remembered Warlord San showing me his scar, too. "Yes," I said impatiently. "You signed a blood compact during my father's war. So did everyone else. It's not half as impressive as you all think it is. A scar is a small price to pay for peace."

"You're mistaken," Ozo said. "This wasn't done when your father was alive." He lowered his arm. "It was after. A second blood compact. I wasn't there for the first, but I made damn well sure that I was for this one."

"And was this second one for my head?"

He laughed. "Enough! You'll bark at your own shadow if you've got nothing else, Yeshin's child. I will not sink to this level." He turned to Rai, as if noticing him for the first time. "You will return her immediately to her quarters, Prince Rayyel, if you don't want your mother's representatives to catch wind of this. It was you who called for this trial. If you were so concerned for your queen's health, perhaps you should've thought twice about what you did in the first place. You don't throw someone into the fire to save them." A shadow crossed his face, and he suddenly looked like he regretted what he'd just said. Without another word, he heaved himself up the stairs.

I watched his shadow disappear from the walls. "I hate that man from the very bottom of my heart," I whispered under my breath.

Rai gave a soft sigh. "You hate them all. You always did."

I cleared my throat. "He was at Agos's funeral."

"What would he be doing there?"

"We should have breakfast first," Khine broke in. "It's not safe to talk out here." I glanced at Rai, who nodded. We followed Khine to the kitchens. Inzali and Namra were at the main table, bent over a pile of books and steaming cups of tea. Such dedicated scholars, the both of them; I could see why my husband respected their counsel.

"About time you got back," Inzali said without looking up. "We were getting hungry."

"Yes, Mother," Khine grumbled. He strode over to the curtained-off section of the kitchens. I heard him grab a pot and step out through the back door.

"Where's the rest of the staff?" I asked, taking a seat on the bench beside Namra. I glanced at the books spread out in front of her and immediately grew nauseated. I could barely get through a history book without dropping it on my face and snoring, and these women were reading two or three at once.

"You don't know what's happening in your own castle, do you?" Inzali asked.

"People have been deliberately keeping me in the dark." I threw Rai a sideways glance. He simply shrugged.

"They've been leaving one by one over the last few days," Namra said. Her face was ringed with shadows of exhaustion. "I believe Warlord Ozo has called for servants from his own holdings. He didn't trust yours, I suppose. Speaking of which—" She excused herself and stepped out to the adjoining hall.

"I must confess," Inzali said, "that I find all of this odd. Servants who abandon their masters, lords who neglect their queen. Such things are unimaginable back in the empire."

"They'll explain it all away as simply being *Oren-yaro*," Khine called over the sound of crackling oil.

Inzali frowned.

I gave a small smile. "I can see what Ozo is doing and why the people support him for it, but I don't have to *like* it." I glanced away. "Maybe that's why he accused me of not being a very good Oren-yaro in the first place. Maybe he's right. I could keep this illusion of power so long as I danced to their music. But now that I openly rebel against their ways, I am no longer one of them. Never mind that I am still my father's daughter, or that I love this land as much as the rest of them claim."

"His presence at Agos's funeral…" Rai began. "It's curious why he would take such a risk. He could be seen either as a sympathizer or, at worst, as someone concocting a plan to betray you. I've never taken him to be so careless."

"And I've never taken him as a traitor before. I wish I could just call him senile and have it done with."

Khine returned with a plate heaped with fried fish and a hunk of cold rice.

"Have you been cooking the meals they've been sending me?" I demanded.

"Since yesterday, after Hessa's replacement went off and left. Ozo's been eating with his men in the barracks down at the square."

"Everything's falling apart." I broke off a fin and popped it into my mouth. It was salty. Apt, I supposed, for everything to taste like tears lately.

"And about to fall apart even more," Namra said, returning with a grim expression. "The rest of the Ikessar council are at the gates. Princess Ryia is with them."

I would have never believed Rai capable of fear, but all the colour immediately drained from my husband's face. Ryia Ikessar—the Butcher's Bane, the Witch Who Defied the Wolf—had come at last. I would have laughed if I didn't know any better.

I followed my husband to the great hall in silence.

CHAPTER THREE

THE WITCH AND
THE WOLF

ᴣᴴ⵿Ɋⴘ

A t the time, as far as Jin-Sayeng was concerned, Queen Talyien had never met her mother-in-law.

Princess Ryia had only visited Oka Shto once after the war, during the betrothal ceremony when I was an infant. The Oren-yaro believed that her fear of Warlord Yeshin kept her away. But even after his death, she chose not to leave her mountain domain, and we saw neither hide nor hair of her. The only reasonable conclusion was that she cared nothing for the land she had fought my father for; almost as if, not having won it for herself, she would rather see it crumble into dust.

And yet here she was. I couldn't really blame her; her son was neck-deep in conspiracy after years of being away…surely a mother's concern eclipsed disdain for an enemy long dead.

We waited for her by the throne. I could hear Rai breathing deeply, could see his hands clenched into fists. Anticipation, dread? Expressions I never imagined he was capable of. His face was still very pale. He hadn't spoken a word since Namra's announcement. I tried to imagine what he was thinking. If my father was still alive, knowing he was on his way right after I had made a terrible mess of things would be enough to tear my spirit from my body. Rai had every reason to fear his mother. Even if they never openly acknowledged it, his actions had brought just as much shame to his clan as mine. Princess Ryia had swallowed her pride and allowed her son to be betrothed to her rival's daughter to save the land. To save *his* life. For our parents, two of the fiercest figures in recent history, to lay down their arms for our marriage would have required a remarkable amount of patience.

And I was willing to gamble it took more for her than my father. Yeshin had been an old man, fading fast and consumed with nothing but hatred over what was taken from him. He was convinced the Ikessars lured him into causing his own sons' deaths by fooling him into taking that first mad dragon into Orenyaro and releasing it there. But Ryia wasn't his real enemy. He hated her family, what she stood for, and the incompetent governance of monarchs too weak to turn Jin-Sayeng around. He hated what she represented, but the woman behind the mask would've been just a passing concern.

Ryia, on the other hand, had been young, at the prime of her life when the war broke out. My father massacred her family, including her two elder sisters. The War of the Wolves was a personal affair for the youngest and only remaining daughter of her line. She had been raised a priestess; my father's actions forced her to become a warrior. That a woman of a dying clan could stand head-to-head with a powerful warlord was a feat in itself. She had Kaggawa's family to thank for that—they supplied the assassins and spies that made the Ikessars a clan to be feared once more. For her to give up the chance to rule, after all of that...

The doors opened. I straightened myself as Ryia strode in—no pomp, no ceremony, no announcement. She was dressed in simple red robes, unadorned save for jade earrings that reached down to her shoulders. I was surprised to see how young she looked. She was close to Ozo's age, but they would seem twenty years apart if you had them side by side—the sort of person for whom age was simply an inconvenience they could brush off. Her hair, which reached all the way to her waist, only had the faintest streak of silver—a stark contrast with her son, and strange for an Ikessar.

I was even more surprised, however, by her beauty. A failure on my part to realize that the books in our library were written by her enemies, who would at turns call her a hag and a witch, a woman more hideous than an *anggali* with half its body cut off. Perhaps men wouldn't write poetry about her—they didn't, as far as I'm aware—but an aura of power emanated from her, one that could turn heads just as well as beauty. Were the historians so threatened they failed to mention this?

"Beloved Princess," Rai said, reaching to take her hand. He pressed it on his forehead.

She allowed the gesture of respect, but when I tried to do the same thing, she pulled her hand away, as if I didn't exist at all. My newfound admiration dissipated. Her mouth was a thin line as she regarded her son. "Is this how I raised you, Rayyel?"

"Mother—"

"Your envoy arrived *after* you made such a remarkably careless announcement. You never consulted me beforehand. Years, you said—you knew this for years. I should've known your ridiculous refusal of the Dragonthrone was more than a religious crisis. Jeopardizing everything because of your damn pride—are you trying to get us all killed?"

"Mother," Rai repeated, drawing a deep breath. "It was a necessity. The Zarojo were headed this way. I was hoping it would stop them."

"Did it?"

"I—"

"A *no*, then. I expected better from an Ikessar. I expected better from *my son*." She turned away from him to glance at me for the first time. "And is it true? This woman was unfaithful to your marriage bed?"

Rai turned red. "Beloved Princess—"

"Answer me, Rayyel!"

"The trial—"

"A pointless trial," Ryia finished for him. "You dare rouse the whole nation for a problem easily solved. I can kill her for this now while we search for that bastard child of hers." She drew a sword from her belt and rushed towards me.

"Beloved Princess—!" Rai screamed.

Ryia stopped a foot away, the blade on my neck. I thought I felt a trickle of blood down my clavicle. "What do we need a trial for?" she asked, looking into my eyes. The softest of smiles flitted across her lips. "You're guilty. You would have fought back if you weren't. That *is* your reputation, isn't it, Bitch Queen? Yet look at you standing there. So straight, not a shred of shame in your eyes. Like you're just begging me to put you out of your misery."

"Did you come here just to cause trouble?" I asked, keeping my voice calm. "I was hoping for more. This *is* our first meeting, *Mother*."

A shadow of revulsion crossed Ryia's face. She sniffed as she slid her sword back into her belt. "I came here to try to salvage a land I sacrificed too much for. You children have no idea what you're doing. I should've claimed the throne when I had the chance. Entrusting it to the shoulders of Yeshin's whelp was a step too far. But she convinced me. She said—"

"She?"

"Kaggawa," Ryia replied, in a voice that told me she didn't mean the man waging war out west. Her eyes flickered. "Yesterday's regrets. The Dragonthrone could have been mine. But saving thousands of lives was more important to me, and so I made the proposal to your father with every intention of ridding this land of its ills once and for all. I believed his sincerity when he accepted it. I thought he, too, was done with the fighting. Now I am hearing rumours that I have been tricked, that your father was as wily a wolf as ever and never meant to see you wed to my son."

I was silent for a moment. "My father did what he thought was right, even if he was wrong," I said at last. "Given the opportunity, you would have done the same thing."

"Listen to yourself. You are defending a tyrant sixteen years dead."

"I know what he did," I snapped. "I know he deceived us all. But you said it yourself. He's sixteen years dead. What he wanted then doesn't make much of a damn difference now. I can respect my father and acknowledge his mistakes without following his footsteps."

"You are a fool, Talyien Orenar, blinded by your love for a man who is now—if the gods are kind—rotting in the furthest reaches of hell."

"They said the same thing about me with your son," I said. "I have been criticized for how I choose to feel all my life, but I'll say this much, *Princess*—you will not insult my father's name in his own halls."

"*His* halls?" Ryia asked, amused. "Aren't they yours, now?"

I fell silent and watched her make her way to the Akaterru alcove along the western wall of the great hall, her earrings swaying with each step. One of the candles had gone out. She tilted the wick to the nearest lit one. The flame rose, making the powder on her face sparkle with the light. "Good intentions are like a single lit candle in a dark sea," she said, inclining her head towards me. "It won't do you much good for long."

I stared at her in confusion.

"My sisters used to tell me that," she said. "Back when I was young and softhearted and I didn't know the cruelties of this world. I should've listened to them. Your father killed them at the onset of his war."

"A war that happened well over thirty years ago," I replied, stepping towards her. "Young men and women who survived it are now saddled with grandchildren. Beloved Princess, isn't it time for us to move forward? Jin-Sayeng is on the verge of collapse. Foreign invasion, civil war...we have more pressing concerns than these tired old arguments."

"Why," she said, "should I listen to you?"

Her voice sent a chill down my spine.

"You wouldn't exactly make the most trustworthy ally," she continued. "You seem to have enough problems staying a trustworthy wife."

"Princess—" Rai tried again.

She glanced at him sharply. "You'd correct me, boy? It was *your* accusation that brought light to this. And now you're defending this woman?"

"She's my wife," Rai croaked. He sounded exhausted, despite only having managed to get those first few words in. I would've found it amusing under any other circumstances.

"Some wife," Ryia said. "I expected better."

"You expected Yeshin's daughter," I managed.

"As I said. I didn't expect Yeshin's daughter to be so dim-witted." She gave a dismissive gesture and made a show of looking around the great hall. "Where *is* this man then, this lover of hers?"

Rai's face flickered. "He's dead."

"Good," Ryia said. "I can't see why *you* didn't execute him yourself. You knew for *years*," she repeated, as if it was a source of irritation that her son would keep secrets from her. "You think me harsh, but look at what your fumbling foolishness has created. Some Dragonlord you'll make—you're as weak as my brother had been. Did you take care of the others?"

Rai stared at her blankly.

A line of irritation appeared on her forehead. "Rumours abound on her activities. I dismissed them as idle gossip until you proved otherwise. You wouldn't lie, Rai—I know that much. And one truth will reveal the rest." She turned to me. "Did you think you could run this nation to the ground and get away with it? All your father's secrets, Talyien, and all of *yours*...I will find them soon enough." There was a cold smile on her lips, and only then did I recall it was her men who killed Agos. For all I knew, she ordered it herself.

The chill worked its way into my heart.

I don't remember how the conversation ended without one of us dead. Somehow, I managed to avoid attempting to take her head off, and Rai himself escorted me back to my chambers. He looked apologetic.

"She can't be here," I blurted out as he turned to leave.

He tightened his face. "I can't exactly send her away."

"Have you *tried*?"

He gave me a pained look.

I sighed and walked to the window. I pulled the shutters close. "The woman didn't even ask about Thanh."

"I don't understand why this is important."

I struggled to keep my voice even. "She didn't ask about Thanh. She's never once visited him, not when he was born—never. You've kept away all these years and I think I can understand *why* now, but—this isn't a matter of pride for her. In all the times you've been to the Citadel since Thanh was born, has she ever once mentioned him?"

Rai swallowed, panicked eyes darting away from me. Which told me she had, but not in a way that I would appreciate hearing about. "You need to worry about the trial," he said. "Let me handle my mother."

"She has no intention of letting the trial determine anything. Didn't you hear her out there? She regrets this arrangement. She will not want things back the way they were. She never wanted it in the first place!"

"Let me handle it," he repeated.

"You stubborn, inept man—don't you understand? We're powerless here. Both of us. If we let them, they'll have our heads decorating the courtyard by dawn!"

I didn't know what I expected from raising my voice. It always irritated him when I did, and nothing had changed. He walked away, slamming the door behind him. I dropped to my mattress, hands balled in frustration. I wasn't sure why I was angry. *I* didn't want things to go back the way they were. I didn't want this prison, this shadowed chamber with its empty walls and cold bed. There was a knot in my stomach threatening to split me open, and I was suddenly tempted to go stomping after Ryia and tell her she could have the throne. She could have all of it if she would just leave my family alone.

I took a deep breath, staring at the ceiling to calm myself. She would kill me after such an admission. The land that had supported her pact with Warlord Yeshin would not let her just *take* it all back; she'd still need my head to convince them of my guilt, for a start. I had no intention of letting her have it.

I didn't know where my conviction was coming from. Death was a given in the life I led. I ordered it of others, decreed so easily that the loss of their lives was important for the greater good. And I always knew mine wasn't an exception. Trial or not, I was guilty. I *may* have planted a false heir on the throne. In the nation's eyes, I also committed infidelity. All that remained was whether they could prove either. If I was truly as loyal to my duties as I once thought I was, if I was a true Oren-yaro, I would tell them now, and let them do with me as they will.

But the despair that had taken me from the Zarojo Empire and all the way back here seemed to have faded, replaced by something I didn't understand. I felt like someone still swimming in the ocean, but instead of a black sky, I could now see stars. Not much, not even enough to light the horizon, and yet they gave me something to gaze at, something to remind me that brightness could exist elsewhere. Maybe not in the world I lived in, but somewhere far away…

I swallowed, remembering what had happened that morning in the rain. A second kiss, thoughtlessly given. I couldn't even call it unexpected. I suddenly understood my restlessness. *All your secrets…*

I fell asleep—that sort of wretched sleep that brought very little rest and nothing but a blessed numbness for a few hours—only to wake up to the sound of frantic knocking. I rolled off the mattress and opened the door.

"Beloved Queen," Namra said, taking my hand and pressing it against her forehead.

"If Princess Ryia finds out a Kibouri priestess is offering me respect, she'll throw a fit."

"She can do that if she wants. Will you come with me?"

"Where?"

"To your father's study."

I stared at her, at this woman who had been my husband's companion longer than we had been married. Was she truly his, or was she his mother's creature? "Ozo lets you walk around like that?" I asked, trying to keep my suspicions at bay.

"Warlord Ozo does not need to know everything that transpires behind these walls," she said with a small smile. Few things seemed to bother her—a necessary trait to be able to withstand the company of my husband for long. My complete opposite in that. I might have been jealous of her when we first met, even though Namra was the sort of plain-faced, unassuming woman one normally wouldn't be jealous of. It's not supposed to be an insult. But she was no Chiha Baraji—her eyelashes didn't flutter with her every breath, nor did she have a cleavage that could draw attention from across a crowded room. Neither did she have the kind of electric personality that I'd come to associate with women who attached themselves to men with the sort of perceived power my husband had. Still, by all rights, I shouldn't trust her. And yet I did.

I grabbed a shawl to ward off the sudden draft and found myself following her up the stairwell, crossing over to the other wing. The only movement through the empty corridors came from the chilly breeze wafting through the half-open windows. I wondered how long I had been asleep. It must be late at night, now...the hallways were empty and our footsteps sounded like a crowd's. "Ozo is in my father's chambers," I reminded her. "I'm surprised he hasn't caught you yet."

"He is not, Beloved Queen," she replied. "He's been staying in the guest quarters this whole time. I haven't seen him on this entire floor since we arrived."

It was an odd thing to learn. You would think Ozo wouldn't have the same qualms about taking my father's bedroom as I did. Sixteen years dead and Oka Shto remained ruled by a ghost. I shivered. "Why do you serve Rayyel?" I asked, in an effort to change the conversation.

She cocked her head at me. "Is that truly the question you are asking?"

"Maybe not," I admitted.

"You want to know if I have a relationship with your husband."

I shrugged. "He once said there was a woman, and I'm assuming that means there could have been more."

"And as intelligent as you are, you took the bait?" She smiled. "Dragonlord Rayyel is not that kind of man."

"I'm starting to fear you're right."

"His devotion to you is true, though I can admit his way of showing it is... unconventional. But I believe you, and you alone, have been on his mind all these years. There has been no one else." She paused, reading the look on my face. "This isn't what you wanted to hear, is it?"

I kept walking so I wouldn't have to answer her. Unconventional, indeed. The bitterness was still there.

"My father served his mother," she said, at length. "A long time ago, during your...during the war. My father died when I was young, and I do this to honour his name."

"Ah," I said. "I think I can understand that."

"You, more than anyone I know."

"I can see the shadow behind your smile, priestess. You wonder, like they all do, why I would want to honour a tyrant at all."

She clasped her hands together. "I make no presumptions when it comes to you, Beloved Queen. But please, speak your mind, and I will listen."

"Warlord Yeshin was created by a land at the cusp of war," I said. "I'm not. My birth was supposed to bring peace. My father may have been cruel and ruthless in so many other circumstances, but this one thing, he did right."

She nodded but, true to her word, didn't say anything.

"I know, Namra. He made a grave error. He chose to trust a foreign prince over upholding his alliance with the Ikessars. But the intent is there. He *did* promise the land peace. I was supposed to bring it. Could I not continue to work towards that? Can I not try to undo his mistakes, and mine? I want to be a good queen, Namra. I want to do right by this land. It has already seen too much suffering. I just want to set this all aside and continue to fulfill my duties, even if I have to do it my way. I'm not him. I don't have to try to be like him. I can carve my own path in this world without spitting on my father's name. I can still honour him without being him."

"Carving your own path and honouring your elders do not exactly go hand in hand," Namra reminded me gently. "Their word is law, as far as the gods are concerned. This has been drilled into us since birth."

"I know," I said. "But I am a stubborn woman."

"In that we can all agree, my queen."

I fell silent as we found ourselves at the door leading to my father's study. Namra placed her hand on the knob. The door opened, even without her turning it.

"Opening doors without taking precautions is ill-advised in Dageis, where I was educated," Namra said. She ushered me in. It was suddenly very warm, almost hot. Strange, because I couldn't see a fire anywhere. I shrugged out of my shawl with a soft sigh, draping it over a chair.

"What do you mean?" I asked, turning back to her.

"Dageis is a land of mages. Almost everything is laced with spells and counterspells; some could obliterate you if you walked into the wrong room. But this is Jin-Sayeng, where everything is so...archaic."

She began talking about the intricacies of Dageian spells, but her voice faded in the background as I found myself staring at my father's vast bookshelves.

I allowed myself to breathe. The last time I was here was before his death. I caught a whiff of the scent that I used to associate with him—the smell of the oils used to preserve the covers of his books, moldy leather, and maybe a touch of *him* as he was. Perhaps sixteen years wasn't that long ago after all.

I turned my attention to his desk. There were scattered papers, as well as a jar of ink with a pen inside. The ink had hardened around the pen. I suddenly remembered that he had been here the day he fell ill. I was sitting in the corner next to the window, trying to force myself through a book Arro wanted me to finish by the end of the moon. I remember turning to Yeshin to ask him a question—I couldn't remember what—just as he collapsed, one hand on his chest. I still feel a twinge of shame over the fact that I didn't rush to him immediately. That I watched him longer than I should've, afraid it was a test of some sort...that if I panicked, I would fail. I stood there, a girl of eleven, staring at my weakened, convulsing father on the floor, at the spit that dribbled down his chin. Staring at him die.

"Your father was a busy man," Namra said.

"Until the very end." I placed my fingers along the edge of the parchment. The ink had faded to a faint brown over the years, but I could still make out the straight block script my father liked to write in. He took pride in his clear handwriting, and always made note to mention how he didn't scribble mindlessly like some officials he knew. Everything he did was precise, calculated. "I can count on one hand the number of times I've seen him engage in anything that could be considered recreation. He was always working on something—drafting up elaborate plans, conducting meetings. If he took walks, it was always for a patrol or an errand."

"I always thought royals had plenty of hobbies, my queen. But after meeting Dragonlord Rayyel, I think I could believe that rest is a luxury for many of you."

"You misunderstand me, priestess. My husband has his quirks, but I've seen him read for pleasure or engage in moments of silence with a cup of tea. No... my father *never* rested. In retrospect, that should have been the first clue that my betrothal wasn't as it seemed. My father wasn't the sort of man who would willingly lay down arms in front of his enemy—not unless it suited him." I sighed. "What did you want to bring me here for?" I asked, to change the subject. Reflecting on my father while sitting in his very study brought back too many fraught memories.

Namra strode over to the bookcase, which took up the entirety of one wall. My father wasn't the kind of reader Rayyel was, either—he consumed books only when he needed to, as opposed to letting them take over his life. But he had amassed quite a collection over the years. The man valued knowledge as much as his time. "Your father—I was told he was a traditionalist," Namra said, "and that his war was partly fuelled by his desire to return Jin-Sayeng to its older ways, because he felt the Ikessars had become misguided."

"He was as traditional as they came," I said. "Why do you ask?"

"Because of this." She pressed her hand on the edge of the bookcase. It glowed before sliding open, revealing a narrow staircase. Something about it seemed to swallow the light—the shadows that crept along the sides felt alive.

My stomach curdled. "What is that?"

"The sort of spell I was telling you about," Namra said. "Be straight with me, Queen Talyien. Did your father have a mage on staff?"

CHAPTER FOUR

BLOOD WILL TELL

ᜀᜈᜒᜆ

I almost didn't understand her question at first. It was so much at odds with the sort of man my father had been that she might as well have asked me if my father rescued orphaned kittens and embroidered dresses on the side. What I knew of my father was that he detested talk of the *agan* and mages. He was a believer in the old ways, which found magic beyond abominable—it was a transgression to the gods. This was, after all, the same man who beat Eikaro Anyu bloody for revealing his gifts and blackmailed the boy's father in exchange for his silence.

But before I could protest, I remembered the night of Agos's death, when we had come in through the tunnels. I remembered the bottom of the stairwell, which lit up with *agan*-wrought runes as we passed, and the rusted cage once laced with spells. I should've known I had barely scratched the surface of my father's lies.

I stared at the gaping darkness at the bottom of the steps. It felt like staring down into a creature's maw. "How did you discover this?"

She bowed. "It was at Dragonlord Rayyel's behest. Jin-Sayeng has lived in denial about the *agan*, and yet it is the very essence of life as we know it."

"Our gods forbade magic. Affected children were put to death."

She placed her fingers on her forehead. "A fallacy of thinking. Jin-Sayeng has been led astray. One way or another, we are *all* connected to the *agan*, Beloved Queen—everything that is living or was once alive. Those of us who train as mages can see the threads invisible to most. We hone our skill to manipulate it, to channel it like water where we need it, to etch spells on the physical world like ants embroidering on a giant fabric. You see why Jin-Sayeng's ignorance is dangerous. You have few among you who can see the damages that can be caused by the careless.

"My lord suggested I start with Warlord Yeshin's study. If there is anyone who would have gotten a head start in this research, it would have been your father. The mad dragon that destroyed Old Oren-yaro and killed your brothers was made by a mage—a corrupted, unholy thing created by someone who knew better and chose to break the rules anyway. In the face of that, even a traditionalist like your father couldn't remain in denial. And Lord Rayyel was right. More than right. Beloved Queen, I knew the moment I stepped through the doorway that mages had been here. The very foundation of this castle is steeped in spells."

"I know," I said. "I saw them when we entered the castle from the tunnels. But I didn't want to think about it. We have more problems here than the sort of builders my father chose to hire."

She pressed her lips together, choosing not to comment.

"What's down there?" I turned my attention back to the staircase.

Namra gave a sheepish grin. "I haven't explored that far, my queen."

"Why not?"

She shuffled forward, leading me to the side. I watched as she approached the doorway, framed by the bookcases, and placed a hand on the wall.

A flurry of arrows struck the column directly across us.

Cold sweat dotted my forehead. I turned back to Namra, who had a streak of blood on her cheek. She wiped it away with a nervous chuckle. She looked like she was going to faint.

"There was less the last time," she croaked. "I was telling you about certain spells meant to keep intruders out. You've just seen one. I think if you want to know what your father is hiding, it's best that you venture down yourself."

"Thank you, Namra, but I'd rather not."

Namra smiled. "The spells are reacting to me, an intruder. You, on the other hand—I believe you will be allowed to descend unharmed."

"You must be mad. Why by all the gods do you think *I'd* be so foolish?"

"Your father built this," Namra said simply. "He wouldn't put up spells that would hurt his daughter."

I stared at her. Did I believe that? Had she asked me before I went to Anzhao City, I might have had a better answer. I swallowed. The darkness beckoned, bringing back memories of Yuebek's dungeon. I imagined my father waiting below, arms folded, with that ever-vigilant, appraising look on his face. *What's the matter, child? Lost the throne, did you? Everything I worked so hard for, nothing but dust now. All because you couldn't keep your legs closed?*

I closed my eyes, my senses whirling. Those, of course, would not be the sort of harsh words my father would've used—at least, not to my face. But he was more than capable of them. More likely he would simply lift his eyes and gaze at me long enough for it to be uncomfortable. And then, he would sigh. That sigh would feel like a knife in my gut, twisting, preparing myself for the onslaught of whatever judgment he felt like passing.

"My queen," Namra continued, breaking my thoughts. "You grew up here. You've been in this room before. Has your father ever forbidden you from venturing to that corner?"

"He'd rather I didn't touch his things with my dirty hands," I said. "He never forbade me from doing anything here."

"Did he seem oddly protective? Concerned?"

"No. Just annoyed."

"Because he would never hurt you."

That's a lie, I thought. But I bit my lip and took a step forward. To hell with it. Yeshin's scheming had already doomed me. One foot in the funeral pyre—I might as well throw my whole body in. I grabbed the lantern from the wall and strode down the steps, not even stopping to see if I had triggered anything. Arrows could've been zooming above my head for all I cared.

Somehow, I reached the bottom in one piece. Runes glowed along the walls.

"Are you alive, my queen?" Namra called.

"Thank you for your concern, Namra," I said wryly. "I'll let you know in a moment or two."

"I'll be waiting right here."

I smirked. The priestess had a glorious sense of humour, though it wasn't obvious to the naked eye. She must've developed it since she'd started travelling with my husband. Sit beside a man like that long enough, you're bound to find ways to amuse yourself. I saw a hook on the wall and stood on tiptoe to hang the lantern.

I heard a clink. Blue light flooded the room. To my horror, I saw the walls begin to shift and the floor to rotate. The passage behind me disappeared.

I didn't even have time to call for the priestess. I stood at the doorway of a cavernous hall, with ceilings that seemed to stretch to the skies. A single chandelier hung below the rafters, swaying slightly. The hall was lined with arches, with sconces on every column. The stale air in my father's study had disappeared.

I walked forward. The torches lit in flames as soon as I passed them, an effect that sent chills up my spine. I tried to ignore the feeling of dread by focusing on my surroundings. Red carpet, rimmed with gold, lined the floor. Each step felt like sinking into mud.

I reached what appeared to be the middle of the room, where the ceiling gave way to a glass-covered dome, held up by metalwork in the shape of petals. Sunlight pressed through the glass, still tainted with blue. Beyond, on the horizon, mountains rose like jagged teeth, capped with white. It looked nothing like the low-lying hills and rice terraces around Mount Oka Shto nor anywhere near Oren-yaro. If anything, it felt like I was looking through the window in the Sougen.

I turned away from the ceiling. Up ahead, the light revealed a single throne, carved from thick *kamagong* wood. Snarling wolves circled the base. A crown sat between the armrests, with two golden links falling on each side and more wolves engraved along the surface. Their eyes were inlaid with clear jewels. One last wolf stood above the others, embodied with a steely gaze that seemed to bore a hole into my soul.

My mouth felt dry. A throne and a crown fit for a king—for an Oren-yaro Dragonlord. Did my father have this throne room made in the event he won the War of the Wolves? He had always been two, three steps ahead. Perhaps he was so sure of victory he couldn't help himself. He never liked Shirrokaru, but the great hall in Oka Shto was small—it made sense to have a proper throne room built. And it made sense to have it hidden away after my betrothal to Rayyel, because such a throne and crown, designed with symbols of the Orenar clan, were presumptuous enough to result in another war.

I picked up the crown. It was lighter than it looked. I turned it around and felt an odd lump in my throat. The crown couldn't have been made for my father—it was too small, delicate. A woman's crown. I placed it on my head.

It was a perfect fit.

An ironic smile flitted over my lips. I turned and seated myself on the throne, my fist on my chin as I gazed at the empty hallway in front of me. Specks of dust floated along the blue sunlight like quiet courtiers, drifting between the shadows and my vision. For a time, I felt like a true queen—one who didn't need to pander to the warlords, who ruled because I wanted to, not just because I *had* to. A true Dragonlord, exactly as Yeshin would've wanted.

———♦———

Footsteps echoed from the other end of the hall. I didn't shift from my seat, but I would be lying if I said I didn't feel an odd mixture of fear and anticipation at the thought that I might see my father's ghost again. Queen or not, in his presence I was reduced to a child of seven.

So I didn't know if it was disappointment or relief that rushed through me when the figure appeared and it was only a servant. A woman, short of stature, with black hair bound at the nape of her neck. She looked startled. I pretended I didn't feel the same way. "You—what are you doing here?"

She made no motion to pay her respects, not even to bow slightly. Which meant that even with the throne and the crown on my head, she didn't know me, which was odd.

"I should be asking you the same thing," she finally said, gathering courage. "You're not supposed to be here. No one is."

"Ah," I replied. "Except you?"

She fidgeted, hands in front of her belly. I narrowed my eyes. She could be anywhere from my age to her late forties—there was a timeless quality to her complexion that made it difficult to tell in the blue-tinged darkness.

"Do you live in the castle?" I tried again. "Else there must be a tunnel that connects this place to somewhere."

"There is no tunnel," she said at last.

"You're lying," I replied. "Your eyes dart away when you speak."

"It's not a lie."

"Well, then—"

"My queen!" a voice called from the end of the hall.

The woman turned to run.

"Hold on—!" I cried, reaching for her. But the priestess appeared from the shadows and when I turned, the servant was gone. I blinked, feeling a cold sensation in the pit of my stomach. It was as if I had been dreaming and now—only just now—woken up. I couldn't even recall the servant's face. Trying to revisit the last few moments felt like trying to vomit on an empty stomach.

"Is everything all right, Beloved Queen?" Namra asked.

"How did you bypass the wards?" I asked, trying not to think of the servant.

"Here." She handed me my shawl. "There was blood on it. Yours, I assumed." She glanced at my bandaged arm, injuries from seven days ago. Only seven days. Gods.

I took the shawl and settled back into the throne. "Welcome to my court, lowly vagrant," I said out loud, trying to gather my senses. The cavernous hall swallowed my voice. "If you play your cards right, you might get to keep your head."

"The Bitch Queen." Namra stared at the throne.

I didn't know whether to tell her about the servant or not. Something about it didn't feel right. "It's beautiful, isn't it?" I said distractedly.

"The throne? Or the title?"

I smirked. "The throne *is* lovely. Magnificent, even. But the title! I've always thought it was a thing of beauty. Acknowledging my father's prowess *and* insulting him, all in one breath!"

"My understanding, my queen, is that it's meant to insult you both."

"I can see why Rai keeps you around," I said.

She gave a small bow. "Coming from you, I will take that as a compliment."

"I just called you a vagrant."

Namra smiled. "You're right. I shall retract my statement at once."

"I haven't been queen long enough to know, truly, whether people are responding to my reputation or my father's."

"With all due respect—six years is substantial even within the context of the Dragonthrone's history. Many sovereigns have found themselves succumbing to poison or assassins within the first. As you said, you have been here...long enough."

Long enough that you shouldn't really blame those before you. I leaned back against the throne and took the crown off my head. I placed it on my lap and turned it so that I was looking at the wolf again. The she-wolf, the bitch. Did my father commission a craftsman to make this after the war? Or was he so arrogant he knew all about the child in his young wife's belly before she was born? I wanted to throw it on the walls, but it was too pretty and I would feel bad if it broke.

"How do you think Ryia will react if she learns of this?" I asked.

"Not well," Namra admitted. "I've heard stories."

"I believe she was fond of upside-down crucifixion. But maybe she'll have something more special for me. Death with bamboo spikes, perhaps." I cleared my throat, my hand momentarily drifting to my belt. My sword wasn't there, but I had a dagger that would serve me well if needed. "You serve Rayyel because your father served the Ikessars."

"My queen?"

"And yet you still call me *queen*, while showing more disdain for the woman you're supposed to be serving. Rayyel isn't the head of the Ikessar clan, not while his mother is alive. I'm still not sure what to make of you, Namra."

She bowed again, low and deep. "My father served the Ikessars because he believed theirs was the way to achieve peace. Your father, unfortunately, didn't inspire such confidence. But..." She craned her head to the side, folding her hands together. "My father changed his mind before the war ended. The Ikessars hid behind pretty words, but their actions were just as merciless. Warlord Yeshin, at least, did not pretend to be something he was not."

She sounded sincere. I removed my hand from the dagger and gestured at the throne room. "I beg to differ."

"He never hid his nature. You and Dragonlord Rayyel are the same—you have honesty within you, rare traits for people in your position. My father wanted peace for this land. I do, too. I believe the best way to achieve that is to put it in the hands of those who want the same thing."

"You choose to judge intention, rather than competence?"

She gave a grim smile. "Competence can just as easily mask corruption."

"I do not disagree. Yet if these metrics of leadership are all we have left, we've sunk very low, indeed."

"Perhaps. But to me, you remain queen, just as Lord Rayyel is *Dragonlord*, uncrowned or not."

"Such simple honesty is as deadly as naivety. Was your father a soldier?"

"A banner-maker," she corrected.

"A banner-maker," I repeated with surprise. "With a daughter skilled in the *agan*. In an attempt to remove you from my father's bloody rule, he brought you to Dageis to save your life. And what do you do? You *return* to save that wretched land in his memory." I tapped the crown, petting the wolf's head. "It is difficult to shake that shadow off of you, isn't it? We are forever our fathers' daughters, whether we like it or not."

Namra stared at me in silence. It was the first time I'd ever seen the priestess startled. I wondered how deep of a chord I'd struck. Maybe it was always easier for me—I who had grown up torn between terror and the desire for my father's approval. I cleared my throat by way of apology and got up, returning the crown to the throne.

"Can we go back the way we came from?"

"I'm not sure," she replied. She stared at the dome. "This is a strange place. The runes are different... Zarojo-make, if I'm not mistaken. Cruder than what I'm used to."

"This doesn't seem very crude to me," I said, indicating the arches.

"Perhaps *crude* is a bad word. Inelegant? Superfluous?"

"Give me some credit. You're not talking to Rayyel here, priestess."

"The secret entrance, the wards, never mind the inconvenient trek up the west wing and *through* Warlord Yeshin's study... this was never meant to be a proper throne room for receiving one's subjects." Namra strode up to the nearest column to scratch the stone. She lifted her thumb to show me blue flecks of what appeared to be sand. "This entire place was *agan*-wrought. More than that—the spells are unsophisticated, scattered. Look at those two." She pointed at a rune, before drifting down to another.

"I'm a poor judge of these things, priestess, but they look the same."

"They are." She gave me the impatient look of someone who expected a better reaction, and then realized too late that I had a child's understanding of her world. She jabbed the second rune with her finger. "They cancel each other out."

"If you say so."

"This entire chamber was built as an exercise, such as mage-builders often engage in when they're in training."

"Mage-builders?"

"We call them that in Dageis. They're mages who go on to study with builders. Steeping a structure with spells is not as simple as making scribbles on the walls. You are, after all, imbuing inanimate matter with connections intended for the living, so that they can naturally channel the *agan* on their own. If you want the spells to hold up, to *last*, you begin from the ground up, right into the very foundations and material. That's how mage-builders often go on to create elaborate structures that can't be achieved by builders alone. They make airships, too, and roads and bridges that span impossible lengths, and..."

"I get the idea." I touched the wall. The surface was warm. I wasn't sure why, but for some reason, I got the impression that it *hummed*. Not a vibration, but a sound reminiscent of the rumble in my father's chest when he sang me lullabies. It felt alive. "So somebody was out here practicing their spell-making ability and created this rather...unsubtle place. Are the throne and the crown also *agan*-wrought?"

"No, my queen. Those are inert, and seem to have been crafted by a rather masterful—and *agan*-blind—artisan."

"Commissioned by my father, of course." I glanced at the ceiling. "And it almost feels like we're not in Oren-yaro anymore."

"That's impossible. I didn't detect a portal when I came through. We're still very much in the palace, my queen."

"Then how do you explain that?"

"My best guess is that it's a mirror."

"It doesn't look like any mirror I've seen."

"It's an *agan* mirror. They're common in Dageis. You can talk to people through them. This one looks like it functions as a window—we're looking at a very real place, even though we're not standing there."

I frowned. It sounded like something straight out of a book. I stared at the mountains again. The treetops—many leafless or touched with red and yellow overtones—swayed with the breeze. They looked familiar. I realized I'd been there before.

"Those are the mountains around the Sougen," I breathed. "To the north. We're looking north. There was less snow when I was out there, but that was summer. We're well into autumn now. Look at the leaves. This is—"

I fell silent as a large shadow passed over us from behind the glass. A dragon appeared, circling the treetops before it made a swift landing on an empty field. The air around it sparked, and I heard Namra gasp just as a flash erupted around us, knocking me off my feet.

I caught my fall and somehow managed to avoid hitting my head on anything. My ears were ringing as I crawled along the floor. I found a column and pulled myself up just as the flash disappeared. On the dome above, the dragon reared on its hind legs and roared. Saliva dripped down its fangs, followed by a short burst of flame. It flapped its wings and took flight. As it approached the sky, more sparks appeared beyond the clouds.

"You don't see it?" Namra called through the noise. She pointed at the sky over the mountains, not the dragon.

I felt the breath catch in my throat as I beheld the gash on the purplish-grey sky, a long, ragged hole that blinked like an eyeless socket. I didn't need her to tell me where the flash had come from. Something told me I was looking at the heart of Jin-Sayeng's problems.

"It's spreading," Namra continued.

She was right. The diseased-looking sky stopped along an edge, where small tendrils touched the untainted blue, like drops of ink spreading in a basin of clear water. "This is what Kaggawa was warning me about. He said the mages from Dageis had thrown up spells to try to seal the fabric, but the spells were weakening and *agan* was spilling from the other side over here."

"It's infected flesh," Namra continued. "Rotting, putrid. You don't just bandage a wound like that. You have to clean it first, cut out the parts that can't heal."

"Lamang's got a worthy apprentice in you. You should've been there to tell them. That rift...it wasn't there the last time. The tear in the fabric has grown that big in a matter of weeks."

"This spells chaos. The larger this rift gets, the more unstable the land under it will be. It can only grow worse from here."

"Kaggawa tried to explain it all to me. Layers and fabrics and...Dageis is involved, somehow?"

"It would be," Namra said. "The Empire of Dageis is involved with just about anything to do with the *agan* on this continent. In this case, it looks like they were until they didn't want to be."

"They don't care about Jin-Sayeng. None of the empires or larger nations do. Most don't even bother to learn the name of a feeble nation attempting to stand by itself." Staring at the rift made my eyes water. "That's the thing, isn't it? That's the thing creating mad dragons that burn our rice fields. Now it's turning our people into mindless monsters, as mad as the dragons themselves, and if we don't do anything it's going to engulf us all. Jin-Sayeng will become a living hell."

Namra didn't answer. She stared at the dome, unmoving, confusion dancing in her eyes.

"You're the trained mage," I whispered. "Tell me what we're supposed to do."

"My queen—"

"There has to be a way to repair it. There *has to*, Namra. Would the gods be so cruel as to destroy our land and our people this way?"

She shook her head. "This is beyond my comprehension. If we make a petition to Dageis, maybe they can send another team of mages down here to investigate. I'll have to go to my old school, beg my professors for an audience with a Dageian official, which would take months, if not years, if it happens at all. They've done it before. I don't see them wasting resources for yet another failed attempt." She didn't look overly thrilled with the idea.

"That will mean sending you away, too. I need you here."

"I'm glad you think so, my queen. At any rate, it's a reach. I don't have those sorts of connections. I studied, as best as a poor Jinsein immigrant could, and was sent on my way. I know no one of power in Dageis, and even if I did, as you yourself said—they won't care."

"Even if this will eventually spread to their lands, too?"

"They will watch it consume Jin-Sayeng before they lift a finger."

I swore under my breath before I turned back to the dome. "A mirror into the Sougen, right in the path of dragons," I murmured. "This view…" I suddenly recognized exactly what I was looking at. It was as if I was at the very top of the Anyus' dragon-tower, overlooking the ridge. If I squinted hard enough, I could make out the faint outline of the road below. "This room somehow connects Oren-yaro to Yu-yan. The Anyus have a new dragon-tower there."

Namra rubbed her chin. "For this to work at all would require another connection from the source, spells created on purpose to link that area to the mirror. Your father must have wanted a way to see out there. Why, though? I wasn't aware he was that interested in the west."

"He wasn't," I breathed. "If anything, he went on as if the west didn't matter. The Anyus lit their own funeral pyres during the War of the Wolves when they seized the Sougen for themselves. Let them deal with the angry landowners used to centuries of self-rule! Their concerns were nothing to him. But this— we're looking straight from their tower." I turned back to her. "Look at it, clear as the wretched day. Can you only see it from behind this glass? Is my son out there right now, sitting under this very tear, waiting to die with the rotting flesh of this land?"

"Do you need to sit down, my queen? You're shaking."

"He must have known everything. He wouldn't have built this chamber if he didn't. But why didn't he say anything? Why did he keep this all to himself, the knowledge of what is happening to our land? He could have brought the other warlords here to see…he could have told them to stop fighting and *look*. Look, gods be damned! How can you see that and not drop everything? How could you let your own home burn?"

"With all due respect, my queen…both Kaggawa and Anyu live next to this, and yet they still wage war on each other."

"They cannot agree on *how* to fix it, and so they fight. If those who live with the consequences can't find a way, what chance do the rest of us have?" I looked down at my shivering fingers. "Find us a way out of this place, priestess."

Namra walked away, and I slumped down on the floor near the edge of the throne, trying to work my mind around yet another of my father's untruths. I tried to tell myself it didn't matter. His plans died with him. I needed to focus on mopping up the mess, not getting to the root of it. My father had ambitions grander than I could've imagined—what more did I need to know?

The sky on the other side of the dome flashed again, filling the room with another burst of white light. I stared until the corners of my eyes watered, trying to make the vague shapes in the distance yield more than what I could see.

"Thanh is out there," I said as the light receded. "Gods forbid that he is frightened and alone. Let him be cared for, at least. Let him be alive."

"My queen." Namra didn't look up from examining the runes running along the base of the wall. It was almost as if she was ashamed she had no answers. Ashamed, or afraid.

"Kaggawa would have taken him straight to the Sougen. The region is the heart of his rebellion, after all, and he wants to use my son to legitimize whatever governance he means to start himself." I pressed my fingers over my forehead and stifled a groan. "Has your Dragonlord allowed you to tell me the council's thoughts? If they catch my boy, will they kill him?"

"Belfang is trying to find a way to compare your son's blood with that of one of Agos's trueborn sons. The runes that protect this room—Belfang knows of a similar technique to craft a spell using Prince Thanh as a base. If it responds to Agos's son, then it means they share the same blood."

"This is ridiculous. Why bring his children into this? Couldn't you use Rai?"

"He has managed to convince the council to openly allow the use of *agan* in this instance, my queen, but the Ikessars will not risk Dragonlord Rayyel."

"Yet they think it's all right to risk a young boy."

Namra got up. "My queen, this is not my will," she said.

"I know," I said. "I know it's not." I curled my hands into fists. "I need to learn to stop doing this. Blaming Rayyel. Blaming my father. It's all we do."

She pressed her lips together. "Ridiculous as you may find this charade to be, my queen, please see the bright side in all of this. If Thanh is proven to be Dragonlord Rayyel's son, then you may call on your warlords to rescue him from Dai Kaggawa. If he *isn't*—he will be safe from the warlords' fury. You said Kaggawa is interested in him because of *your* blood, not his father's. He remains a valuable hostage to the man regardless what happens here."

"Your idea of a *bright side* only deepens the pit inside my stomach." I took a deep breath. "And Princess Ryia...who knows if she'll even let it get that far? We know nothing plays out like we want it to and now she's here, breathing down my neck. She's got something up her sleeve—I just know it. Her discovery of this room alone will be enough for her to convince every other warlord to stick a spear through me. Any luck with that exit?"

Namra pointed at the throne. "The crown, my queen. Set it back the way you found it. I believe it's a key of some sort."

I frowned. The crown was already sitting there. But I suddenly remembered it was facing me when I first walked into the hall. I angled it forward. As soon as it was in the right spot, I felt my fingers tingle, followed by the sound of metal clicking together. Light—real light, not the artificial blue glow around us—touched the far end of the hall, chasing away the dream-like haze of our surroundings.

We returned to my father's study. I noticed my hands beginning that tired old trembling again and moved to tug the curtains half-open to distract myself. The sun was barely peeking past the hills in the distance, christening the rice terraces with a crown of gold. "Perhaps you should make your way back to your chambers," Namra suggested. "The rest of the castle will be up soon, if they aren't already."

"The guards don't even make their rounds through my hall," I said.

"Dragonlord Rayyel does," Namra replied. "He'll be worried if you're not there."

I didn't know how to respond to that information and turned to counting each of my steps along the chilly corridor. We met no servants along the way. At the door to my room, I turned to her. "You've been good to me, Namra," I said. "Even when I haven't been to you."

She bowed. "I will continue with my investigations, Beloved Queen, if that is your wish."

"We need to learn what else we can before Princess Ryia does. But if I can be honest with you, Namra... it's *what* we will learn that frightens me the most." I smiled. "I hate to disappoint you."

"I don't understand."

"Intentions mean nothing without competence. If you believe I am the rightful queen of this land, then surely you must have some confidence in my abilities. I am sorry to tell you that I am not my reputation." I showed her my hands. They were still shaking. For me to bare my neck to a woman I once considered an enemy... my father would have considered it the last straw, an insolence that dwarfed the rest. But the people who would serve me needed to know what I was—and what I wasn't. It was the first step to carving my own path.

She pressed my hands together and touched the back of them to her lips. Without another word, she turned and left me with my thoughts.

CHAPTER FIVE

THE TRIAL

ↆ ↑ ↆ ꙮ

I entered the room, wrinkling my nose at the draft. The air felt like the full embrace of winter, the sharp cold deepened even more by what I had just seen in my father's study. As I closed the door behind me, I noticed the windows were gone. Not open—*gone*, ripped out from the hinges. Khine sat on the edge of the sill, a tired expression on his face.

"You locked it," he said as soon as I appeared. He wrinkled his brow.

I glowered at him. "Did you by any chance miss our latest arrival?"

"One more princess to keep track of. I don't see—"

I came up to clamp a hand on his mouth. "You're too loud."

"I am?" he asked, voice muffled.

I pulled away with a sigh. "My mother-in-law, Princess Ryia. She has a reputation of her own, too, one that matched my father's. I wasn't sure I believed them until I saw her yesterday."

"That doesn't explain the windows. I thought the worst. You said you'd keep them unlocked in case you ever had to escape. I thought someone had gotten in, and—"

I stared at him. "Khine…"

Khine's face darkened. "Your burdens aren't all *yours* to bear, you know."

"That's not what I'm worried about," I said. I took a deep breath. "Her men killed Agos. I cannot lose you, too."

"You won't lose me."

"You cocky bastard. Agos could break a door down with one kick and look what they did to him."

"Agos died because he didn't realize what he was getting himself into," he said, his voice growing serious. "I told you that I don't blame him for his senti-ments, but he was ill-prepared for the repercussions. What did he expect? He was in the process of hacking the king to pieces!"

"Rai's not really—"

"Details," he told me. "You get lost in the details too much. Dragonlord. Warlord. Uncrowned king. I've been here seven days and haven't gone a single step without hearing an argument about something irrelevant. You've got other things to worry about, yet here you're all but ready to butcher each other over trivialities. Tali, look at me."

I faced him reluctantly.

"I'm the last person you should worry about. You need to keep your head afloat first."

"That's not going to happen if she uses you to hurt me."

He took a deep breath, eyes ablaze. I felt my skin prickle, as good a sign as any that he had overstayed his welcome.

"Please leave." I turned my head away. "I don't want her to catch you here."

"Is that what you really want?"

"Please, Khine."

He hung back another moment before he finally stepped away.

I felt my insides tighten. "Wait," I said, before he could disappear.

He glanced at me, the wind ruffling his hair.

I scrabbled for something to say. "You said something about arguments. What did you hear?"

"The officials are having a meeting in the great hall," Khine said. "At least, I assumed it was a meeting. They looked like Shang Azi thugs at the cusp of a brawl."

"And of course the bastards didn't even invite me. Typical. Let's go there."

"Are you sure?"

"A live show is better than reading Rai's boring transcripts."

He conceded, and we made our way to a ledge built directly adjacent to stained-glass windows overlooking the great hall. The glass itself was cracked, which allowed me to peer through and see what was happening below. The great hall was bursting with dozens of officials, all lined up in two rows along the walls. I recognized some, but there were also fresh faces, each bearing robes marked by the banner of their ruling lords and ladies. In the middle of the hall sat members of the council from the wider province of Oren-yaro, the capital city of Shirrokaru, and the Citadel, the mountain city where Ryia reigned.

The balance of power was always tipped in favour of the Oren-yaro and the Ikessar-influenced lands to the north, which made this the largest gathering of the highest-ranking bureaucrats in the land since my coronation. Larger, had the other warlords and their council representatives bothered to pay a visit—but only Warlord Ozo was in attendance, and he didn't look particularly thrilled to be there in the first place. He refused the tea a servant came to pour for him and sat with his legs crossed, his hands on his knees, glowering at Princess Ryia.

Her position in the circle was interesting. Because the Ikessars had sat on the Dragonthrone for so long, they didn't have a warlord in those lands. There was no need. Yet every official there accorded her the respect that would rightfully belong to someone of that stature, perhaps even more. She was a living legend, a tiger from the mists.

"I wonder how Lo Bahn is doing," I said. "If he's still alive."

Khine's expression grew pensive. "We're a whole sea away. Don't tell me you actually miss him."

"You call him Lord Han. He's not even truly a lord, if I understand Zarojo politics correctly. And yet he would look better down there than I ever could."

"You've lost me. Lo Bahn isn't half as pretty as you are."

"Khine…"

"I know," he said in a more sombre tone. "I just don't like it when you go down that road."

I turned my attention back to the meeting. I couldn't hear what they were saying at first, not with the muttering of the officials behind them. But Ryia eventually stood up, and the crowd fell silent. "I came here to see the shambles this nation has fallen into." She turned to Ozo and pointed at him. "The queen was missing for nearly a year and this man *knew*. You knew, you cantankerous old fart, and yet you did nothing! You didn't think the rest of Jin-Sayeng would care to be informed? A missing queen—"

"A missing Dragonlord," Ozo said easily. "Now, where have I heard that before? Between your son and your brother before him, you'd think you could be more lenient when it comes to other people's failings."

"What did Warlord Ozo's reports say about the queen's whereabouts?" she snarled.

An official cleared his throat and stood up, a scroll in his hands. "On the summer of the Fifth Year of Queen Talyien's reign, an emissary from the Jeinza clan was sent to Oren-yaro to discuss Sutan road conditions with the queen. Lord Ozo—"

"Warlord Ozo," the old man corrected with a frown.

"You were only a lord at the time," the official said, turning back to the scroll. "*Lord* Ozo aren dar Tasho," he continued, without missing a beat, "claimed the queen was spending a few weeks by the sea for her health."

Ryia laughed.

The official cleared his throat. "He met with the emissary and signed papers using the queen's seal."

Ozo gave a snort and turned away.

"In late winter of the Fifth Year of Queen Talyien's reign," the official continued, "it was confirmed that she had travelled to the Empire of Ziri-nar-Orxiaro the previous summer. *Lord* Ozo pretended to be ignorant of the entire thing and laid the blame solely on the queen's shoulders. '*Off doing her own thing, like always*,' he said. '*Pup never did know what was good for her.*' "

"Don't put words in my mouth," Ozo said.

"I am merely reading the transcript," the official pointed out. "Or are you denying what the scribes have written?"

Even from where I was, I could see Ozo's face turning red. "I wasn't aware I was the one on trial."

"We need to uncover everything from the beginning," Ryia said. "My greatest of apologies if it offends you, Warlord Ozo." Her words were anything but sincere—the sarcasm was so thick, you could scrape it off with a spoon.

"So you *do* recognize my authority."

"I recognize that you felt the need to intervene only *after* my son announced what has truly been happening in this region. Infidelity is a grievous sin, Warlord Ozo, particularly when an heir is involved. The queen proclaimed her son, this supposed grandson of mine, as Rayyel's trueborn. She presented him to court days after his birth, right in the very halls of the Dragon Palace. Is this not true?"

The officials nodded solemnly at each other.

"If it is found out that you assisted in hiding the truth from the rest of us..." She let the ensuing silence carry the weight of her message. The woman wielded power with more viciousness than I ever could.

"And now," an official beside her announced, "we have war in the west. A farmers' rebellion. Would commoners have had the audacity to rise against their warlord if the queen had been around to rule, as she should have? I can hardly blame them for taking advantage."

"Soon we'll have more of these rebellions, more commoners foolishly think-ing they have what it takes to rule," another official snapped. "And of course the Oren-yaro don't care. *Their* commoners are as frightened of them as bleating lambs. What did you expect from scum?"

Ozo's hand dropped to his sword. "You're *surrounded* by these Oren-yaro scum, boy. Learn to pay your respects before I give you a close shave!"

"Stand down, Warlord Ozo!"

"And you, Princess Ryia, if you weren't a woman…"

"Are you threatening me, Warlord Ozo? Why does my sex still your hand? Your own queen would eviscerate you given half the chance."

"I'm giving you advice!"

I pulled back from the window and made my way to a shadowed corner of the rooftop. There, I let out a soft sigh. "It's like being around children. Only you can at least distract children with sweets."

"This happens a lot, I'm guessing."

I prodded a loose roof tile with my foot. "Enough to drive anyone insane."

Khine smirked as he put the tile back into place. "I think I can understand why they don't want you to sit there until they come to a consensus. Which doesn't seem like it will happen any time soon."

"Does this amuse you?"

"I—"

"Because it shouldn't. Ridiculous as they appear, they have power, and power does not always belong to the wise. Ironic words, coming from someone who was queen. But you've seen how it really is. You're wrong about Agos. He knew what he was dealing with. We both grew up here. Khine—"

"I'll be careful," he said under his breath.

"It's not just that." I inclined my head towards the meeting below. "I told Rayyel I don't believe his mother has any intention of letting tomorrow's trial run unimpeded."

His brow furrowed. "Has she made threats?"

"Thinly veiled," I said. "But you can tell. She isn't here out of concern or the goodness of her heart. She's here to dig me a grave, and she means to push me into it herself." I glanced back at him. "Whatever happens tomorrow…when they proclaim Thanh as a bastard…"

"You're not sure, are you?"

"It doesn't *matter* what the truth is. Don't you see? She'll have made the arrangements. Ryia has no desire to prove my innocence. Do you think for even a moment that we could trust Belfang, of all people?"

"Of course not," Khine scoffed. "The man hasn't changed much since we were boys."

"Ryia's got her claws into him. I just know it. Rai thinks he can do this the right way—the *proper* way. He's still counting on Belfang's help. I think there's a limit to how much scheming that man's brain is capable of, but he's too stubborn to say otherwise. I know better now." I placed a hand on his arm. "When they declare my son a bastard—"

"We don't know that yet."

"*When* they do," I said firmly, "I need you to be on a horse heading to the Sougen. No matter what happens to me, find him before they do."

I think he wanted to argue that it wouldn't come to that, but I saw him hesitate. "I will," he finally said.

"Khine—"

He placed a hand on the back of my head while his other brushed my cheek. "I will," he repeated. "I promise." He suddenly looked like he wanted to kiss me, and I saw him stop himself again.

I gazed into his eyes. "This isn't about debt," I told him. "You know if I didn't want this, I'd say so."

"I know," he whispered. He kissed me then. *Third time*, I thought, before wondering why I was counting these. His lips were fire; I felt his tongue brush briefly over my teeth, felt myself sinking into his arms.

He said nothing when he pulled away, and not a word the entire time he walked me back to my room. At the window, I paused. I wanted to invite him in, to shut the world out for just a little while. Imagining what it would be like to drown out the darkness in his heat and scent made the ache to touch him again so tangible, my fingers trembled. But the memory of Ryia's threats burned even more than my desire, and I stood there, racked with indecision. I knew I couldn't. Not now, if ever at all. I also knew I loathed the idea of being the one to let go.

He broke the spell by allowing his gaze to wander over to the broken window. A shadow crossed his face and I realized why he had been hasty. They were locked. The curtains had been closed. He said he feared I was in danger, but was it more than that? Did he think I called for my husband and betrayed *him* somehow? Was I even in a position to betray him at all? Whatever it was,

I could tell from the look on his face that he was sorry—that he knew it was uncalled for.

We spent the next hour putting my windows back together, trying to find where we fit in the grating silence of it all.

The days passed at a snail's pace, filled with seemingly endless hours of politics and meetings and ironing out minuscule details that seemed to have nothing to do with what was at stake. The morning of the trial, I watched my hand-maidens' faces as they scrubbed me in the bathhouse. "Yayei," I said, out of nowhere. "And Ingging."

"My lady?" the one called Yayei asked.

"I'm reminding myself that I know who you are," I replied. I remembered when I didn't bother, because I was taught such concerns were beneath me. But so much had changed in a year, and I was determined I needed to begin setting myself apart from my forefathers. They may have taken the crown from me, but deep inside, I was still queen. I had always cared for my people—I just didn't know how to show it. It was time I learned how.

"But you do know," Ingging said with a laugh as she polished my fingernails, brushing dirt out with expert ease. She had been taking care of me since she was a girl and knew exactly what grooming habits I lacked.

"Sometimes, I wonder. I'm lady of this castle, and yet I know so very little of what's going on inside it."

"My lady," Yayei said. "It's not your duty to pay attention. We take care of you, and you take care of the land. It was ever how it should be."

"Although you *should* take better care of your hands," Ingging added. "They've been getting worse over the years. Callused fingers are so unseemly for a queen."

"I'm not queen anymore," I reminded her.

"Callused fingers are unseemly for *any* lady," Ingging corrected, shaking her head at me. "Have you been digging through the mountain with your bare hands? Lord Rayyel's fingers look far lovelier."

"Of course they would," I grumbled. "His hair's better, too."

Yayei pinched my drab locks in agreement.

"How are you doing, Beloved Princess?" Ingging asked, growing serious.

"Well enough." I stared at the water.

"We didn't know how to talk to you after…after everything that had happened." Ingging snipped off a hangnail before handing me a towel. "We were all in mourning, Beloved Princess. Our poor Agos…"

"Ingging—" Yayei warned.

The older handmaid made a sound in the back of her throat. "You didn't grow up here. Both of them did. It doesn't matter what cruel words they throw about outside of this castle, what those strangers think of the princess. We take care of our own. Princess…" She took my hand again, this time to press it between her palms. "We saw you at Agos's funeral the other morning. Between everything that had happened and Lord Ozo's command to keep out of it, we didn't know what to believe anymore."

"Ozo told everyone to keep away. To keep me in the Zarojo Empire," I said.

Ingging looked embarrassed. "He assured us your soldiers would take care of you."

"But it's not as if you were alone," Yayei broke in. "You found Lord Rayyel, didn't you?"

"I did. And he's the same as he ever was."

She gave me a knowing smile. "His attendants say he refuses to let them serve him. A shame—Jing's missed him. He was looking forward to his return the most."

"Poor Jing," I said, shaking my head. "Still, Rai keeps himself relatively neat these days."

"He must have learned how to brush his hair himself." Yayei cleared her throat. "And what about the young foreign man who speaks our language so well, and goes around asking about you every chance he gets?"

I felt myself grow serious. "A liability."

"Such a lovely liability. Have you—"

Ingging clicked her tongue. "That's enough, Yayei. They're waiting for her."

We left the bathhouse and returned to the east wing and my chambers. I stood over the edge of my mattress and for the first time in over a year allowed myself to get dressed by others. As Ingging slid the sleeves over my shoulders and tightened the belt around my waist, I watched the wind chimes hanging beneath the eaves outside and thought about Khine. If my handmaidens saw it, who else did?

"There," Ingging said, breaking my thoughts as she took a step back to view her masterpiece. "That's lovely, my dear. You do clean up so well. Look at you."

She held up a mirror. The flash from the jewellery threatened to blind me. Golden earrings, so delicately wrought they looked like lace, streamed down to my shoulders. I wore a golden necklace with a plate beaten with a pattern unique to the Orenar clan, as well as plain gold bracelets on both my wrists. Even my red dress was threaded with gold, all along the robes and the sleeves that were cut short near my elbows. The only thing missing was the crown. It had been replaced with a corded golden rope that kept the hair out of my face. My head felt bare, made all the more obvious because they didn't scrimp on all the other ornaments.

"If only you had tattoos..." Ingging continued, touching my unmarked arms. "But the Ikessars wouldn't hear of it. They thought it made us look like savages."

"Could you imagine Rayyel with tattoos?" I asked. "I'm surprised my father didn't fight them for it."

"He had to pick his battles. Still, you do not look half bad. You almost look presentable," she added, with a smirk.

Yayei cocked her head and made a sound. "They'll ask where we've been keeping this one, and what happened to the stray dog we called princess—"

"Hush," Ingging chided. But I could see something in her eyes, a reflection of why it seemed so easy for her to talk to me now. I was a child to her once more, the same one she used to wrangle into frilly skirts—not the precious queen upon whose shoulders rested the fate of the nation. She couldn't ruin me any more than I'd already ruined myself.

"Did you know my mother?" I suddenly asked.

Ingging didn't even look surprised. She finished patting my dress. "She was such a beautiful girl."

Girl. She said it deliberately.

"What was her name?" I asked.

This time, she kept her mouth shut. I suspected Yeshin had forbidden them to speak of her in my presence. I wondered how much of my father remained hovering over us all.

"We didn't just lose lives in the war," Ingging finally said. "We lost homes. Lands. Fields. Entire families of loved ones who decided it was better to seek peace and security elsewhere. And so many of us, your mother included, lost their innocence. She came here against her mother's will thinking she would get to meet a prince, and instead..."

"I thought my father abducted her."

"He might as well have. He courted her openly. She cherished the flattery like you wouldn't believe. The letters, the gifts...not strange, I suppose, for her age."

"They said she was very young."

"The rumours exaggerated her age, but she was young enough. Young enough to think she knew better."

"Did she know...what he was?"

"She was warned that he had been her own mother's husband, that *she* fled him for a reason, but she wouldn't believe anyone. She wouldn't believe *me*. I went with her all the way out here hoping I could get her to change her mind, but even after she saw what she was getting, she decided to follow through. You and her are alike in that. Stubborn." Ingging passed me a wistful smile.

"I didn't know you were her friend."

"I still am."

I turned to her in confusion.

"Come," Ingging said, tugging my sleeves.

I rose to follow her. We walked in silence, a handmaid on each side. Back on the grounds and towards the main doors of the great hall, under the arches on the stone path, I stopped. Khine stood near the steps. His eyes fell on me, but he didn't crack his usual smile. We hadn't talked since that morning on the rooftop. Between the sudden flurry of officials and my own mother-in-law's presence in the castle, I could argue that I just didn't have the opportunity. But the truth was I was deliberately avoiding him. With Ryia's snakes around, the last thing I needed was to be looking longingly at anyone. I glanced away before realizing he was approaching me.

Startled, my handmaidens stepped aside to give him room. Khine bowed and took my hand.

"Beloved Queen," he said in that deeply accented Jinan. "May the gods favour you today."

"You are too kind, Master Lamang," I replied smoothly.

He pressed the back of my hand to his lips before he looked up.

"You are..." he began, gazing into my eyes.

I pulled away, flushed, and returned to my handmaidens, every step echoing with my beating heart.

An Ikessar retainer announced my arrival with about as much enthusiasm as a servant informing his master that his least favourite dog has been found at last. I glared at the man as I walked past him, wishing they'd let me carry a sword. The council didn't think it was wise for me to carry a weapon, which was hilarious given everyone else had, at the very least, a ceremonial blade shoved through their gold-threaded belts. It wasn't as if I owned anything like my father's sword, one that had cut its way through Jin-Sayeng's history as easily as a knife through paper.

"Does she always smile to herself like that?" Ryia asked, her voice—for all its natural softness—stinging like a whip.

I gazed at her in stunned silence. She had directed her question to my husband, who was sitting cross-legged on a cushion beside her, on the dais where my throne had once stood. It had been removed for the occasion, to give room for all the officials. She didn't turn to greet me, even when I strode close enough that I could smell the perfume on her skin.

Rayyel ignored her question with his characteristic blank-faced expression. It gave me a measure of satisfaction when he greeted me with more warmth. "My lady," he said.

I said nothing to him and turned towards Princess Ryia, reaching for her hand to press it on my forehead. They may have chained Yeshin's bitch pup, but I still carried every trick my father had ever taught me. Everyone would have seen how I ignored my husband and deferred to Ryia first. Every single man and woman in the great hall grew silent. All eyes fell on her.

Jinsein politics worked in harmony with Jinsein decorum. Respect for elders is always appreciated, no matter what the situation or the context. Respect for one's matriarchs is upheld to the point that a warlord's grandmother could walk into a meeting and drag him out by his ear, and no one would think twice about it. They would berate him in private, perhaps, for bringing the old woman along in the first place, but one didn't question her right to punish her grandson as she saw fit. And while loyalty to your warlord was praiseworthy, loyalty to clan, to family, was universally understood by royal and commoner alike.

So what people saw in that moment was a daughter-in-law accepting her mother-in-law publicly for the first time. An appeasement coming from *me*, when everyone knew she was the one who failed to appear at my wedding, she who wouldn't recognize me or my son. They all watched, waiting to see how she would react, if she would accept the gesture.

Ryia retracted her hand with a quick incline of her head. From the swiftness of it, I could tell she knew what I was doing. It didn't seem like she cared. "Talyien aren dar Orenar," she said, dropping the words like they were steel knives. "Your father named you in defiance of me. I came here with my son for your betrothal, believing Yeshin's intentions pure. And then he announced your name in front of the warlords, the first time I ever heard of it. Talyien. Named for Warlord Tal, hero of the Oren-yaro, the man your people use as an example of why the Ikessar Dragonlords should've never been given this land."

I would have expected such directness from an Oren-yaro—not from an Ikessar. "Have I offended you, Beloved Princess?" I asked. I glanced at the crowd, enjoying the effect of this elaborate show. "Perhaps I should excuse myself. If I have displeased you in any way—"

"You've a golden tongue, Yeshin's child," Ryia replied. "So like him. A ruthless murderer on one hand, a charming courtier on the other. You look surprised. You think everyone is as easily fooled by this show as my gullible son? You are *too* much like your false-faced father."

"One thing at a time, Beloved Princess," Rai spoke up, though his voice remained subdued. It was clear that he didn't want to confront her. "This trial concerns Prince Thanh. We will worry about the rest later." He didn't look at me now, either.

An official came to lead me to a corner of the great room. It was a significant distance from the rest of them, as if they were afraid that I was capable of decapitating someone with my bare hands. Well—maybe it was a good day to find out they weren't wrong. I sank into the cushion, imagining myself adrift in a sea of sharks. I reminded myself to be careful. One slip, and then who would pay the price? I didn't want to find out.

The trial began. I had every intention of listening to all the details, to commit to my memories the reaction of all the members of the council the way I used to in all my years in this court as queen. Who remained sincere, sympathetic to my cause? Which ones were treacherous bastards? Such insight was valuable for a ruler. The wisest know how to play the game even with the odds stacked against them.

But I didn't.

Instead, I looked at Rai, at my husband and how he listened stern-faced, straight as an arrow, to the accusations *he* himself had thrown out to draw attention from me. Or so he claimed. I tried to remember how I had once loved him so much that I would've thrown myself into the ocean for him. Why? Because I thought my father had told me to. His command. Marry your prince. Become queen. He had drilled them into me as far back as my earliest memories. Marry your prince. Become queen. Bring peace to the land. *I did it all, and more.*

Ears ringing, the crowd seemed to fall away, the garbled arguments receding to the back of my mind. A memory surfaced. I was chasing a puppy down the hall, hoping to catch it before it piddled on the imported Zarojo rugs.

"Tali."

My father's voice. I hurled myself after the pup with renewed speed, and it dashed underneath the stairs, disappearing into the shadows. I turned around. My father had crossed the room and was now sitting on the bottom of the dais, his elbow on his knee.

"Come to me, my heart."

Like a chastised pup myself, I slithered towards him, flooded with shame. I really wasn't supposed to be letting the dogs loose from the kennels in the first place. I sat beside him. He stared at me for a moment before reaching out to pick me up and place me on his lap.

"How old are you now?" he asked. "Remind an old man."

"Five," I said, holding out the exact number of fingers.

He chuckled. "Only yesterday you could fit in the crook of my arm."

"Soon I can ride Whitewind!"

"If she's still around by then. I'm afraid the old thing won't last very long."

"She rode with you to war, didn't she, Papa? Did she fight off the enemy, too, like a true wolf of Oren-yaro?"

"Even if she *is* just a horse." Yeshin gave a snort before gazing down at me thoughtfully. "I may not live long enough to see you ride any other horses, either. Or rule as queen."

"Why not, Papa?"

He clicked his tongue. "I'm old, too, child."

"You're not old."

"You don't say?"

I reached up to squeeze his cheeks and look into his eyes. They were dark, as dark as mine, though the whites were streaked with blood and the edges rimmed with sagging yellowed flesh. But the fire in them was unmistakable. "Well," I told him, wrinkling my nose. "Not *that* old."

"But what I would give to see that day." He embraced me, his hand on my head as he pressed me to his chest. "What I would give to see the land bow to you, Ikessars and all. You are the Dragonlord we've all been waiting for."

I opened my eyes to flickering shadows and solemn figures, and the bare stone walls of the hall—no tapestries for this occasion, none that would suggest disrespect to the Ikessar clan. It was Rayyel's turn to talk. He cleared his throat and straightened his robe before he got to his feet. "We have presented the evidence to the council," he began. "Lady Talyien's relationship with her guardsman Agos was discovered by the innkeeper himself, information that he later relayed to his family. It has been verified that Lady Talyien was indeed in town the night she broke her vows."

For some curious reason, the words didn't seem to affect me. Nor did they elicit the usual response in my head: *You broke yours, too, you bastard.* In light of everything, they were just words now, nothing more. I wondered at how Rayyel could say them so effortlessly. If I didn't know better—that is, if I didn't know that he was the kind of man who forced his emotions behind a steel cage—I would've sworn he was manipulating the crowd. It was just the sort of thing Yeshin would've loved.

You were wrong about him, too, old man, I found myself thinking. *He could have made a good king—if you had chosen to support him instead of continuing to pit us against each other. You talk about peace and prosperity, but all that ever really mattered were your petty grudges.* All I had to do was look at Princess Ryia to know how deep those wounds still ran. My father had killed her sisters, while her brother had caused my own brothers' deaths. An endless circle of hate, like a dog snapping after its own tail. We never stood a chance.

Another announcement, this time from a servant standing by the door. I sat up as Belfang strode in, dragging a small boy across the floor. I bolted from my seat as I recognized Agos's eldest son. "This is a step too far, council!" I called. "Have we sunk so deep into the mire that we would hurt a child to prove a point?"

"You *would* protest," Ryia remarked, her voice echoing through the hall. "Were you not aware that silence best proves your case here, Lady Talyien?" The officials murmured in agreement.

She looked at me with the same sort of expression a cat gives a mouse before it dashes out of its hole. I realized *I* was the very reason that Princess Ryia stayed in the Citadel all these years. Her absence from court threw doubt on my capabilities; if she could not be seen even just acknowledging me, then I must be the one lacking. And now with my name tarnished beyond repair, she was certain everything would fall into their favour. The Ikessars could seize control of the nation once again. I had made enough mistakes—all I needed was one more. I bristled. She may have been confident in my defeat, but did she really think I would roll over and wag my tail for her?

"The gods can spit on this charade for all I care. If you think I'm going to sit here and watch you hurt an innocent child, then you *really* must've forgotten whose daughter I am. Since you people wouldn't let me have a sword, how would you feel about a fist in your gullet?"

In the shocked silence that followed, I heard Ozo begin to laugh.

"My lady," Rai said. "Please sit down."

"I'm done with this," I replied. "You decrepits have stretched my patience thin." I approached Belfang, who seemed to recall the circumstances around the last time we had seen each other in the Shimesu temple in Phurywa. He shrunk back, revealing a small sword in his hand.

Blinding fury replaced my irritation. I grabbed the boy, wrenching Belfang's hand loose from his wrist. I reached for the sword. Only then did I recognize it as Thanh's—the same sword he received as a present on his last nameday. There was caked blood on the bottom edge.

"Lady Talyien," Belfang said, holding the sword as far away from me as possible. "A moment of patience. It took me days to locate something of your son's that we could use for the spell."

"That blood..." I began.

"A training accident just a few days before. They assured me at the barracks."

"Since when did he start training?"

"I can answer that for you, Lady Talyien," Ozo said, coming up towards the center of the hall. "Your boy had yet to learn how to hold a blade. We needed to start somewhere. I can confirm the blood is his."

"Why would you even care about Thanh? You took advantage of this whole thing to seize Oren-yaro from us!"

"He's your father's grandchild," Ozo said. "I needed to do right by him, no matter what his mother has done. But now we're here. Listen to the Ikessar brat. Hand the boy over and let's finish this before the night is out."

"I've seen what Belfang can do to his victims," I said. "Zarojo witchcraft, you would've all called it once. I can understand the Ikessars accepting it. *You*, Lord Ozo? I didn't realize the Oren-yaro have sunk so low."

It was a trap, meant to force Ozo to reveal everything, and he knew it. His lips turned upwards. But he didn't fall for it. Yeshin's general against Yeshin's daughter—we were both trained by the man far too well. While I was waiting for his reply, he turned and jabbed a knife right above the boy's elbow. Agos's son screamed. "Stop crying, you snot-nosed little shit," Ozo snarled, holding the bleeding arm up towards Belfang while blood gathered between his fingers. The priest wiped it all up with a piece of cloth. It took half a second, and then Ozo flung the boy back towards me. I placed my arms around him as Belfang began to draw the runes for the spell, with Thanh's sword in one hand and the blood-soaked cloth in the other.

The boy's sobs died down as he stared at his wound with fascination. I could see Agos's stamp on him, plain as day—the eyes, the forehead, the lips. "What's your name?" I whispered.

"Kisig," he croaked out. "Are they going to kill me?"

"Not unless they kill me first," I reassured him.

He gave a soft smile. Agos's, too, without a shadow of a doubt. Strange how well we leave these ghosts of ourselves in our children. How much of myself had I unwittingly foisted on Thanh? And my father? How much of *him* did I still carry? I was once convinced I was nothing like my father—the very implication was an insult to my ears. Now I wasn't sure. Something about Ryia's accusations lingered like a dead rat's stench. There was one thing I knew for sure: The child in my arms was nothing like my own.

Belfang dropped the cloth into the spell on the floor he'd created. I glanced behind me and watched as it burst into flames. I knew what he was going to say before he opened his mouth.

"The ward didn't respond. The boy does not share the prince's blood."

There was an outcry, followed by others, until half of the crowd was arguing and the other half was clamouring for order.

I stopped listening to them as I held the boy in the same spot where I cradled his dead father seven days before. Thanh was Rayyel's. Somewhere deep inside, before those events in Ziri-nar-Orxiaro upended my world, before he left us, I always knew.

So why were there tears in my eyes?

CHAPTER SIX

HARD TRUTHS

ㄒㅈ⑩

I didn't know how long I knelt there. My legs felt like a thousand ants gnawed on them, and the boy was looking at me in concern as he wondered, perhaps, if I'd grown as mad as the rest of that court. I could feel the breeze on my arms, the sweat under my nose. Behind the hollow silence, sandals clicked on wooden floors and wind chimes tinkled between the susurration of souls convinced they were going to be rid of me.

"Beloved Queen."

The words were dropped in unison. They must've come to yet another consensus while my back was turned. So quick on their heels, this council. Well—a good majority of them represented the Ikessars. I supposed they had to save face somehow.

"Queen again," I said bitterly, wiping my face. "Bastards, the whole lot of you." I slowly got up, my joints creaking. I felt like I had aged twenty years. "Someone come here and take this child back to his mother. Where is Namra?"

"My queen." The priestess pushed past the officials, reaching for Kisig's hand.

"Make sure the fool priest didn't curse him."

"It doesn't work that way, my queen. But yes—we will make sure the boy is unharmed."

"Get Khine to look at the wound. We've done too much to that family. Give the boy and his mother everything they need to get the hell out of here. *Everything*, Namra."

She bowed.

I turned to face the court as queen for the first time in months. Anger bubbled beneath the surface of my skin. I wanted them all executed, tortured, sent away in pieces inside little barrels. Did the Zarojo pay good money for pickled councillors—the doubting, traitorous, easily bribed kind?

I heard footsteps. Ryia walked towards me, sword drawn. It trailed along the ground, cutting a long line through the soil. There was murder in her eyes. With no way to defend myself, I was at her mercy. Perhaps I could overpower the old woman, but I knew nothing about her prowess with the sword. She'd survived my father. An enemy like that can't be taken lightly.

"Beloved Princess!" Rayyel called.

She stopped—not, I imagined, because her son asked her to, but because it gave her satisfaction to see me unnerved. "Infidelity is still a sin," she said. "The gods demand penance."

I met her gaze. "Do you want a duel?"

"You've barely just gotten your crown back, Queen Talyien. Is your first act to kill me? Don't think Jin-Sayeng doesn't know how the Oren-yaro prefer to rule." The bitch was baiting me.

"Bite me," I snarled, refusing the challenge. I turned to Ozo, and she let me walk past her towards him. He froze for a moment before dropping to his knees, saving me the trouble of having to order soldiers to do it for him. I wasn't sure if they'd obey me, anyway. "Send out a search party to find Kaggawa and Thanh."

"I already have, Beloved Queen," he replied. His eyes remained downcast.

"Presumptuous son of a bitch. Any reports?"

"Sources believe he has taken the prince straight to the Sougen. There are rebels making their rounds. They've made it difficult to get clear information. We've lost at least two scouts. I need time to hear back from the other riders."

"At least you're not fully incompetent. Remember to drag my throne back here yourself before you vacate Oka Shto." I turned back to the other officials. "Are we finished with this show? Don't you all have families waiting for you? Lands to rule? Rooster fights to bet on?"

Ryia began to clap her hands. "Well done, Queen Talyien," she said. "Well done. You truly are your father's daughter."

Some of the officials grumbled in agreement, but I could barely discern it. The energy in the great hall had changed—I could tell they wanted to leave before I decided to retaliate. I was willing to bet that most would be gone from Oren-yaro by nightfall.

The only exception was Rai. He remained quiet, staring at the ceiling, arms folded over his belly—still looking every bit like the scholar of our youth. To the untrained eye, he looked almost calm, unaffected by what had just transpired. I knew better.

"Go back to whatever hell spawned all of you," I told everyone that remained in the hall. "I will speak with Lord Rayyel alone."

"Dragonlord Rayyel," Ryia corrected. "Your anger makes you forget your manners."

"*Lord* Rayyel," I repeated. "And he will remain so until he gets that crown formally placed on his head. I invite you to make the arrangements. We had dancers at the one he missed—let's have jugglers next time. Or how about flowers? I hear you Ikessars are fond of pretty things."

She smiled. "You proved your bastard has no relation to the boy. Good. But that is *one* guardsman, and rumour has it you've had many."

"Then get the priest to check again. I'm sure my dear husband won't be opposed to what you just put a little boy through."

Rai heard and got up.

"Not one step," Ryia snapped. Rai stopped in his tracks.

"There was only one accusation, and it's been disproven," Ozo broke in. "If there are more…"

"I will find more," Ryia said.

Belfang approached us, hands held out. "I'm afraid we're all out of your son's blood. The spell consumed all of it."

"That settles the matter," I said.

"It settles nothing," Ryia replied. "This is a hollow victory. How long do you think the nation will support a loose, amoral leader?"

"Perhaps long enough to see me dance on your grave." From the corner of my eyes, I could see Oren-yaro soldiers entering the hall to displace the Ikessar guards.

There was a short period of silence. And then Ryia smiled—a cold smile, one that seemed to affix itself permanently to her face. "Talk to him then," she said. "He is *your* husband, after all. The love of your life. Isn't that right? You've no others skulking about the castle grounds?"

I returned the smile, though I could feel myself grow numb at her words. "Search away, Princess Ryia. I don't know what you think you'll find, but *do* let me know when you do. It'll be nice to be with a man again. Your son *was* gone for years. Isn't neglect of duty grounds for absolving a marriage? I'm sure we can find priests who will agree."

I felt the satisfaction of seeing her look like she wanted to rip my throat with her teeth. Without waiting to see what she had to say, I gestured at Rai, who bowed to his mother before he followed me.

"You shouldn't antagonize her," Rai said as soon as we reached the safety of my father's study.

I slumped down into my father's chair. "I know she's your mother..." I started.

Rai sighed. "Believe me, Talyien, that is not what I'm concerned about." He turned towards the window. The sun was sinking on the horizon. He stroked the curtains, a thoughtful expression drifting over his face. "Thanh is...my son, after all."

I gave a weak smile. "Didn't you hear Ozo? The boy cut himself on his sword the first day of training."

"That's..."

"He sure as hell didn't get it from me. I'm not sure how, either. The damn thing was dulled. I was afraid he would drop it on his toe. *Your* son." I took a deep breath. "Through and through."

Rai didn't reply. There was sorrow on his face, like a man from whom a burden had been lifted only to find out there was more to be piled on. The crack on his own facade. He must have thought a stiff front was all he needed to solve this problem. That once one matter was settled, everything else would fall into place.

I turned my attention to other things. "How do we get rid of your mother? She can't stay here a moment longer. I'm surprised she hasn't found this study yet."

"Namra placed spells on the door, I believe. Her people would've missed it if they didn't know what they were looking for."

"She's a complication, and the last thing we need is a complication."

"Are you suggesting I have my own mother assassinated?"

"If I asked, would you do it?"

He looked confused.

"I'm jesting," I said, because the thought was tempting. "Tell her to go home."

"If it were only that easy. She won't listen to me. Why would she?" He tightened his jaw. "She hates...everything that had to do with your father.

She didn't think he'd ever attempt to negotiate a treaty, much less consider a betrothal in the first place."

"She said *Kaggawa* had convinced her."

"Sume Kaggawa," Rai said. "A close friend of hers, at least for a time."

"Where is she now?"

He clasped his hands behind his back and paced along the wall. "Who knows? She has family outside of Jin-Sayeng. She could be anywhere."

"If your mother listened to her counsel, maybe she's not entirely hopeless. Maybe we can convince Princess Ryia I'm not the enemy here."

"She agreed to Kaggawa's resolution, but they didn't part on the best of terms. I don't even know if she's still alive." Rai took a deep breath. "Anyway, I've tried that already. I begged my mother for years to see you as you are and not as Yeshin's child. But it was like talking to a wall."

"Ah. A family trait, I see."

He ignored the jibe, taking one hesitant step forward. "My lady," he began. He swallowed. "I promised you back in the empire that once we put this matter to rest we could…start anew. We can guide this land as our right, no matter what our parents may have truly wanted."

Rai looked at the ground as he spoke. I realized they weren't easy words for him to say. It is frightening how perspective can change once all the emotion has been taken out—drain the pus out of a wound and it hurts less, can start healing. Or so one would think. I was standing exactly where I wanted to be all those years ago, after he first left. He was here, we were together. He now knew the kind of gaping hole he left behind when he walked away. I felt that if I wanted to ask him to do anything now—apologize, grovel, admit to every single wrong he had done to me and my son over the years—he would, without question. I could even ask for his death like an aggrieved Zarojo. Except I would rather be anywhere but there. I didn't want to hear him say these words.

I didn't want to heal.

Why are the heroes in stories always kings and queens, princesses and princes, lords and ladies? Once in a while, a peasant makes their way to the books, but it is always someone who climbs to the top, who turns the tide because of the power of their wits or strength or charm. Why do we not care for the troubles of a lowly housewife or butcher or a farmer unless they leave their home to save their land from dragons? If I do not write of Mei Lamang and her sacrifice, who would remember her once her children had passed?

It is the desire for illusion that sustains us. We want to believe there is a happily-ever-after and it involves those who cannot possibly be as we are. And so if we cannot be heroes... if we feel we cannot make a difference or make our words carry weight... we create them—idols we praise to the highest heavens, sparkling figures who can do no wrong. We hold them as examples of what we could never be and use them to explain away our own deficiencies, tell the world we won't bother because of what we are not. We create heroes so we never have to try ourselves.

Or at least that was how Khine explained it to me after I asked him why a woman in my position had difficulties garnering sympathy. He said it is simply because people do not want to believe someone like me can have the same problems they have. I was queen: blessed, chosen, anointed. That I could get lonely, or make mistakes, or want something as simple as the kind of love they speak of in the stories—one fierce and true and unending—was unimaginable for people who live with suffering every day. "Hunger," he told me with gravity, "can be all it takes to erase compassion. It isn't your fault, but you cannot expect others to offer sympathy when their own lives are fraught with the pain you've never felt in yours. Hunger, helplessness, the soul-crushing realization that you are but a speck of dust in the grand scheme of things. You are supposed to be infallible. It is supposed to offer comfort in a world where most have nothing."

I know the complications of my life do not belong in history books. There will be a chapter outlining my failures, and then another where they will talk of a crisis averted and how the Ikessar blood remained the center of the king-dom, this wretched nation of Jin-Sayeng where no one ever learns. And they will discuss, at length, the tumultuous relationship between the Ikessar and the Orenar, because nothing ever changes, does it? We want those patterns. We want heroes and villains, we want explanations, we want conclusions, we want to make sense of the turmoil even when the only way to do that is to lie through your teeth. Delineations do not exist in the real world. I wonder what part they would say I played. I know most would call me the villain—many already do. Heroes are allowed to make mistakes and grow; villains can only survive what they've already done.

But I was finished with illusions. I had lived with the pain for so long that I was afraid of what I would be without it. If Rai had never left, I would still be as I was, blindly following the path my father had set for me. Without the pain, I wouldn't have learned that more could lie beyond. I thought of Khine staring back at me from the window he had torn apart. Lovers are easy to find for some-one in my position, but this had nothing to do with that.

"I loved you against my father's will, did you know?" I whispered, drifting to the corner, where the oppressing shadows of the study all but cloaked me.

Rai stared back in silence.

"I didn't, either," I continued. "Not back then. He always spoke in layers. *You will marry that boy and you will try to love him. You may not want to.* Those were his words. *Try.* I used to wonder why he would say it that way. Why the uncertainty? He knew I would obey him. In those days, all he ever needed to do was ask, and I would...without question..."

The edges of his mouth twitched.

I swallowed. This newfound honesty with my subjects, with him, did not come easily. But I forced myself to continue. "Then I remembered recently that one of your mother's representatives was there that day. Was he sending me a message? Trying to tell me something because he was losing time? Back when he was stronger, he would always tell me *never* to bow to my prince—I was an Orenar first and could never be an Ikessar. The fate of the nation, the burden of its rule, rested on me alone. I didn't...understand. But I managed to love you. I didn't have to try very hard. What girl wouldn't fall in love with her prince when it was someone like you?

"Seeing you with Chiha had made me realize how little I knew of the world, that love wasn't what I thought it was or what I wanted it to be. I married you with every intention of treating love as duty. *Duty* I knew, even if I couldn't make you see me the way you saw Chiha. I told myself I could love you even if...even if I couldn't make you love me."

I fell silent. The Rayyel of my youth, the husband from my memories, would have dismissed what I'd just said. He would have told me to control my emo-tions before pointing out that the fate of the nation mattered more than what I felt about our arrangement. But if I had changed over the years, so had he. His expression was marred with rare self-reflection.

"We are still married," I said, when I realized he was at a loss for words. "There is nothing I can do about that. But whatever I was drawing from in the years we were together and the years we were apart...it's all empty now. I know what you thought you did for us. I know you felt I would just accept your explanations because they made sense to you. But I am *not* an Ikessar. I can't sit in some cave for three years and pretend I'm made of stone."

"I never—" he began.

"You did," I said. "You thought I could harden my heart just as easily as you harden yours. That I could listen to you throw words like *bastard* and threaten my son—our son, Rai, *our* son, like I've told you a thousand times!—and I would forgive you as soon as you dropped it. You thought you alone had the right to make decisions for this family. Did you think you could decide to tarnish our names and once it's all over I would come running to you with open arms? I know this is the life we lead, these lies, this trickery, using each other all while pretending it's for the best. But I would have preferred you showed your hand, even if it damned our lives. Politics should have never come between us. If you loved me, you should have screamed it from one corner of the nation to the next. You should have left me with no doubts. You should have fought for us, damn you.

"And maybe I'm to blame—maybe I built this image of myself so well you thought the things you did couldn't possibly break Yeshin's daughter. You're right about one thing: *You* didn't break me. But the woman who waited for you for five years is already dead. I don't know when she died. I just know that I can't do this anymore. I am still here for Jin-Sayeng. I am still here because I am her queen and I swore an oath when I was crowned, but…" I took a deep breath.

His face was chalk white. "But you don't love me anymore." He spoke as if he was trying to avoid walking into a pit. As if he had never considered the possibility before and now that he was looking right at it, he didn't know how to cope.

"How can love survive in our world? These are not fertile grounds we could sow seeds on. That Thanh came out of it at all still feels like a gift from the gods."

He placed his hand on my arm. I stared at his smooth fingers, at the shade of his skin, a touch paler than mine. "Can you learn once more?" he asked. "Given time? If…if I try hard enough? My wife…"

No, I wanted to say, hating the familiar twinge that came from hearing those last two words. *Your wife, Rai? Yours? But when was I ever yours? You take care of what is yours. You cherish it until the day you die.* I felt a lump in my throat, not knowing what to do with my anger. I didn't know what I expected after my outburst. Anger, in return. Indifference. Not sincerity. Gods. I thought I knew him. Then again, I thought I knew myself, too. Shards of glass remained where our life used to be, and I didn't know what to do with them.

"Because I can try to make it up," Rai continued. He curled his hand into a fist and placed it over his chest. "To you and Thanh. I know I have missed much. My son was still so little when I left. I thought I had all the time in the world, and now—now he's grown. It's not too late, is it?"

I pressed my lips together and avoided looking into his eyes. I had my answer already, but I didn't want to be cruel. "We have to find him first."

I went to bed alone. Rayyel didn't press the issue about our marriage arrangements, and I felt guilt over how relieved that made me feel. I woke up the next morning before dawn and got ready before my handmaids came for me. It felt good to be able to walk out of my own quarters without being accosted by Ikessars, to see Oren-yaro guards in the halls once more. They even saluted as I passed. If I didn't know any better, I could pretend everything that had happened was a nightmare. But was it right to want to go back to sleep? To prefer the nightmare over what else awaited?

My feet took me to the kitchens. If anyone saw me, I could claim I needed a drink of water. Just as I expected, Khine was already awake. Even after months on the road, I still recalled his daily routine from the time I stayed with him in Anzhao. He told me he liked getting up early to spend time with his own thoughts before it became too noisy to hear them. It was a habit he had picked up living in such close quarters with three siblings.

He was behind the curtains when I came in. I settled into the bench and listened to the sound of him getting the fire started—the rhythm his feet made on the stone, how he hummed to himself as he stacked the logs. Once the wood began to crackle, he noticed he wasn't alone and came around to see who it was. A sad smile flitted on his face.

"Can I tell you something?" I blurted out, before he could say anything. "I wanted him to be Agos's."

Khine strode past the curtains to sit beside me. I was facing the table—he was facing out. It helped that we didn't have to look straight at each other. "Why?" he asked, after a length of time.

"It . . . it would have been a way out."

"Ah."

"Wishful thinking. Ryia would've had me executed on the spot. Ozo would've jumped at the chance to ruin me, too. But for a moment there, I was ready to throw it all into the fire. To say yes, I failed, I fucked up. Do I get to walk away now? Am I no longer responsible for anything that happens after this?"

He didn't reply.

I glanced down. "What do I do, Khine?"

"I don't know why you're asking me."

"I never really imagined I would get this far—that I would have, if nothing else, my husband's full support at last. He spoke to me last night in earnest. He says he wants to fix things, to assist me in every way, and not once did he mention his pride or any of the retorts I imagined he was capable of after everything that had happened. All of it is…unexpected."

Khine cleared his throat. "Only a truly skilled actor could pretend in these situations, and from what I've seen of your husband, he is far from one. Misguided though he may have been, he is a good man. Direct, but honourable. Whatever he's done over the years is merely a reflection of the expectations put on you by your elders. You of all people should understand how that feels."

It wasn't the answer I wanted to hear. I glanced at his hand. After a moment's reflection, I placed mine on my lap. "He wants things to return to the way they were before he left," I whispered. "Once we get our son back, and we've stabilized everything…"

"It's all you ever wanted."

I swallowed.

"I mean, what's there to consider?" Khine continued. "He's the only ally you've got left. With him on your side, the Ikessars can't get rid of you so easily. Whatever their feelings about you, they're obligated to help Thanh, now."

"Thanh isn't safe with those people." I found the courage to meet his eyes at last. "There is no going back to the way things were. I look around me and see the same world I left behind. The same arguments, the same games, except I no longer see myself as part of it. This must be what a ghost feels like."

"You have also told me, time and time again, that your feelings hold no sway over these matters."

"To dissolve our marriage would require…one of us to admit to our wrongdoings. One of us will be sent to prison, possibly executed."

"And for all the troubles he's caused you, you're not the kind of woman who will wish him ill. You could never harm him." He said it matter-of-factly again, as easily as whenever he discussed my relationship with Agos. *Only a skilled actor*... of course he knew what skilled acting looked like. He had acted all his life just to get by. By necessity, he knew exactly how to phrase his words or smile even though he was clearly hurting.

"We've already shook the boat enough," I replied, trying to avoid what I think I wanted to say to him. "More will be reason for them to tip us over."

"You're probably right." Khine got up. "The water is boiling." Despite his light tone, his feet dragged, and he returned to the stove with a sigh. He removed the pot from the stove before turning around to begin slicing a tomato. There was nothing precise about the way Khine made meals. The onions he had dropped in hot oil were chopped into different sizes, and the ginger that followed was half crushed instead of diced. As far as I was aware, he followed no recipes—he cooked with whatever was available and simply tasted what he was making as he went. If Hessa was around, she would've screamed at him to get out of her kitchen.

But I couldn't draw my eyes away. I watched how his jaw tightened each time the knife came down, his face locked in concentration as his fingers curled over the handle. The tendons in that arm still bothered him. He had avoided stitching my latest wounds, stating he didn't trust himself with a needle anymore. He never mentioned the reason, of course. His silences often spoke louder than the words that fell from his lips. There was talk he avoided altogether.

It was a pattern I'd fallen into the past few months—observing his movements, trying to guess at what he was thinking. I used to do the same with Rayyel, but there had always been a thread of irritation over the fact that he left me no choice because he never told me anything. With Khine, even when I was grappling for answers, even when I could feel the uncertainty bearing down on us like a windstorm, I didn't want to be anywhere else.

"I'm sorry, Khine," I said.

More silence. And then, "For what?"

For what, indeed? Unsustainable, this dance we had going on. Surely he knew it, too.

"I am queen again," I said, changing the tone of my voice to something resembling what it was if I was in front of my court. "Should you desire to return to Shang Azi, I can make sure that your debts are paid in full and that—"

"Don't start with this. Not again. You know that's not what I want."

"What are you going to do about it?"

"Duel you, maybe." His voice was flat, polite.

"Your swordsmanship has improved, but if you think you can defeat me…"
I forced myself to laugh.

"Mmm. I never said I could. But maybe I don't need a sword. I make your
food, remember?" He waved the knife.

"You'd stay here, as a servant?"

He turned to wipe his hands on a dishcloth. "My sister is working for your
husband. The pay he's offered is much better than anything she'll get in Shang
Azi short of becoming Manshi Ziori and running a whorehouse herself. Lo
Bahn is—we don't know what happened with him, but he's ruined, regardless. Even if he's alive, I don't know if he'll want me back. I made a terrible
henchman."

"What about your younger brother and sister?"

"They're old enough to take care of themselves. Tali, if I can be honest… I
just can't see myself picking up where I left off. It isn't—without my mother, it's
just not *home* anymore."

"It won't be the same as before here, either," I said. "The council will appoint
me new advisers in place of Magister Arro and I will return to having my every
movement, every action, recorded. Rayyel will be crowned Dragonlord. If we
stabilize the nation, they… they will desire more heirs. What happened with
Agos… I don't want it to happen to you. You heard Ryia. I can't… this thing
between us…"

I faltered. I didn't know what I was saying. Or, more precisely—I knew, I
just didn't know what I expected to come from it.

"I am content as I am," he whispered, a better liar than I could ever be.

I heard footsteps outside the hall and turned to see one of the guards step
in. "Beloved Queen," he said with a bow. "Messengers from across Jin-Sayeng
have arrived. Lord General Ozo had requested they not interrupt until after the
trial…"

"So now he's let them loose, upended on me like a bucket of piss. Typical."

"They are waiting in the great hall, all but one. He simply asked me to give
you this. It's from Warlord Lushai." He handed me a sealed letter.

I removed the wax. I read it once, and then again, the words blurring before
they struck like a knife. My heart dropped.

"What is it?" Khine asked, drifting back to the tables.

"Warlord Lushai is inviting us to Bara for a feast to welcome his most honoured guest," I said. I turned to him. "The Fifth Son of the Esteemed Emperor Yunan..."

"The bastard," Khine whispered. "So soon?"

I stared at the letter without replying. Governor Qun had warned me he was on his way. I wanted to believe it was a bluff, the last-ditch effort of a doomed man to strike fear in the heart of his enemies. At the very least I thought I would have more time to prepare.

Always amusing, how the gods shit on our expectations.

CHAPTER SEVEN

A QUEEN'S GAMBLE

Too many nights I had woken up in a cold sweat, afraid I was back in Yue-bek's dungeon or that I lay on the streets of Zorheng while his wife bled a foot away. And too often I dreamed of striking him with a sword until my own fingers bled. *Your father wanted this, Beloved Queen,* he would sneer, trading every blow with laughter. *Why do you resist? You know you are powerless when it comes to his will.*

I tried to remain expressionless while I sat on the throne in the great hall of Oka Shto, listening to the messenger with growing trepidation. He was one of many waiting to seek audience with the newly reinstated queen. This one claimed to have come from the Sougen, the third so far. "Not all the farmers support Kaggawa's war," he said. "My master personally wants you to know that he is sincerely waiting for the Dragonthrone to intervene in these affairs."

"Why not implore Warlord Ojika?" I asked impatiently.

"He has holed up in Yu-yan. He never cared about the farmers, Beloved Queen—only the city."

"Farmers keep him fed."

"The Sougen keeps most of Jin-Sayeng fed," the messenger said with a small grin. "And yet it has been burning all these years. Mad dragons have made short work of much of our fields—has the Dragonthrone sent anyone to take care of them? But Beloved Queen, my master is not looking for reparations for the past. It is all done with, and he has always supported you for the throne. All he asks is that you do something *now.*"

"Dai Kaggawa believes himself a representative of the Sougen landowners," another messenger broke in. "This is furthest from the truth. He is an adopted son of the Shoho clan. He may speak for *them*, but..."

"His mercenaries are wreaking havoc on the countryside," the first one agreed. "They are foreigners who hold little respect for the people of Jin-Sayeng. They will bring as much destruction as the mad dragons have done all these years. He thinks this will bring us freedom? That he can save Jin-Sayeng from what the royals have neglected *this* way?"

A woman stepped out from behind the others and walked towards me, baring her shoulder as she did so. There was a long wound there, barely held together with stitches and caked blood. The rest of her arm was covered in a mass of purple bruises. The look in her eyes dared me to show pity, to express my horror in fake sympathy. But the extent of her injuries only numbed me to silence.

"Kaggawa's mercenaries go too far," she said. "You've let us suffer all these years, Queen Talyien. Now you will let us suffer even longer, all for an argument that could've been resolved overnight."

"All of that is over now," I said. "We are in the process of finding a solution to—"

"Fuck your processes!" the woman roared. My guards started forward, and I held out my hand to stop them. "Fuck your solutions! Fuck all of you!" she continued, turning around. "You and your eastern cities that have yet to see *famine*, who haven't had to deal with dragons razing your fields every day..."

"Both Shirrokaru and Oren-yaro have been burned down by a dragon," I reminded her.

"Once," she hissed. "Once in thirty years. Don't even dare bring up your dead brothers, *Beloved Queen*. My brothers have been killed by dragons, too, and it didn't end there. Do I get to go overseas for a year, like you did? Do I get to lie down and give up on my farm? We still have to feed our children, Queen Talyien. We still have to feed the *rest of you*."

An official came up to whisper in my ear, something about allowing such insolence to go unpunished. I waved him off. He looked surprised, and only then did I remember why. Last year, anyone who dared speak to me that way would've been executed on the spot.

"I am listening," I said, looking straight at the woman. "I've been to the Sougen. I know what you are dealing with—I have seen it with my own eyes."

She stared back, unblinking. She didn't believe me.

"Your mad dragons are mad because of a corruption," I continued. "A tainted soul, trying to take the place of the existing. Two souls in one body." I glanced at the official, who now seemed at a loss for words, and pointed at him. "You can write that down, Councillor. What happened to the mad dragons is now starting to happen to the people in the Sougen. Is this not true?" I glanced back at the woman.

She slowly nodded.

"This is preposterous," the official grumbled. "I can't write hearsay down."

"Hearsay, Councillor? From your own queen's lips?"

"They will think you are talking blasphemy."

"Ah," I said. "Blasphemy. Like the *agan*."

I think if he could have chosen to disappear into thin air, he would have. He glanced at the others in the great hall before his eyes flicked downwards, as if to see if my fingers were on my sword.

"I will spare you the trouble of pretending you disagree," I said. "That's what this is all about. The *agan*. We deny its existence while it rips our nation apart from the edges. Why do you look so frightened, Councillor? Are you afraid your peers will hold you in contempt for my words? They shouldn't. It's about time we start saying things for what they are!"

"What's happening here?" a voice boomed from the other end of the hall.

"Mind your own business, Ozo," I snarled.

He stomped in, dismissing the messengers with a snap of his fingers. I bristled at how quickly my guards stepped up to drag them away, but I didn't want to risk asking them to stay. If they disobeyed me, it would make my already shaky position look even weaker. I had *just* regained the crown; I wasn't about to throw it away.

Ozo turned to the official and quickly snatched the piece of paper from his hands. He tore it in half. "Burn it," he said, handing the pieces to a guard beside him.

"Do you want a duel for the throne, Lord General?" I asked. "You seem to want to defy my authority so much. Why not just fight me, and be done with it?"

"You'd like that," he said. "You know very well I can't lift my hand against Warlord Yeshin's daughter. I still obey our laws, even though *you* seem to have forgotten them."

"I've no desire for this right now." I got up and left the dais.

"Queen Talyien," he said as I walked past him. "You will learn that you cannot change what is just because you want to. Things are the way they are for a reason."

"Does it have anything to do with your fat rump, I wonder?" I grumbled. He didn't reply.

I cornered the woman outside the hall, grabbing her by the wrist. She looked startled. "We *will* liberate you," I told her. "But understand that I cannot do anything until I've gathered my own forces."

"I understand that you can't get your shit together out here," the woman said. "There are rumours that there are Zarojo ships on your eastern shores. Are they making you deny this one, too?"

"It's true," I said, after a moment's pause.

She gave a grim smile. "If there's anything I've learned from Kaggawa's men, it's that foreigners don't belong on Jin-Sayeng soil. I'm just a farmer's daughter, Queen Talyien. I can't tell you how to manage your affairs, and it looks like you've got more on your plate than you're equipped to deal with. But I will say that the thought of invaders left and right fills me with unease. I hope you know what you're doing. I hope you remember you're our queen. I hope you never forget that your people are at your mercy."

Apart from Belfang, I met with everyone who had arrived with me from the Zarojo Empire in the false throne room my father had planted in his study. After our last excursion down there, we had learned we could bypass the wards if I cut myself and covered the spell runes with my blood. Rai looked around in wonder, absorbing everything as matter-of-factly as if the knowledge that Yeshin dabbled in this sort of thing wouldn't set the whole kingdom aflame. For some reason, I now couldn't get Thanh's resemblance to him out of my mind. My boy carried the same levelheaded curiosity. Would he look more like Rai when he grew up? *If he ever grows up...*

"So," I said, as soon as I heard the door mechanism turn and it shut itself above the staircase. I strode to the middle of the room. "We have to somehow deal with the Zarojo without arousing everyone else's suspicions about my father's *grandiose plans* for my future. We want to get rid of his great Esteemed Prince Yuebek, may he rot in the deepest bowels of hell, without setting the rest of Jin-Sayeng after me, because I will *need* their support afterwards to deal with the problems in the Sougen. I don't know if the Oren-yaro army is enough or even that they will follow any of my orders. They're Ozo's, as far as I'm concerned. Does everyone agree with me so far?"

"Yes, Beloved Queen," Namra said from across the other side of the room. Inzali gave a short nod, while Khine grunted in acknowledgment.

Rayyel didn't reply. He was staring at the glass dome and the mirror. "Is that the Sougen?" he asked.

"Rai," I said, snapping my fingers. "Focus."

He turned back to me with some difficulty. "I heard what you said."

"So you agree we need to accept Warlord Lushai's invitation."

He didn't even hesitate. "Of course. Rejecting such a well-worded invitation would bring more trouble."

"I see," I said.

He must have noticed me staring at him, because he suddenly looked like he'd been dipped in hot water. "Unless you would rather not..." he began.

"Oh, I would love to. Chiha and I need to compare notes...on recent events in Jin-Sayeng." I took a moment of satisfaction in seeing his ears turn red before I glanced at everyone else in the room. Inzali and Namra were both oblivious to the exchange, but I caught a faint smile on Khine's lips. He scratched the side of his head and finally glanced away. "There is, however, no way we can ride to Bara without Princess Ryia finding out. Woman's probably got her ear pressed on the walls as we speak. We need to trick her."

Rai sighed. "I'm not sure how that can be done. Your own father couldn't defeat her, if you recall."

"Can you distract her somehow?"

"Our conversation during her arrival was the first time I had spoken to her in years."

That took me by surprise. I didn't know what was worse—that he could say it with such a straight face, or that he didn't think this was important to mention at all. It made me feel ashamed of my recent outburst. "Does she know we are not as...hostile to each other as we make ourselves appear in court?"

"I don't believe my mother ever looks at me long enough to think such things," Rai said. "In any case, it is dangerous to rely on this. She will find out, sooner or later."

"This is where you come in, Lamang," I said, cocking my head towards Khine.

"Me," Khine repeated.

"The most brilliant con artist ever to grace the streets of Shang Azi." I grinned.

He frowned and crossed his arms. "You make me sound so accomplished."

"You really do," Inzali broke in. "He's not even a famous criminal—just a two-bit thief who shakes pocket change out of the occasional gullible fool."

"You're so supportive, dear sister. Whatever will I do without you?"

Inzali sighed, placing a hand on his shoulder. I wasn't sure if she was squeezing it or threatening to throttle him. "Dear brother, if this nation has to rely on *you* for any reason, it really is doomed. We're not talking about idiots in Shang Azi here. Princess Ryia is the one woman in history who was able to make a stand against Warlord Yeshin. You *have* brushed up on your history lessons in your attempts to impress the queen, yes?" She pinched his chin to turn his head towards her.

"Choke on your barbed tongue," he grumbled. He cleared his throat. "Why do we need to trick her? Sometimes the best plans are the simplest."

I stepped closer. "Go on."

He waved Inzali away. "A smart woman like that—there's no sense in hiding it. So have her where you can keep an eye on her. Invite her to come with you as an honoured guest."

I blinked. "You mean—take her with us to Bara?"

Rai flared his nostrils. "You don't know what my mother is capable of."

"What's that saying? An enemy of your enemy is your friend." Khine tapped his foot, a thoughtful look on his face. "It's better than leaving her here, alone and free to roam the castle to her heart's content. Who knows what else she'll find? This very room contains knowledge she can use against you."

"That's tempting, though," I said. "I have an image of her in my head with arrows through the face. It's oddly comforting."

"Let the cat fall into the mousetrap," Inzali mused. "I like it."

Khine grimaced. "Putting aside how frightening it is when you both agree on something, it's not a good look to have the Ikessar princess dead in Warlord Yeshin's room, is it? So continue where you left off yesterday. Formally invite her as part of the procession to Bara...I'm sure she won't refuse. And so she becomes not just a guest, not just a hostage, but a distraction, because this Lushai and your mother are none too fond of each other, yes? Remnants from the war? And this Lushai has an army. Yuebek has an army. Everyone in this jovial land has an army, and assuming they all consider each other a threat and are only out for themselves... *you* will become the least of their concerns. When buffalo clash, the lowly ant can walk right by..."

I smiled. "Last-century poetry?"

"No, I made it up just now. But I'm flattered you think so. Maybe I should be a two-bit poet instead of a thief."

"I'm being polite. I was going to ask if you heard it from a passing drunk."

"You *really* know how to hurt a man's feelings."

Rai cleared his throat, and I realized Khine and I were doing it again— slipping off into our own little world. I stepped away from him and pretended I was gathering my thoughts. "Speaking of Lushai," I began. "Rai and the warlord of Bara are friends, I believe."

Khine glanced at Rai and then back at me before deciding to keep his mouth shut.

"I am as in the dark about all of this as you are," Rai said. I couldn't tell if he was responding to my slight or not. "He has been kind to me in the past. It doesn't make us allies. To hear that he has opened up his home to Prince Yuebek, of all people..."

"It's obviously a trap," Inzali said. "A man like Yuebek doesn't parley."

"And the ease with which he found his way into Bara reminds me of how easily Oren-yaro embraced Qun and his delegates," I said. "What are the bastards up to?" I glanced at Namra, who was still walking around the edges of the throne room with a glazed look on her face. "And what are *you* busy with there, priestess? I know I should've laid out tea, but come and join us."

"Tea *would* have made this meeting more pleasant," she said, lifting her head. "I'm mapping the spells in this place."

"Maybe we should wait until we've gotten rid of Yuebek to worry about that. One problem at a time, priestess."

"I don't believe you get that luxury," Namra replied. "It's all connected." She crossed the room towards the throne, draping her fingers along the smooth wood. "Your father has been dead sixteen years. Did you not wonder why this chamber is clean? Why the throne isn't caked in dust? Someone else has been here recently. Someone who cared enough to sweep this whole place and wipe the throne from top to bottom." She paused over one of the wolves and flicked her finger along the crevices, showing a lump of dirt at the tip. "Yes. Only recently. They missed *some* parts."

I remembered the servant the last time I was here. I'd been convinced she was a hallucination. Now I wasn't sure, and the uncertainty multiplied my discomfort. Did I want the illusion to remain an illusion, even if it meant I was the one going mad?

Silence fell across the room as the shadow of a dragon descended from the sky. It drifted along the treetops before disappearing behind a blanket of fog. I held my breath and waited; predictably, the white flash came. I heard the others cry out, but I simply closed my eyes, waiting for the buzzing, for the hair-prickling sensation to pass.

"Fuck," Khine finally said.

"Should we walk willingly into a trap?" Rai murmured.

"Do we have a choice?" I countered. "Look at that, Rai. We need to free ourselves here so we can take care of that. You and I are both Dragonlord. It's our duty."

"I know," he whispered. "Believe me, I know."

"Maybe you can refuse the invitation," Inzali said. "This Warlord Lushai has no power over you. Tell him no. Let them come up with something new."

Khine cleared his throat. "Maybe the trap lies with her refusal. The way Yuebek's mind works—you don't want to be waiting for his next move. This is a man who orchestrated the machinations of an entire city just so you could be delivered into his arms. No—so you would willingly throw yourself *into* them. Remember when he wanted you broken just so he could be the one to put you back together? Who knows what he's got up his sleeve now."

"That wasn't all Yuebek," I found myself saying. "My father played a bigger part."

Rai frowned. "He's dead."

"Yeshin scoffed at death," I replied. "You didn't know him, Rai. He never believed he was old, never listened to his advisers telling him to slow down and appoint trusted officials in his stead. When he fell ill, he wouldn't believe he was dying."

As soon as I spoke, I gazed up at the ceiling, mulling over my own words. I remembered how fast my father had faded after his collapse. The healer had declared him close to death, and he called the man a lying dog from the corner of the province. "A corner I should've handed over to the Baraji!" he had screamed, shattering clay pots full of herbs and strong-smelling poultices against the wall. The servants walked on eggshells around him until he was finally too weak to do anything but lie there, breath wheezing from his body like steam from a leaky kettle, as if he was falling apart at the seams. I remember sitting beside him and holding his hand for hours. Despite his weakness, his grip remained firm, like I could somehow be the link that would stop death from claiming him.

I didn't think the others understood.

They left to carry out preparations and I found myself alone in the throne room, staring at the crown, at the empty, jewelled eyes of the wolf. "What kind of hell have you dragged us into, old man?" I asked out loud.

If the wolf had replied, I wouldn't have been surprised.

Rai delivered the news to his mother during breakfast like a priest doling out a litany.

Princess Ryia turned to me as soon as he uttered the words. "*We* are inviting you to Bara with us," Rayyel had said, but she knew exactly whose idea it would've been. A servant arrived with tureens of rice porridge over which she dropped balls of dark cocoa. Ryia continued to glower past the steam and fragrant smell of coconut milk.

"All these distractions," Ryia said, as soon as the servant stepped away with a bow. She tapped the edge of the porcelain bowl with an exquisitely long fingernail, her expression almost wistful. I wondered if she was imagining stroking my skull. "If you want me to believe your sincerity, *Queen* Talyien, you should've opened this conversation with an apology for your actions over the years, followed by details of my son's impending coronation."

"I was under the impression Rai was not important to you," I replied, stirring my porridge into brown and cream swirls.

"Says the woman who has yet to find *her* son." Ryia's cool detachment was well-practiced. It was almost enviable.

I laughed in response. The approaching servant dropped a fork. I got up and picked it up for her. She placed a dish of dried mackerel at the edge of the table before scampering away. I twirled the fork under the sunlight. "The fondness you Ikessars have for Kag things is undeniable," I said. "It was your father, wasn't it, who wanted to reverse Zarojo influence by embracing yet another culture? It seems as if Jin-Sayeng is incapable of remaining Jinsein."

She gave that tiger's smile, the one I was starting to get used to. No falcon, this one; my father's war did this to her. "And yet if you Oren-yaro had your way, you would have us pandering to the Zarojo once more. Isn't that why this prince is here now?"

"He is mistaken," I lied. "He thought my father and he had an agreement. My father was using him."

"Your father used everyone. Who do you think you're fooling, girl?"

"No one, Beloved Princess. But I was hoping you could understand...it's all politics."

"Provincial politics."

"Provincial politics," I repeated with a smile. "So why concern yourself over them, Beloved Princess? Perhaps Ozo thought he could extend that farce on the off chance that your son's tantrum would cause more trouble than we could handle." I glanced at Rai, who was looking at his teacup intently, even though the servants had yet to pour us tea.

"So you decided to pre-emptively prepare for civil war," Ryia said. She folded her hands on the table.

"Wouldn't you?"

"And now you've changed your mind."

"We're all getting along now, aren't we?" I asked, smiling. "Family, and all that. So we should all go up there together to tell him he's not needed anymore. As family." I took Rayyel's hand and lifted it up for her to see.

She stared back at me, unamused, with eyebrows that looked sharp enough to cut a finger off.

"So you're agreeing to accompany us," I drawled, stopping to break salted fish into my porridge. Rai still looked confused. Nothing in the man's life had prepared him to be in the midst of an argument between his mother and wife. I think if someone had offered him a pillowcase, he would have gladly crawled inside.

"I won't have you make a mockery of the throne any longer," Ryia said, her voice growing more sombre. "For all I know this Zarojo prince is waiting to murder my son as a wedding gift to you. *Do* remember that if that happens, you forfeit your claim to the throne. Your animosities have been recorded. This land cannot be yours if it is not also his."

"A point, Beloved Princess," Rai finally broke in. I was wondering if he had somehow lost the ability to speak. "The throne belongs to whoever the people support."

"And who do you think that is?" Ryia asked. "It can't be her. Only the structures that *put* her on that throne are keeping her there."

"If she is assassinated, it cannot be mine alone, either."

I looked up with a start. Hearing barbed words from Rayyel was rarer than hen's teeth. I glanced at him, and then at Ryia sitting directly across him. One stern-faced, the other still carrying that cold smile.

"Are you suggesting something untoward, dear son?"

"I am suggesting that my wife's death will not secure the throne," Rai said.

"No. You are accusing me of wanting to kill your wife. Your own mother—!"

"You've not exactly hidden your disdain."

"And so you've decided it's time for you to speak up? To slap me in the face with this discourtesy?"

"You've been just as discourteous to her," he said. "This goes both ways, Beloved Princess."

Fury now danced in her eyes. "I didn't realize I raised you to be so uncivilized. To bandy such careless words around…"

"They aren't exactly careless," Rai said. "Unless you would also deny that you attempted to botch the trial."

Ryia's face turned white.

"You paid Belfang to claim he was the boy's brother," Rai continued.

"You'd take the word of Xiaran scum over your own mother's?"

"I would take the word of someone who risked his own life to travel here with me," Rai said evenly. "Consider that I am not using this knowledge against you, Mother. I am only trying to show you that it is futile. Why are we fighting with each other when we have enemies waiting to tear what's left of us apart? You heard Talyien. We're family."

"Does she really think that?" Ryia asked.

"Don't turn this on me, old woman," I snapped.

She sniffed. "So the pot calls the kettle."

"You're the one who tried to buy off Zarojo scum. How much of a penny-pincher are you that someone like *him* would turn you down?"

"He didn't turn her down," Rai said. "She fully believed going into the trial that he was working for her. You wouldn't have been there otherwise, would you, Mother?"

"And he turned on her at the last moment," I concluded.

Rai nodded. "He said his honour would not allow him to sink to such depths."

"He said..." It was my turn to frown. "Rai—*Belfang* said this?"

"The man is atoning for his sins," he said. "He deeply regrets what happened in Phurywa and the part he played in those elders' deaths."

"I will not be insulted by children any further," Ryia stated. She walked away from the table, leaving her bowl of porridge untouched.

I didn't even give her the courtesy of being offended. I turned to my husband. "Rai, that doesn't sound right. I knew he came here with you because we burned that temple down and the villagers would've skinned him alive, but... for him to betray Princess Ryia for *honour*?"

He blinked at me. "Perhaps he is a more loyal man than we gave him credit for."

"No," I said, remembering the man who happily bled his own elders back in Phurywa. "Not *this* one. I need to talk to Khine." Before he could respond, I rose from my seat and strode out of the dining hall.

I went in search of Khine and found only the kitchen staff, most of whom had returned in the aftermath of the trial. One of the cooks, upon further prodding, remembered she had seen him lurking about the east wing, where the main libraries were. I dashed up the stairs, two steps at a time. Oka Shto Castle was high up enough on the mountain that you could see the ridges on the horizon from the first level. I reached the second floor, turned down the corridor, and saw the door to the library wide open. I caught sight of Belfang on a chair, his feet on the table. He didn't see me arrive. "This is a nice, cushy position you've found yourself in, Khine," he was saying.

I drifted to a corner, as close to the wall as possible.

"And it doesn't look bad from my end, either. You ever imagine we'd find ourselves here? Royalty feeding off our hands. Look at you. You've got the queen wrapped around your little finger, don't you?"

"Get your head out of the gutter."

"It's not mine that's there, Lamang. Spirits, you've got quite the appetite for danger. Even after what happened to her last one, you're still going after her? What kind of treasure lies between a queen's thighs, anyway? Just grab a whore or two in a back alley and take care of it. You can even pay them to pretend to be her for a spell."

"I'm not in the mood to be insulted."

"You humourless bastard. You can't even share a joke or two, for old times' sake?"

"You make it sound like we were friends."

"I wouldn't make that kind of mistake! When was lowly Belfang ever friends with the golden boy, the grand, clever scholar Khine Lamang? Oh, I'm sorry. It's not that anymore, is it? Hasn't been for the longest time. Now you're nothing but a fraud and a thief, and you're after the ultimate prize. Not that I blame you! Seems like just about every ambitious man's got his eye on that tasty title of hers, and you're just being smart, taking advantage when she clearly favours you. I get it. I might've done the same thing if she was my type."

"Go bother someone else before I split your skull open."

Belfang laughed. "Bedding the queen won't do a damn thing, Lamang. It won't make you who you once were and it sure as hell won't fill that hole inside of you. You'd fill hers, no question about it, but—"

I heard a snap and saw Belfang topple backwards as Khine's fist slammed onto his chin. Instead of crying out in pain, Belfang chortled. "All right, I'm leaving," he said, his face red. "So much for trying to watch out for you. Your temper hasn't improved all these years, I can tell you that much. Maybe Inzali would be less hostile, hey?" He walked away without so much as a backwards glance. He looked flustered.

I waited a moment before walking inside the library. Khine glanced up and looked slightly embarrassed. "You just missed Belfang."

"He's...ah, the reason I came looking for you, actually," I said. "Should we really be letting him run around the castle without a guard, at least?"

"Are loose lips a crime in Jin-Sayeng?" He flexed his fingers with a frown. "No, I don't trust the man, if that's what you're saying. I never did."

"Rai says he's confessed to taking bribes from Ryia."

"He did seem oddly confident on their way here," Khine admitted.

"But then he turned on her anyway. She paid him to botch the spell and he didn't—he made it work exactly as Namra explained it would. And then he fed Rayyel this nonsense about honour and atonement..."

"That's bullshit."

"You don't say."

"When we were children, he would get the other boys to pay him to kiss his younger sister. They happily obliged."

"What?"

"I'm not sure if things went further than that. I told the other boys to stop and…" He shook his head. "She ran away the next summer and never came back. I can tell you right now: The bottom of a chamber pot has more honour than Belfang."

"Then it's clear as day. We thought we picked up a stray puppy and it turns out it's Yuebek's rat."

"It's starting to sound like it."

"But why come here at all? Why *help* our cause?"

"I don't know," Khine said. "Perhaps Yuebek needed to clear your name."

"He was counting on *my disgrace* so he could swoop in to save the day."

"Was he, really?" Khine asked.

"What do you mean?"

He tapped the table. "I've been thinking about all of that. From the very beginning, Yuebek's plans have evolved in his attempt to ensnare you. Back in the empire, he tried to fool you. Later, he tried to break you—threatened to take it all away with one hand, and offered you salvation with the other. It stands to reason that he's changed his stripes yet again. He's found something else. Something new. Why else has he been silent this whole time? Let Belfang run around like the rat he is. I'll keep my eye on the fool. As for Yuebek, I think we'll find out more when we see him."

"*We*," I repeated.

He scratched the side of his cheek. "Did…you not want me to come?"

"I…that's not how I would phrase it. But…"

"You're with your mother-in-law and your husband," he finished for me.

I flushed. "Namra will be with us. And Inzali. Rayyel has officially made them his advisers. A Dageian-educated mage and a celebrated tutor from the Zarojo Empire—"

He laughed. "Celebrated? Inzali?"

"Mayor Feng of Phurywa had her registered. Rayyel is extremely thorough, if nothing else. She's also functioning as the official translator for the Ikessars."

"Her Jinan is poorer than mine. And anyway, if you leave me behind, what are the chances you'll walk into that other castle and I'll be right there?"

I closed my mouth.

He placed his hands on top of mine. "I told you. I'll be careful."

I glanced down. "That's not being very careful."

He pulled away with a shadow of a smile on his lips. "When do we leave?"

"Tomorrow," I murmured. "I'll...I'll have a horse ready for you. If anyone asks, you're Inzali's assistant." I cleared my throat and got up. He looked troubled as I left.

CHAPTER EIGHT

THE BARAJI CIVET

ᴛᴜᴍ

The day we took to the road, I found myself glancing back once from the city square. I beheld the castle nestled on the slab of rock, the fringe of trees, the clouds that drifted along the mountaintop. Everything my father had bequeathed to his only child...and I felt nothing. It made me wonder what kind of daughter that made me. It wasn't that I was ungrateful, but if they knew what I felt, the rest of Jin-Sayeng would see it that way. If the very act of trying to be a good queen meant I was a bad daughter, then so be it.

I didn't get to travel by saddle like I wanted and had to share a carriage with Rayyel, where I endured long hours of silence, staring at him while he perused through the books he had decided to bring along for the journey.

"Jin-Sayeng royals have a long history of intermarriage with the Zarojo, do you know?" he asked, at length.

I narrowed my eyes. "Where the hell are you going with this?"

"Just a thought," Rayyel said.

"Is it a *useful* thought?"

"I suppose not," he conceded. "Nevertheless, your father's rationale is not entirely unwarranted."

"Sometimes I wonder if you really do have a morbid sense of humour instead of just being blindingly oblivious."

He stroked his beard into a point. "I was...trying to comfort you. About your father's decisions."

I turned away. "I've no need to be comforted over them. He was a ruthless man. A wolf will always be a wolf, he used to tell me; and so why should I be surprised it came down to this? You with your precise logic ought to know." I took a deep breath. "I understand, perhaps, why he did what he did. He had betrothed me to his enemy, and he always considered your clan the weakest of all. Well—that's a given. He wouldn't have started his war otherwise."

Rai nodded. "It's in the books."

"And he had no way of knowing Prince Yuebek is...as he is. I can't fault a dead man for decisions he made during a bloody war. But I'd like to think I am capable of more. It frightens me that I might be mistaken. When I met your mother for the first time, all she could say was how I remind her of *him*. I don't even look like an old man, do I?"

"I don't think she means anything by it."

"That's bullshit and you know it. Yeshin had that presence. He wouldn't have gathered so much support if he didn't. An unforgettable friend, and an even worse enemy. Even after sixteen years, he won't die. What do I have to do to get rid of his ghost? Why do they continue to see *him* and not me?"

He folded his arms across his chest. "They see what they want to see. It is easier to hate someone than to try to understand them. To turn them into something they're not. I have made the same mistake."

I fell silent, realizing what he was trying to say. The sound of the wind rushed past us, interspersed with the creaking wheels underneath. Moments passed.

"We've been on this road before," Rai said, pulling aside the curtains from the window of the carriage. "It was not long after our wedding. Do you remember?"

"I would remember if you took me to visit the Baraji."

"We were going to Sutan and took the long way. You wanted to see the ocean from the edge of the Bara Plateau."

"That sounds like something I would do." I still had no recollection of it.

He smiled. "We never made it. You...weren't well."

"Oh." Now I had a faint memory of feeling ill while staring at that same forest of maple trees. They were red then, too; fuller than the trees in the distance, which were nearly bare. "I suppose I found out I was carrying Thanh not long after."

He nodded. "Three days later, in fact."

"I didn't know you kept track of these things."

He smoothed out his trousers to avoid looking directly at me. "I keep track of a lot of things. I do not always find the opportunity to bring them up in conversation."

"That tends to happen when you don't speak at all. Still, you've spoken to me more these past few weeks than in all the time I've ever known you. Miracle of miracles."

His brows knotted. "I believe...that the last year has done much in making me feel more at ease in your presence. It is a touch presumptuous for me to say so, I know. And I realize there are complications to this arrangement and do not wish to dismiss your feelings on it. But to me, you are my wife. You are still my wife."

I felt my ears tingle as he spoke and turned my eyes away from him. His cold detachment was easier to handle than this. My upside-down world was back in order, but now it was unfamiliar, unrecognizable. I felt like a stranger in my own home.

The carriage drew to a stop.

"That's odd," Rai said. "I didn't think we were there yet."

"Maybe one of the guards—"

Before I could finish, something crashed against the carriage, sending it toppling to the side.

I managed to brace myself. Rai tumbled to a corner with the cushions. Outside, horses screamed in panic. I grabbed my sword as I rushed to him. "Are you all right, Rai?"

"I split my lip." Blood ran down his chin. I wiped it with my finger and then motioned for him to stay. I turned to jump up the window.

He grabbed my leg. "Don't! If those are bandits..."

"All the way out here?"

"I've heard they've spread all throughout the last year. They're right about the commoners taking advantage when the Dragonthrone is in turmoil."

"Well, I'm not going to wait for them to unwrap me from a box." I struck the doors with my fist and pulled myself out of the carriage. One of the wheels had been ripped off, and the horses had been cut from the traces. In the distance, I could see my guards in a heated battle with intruders on horseback. I turned to the sound of a loosed rock just in time to deflect an incoming spear. A youngster, awkwardly flailing about with a weapon too heavy for him to hold properly. He must have thought I was easy prey. I struck his leg, right below the knee—not even enough to cripple him—and watched with satisfaction as he turned tail.

Rai crawled out of the carriage just in time to see the bandit scramble away.

"I told you to stay inside," I said.

"What would they think of me if I hid while my wife went to battle?"

"They'll sing stories until the end of time, I'm sure."

"Tali!" Khine called from the distance, thundering down towards us on his horse.

"Where's Princess Ryia?"

"The bastards cut us from the rest," he huffed, pulling his horse to a stop. "You think this is her doing?"

"It can't be," Rai replied.

Khine scratched the stubble on his face. "I know she's your mother, Rai, but—"

"Why are we on familiar terms, Lamang?"

"Bandits are common around here," I interrupted. "There's more of them at the northern border of the Oren-yaro province. Rebels who don't recognize any lord and raid royals whenever they get the chance. I need a horse." I picked up the spear the bandit had dropped.

Khine tugged at his horse's reins. "You've barely recovered from your injuries...don't tell me you want to fight *now*."

"I don't think they care about that." Truth be told, I was itching for a fight. The last two weeks had felt like a lifetime. If I could pour my anger out on a bandit or two...

A horn trumpeted in the distance.

I couldn't tell how many of our attackers there were, or if our own guards were overwhelmed. Two Oren-yaro soldiers came thundering down the road. "Beloved Queen!" they called out. One jumped from his horse. "We need to leave!"

I grabbed the proffered reins and swung into the saddle.

"Consider," Rai broke in, "that they know you're here and want to capture you. Remember what happened during Thanh's birth."

"Where would we run to?" I asked. "The edge of the plateau is right behind us."

"Into the forest..." one of the soldiers started.

"Deeper into unknown territory? Towards how many of them are waiting for us there? We have to fight our way out." I lifted the spear, testing it. The muscles in that arm were sore. It had been weeks since I had battled the dragon in Kyo-orashi, but Khine was right—injury after injury made my body feel like a traitorous, lumbering creature.

"Just along the fringes, then," Khine said as the other soldier gave up his horse to Rayyel. "Don't rush headlong into them."

I laughed. "Me? I don't rush into things."

"That's an understatement," Rai commented.

"An outright lie, more like," Khine added.

"Both of you," I said, "can go to hell."

I turned the horse and drove into the cloud of smoke and dust. The bandits had chosen to attack at the narrowest part of the road. A few caught sight of us trying to sneak past and gave chase. I drove my spear into the first, catching him clean on the breast. Beside me, Khine managed to unseat a bandit.

Somehow, we fought our way past the choke point and made it past the bridge. The land rolled sharply downhill from here, winding back towards the eastern fork of the River Agos. If we could break from the forest, we'd be able to see the city of Bara down below.

Another horde of bandits blocked the way. I yanked my horse to a stop, sweat pouring down my face. Where were the soldiers ahead of us? Why hadn't they turned back to assist?

"Queen Talyien," a bandit spat.

"She's here?" I asked, feigning surprise. "Where?"

"You, ah—you're still wearing royal robes," Khine whispered behind me.

"Not my crown," I hissed back.

The bandit pointed at me with his sword. "Capture her alive!"

I readied my spear. But before they could even take a step towards me, another group appeared behind them. I caught the black flash of the Bara city guards' armour. I pulled my horse back and watched as they ran through the bandits. The ones they didn't drop on first impact were routed and fled downhill.

A woman in armour rode towards us. "Is that all that's left of you?"

"We got separated," I started. And then I paused, realizing who had just spoken. The woman. Chiha aren dar Baraji, with her red lips and full figure, and eyes you could get lost in for hours.

My fingers twitched.

I don't know how it was possible for Chiha to look even more beautiful now than she did all those years ago. The bloody woman had aged. She must be over thirty now, though Akaterru knew, I had long stopped trying to learn what I could about her—her hobbies, her level of education, what she liked to eat, her least favourite way to die.

"Unhealthy obsessions," Arro told me once, interrupting me in the study. He pointed at the book in my hands. "If you spent all this time reading what I asked you to instead of Baraji gossip, you'd actually learn something."

"It's a history book, Arro."

"It's garbage pretending to be a history book. I don't even know why your father has that in his collection."

"It amused him."

He plucked the book from my hands and slammed it shut. "*The Dragonlords of Bara*," he said, reading the title out loud. "What a joke. The day those Baraji goats get the support to sit on the Dragonthrone, I'll shave all the hair on my head and get ordained at the nearest Kibouri temple. What do you think you're going to do with this information, anyway?"

"Nothing," I grumbled, looking down.

He paused. "You've been here two weeks and in all this time you've done nothing but mope and read this filth. You're returning to the Dragon Palace soon—tell me what's bothering you, Princess."

"There's this girl," I said at last. "Chiha."

"The Baraji princess? I didn't realize her father sent her there."

"She and Rayyel seem...close. Really close." I swallowed and glanced at the floor.

Arro paused.

"It's nothing," I quickly said. "I'm—I'm being fearful for no reason. My betrothed is allowed to have friends, isn't he? Of course he is. I'm—"

He knelt beside me with a thoughtful expression. After a few moments, he said, "You know, I've heard they have new puppies down at the barracks. Let's take a break for now, shall we? Tell the captain you have my blessings." It was the first and last time he had ever allowed me to step away from my responsibilities.

The memory receded. I glanced at Rayyel now, who looked away with discomfort. Of course. He was always like that around her. Even back when we were students in Shirrokaru, he couldn't be in the same room as Chiha without reacting somehow. Sometimes it was a simple cough—sometimes he would leave as soon as she walked in. Signs enough. The man claimed to love me, but it always stung that he never looked at me the same way, that he didn't act like I took his breath away. Such feelings were beneath Yeshin's daughter, so I endeavoured to bury them over the years.

I was no longer that young girl, with those jealousies turning cartwheels in my head. It was strange—had it been any other woman, I would've happily thrown Rayyel at her. I would've asked her to please—*please*, take him, with my blessings. But I suppose we don't really grow up even when we grow old. The mere sight of her brought back memories, the sort that sent spasms of hate from my spine up to my eyeballs.

Arro ought to be proud of me. She came closer, and all I did was smile. "A pleasure, Lady Chiha," I said. "You came just in time."

"Beloved Queen." She took my hand and pressed it on her forehead. Her fingers were cool, her grip loose. "A scout came by with news of the attack."

"You didn't see my mother?" Rai asked. "They were riding before us."

"They must've taken the other road," Chiha said. She bowed, her face perfectly calm as she accorded him the respect befitting of his stature. "Lord Rayyel." Her voice changed, deepening slightly.

Lord. Not Dragonlord. It was odd for her to avoid an insult when I knew she was capable of throwing them like darts. I could *still* hear the sneer in her voice the last time I was down here, could still see the shadow of the amused smile on her face. *Missing a husband, Queen Talyien?* I remembered wanting to ask how someone could find joy in another's sorrow, why she couldn't see how it had turned my life into a living hell. Did she want him so much she was willing to tear my family apart? Why didn't she fight for him the way I did?

"That one leads straight to the city of Onni to the north," Rai said, not returning the greeting. There seemed to be an ice wall between them. An act? If Rai hadn't seen his mother in years, what about her? I was once so convinced they'd rekindled their relationship, I would have bet my life on it.

Chiha gave a small smile. "Time has not been kind to you, Lord Ikessar," she continued, answering my questions for me.

Rai's eyes darted to just about anything but the two of us beside him. He looked hopelessly out of his element.

"It'll be another hour or two for them to get back here," I broke in, taking pity.

"They must be backtracking to avoid the attacks," he murmured.

"And not send us help?"

Rai didn't reply. He turned to Khine. "Ride back and find them, Lamang," he said.

Khine's face twitched. "I'd rather not leave the queen, if that's all right with you."

"Your sister is with them. Aren't you her assistant?"

"She can take care of herself. It's what's ahead of us that I'm worried about."

"What's ahead," Chiha repeated with a small smile. "Who is this man? His Jinan is exceptional."

"A translator overstepping his bounds," Rai commented. "I gave you an order, Lamang."

Khine's eyes skipped towards me, and I caught a flare of impatience on his brow. This was a man who found the concept of royalty laughable, who considered working for a gambling lord the lowest point of his life. It felt like he was daring me to override my husband's words. But after a moment's hesitation, I gave a small nod. There was no point stirring trouble, especially not in front of Lushai's daughter. Khine frowned before turning his horse around. Chiha gestured at her soldiers, and a group split from us to follow him.

"As it were," Chiha said, her voice rising as they disappeared around the bend. "I'm glad to have heard the news that you and our Beloved Queen have reconciled at last. The years of your separation have been rough for all of us, as I'm sure you're well aware. I assume your coronation will be on the horizon soon?"

"The Beloved Princess Ryia has discussed it with the council," he replied.

"Well, when it happens, send me an invitation. I wouldn't miss it for the world," Chiha said, her hands on the pommel of her saddle.

I wasn't the only one trained in diplomacy. We all were. Tittering puppets in a play, acting out roles picked for us before birth. But our troubles had done their share of wearing us down over the years. We rode down to the city in silence, without bothering to exchange more pleasantries. We dismounted as soon as we arrived at the gates.

Music greeted us on the road leading to Toriue Castle. Shirtless men with painted faces and bright-purple headbands were beating large drums in true Bara fashion, bronzed skin glistening with sweat. Various crops—plantain, eggplant, and bitter melon, among others—decorated each house like ornaments. They were strung outside the walls with coloured paper shaped into fans and flowers, which made the street look like a scene from a stained-glass window, a mosaic come to life.

"So Prince Yuebek arrived just in time for your harvest festival," I told Chiha.

She kept a straight face. "As did you, Beloved Queen. A shame you missed Oren-yaro's last summer. I was there, as it happened. The plays retelling the stories of your heroes were particularly well-done this year. The people remain in high spirits, despite our recent troubles." She was very good at skipping past what these troubles were—she paused long enough to pluck a mango from a fence and hand it to me. I wasn't sure if this warm politeness of hers was easier to take than her usual cold courtesies. I dug a nail into the side of the mango and started peeling. My horse, smelling food, nibbled my shoulder. I took a bite before allowing him to have the rest.

"I trust this means the harvest has been good this year," Rai said.

"It's been good *here*," she replied. "I'm not sure elsewhere. I've heard the Oren-yaro have been busy building their army. No need to look concerned, Beloved Queen—you're with friends here."

"Am I?" I asked in a low voice.

She smiled. "And it's not as if Lord General Ozo tried to hide it, either. We do know how the nation tends to respond when the Oren-yaro army grows bigger, but…clearly these are troublesome times, with the war in the west, and these pesky bandits…"

"So you've dealt with this before," Rai said.

"Shirrokaru has been lax with its patrols. Not that you can blame them. Princess Ryia wouldn't allow the council to appoint a regent in the queen's absence. We've all been effectively functioning as in the old days: to each their own, province before nation, and clan before all else."

We reached the gates leading to Toriue, where guards arrived to relieve us of our horses. The Baraji castle was about twice the size of Oka Shto, with grounds that went much further. It wasn't always theirs, of course. Back in the day, the province was called Laiong before the Baraji took control, renaming the city and the entire region after themselves. A common enough occurrence in that war-torn land; but the circumstances with which they won the castle for themselves were particularly noteworthy in that they tricked an entire family under the guise of friendship before murdering them in their beds.

Given that story, showing up at that castle's doorstep probably wasn't the wisest thing in the world. The words *I knew better* came to mind. But the risk of insulting Warlord Lushai when we *knew* that he knew more than he let on was just as great. I wondered why Rayyel continued to insist that he found Lushai trustworthy. I never did like the bastard. Most days, my father considered him a blubbering fool who would stab an ally given half the chance. Not just in the back—anywhere he could reach him.

We entered the great hall, which had the appearance of the Akaterru temples up in the foothills. Sunlight streamed through the windows from right under the ceiling, forming a circular, flower-like pattern on the floor. Warlord Lushai stood on the raised platform, arms folded over his chest. His long whiskers seemed to curl at the sight of me. "Queen Talyien," he purred. "It has been far too long since you graced these halls with your lovely presence. I was surprised you answered my summons almost immediately. Pleased, but still, surprised. What was it you said, Nijo? Something about buffalo sprouting wings?" The layer of indignation was hard to miss, even as he tried to mask it. He stepped down to meet us.

I allowed him to take my hand. He had a limp grip. Combining that with the way he looked at me gave me the sensation of cold slime, one I wanted to scrub off with a rock under running water. I was almost relieved that he didn't kiss it. He pressed the back of my hand against his forehead, the sort of thing that an elder like him would only give to someone in my position. I pulled my hand back immediately—I could still feel the oil of his sweat on my skin.

"You had a guest, you said."

He sniffed. "I did say. Unfortunately, it will only be me and my son entertaining you for now." He bowed, glancing towards the heavyset young man beside him, who took a step towards me. Lord Nijo, his eldest, and Chiha's brother. He didn't touch me at all, choosing to perform an elaborate bow in Zarojo-fashion.

"So where is Prince Yuebek?" I struggled to keep the irritation out of my voice. To be dancing around the biggest threat our nation had faced since Yeshin's war seemed like the sort of thing they would be mocking us for in the years to come.

Lushai gave that crocodile smile of his. "He is . . . indisposed at the moment."

If you don't know Warlord Yeshin's history with Warlord Lushai, I suggest the book *Memoirs from the Beginning of the Wolves' War* by Ichi rok Sagar, with caution. It has created a myriad of controversy because of his portrayal of the women involved, but the tome also contains some fascinating details about both men and the arrangements that helped fuel the war.

Of course, I've never gotten past the first chapter. His account of Sume alon gar Kaggawa, one of the key figures of the war, is rather distasteful, especially considering she was supposed to be an ally of his. Perhaps it is a pity that I chose to let my personal aversions get in the way, because it's supposed to be a well-written, well-researched piece, at least according to Rayyel.

In any case, I recommend you read *something* other than these tattered notes, because I never thought much of Lushai from the beginning. I knew his history with my father, and I knew that he played just as important a part in the War of the Wolves as Yeshin did. But I could only see him with Yeshin's eyes—as nothing more than a man who would doggedly chase after the first shiny object so long as he knew the consequences wouldn't be damning for him. When he agreed to support my father's cause, it was with the understanding that he would lay all the blame on Yeshin should they ever lose and be put on trial. My father had accepted this with a bark of laughter and an open invitation for the opposing warlords to try their best. So while the rest of the land saw them as close friends—blood brothers, even—I saw only a man who would use grief for his own gain. Did he even believe in my father's cause? If you asked him, he would say *yes* with conviction. If you asked me...well. I would sooner trust a crocodile not to tear my arm off.

"Indisposed," I said, echoing Lushai. I glanced at Rayyel. I noticed they didn't greet him. It was almost as if he wasn't even there.

"The weather, he said, is too humid. He sends his deepest regrets."

Too humid, no doubt, for that clay-scarred face. "Lushai. Please don't tell me that I took all this trouble to respond to your invitation, gathered my people—the Beloved Princess Ryia aren dar Ikessar is on her way here as we speak—*just* so you could tell us that we wasted our time?"

Lushai's face barely registered a flicker. He was used to my father's outbursts. "We've prepared our best chambers for you," he said, clicking his fingers. "I'm sure you've had a long journey. Food will be sent to your rooms."

The insubordination was so clear in his tone that my hand dropped to my sword almost instantly. Just as quickly, I felt Rayyel's fingers around my wrist.

"Thank you, Warlord Lushai," Rai said.

I still managed to clink my blade against the scabbard. "If you try anything, do remember that Bara has never once fought against Oren-yaro and won."

Lushai gave a pained grin. "Your distrust wounds me, Beloved Queen. Consider this your home. Enjoy everything Toriue Castle has to offer."

I followed Rai in silence. It was clear from his familiarity with the servants and the turns that he knew this place well. Too well. We reached a solarium, surrounded by the remnants of what were once hibiscus bushes. A fountain in the center struggled to gurgle water past the thin layer of ice on the surface.

"What is going on?" I asked, whirling around to face him.

He let go of my arm. "You were too distracted on the way up here."

"Is that a problem?"

His face tightened. "Chiha took the news of the bandit attack as an opportunity to meet us first. She wanted to warn us. Her father is... acting strangely, and she needs our help."

"When the hell did she tell you this?"

"She whispered it to me right as we entered the city."

"Is this really the time? The woman's just appealing to your chivalric nature."

He looked confused.

I struggled against the wave of anger. "Spit it out."

He pressed a letter into my palm. "It's an address in Bara. She wants to meet us there tonight. She says it's urgent."

I barely glanced at it. "Listen here, Rai. I'm not going to run blindly into a trap set by an old lover of yours."

"I did the same with Agos for you." Rai said it matter-of-factly, but it filled me with a momentary flush of shame. I fell silent.

He placed his hand on mine, the one still loosely grasping the letter. I think he wanted to say more, but words had never been his strong suit, and he seemed to change his mind and cleared his throat. "The guest quarters are out that way," he said, indicating the hall with a quick gesture. "I will speak with Lushai alone. I feel perhaps that your presence intimidates him."

"A snivelling dog like that? I'm not surprised." But I saw the value in his suggestion and allowed him to walk away. Only when he had disappeared around the corner did I look down at the note. It was barely legible, scratched in haste. For a moment, I was tempted to tear it apart. I owed this woman nothing.

Instead, I tucked it into my pocket and continued down the path.

CHAPTER NINE

OLD GAMES

ᛁᛏᚬᛩ

A servant emerged to lead me to a walled-off portion of the courtyard and down to a group of single-room dwellings, surrounded by stone paths. Guards in the Oren-yaro armour were waiting for me, none of whom I recognized from the march. The captain stepped forward with a bow. "Lakas asor arak Parang at your service, Beloved Queen." He was a big man with a round belly, with the darker skin of someone from the southern islands—Akki or Meiokara. I couldn't tell from the accent. But I knew the name.

"Lakas," I repeated. "You're Captain Nor's husband."

He bowed a second time.

"Your wife—"

"General Ozo has asked me to serve you in my wife's absence," he said, deflecting the impending question of his wife's abandonment of her duties with ease. "He sent me ahead to ensure your safe arrival. We didn't anticipate a bandit attack so late in the season—it's the first in these parts. You have my apologies for that."

A formal man. I stared at him for a moment, wondering if he was one of Ozo's dogs. He had to be. They all were, as far as I was concerned. "Is there news from the others?"

He paused for a moment before nodding towards the door, which the guards opened. He gestured for me to step inside. As soon as I had walked past him, he carefully closed the door. "Truth be told," he began, "we purposely gave you fewer guards to see what she would do."

She. Princess Ryia. I cleared my throat. "And she took the bait."

He nodded. "I'm glad to see you unharmed. Unfortunately, we couldn't capture any of the bandits alive. The only proof we have that Princess Ryia was involved at all was that no one dared approach Lord Rayyel. We were counting on your close proximity to his presence to keep you safe, but this won't convince the council of her treachery, especially a council heavily influenced by the Ikessars already."

"I didn't know you were a politician, Captain Lakas. We're nearly kin—be straight with me. Was this a promotion or a demotion for you?"

He frowned. "You are our highest priority at the moment. Ranks don't matter—you need to be kept safe."

"Was that in your pamphlets while I was running for my life in the empire?" Lakas frowned.

"If Ozo wants to seize power, he can stop drawing this out. If he wants the throne, let him face me in combat! You have given me the title of queen, but you've made it clear it means nothing unless I carry out my father's will. Yet it's not Yeshin sitting on the throne, is it? *I'm* Dragonlord. Either you're with me, or you're against me. Which one is it, Captain?"

"The title…" Lakas began, his eyes on the floor. He took a deep breath. "The title is a reflection of what you can do for your people, not what they can do for you. This… this isn't about you, Beloved Queen."

Just at that moment, someone knocked at the door, and Lakas, looking slightly embarrassed at having lectured me, went to open it. A guard came in to whisper something in Lakas's ear. He turned back to me. "Princess Ryia has arrived," he said. "None the worse for wear."

"What does Ozo intend to do from here?"

"Nothing," Lakas replied. "We were hoping she would show her hand and we would have an excuse to ride against her. But as it is now, we don't have anything."

"We already know she's out for my blood."

"We've always known that. But you have nothing to fear. General Ozo is a devoted servant of Jin-Sayeng and will ensure your safety at all times." His eyes were distant as he spoke, and I felt that same old sting, the one that I've carried with me all these years. I could see it now, name it even. How can I serve Jin-Sayeng from inside this cage? My own people—my own family—have kept me at arm's length my whole life.

Khine appeared at the end of the courtyard. Lakas sniffed and went to intercept him. "I'm Inzali Lamang's assistant," Khine said, showing his empty hands. "I need to speak with the queen."

"We know who you are." Lakas's fingers were on the hilt of his sword.

Khine frowned. "I'm sorry, I don't—"

"If you think the queen is so friendless that she has no choice but to entrust her life to the hands of a foreigner—"

"Captain," I broke in.

Lakas tightened his jaw. "I can't stop you from congregating with scum," he said, turning to me. "But General Ozo wanted me to remind you who you are. You're not Zarojo. You're not an Ikessar. You're a wolf of Oren-yaro."

"There's not a damn moment in my life that I've forgotten that," I replied, keeping my voice low. "Now leave."

He bowed and left without a reply.

"Your people seem awfully fond of you," Khine said, following me inside the guest quarters.

"He's Nor's husband."

"I should've recognized the scowl. They say when a couple spend too much time with each other, they start to look alike."

"Good thing Rai left after three years," I grumbled. "I remember Lakas being more cheerful than this. Whatever's weighing on their minds must be a heavy enough burden. If they could just *tell* me, maybe it wouldn't be so hard."

"Clearly they support Yuebek's claim," Khine said. "Ozo didn't seem very happy to learn that you killed Qun or that Rai let Ikessars into your castle. Of course, he wouldn't be so vocal about it—not with Princess Ryia around."

"You neglect honorifics with just about everyone but that witch. What gives?"

He paused. "She looks like a princess."

"And I don't?"

"Do you really want me to answer that?"

"You know, Lamang, behind that ridiculously charming smile, you're just as vicious as I am."

"I think you're wrong, but I'm glad you think I'm charming." He grew serious. "Whatever Ozo wants lies in what he's keeping from you. He must know how you don't appreciate the dishonesty. I don't believe that he's abandoned this Yuebek business just because you're back home. They'd prefer if you offered yourself up to him on purpose, of course, but barring that..."

"They know I can't just set Rai aside."

Khine shrugged. "The dangerous part is how quiet they are. They've got something up their sleeve."

"So I'm trapped between my people, who want me to marry a monster and reclaim the power my father had given up for peace, and my husband's people, who would see me dead for that same reason." I sat down beside him with a sigh.

His lips twitched. "If I had an answer for you, Tali..."

"I'm not asking for one," I said. "Chiha...went under her father's nose. She wants to meet me and Rai somewhere in the city."

"Remind me again what happens every time someone hands you a note and arranges some clandestine assembly. Assassins, was it?" He crossed his arms. "Your husband is quite the prized possession. I'm a little envious."

"It's all in the grooming. Would you happen to know what a hairbrush is for?"

He tried to smooth his messy hair back into place. "That impressive moustache, I'm assuming. Maybe I should grow my beard out."

"You...maybe you shouldn't."

"Why not?"

"And Yuebek—he didn't meet us at all. *Indisposed.* Like I'd believe that."

"Namra told me to let you know that she doesn't think Yuebek is in the castle. He's a mage, with enormous power and a connection to the *agan* that is difficult for other mages to miss, at least in a land as barren of mages as Jin-Sayeng. She told me that she should, at the very least, detect a faint wisp of it in the air. Unless Yuebek's trying to mask his scent on purpose, but...she doesn't think he would bother. We *know* he's in Jin-Sayeng. Why try to hide?"

I sighed. "Rai wants me to go with him."

Khine squinted. "He wants you to trust his ex-lover?"

"Evidently."

His face twitched. "And, er—he doesn't think she's going to smash your brains in with a brick and drag you to a back alley?"

"She's a princess."

He smirked. "So are you."

"You're really not going to stop with these jokes, are you?"

"I'd make them forever if you'd let me." There was a note of longing in his voice. I wanted to catch it the way I caught seed fluffs in the wind when I was little. *Those carry wishes*, Agos had said. *If you hide them in your palm and whisper your life's desires, someday the gods will grant them.*

The door opened and one of the guards returned. He saluted without really looking directly at me. "The captain wants to inform the Beloved Queen that official translations are not needed at the moment and that Anong Lamang will be most welcome in the servants' quarters, if it's not too much trouble."

"It is," I growled.

The guard still wouldn't meet my eyes. "Captain Lakas believes it isn't appropriate for you to be left alone with the foreigner for very long."

"Tali," Khine said in a low voice. "This isn't a battle we want to fight."

He was wrong about that, but I decided not to argue. He walked away, allowing the guards to lock the door behind him.

I dreamed of a child that evening—a girl with long hair and Agos's eyes. Not a memory, not a ghost—nothing but a dream conjured by an exhausted mind. But she smiled as she reached for my hand, and the grief I wasn't allowing myself to feel broke loose. I woke up in tears, my belly aching, a gnawing sensation that reached into the depths of my soul. I curled into a ball as the images from the dream faded into nothingness. It was strange to feel loss when nothing had truly been ripped away from you. I felt like an intruder prodding at a sorrow that wasn't mine. When the haze receded and my thoughts became clear, I thought—as I had hundreds of times since his death—about what I did to Agos. I thought about what I could have done differently and if there was anything I could still do to make it right. I let my mind play over the memory of his mangled body on the floor, all those details burned into my brain—the sweat on his stiffening body, the blood on the floor—so that I could never again forget how power could turn a lapse of judgment into a hole big enough for a grave. If I was careless yet again, there would be room for a thousand more.

Three knocks sounded at the door. I rolled over to grab my coat before answering it. Khine and Rayyel stood outside, huffing into the cold air. My guards were nowhere in sight.

"How did you chase them off?" I asked.

Rai grumbled something under his breath.

"You really don't want to know," Khine said. "They'll be back soon."

"It was a step too far, Lamang," Rai managed, his face beet red.

"I merely implied that the queen and her king might want a moment's privacy, and if they want to just do a quick patrol for a few minutes…"

"His mouth ran ahead of him," Rai growled.

"It always does. Let's go before I have to come up with a better excuse."

We made our way through the gardens until we hit the end of a wall. Khine vaulted up first—I scrambled after him before turning around to help Rai. He already looked like he was regretting the whole thing. The castle walls were covered with vines, which helped with every drop-off. We reached a section that ran downhill, over another compound where I could see fires and pavilions.

"My mother's camp," Rai said under his breath.

"She refused Warlord Lushai's hospitality? Typical Ikessar."

He stared at me.

"Sorry," I grumbled. "Bad habit."

"It is likely that she'll entertain him if he begs long enough," Rai continued. "She'll want to see him begging. The war left plenty of wounds. Warlord Lushai has committed his fair share of atrocities."

"And yet you still trust him?"

"He maintains that it was your father who…" Rai stopped talking, as if realizing he didn't want to bring up my father after all. I didn't remember having been around him this long without an argument. It occurred to me for the first time that he was afraid of *me*—not because I was Oren-yaro, but because I was his wife, the woman who shared his bed for years. I wasn't sure how to feel about that. It wasn't the sort of thing a bride would ever want from her husband. I didn't even want it from my people.

Khine paused up ahead. He turned around, gestured sharply, and slid down the wall. I dropped down after him, landing behind a tall bush. Just as I heard Rai amble after us, I heard a familiar voice from behind the gate.

"You implied I had a choice, Beloved Princess." Belfang's. I felt my blood curdle.

"I have never met anyone so daft," Ryia replied. "What were you hoping to gain?"

"Didn't you want to see for yourself if the Beloved Queen Talyien was true or not? If her heart is false, or simply misguided?" Belfang asked. "I did. I thought this was what you meant when you said—"

"Consider yourself lucky…you assisted my son in the Empire, and for that you may keep your head. But I might no longer be generous should I see or hear from you again. Go."

I saw Belfang's figure shuffle forward in an awkward bow. "Beloved Princess," he said before he left. I caught a hint of something—a shadow of a sneer.

I turned around. "We need to follow him," I whispered.

"But Chiha..." Rai began.

"I feel like I'm going to regret this, but...you need to go to her yourself. Take Namra, for safety's sake."

"And you?"

"Khine and I need to see what that man's up to," I replied. "He works for Yuebek and Yuebek is hiding from us. Why would he hide? None of this feels right."

Rai grabbed my sleeve. "Beloved Queen," he started. I thought he was going to argue. Instead, he tilted his head down to kiss me.

The movement caught me by surprise. I flinched and pulled away as soon as his lips touched mine. "We need to go," I said.

"Please be careful."

Khine ran a hand through his hair as I caught up with him. "I think he went that way," he croaked out. His eyes looked distant.

It was tricky trying to stay as far away from Belfang as possible without losing sight of him. The road became darker the further from the castle and camps we got, until eventually the only source of light came from the moon shining over the right fork of the River Agos.

We went around the low road, the one that led straight to the river docks. Rain from the past few days had near-obliterated the path, blanketing it with a sheen of frozen mud. It was the sort of thing I should've noticed if I visited the province more often. The Baraji openly pilfered from their coffers, so that coin needed for infrastructure repairs often went to their own castle instead. This was somehow always reported as public maintenance or somesuch nonsense. I knew about the fraud, but my quest for Rayyel in those days left me little energy to argue with this particular clan. It was the way they had always done things, Arro told me—a privilege Lushai took advantage of because of his close ties with my father. And I hated dealing with Lushai, hated having to be in the same room as Chiha. It was just easier to sign the papers and pretend all future problems were theirs alone. Now that I could see the results of my own neglect, I wondered if I was lying to myself about doing better as queen. The last year had left me a shadow. Could I be what I never was?

I turned my attention to the river, swollen to twice the size it was when I first came home. The street sloped downhill, and we came upon an alley connected to a strip of dock. Sudden laughter obscured the current, and I smelled smoke laced with cloves and incense. There was a small shrine to Akaterru in an alcove, where thin candles hung from metal grilles, lit by the faithful in the hopes that the god would grant them blessings and good fortune.

"Shit," Khine murmured. "I can't see him."

"Figures," I replied. I stuffed my hands into my pockets, my breath turning white as I glanced around. Despite the cold weather, laundry was flapping above us, rags forgotten for the night. A cat peered back at me from the rooftop, yellow eyes gleaming.

I strode up the steps leading to the alley, following the sound of laughter to a row of gambling houses. Men were gathered in groups out on the street, playing dice and cards in lantern light while drinking from clay jars. Women with painted faces hung about, tittering as they draped over the men. Despite the cold, their robes were half open.

"Why do I always find myself in places like these when I'm with you?" I asked.

Khine gave a soft smile. "That's what I feel about you and dragons."

I scanned the buildings and spotted a noodle house. Tables of various shapes and sizes were scattered on the street, right outside the windows. Belfang was on the other side of the glass, standing between two other patrons. I started after him.

"Hold on, lady," one of the men from the tables called out. "You look like someone I'd spend my money on. How about you give us a second here?" He tried to grab my sleeve.

I drew my dagger, turned around, and stabbed the table right between a bowl of peeled sugarcane and his arm. "Damn," I said. "Missed."

The man pulled back. "You fucking cunt. If you think you can get away with this—"

I glanced through the window. I could see Belfang sitting down and ordering a meal, which gave me time to think. If this commotion continued, he could very well just slip out and run off again. And I wasn't sure if I wanted to tail him through these streets the whole night—it was too easy to lose sight of him. I swore under my breath before turning back to the man and giving my sweetest smile. "I'm sorry," I said. "Was that rude of me?"

"Bitch," the man hissed. "Do you want me to call the guards?" His companions grunted in agreement.

I grasped the hilt of the dagger and, without extracting it from the table, grabbed a stool with my other hand and sat down.

"What are you doing?" Khine hissed behind me.

I ignored him. "What are you playing?" I asked.

They threw dubious looks at each other. "Monkey-hands," one finally said, glancing at the man I'd accosted with an expression that was almost apologetic.

"Perfect," I said. "I *love* Monkey-hands. Let me join in."

Such a reasonable request, coming from a woman brandishing a dagger, was more than enough for them. One of the men began dealing the cards, and we placed bets. I named a substantial amount. Eyes bulged. Some of the whores, drawn by the talk of money, approached cautiously. When they saw me playing, they began to insult the gamblers, daring them to match my wager.

"Let me rephrase what I just said," Khine grumbled, waving a woman away without even looking at her. "What the *fuck* are you doing?"

"I'm playing, sweetness," I said. "Be a dear and keep away from the window."

"I'm trying to block you from the sun, my love."

I pointed at the sky. "It's the dead of the night."

"With your complexion, dearest, I didn't want to take chances."

The men were looking at us in confusion. I smiled. "We're tourists," I explained.

"And you came to Bara, of all places?" one asked. "What's this shithole got that's worth coming all the way out here for?"

"Sutan's the spot," another sniffed. "Better streets. Nicer bridges. Warlord Buhawi's a half-decent lord, too. An improvement over his father."

"And in the meantime, old Lushai's just getting fatter and richer every year," a third barked. "We're hoping he dies soon, but then Nijo's not much better than him. The best we can hope for is that he steals *less* from public funds. Thank the gods the queen is back. Hopefully she puts those bastards on a leash. I was worried for a while there, thinking we'd go back to the way things were."

"The war, you mean?" I asked casually.

"The war was shit," the man said, chewing off a huge hunk of sugarcane. He ground it between his teeth. "I was just a kid, but—the damn royals, dragging us along with their problems! Why can't they just get along?" He spat to the side, sending bits of sugarcane flying.

"You know what I think?" the first man broke in. "Queen's not going to do a damn thing. She never did. She spent all of five years doing nothing but obsessing over her husband."

I felt my face twitch as I shifted the cards in my hand.

"They're together now," his friend replied. "Maybe things will be better with Dragonlord Rayyel around."

"You never know with the bastards."

We played the cards. I won. I bet higher, and talk turned away from the royals—to my relief—to the weather and the price of rice and rooster fights. On purpose, I butchered my play; the money I lost drew attention. Players from the other tables crowded around us.

"Damn," I said. "I don't have the coin to pay that back." I turned away half a cup of clear coconut liquor, offered in sympathy.

"Shouldn't have bet so much if you didn't," one of the men snarled.

I shrugged. "I got carried away. Will you take something else in exchange? Something worth more?"

The men traded glances. "Like what?"

I pulled the dagger out and ran my fingers over the blade before I replied. "A mage," I said in a low voice.

Their eyes flashed, but they kept their mouths shut. I smiled.

"We're in Bara," I continued. "Warlord Lushai, like the departed Warlord Yeshin, is a traditionalist. His stance has always been to maintain Jin-Sayeng according to the old rules. Mages aren't welcome here." I slid the dagger back into its sheath. "A mage will fetch a fine price with the city watch. I know for a fact that they offer rewards for turning in persons of interest to the warlord. What if I deliver a mage into your hands?"

"That's ridiculous," one of the men eventually said. "Even if you know such a person, how can you prove that they *are* one?"

I got up, lifted the heavy wooden stool, and flung it at the window behind me.

Glass exploded as it flew straight at Belfang, who was just about to sit down to enjoy a second bowl of noodles. He threw up a shield spell before he realized what was happening. The stool slammed against the thin blue barrier and shattered into pieces upon impact.

The men roared. Belfang's eyes fell on me, but it was too late. I hung back as they thundered through the door after him.

"You're evil," Khine commented as we followed the mob down the street.

I smirked. "He'll talk now."

"What makes you think that?"

I placed a finger on my lips before motioning for him to stay back. I crossed the threshold to the jailhouse, where the city watch yelled at spectators to go home. I caught sight of the gamblers grinning amongst themselves.

"You've a good eye, woman," one said, showing me a hefty purse. "Consider your debt paid."

"Next time I'll sweep your pockets clean," I promised.

They laughed and strode back out to the street. I glanced behind me. Belfang was in chains, his face like a garden in mid-May—decorated in an explosion of red and purple. Even his fists were bruised—he had been foolish enough to try to cast another spell as the men bore down on him, and they had responded by attempting to break his wrists.

He looked at me, seething, a trickle of blood dripping down one side of his cheek. His hooked nose looked broken. I gazed back, unaffected. I couldn't look at him without remembering Khine's mother and what he had done to the villagers back in Phurywa. I liked to imagine that if I had my way, I would use his head to mop up the same blood he helped spill.

I walked up to the captain. "Are you transferring him straight to Toriue?"

"In time," she said without looking at me. She was bent over her desk, scribbling over paperwork. "Move along with the rest of them."

The lobby was mostly empty now, save for two other guards and another prisoner in the single cell in the corner. I cleared my throat and took one step closer to the captain.

She looked at me in irritation. "I said—"

I flipped my hand palm-side up, showing the wolf's-head ring that iden-tified the warlord of Oren-yaro. I had worn it upside down since leaving the castle. The captain's eyes widened. I was suddenly glad to be back in the part of the world where the symbol still meant something. Her lips quivered, as if she wasn't quite sure if she believed it or not, but a moment later she dropped her head in a quick bow. "My lady," she started. "Beloved Queen…"

"I'd like to take custody of the mage."

Belfang lifted his head.

"That is—if he promises to cooperate." I turned to Belfang. "You're still work-ing for *him*, aren't you?" I said, switching to Zirano. "I want to know everything."

Belfang looked away. He never really did like looking straight at me. "Just leave me be."

I strode up to where he was chained and sat down on the closest bench. I crossed my legs. "You and I haven't really spoken."

He chuckled. "What's there to talk about? You were convinced I was a villain the moment you laid eyes on me."

"You don't consider the things you've done villainous?"

"Says the queen famed for her decapitations and torture," he sniffed.

I continued smiling back at him, inwardly wondering whether the accusations would ever lose their sting. "Meting out justice is not the same as using helpless elders who *trusted* that you only had their best interests at heart," I replied. "But that's all done now. Nothing we do can bring them back. But you—right now, you can help prevent a bloodbath."

"What do you think I'm trying to do?" he asked.

"You think that you can achieve that by continuing to work for someone like Yuebek?"

"I told you. I have nothing to say to you."

I clicked my tongue. "Maybe you think he can help you. That he'll hear about what the crude Jins have done to one of his servants. A pity that he can't lift a finger if he doesn't know what happened to you. The riot back there—how many of those happen every night in these streets? Do you honestly think word of it will ever reach the Baraji? You must've seen how little they care for their own."

That got his attention. "What are you saying?"

"I'm saying that if you disappear within the bowels of the city, no one's going to be the wiser." I crossed my arms. "I can order them to dispose of you now if I want to."

"Your laws..."

"Are you really going to take your chances with—as you said—a queen famed for her decapitations and torture?"

He licked his lips. "Damn you."

I glanced at the guards. "I'll be taking him now."

"My queen, he's a mage," the captain breathed.

"If he turns me into a toad, you can string him upside down in the square tomorrow."

She nodded, and a guard stepped forward, hauling Belfang to his feet. He handed the chains to me.

We stepped out into the street, Belfang a foot from me with the tip of my sword at his back. We walked in near-darkness until we reached a quieter neighbourhood at the edge of the city. There, he led us down a series of steps leading back to the river, to the mouth of a sewage tunnel.

Khine held the lantern over our heads as we ventured down the path along the side. It was rough, moldy, dug centuries ago, stone jutting out from every angle. It opened up to a tangled maze of tunnels, more elaborate than what we had in Oren-yaro. Bara was an older city, and I could spot the Zarojo craftsmanship even on the grates. We could deny it as much as we wanted, but we were too intricately tied to the empire.

"I mean, you're really more foolhardy than you're smart," Belfang said out of nowhere.

"Did I say you could talk?"

"You *know* who I'm working for," Belfang continued. "What can I tell you that you don't already know?"

"Whatever you're hiding," I said easily. "Whatever *he's* hiding, to be precise. That is why we're here, right?"

We were interrupted by the scrabbling sound of what could only be rats scampering up ahead.

"Maybe he's taking us to his family," Khine mused.

Belfang attacked.

I didn't have time to wonder how he managed to loosen the chains enough to dare. But he didn't go for me. Too loyal of a servant, even away from his unseen master; it was Khine he lunged for, aiming for his weak arm. I turned to fight and saw Belfang fall.

Khine pulled his sword back. Belfang rolled along the path, blood pooling on the ground underneath him. His lips twitched into a smile. "To be killed by holier-than-thou Lamang," Belfang croaked.

"You should've left my mother alone," Khine said.

"You had it in you after all. But then again, you've always hated me. Back when we were kids, the way you looked at me…" He spat out blood. "Is it because *we* were willing to settle, while you, for all your hard work, couldn't get close to your lofty dreams? That's why you're *with* her, isn't it? She's your key out of your hellhole. Because underneath that act, you're just a good-for-nothing dog like the rest of us. You—"

I stabbed Belfang myself before he could open his mouth again, a dagger straight into his heart. Khine watched as I yanked the blade out of the body.

Blood dripped down my arm and next to my boot. We stood there for several moments, the silence interrupted only by the sound of dripping water above us. I slowly sheathed the dagger.

"Yuebek will be here somewhere." He shrugged away from me.

I grabbed his arm. "Khine..."

"This isn't the time."

"You don't even know what I was going to say."

His jaw tightened, and his eyes danced as he considered me with an expression I had never seen on him before. One part hunger, another part regret. He turned his head before I could do anything about it.

We ventured deeper into the shadows, which was vastly preferable to confronting what we didn't have the power to change. It helped that the path was straightforward from here on out. There was the possibility that Belfang had been trying to lose us out here, but I didn't want to dwell on that. He *had* to have brought us here for a reason. The man had seen an opening and decided to take it, but if he hadn't...

I stopped in my tracks as I saw the path widening up to a series of flat steps and a ledge overlooking a trickle of storm water. There was a single door at the far corner.

"Old cities, old secrets," I said out loud in an effort to chase away the silence. "I would love to know what Chiha wanted to tell us, but then that rat would've been slinking around, doing the gods know what..." I shivered slightly as Khine strode up behind me. His eyes were on the door.

"Let's end this," he said. He kicked it open.

CHAPTER TEN

WILTED ROSES

ʊɔ͡ɾɪ͡ɾ

There were candles in the hallway we found ourselves in, which sputtered slightly at the sudden draft. A feeling of dread hung in the air, like a musty scent. Thicker than what you'd find in an old room. Thicker than mud. I was starting to recognize it.

"I suppose there's no point asking you to let me do this alone," I said.

Khine gave a cold smile. "Absolutely none."

I made my way down the corridor. The candlelights danced as I passed them, the flames turning a deep blue. "I guess it doesn't matter," I grumbled. "He already knows we're here. The bastard has his claws in everything. Dear Esteemed Prince, perhaps a guide to save us the trouble?" My voice echoed down the hollows and dead spaces between the walls.

The hall ended, revealing a door fringed with cobwebs around the frame, most of them gathered in bunches around the hinges. There were none on the knob. I placed my hand on it and found it warm. The door opened with no resistance.

We found ourselves in a small courtyard with a square pond in the center, decorated with crumbling statues of Saint Fei Rong and Akaterru. Vines crept around the bases and through the figures' mouths and eyes, like snakes creeping up the stone. I glanced at the water, a murky brown with a thin layer of foam. I thought I glimpsed tadpoles, which was strange given the time of the year. The cold water should've killed them.

"That bastard is playing with us," Khine said, breaking the tension. He struck one of the statues with a closed fist, sending a chunk of stone flying into the pond. The change in his mood was palpable.

I saw a light from one of the windows directly across from us. "Up there?" I asked.

Khine gave a mirthless chuckle. "Perhaps he wants a tryst."

"That's not funny."

"I wasn't joking."

I tried to shrug off the feeling of dread crawling over me like dozens of trailing fingers. At that moment, I wanted nothing more than reassurance, but I wasn't sure who was capable of giving that to me anymore. I turned to a memory of myself as a child sitting astride my father's shoulders, my hands in his as I viewed the city of Oren-yaro from up high. "Yours," he told me. "This whole kingdom is yours." He laughed, his eyes disappearing into the folds of his face as he held me to the sunlight. Other memories of my father pressed against the corners of my thoughts, memories that hurt simply because they existed. Memories that shouldn't sting, that for most other people brought joy and warmth, a sensation of having been loved once in their lives. Of having been loved enough.

I pushed the feelings away, along with the tears. I was a grown woman, a queen; in light of my responsibilities, it didn't matter how many pieces of myself were missing. I gathered my courage as we left the courtyard and stepped under the covered platform. A single door beside a lit window beckoned. This one, too, was unlocked.

We were now inside the first floor of a Kag-style apartment. There was a boy sitting on a velvet chair near the brick fireplace with his back to me—black hair tied above his head, a familiar height and shape.

"Thanh!" I cried.

The boy turned.

I knew my mistake as soon as I saw his face, but there was a moment where I told myself it was just the light. This *had* to be my boy. The turn of his nose, the shape of his features…If the shadows had loomed a little closer, I would've sworn it was my son. I wanted it to be him.

But it wasn't. "Yes?" the boy asked, a voice that was a touch higher than Thanh's. It was different enough that it broke the illusion.

I took a step towards the child before noticing that Khine, too, had been holding his breath. He didn't know what Thanh looked like.

"It's not him," I said.

He drew his brows together. "Perhaps you should stay away, then."

"What do you mean?"

"Who knows what things that man could conjure?"

"It's just a boy," I muttered.

"I made that same mistake in the Sougen once, if you recall."

I noticed a line of worry over the child's forehead. "We're not here to hurt you," I found myself saying, despite Khine's warning. "We're looking for someone else."

"Do you know where my mother is?" he asked.

I shook my head. "I haven't seen her."

Khine cleared his throat. "Who's your mother, child?"

He suddenly looked frightened. "I . . ." he began. He wiped his face.

"Anino!" a woman's voice thundered from the stairs.

The boy shrank back. No—not my son at all. Thanh would've simply scoffed at such a tone. He was dressed in royals' robes, with the pale complexion of a child who had been kept out of the sun. As I mulled over this, I turned my head in time to see a woman appear around the corner.

"Who are you?" the woman asked.

I struggled to keep my focus. If the boy looked familiar, so did she. But I couldn't put a name to her face. She was either younger or older than me, with plucked eyebrows and painted lips, which told me that if they were prisoners here, they hadn't been for very long. "I think I should be asking the both of you that instead," I said.

She caught a glimpse of my ring, which I made no effort to hide. Realization dawned on her face. "Beloved Queen," she managed, before dropping to the floor, the bow of a frightened commoner. It was an extreme reaction. I glanced at the child, who managed to get to his feet before the woman dragged him back down. She forced his head to the floor.

"The boy." I nodded towards him. "He's a royal."

She didn't try to deny it. "My queen," she said, keeping her head low.

I turned to the walls of the apartment, decorated with Kag-style paintings, the sort that favoured rich oil paints. "Whose house is this?" I asked.

"My queen," she repeated.

"I'm guessing they live here," Khine spoke up. "I noticed shoes at the door."

"Is that right?" I frowned. "A child who would not tell me about his mother, and a woman who will not say who she is or what she's doing here. Strange." I now stepped towards the child again. His face was completely white, the fear dancing in his eyes. "Didn't I tell you I'm not here to hurt you?" I asked.

He nodded.

"Then why don't you believe me?"

"You're...you're the queen," he gasped.

"Anino," the woman said. "Please."

"I was speaking with him," I replied, a tad irritated.

The woman fell silent.

"Continue," I told the boy.

"They said that if you ever find me, you'd kill me," he stammered.

Why would I kill a child? I knew my reputation was tarnished, but I didn't think it was ground so deep into the mud that people actually thought of me as some witch who stalked helpless innocents in the dark. Unless...

I felt my senses darken. I turned to Khine, who had his arms crossed as he considered the situation, and then to the woman, who remained on the ground, her face a mask of both terror and appeasement. "Who *are* you?" I repeated.

She mumbled something incomprehensible.

"There's no sense hiding it," I snapped. "I left Toriue Castle this evening at Chiha Baraji's urging. This must have something to do with it."

The woman's face flickered at the name. The boy, Anino, started weeping.

"I knew it," I whispered.

"Rayyel's bastard?" Khine asked, coming to the same conclusion at the same time I did.

"My husband's stamp is all over the boy," I said. "And believe me, I *know* now, after everything that had happened the last few weeks. I've spent days going over any resemblance Rai may have to my memories of my son. And now this..." I found myself sitting down, shaking my head. I didn't know how I was supposed to feel. I turned to the woman. "Get up," I ordered.

She rose slowly. I gazed at her face and saw that she wasn't afraid of me for herself. It was the boy that made her compliant. "Are you an Ikessar?" I asked.

She shook her head.

"But this apartment *belongs* to the Ikessars, correct?"

She shook her head again. "An old Ikessar supporter," she finally croaked out. "A merchant, or a merchant's wife. I...don't know the details, my queen."

"She looks like Rayyel, too," Khine reflected.

I saw it now. "Gods. Another bastard?"

She shook her head a third time, her hair falling over her face. "No, Beloved Queen. I'm...Karia aron dar Hio. Lord Rayyel's older sister through our father, General Shan. My mother was his natural wife."

I had never heard the name before. But I wasn't surprised. Princess Ryia's affair with General Shan was considered a mark of shame. That it resulted in the only direct Ikessar heir was reason enough to try to erase Shan's history from the record books; the less said about the whole situation, the better. "So we're looking at a family reunion here," I said, clapping my hands once. "Anino is Chiha Baraji's son, I presume?"

"Yes, Beloved Queen," Karia replied.

"And of Thanh's age. Lovely." And if my guess was correct, I was a witness to the boy's conception. I pushed away the memory of walking in on Rayyel and Chiha that fateful afternoon, the one that I tried to drown in the dredges of time with anger and my own mistakes. "I suppose they've tasked you with keeping him away from the court's eyes. Have you been living here this whole time?"

"For the last few years."

"Does Warlord Lushai know?"

Karia dipped her head. "Yes, my queen."

"Princess Ryia?"

"No."

I took a deep breath. "My husband?"

A long pause. Long enough. I felt my chest tighten.

I didn't love Rayyel anymore, but that doesn't mean scars can't bleed.

It all went back to illusions. To wanting something that still made sense because none of us can grasp at emptiness for very long. I wasn't angry with Rai the way I would've been if I had learned this even a year ago. But there was something else there, one that went full circle. I could see our lives panning out like a play, a theatre of the doomed and damned. Only now, I wasn't a player, but the audience, and I wasn't amused. All I could think of was how much of a fool I'd been putting my trust in people who would use me, who would lie to me, even as I knew that there was nothing I could've done to ward against their deception.

When the door opened and Yuebek walked in like a welcomed guest, I wasn't even surprised.

He had changed from when I had seen him last, looking closer now to the pristine prince I met nearly a year ago in Zorheng City. A well-trimmed beard, eyes that twinkled, a face that looked like it had been scrubbed several times with a strong brush before getting a layer of bright paint over it. A silk hat, robes threaded with real gold and silver and probably worth more than a village or two. Black hair without a single trace of grey, skin so shiny it looked porcelain. He was almost *too* perfect.

I didn't bother greeting him. I simply drew my sword and attacked.

I hoped the element of surprise would be enough to turn the tide. To have two against one, at least; he was alone, with not even a shadow of a scabbard on his belt. But my sword struck empty robes, shattering in a spray of metal shards. The robes dropped to a pile at my feet. Yuebek somehow appeared beside Anino, a naked dagger in his hand. He grinned, perfect teeth showing.

"My queen," he said as he brandished the sharp edge along the boy's neck. "You look lovelier by the day."

"Let him go, Yuebek. I'm the one you want."

As an answer, he pulled the blade up. Anino whimpered as a streak of blood dripped along the edge. I felt my insides knot.

Yuebek's eyes lit up. "They were right about you and children! But this one? Isn't this one the most worthless of them all? Come, now. Don't tell me you still want it alive after everything you've learned? Wouldn't you want to sink this blade into this soft, young flesh yourself? Living proof of your husband's treachery, as if you haven't had to live with it all these years already. Living proof that even as he tries to make amends, he continues to lie to you still!"

I didn't answer, and he began to laugh.

"Perfect," he said, sliding the blade across the boy's throat a second time. Another streak of blood. The boy continued to cry, though to his credit, he didn't try to run. "Just perfect. But you do realize what keeping him alive means, don't you? It means that the little show your husband started to thwart *me* is now going to be his doom. There is no need to *prove* this whelp isn't his. They've hidden it this whole time, right under your nose, Beloved Queen! This hypocrisy, stirring the land for a fault that was his all along, is enough! Grounds for an annulment! The Dragonthrone, well and fully ours!"

"This is what you've been sitting on this whole time."

He chortled. I thought I could spot tears leaking from the corner of his eyes. "I wanted you to see this for yourself," he said. "I've been here the last three days. Karia has been—*most* hospitable." He gave a quick glance at Rayyel's sister, who hung back another step. "But you've interfered with my arrangements yet again. Couldn't you have waited for my invitation, for the grand party that will announce not just the dissolution of your marriage to that bastard but our own, happy betrothal? I was going to hire dancers."

"I'm sorry," I said. "I must have missed the part where I agreed to these proposals."

"You won't get rid of your husband even for *this*?" Yuebek picked Anino up by the collar and flung him to the side. The boy gave a soft cry. Karia rushed to him, nearly stumbling into Yuebek along the way. The prince barely gave them a second look. "Just as your marriage was not your choice, so will you be unable to stop this from happening. If anything, the presence of this runt should remind you what others have done to take what is rightfully yours. Did you think your husband's affair was born from love?"

He slapped his knee with glee, turning around to the quivering Anino and Karia as if inviting them to join in his merriment. "Qun—you remember Qun, don't you? He went missing, I believe, not that *I* care..." His eyes twinkled, which told me he knew exactly what had happened to the Anzhao governor. "I told Qun how surprising it is that a man like Yeshin would bear a daughter like you. For your position, for your education, for all that your father must've taught you, you remain so trusting, and so inconveniently...ignorant. That one..." And here, he pointed at Khine, as if just noticing him for the first time.

Khine didn't move. He was holding his scabbard across his body, sword inside, as if afraid that to draw it now would be to lose the only weapon we had between us.

"Yes," Yuebek continued, eyes narrowing. "The Shang Azi dog. What happened to the rest of your companions? Let me guess. Out of all, this is the only one that's left. This one! A dead mother, debts piled higher than your dragon-towers, and you'd entrust him with your secrets? A con artist, of all people?"

"You're rambling," I snapped. "The boy, Yuebek. What do you need from him?"

He laughed and straightened himself. "Your husband's bastard's mother was planted in the Citadel," he continued, his voice growing serious. "Her father was your father's closest friend, wasn't he? For him to have his daughter live amongst people who would've once roasted his liver over hot coals, simply so she could get close to your betrothed, is so brazen it's almost admirable! And your husband! Your sweet, foolish bastard—quite your match in many ways, isn't he? Just as simple-minded. Just as easily trapped. Fell for the bait like a hound, driven to lust like any man with a whore. What?" he snapped, raising his voice as Karia tried to cover Anino's ears. "You don't want the brat hearing about how he was made? You Jinseins are so sentimental."

"So Lushai worked behind my father's back," I said, taking a deep breath. "Like you expected me to be surprised. And now I suppose you're using *this* scandal to blackmail him into compliance. All well and good, Yuebek. So you've got a handful of warlords leashed. You don't think the Ikessars will try to preserve what's been theirs for all these centuries?"

"The Ikessars and what army?"

"The same mistake my father made," I said, my eyes locking with Khine for a moment. I pressed my lips together. "The Ikessars may not have a sizable number of soldiers, but one word and you'll have the rest of the nation united against *you*. I know you once told me you had an army, Yuebek. Twenty thousand, you said, along with the rest of the warlords who would back this nonsense. But that still leaves thousands upon thousands of minor lords and common men who would oppose you, not to mention the proud and haughty warlords you can't blackmail. You don't know how Jinseins think. They would sooner burn this whole nation to the ground than submit to a foreign master. Besides..." I clicked my tongue. "I don't see your soldiers anywhere. A pity. Mine are on their way as we speak."

"I admire your fire, but did you really think I would fall for that?"

Of course I knew he wouldn't. The bastard was *too* much like my father. He enjoyed the verbal sparring, was in love with hearing himself talk. So while his eyes were on me, waiting for an opening to beat me down and prove me wrong, Khine had inched his way to where Anino and Karia cowered. All three were on their way out of the door before Yuebek saw what we were doing.

The prince's eyes widened, the mad look in them turning vile. Even though he always appeared to be one step ahead of me, I was starting to recognize whenever I had momentarily outwitted him. Khine's diversion gave me time; he threw his sheathed sword. I caught it in mid-air. I whirled around, drawing the blade just as Yuebek lunged for them, and cut down, grazing the man across the thigh. He howled in pain. I caught a whiff of foul-smelling blood dripping down his open wound, one that *didn't* close in on itself like the last time I fought him. Did it have anything to do with the place, or the lack of mages around? It reminded me of when I thought I'd almost killed him—despite the power he displayed, he wounded as easily as any other opponent I've had. I pulled my lips back into a grin as I stepped to the side and braced myself for his counter-attack.

There was none. With an irritated sigh, Yuebek lifted his hands. Just as Khine stepped through the doorway, Yuebek dropped them, and the door slammed shut with such force the floors shook. I heard Khine try to tear it down from the other side.

"What did you think that would do?" he asked, turning to me.

I opened my mouth to respond. *Now* his attack came, a spell that came hurtling at me from out of nowhere, that filled me with the sensation of crashing into a window. I realized, just before I struck the ground and darkness set in, that this man was ten times more powerful than we thought he was. Loathing him was not enough.

I should be terrified.

The smell of mothballs was the first thing I noticed.

Mothballs, so strong I nearly had trouble breathing at first. My hands and feet were bound. I reacted by straining against the silken rope, attempting to kick out; I managed to turn to the side and saw Yuebek lying beside me, a book in his hands. He casually turned a page.

"You—" I hissed.

"You're not naked," he pointed out. "I didn't touch you."

"—if I get out of this—"

"Exactly why you're all tied up. You're unbelievably troublesome, my dear." He now glanced at me, pulling himself up to cross one leg over the other. He, too, was fully clothed, which didn't really do much to suppress the shudder of revulsion that ran through me. The smell of mothballs was coming from him.

"Your language is so unbelievably primitive," he continued, waving the book around. I caught the writing on the spine—a Sagar book, though it was too dark for me to tell which one. Not that it mattered. I tested the rope again, twisting my wrists.

"You can't expect me to stay bound forever," I said evenly. "At some point, you'll have to let me go. And then I'll kill you. And it goes without saying, but I will enjoy every minute of it."

"I know," he replied in the most sombre tone I have ever heard. He flashed me a smile. "A shame, really. I was looking forward to a proper marriage match, a world of difference from the last one I was forced into. Of all the people in the world, I thought, *this one*, this woman would understand the allure of power, even as it seeks to isolate you from the world!" He reached out to cup my chin. I tried to push against him, against the muggy scent rising from his pores—there was a touch of corpse-stench to it, almost sweet, which made me gag more. I was afraid he would kiss me and prepared to attack him for it.

But Yuebek knew that I would. Mad, but not a fool. He simply pressed his fingers into my jaw, nails digging into my skin. "You act so virginal," he lamented. "I was looking forward to... *more*, when I heard of your repute. Zhu was an utter failure in that, too. Used to lie on her back and count the lizards on the ceiling. I had to get up and stab them with the fire poker to get her to pay attention. Well. One can't have everything, I suppose. You realize I could *have* you if I wanted to. But I'm learning to control my urges. It's been pointed out to me, more than once, that raping you would have dire consequences in the eyes of this abominable nation."

"How thoughtful of you," I hissed.

He let my jaw go, pushing away with a snort. "I can't just take over—I have to *win* the hearts of the people, too. I don't know how Jinseins think, you said. You continue to underestimate me. Another disappointment. You're going to have to stop undermining me when we're married. Don't you understand?" This time, he grabbed my shoulder, pulling me to him. He pressed his head over mine and lightly stroked my hair.

I struck his chest with the ropes. He only laughed; his embrace was like a vice. If he wasn't using spells, I might've been able to wrap my arms around him and strangle him with my own bonds. As it was, I could only writhe in his grasp. "You and I, we were meant to rule together and create a legacy that will carry us through time. Your father knew it! Ahh, he knew it so well. Did I tell you I was skeptical when I first met him? My mother had told me everything, about their plans, the offer they had agreed to in the past... but all I saw was this old, wrinkled man. My own father, I thought, could *crush* him with his little finger. If he had come to me grovelling like an ant like every other official I've met, I would've done it myself. Poisoned his wine and danced on his corpse. I have no patience with bootlickers.

"But the arrogant bastard seemed incapable of understanding the difference between your small nation and my father's empire. He didn't quiver. He didn't beg. He was courteous—he acknowledged the strength I could bring to this land—but he seemed like he would've taken my rejection just as easily as my cooperation. A proud man, Yeshin, but he made me *see* how dedication and persistence can catapult one into greatness."

"How much greatness can you achieve taking over a *primitive* nation?" I managed.

Yuebek looked me in the eyes. "You see? This is where I lose you. My lovely queen, if the Jinsein people can be made to follow your father's footsteps, if I can make them *see* reason, imagine. We could grow. There are instabilities to the north, past the borders. The Gasparian warlords are at each other's throats, divided into their own states. Anarchy! With an organized force, we can capture their lands for our own, and in time, we could have our own empire, one that can rival even my father's! And he'll have to see, then—he'll have to acknowledge how wrong he was for overlooking me, for choosing my brothers over me...!"

He began to laugh. Tears poured down the side of his face. I don't think he even noticed. "You know, don't you? You know what it feels like. To have so much potential, but be ground under the heels of the lesser, of people who haven't done an ounce of the work *you've* had to do! I admired your father, but I could see from the beginning how he thought so little of *you*, too, that he would need *me* to make you whole! I know, I know! But don't fret, my darling. Time is on our side. Everything I need to make this happen for us is in the palm of my hand. Years of planning have finally led me here!" His eyes sought the curve of my shoulder.

I struck the spell again, shaking myself free. He dropped the shields and I fell back into the mattress, my head on the silken pillows that smelled of death.

"Time..." Yuebek repeated, rising from the bed. "First. The dissolution of your marriage with that bastard. Jin-Sayeng will understand what they've been doing wrong this whole time, appointing such men as rulers. Weak, spineless worms, and for all their talk, incapable of fighting *their* own desires. See who supports him now when they realize he has neither power *nor* virtue. Your little trick down there only delays the inevitable. We'll find the boy yet, and once we have him, once all of these treacheries have been exposed, we'll take over. We'll rule, my queen, side by side."

He rang the bell by the door. I sat up as servants entered, bowing first to him, and then to me. They untied the ropes.

"I can't make you love me," Yuebek said with the sort of wistfulness that would've drawn my sympathy had it come from anyone else. But he said it with that manic look in his eyes, and it was all I could do not to choke on my own vomit. "Qun had his own ideas about how to make you more compliant, but the fact that you're still here and *he's* not tells me there's no sense pursuing them any further. You've proven your point. But we're close, my dear. Too close. You don't shit where you eat."

The servants stepped back as I found myself freed. "Clean up and rest," he continued, stroking his trimmed beard. "I hope you've had enough of scuttling through the sewers with rats. I'll tolerate no more of it, not from the woman I have to rule with. We're royalty. We need to be better than the common folk."

"Ironic for a man who killed his wife," I said, getting up. I started scanning the room for things to throw at him. But other than the bed, the room was bare, and there were three servants between us.

"It was a most efficient thing," he replied easily. "I wish I could've made you see just how efficient. Then your precious Rayyel would be dead now. But no— this *would* be harder if we had killed him. It all turned out for the best. Disgracing him is better. You see? I can admit mistakes, too." He giggled. "Tomorrow, you'll meet my council. Perhaps if I can't change your mind, they can."

"I don't see how. You said it yourself, Yuebek. You can't *make* me do anything I don't want to."

His eyes narrowed. "I still haven't tried fucking you into submission," he chortled. "We'll get there, my queen. Who knows? Maybe by then you won't hate it." With one last barking laugh, he left.

CHAPTER ELEVEN

THE COURT OF THE MAD PRINCE

ᜆᜈ᜔ᜆᜈ᜔

I tried to learn what I could about my new prison in the ensuing hours. Once the initial shock had passed, I was almost calm. Knowing Yuebek couldn't be more than a few paces away was unsettling, but then so had been knowing the madman was coming for me. Why fight the inevitable? I lacked the power to stop him, certainly not when I was his prisoner.

So I turned to the only activity that made sense—I studied the walls. Namra had done the same in my father's secret chamber. Although I was what she called *blind to the agan*, imbuing spells still left physical traces. My search revealed faint etchings of runes near the floor, ones that looked like nothing more than a child's scratches. They glowed when my fingers touched them.

More marked the windowsill. I ran my nails over the rough edges before I turned my attention to the street below. It was too dark for me to make out any details, but I recognized the rooftops well enough to know we were still in Bara. I wondered if the runes made a spell that would stop me from breaking the windows. Perhaps Yuebek wanted to impress me at how much he'd thought things through.

He was going to have to try harder.

Namra told me that the runes in Oren-yaro were built right into the walls to stop people from attempting to tamper with them. I walked around the room and spotted the book that Yuebek had left on the bed. I picked it up and returned to the window. "Sorry, Magister," I said as I struck the runes with the hard bamboo along the book spine, sending splinters flying.

The runes were still there. I frowned and tried another angle. More splinters, exploding with a scent of iron—or blood. The runes began to give off a frantic glow. I took that to mean that my assault was working and put all my strength behind one last blow, hoping I could take a huge chunk off and render the spell inert.

The next flurry of sparks was followed by darkness. My mind fell blank.

When I was able to gather my thoughts again, it was daylight. My eyes skipped towards the bed.

It had changed from a flat, Zarojo-style platform to a familiar four-poster bed set over velvet rugs. I took a quick glance at the wide expanse of the room, clearly not the same one I had just been in, before tearing for the door to confirm my suspicions. It swung with one tap, as if it had just been waiting for me.

Somehow, inexplicably, I was back in that room in Yuebek's dungeon. I spotted the piano, the arrangement of sofas, the *Hanza* game, pieces still intact. The bonytongue swam in the tank, unperturbed. It stared back with one eye as I peered through the murky water, its mouth opening and closing. I wondered why it was still alive—the water seemed dirtier than last time. I made my way to the piano, my hands drifting over the ivory keys. They were warm.

"Taraji," I called.

There was no reply. I felt relief at first, followed by a tinge of disappointment. Seeing apparitions might be a sign of a fevered mind, but I was starting to suspect that madness was much better than loneliness. The brother I had never known was company at least, a hallucination that wouldn't try to hurt or betray me. And unlike walls, he talked back.

I found myself drifting to the door, which I remembered led to the library that led down to the dungeons. The handle wouldn't turn. "Good," I grumbled. "I didn't like that place, anyway. Are you listening, Yuebek? Your tricks aren't going to work. You should learn by now." Not that I expected *him* to respond, either; he would know how much I preferred lively arguments to hollow silence.

The bonytongue rose to the edge of the tank, gulping at something on the surface of the water. I returned and noticed the bodies of smaller fish, floating along a trail of slime and foam. The bonytongue snapped them up greedily, its low jaw quivering with each bite.

I drew away in disgust and noticed a new door directly across the library. It was painted red. Boredom won over caution. The knob turned this time.

The door opened to a hallway, lit by torches with *agan*-blue flames dancing along the edge. At the end, it curved into a chamber lined entirely with glass. Light barely made it through the murky green water on the other side. As I wondered how it was possible to have so much water in that tank, a huge shadow lunged at me. A creature twice the size of a grown man struck the glass from the other side, just strong enough to make it quiver without breaking it. I wasn't sure if it was a fish or a reptile—the shape reminded me of the crocodiles that would sun themselves along the banks of River Agos. A sea serpent, perhaps. I found the courage to peer closely, but it was gone.

Another shadow crossed the water, revealing a monstrous carp. Its skin was a dull pink, flecked with spots. It turned on its side, struggling to swim through a cloud of mud. Before it could turn upright, something leaped out from the sand to grab it.

The attack was short-lived. The carp's mangled body flopped between the jaws of an eel, equally gigantic. It turned to the glass as it chewed, razor-sharp teeth scraping the carp's pink flesh. The stripes on its face glowed. There was an almost human quality to its eyes—it reminded me of how the warlords looked at me sometimes, which was disconcerting.

I backed away and returned to the main hall. The bonytongue was still feasting. I suddenly remembered that my father kept one in a tank outside his study for the longest time. Paler than this one, so big it could swallow a kitten. My father claimed to have inherited it from his eldest brother, which meant the fish was a good half a century old. It died right before Yeshin's own passing. Because of my father's illness and the chaos at its heels, nobody discovered it until after the funeral, when one of the servants found it bunched up in the corner of the tank like tattered linen, covered in white fungus.

Prodding at that memory brought a conflicting mess of emotions, of grief and bitterness, but also a yearning so strong it felt like a fire inside of me. Where was my father? He was here the last time—he would know what to do. You could say every cruel word about my father and I wouldn't disagree, but deep inside I knew he would not begrudge me answers. The man who had sold me to a monster, a man who was very much a monster himself, was still my father. He was my only father.

I knew that there was no sense trying to escape; the only way I could is if that was what Yuebek wanted from me, and I didn't want a repeat of last time. I returned to the bedroom, crawling into the mattress and pulling the covers over my face. I forced myself to sleep, drifting past the aching emptiness and the dreams of large fish getting eaten by even larger fish and towards the memory of myself as a child on Yeshin's shoulders, overlooking the world.

"Beloved Queen," a voice whispered in a thick Zarojo accent. My eyes snapped open. I was back in that first room in Bara, a broken book in my hand. There were streaks of blood along my fingers and under my nails.

A servant approached, taking the book from me. She placed a basin of water next to the mattress and took out a wet sponge, which she ran over my skin, taking dirt and blood along with it. I flinched; scented oils had been dissolved in the water and it stung the wounds I had no recollection of acquiring. The whole time, she didn't say a word. If she was Yuebek's servant, perhaps this was a common thing.

Or perhaps...I cleared my throat. "I remember you from Zorheng."

"You are correct, my queen," she replied. "I was one of Lady Zhu's hand-maids." She said this with her eyes downcast, never once glancing at me.

I kept silent as she turned to sponge the rest of my skin. When she was done, she showed me the dress she had brought. I frowned. "I know you'll say I *have* to wear it—" I began.

"The prince was most adamant," she gasped. I could see her inwardly pray-ing I wouldn't resist—at least, not out loud.

I picked it up, thumbing my fingers over the fabric. It was old-fashioned, the sort of dress that was in style before the Empire of Ziri-nar-Orxiaro and Jin-Sayeng's relations had dissolved into dust—dull gold in colour, with lace patterns, loose sleeves, a pleated skirt, and a collar that went a little lower than I was comfortable with. I frowned even more.

She must've noticed the look on my face. "Making the prince angry is...not advisable." She said this in Zirano, which was accented.

"You're Jinsein," I said. Khine had taught me to pay more attention to lapses in speech; Zirano wasn't his first language, either.

She paused. "I was...brought to Zorheng when I was too young to remem-ber. My father was an emissary."

"An emissary brought his child...and left her there?"

She nodded. "It was right after the end of the war. My father never returned to Jin-Sayeng. We were ordered to serve there."

I pressed my fingers against my temples. "But that must've been before Yuebek's marriage to Zhu Ong."

"It was right when their betrothal was announced."

Ah, I suddenly thought. The emissary was sent as an appeasement. "What did your father do there?"

"He worked with Governor Radi Ong to maintain relations with Jin-Sayeng. I'm not sure of the details, Beloved Queen. They sent a half-Jinsein back to Oren-yaro in exchange."

I blinked. "Arro. They sent Arro in exchange."

She bowed. "If you mean Arro rok Ginta, then yes."

"He's a Zorheng native? But I thought he grew up in Jin-Sayeng."

"I don't know about that, Beloved Princess. He had a Jinsein mother. Perhaps he found it easy to pretend he did."

I tried to push away the memory of Arro warning me of my interest in Zorheng. It was one thing to slowly come to the realization that my own father had trapped me into this, and quite another to believe that Arro would've ever agreed to it. The thought of the latter was so painful that since my return to Oka Shto, I'd avoided trying to unearth anything that had to do with Arro. I had so little left to believe in.

Yeshin. A thought came, unbidden. It held the sting of Ryia's voice. *He trusted no one but himself. He didn't believe in people—he hated them and used them instead. You can be smart and go down that road, Talyien. Be Yeshin. You're already one step in the right direction.*

The maidservant cleared her throat. I wanted to argue again, but it occurred to me that she would probably pay more for my refusal than I would. I conceded and disrobed, allowing her to put the dress on me. Later, she led me out of the room and through a passageway that overlooked a cavernous entrance. There were guards down there, dressed in armour that reminded me of the Zarojo imperial regalia, only their shoulderplates ended in points and there was an etched arrowhead in the middle of their breastplate. The metal was also a light silver, nearly white. "Yuebek's Boon," I guessed. The maidservant's continued silence told me I had it right. Had the Zarojo emperor finally allowed him full access to his army?

We stopped in front of a wide entryway guarded by more soldiers. They pulled their halberds to the side to let me through, leaving the maidservant behind. I entered a great hall with a single chandelier hanging above. There were men seated on individual platforms—I spotted Yuebek at the far end, his hands folded on his chest. At the sight of me, he jumped, scampering over the food tray and rushing to me with all the eagerness of a year-old dog.

"My queen joins us at last!" he cried, grabbing my hands, which I tried, unsuccessfully, to hide behind my back. He dragged me up to the seats, all but pushing me onto the mat beside him. I recognized half the men in that room. Radi Ong was the closest to us, his head bowed deferentially. There were three others whose names I couldn't recall, but they were most definitely from Zorheng. And then at the far end, two faces I didn't think I'd ever see again: Jiro Kaz, the bandit leader from the foothills near Anzhao and Anya Kaz's husband, and Han Lo Bahn, lord of the slums of Shang Azi.

Yuebek must have been counting on me to react and couldn't wait for me to do it by myself. He grabbed me by the sleeve. "Look!" he said, pointing at the last two. "Don't you recognize them? Old friends, I believe! And men who hate each other, on top of all of that! What do you think, my queen?"

"I think," I said, without taking my eyes off them, "that you must've run out of people to trust, Prince Yuebek, if these two form part of your *council*. Scraping the bottom of the barrel, are we?"

"Pah!" Lo Bahn snorted. "You'd say so."

"I thought you were in prison, Lord Han," I replied.

"I was," he said. "How did you think I got out?"

"Did you have to crawl under Governor Hizao's desk?"

"You've a sharp tongue."

"Was that what Hizao told *you*?"

He laughed. "Your prince there gave me an offer I couldn't refuse."

I fixed my sleeve, hoping the wet spot on it wasn't Yuebek's drool. "Loyalty doesn't mean a damn thing to you, I suppose."

"I risked my neck to get you back home, didn't I?" he replied easily. "Loyalty enough when it wasn't even mine to give." He tugged at his beard, which seemed to have been groomed for the occasion.

"*This* is your famed friendship with the queen?" Jiro Kaz broke in. *He*, despite his clean robes, looked just as rough around the edges as ever. "I should've known better than to believe you."

"I'm surprised your wife let you come here," I told him. "Last I recall, she was upset with me for what had happened in Anzhao."

"Lord Han asked for my help. The prince needed people, and some of them had to be smuggled through the empire. My specialty."

"I thought you hate each other."

"I don't hate money." Jiro flashed Yuebek a grin.

Yuebek tugged at my sleeve a second time. "There'll be time for making acquaintances later," the prince huffed. "For now, there's still the matter of the missing brat." He glanced at Jiro and Lo Bahn. "I thought you said you had it under control. You know her dog escaped with him, don't you?"

He was talking about Khine. I managed to peel his fingers off my dress before he ripped it and pretended to touch the food in front of me. There were rice balls dotted with black sesame, pickled cabbages, and sliced raw fish with the head intact. The fish must've been killed mere moments ago—it stared back at me, jaws quivering. I remembered the monsters in the tanks in Yuebek's dungeons and suppressed a shiver.

"He's hard to find if he doesn't want to be found," Lo Bahn said. "I don't want to arouse his suspicion."

"We can agree on that," Jiro added. "We need to take our time. If we go straight to him, he'll be suspicious."

"Mundane details," Yuebek snorted. "The boy—we can't stroll into Toriue Castle without the boy. I need him to announce our betrothal. It would make for such a grand entrance." He tried to reach for me again, and looked irritated that I had moved too far away.

"Princess Ryia is still in Toriue," I reminded him. "You'd really make such a bold claim in front of her?"

"Why do you think I sent Belfang?" Yuebek asked. "I *wanted* to lure the witch here. She represents the most powerful clan in your puny little nation, and the sooner we can knock her down, the better. Belfang pretended to assist in your humiliation to ensure she would be tempted to leave her sorry little hole."

"The Esteemed Prince's wisdom exceeds all," the men in the room—with the exception of Lo Bahn—uttered together. They clasped their hands and bowed.

I stopped myself from laughing.

"Dangling what someone wants the most in front of them," Yuebek continued, "is the best way to ensure you get what you want. Isn't that right, my queen?"

I didn't say anything. My son was safe from him, so long as he stayed with Kaggawa.

He smiled at my silence. "You must think I'm daft," he said. "You must think you've got it figured out. From what I understand, he's with rebels. Who's to say they won't stick him if I, say, offer them a reward?"

I felt cold sweat trickle down the back of my neck.

"They say he is with a man called…Dar…Dan…Kaggawa, is it?" He pointed at one of his servants, who rushed forward with a bamboo scroll. He flicked it open and snorted. "Dai Kaggawa. A merchant. Merchants only care about money."

For the first time in weeks, I found myself suddenly glad that Kaggawa *was* as pompous of an ass as he was. No—Yuebek didn't know people as well as he thought he did. Intelligent, but shortsighted where it mattered the most. I strove to remember that and watched as he handed the scroll over to Ong, who bowed as he took it. "Let him know how well I'm willing to pay for *that* brat, too," Yuebek said. "Give it to your bastard Dragonlord to know how to do one thing right, Beloved Queen: make more bastards. I can't wait to rid this nation of them. The fewer potential heirs to compete with ours, the better. I *told* Qun to take care of him, but the damn fool thought he could use your boy to ensure your compliance. Showed him—you took care of him instead, didn't you? How did you do it? They said he fell off the ravine."

"If you hurt my son, what makes you think I won't murder you in your sleep?" I asked in the smoothest voice I could muster.

It was amazing how nearly every person in that room didn't seem to hear me or the venom that dripped from my tone. Only Lo Bahn glanced away. Yuebek, though—Yuebek simply responded with his usual howling laughter, as if I had done nothing but threaten to caress his head. Bile crawled up my gullet. "Your fire has always amazed me," Yuebek said. "Let's see it in a more useful form." He clapped his hands.

A servant approached us with a tray covered in silk cloth. He bowed as he placed it in the center of the room before pulling the cloth back, revealing a *Hanza* set. With another elaborate movement, he picked it up again and deposited it in front of the prince. "Your father's favourite game," Yuebek said, drawing his sleeves back to show his hands. "Mine, too, incidentally enough. As it turns out, we're all cut from the same cloth." He gestured, offering me the first move.

I almost didn't want to give him the satisfaction of bullying me into providing entertainment. But I was also curious. *Hanza* had always been the easiest way for me to see how my opponents' minds worked, and so I moved the obligatory piece.

Yuebek barely glanced at me. His attention drifted to Ong, who cleared his throat. "With all due respect, Esteemed Prince," Ong said, looking up from the scroll in his hand. "It is my understanding that Kaggawa is currently embroiled in a civil war with the local warlord. Sending a message to him might prove to be problematic."

"Jinseins and their petty wars." Yuebek laughed as he made his move.

"We do like them," I said as I matched his piece. "Ojika Anyu and Dai Kaggawa have been at each other's throats for years. Anyu has enough loyal bannermen and an army of six thousand the last time I checked, but Kaggawa is supported by many of the landowners, who have resented the royals' intrusion for decades. I'm still not convinced this is the sort of trouble you gentlemen are equipped to deal with."

"My queen believes she knows politics," Yuebek giggled. "You Jinsein women *are* truly something. I'm not surprised your men allow you to lead." He captured three of my pieces before settling back with a satisfied grin.

I could've protected them better and silently kicked myself for being too distracted. "I know my own," I bristled. "When will you learn that your primped Zarojo eccentricities count for nothing here?"

"Nothing," Yuebek repeated, his eyes gleaming. "Do you not recall how I've secured cooperation from at least three of your warlords already? More will fall, in time." He gestured at the *Hanza* set. I glanced down. In the process of capturing those pieces, he had set himself up so that my next move would sacrifice whatever piece I played.

I gritted my teeth and stared at the board. I had made a fatal error; my father would've shaken his head in disappointment had I done it in front of him. I was tempted to stop drawing it out and admit defeat. But I glanced up at Yuebek and realized this was what he wanted. He could read the devastation on my face—I could see the celebration on his. He might as well have been licking his lips.

"Cooperation," I stated, making a pretence of glancing across the room. "I assume these three warlords are Ozo, San, and Lushai. Do you think the other warlords would fold so easily?"

"If I asked her to be silent, would she?" Yuebek asked the men.

"I believe the queen is simply—adjusting to her new circumstances," Ong said, clearing his throat. "Jinsein women are allowed too much power in these parts. I've been told it was not a problem in the past, when the Zarojo influence was still strong. Even the Ikessars' trusted adviser Ichi rok Sagar would rather her father become Dragonlord than Princess Ryia. Of course, Warlord Yeshin preferred to do things his way, and in the end Magister Ichi had no choice but to put his full support behind a woman. The reality of the political climate in this region... the Esteemed Prince may have to... teach the queen the true meaning of subservience..."

"The same subservience that saw your daughter stabbed in front of your very eyes, Ong?" I asked.

Ong had the decency to flush.

"Womanly subservience or not, you were still her father," I continued, fixing him with a stare. "You betrayed her trust in you. A child who must've looked up to you, who loved you, who didn't think twice about your intentions... this man *killed* her in front of your very eyes, and what do you do? Grovel and continue to worship him."

Sweat poured down his face.

"I don't see what you hope to gain from insulting my men," Yuebek said. "Ong will readily admit he's a bootlicker if you hit him long enough. Won't you, Ong?"

"I am ever my prince's servant," Ong said, bowing so low it looked like he sank to the floor.

I moved the queen piece forward. Yuebek's eyes danced. "Giving up already?" he laughed. "And you couldn't just say it, could you? First you needed an elaborate show...!" He lurched forward, grabbing the piece, along with the three soldiers behind it. I was almost out of pieces, all but defeated. Most people would walk away.

I blocked his king with mine, calling a draw. A pointless maneuver. You were still scored by how many pieces you had left on the board. But my refusal to submit turned his face sour. It contorted like a child on the verge of a tantrum. He grabbed the edge of the board and flipped it upside down before he stepped on it, pieces and all. I could hear the shells crack under his boot.

In the ensuing silence, rain began to fall, crashing on the roof with the sound of crackling oil.

"Speaking of women," Lo Bahn finally broke in, his voice booming like fireworks in the great hall, "I've procured quite a few talented beauties as a gift to our gracious prince for all he has done for us." He clapped his hands. The doors opened, and about a dozen half-dressed young women filed into the room, throwing themselves at the men. Most looked pleased at the interruption, with the exception of Jiro, who shrugged away with discomfort, and Ong, who remained on the ground, forehead on the floor.

Two made their way towards us and had the decency to curtsy first. "Perhaps the Beloved Queen will want to retire before you continue with the rest of the talks?" Lo Bahn asked in a voice that was unusually polite, coming from him. "I don't believe she is relevant for the rest of it. If I may be allowed to escort her back to her chambers..."

Yuebek, still scowling, turned away from the broken *Hanza* set and motioned with one hand.

I followed Lo Bahn in silence, fists clenched. Only out in the hall, well away from the guards, did he give me a cursory glance. "You'd think you would at least have the wisdom not to make him angry." We stopped in front of a window protected by a rusty iron grate. The glass was tinted with images of dark-furred civets scaling a mango tree with red leaves.

"I was trying to see what I could get out of him," I said, prodding the grate with my finger. It was solidly built.

Lo Bahn stroked his beard. "I'm aware that's one of your tactics. Anger makes some men babble. It doesn't work well on Prince Yuebek. Believe it or not, he is as honest as they come. He's even more honest than Khine Lamang. What did you want to learn, anyway?"

I sighed. "Where the rest of his army is, for one thing."

"You could've just asked me. They're waiting an hour from the port of Sutan in the east." Lo Bahn snapped his fingers. "One word and they'll come riding here within the day."

"You've got Warlord Buhawi wrapped around your little finger, too. Why don't you people just take over the whole nation for me? Save us the trouble of this charade."

"Don't play the fool, woman. Even if those warlords fully supported us— which it's clear they won't, even if they let us walk through without batting an eyelid—wouldn't you rather do this the peaceful way? Twenty thousand soldiers can do quite the damage to your villages and towns."

"I thought Yuebek wasn't allowed to have those damn soldiers in the first place. Something about keeping his ambitions in check."

Lo Bahn sneered. "You helped with that, actually. Your attack at the temple of Phurywa gave Yuebek the chance to convince his father that Jin-Sayeng was a threat. He released Yuebek's soldiers to him."

I leaned against the windowsill. "I'm flattered he would think it was an attack. We just stumbled into the damn place."

"You're a gnat compared with the empire," Lo Bahn said. "Twenty thousand soldiers is nothing. The Esteemed Emperor has hundreds of thousands at his disposal. It doesn't look like it, either, but he favours Prince Yuebek, if not publicly. I believe the man *could* obliterate your nation if he wanted to, just like he did to that *Hanza* set. But he doesn't want to. He doesn't want a pile of bones and ashes—what he wants is a kingdom for himself."

"Who else is working for him?"

Lo Bahn started walking again. I walked a step behind him, wishing I could shed the frilly, uncomfortable dress while hoping I didn't trip and land on my face. He finally paused mid-step, folded his arms, and sighed. "You want to know who you can or can't trust."

I poked his shoulder with my finger. "Obviously."

"Trust no one," he suggested.

"Oh, if only it were that easy. Give me a sword and an open door, Lo Bahn, and maybe I can take over the world. What the hell did he do for you, anyway? Those women couldn't have been cheap. Last I was aware, you couldn't afford a troupe of monkeys, let alone paid entertainment."

He sniffed. "Shows what you know. Monkeys are fucking expensive. Have to pay the trainers, too."

I strode past him so I could look at his face. "I don't know what to make of you, Lo Bahn."

"I'm a marquis of Zorheng province now," he said with a satisfied smirk.

"Ah. Your knees must be scabbed from all the grovelling."

Lo Bahn rubbed his hands together. "What else do you want me to say? You know the stakes. My parts would be rotting in the streets of An Mozhi if I didn't bow to the beast." He said the last part almost in a whisper, as if he was scared Yuebek could still hear him.

"A paid title in exchange for your cooperation. How droll. And I suppose next you're going to ask me the best way to find Lamang."

"You *would* be the best bait," Lo Bahn said, tugging at his beard. "Probably one word that you're in trouble and he'll come running for you."

"He'd know it was a trap."

He kept his smug expression. "The beauty of it is that it doesn't matter. He'll come, anyway."

"Why would you think that?"

Lo Bahn gave me a curious look. "I'm not a young man anymore, but I can still recall how it is to be in love."

I turned my eyes away. "You overestimate Lamang. He's still got his debts. The best way to draw him out is to promise money in exchange for the return of Chiha's son."

"You think that'll fool me? Pah! But I understand. You don't want Yuebek to catch on. Don't worry; I know very well what I've gotten myself in. Help us get your husband's son back and there'll be no need for the Esteemed Prince to know all about Lamang's affections."

I kept silent. No one needed to know about mine, either.

"I know you well enough to feel like I could warn you," Lo Bahn continued.

"About what?"

His nostrils flared. "Back there. You didn't succeed, so you're going to try something else. Something foolish. I would bet both my kidneys you're going to try to escape. Perhaps you'd consider it an affront to your gods if you didn't. But where would you go? Your warlords are all but ready to hand you back to him on a silver plate. The bastard's grandfather was the one who met us at port."

"Warlord Lushai?"

"So he said. He made a great show of making sure we didn't forget, either." He sniffed. "And that was *before* the prince discovered the bastard. Ah hah! You didn't know that part, did you?"

I shrugged. "I don't see why that should matter to me."

"You're not the only one who'll suffer if he doesn't get what he wants," Lo Bahn said. He pointed at the empty walls. I squinted and thought I could see runes drawn on random corners.

"Yuebek makes a poor house guest," I suggested.

"Don't you understand?" Lo Bahn asked, exasperated. "Prince Yuebek has laced this place with spells from top to bottom. Fool though he may appear, the man himself can turn you into splinters with one flick of his fingers. If you've got any sense of self-preservation, you'll stop fighting. You couldn't even defeat him in a fucking game."

The maidservant from earlier was waiting at the end of the hall—she bowed as we approached.

"You and everyone else say the same thing," I said under my breath. *"He's too strong. We can't defeat him. Tremble in fear, mighty queen, and let the madman have his way.* But there's one thing you people don't understand. I've known a man just as powerful, and I watched him die right in front of me."

Lo Bahn shook his head as I turned to follow the servant back to my chambers.

CHAPTER TWELVE

THE CAGED WOLF

ᛏᛁᛗ

Four walls, one window, and my father's name made up the extent of my prison. The runes were still there, etched deeper than my scraping could reach. I didn't have the courage to try again. A coward, deep inside; I didn't want to find myself back in that chamber. I was convinced that if Yeshin had showed himself once more in my frenzied hallucinations, it was a sign that he cared. But he didn't, and so I made myself believe he had abandoned me once and for all. Dying wasn't enough. Berating me to my face as a ghost wasn't enough. I had to face his cold rejection all over again.

I could at least see why it was easy for Yuebek to sway people to his cause. He was more than generous when it suited his purposes. I complained about the dresses he made me wear, and the next day simpler, more comfortable ones were procured. When I told him I didn't like the food, the menu changed—from strange Zarojo delicacies to plain Jinsein fare: clean white rice, milkfish soaked in vinegar, sliced green mangoes, and grilled lemongrass chicken.

I didn't see Yuebek often in the following days; he visited sporadically, always in broad daylight. Someone must've warned him not to at night. After his hissed threats that last time, I wasn't sure what was stopping him. He had made it clear he didn't take me as seriously as I wanted him to—what was he afraid of? One of the maidservants implied that it was the prince's attempt at being a gentleman. She said this with a smile—someone who cleaned up after Yuebek's childish tantrums, who had seen what he was capable of and must've noticed the madness dancing in his eyes, the smell of death rising from his pores. His courtiers were no better; even Lo Bahn thought of him as nothing more than an eccentric man spoiled by too much power.

Illusions. Only illusions could allow a monster to walk uncontested in the midst of so many intelligent, educated minds. Only illusions could allow you to worship a monster and entrust your life, and the lives of those you loved, to his hands. Radi Ong had seen his own daughter murdered by those same hands and yet he would wipe the shit off Yuebek's ass with his own fingers if ordered to. I hated him the most. Every time I looked at him, I caught a glimpse of my own father.

I saw what tempted Yeshin in the first place. Yuebek's soldiers were trained, disciplined—warriors to be reckoned with. And his coffers seemed endless—no expense was spared. Every meal felt like a feast, and each of the staff seemed well-paid. In the few meetings I attended with his council, Yuebek threw bribes around like a priest sprinkling holy water.

It hurt to imagine my father drawn by these same things. That for all his talk about putting the land above personal interests, he was no better than the rest. Was I such a failure as a daughter that the old man, teetering on the edge of death, finally gave way? Did my weakness make it possible for that deep-seated, inexhaustible ambition, spreading like a disease, to be my father's last gift to the nation?

Lo Bahn tried to convince me a thousand different ways. He insisted that if I was a little more compliant, if I was willing to speak with the warlords about my husband and his own infidelity, then we wouldn't even *need* Chiha's son. Yuebek's greatest mistake was letting things come this far. You cannot respect Yeshin and then underestimate his daughter.

The day arrived when a messenger came, claiming that Anino had been found by none other than Warlord Lushai himself. The boy was inside Toriue Castle. Yuebek laughed, hearing the news. "The man knows his true master!" he told me, grabbing my hands and breathing into my face. He chewed mint leaves to mask the death-scent of his mouth, but I could catch a whiff of it all the same. "He's making the arrangements now; we'll head to the castle and denounce your husband right in front of his precious mother!"

"I'm surprised she's still there," I said. "You took your damn time."

"Don't you fret, my dear!" Yuebek laughed. "She's been looking for you, too. Do you know how many of her agents we've had to kill the past few days?"

Preparations were made, and I soon found myself sharing a litter with Lo Bahn, which I would've never imagined I would find as a relief before. "He doesn't trust you," Lo Bahn snorted when I saw him instead of Yuebek in there.

"Probably remains convinced you'll stab him in the balls once you're alone with him. Hell, I'm not convinced you wouldn't try to do the same thing to me."

"I'm not going to bother," I said. "When it comes down to it, I'm pretty sure you don't have any."

"Do you know why Lamang is fucking obsessed with you? The both of you don't do much else but think of ways to insult me."

"We don't really have to think, Lo Bahn, the opportunities just present themselves."

"Bah! There you go again. You've slept with him already, I suppose. You must've."

"Why the hell should I tell you about my personal life, Lo Bahn?"

He snorted. "Because this is going to be a long road and I like gossip as much as my wife. I'll tell you about mine if it makes you feel any better."

"No thank you. You must miss Khine more than I thought if you're willing to spend this whole trip talking about him. If Lushai found his grandson before you did, your efforts must've been a failure."

"I did see Khine," Lo Bahn said, growing sombre. "The boy was gone from his care by then."

I glanced away.

"Not going to ask about him, are you?"

"Did you kill him?"

"Of course not! I'm too much of a softie and his head's not going to win me a kingdom." Lo Bahn crossed his arms. "Cornered him in the markets. Rented room above a tavern and some shop that sells that kind of disgusting soup you Jinseins love. Goat tripe, is that right? Goat tripe soup. That fucking stench. Asked about you. Told him the truth. Said you were well, but nothing short of the heavens opening up and smiting Yuebek where he stands is going to stop this marriage from happening."

"You're all assuming I'm going to agree," I bristled. "I have to agree first before Yuebek gets anything. I had to agree to marry Rayyel and the gods know the entire nation was behind *that* one. And you have nothing on me. Qun had used my son, but none of us know where he is now."

"He's in this Sougen region," Lo Bahn sniffed. "We'll find him."

"So until then, nothing happens."

Lo Bahn frowned and was silent.

I watched the streets unfurl in front of me from behind the curtains. It was the middle of the day and we were crossing the market, thick with the smell of dried fish and herbs. People stopped to stare at us. This kind of parade, of extravagance, was not common among the royals except for those of us surrounding the Dragonthrone; Yuebek wasn't trying to hide my presence at all.

"He'll hurt your husband," Lo Bahn said. "Torture him. Find him a fate worse than death. Have you considered that?"

I shrugged.

He curled his lip. "I mean, you *were* madly in love, as far as I could recall."

"How much in love could you be with a man after discovering he's been keeping a child from you the past eight years?"

"You Jinseins are such a sentimental lot. I tried to study your poetry during the trip here. It hurt my head."

"It would. Our language is more poetic than yours. I could insult you better if you knew how to speak Jinan."

The litter stopped; the curtains parted and a maidservant peered in. I recognized the one from Zorheng.

"There's Baraji soldiers passing in the road ahead," she said. "They've asked me to tell you to be patient, Beloved Queen."

"I have to use a chamber pot," I told her abruptly.

"Really?" Lo Bahn barked. "Now?"

"Well, since *you* didn't have the foresight to bring one…"

"Why the fuck would I bring a chamber pot inside a litter?"

I rolled my eyes. "Lord Han has always been insensitive to the needs of our sex. If you'll accompany me…?"

"I know you. You're not going anywhere without a guard," Lo Bahn said, bristling.

"It's the middle of the day, Lord Han, and you've got enough soldiers to burn the whole city down even while they still keep watch on me. A moment of privacy isn't *too* much to ask."

He bit his moustache, his face red. "There's nowhere to run," he managed. "I'm going to keep count. If you're not back after a hundred, I'm going to send soldiers after you."

"Spare them the trouble and do it yourself, you fat old man," I grumbled as I clambered out of the litter.

"You're running out of insults!" he snarled after me.

I smiled at the maidservant, who looked confused by the whole exchange.

"On second thought," I said. "The alley will do. I don't want to squat in front of an entire regiment."

Her cheeks turned red. "My queen—"

"You're coming with me, of course. Prince Yuebek trusts you, doesn't he? You're not going to let anything happen to me. It's the middle of the day," I repeated, squinting at the sunlight.

She conceded. We made our way past the guardsmen, who looked too pre-occupied to pay us much attention, and found our way to the nearest alley. The maidservant glanced at me before turning back to the street, as if indicating I should hurry without actually saying so. Subservience—the highlight of the ideal Zarojo woman, if you listened to Yuebek and his ilk. I wasn't sure I believed them. I thought about Zhu and uttered a quick apology under my breath as I darted into the shadows.

Running in skirts was not like what I remembered it to be, but the effort kept me from dwelling on the maidservant's inevitable fate for allowing me to escape. I headed straight for the market, where the crowd and the thick, pungent air made it easier to disappear. The first thing I did was find an unwatched laundry line to pilfer plainer clothes. I made my way to a dark corner, counting on the parade to keep people busy, though a dog did spot me and started barking up a storm while I tried to rip the laces from my back.

I managed to change into the more comfortable outfit and left the dress folded under the clothesline for payment. By now, I could hear commotion down below, though I wasn't sure if it was Yuebek's guards searching for me or something else. I hurried down the streets, and found someone selling roasted cashews by the bag. I pretended to dig through my pockets.

"You wouldn't happen to know where they have goat tripe soup here?" I asked while I patted my trousers.

The vendor whistled. "Well, you're in Bara, and goat tripe is a Darusu specialty..."

"I'm not interested in going all the way to Darusu."

"They have one that almost *passes* for it here, just the one place down by where the river runs up Toriue. It's right at Copper Street."

"Thank you," I said, skipping away without buying anything.

The speed with which I went through those streets surprised me. I didn't know Bara all that well to know where Copper Street was, but I headed to the river like I did. It kept me several steps ahead of my pursuers. The soldiers would be looking for a completely different woman, perhaps someone who *hadn't* left Jin-Sayeng for the Zarojo Empire. A forlorn royal, wandering helplessly about, unsure of how to talk to the common folk. Last year felt like a lifetime ago.

A group of children playing by the riverside gave me better directions, and I soon found myself within the vicinity of the eatery. You could tell which one from the stench—a combination of putrid bitterness that came from the slaughterhouse, and the distinct aroma of roasted goat. I walked around the fence, catching sight of a carcass strung up between two banana plants. A butcher was ripping out its intestines as deftly as if he was peeling fruit.

Someone whistled; the butcher disappeared into the back door, leaving his grass-cutter blade on a rock. I didn't even wait. I slipped my hand through the fence, claiming the blade for my own; the wooden hilt was still covered in goat's blood. It was half the size of my arm.

I circled the eatery, past the tavern, until I found the set of stairs leading up to the lodging. I let my arm hang loosely, a faint attempt at hiding the knife between the building and my body, and slowly made the climb. There were silhouettes behind the curtains. I recognized one of the voices. Lushai. I didn't know the others. At least one guard, and perhaps one of his deputies.

I pressed my back against the wall, right outside the window, and breathed slowly. Their conversation drifted between the day's events until the deputy started talking about Yuebek's arrival in the castle.

"And how sure are you that she'll come?" he asked, appearing right by the window.

"The Zarojo assured me," Lushai replied. It was definitely him; I had spent too much of my childhood listening to the man brown-nose his way through my father's meetings. "He'll drop a bait she can't refuse, he said."

I smirked. *Can't refuse.* Of course. Lo Bahn didn't look like it, but he had gotten smarter, at least when it came to his dealings with me. Too bad for whatever new deal he had going that I had learned my lessons, too. I knew he had been oddly specific about where he saw Khine for a reason. But the joke was on him; all he did was give me a way out. I could take care of the rest.

"Won't Prince Yuebek be angry?" the deputy continued.

"Of course," Lushai chortled. "He needs to learn his place. Having the queen in our custody will shift the tides in our favour, and I can imagine she'd much rather be in the company of her countrymen."

"My lord, I'm not sure I agree with you."

"You don't know the queen half as well as I do. I've watched her grow up. Head harder than a brick, harder than her father's, the only person she ever listened to. You couldn't force that child to do anything. You can lay out all reason for her, tell her exactly why it's important, and she'll do the complete opposite just to spite you. If Yuebek wants to marry her, he's going to have to do it on *our* terms. At this moment in time, Queen Talyien is prime currency, and—"

He paused, and the room fell silent. Long enough that I felt unease stir in the pit of my stomach. The shutters flipped open and I caught sight of the deputy peering down at me.

I sliced him across the neck with the blade.

He uttered a low shriek. I took off just as Lushai and the other guard came barging after me. They were in full armour, and lumbered down the steps at half the speed. I went straight for the safety of the narrow streets. A drainpipe gurgled with water from that morning's rains, and I paused to wash the blood off my hands and my face. From around the corner, I saw the guard's silhouette. The idiots had split up to search for me.

"You...!" he thundered as he approached. "Who sent you?"

I paused. If he didn't recognize me, then...

He took another step, sword drawn. A mere guardsman. I struck him, missed his neck, ended up hitting him under his armpit. The grass-cutter was dull, which didn't stop me from ripping a hunk of his flesh. Dull blades hurt just as much as sharp ones, if not more—you just had to strike a little harder. Reeling in pain, he bore down on me ungracefully, sword in hand, giving me no room to escape. I stepped back as he slipped on a puddle and tripped over the gutter. His jaw struck the hard ground. He groaned and tried to twist himself back up, but he ended up only flopping like a fish on dry ground—the fall must have dislocated his neck. I tightened my grasp around the wooden hilt, making sure of my target, and put him out of his misery quickly with one clean strike across his throat. Blood spurted out like a lemon squeezed too hard, and he slid partly down with the water, leaving red trails in the current.

The assault left the grass-cutter so dull it was useless. I dropped it and picked up the soldier's sword. Without stopping to examine my kill, I raced down the alley and into another, separated by another narrow channel of storm water. Slurries of green slime floated above the surface, smelling faintly of urine.

Lushai was waiting for me on the bridge.

"You irritating, troublesome wretch," he snarled.

I smiled. "I should say the same thing about you, Warlord Lushai."

"I'm not your enemy, Talyien."

"You all say that. Forgive me if I find it hard to believe now." I paused. "Not queen? You can't even *pretend* very well, can you?"

He took a step. "I told your father he should've disciplined you more. Instead, he chose to spoil you."

"Spoil," I repeated in disbelief.

"He gave you the fucking world instead of letting you learn what it's truly like to live in it," Lushai snorted. "Look at you. Running through the streets like you must've been doing the rest of the year, like some common harlot. Dragonlord Rayyel had a sensible plan, and what did you do?"

"You're not even pretending to work with my father anymore, are you?"

"Warlord Yeshin isn't my liege."

"And yet when he was alive you licked his boots better than his own dogs. I see how it is. You're only an ally when it suits you. You don't want the Oren-yaro banding together against you, and yet it would have worked out very well for you if I *had* been assassinated out there, wouldn't it?"

"Don't be ridiculous," Lushai huffed.

"Come on, Lushai. Haven't you always wanted what my father got? Oren-yaro benefitted from the resolution of *your* war, but you? Bara didn't get much more than a couple of fiefdoms added to the region. You wanted *your* daughter to be queen. Your grandson, heir to the Dragonthrone." I stopped in front of him.

"You do recall that marrying Prince Rayyel is not enough requirement to secure the throne," he said. "Otherwise, I would've suggested your father marry Ryia Ikessar and save us all the trouble."

"A suggestion that would've gotten you killed."

"Perhaps." He nodded towards me. "Rest assured, I'm not going to try to take anything from you. All I need is leverage over your new prince, and we can embrace this new tomorrow with open arms. Imagine the possibilities. Trade with the Zarojo Empire once more, and beyond! Riches and powers beyond our wildest dreams. We'd be true royalty, Talyien, not just landowners squabbling over ruins and rice fields."

"You'd let the nation burn because of your ambitions."

"No," he said. "*You'd* let the nation burn because you can't see beyond what *you* want. Clearly, you're here now because you couldn't imagine yourself married to that man. But I suppose your own happiness, your own feelings, take precedence, eh? What did I tell you? Spoiled!"

I attacked; he met my charge like an angry boar. The man didn't look like it, but he had survived the War of the Wolves for a reason. He tore the sword from my hand as easily as if it had been made of wood, grabbed me by the collar, and flung me to the ground like a rag doll. My left rib cage slammed against the pavement. Stars exploded in my vision.

"A spoiled fucking brat," Lushai continued, thundering after me. "My own children wouldn't dare act the way you do. If *Chiha* was queen, I'm sure we wouldn't be in this mess. Wouldn't have the Zarojo breathing down our necks like dragons, for sure! Because she would've been smart—she would've followed every command and never once forgotten her place. You, on the other hand? I couldn't believe what your father let you get away with when you were a child. Talking back to him, building up your own ideas before you understood the way things are... I *should* teach you a lesson first!" He reached me just as I got up and struck me with the back of his hand.

I grabbed his wrist, staring at him with blazing eyes. Lushai tore it away and spat to the side.

"You're coming back with me to Toriue," he said.

"If you want to present a carcass to Yuebek, then be my guest."

"You bring shame to your father's name with every breath you take. Very well, then. I can't bring a carcass back, but your unconscious body..." He lifted his hand again.

It never reached me. Blood suddenly spurted from his mouth, and he turned just as someone stepped away from him, bloody knife in hand. Lushai slumped to the ground, the blood seeping from his belly and around his shirt. His eyes lost light before he could manage another word.

I turned to the newcomer and recognized Sayu, Agos's wife.

CHAPTER THIRTEEN

THE BARAJI EXCHANGE

ay the gods forgive me," Sayu managed to breathe after what felt like
forever. "He was going to hurt you."

"What are you doing here?"

She glanced at the body and walked around it as she came up to me. "That's
Warlord Lushai, isn't it? I just killed a warlord. Gods . . ."

"My question first."

She looked up, startled. I've found that you need to be straightforward sometimes when someone is in shock, and Sayu clearly had never killed anyone
before. I placed my fingers on her wrist and took the knife from her hand. She
surrendered it willingly.

"It was Kisig," she managed as I led her away from the body, towards a corner where she didn't have to look at it. "My son. You remember him? You saved
him during the . . . during your trial. He told me so. We heard you were missing
and . . . he begged me to come here and help you. Begged me. I don't know what
came over me. They would have killed him if not for you. So I agreed."

I took her from the alley and out in the open street, where the canal opened
up into the river. The spray of sunlight seemed to energize her. "I left the boys
in Oren-yaro a few days ago," she said. "There was an uproar in Toriue when
I arrived. The Ikessar priestess found me wandering near the castle gates and
accepted my services. She asked me to come out here today, keep my eyes
peeled. She told me to keep an eye out for him."

Sayu pointed at Lushai. She still looked distraught. I placed my hands on
her shoulders. She turned her head to the side, though she wouldn't meet my
eyes. "Where is she?" I asked.

"Just further down the river," she breathed. "Behind the brewery. Prince Rayyel is there, too, and Lady Chiha. They've been meeting there while looking for you."

I pulled away and followed her as she started down the path by the river. We walked in silence as we crossed a boardwalk that hugged the side of a large rock face, fringed with red and green moss.

"I'm sorry for what I did during my husband's funeral," Sayu said, at length. "I overstepped my bounds. You could've had me killed for that. You didn't. You saved my son instead."

I glanced away. "I should be the one apologizing."

Sayu made a sound in the back of her throat, and we were silent again for a little while. I wondered if she was trying to stop herself from pushing me into the river.

"What they say about you and my husband," she managed. "It's true, isn't it?" She turned around. *Now* she was looking into my eyes, and I saw the tears in hers. She was forcing them not to fall.

"It's true," I replied.

"All of it?"

"Enough of it."

I heard her take a deep breath.

"I did always know about you," she managed. "I knew what you were to him. When I first met him, he spoke of nothing else. But you were so far away, this distant queen of stories, and we...we were *real*. I thought I could make him forget. That I could give him a good life, good enough to wash away his past. But we can't have everything. Did you at least love him? No—don't answer that. I'd rather hold on to the belief that I loved him best."

"Sayu..."

"You *are* sorry. I saw it in your eyes the day of the funeral. You risked yourself to say goodbye. And you protected my son and remember my name even when I can't even say yours without wanting to bite my tongue. Let's...leave it there. To say more would be...disrespectful."

"The court's not here," I said. "Say what you need to."

"Maybe you're testing me. Maybe you'll take my head after I'm done. For what it's worth, I can see why he...what he saw in..." She swallowed and wiped the last few tears from her eyes.

"He had a home with you," I said. "The kind he never had in Oren-yaro.

He was loyal and dependable and brave, and he paid the price for it. I'm sorry, Sayu. He deserved more than this, and so do you. I know it cannot bring him back, but I will be indebted to him all my life. So believe me when I say this: Your services here are not required. Take your sons and go home."

"I don't know what to feel about what you just said," she replied.

"Whatever it is," I said, "you're allowed."

We fell silent again. The sun felt hot on my face. The way it looked so peaceful, hovering over the horizon, you wouldn't think we were at the cusp of war.

"You're right about one thing, anyway," she whispered. "Nothing will ever bring him back." Beside us, gulls shrieked over the dark shadow of River Agos, reminding me that I had not grown numb to the pain—I had simply learned to live with it.

We reached the part of the riverbank that rolled up to the city, to the last patch of buildings right under the shadow of Toriue Castle. Sayu led me through a small gate and stopped outside a rickety-looking door. She knocked twice. I saw Namra from behind the window. Her eyes lit up.

"My queen," she said, rushing out to meet me. She cupped my face in her hands. Only then did I feel the sting of bruises from Lushai's attack. "Oh, my queen. We thought the worst. What happened?"

"Yuebek," I said. And then, realizing she was looking at my injuries, I shrugged. "And Lushai."

"What did he do?"

I glanced at Sayu, who flushed. "Nothing. Tell me what's happening here."

She led me into the dwelling, where Rayyel sat with Inzali and Chiha on mats in the common room, steaming mugs of tea in their hands. "What's this?" I asked, glancing at everyone. "A secret meeting? And I wasn't invited?"

You could cut the ensuing silence with a knife. I took a deep breath and turned to Rai, whose eyes were on the floor the whole time. "I'm back," I continued. "Aren't you going to greet your wife?"

He got up slowly. I could see a flash of relief on his face, but nothing more. That pride again, ever the downfall of the Jinsein people. The pride that kept us all tight-lipped and stubborn. He would rather sit with his pride than even worry about me. Why was I still surprised? It was why we were here in the first place.

"Stop," I said. I sighed. "I suppose there's no point asking for an explanation."

"You are entitled to it," Rai whispered.

"There are scandals in both our lives," Chiha broke in. Her voice was calm. Unlike Rai, she could look at me straight—eyes unflinching, head unbowed. What she had done was not a sin, as far as she was concerned. Perhaps her father had it right. Perhaps if she had been queen, the world wouldn't have erupted in chaos.

"Chiha—" Rai began.

She smirked. "What? After everything that has happened, will you lie after all? Are you going to deny Anino like you've done his whole life?"

"My wife—"

"Is sitting right in front of us and has yet to draw her sword. That ought to tell you something, Rayyel, if nothing else." She turned back to me. "*I* will not apologize. You can carry grievance against me all you want, it won't change the past. We were all children back then, thinking we knew it all, reaching for what wasn't rightfully ours, for all that we think we are entitled to it. Maybe I'm not talking about me. Maybe I'm talking about you."

Anger flashed on Rai's face. "Lady Chiha..."

"No, Lord Ikessar," she said. "You don't get a say, not this time. I warned you this would happen. Nine years ago I begged you to tell her. Tell the child the world is bigger than her own, Rayyel, that your betrothal was a sham, that people are allowed to feel and love outside of her father's wretched plans. Tell her growing up under Yeshin's shadow has sheltered her from the truth. Not all of us are Oren-yaro dogs. But you chose the predictable route. Morals, family, duty—ever the Jinsein way. Now look where we are."

As soon as she finished speaking, Rai walked out of the room.

I pressed my lips together, realizing I had witnessed a lovers' spat, nearly a decade overdue. My hunch over the years was correct. He did love her. He loved her and she loved him back, years before I ever came into the picture. Far from the aggrieved party, I was the wedge that drove them apart. "I'm not here to fight."

She turned to me. "That's surprising. Seems to me like fighting's about all you've done since you took the throne. And you did it without even knowing who the enemy is—a marvel of marvels. How exhausted are you now, Queen Talyien?"

"Very."

She didn't seem surprised by my admission. "That happens. It's hard to be a bitch without a master—you're barking at every shadow that walks across the street."

"You're an admirable woman, Lady Chiha," I said. "And if we were in a better place, perhaps I'd want to speak more about…what we intend to do from here on. Knowing your son's existence is not a reason for me to harm him—far from it."

"If that's true, then where is he?" she asked. "Word has it that he was last seen with a man who worked for you."

I glanced at Namra. "Warlord Lushai…claimed to have found him, did he not?"

"My father lied to flush that Prince Yuebek out," Chiha said. "He spoke about *saving* you from him. And while he claims to care for my son, the people around him do not. His survival seemed to be attached to yours." She paused, her eyes flicking over to my bruises. "My father—what did you do to my father?"

I had hoped to have more time to tell her properly. "I killed the bastard," I said, choosing to give her the easier way—that of anger. Unlike Sayu, I could bear the brunt of their judgment.

Her face grew white. "You…"

"Yes. I killed him. What did he expect? He attacked me. He should've known better, Lady Chiha."

"Misery," she whispered. "You've brought nothing but misery to my life." She lowered herself to the floor as the sobs tore out of her like a wave. I heard Sayu draw a deep breath. I didn't even risk looking at her. Chiha hated me already—another reason wouldn't hurt. I left her to her grief and walked out of the door to my husband.

Mistakes are like spilled wine. Like shed tears. You can revisit the circumstances as much as you want, but there is no returning them to the vessel, no erasing the pain. And yet refusing to face circumstances was a luxury I couldn't afford. What else is there to do? You get up. You wash the wine. You wipe the tears.

"I should have told you," Rai said as I drew close. "But I didn't know where to begin." He remained calm, like a man explaining yesterday's rains or a late harvest and not the existence of a bastard to a wife he had wronged.

"Of course you didn't," I replied. I sat beside him. I couldn't blame him, really. The way he thought I was, he would have believed without question that the boy's life was at stake. Of course he would have kept it from me.

We were quiet for a time, the cold wind whistling around us. It felt strange that it took this long, that we needed to be holding up the mess of our lives before I could finally feel a shred of connection to the man I married. We shared the same shell, the same troubles. And somehow, in that brief span of time we were together, I think we loved each other the same way. Ours was a love born from the desire to do the right thing, to fulfill our duties even if it meant throwing away our very selves.

He looked up, his eyes red. "An apology—"

"I don't really need it."

Confusion crossed his features. "I am glad, at least, to see you safe." He swallowed. "We've…we were just talking. Inzali and Namra have both gone through our options, and believe we only have one left: We need to gather support for ourselves. Our names still mean *something*. If we can gather an army to fight for us…"

"What do you know of war, Rai?" I asked softly.

He opened and closed his mouth. "Not much," he admitted. "I've studied past wars…"

"As I have," I said. "Which means absolutely nothing in the grand scheme of things. We'd be fighting against veterans. Lord General Ozo won almost every battle my father assigned him to. He is older now, wiser, and surrounded by the best generals the Oren-yaro army has to offer—all of whom seem loyal to *him* and him alone. And Yuebek? I don't know what his warriors are capable of, but I'm more than willing to guess they don't skimp training in the empire. Even if we managed to gather the recruits to stand against them, will we have time enough to get them ready?"

"We can't just sit here and admit defeat."

"I didn't say that." I glanced at the sky.

"We are both nothing but children in our clans' eyes," Rai said. "We have only one weapon in our grasp. Yuebek all but handed it to us."

"You mean Anino." I pressed my lips together. "Chiha back there accused you of denying him."

"I never denied him. I found out too late myself. Chiha was…not pleased that he was born after Thanh. You went into labour a month early, if you recall. I believe Chiha may have wanted a contender for crown prince. I could have told her it wouldn't make a difference. I sent Karia to look after the boy, and to keep an eye on the Baraji clan's ambitions."

"You've never met him?"

Rai frowned. "I don't understand these questions."

I gazed at the sky. "They're just questions, Rai. I'm not trying to trap you."

He sighed. "No. I have never met him."

"I'm not sure if I feel better or worse that I wasn't the only woman you abandoned with her child." He had the decency to look embarrassed. I placed my hands on my lap. "As it is, I won't use a child. Don't even start, Rai."

"I've no intention of doing that," he said. "The weapon—no, not the child. I was talking about *us*. If their plan of attack involves discrediting us somehow, then we can match them. We do the last thing they expect us to. We both admit to our faults and let them remove our claim to the throne themselves. With our downfall comes the opportunity to garner sympathy and support, a new banner under which we will unite the nation at last."

His voice was as determined as I had ever heard it.

"This must be Inzali's trick," I finally said. "Take the fall. Play the wounded deer to draw the enemy. She's awfully fond of it, isn't she?"

"It's a sound idea."

"I don't disagree. But how do we begin?"

"I can't say," he breathed. "We haven't thought the details through."

"If we do this, our marriage will be dissolved."

He really hadn't thought it through. I saw him look down, his face a mask of conflict.

"It won't even go to trial," I continued. "Our betrothal hinged on our capability as rulers, on the promise my father and your mother made to the nation. Without that—we are as good as nothing. We will be throwing away every single tool we were given so we could succeed in this position in the first place. It means publicly spitting on our parents' and our clans' wishes to create our own path. Do you understand what this all means? There is no going back from this, Rai."

He remained silent. I found myself gazing at his face to recall a time when the sight of it filled me with joy. Could this be the same boy I hated and loved so fiercely with the same breath? It was akin to remembering my father—echoes of childish whimsy, of love not yet soiled by reality. I couldn't feel a single trace of regret; the five years I wasted in anger were actually spent in mourning, and it had done its part. I didn't really need him to say anything else because I already had an answer for myself.

I didn't want to be his wife anymore.

I watched him sit up and walk a few steps away, his hands balled into fists. "What I truly want…" he began, his voice muffled. But then he trailed off and turned, a scowl underneath his thin black beard, and he looked at me like I had gone insane. No—like *he* was going insane, and the only cure lay in the safety of what we thought we would have our whole lives through. He wanted me to tell him I could still love him, that I couldn't bear the thought of losing him, that I needed us to be together as surely as the sky needed the sun. And once, perhaps, I might have. Or at least I could pretend that I already did, and it was his own fault for not listening. Old, tired games, games we needed to leave behind. We weren't young anymore. Yeshin's daughter and Ryia's son could still fulfill those promises, but on our own terms. If we were to do better than the ones who came before us, we had to start with ourselves.

My silence must've spoken volumes. He returned to me and then, after a moment's hesitation, placed his hands on my shoulders. I thought he was going to try to kiss me. Instead, he placed his forehead on mine. I could feel the warmth of his skin. He took a deep breath, as if trying to preserve the memory of it all.

"We can start anew without trying to build a castle with the ashes of the past," I whispered.

He nodded and walked back to the others slowly, a man resigned to his fate. But he didn't stop; he didn't falter. Maybe it wasn't surprising that it was easier for him than it was for me. I stayed on the bench a little longer and allowed myself a memory: the morning after our wedding night, his hair spilling on the pillows, the sun shining over the white sheets that covered our bodies. *My prince*, I mused while I lay there, awash in his scent, his soft breathing tickling my chin. I touched his face as gently as I could, not wanting to wake him up, but unable to help dreaming I might finally be where I belonged. My prince. My king. My happily-ever-after. He placed his arm around me in his sleep, and I fooled myself into thinking the past could be erased, ripped out like pages from a book. Now I know there is no way to do it without breaking the spine.

I followed him back inside, past the silent women and towards the table where paper and ink were laid out in a neat row. Rai spoke a word to Inzali, who nodded. I pulled a stool towards me, sat down, and began to write a letter of confession. I showed it to him as the ink dried. We switched places, and he did the same thing. Afterwards, we folded the letters and sealed both of them together. He used the little seal he seemed to carry around everywhere; I used my ring.

And just like that, we held the key to the destruction of it all. Our claim to the throne. Our marriage. But my resolve felt hollow. I was filled with a sense of grasping the air, of losing the ground from underneath my feet. Everything I understood of the world had hinged around my father's orders. Could I really move beyond it? It felt like the kind of thing you examined after a long night of hard drinking—something you needed to reflect on, maybe write poetry about like an Ikessar with a belly full of tea. But uncertainty was a luxury I couldn't afford. We didn't have the time. We had to strike at the enemy somehow, the only way we knew how.

I heard the sound of footsteps outside. Heavy boots, on packed ground, with the clink of chain and armour. Somebody began pounding on the door.

"We know you're there." Ozo's voice boomed like a warhorn at daybreak.

I went to open the door, because no one else looked like they wanted to. It swung open, revealing the general and a handful of men.

"You are bloody resourceful, I'll give you that," Ozo grumbled as he considered me, his old, tired eyes boring a hole into my soul.

My hand sought my sword hilt.

He sniffed. "Not going to answer, are you? Did Lushai slit your tongue? No. You would've done it for him; that's why you're here and he's not. The fool. I told him not to anger Yeshin's child." He glanced at Chiha, whose face was the still mask of grief. "My condolences, Lady Chiha."

"If not angering me was the goal, you're not doing a very good job yourself," I said in a low voice.

He sighed again, like a man who had seen too much and wasn't sure why he was still alive to make sense of it. "I could've told you killing Lushai was a mistake. The son is more stubborn and twice as foolish—dealing with the new warlord will be a pain in the neck. But when did you ever listen?"

"I have no reason to listen to traitors."

"Me, a traitor," he repeated. He shook his head, grey strands of hair falling over his forehead. "To have sunk so low. To be called a traitor by my lord's pup."

"You seized my army, Ozo. Refused to help me. Proclaimed yourself a warlord. Actions of an opportunist."

"And yet look at me here, unarmed, speaking sensibly to you. I suppose there's only so much we could've asked from you," Ozo grumbled. He drew his sword. "Step aside, Queen Talyien. We've come to arrest Lord Rayyel."

"No," I said. "You won't do that."

"You're defending the Ikessar now? After everything he's done?"

"So what if I am?"

He glowered. "You impetuous child…"

"Careful, Ozo. Lushai walked down that same road."

"Feel free to kill me. Save me the trouble of having to deal with you."

I drew my sword and charged. He struck me, flinging me aside as easily as a bear swiping a gnat away. As I struggled to recover, I saw him lumber towards the doorway, blocking it with his body.

His soldiers stepped towards me. *His* soldiers, in Oren-yaro garb. "Please, Queen Talyien," Captain Lakas said, holding his hand out. "Fighting only makes this harder for all of us."

"You assholes have made it impossible for me to do anything else!"

"Catch your breath," Ozo suggested. "Why resist? It's Rayyel Ikessar's head on the plate this time, not yours. Did you think Lushai was as careful and secretive as he thought he was? We've known about the bastard a while, even before Prince Yuebek did." He glanced at the others, grinning. "We knew Lushai sent his lovely daughter to seduce the Ikessar prince. Not a hard thing to do. You could play the chaste priest all you want, Lord Rayyel, but deep inside, you're just a man. Just as pliable to seduction as the best of us."

"Is your hatred for the Ikessars so great that you would have us become slaves to the Zarojo to prove a point?" I asked.

"You make it sound like Prince Yuebek left a sea of blood as he marched towards us. He could have—he didn't."

I smirked. "They said you feared only my father back in the war. And yet here you stand, the celebrated Lord General Ozo, bending backwards for a foreign invader! Your ancestors will condemn you. Your descendants will curse your name."

Ozo's face tightened. "You know why you make a poor queen? You let your emotions cloud your judgment. You can't even do a very good job of pretending." He began to fiddle with his sword belt. "This is what's going to happen. Lord Rayyel will be dragged back to Toriue to confess to his infidelities. Lushai lied about finding the boy, but we've got servants who can prove his existence.

Your marriage will be annulled, and then you will marry Prince Yuebek and assume the throne with him as your consort. These were your father's wishes, Beloved Queen, whether you like it or not."

"Impossible," Rai spoke up. "The people will never recognize it. Your Esteemed Prince won't be happy, either—I assume you promised him the title of Dragonlord in exchange for his army. The Zarojo don't like having to bow to their women. To expect the same from an emperor's son…"

"I didn't say it would be easy," Ozo said. "I expect bloodshed from here on out."

"You're talking war."

"Of course I'm talking war," Ozo snarled. "A change of power doesn't happen without war. It's high time we had another. Maybe this time around I'll finally get rid of that mother of yours!"

"Your lust for blood, Lord General, will go down in history," Rai said. He walked towards Ozo, holding his wrists out. "But arrest me if you will. Please." And then he glanced up, meeting my eyes. "Beloved Queen…I leave it up to you."

"So you're working together now," Ozo laughed. "After everything you put us through—"

"Why the hell should I care what you think?" I snapped. "I don't owe you anything."

"You don't have to tell me. I wasn't born yesterday," Ozo said. He curled his lip. "You're clearly going to let yourself take the fall with him. You think the nation is going to be impressed? But since you're going to insist on doing things your way, I suppose there's no harm in letting you know your options. You *could* throw your body down the hole with him. You could do that. It'll go down in time as the ultimate lover's sacrifice or whatever the hell you think that's going to do. I'll tell you now it won't mean a damn thing. Prince Yuebek's men have found the Baraji bastard in Onni. Your servant's being tricky, Queen Talyien, but they'll get them all soon enough. And then it won't matter if you confess along with Prince Rayyel…his sins will outweigh yours. We'll have all their heads strung outside the castle walls by the end of the week."

"No!" Chiha cried. "My son—!"

"There's no point protesting, Lady Chiha," Ozo continued. "Consider it a compliment I'm not dragging you with them. Your father was a piss-poor ally, one with his own damn ambitions, but he was an ally all the same. I'm sorry about your boy, but the gift will appease the Zarojo prince. He's got quite the temper. I'll make it quick."

"I'm not going to let you do this," I said.

Ozo sniffed. "I know you won't. I do know you, more than you realize. Gods be damned, Tali, you are *too* much like your father and you'll end up killing us all."

He nodded towards Lakas, who grabbed my wrist. I turned to strike; the captain twisted my arm, tearing the rusted blade from my grasp. A few feet away, Ozo unstrapped his sword belt, tugging the scabbard loose. He flung the sheathed sword towards me.

It landed near my feet, and I realized my mistake. It wasn't his at all. I recognized the wooden handle, the one carved to appear like a sea serpent's mouth, wide open.

It was my father's sword.

"Take it," Ozo commanded.

"Why do you have this?" I gasped. "I've been looking for it for years!"

"Just take it."

Lakas released me. I reached for the hilt, my fingers trembling, and lifted the blade. It was larger and heavier than I was used to—nearly a two-hander, but balanced almost like a well-made grass-cutter. The blade was broad and notched at the tip.

"Your second option," Ozo said, crossing his arms, "is that you make this easier for all of us. You won't listen if I tell you to stop resisting. You'll tell me to go to hell if I insist you cut off your husband's head yourself."

"Go to hell."

He glowered. "Before you decide to bury your father with this insolence, I suggest you travel to your ancestral home in Burbatan. Go to your father's study in the attic. See for your own eyes what you refuse to listen to with your ears."

"I've been in too many traps to fall into another one."

"Of course you have. You're forgetting that I've no reason to trap you. I already have you here. But if you are who you claim to be—if you truly give a damn about Jin-Sayeng, if you claim about your father's honour *at all*..."

My hands tightened around the sword as I considered the best angle to cut him from.

He saw the movement and gave a grim smile. "You *could* kill me here, if you want. Unlike Lushai, I have no heir. Perhaps the Oren-yaro won't mind my death and you'll get your army back. You'll be able to declare war against the Zarojo now. The Baraji won't fight for you—and hell would freeze over before you get support from the Ikessars and their allies—but maybe you'll have a better chance with some of the coastal lords. And maybe you'll even win. Impossible things have happened before. But then what? Will you be able to stand your ground against what happens after?"

"My queen…" Namra broke in.

"Go to Burbatan," Ozo repeated. "Before you do something we all regret. If your father was alive, he would've said the same thing."

I hesitated.

"Go!" Ozo barked.

I flinched, the sound of his voice somehow reminding me of Yeshin. For that moment, I was a child reprimanded for disobedience, and my senses swam as I tried to recover from the blow. I tucked the sword into my belt and gave Rai one last look before I fled.

CHAPTER FOURTEEN

THE RUSE REVERSAL

᚛ᚔᚒᚋ᚜

I had thought the sword was lost forever. Stolen by one of the staff, sold for a few pieces of coin.

I noticed it missing after the servants had discovered the bonytongue's body several days after Yeshin's funeral. We scoured the castle from top to bottom, though I left it to the staff to check my father's study because I didn't want to step foot in it myself. His loss had sent me spinning, and I didn't want to be reminded of how truly alone I was. I was convinced that the sword would fill up that empty space my father had left behind.

My obsession numbed the grief. I imagined claiming the blade for myself, cutting into my enemies with the comforting weight of it in my hands. I thought of making a show of having it presented to me in court during my coronation—how I would bow to it before they placed the crown on my head. The gesture alone could spark war. Perhaps it was better it never happened. Everything unfolded as it did, the years whirling around me like a hurricane. The sword was forgotten.

To learn that Ozo had it all this time was a light to a corridor I wasn't sure I wanted to explore. It was easier to pretend he simply wanted what I had. The province of Oren-yaro, at least, if not the throne. Yeshin's sword would have been a remarkable addition to his collection, a glorious symbol that he deserved what was mine by right. But for him to just hand it to me, and then to let me go . . .

Go to Burbatan. It was an old town in the foothills, left under the steward-ship of a minor lord. The Orenar clan was said to have been in charge of the town in the past, and we still owned the surrounding land to the north. My great-grandfather had built a house there on top of a hill, overlooking a lake;

it was where my father had spent most of his childhood and part of his youth, when his brothers were being groomed to rule Oren-yaro. Facts from the vestiges of time, stinking like mothballs.

"We have to find Lamang first," I told Namra. "Yuebek's men say he's somewhere in Onni."

"Would he still have the boy?"

"He would never abandon someone under his care."

"If Yuebek's men have already caught up to Lamang, I don't see what else we can do," Namra said. "You need to be gathering support for yourself, Beloved Queen. Make contact with the warlords most willing to listen. You don't have time for anything else."

"They have a reason to kill Rayyel if they find Anino. You heard Ozo. The man doesn't make empty threats. If you care about your lord at all—"

"I care about you both."

"So move a little faster."

To her credit, she tried to.

"I don't know what they want from me," I managed, slowing down so she could catch up. "Ozo. My father."

"Your father is—"

"Dead, I know. We've talked about this, Namra." I turned to her and swallowed. "But you've seen that throne room. It very nearly killed you when you were trying to investigate. You don't see how firm of a grip his unseen hand has on all of this?"

"And yet you're tempted to go to Burbatan, in spite of everything. Beloved Queen, the things Ozo has told you—you don't have to listen. You are not a child anymore, to listen to your father's command. You are *queen*. You can make your own decisions."

"I can," I conceded. "But even you can admit my record is…terrible." I glanced at my father's sword and felt the sea serpent's eye looking back at me, imagined a monstrous orb rolling back in its socket, the piercing light shattering my soul. I swallowed and turned to the cloud of dust in the distance. The sound of hooves was suddenly overwhelming. We managed to make it to the side of the road as thousands of riders appeared on the horizon.

Thousands. It had to be thousands. I had never seen so many horses or soldiers before. I felt my heart in my throat as I gazed up at the ones in front, holding up banners with Yuebek's sigil on them. Their silver-white armour gleamed under the steady blaze of the winter sun. Namra pulled up my hood and motioned for me to cover my face.

"Rai is all alone," I said, offhandedly.

"We have to believe that he will be safe," Namra whispered. "Inzali is with him. And his mother is still there."

"She doesn't seem to like him all that much."

"I've been with the Ikessars long enough to know she'll protect him, even just on principle. An enemy of an enemy is a friend, and this is her *son*."

"I'm not sure how much I believe that," I said. "I'll take your word for it. But blessed Akaterru, that is a *lot* of soldiers." I watched as they stopped right outside the city gates, assuming a formation.

"We'll have to travel off the road," Namra said.

"It looks like they're seizing control. Lushai is dead. Prince Nijo is warlord now. He—"

Namra took hold of my elbow. "Tali," she said.

I found myself staring into her face.

"There are other things you need to worry about. Whatever happens out there…will unfold without you."

Until she said my name, I didn't realize how exhausted I must've appeared. And perhaps she was right. I had been on the run for most of the day, without a bite to eat since that morning. My trembling fingers were still covered in blood. Subdued, I allowed her to take the lead.

I don't think we would've made it through that parade of soldiers as easily without Namra. Although they appeared disciplined enough as they marched down the road, the long journey from Sutan was taking its toll on some of the lower-ranking soldiers. Some of the foot soldiers jeered at the villagers as they passed—a farmer's goods were stolen, excused away as "tribute for the Esteemed Prince," and two young women would've been raped if not for the interference of the company captain. If I was alone, I would have marched over there and used my father's sword to carve my initials into their skulls.

Namra seemed to know what I was thinking and interfered before I could make a decision. She must've been the reason Rai had survived all his years of travel—she knew her way through the city, automatically changing her demeanour around me so as not to arouse suspicion. In my peasant's clothes, I simply appeared to be a serving woman accompanying a priestess to a temple of the Nameless Maker. There were enough such temples around those parts.

Namra and I parted momentarily to find information faster. A mango-seller noted a stronger-than-usual Zarojo presence in a certain district and pointed me to a Kag-style tavern bearing the name of the Owl and the Granny in the distance. "I heard there was at least one Zarojo staying there," he told me, pocketing the coin I gave him. "Foreigners seem to like the place." He returned to slicing mangoes.

I crossed a dirty street, past a buffalo dragging behind a cart of wicker goods. A hairy, red-headed man stopped me at the entrance. He said something in Kagtar. I understood it in theory, but real life was making a fool out of me and I couldn't make out a single word. I made a show of patting my pockets.

The man didn't look like he believed me. He grabbed my shoulder. I sidestepped, pushing him into the wall. He was a big man, which meant he hit it with a satisfying crack before he tripped over a crate of cabbages.

Somebody whistled from inside the tavern. A woman stepped out, hands on her apron.

He lurched to his feet, spitting blood. He gave me a dirty look, but the woman walked past him to take my arm. I tore myself from her grasp before she could even wrap her fingers around me. I extended my arms past my cloak, revealing my sword. She must've gotten the idea, because she took a step back before gesturing to me again.

I stepped inside the tavern. There was a single patron there, sitting on the counter, nursing a mug of dark beer.

"You own business in the city now?" I asked, striding casually towards Khine. "I didn't even know you speak Kag."

His body tensed as I took the stool next to him, and he looked away for a moment before replying. "I'm glad to see you safe. But you need to make it a habit not to make a scene everywhere you go."

"I'll have you know, that was the first since walking into town. Are you going to explain your new friends? Or have you always secretly been a Kag merchant of some sort?"

He laughed, more for his benefit than mine. "Nothing of the sort. They're closed today, but they let me sit around and watch them dust the chairs or whatever other chore they need done. If that's friendship, my standards have dropped even lower." He nudged his plate towards me.

I grabbed the bread. It was drenched in butter and stuffed with some sort of soft, white cheese, the sour kind they made from buffalo milk up in the foot-hills. I broke it in two and handed the bigger piece back to him.

He shook his head. "You eat. I'm full."

Without waiting for a second bidding, I crammed the bread into my mouth. He passed his beer over to me.

"I speak a little bit of Kagtar," he said as he watched me attempt to juggle bread and beer without making a fool of myself. "Not enough to get by."

"Where's Anino?" I asked.

He hesitated.

I turned to him in surprise. "Khine—"

"It's not that I don't trust you. But…"

"I see." I swallowed.

"They're safe," Khine continued. "That's all you need to know." He paused, frowning as he gazed at my face. "You look exhausted. Did he hurt you?"

"Yuebek? He always does things that make me ill, but no. Not as you think. I escaped him just this morning."

"And knowing you, you've been on the run since then." He got up, holding out his hand. "Come. They gave me a room downstairs. You need to sleep."

"Namra's still out there."

"I'll go fetch her later. Kaz's men are everywhere."

"Jiro?"

"His wife, Anya. She's knows I'm around. I've been lying low, hoping to keep her here to give Karia and Anino a chance to escape." Realizing I wasn't moving towards him, he reached for my hand himself.

My heart leaped to my throat. I didn't know what to tell him, didn't know where to start about everything that had happened that day. His hand was warm on mine as I followed him down the steps.

The room was barely a closet, with only a single potted cactus on the windowsill for decoration. As soon as I walked in, he took a step back, an unsettled expression on his face.

"Is everything all right?" I asked.

"It's nothing," he lied.

I took a deep breath. "Ozo admitted they were close to capturing you. I was worried."

"You shouldn't be," he said. "You know I can slip past the best of them."

I paused for a moment before sitting on the edge of the bed. "It's over,

Khine," I finally said. "Rai and I can forfeit our claim to the throne without having one of us in a position to be used against the other. That damn Chiha gave us all a way out, after all."

He was silent for a few moments. "Do you really think it'll be that easy?"

"It won't. If I do this, I will have to claw my way up from the bottom—become queen on my own merits," I said. "I've no accomplishments on my own. These people won't follow me for me. Without my father's name or my marriage..."

"You'd still be you." He craned his head to the side.

"And is there value in that?" I asked. "A hot-headed woman who can fight better than she can rule...I'm not sure I've ever thought of finding support on my own before. I didn't even think it was an option."

"Would you rather obey your father's will?"

"Of course not," I said.

"And yet you don't seem angry with him. You are angrier at the personification of his orders than at the man himself."

"Because there is no sense in getting angry over a dead man," I said. "Ozo, on the other hand, is very much alive, and has chosen to obey that dead man rather than his own queen. He wants me to go to the foothills, to my clan's ancestral home first. He says I will regret it if I don't."

Khine frowned. "That's an odd word to use. *Regret.*"

"Why do you say that?"

"From what I've seen of Ozo, he's as blunt as they come. Reminds me of Agos, really." He chewed his lip. "Do you intend to go?"

"He's not exactly the epitome of a man you can trust." I closed my eyes for a moment. "What," I murmured, "do I do?"

He looked flustered. "You're asking me? I'm not really your adviser. The crowning glory of my life is making my last boss lose all his money."

I recalled Belfang's words. They must've struck deeper than I imagined. "Your counsel has kept me alive this whole time. That's—"

"Nothing," he replied easily. "Survival is easy, Tali. Beyond that...it's something I've never had to worry about. Your husband would be more qualified to comment."

"He won't be my husband for long."

"For now, he still is." Khine scratched the side of his face. "Don't forget about your son."

"Kaggawa needs him. He'll protect him."

"Not if you give it all up." He scratched his head with a grimace. "I've spoken out of line again. I'll go look for Namra before I dig myself a hole." He lingered at the hall for a moment before slowly closing the door. The sound of his boots hung as heavy as his absence.

I fell asleep. That is, my body did; my mind remained awake, drifting down a corridor that led to that blue-tinged throne room underneath my father's study. I felt myself running, felt myself wanting to run faster than my legs would let me. As I reached the gaping blackness of the far end, I turned to see a dark figure approach, sword in hand. Yellow eyes gleamed from the shadows. A shot of fear ran through my veins and I started barking.

I woke up. Blinding orange light seeped through the windows, as bright as those eyes.

The woman who worked at the tavern came down to give me breakfast, which was nothing more than a plate of hard-boiled eggs and a cup of strong coffee, sweetened with brown sugar. I managed to convey a question on Khine's whereabouts, and she spoke the Jinan word for "market" before handing me my cloak. Khine, it seemed to me, had the same penchant for making friends as I did enemies—she seemed oddly concerned about my well-being. I left the inn not long after, winding my way through the back alley that led to the marketplace.

It was crawling with Zarojo.

I could see them wandering through the stalls, harassing the shopkeepers in broad daylight. A guard passed a group, and I noticed that they conveniently looked away. It didn't matter that their warlord was dead; word must've come from the castle telling them to leave the foreigners alone.

Something tugged at my shirt. I turned around and saw a little girl. She placed a finger on her lips. I followed her to the back alley where Khine was waiting. He flipped a coin at her.

"You should start your own crime syndicate," I said, stepping to one side as the girl dashed off. "You'd own half the city in no time."

He didn't look amused. "Anya's in the neighbourhood. It's time you leave. Namra's staying in a shop near the river. If I draw Anya's attention, I don't think she'll even realize you were around."

"I came here for you, Khine. I'm not going to leave you to her mercy."

"Why?"

"What do you mean *why*?"

He glanced away, looking discomfited. "I'm not worth the risk."

"I've—"

"Your son, Tali. You need to get to him. You can't afford to give your enemies that kind of power over you. They'll use the people you care for, and then—"

"That's *exactly* why I'm here."

He stood there and stared.

We were distracted by a sharp whistle from the end of the street. Khine placed a hand on my shoulder and led me to a roof deck in the building behind us, where a group of older children were taking care of a flock of pigeons. He greeted them, throwing more coins into the air. "Give me and my lady friend a moment alone?" he asked. The children laughed as they grabbed the offering and fled down the steps. I walked past the pigeon coops, towards the railing where I could see the entire district.

He stepped towards me. "Tali…" he started, and then trailed off. Did I want to know what was really on his mind? The truth that lay hidden between the pauses, these silences, the things we weren't willing to say out loud—perhaps it was best to bury it.

"Yuebek made Lo Bahn a marquis, did you know?" I asked.

He gave a soft smile at my attempt to change the conversation. "A poor decision. The man will bankrupt the province within the month."

I heard laughter again, louder than from the street. I turned around and saw the little girl from earlier. She was holding a crumpled piece of paper in her hands. She gave Khine a furtive glance before rushing off to envelop me in a hug. "She's taken a shine to you, hasn't she?" Khine asked.

"I'm good with children," I replied, patting the girl's head. "Life with Rai prepares you for that kind of thing."

"The Lord Ikessar isn't a big baby," Khine said, shaking his head. He leaned over the railing. "More like an awkward teenager after a growth spurt."

While Khine was looking away, the girl took my hand and pressed the piece of paper in it. I felt something hard inside, almost like a bone. A bone, covered in flesh.

I felt as if my blood had turned to ice. I walked to the other end of the roof-top, pretending something in the street below caught my eye. In truth, I was unwrapping the object. I forced myself to stop thinking as I stared at the finger, at the clean cut of bone at one end. It reeked of spirits.

The paper was a letter.

Kaggawa doesn't have your son, it said. *Go to Burbatan if you want him back.*

I stared at the finger. It was the left ring finger, so grey it must have been cut off some time ago. A little boy's. If I squinted, I could pretend it was any other's.

Like many mothers, I know my own child from head to toe. I held my son's hands a thousand times before, from when they were so small they could fit neatly into the palm of mine. I knew the shape of his knuckles, how his fingers were long and slender like his father's. Every line, every scar, the way he chewed his fingernails so much he left only small slivers of them, the thin black dot of pigmentation on the nail itself. And there was no denying the indentation around the base, made by the royal ring Thanh wore at all times.

I closed the letter over the finger, my heart pounding. Ozo? Could he be so desperate that he would fake Thanh's presence in Oren-yaro? Was it another boy's finger? *You know it's not. You would know your boy in your sleep. Your soul would recognize him long before the rest of you.*

Did he have him? Was he lying? But the look in Ozo's eyes when he gave me the sword was the look of a man who knew he was at my mercy. He could have given me this, then. So this was someone else, something far more sinister. Yuebek, perhaps, except...

"Lamang!" Anya Kaz's familiar voice thundered, streaked with irritation— the sound of a hound scratching at the den where the fox lay waiting. "Spirits above, Doctor, what's the use of this? You're wasted on that woman!"

I glanced around for the little girl and noticed she had disappeared. I pocketed the finger and returned to Khine, pretending the last few moments hadn't just occurred. I didn't want to tell him. If I didn't talk about it yet, I could pretend nothing was wrong.

We spotted her down below, dressed from head to foot in leather armour. She glanced up at the roof deck. We were too far away for her to see us, but I realized it didn't matter; she knew exactly where we were.

Khine didn't move. There was no hint of surprise on his face.

"Didn't you think I would catch on to your tricks, Lamang? I've got men on every side of the street. There's no escape!" She held out her hands. "But why would you want to? Have you forgotten we're family, Khine? All of us from the streets of Shang Azi . . . we're all here for the same reason. We got caught up with the bitch and now we're paying the price. Why stay with her? She'll cut your throat herself if she thinks it's right. Don't you want to finally be a physician? It's nothing for Yuebek to force the guild to sign you in. Imagine rubbing Reng Hzi's nose into that!"

Khine grunted.

"She's just a warm cunt, Khine," Anya continued. "You know she's done for. When the time comes for the Esteemed Prince to take over the world, you don't want to be on the wrong side!"

"I'm sorry you have to hear this," Khine said. "You know how they are." But he looked troubled at her words. I turned to gaze at the sword on my belt, at the carved sea serpent on the hilt. At the notches in the dark wood that had once been soaked in the blood of my father's enemies. And then I felt the finger in my pocket, heavy as the world.

Bury it, Talyien. The thought felt like a blow, with a strength to make a warrior fall to his knees. *Do you want another sacrifice at the altar of your worship? How shall his story end? Split open with arrows like Agos? Dragged into a prison like Rayyel? Learn from your mistakes. Let him find happiness and meaning elsewhere, in a world where the shadows that haunt you cannot follow.*

I noticed a blur of movement from the distance. It was the children. They streamed behind the bandits, as if to ask for alms. One brushed close to Anya before retreating. A moment, and then a vendor whistled. A big man came up to one of Anya's, pulling out an item from his pocket. From the look on Anya's man's face, he didn't know how it got there. It didn't matter. The townsfolk tolerated harassment, but not theft. A fight broke out.

"That's our cue," Khine croaked.

The commotion grew louder, drawing the attention of the guards. We emerged near the district gate, where horses were hitched along a fence. As soon as Khine untied one horse, I grabbed it from him and swung into the saddle.

"What—" he started.

"I'm just returning the favour," I said. "All of them, actually."

His eyes widened. "You're not going to do this to me again. Tali…"

"I need company in Burbatan and Anya would be perfect." I gave a soft smile. "Have a good life, Khine."

He grabbed the horse's bridle. The glimpse of his face—the clear lines of worry, of anger—was both soothing and painful. I vowed to hold on to that image forever. I yanked the reins from his hands and sank my heels into the horse's belly. Anya and her men were still arguing with the vendors as I cantered down the street, and the guards were knee-deep in their attempt to control the crowd. "Kaz!" I called, nearly laughing.

She stopped and turned. Realization dawned on her, and she called for her men to chase after me. Their horses were still hitched near the gates. I cut their reins as I rode past them. Panicked neighs and thundering hooves blocked the path behind.

I lurched full speed onto the road.

ACT TWO

THE PLAY

CHAPTER ONE

THE WILDS OF OREN-YARO

ᴊᵧʊᵧ

When I was a child, I knew what my father thought of cowards from the ease with which his sword hacked heads off men who simpered and lied to protect themselves. I remember one such occasion: an old lord from one of the southern holdings who had been accused of sending bribes to the Ikessars. Yeshin had pounded his fists on his chest. "If you want to betray me," he snarled, "then do it to my face!"

The old man continued to deny the allegations, his words running over each other—as if he thought the more frightened he was, the more likely Yeshin would take pity on him. The hooked end of Yeshin's sword caught at his throat first, ripping the skin out like a ragged piece of canvas. As he wrapped his bony hands around his neck in a faint attempt to stop the blood, my father stepped on his back and finished separating his head from his body.

The son fell to his knees and immediately admitted to the crime. My father never batted an eyelid. Still carrying the bloodied sword, he pulled the young man to his feet and embraced him. And then he carried on with the rest of the meeting as if nothing had happened.

I watched the scene unfold from the stairway, though I can't say if it was fear or fascination that kept me staring at the decapitated head on the floor, seemingly forgotten by the droning old men and women around it. A goldfish in an earthen pot would have gathered more attention.

"Come away, child," a soft voice had called out to me from the landing. "It's time for your lessons, and you shouldn't have witnessed this thing."

I gazed up at Arro. "Why not? Isn't this what warlords do? I should get used to it."

His brow creased. "No."

"But..."

"One shouldn't get used to death and killing, child."

"They are," I pointed out.

He glanced at the great hall in the distance before placing a hand on my shoulder. "You're not them."

"I will be someday," I whispered.

He looked amused by my words—Arro, who was rarely amused. I wondered what he would think of what had happened over the past year. I knew precisely what my father would've said, but Arro had never expressed his disapproval in the same manner. It still seemed odd to me how simply people slipped in and out of our lives. One moment a constant, like the sun or the stars or the sky; the next, gone like a gust of wind. Saying goodbye to Khine was the most difficult, but it had to be done. Lingering over whatever I wanted was a pointless exercise.

Clarity, if not courage. And it didn't come like a shaft of light breaking through the clouds. I sought strength from my father's sword. Maybe I even prayed to it. The man survived onslaught after onslaught of the Ikessars. Even if Yeshin had hated Thanh as much as Ryia did, he was still my father, and surely my own father could lend me the strength to save my son. *If he is still alive. Please, let him be alive.* I still had my son's finger with my things. I didn't know why I held on to it. I didn't need a reminder of what was at stake. But throwing it away felt like giving him up for dead.

So I rode to the foothills with barely a thought for my own safety. I owned much of those lands—even if I wasn't queen of Jin-Sayeng, I was still Yeshin's heir. Jin-Sayeng had always considered it a flaw, but now Rayyel Ikessar's open support might make all the difference. And yet the exact same thing that would cause the rest of Jin-Sayeng to reconsider their view of me would cause me to lose the Oren-yaro for good. To stand beside an Ikessar while wielding my father's sword was unthinkable. How would I approach the Oren-yaro royals to gain their loyalty? How could I discredit Lord Ozo, decorated war hero and defender of the province, and get them to follow me instead? They all saw me as nothing but Yeshin's bitch pup.

The evening darkened, the road lit only by the soft glow of the moon above. Breath fogging around my lips, I caught the sight of fireflies dipping in and out of the rice fields and felt loneliness hit me like a battering ram. I hardened myself to the feeling. I was my father's daughter, whatever that still meant. To be born to the quivering thighs of war meant that happiness and love and joy were afterthoughts. I could rail out in anger, but then what would that do? Are we given what we want simply because we want it? Even children know better.

A group of people were marching south from the first fork on River Agos. I slowed my horse down. "A strange night to be moving, Anong," I called to one of the elders.

The old man jerked a finger behind him. "Bandits," he said simply.

I narrowed my eyes, counting the torches further up the road. "It looks like you're moving a whole village. Are the rebels so brazen now?"

"Deng Kedlati's bandits have always been brazen," the old man replied. "Their territory used to be further north, but ever since the queen disappeared, General Ozo's patrols seem to have disappeared with her, and they've been pushing south."

"Don't the Ikessars have patrols?" I asked. "The bandit territories border both our lands."

Another villager laughed. "We think Ryia's been turning a blind eye on purpose."

"A blind eye?" someone else called. "You mean she's *paying* them. That's the only reason they've been able to get a foothold in the first place. She hasn't forgotten her war. If it means burning the whole nation to the ground with her in it, she'll do it happily enough."

People grumbled in agreement. I couldn't say I was surprised; royals never have a problem finding disgruntled commoners to cause havoc in their rivals' lands. It usually didn't cost much, either. I glanced back at the old man. "You can travel with us if you want," he said. "We're heading to Oren-yaro."

"I'm on my way to Burbatan," I replied.

The old man clicked his tongue. "That's where we came from. The rebels have the whole town under siege."

I paused for a moment, racking my brains to recall who oversaw the town. "Lord Ipeng," I said at last. "Doesn't he have the soldiers to take care of it?"

"His barracks are all but empty," one of the young men broke in. "Lord General Ozo pulled the younger soldiers out in the beginning of the year. My brother's one of them."

"And it's not just a handful of bandits," another added. "It's a whole army of them. General Ozo will have his hands full—especially with all the troubles he's already dealing with."

Shaking their heads, they all began to walk again. "Be careful out there," the old man said, waving goodbye.

He didn't get far. He had barely walked two steps when an arrow took him in the throat.

The bandits appeared on the edge of the road, running right into the line of refugees, who scattered. One of the young men tossed me a spear, which I caught in mid-air. I charged the closest bandit, gritting my teeth as my spear found its mark in his neck.

The first kill is always the easiest. I'd barely gotten a breath in when a second bandit drove his horse into mine. I fell from the saddle, skidding through the mud. I couldn't draw my sword in time. The bandit was on me, his hands around my neck as he tried to choke me into unconsciousness. My senses were slipping as one of the refugees arrived, sword in hand; the bandit turned and slashed his belly.

I watched as his guts tumbled out of his body and onto the ground. The man looked surprised, and his hands made an involuntary motion, as if he wanted to stuff his entrails back into the wound. But he never got that chance. Anya appeared behind him, taking his head off with one clean stroke.

"Took you long enough," I managed to hiss as I tried to tear the bandit's hands from my neck. He simply turned and struck the side of my head with a closed fist. Then he lunged at Anya, who killed him, too.

Ears ringing, I stepped back. "What's this?" I asked. "These assholes aren't yours?" I paused when I saw her face clearer in the moonlight. She had a split lip, and there was a bruise on her chin and above one eye. I laughed. "Straight from the frying pan and into the fire, I see."

"Your land is crawling with vermin," she spat. "If you're smart, you'll hand over your weapon now and come back with me. Prince Yuebek offers solutions, not problems."

"Haven't you asked around before you committed to this? You know I won't bow to your emperor's son. Ask everyone who's tried to make me." I paused. "Oh, that's right. Most of them are dead."

"He'll bend your knees if you don't do it yourself," she said simply.

"I thought you made your own rules. Why are you working for him now?"

"Weren't you listening? The man can make you bend your knees. Maybe a pampered cunt like yours won't understand. Look at you, leading bandits straight into helpless villagers..."

I struck her. She doubled back from the blow, allowing me to crawl up.

"Did I hit a nerve?" Anya laughed as she got to her feet. She wiped a streak of blood from her mouth. "Come on, Queen Talyien. I don't think the aches of the common people have ever occurred to you. We don't care what side we're on so long as our bellies are fed."

"A bandit has no right to lecture me."

"Maybe not, but then again, you don't become a bandit out of principle, Queen Talyien," she said.

"The allure of gold and shiny things..."

"You've been around Lamang too long. You even talk like him."

I drew my sword. "You helped me once, Anya, and I'll never forget it. But now you're in my way."

The smile on Anya's face grew cold. I wondered if she thought I would surrender just because she'd caught up to me. Holding her scabbard above her chest, the hesitation was clear in her eyes. She had seen me fight. And she was a smart woman—she knew the advantage lay with me because I didn't need *her* alive. I had qualms about killing her, but I could shed them easily if we came to blows.

Then she glanced behind me. I didn't follow her gaze immediately—it was a cheap tactic, one I'd used far too often in the past, and I wasn't about to fall for it. Most of the bandits were far down the road, chasing after the fleeing refugees. The ones who stayed behind to fight were already dead.

The shadows of more appeared from the forest. A sea of torches. I heard Anya give a soft sigh. "This is what they call...what was that word? An impasse?" she asked, almost calmly.

"What would you have used otherwise?" I replied, sweat dripping down my brow.

"Fucked."

"Ah," I said. "I agree."

"What do we have here?" A man I presumed was the leader of the group approached us, lamp in hand. He had an eyepatch and a long scar that rolled from behind it to the back of his shaved head. He grinned behind a thick beard. "Two women arguing in the dead of the night. You don't see that very often."

"Don't *you?*" one of his companions asked. "I could've sworn I heard it the night your mistress followed you home."

The man laughed, throwing a hand out. One of his thumbs was missing. "I stand corrected. Two women arguing in the dead of the night—something that occasionally happens to the best of us. So which of you slept with the other's husband?" He trailed off as he stared at me. I remembered I still had my blade drawn and quickly slammed it back into the scabbard, but it was too late. "That's a royal sword," he said. "Go take it, Noerro."

"*You* do it, brother," the man who had spoken earlier replied. "She doesn't look friendly."

The man in the eyepatch frowned. "Come and hand me that before someone gets hurt."

"If it's all the same to you, I'd really rather not," I said.

"It's not all the same to me," he hissed. "Your accent..."

"She's from the city," Noerro piped up. "Oren-yaro."

"What if I am?" I asked.

"You were talking in Zirano earlier."

The shadows drew closer. I found myself back-to-back with Anya. She was breathing through her mouth. "Too many for us to fight," she mumbled.

"Royals speak Zirano," the man continued.

"You're a smart one," I said. "Your mother must be proud."

"I'll shut the bitch up for you, Deng," one of the men said, approaching us.

I tightened my grip around my sword. "Deng," I repeated. "Deng Kedlati."

Eyepatch man smiled. "You know me. But of course you do. My reputation precedes me." He stared at the sword some more, and the grin grew wider. "And I know *you*. Grandmother was right. Talyien Orenar, she said, would never turn her back on her son. I take it you received my package."

"You," I said. "You sent the finger."

He bowed.

"You have my son." I didn't want to ask. I didn't want to beg. He might have a blade to my neck, but I didn't want to give him the satisfaction of twisting it further. I untied the sword from my belt and dropped it. "Bring me to him."

He picked the sword up and smiled. "As you wish, Beloved Queen."

The bandits took me further north, deeper into the lands the Kedlati Faction had staked out for themselves. A stone's throw from Burbatan. I gazed up at the hills and the terraced rice fields, the numbness spreading inside. The thought of what awaited ahead burrowed like a tick, feeding, growing fat on my fears.

We were on the road for a few days when we chanced upon the first merchant caravan, on the main road leading to Shirrokaru. The bandits wasted no time driving the horses straight into the road, blades flashing. As the blood scent drenched the air, Anya approached me, balancing herself perfectly as she nudged the horse with her legs. Unlike me, they had bound her hands behind her back. "If you want to escape now…" she began.

"They have my son," I said.

"You know that's a lie."

I closed my eyes before reaching into my pocket. I handed her the finger without a word.

Anya's expression barely changed. "So?"

"It's my boy."

"If they had a boy with them, wouldn't you have seen him already?"

"Deeper in their lands, then. In some town they own. I can't take the chance."

"You've got to ditch your wretched offspring," she said. "He's a weakness, don't you see? They take him from you and tell you anything they want, and you'll listen in the hopes they have what you seek. It's almost too easy. You're a queen. Take control."

How? I wanted to ask her. *With what power?* "If I try to escape, I don't know what they'll do to you," I said, to stop myself from falling into despair.

She smirked. "You do care about me. I'm touched."

"Don't be absurd. I just think your squealing would be very unpleasant."

She leaned over the saddle. "I'm surprised by how your sense of duty now extends to me. I would've dragged you back to the prince by your hair. No wonder Khine is so conflicted."

"I'd rather not talk about him."

"You wouldn't?" Such words, of course, seemed like an invitation for her to do exactly that. She drew her horse closer.

In the distance, the sound of battle continued.

"I've known that man longer than you have," she continued. "Since he was a boy, all fuzzy-lipped and acting older than his years. Jiro always found him amusing. Little Philosopher, he'd call him. There was a time he wouldn't be caught dead associating with people like you."

"You mean royals."

"Nobles. Politicians. Privileged folk who don't think twice about turning the lives of us lesser folk upside down while they get *their* affairs in order." Anya nodded over to the dying merchants, a smile on her lips.

"I never wanted this," I said.

"And yet you're still here. You knew it wasn't clean hands that put you on that throne and you're still here. But then why shouldn't you be? Why give it up when the whole world already revolves around you? Beloved Queen, precious princess... even when you mean well, you barrel through without realizing what *you* do to others. You want to rule as queen, and you want to say it was the goodness of your heart and the purity of your intentions that got you there. I get it—I respect that. Fuck, I don't think I know a woman who wouldn't want to be in your spot in a heartbeat. But yours isn't a life earned, and you don't seem to understand this. It was clear as far back as Anzhao. I tried to warn Khine, but he wouldn't listen. The man both hates and admires you so much he doesn't know what to do about it. You should've just put him out of his misery and fucked him already. If you had seen him when you left him there in Onni..."

I turned away from her. "You're really cutting it close, Anya," I grumbled.

"Of course I am," she laughed. "But isn't it inconvenient? Look at me. I just do what I want. Maybe it'll be easier for you if you do the same thing. If you're going to take from people, if you're going to make their lives miserable to make yours better, don't wrap it up in all these justifications. I steal, and I call it stealing. I kill because I want what isn't mine. And if I die in the attempt, so what? I've lived a good life. Jiro will burn a candle for me and the children we've lost and then go find himself a young tart to marry again, hopefully while he can still get it up. And so life goes on."

"Anya..."

"I have no intention of wallowing in sob stories," she sniffed, before cocking her head to the side. "I believe we're being followed by one of yours. I caught sight of her when I was making water this morning. Thin, plain woman, dressed in strange robes. Face like a horse—"

"Namra." I frowned. "And don't say that. She must've guessed I was headed this way."

"Damn woman sure knows how to keep herself out of sight. I don't think these idiots have noticed her."

"She would. She's a mage," I said.

"I've never been too fond of mages, but suddenly I'm thankful you've got one on your side."

"I don't know how much good she'll do us now." I fell silent as the bandits returned from the road, joyous faces streaked with blood. A good day for them, a sign that they were blessed by the gods. That murder and robbery could be seen as a blessing was more than blasphemous, but I couldn't very well tell them that. The nation was broken everywhere I looked. One more crack was nothing.

The sun was halfway up the sky when we finally reached the bandits' village, all stinking of sweat and dirt. A young girl came to take my horse. I all but stumbled off the saddle.

"Don't accuse us of forgetting our manners," Deng said, patting my back as he undid my ropes. "You're a guest here, Queen Talyien."

"My son," I said. "Where is he?"

"In due time," he replied with a smile.

He led me down to the middle of the village, where a feast had been laid out in anticipation of their arrival. The food was plain, simple fare: rice with boiled eggs and smoked, sweet sausages, snail stew in a peppery gravy, and roasted wild chicken so tough it could cut your teeth. I barely touched anything.

They led me to my quarters, a small hut overlooking a creek. Judging from the upturned clay jars in the common room and the unwashed dishes, still dotted with grease and dried grains of rice, it looked like it had been vacated hurriedly by some family for my purposes.

I heard scratching coming from the window on the other side of the hut. With a frown, I cracked the shutters open. Anya whistled. "What did I tell you?" she said. "No sight of a little royal boy anywhere. I looked around."

"They let you out of their sight?"

"They don't seem to care what I do here," she said. "Probably convinced I won't escape. I've been working on that leader of theirs, Deng. I bet I can have him on his back in half an hour if I wanted to."

"What would your husband say?"

"That it's a necessity, born from troubled times, and it's only a pity that his poor angel would have to go through—"

"Forget I said anything."

She laughed, before growing serious. "That day you used yourself as bait so I'd leave Lamang alone—you really didn't think I would hurt him, did you? All we needed from him was the bastard. Prince Yuebek doesn't give a damn about him. I *do* consider him one of ours, and we protect our own."

"Who knows what I believe anymore," I said in a low voice.

"You must've believed his life was in danger for you to do what you did. I didn't realize you cared for him so much. I mean, I'd *guessed* it, but..."

I cleared my throat. "I didn't think you cared about what I thought."

"It just occurred to me to check if you're holding any grudges before we go through with this." She gave a soft whistle. I heard rustling from around the hut; the door opened and Namra walked in like an invited guest.

I slammed the door shut and dragged a stool to keep it in place. Behind me, Anya jumped over the windowsill, landing on the floor with a soft thud.

"Beloved Queen," Namra said. "I'm glad you're not hurt."

"Namra, I can't leave. Thanh—"

"Is not here," she continued.

"I told her everything," Anya added. "She agrees with me. No boy, nothing. They're manipulating you like a puppet on strings. We have to get out of here."

I swallowed. "The finger—"

"Let me see," Namra said.

I went back for my things and found it. I couldn't even look at it anymore and turned my back as Namra inspected it.

"Perfectly preserved," she continued. "You're sure it's Thanh's?"

"As sure as the woman who birthed him."

"I won't argue. But my queen..." She approached me with the finger folded inside a cloth and bowed. "There are better ways to find out. You have to be where they don't want you."

I took the cloth and placed it back in my pocket. "What do you mean?"

"Deng Kedlati is here now, but they've had the town of Burbatan under siege for days. They have another leader."

"You think we should go there, on our own terms."

Namra nodded.

"We'll have to find somewhere to hide first," I said. "Until we come up with a plan to break through the siege. There's a temple near the town."

"Is it safe?"

"I've been there before," I said.

Namra pulled her sleeves up, revealing her thin arms. "We shouldn't waste time. Anya, do you have everything?"

Anya reached back over the window to fetch a wooden bucket filled with water and two candles. I frowned. "Do I wear that bucket on my head and pretend they can't see me?"

Anya burst out laughing. Even Namra managed a small smile. "I'm going to cast a spell, one that will tear a small hole through the *agan* fabric and allow us to walk straight through to a spot I've prepared on the other side. It wouldn't be far from here, and it's right on the path leading to the temple of Akaterru at the base of the hill."

I frowned. "Let's pretend I actually understood any of that. I'm not sure I'm comfortable with what I just heard."

"I'll be right beside you the whole time, my queen, and I've done this before. Once."

"You're not helping ease my mind here, priestess."

"Do you happen to have any other ideas?"

"If you can grab my father's sword from Kedlati…"

"There are situations where it is safer for you not to have any sort of bludgeoning tool in hand."

"Excuse me, priestess, but you don't bludgeon with that sword."

"I'm almost sure *you'd* find a way, my queen." She turned to Anya. "I can only take one person through. You'll have to make your way to the temple by yourself."

"I'll get the sword," Anya said. "I've seen where they keep it."

"Knowing you, you'll run off and sell it first chance you get."

She smiled. "You'll just have to trust me. Do you want to stay here forever?"

I didn't reply and turned to watch Namra sit in front of the bucket. There was a blue glow on her fingertips. I found myself transfixed. I had only been around so many mages, and they each had different techniques. Yuebek's magic was like a charging bull, while Eikaro was a little child playing with blocks. Wily Belfang treated it like a game of cards, something he had to win. But the fundamentals, from what I could gather, were the same. It was like working with thread—if the strands were attached to your fingers. Those blind to the *agan* only see the glow; those with the gift, on the other hand, can see more. And if they're skilled enough, they can coax out those strands and form connections to mask, or create, or destroy.

I didn't know what she was doing this time. Her hands were hovering over the water, and I got the sense that she was using it to amplify the connection. I felt a touch of something in the air, a little like the prickling of the hair on your skin before a lightning storm. My senses began to blur.

And then I noticed I was staring at a hole in the middle of a hut. It gave me the impression of staring down at the bottom of a well. I thought I could even smell the damp scent of water coming through it.

"I'm not so sure about this, Namra," I said. "I can't. I need the sword—"

The hole grew bigger and I heard a bang, deep inside my head.

"Tali!" Namra cried, just as the blue-touched blackness overtook me.

I was running through the shadows, weaving through the ghostly blue radiance. Someone was screaming at me to keep my feet moving. *Don't stop, don't turn around.* I forced down the whimper building up inside my throat. My breath felt like a knife inside my chest.

I skidded around a sharp corner, my legs buckling underneath. Against all warning, I looked up.

A sword was bearing down on me. I caught a glimpse of the handle, the open-mouthed serpent. I screamed. The sword slipped past me and struck the head clean off a man nearby. I blinked and found myself in a battlefield, amidst soldiers hacking at each other. The smell of blood and urine filled the air. "Don't let the Butcher through!" someone cried. "Kill him! Kill the bastard! Free Jin-Sayeng!"

A horn sounded. I turned and saw Yeshin on his horse in the distance. I felt my mouth go dry and the knife wrenched through my throat—I didn't think it was possible to feel both fear and longing at the same time. "Father—" I started.

Someone grabbed my wrist, tearing me away from the street. "You shouldn't be here!" a woman all but screamed at my face. "Didn't you hear them? Run! We have to run!"

"My father's there!" I cried. "I can't leave him!"

"He'll be dead soon, child! Mourn him when this is over!"

I wanted to argue that he wasn't dead. What could kill a man so powerful? I heard the sound of panicked neighs and looked up in time to see Yeshin fall from his horse in the distance, a spear through his shoulder. Blood foamed around his mouth and dripped down his white beard.

I screamed. Yeshin got up and broke the base of the spear from his body. A man came running for the kill, and he turned around, still skewered, and all but crushed the attacker's jaw with his sword. "Ozo!" he snarled. "Where the hell are you?"

A hand covered my eyes, and I felt myself being lifted over somebody's shoulder. I struggled before turning around to bite it. There was a cry of pain; I bit harder, hard enough to draw blood before I spun around to look into my captor's eyes.

It was the woman from the throne room.

"This is all I need you to know," Yeshin once said when I was still so small he could hold me in his arms while we sat underneath a single woolen blanket, staring at the stars. "You and I, we are enough."

He loved such talk—just out of nowhere, as if picking up from a conversation that I hadn't witnessed. I remembered pulling the blanket closer. "We don't need them, Tali," he would say, holding me in an embrace so fierce I couldn't tell which was his heartbeat and which was mine. "*You* don't need them. Why would you? They never cared. That's how some people are. They'll flatter you and fawn over you for as long as they have to, and once they've gotten what they can, they'll discard you like a useless husk. These people have no concept of loyalty, or integrity, or honour! They think loyalty doesn't pay, that honour can't put food in their bellies. And integrity? The price of one's self pales in comparison with shiny baubles." His eyes turned to me—deep brown, almost black, the depth a stark contrast with the glow of the stars around us. "You are..."

Enough, I repeated to myself as the memory receded. I opened my eyes to a flood of sunlight. Namra was bent over my body, a look of concern on her normally placid face. "My queen," she said. "How do you feel?"

"Like I've fallen off a dragon," I grumbled, "and landed on my head." I turned to her, my eyes focusing. "And that nearly happened once already."

"My apologies. I don't know what went wrong. I wasn't even finished casting the spell."

I swallowed my own spit. I could taste blood, and wondered if it was mine or if I was still imagining it from the dream. The woman had looked so frightened...

"How far did it take us?" I asked.

"Far enough," she said.

I glanced behind me. "Anya?"

"I have no way of knowing." She cleared her throat, as if she knew what I was thinking. "With all due respect, Beloved Queen, your father's sword is of little importance right now."

I sighed. "Just tell me if my head is facing the right way."

"It...appears so."

I groaned as I got up. The blood was coming from my own nostrils. I wiped it off before turning to Namra. Her expression held more than concern. She looked like she had seen me die.

"What happened?"

"I made the spell. I'm sure I did it correctly. At worst we would've ended in a completely different spot than I wanted to, or perhaps...we might've gotten stuck in the fabric. But we merely crested over the surface of it, and—"

"Say things I can understand."

"*You* reacted," Namra said. "Something threatened not just to undo my spell, but to try to drag us with it. I stopped it long enough to lead you through the tunnel, and it stopped as soon as I closed the tear behind us. But then you wouldn't wake up."

"I'm awake now." I got up, swaying slightly, and stared out at the familiar hills that crested the borders of the Ikessar and Orenar ancestral grounds. Leafy forests rose over the mountains behind the terraces, broken with steep faces of limestone. "We're in the right spot."

"At least, my queen." She flushed. "If I had gotten you killed, I don't think Dragonlord Rayyel would've forgiven me."

"Oh, he would if you explained it well. What happened in Bara?"

She nodded as she helped me walk down the road. "My lord admitted to everything. They threw him in the dungeons. I don't know what Ozo told them, but they're waiting for you to return and give your testimony."

I paused. "He...what? But what about the letters? The plan was for us *both* to be under scrutiny."

"My understanding is that he embellished his confession, too. He claimed to have sired the child after your wedding, which is why he was born a few weeks later than your own."

"Rai couldn't have—he never left my side the first few months of our marriage." I coughed, wondering at why I was suddenly defending a man who *had*, by all rights, betrayed me. But there was truth in my words. He was in Oka Shto all those months. "And Thanh—was born early."

"So I've heard. Embellished, as I said."

"Rai's not the sort of man who could lie so easily."

"Lamang must've goaded him into it."

"Lamang?" I asked.

She looked at me curiously. "Inzali."

"Right. I should've guessed. I told Rai she favoured the wounded-deer stratagem—maybe she favours it *too* much. What would his head on the chopping block do for us?"

"My guess is she did it to keep Princess Ryia at bay, to keep her away from you somehow." A smile flitted across her lips. "The Lamangs are fairly educated, considering where they grew up. Regardless of what you think, her plan seems to have worked: I've heard Princess Ryia has retreated to a town in the north, to the holdings of an Ikessar sympathizer. My lord's trial will be postponed until your return—hopefully with the beginning of an army at your back." She craned her head towards me.

I turned in discomfort at the hopeful look on her face. "What of Yuebek?"

"I haven't heard anything from the Zarojo other than the rest of their army's abrupt arrival in Bara. I can imagine the newly appointed Warlord Nijo has his hands full." She took a deep breath. "It is all up to you, Beloved Queen. You must gather your allies. I believe that Inzali has your letters on her person and will dispatch them as soon as you make an announcement. That alone will still Princess Ryia's hand; your own confession will prevent Yuebek's claim."

"I cannot move without knowing my son's fate," I whispered. "A weakness, Anya said. I don't disagree."

"You love your son," she said. "Love isn't always a weakness. Could I trust a leader who doesn't care?"

"But do I, really? Or am I cloaking my intentions with just the right words, at just the right time?" I swallowed. "The truth is if you told me my son lay on the other side of a thousand innocent souls I have to cut down, I'd be tempted. I would certainly lift my sword, at least. And that...doesn't make me all that much better than the rest of them, does it? I feel like all this time I thought I've been looking through a window, seething at what I saw on the other side, only to find out it was actually a mirror."

She took my hand and pressed it against her forehead.

"I'm a coward," I whispered, letting her pay her respects without taking comfort from them. "I may not have what it takes to stand with the whole nation to crush my enemies into dust. I can't be the leader you're looking for—I don't even know who my enemies *are*. But I know what I am. I am still Yeshin's, still of his blood. Doesn't that frighten you?"

"Beloved Queen..."

"Because it frightens *me*. Queen. Bitch Queen. I could smash the image with a hammer a thousand times and the pieces of that mask would still stick to my face. Every time I try to move from it, I feel as if I'm digging myself a grave, dragging everyone I care about with me."

We fell into a deep silence, my confession hanging above us like a noose.

"I may...have already begun correspondence," Namra said, at some point. "Letters sent to Lord Huan and Lady Esh—those most likely to be sympathetic to your cause. I believe Lord Huan is the best candidate for you to seek shelter with. Not only are you friends, but the Sougen is the least traditional of all the provinces, owing to his family's recent rise to power. He can bolster your new claim, lend you the resources to begin your campaign."

"You're forgetting he's at civil war with Dai Kaggawa."

"We were hoping if we assisted them, we might put an end to it soon. If we can deal with their war fast enough, we can deal with the other, impending one."

I crossed my arms. "When did you send these letters?"

"Weeks ago, not long after our arrival in Oren-yaro."

"I see. Do I have to worry about you, Namra?"

"It was Inzali—"

"Right. The sister is even craftier than the brother."

Namra cracked a smile. "She told me that one of their childhood games was trying to outwit the other. She'd usually win."

"I'm not surprised." I swallowed. "Khine...did you see him in Onni before you left?"

She nodded.

"Is he well?"

"He's alive," she said. "But he—"

"That's all I need to know."

We came up into the thicket, past the ratty signpost pointing out the direction of the temple, and I turned my thoughts to other less upsetting things. I remembered arriving on this same path the day after I gave birth to my son, memories that seemed to come from yesterday. Cradling Thanh in my arms, still so small I was afraid every jostle would break him, I limped in silence behind the handful of soldiers we had left. Agos walked close, his protective shadow hovering over us.

"Don't you want me to carry him?" Agos asked, leaning on his halberd as if it was a walking stick. His shirt was soaked in blood and sweat.

I was so distracted by the flutter of Thanh's heartbeat against my chest that I almost didn't hear him. "No," I replied.

"But your wounds—"

"He's sleeping."

Agos laughed. "You hear that?" he asked one of the guards who walked past. "The little prince is sleeping. Breathe through your damn noses."

"Tell yourself that, Captain," the guard grumbled.

As soon as the rest of the guards walked by, Agos glanced back at me, one hand on his head. He looked like he wanted to say something else. Instead, he said, "Motherhood suits you, Princess."

"I don't know what you mean. I'm all ripped up and I can barely walk."

"Then let me carry him."

"I didn't say that."

"Then what—"

"You're starting to nag worse than Arro. Go up ahead. Stop worrying about us."

He grinned. "Hard not to, after the last few days. Seems like bad luck has a way of tailing you everywhere. Hey, Princess. Are you even listening to me?"

But my eyes barely left my son. The feel of him in my arms contained traces of what it felt like to carry him in my belly—a sensation of oneness, of sharing my life with another living thing for the first time. *See here*, I could remember thinking as Agos's voice faded into the background. *Those are maple trees. In the fall, they turn red, and these forests will be patched with red and green, like the tapestries in your grandfather's study in Oka Shto. Someday—when the nation is truly at peace—we'll come back here and have a picnic, just you and I.*

I let the memory fade as we entered the canopy of trees, and along with it the echo of my words, so much like my own father's. Too much like his. In life, in death, we were bound to each other.

CHAPTER TWO

THE ACOLYTE

ʋȝȱɾɟɾ

The temple was exactly as I recalled eight years ago—still made of the same weather-beaten stone, with a single bell tower on the south side. There were figures carved straight into the walls and pillars, carved depictions of all the various gods and deities in Jin-Sayeng: Sakku of the Seas, Omionoru the War God, Aniuha the Snake Goddess, Immiresh the Warrior-Poet, Bathang the Trickster, and others. The alcoves, however, were reserved for statues of the god Akaterru, patron of the foothill and riverland provinces.

We strode up a flight of stone steps and reached a railed platform overlooking the hills and treetops of the forest below. The temple itself was not much of a climb, but from there it felt like you were on top of the world—a contrast with Oka Shto, which was nestled so deep into the mountain that you could only see the rest of the city from certain spots. A peddler ventured towards us, beaded necklaces and bracelets hanging around her arm.

Namra reached into her pocket and paid for one. I watched curiously as she snapped the Akaterru necklace around her own wrist. "I thought you served the Nameless Maker," I said as the peddler drew away. "Doesn't the worship of him automatically preclude the rest of Jin-Sayeng's deities?"

"Can we not live in harmony, regardless of who we worship? I look forward to the day when I see the Nameless Maker acknowledged on these same temple walls."

"Would that everyone thought the same way."

"I'm aware they don't, Beloved Queen, and that likely they never will. But a mere trinket can bring comfort." She nodded over to the distance, where a priest was standing by the open doors.

"Welcome," he said as we strode inside, leaving our shoes by the entrance. He was middle-aged, balding, a furry moustache on his upper lip. "Be embraced by the grace of the Blessed Akaterru."

"I remember you," I said. "You were here when I arrived with my son."

"Many mothers have sought shelter with us over the years." The priest gave a quick nod of acknowledgment.

"We came in after a bandit attack. You gave us swaddling cloths and blankets. You helped me give him his first bath."

Recognition now stirred in his eyes. "Ah," he said. "Your little one. The birthmark on his back. It looked like Jin-Sayeng upside-down. A good omen, I remember telling you."

"You did."

"He never uttered a single cry. Such a brave boy. Where is he?"

"He's with...family," I lied quickly. We had hidden my identity the last time we were here. We were technically still in Oren-yaro, but towns switched allegiances quickly during turmoil. I couldn't afford to give a place of worship an exception.

"He is well, I hope?"

"As well as could be."

"Blessings of the god," the priest said, invoking the sign of Akaterru. "May he be praised for all of time. What brings you here?" He finally turned to Namra. Her robes still marked her as a priestess of the Nameless Maker. Most temples were tolerant of the worship of other deities, and many even encouraged worship of all—it was the Nameless Maker's priests and priestesses who preferred exclusivity.

"We're here to seek shelter again. The bandits are everywhere these days, Father."

The priest frowned. "They've grown bolder over the years, and Oren-yaro no longer sends soldiers on patrol in these parts. Times were easier when Warlord Yeshin was alive. His daughter tries her best, but—"

There was the clatter of dropped candles from the altar. "No, Liosa!" the priest called. A woman in acolyte's robes fled down the hall like a startled cat. The priest rushed to the altar to pick up the scattered things; afterwards, he excused himself and turned to follow the woman, leaving us alone.

I walked to the center of the hall, to the mosaic of Akaterru on the floor. Named as the River God, he was commonly depicted wrestling crocodiles along the riverbank. The blue of the river in this one had turned deep purple with age, and most of the tiles on the god's face were cracked with faded paint. Namra watched as I walked along the edge of the mosaic, tracing my bare feet along the grooves. After counting the correct number of steps, I stopped and knelt in the center, knees on the ground, hands folded under my chest. I pressed my forehead on the cold floor and closed my eyes.

"I didn't know you were religious," Namra said, after I finally lifted my head.

"Only when it suits me," I replied, giving her a wry smile. "I was praying for my son. I did that the last time I was here and it seemed to have worked so far. Perhaps the god was pleased with him then. I would like to believe that he continues to be pleased and will protect him as a result."

"Is that how you think prayers work?"

"You forget I am married to one of yours. I'm well aware of your Kibouri's teachings, priestess. How you believe it is not the god's but our own actions, that prayers should govern. And perhaps I even agree. But give me this. If you can have your comforts, leave me with mine."

We were interrupted by the arrival of the acolyte from earlier. She was middle-aged, perhaps no older than Anya, with a single streak of white hair on her head. Her expression, however, was young—like someone who had stopped aging at a certain point and just never absorbed the world's troubles since. She was holding a tray in her hands, sweet cakes wrapped in coconut leaves.

"Eat," she said, smiling.

"Liosa," I replied, getting to my feet. "I remember you."

She continued to smile politely, nudging the tray towards us. "Eat."

I thanked her and took two cakes, handing one to Namra. The priest returned, hands folded over his chest. "We do have spare beds," he said, "if you don't mind sharing a room with Liosa. Blessed by Akaterru, despite everything, and since you don't have the boy with you, I'm sure she'll be more agreeable than last time."

"Last time?" Namra asked.

The priest smiled. "She was young, and everything terrified her in those days."

"Babies distress her," I added. "When she saw Thanh, she began screaming, as if he was some sort of monster instead of a helpless babe."

"I know a few grown men who would react the same way," Namra replied.

"Don't I know that," I sighed.

"Show them your room, Liosa," the priest intoned.

She smiled as eagerly as a child in the presence of new playmates. We followed her down the staircase and past the dark halls of the sleeping quarters to a room at the furthest end. As I went to tug at the curtains, letting in a flood of sunlight, Liosa reached for Namra's robes. Her fingers traced the patterned stitching, a look of fascination on her face.

Namra took a seat and patted the mattress beside her. "There's a story in that, about the Nameless Maker," she said. "Do you want to hear?"

Liosa nodded, her eyes bright.

I turned to open the rest of the windows as Namra told Liosa a tale that I remember reading from one of the books in Shirrokaru, one I had tried to memorize in an attempt to impress Rayyel. It was about Thanh, the first Kibouri priest, who arrived in Jin-Sayeng from one of the nations south of the empire. A foreigner, bringing foreign ideas, which the Ikessars embraced readily enough because...I don't know why. For the slim hope, perhaps, that it would bring change to a land doomed to repeat history. It felt odd to think that I named my son thus. If my father had been alive, he would have demanded something completely different.

"Trying to convert the Akaterru acolyte?" I asked after Namra had finished. "I'm surprised you didn't catch on fire the moment you stepped foot in the temple."

"You said you were well aware of Kibouri's teachings," Namra said with a smile. "In any case, she doesn't seem to care one way or another. She looks like she enjoyed it."

"I'm sure she did. Rai tried to tell me the same story once. I fell asleep as soon as he started speaking. His voice has that quality, doesn't it? Almost a gift. He'd make an excellent nursemaid if he wasn't scared of infants. No—" I quickly added, as Liosa approached me. "I don't know any off the top of my head myself. I can never remember the details correctly. Thanh always hated that. He said I kept changing things."

"Come now." Namra grinned. "After the life you've led? Surely you can conjure a personal tale or two."

"What life?"

"Well, there was the time you encountered a mad prince and his dolls..."

"Bad memories don't make good stories," I intoned. "And I don't think she wants to hear about my disastrous marriage. Nobody does."

"If Warlord Yeshin's daughter thinks her life is boring—"

Liosa uttered a small shriek and fled the room without warning. I frowned. "You've upset her."

"Me, Beloved Queen?"

"You called me boring. Maybe she's furious for my sake." I peered between the shutters, looking down at the yard below. I spotted a number of chickens milling about, pecking the ground for bugs and stray grain. "I wonder where Anya is."

"Are you concerned about the bandit, or your father's sword?"

I turned away, not wanting to admit the truth of it. I could still see its blood-drenched hilt in my dream and longed to have it back in my hands. False courage. I didn't know how I could make her understand. "I'm impressed at how nothing seems to worry you," I managed, trying to make light of the situation.

She smiled. "I find worrying to be an oddly useless activity."

"I'm the complete opposite. I feel as if I'm wasting time if I'm not worrying. Everything worries me. Needling, burrowing endlessly, like worms in my brain." I folded my hands behind my back and walked to the far end of the room before I turned to her with a sigh. "Do you think my father knew exactly what he was leaving me with?"

Namra pulled her chin up to give me a painful smile. "I cannot say, Beloved Queen. I'm not privy to a dead man's thoughts."

"Pretend."

She pressed her lips together. "*Forever our fathers' daughters.* You told me this back in Oren-yaro."

"So I did."

"Perhaps he wasn't thinking of what he was leaving *you*," she said. "Perhaps he didn't consider that you were just a child hanging on to his every word. The folly of most parents—to see their children as extensions of themselves. *You are me. You are my legacy. You are capable of everything I am not.* It removes the responsibility of actually having to do anything for themselves, leaving it all on the shoulders of the generation after."

"In almost every other aspect, my father had me convinced that he had everything under control."

"Even a man like Yeshin can have his oversights."

"I..." I swallowed. "I'm not sure how I feel about my father anymore. Hearing your words right now, for instance, I still have to fight back the indignation that you could say such things. That my father could've overlooked *anything*."

"Your father made many mistakes during the war, Beloved Queen. As did Princess Ryia. As did all of them." She craned her head to the side. "Perhaps it is time you accept that the man…isn't as intelligent as you believed. He was as much a fool as the fools he hated. He made the mistake of dealing with Yuebek and Princess Ryia at the same time and pandered to both to keep them off his back. It is what most would have done. There is no shame in admitting your father was human, too. What you need to worry about is right in front of you and Lord Rayyel."

"Priestess, even if we manage to kill Yuebek this very instant, one scandal after another does not bode well for a joint rule."

"Then you will both still have to decide what happens to the nation after," she said. "Your allies will want to know what they are fighting for."

I swallowed. She was right, of course. But I'd committed the same folly—I, too, saw myself as an extension of my father. To let go of him would be like reaching blindly into the void. I wanted to do it, but I didn't know if I could.

Namra looked at me and mumbled an apology under her breath. She bade me to rest and left the room in search of our hosts. I stepped over to one of the beds, wondering if it was even possible to sleep at this rate. My foot got caught on the side of a box that had been kept in the dusty shadows. I pulled it out and noticed it was filled with old books—children's stories, most of which were popular in Oren-yaro for a time. I picked one up.

I heard the door creak open. Liosa returned warily, her eyes darting across the room as if in search of a hidden enemy. She spotted me with the books.

"Is this yours?" I asked. "I apologize. I didn't know."

She came up, plucked the book from my hand, and turned it several pages.

"Now I think *you* want to tell me a story," I said with a smile.

She pushed my cheek, forcing my eyes back to the book.

"Or maybe you want us to do this together…" I grumbled. "Well, let's see what we have here." I began to read the story out loud. It must have been one of her favourites, because her eyes danced as I skipped past the sentences. She didn't seem to mind my inadequate reading, though she did make me re-read a page or two with an intensity that reminded me of Thanh. After I finished, she took my hand and eagerly pulled me down the hall, as if to invite me to take a walk. She looked like she held no memory, no qualms, of our last encounter. Despite my exhaustion, guilt made me get up and allow her to take the lead.

"That's Liosa," one of the priestesses had told us that day. "Don't let her scare you. She's harmless."

The woman was feeding ducks at the pond in the back of the temple. The priestess gave her a dimpled smile before gesturing towards me. I wrapped a swaddling cloth around the baby's bare back before walking around the bamboo grove to join her.

"How long has she been here?" I asked.

"Too long," the priestess replied. "She was so young, just this thin waif of a girl. I wasn't here then—the head priestess told me everything—but they said she was much worse in those days. They had to tear her away from her old mother...she was crying like a baby. No insult meant to this little warrior, of course," she added, glancing down at Thanh, who blinked quietly at the sunlight. I was convinced volcanoes could erupt and he wouldn't utter a sound.

"I think he's mesmerized by the clouds," I stated offhandedly.

"I think he's passing gas," the priestess chuckled. "May I?" She held out her hands.

I hesitated for a second. I still wasn't comfortable letting others hold him. But the woman's face was so bright, and Thanh so calm, that I conceded. She took him from me carefully, the fragile thing, precious gem, and began swaying.

"My sisters had so many babies," she explained with a laugh. "Now they're old and stinky and wouldn't be caught dead in my arms. They grow up too fast."

"None for yourself?"

"Goodness, no! They're easier when you can give them back." She grinned before stepping towards Liosa. "Look at what we have here, my dear. Look at this little one. Isn't he lovely?"

Liosa looked up, the ducks waddling around her. She couldn't see what the priestess was holding at first and approached curiously.

"He's newborn, so you can see how soft his skin is," the priestess said. "And those eyes! Have you ever seen such beautiful eyes before?"

Liosa peered down at the bundle. As soon as she saw him, her face contorted. I was about five, maybe six paces away, but something told me I needed to *move*, even with a body bruised from childbirth. I grabbed the priestess's arm just as Liosa's fingers tore the swaddling cloths from my son's body, twisting it so that he dropped safely into my arms.

Liosa screeched, a sound that tore itself out from the bowels of her soul. I backed away.

"She's just curious," the priestess managed, trying to hold her down. "Liosa—listen to me, Liosa. It's just an infant. She just wants to see—"

But I didn't believe her. The look on Liosa's face was that of a wild animal that wanted to rip my infant son apart. I covered his head with one hand and fled to the safety of the temple just as the other priestesses and the head priest arrived to our aid. I didn't know what happened after, but they told me she was inconsolable and that they had sent her down to the village, to be kept there for the entirety of our stay. They all seemed very apologetic.

The woman I followed up the stairwell seemed nothing at all like the one in my memories. There were lines on her face that betrayed her years, but she moved with the grace of someone who hadn't aged much inside. I remembered asking Agos to watch the door and kill Liosa if she ever came near my son again. If she had shown her face I might have run her through myself; I was young then, too, and couldn't see past the need to protect my child. The recollection filled me with shame. I could have been kinder.

She laughed with the clear sound of bells as we walked past the kitchens. "I was about to call you," Namra said. There were bowls of chicken and papaya soup and plates of steaming rice on the table. "Come and eat."

"I think she wants me to see something." I glanced at Liosa, who had yet to let go of my hand.

"She's curious about one of the villagers," a serving woman commented, passing by. "Just came in for a healing. She always wants to look but she won't go alone and the priestesses don't have time to entertain her."

"I'll go with you," I told Liosa.

She must've understood my words, because she looked ridiculously happy. Namra abandoned the food to join us. We made our way to the temple grounds, past the pond and through the tilled plots of tomatoes, eggplant, and bitter melon. A bamboo hut was built right at the edge of the vegetable garden.

We heard screaming as soon as we came up the path. Liosa's hand tightened around mine.

"A healing," Namra said.

"I know what you're going to say, priestess."

"I mean no offense." She nodded towards the hut, where we could see a woman on a woven mat, hands and feet bound. The head priest and priestess dabbed oil on her forehead while murmuring prayers. "The servants of Akaterru are servants of the people. It's ... comforting, in times like these."

"You're a priestess yourself. To guide the people in times of trouble—isn't that ultimately the goal of servitude to whatever deity you're sworn to?"

She smiled. "As with you."

"Religious dogma is hardly like politics."

"I disagree. There's a reason Dragonlord Rayyel decided to have himself ordained, just like his uncle Rysaran before him. Servitude to the people can come in many forms. Sometimes we must appreciate the intent, even if in practice it is ... flawed." The woman inside the hut started screaming again.

"So the healing doesn't always work," I started.

"If it even works at all. Without treatment, how are prayers supposed to heal?"

"We're in Jin-Sayeng. It's not like we can afford a ship or two of Zarojo physicians to offer to the common man."

She gave a wry smile. "If the warlords would agree to cut their armies in half, perhaps, or do away with them altogether ..."

"—and donate the coin to the Dragonthrone to spend on *commoners* ... I don't think so, Namra."

"As I said." She pressed her lips together. "Comfort. I do understand."

Our conversation was interrupted by a priest who came running down the steps, paying us no heed as he raced back to the temple. Inside the hut, one of the priestesses began to pray out loud, a note of panic behind the chant.

"Back," Namra breathed. "Step back!"

I dragged Liosa away from the hut just as the ailing woman threw herself off the window. Her head hit a garden statue and cracked open like a watermelon, splattering blood across the ripe tomatoes. Her bonds had been gnawed off.

Bile stirred in my throat. I found myself staring at the body as the priestesses flocked around us. She had died on impact, but she seemed to be staring right at me, the whites of her eyes flecked with blood. Eventually, someone draped a mat over her, and I found myself able to breathe again.

"Blessed Akaterru, you shouldn't have been here," the head priest told us.

"This isn't the first time this has happened," Namra said. It wasn't a question. The priest stared back, his eyes watering.

"There's no sense denying it, Father," Namra continued. "You all seem oddly calm about it."

"The fifth since the turn of the moon," the priest finally stammered. "This is the second who was too far gone. The others...we were able to convince the spirits to leave them alone."

"Spirits," I drawled, drawing away from Liosa.

"Spirits, yes," the priest said. "These people attracted the attention of bad spirits somehow. It's been making them sick. Making them mad."

"Is that what happened to Liosa?"

The priest made a sign. "We don't talk about these things."

"Father," a priestess called.

The priest looked startled. "Please," he repeated. "We appreciate the concern, but we have this under control."

A strange look came over Namra's face. "I understand," she said in a voice that didn't match her expression. "Thank you for your service, Father." She glanced at me. Taking the cue, I followed her down to the pond. Liosa, seemingly unaffected by what had just transpired, abandoned us in search of breadcrumbs for the ducks.

"You're thinking the same thing I am," I said as soon as we were alone.

"The things you saw in the Sougen," she said. "People turning into monsters, as mad as the dragons themselves. But it couldn't have spread this far. I don't feel anything in the air. Look at that sky. It's blue, not like the sky we saw in your father's false throne room."

"What else could this be?"

"*Agan* ailments can happen in other circumstances," Namra said. "Just because you don't accept these things in Jin-Sayeng doesn't mean the rules have changed. Connections can still be made—mages can still do their work here. You've seen it with your own eyes, in your castle. Did you see how the priest reacted when you asked about Liosa?"

"Of course he would do that. Talk of the *agan* in Akaterru's holy grounds..." I made the same sign the priest did, and I wasn't sure if I was doing it in earnest or in mockery.

"In Liosa's case—I've seen it before back in Dageis. She must've been in the presence of a spell gone wrong. It's not easy to reverse—you'd need to re-create the conditions, readjust the threads, *understand* what you're working with in the first place..."

"I hardly think anyone is casting spells out here in the middle of nowhere," I said. "Maybe it's an isolated case, caused by that rift all the way in the Sougen mountains. Maybe we'll see more of these in the coming days. We must be among the few who know not only the cause, but also the effect. We need to do something about this, Namra."

"How do you fight what you cannot see? How do you fix something you cannot reach?"

"Welcome to what keeps me awake at night," I told her in my sincerest voice.

Later, I kept an eye on Liosa as she slept. The priestesses didn't seem concerned. "Nearly thirty years she's been here," they said when they brought extra blankets, and caught me wide awake and conveniently situated as far from her as possible. "She won't be flying out of the window any time soon." I was more worried about catching her chewing the legs clean off my body.

But nothing happened. The woman lay on her bed, curled up in a nest of pillows as peacefully as if nothing was amiss. Even in her sleep, she remained child-like. I crept up along the shadows to watch her breathe slowly, her eyes flickering every so often, as if she was deep inside some pleasant dream. I grabbed the edge of her blanket to straighten it, tucking it close to her chin. She made a soft sound and curled towards the warmth like an infant.

"Are you planning to kill her?" Namra asked, appearing by the doorway.

"Of course not," I huffed. "Is it so hard to believe I won't?"

Namra laughed as she approached, a jug of wine in one hand.

"Please tell me you didn't steal that from the kitchens."

"I didn't," she replied. "The priest had a stash in the back of the altar."

"Gods be damned, Namra, they use those for ceremonies."

"Even better." She uncorked it.

"You're really pushing this *not bursting into flames* thing." But I took the jug when she handed it to me. "I'm sure you don't get the chance to be like this around my husband." I swallowed a mouthful, biting back the sour, acrid taste. Holy wine didn't taste very holy.

She started to say something polite, shook her head, and laughed instead.

"I'm sorry. My lord is a good man, but he is as stiff-lipped as they come. We once subsisted on nothing but plain bread for two moons just because—well, I don't quite remember. But I recall thinking it was silly."

"He doesn't believe in drinking. Likes to keep his head clear. As if that makes things better. His worst decisions were made with a clear head." I handed her the jug. She accepted it with a bow before taking a swig. "A good man," I repeated. "You know what amuses me? That back when I needed him, when I would have given the world to have him by my side, I wouldn't have agreed so easily. But now I do."

"Because now you don't love him."

I took the jug back and had another sip. "Do we need a discourse? *What is love*, the priestess asked the queen, and she said..."

"She doesn't know what love means anymore," Namra replied, refusing the wine when I tried to return it to her. "That is, at least, what my lord thinks. And he is shattered by it."

I stared at the glimmer of moonlight on the rim of the bottle. "He talks to you?"

She shrugged. "Occasionally."

"He must trust you quite a bit. Rai hardly talked in the three years we spent together." Well—maybe that wasn't always so true. But it was hard to sift through memories after anger had distorted them.

"We knew each other briefly as children," Namra said. "He is my lord, but he was also once shorter than me. I believe he thinks that since I'm also a woman, I can offer him the deepest of insights about how women think. As if I know! It would take too long to disagree, so I humour him when I can."

"Did you tell him that disappearing for five years all while refusing to acknowledge our child and then later threatening to kill him isn't endearing for *anyone*?"

"I may have," she said with a smile. "Repeatedly."

"Good."

"I may have also told him that you care about this land more than your dissenters would have people believe," she continued, growing serious. "And so even if your method of ruling was never to his liking—you with your threats and rage, a wolf of Oren-yaro through and through—it doesn't make it *wrong*. You can be two sides of the same coin. He can offer stability, levelheadedness, and the age-old comfort his clan's name brings. You? You could ignite fire in the coldest of hearts while striking fear in your enemies'. The perfect pair to bring this nation to harmony."

"I've heard that all my life."

"Not in this way, I'm sure." She gave a small nod. "Forgive me. I'm an idealist. I can't help but see the world as it *could* be. It's inconvenient."

"It's admirable."

"But I must admit that after everything that transpired . . . I'm just surprised you didn't run off with Khine the first chance you got."

I drank more wine.

"I mean, you could have," she continued.

"Gods," I whispered. "Is it that obvious to everyone?"

"An admission?"

"A rhetorical question."

"I'll answer it, anyway. My lord remains blissfully unaware, and Inzali thinks her brother is a fool and doesn't care what he does with his life, but . . ."

"Yes, I see."

"Throughout history, in the other nations, many queens have kept lovers on the—"

"Namra?"

"Yes?"

"You can stop now."

"Gladly."

I heard something click outside the window. I placed the jug of wine on the floor and went up to the single candle I'd left on the sill. I removed it and pushed the shutters open. Anya heaved herself in, clothes soaked in rain. She looked exhausted.

"Some signal you have there," she grumbled.

"Something you're not telling us, Anya?"

She placed my father's sword in my hands. I felt a surge of relief, one that lasted all but a few moments. "The bandits know you're here," she said.

"They won't attack a temple. These bandits rely on the goodwill of the common folk. The moment they start attacking temples, it's their loss."

She shook her head. "No. You don't understand. They're not even worried. When I tried to steal your sword back . . . Deng caught me. He *let* me have it. And then he said that you're exactly where they needed you to be. He said it was time you met their leader, someone by the name of Peneira. That's why they haven't come for you. Not because they're scared of holy disciples. They meant to take you here after all."

"Never give the enemy what it wants," Namra said, reaching under the bed for our shoes. "We have to leave now. Open up the window."

I stared at the scabbard in my hand.

"Tali," Namra began.

I turned to her. "*Why* would they want me here?"

"It doesn't matter. It's not—"

We heard footsteps outside. Anya melted into the shadows and I dropped a blanket over my father's sword, though I kept my hand on the hilt. The door opened, revealing the head priest. He was holding a candle in one hand. "Liosa?" he called. He turned, startled at the sight of me. "Oh! For a moment there I thought... but never mind. I didn't realize you were still awake. I'm just here to fetch Liosa."

"It's too early in the morning, Father."

"She has a visitor," he said. He drifted to the side of the woman's bed and carefully shook her. "Liosa? Your mother's here."

"Her mother?" I asked.

"Yes," the priest replied. "Ah, she's awake! Come on, my dear." He held out his hand. Liosa, eyes still barely open, took it. The old man gently led her out to the hall.

"You can go back to sleep," he told me, turning back. "Old Peneira often stays for several hours. Liosa is her daughter, you know. The temple is the safest place for someone as fragile as the poor girl. And after what Warlord Yeshin did to them—"

"I'm sorry," I broke in. "What about what Warlord Yeshin did?"

"They were both his wives. The mother first, and then the daughter. A great blasphemy. A tragedy." He turned, the shadows dancing with the candlelight.

I stood there, ears ringing, fingers still grasping the sword handle, the etched sea serpent. A moment, stretched on forever.

Eventually I turned to Namra, whose face was completely white. I wondered what mine looked like. Everything was folding together in a sea of haze. The information was there, but I didn't know what to do with it. Liosa, the woman I was just reading stories with. The woman who nearly ripped my son from my arms. Liosa, Warlord Yeshin's wife. My mother.

No. *No.* My mother was dead. My mother, whose name I didn't know, because her death upset Yeshin so much that—

No. That wasn't it. He talked about my brothers more than her. It was my brothers' death that brought him pain, my brothers that he loathed talking about. My mother was a blank page in my life. I never even knew her name. But he said it didn't matter because she was dead. *Was that really what he meant? You should have stopped being surprised by your father's lies by now.*

I felt Namra's hand on my arm. "Breathe," she said.

I took one breath, tears stinging my eyes. It felt like there were shards of glass running through my veins.

You and I, we are enough.

Gods, I thought. Gods. We should've been.

CHAPTER THREE

THE SWORD

ʋ ʒ ʋ ꒦

In those five years Rayyel was gone from our lives, Thanh yearned for his father with a child's fervour. He would sometimes wake up in the middle of the night and speak of a nightmare, of seeing the father he had no memory of dying somewhere cold and alone. "I want him home, Mother. He'll be safe with us, won't he?" His face wet with tears, he would curl up beside me, whispering, "I want my father. I want my father," like a refrain. A prayer.

I never longed for my mother the same way. Hard to believe, perhaps. I thought about her often enough, had questioned her existence the way one wondered why the sky was blue. "Because the god spilled his tears across the sky," Yeshin said. "And you don't need a mother, child. You have me."

The rain poured like the world was ending the night I learned she was alive after all. Alive, and unaware. I almost envied her. I sat on the edge of the bed, turning this new knowledge in my mind until all the emotion had been drained from my body. As the pleasant numbness began, I got up, my father's sword in hand.

"Tali..." Namra said. "Nothing has changed."

"We can leave now and pretend this never happened," Anya added. "My mother was the kind of whore you could buy with a *rean* and a packet of pipeweed, and look how I turned out."

"I don't think—"

"Yes, I heard it, too." Anya sighed and rubbed her forehead. "Let's start again. It doesn't matter. Didn't you hear the priest? Peneira. That's the name of their leader. The bandit leader and Liosa's mother are the same person."

"Tali," Namra repeated. "They could be lying. She's right. This is a distraction. You have other worries."

I understood what she was saying, but I walked out of the door without a word. What other choice did I have? The bandits knew I was there. Likely this Peneira had ordered her men to surround the hill. Escape down a watched path would be pointless. And anyway, I wanted to see my mother.

I walked down the shadows of the narrow staircase and entered the main hall of the temple. It was still dark outside, and the only light came from the alcove, where a few candles had been lit. Liosa was on the steps, her head on an old woman's lap.

She looked nothing like me. *Beautiful* was the first word that came to my mind. Maybe it had something to do with the shadows and how they softened her madness. Her dark hair framed her face with curls, and I saw a woman who could turn heads even as she was, who could render men speechless in their tracks. In contrast, the old woman stroked her hair gently, smoothing it over her cheeks like she was still a child. I felt like an intruder coming across a memory, one that had nothing to do with me. I had grown up thinking both had long ceased to exist in my world; but in truth, *I* was the ghost. I was the outsider. I was the one who didn't belong.

The sound of my footsteps broke the image.

"There she is," Peneira said without turning towards me. "The demonspawn herself, that vile waste of air. Won't you pay your respects, child?"

I drew closer, my hand on the hilt of my father's sword.

She knew the movement, even if she wasn't looking directly at it. "You *would* threaten your own grandmother. I shouldn't be surprised."

"Grandmother," I repeated. "You've been alive all this time." *Why have you never come for me?* But I didn't say it out loud. Ryia didn't come for her own grandson, either. In our world, pride meant more than love.

"I have little choice on the matter," Peneira replied. "Given the chance, I would've drowned you in a barrel the moment you were born."

I tightened my grip around the sword handle and took another step. I didn't know if I was really going to attack her. I couldn't take my eyes off Liosa, over how serene she looked. If moonlight broke through the windows, I was sure it would shine only on her.

I heard a sound beside me and I managed to draw the sword in time to meet Deng's swinging blade. I didn't know when he'd walked in. "Not here!" he called. "Not in the temple. Your whole family has blasphemed enough."

"*I've* blasphemed?" I asked. "You're the one who sent me my own son's finger. Where is he? Is he still alive?"

"That would be a sight to see," Peneira called from the altar. "An apt revenge."

"I've done nothing to you, old woman!" I snapped. "Where is my son?"

"He's not here," Deng said. "I told you. Cooperate, and we'll tell you."

"See, something now tells me you're lying." I met the blows, even with the weight of my father's sword dragging me down like a ball and chain. From the corner of my eyes, I saw the rest of their men closing in from every entrance. They approached, shadows dancing in the darkness.

"Stop fighting, Queen Talyien." He smiled. "I know it's too much to ask from Yeshin's child."

"It is," I agreed. I turned and lunged for Liosa.

I wouldn't really have hurt her or the old woman, but Peneira had no way of knowing that. She threw herself at me, hoping she could shield Liosa from my assault. But instead of striking her, I simply ducked out of the way and grabbed Liosa by the arm. Even in her panic, she recognized me and allowed me to lead her from the altar. I picked out Namra's voice calling for me from the adjoining hall. She held her staff across her body. She was in the middle of casting a spell; a blue glow hovered over her fingertips.

Liosa and I made it past her just before Deng could reach us. Namra slammed the door shut, striking the wood with both her palms. The glow left her body, streaming down into the door cracks. "That should hold them for the time being," Namra said. From the other side, Deng struck the door with his sword, screaming for his men to do the same.

"Maybe she knows how to get out of here?" Anya asked. She nodded towards Liosa, who was staring at us. The fear was growing in her eyes.

"Anya's right," Namra said. "She knows this temple. Could you please...ask her to help us?"

My mouth turned dry. "Why me?" I retorted. I didn't think I was ready to talk to her.

"I have to hold the seal. As soon as I stop, they'll break through."

I swore under my breath.

"Beloved Queen, please..."

"All right, all right," I mumbled. Pushing away my misgivings, I turned to the woman who had birthed me and tried not to think about it that way. She was just a person. Only a woman I needed to ask for help. "Liosa," I managed to croak out, "is there another way out of this temple?"

She pressed her back against the wall, lower jaw quivering. I took another hesitant step, close enough that I could look her in the eyes. "Liosa," I repeated, trying to ignore how much effort it took just to speak calmly. "There must be a back exit."

Liosa glanced down. She was looking at my father's sword. I caught a glimmer of recognition on her face. I was afraid it would enrage her.

Instead, she pulled away with a brief gesture. "Come," she said. We followed her into the darkness.

Liosa brought us to the stairs at the far end, which spiralled down into a dusty hallway fringed with cobwebs. At the very bottom, a ratty wooden door hung askew on rusty hinges. It creaked as Liosa tugged at the handle with the haphazardness of a child.

We found ourselves in a tunnel. Namra turned around to cast another spell. "It's too dark," Anya said, tugging at her shirt collar. "And hot. Does she know what she's doing?"

Namra appeared beside us, her hand glowing. A soft blue light surrounded her. "That's convenient," I remarked.

"There's a *don't-look* spell on that door right now," Namra said. "With any luck, we'll have more time while they search for us."

We continued down the tunnel, Liosa ambling awkwardly ahead. "She remembers my father's sword," I whispered to Namra. "I saw it in her eyes. She...she must still be inside that body somewhere. Her true self."

"Perhaps. But there's nothing we can do about it."

"I know. It's just..." I swallowed. *My mother*, I thought, testing the words again. They wouldn't stick. I was Yeshin's child. I had no mother.

The mouth of the tunnel was half-covered with a curtain of vines. It opened up to a bubbling swamp, covered in a layer of dead brush and black mud. We crossed branches and debris to get to hard ground, which sloped down to a series of stepped cliffs. Liosa remained undaunted; she started to make the climb down, seemingly knowing every root she could grasp, every ledge she could sink her feet into. I hesitated at the edge, watching her.

She reached the bottom, paused, and then turned around to look back at me. "Come," she said again.

"She knows exactly where she's going," Namra said.

"We don't have to follow her," Anya commented. "If we go around that side..."

"The hag would've sent her men around the temple to look for us," Namra replied.

"Where are you taking us?" I asked.

"Come," Liosa repeated. "Talyien."

My insides knotted.

We walked a long way from the bottom of the cliff and reached another temple. This one was older, smaller, half crumbling. No towers—just a building no larger than a hut, with a tiled roof overgrown with moss. Behind the fence, an old man chopped wood with a rusty cleaver. He looked up as we approached.

"Liosa..." he began.

She came running towards him, pointing at the temple up the hill. A shadow crossed the man's face. "What happened at the temple?" he asked, turning to us.

"Deng Kedlati's bandits," I replied.

He spat in distaste. "Those scoundrels. And you? Who are you?"

"We're...travellers. We were seeking shelter in the temple from the bandits, but they followed us and attacked."

"I can't believe they attacked the temple. The old woman must've gone senile at last." The man wiped his face with a towel, setting his cleaver to the side. His eyes skipped towards the women behind me and then back again. "Who *are* you?" he repeated.

"Talyien," Liosa said, laughing. "Talyien. Talyien!" But she didn't look at me. The word was empty, meaningless to her. She skipped past the man, squeezing his arm as she went, before disappearing into the temple.

The man's eyes were wide. "Gods," he stammered. "I would say it can't be, but that's his sword you're holding. Queen Talyien. Yes. It has to be. You have his eyes." Before I could reply, he stepped towards me, hands folded on top of each other. He bowed. It was a Zarojo-style bow, one knee on the ground.

"I should be asking who *you* are."

"No one of consequence," the man said. "They call me Parrtha. I served Warlord Yeshin. I still do."

"Is he—" I began, before correcting myself. No. I wasn't going to go down that road again. The man was dead.

Parrtha saw my confusion and cleared his throat. "His memory, my queen.

His last order to me was that I go to this place to watch over her and to await…
the inevitable. To await the day you come at last."

"You mean the day I came looking for her," I said.

"So it seems." He gestured to us, welcoming us deeper into the ruins.

I suspected it hadn't been in use for over a century. The inside was in bad
shape, as if someone had taken last-century architecture, allowed it to rot under
rain and sun for several decades, and then regurgitated it onto a grassy patch.
Somehow, Parrtha had made a home out of it—I spotted a cooking fire at one
end and a curtained-off bedroom at the other. Liosa ventured to where the altar
would've been, her attention drawn to the broken stained glass.

Parrtha bade us to make use of the mats near the fire, under which a small
pit had been dug. A pot of stew simmered, filling the air with the scent of boiled
roots and marsh cabbage. "Would you like some tea?" Parrtha asked.

"Anya, Namra—keep watch outside," I said.

They bowed and drew away, leaving us alone.

"Let's not mince words," I continued, turning to Parrtha. "My father knew
that she wasn't dead. He knew she was like this."

Parrtha gave a soft sigh. "A most unfortunate circumstance."

"Unfortunate," I repeated. "You make it sound like she went for a walk and
got hit by a wagon."

"It was an accident."

"You're doing it again, Parrtha. How does one accidentally grow mad?"

He hesitated, his eyes glancing briefly on my father's sword. "It was a difficult pregnancy. Liosa was very young and didn't always follow the midwife's
instructions."

"Do you think I was born yesterday? Childbirth doesn't cause madness."
When he turned his head away, I grabbed him by the collar of his shirt. "This is
an *agan* ailment. There was another madwoman yesterday at the temple—that
can't be a coincidence. Now that I know what to look for, everywhere I look I
see signs of what we once adamantly insisted could not exist in Jin-Sayeng. My
father had mages in Oka Shto. Did one of them cause this?"

Parrtha was sweating. "Beloved Queen…"

"Did *you*?"

He swallowed.

"You're Zarojo. I've been around enough Zarojo to know your accents,
even if you try to hide it. You're one of them. No—it *has* to be you. My father

wouldn't have inflicted this sort of punishment on just anyone. You were responsible for this."

"That...that is correct, Queen Talyien."

I pushed him away in disgust. "I thought so. You all treat me like an idiot. All of you who once worked for my father. I don't understand. If you were all truly loyal to him, then why lie to me? Am I not his heir? Isn't it your duty to tell me these things?"

"It's not that simple."

"Then explain. Start with what happened to Liosa."

"Oka Shto Castle was partly built by mage-builders. We used the *agan* to strengthen the foundations. Warlord Yeshin wanted it to go up fast, to give the impression of power; he had no desire to rebuild the old keep, where his children died." He nodded towards Liosa. "She married your father and lived in Oka Shto while construction was still going on. Most of the castle was already up, but there were rooms we were working on that needed...more time. I was working on one—your father's study. I was there two days after you were born, incorporating last-minute changes to the runes..."

"You were instilling them with the memory of my blood."

My guess caught him off guard. He nodded, as if glad he didn't have to explain. "I was down in the stairwell when I heard the door open. I had forgotten to lock it. That shouldn't have been a problem—nobody but your father goes up there, and the runes had already been adjusted for him. But it was Liosa. I believe they were having an argument."

An argument. An argument—like some old, married couple. But everyone always said my father had stolen Liosa from her mother and kept her locked up, the greatest blasphemy he had ever committed.

"She was carrying you," Parrtha continued, his eyes growing wet. He rubbed at it. "She saw the stairwell and became curious. Stepped over the threshold..."

"And the runes reacted."

"Precisely."

"She didn't die."

"I heard her and threw a spell to try to counteract the runes as soon as it all happened. I...I panicked. It was too strong, the wrong kind. The arrows shattered before they reached her, but she lay crumpled on the ground, a wreck, by the time I got to her. She had dropped you and you were crying and the only thing she could say was..."

"Talyien," Liosa called from the other end of the temple. The weight of the name hung as heavy as the silence that followed.

My face was wet. I closed my eyes, allowing the rest of the tears to fall.

In my mind, I turned the gem again to find that the shadows weren't where I once thought they would be. The sunlight had chased them away, but I didn't know if that was a good thing.

Yesterday, I accepted the knowledge of who my father was and what I had to be as a result. A shelter in the darkness—I was only Yeshin's daughter, however much that doomed me. There was no Liosa's daughter, never had been.

Parrtha told me the rest of the story, and it was difficult not to see it unfold in my head with every word. I saw my father come thundering into the room and imagined how his face contorted in horror at the sight of his blood-drenched wife shrieking at the top of her lungs. A man who had seen his sons die—it was a wonder he could still think straight afterwards. He must've assumed the worst. Perhaps he imagined the fates had finally arrived to punish him for his transgressions.

He spotted me on the ground. When he attempted to get close, Liosa attacked Yeshin like a wild animal; Parrtha himself had to hold her down so that my father could reach me. Parrtha said he had never in his life seen a man so devastated. Every wall, every armour that my father had built up came crashing down, and the terrible Warlord Yeshin, Yeshin the Butcher, seemed to disappear in an instant. He picked up my still form and carried me to the corner, where he rocked me back and forth in his arms, sobbing like a little child.

But I was unhurt. When Liosa had dropped me during Parrtha's spell, I landed on the curtains, the part that trailed along the floor near the corner of the room, and somehow that cradled my head from the impact. The blood was Liosa's. My father's warmth must've woken me, because I started crying at the top of my lungs. Yeshin screamed, then, his voice thundering through the hall as he ordered the guards to take Liosa away. They said she howled in her chambers all night long, tearing the sheets and curtains with her bare hands and eating her own filth. The servants wept for days.

Yeshin nearly had Parrtha beheaded for his error, but because he had inadvertently saved me—the arrows would've pierced both me and my mother otherwise—he allowed him to try to find a cure. As a mage-builder, Parrtha had no knowledge of the healing parts, but he eventually found a Jinsein herbalist who also claimed to be a witch within the right company. She gave Liosa a sleeping draught, which allowed her to examine the young woman closely. By then Liosa was so thin you could count the bones on her spine.

She was asleep for several more days after. The herbs, or the spell, or a combination of all those things must've done something to her, because when she finally woke, her mind was blank. She uttered nothing but simple words, a child once more. More than that, though—the sight of her own infant sent her into a foamy-mouthed frenzy. Yeshin had her sent to Burbatan with Parrtha as an escort. On the road, the caravan was intercepted by Peneira's bandits, who dragged Liosa up to the temple instead, hoping the priests and priestesses might figure out a cure. Enraged, Yeshin decided to leave her to her fate, though he ordered Parrtha to stay in the temple to keep an eye on her. In the meantime, he claimed his wife died during childbirth, closing that chapter of his life forever.

"They all knew this," I said. "The servants. Everyone in the castle. And they all kept it from me."

"To protect you," Parrtha replied.

"Protect me?" I hissed. "I was to be queen, not some helpless milkmaid!"

"If the Ikessars had known—"

"He didn't even really want me to marry Rayyel. You knew that, too, didn't you? Let me guess. Prince Yuebek supplied you to him."

Parrtha shook his head. "I don't know anything about that. I don't know the man."

"Then maybe you know the purpose of my father's study. Why the spells, Parrtha? Why did you have to make them in the first place?"

He dropped to a bow by my feet, his head on the ground. "Forgive me. I cannot say. Forgive me."

"You're afraid of Warlord Yeshin," I said. "Why?"

"Forgive me."

"The man is *dead*. *I'm* queen. I order you to tell me, on pain of death. Tell me!"

He didn't even flinch. "Forgive me," he repeated, banging his forehead against the ground, as if he was begging for it to open up and swallow him whole.

I took a deep breath. "What's there to forgive?" I finally whispered. "We're still all his puppets somehow." My gaze turned to where Liosa sat, mesmerized by the sunlight. If I didn't know anything about her, I would've only seen a woman—not that old yet, and still so beautiful for her age. She noticed my attention.

"Leaving?" she asked brightly.

"Yes," I managed, choking down the rest of my tears.

"Come back," she replied.

I couldn't think of an answer. I knew it wasn't her fault, but I could've lived without ever having met her. I wanted to push away this new knowledge and forget it ever existed.

I stepped outside with every intention of leaving it all behind me. But it seemed as if I wasn't allowed even a moment's rest. Deng and Peneira had caught up with us at last. They stood by the fence with their men, swords drawn. From the look on their faces, it was clear they had been listening to Parrtha's story the whole time.

Peneira broke into laughter. "And now you know everything."

"We need to put the past behind us," Parrtha said.

"How do you expect me to agree to that after everything her father did?" Peneira hissed. She took a step towards me, her finger shaking as she prodded my chest. "Your father was a sick, depraved old man who snatched a girl from her mother's side. She could've had her pick of the young men in every city— royal princes could've been fighting over her if I had the time to present her properly in court. Instead, Yeshin ruined her. He ruined my daughter's life!"

I swung my father's sword just as the words dribbled out of her mouth, pressing the blade on her neck hard enough to produce a trickle of blood on the wrinkled skin.

"Kill me if you want, Yeshin's daughter," Peneira said, her eyes blazing. "It's nothing to me."

"You're not worth it."

"You don't think so?" she asked. She turned her head. The commotion had attracted Liosa to the yard. There was a concerned look on her face, anxious, even though there was no possible way she could've understood what was going on. "My daughter is, though," Peneira added in a low voice. "Deng!"

Deng moved quickly. I braced myself, but instead of going for me or my companions, he went straight for Parrtha. He twisted the mage's arm, forcing him to his knees. With another swift motion, he sheathed his sword and pulled out a dagger.

The rest of their men drew closer.

"What do you really want?" I asked, staring into Peneira's face.

I had never seen so much anger in someone's eyes before. "I want my baby back," she snarled.

CHAPTER FOUR

THE ECHOES OF BURBATAN

ⲦⲒⲘ

I learned when my son was born right in the midst of that blood-drenched battleground that it was possible to feel like you could rip the whole world apart with your bare hands, if only to save your child. I recognized the timbre in Peneira's voice and knew there was no fighting it. Nothing in the world could quench the fire of a mother's anger.

"I was just told there's no way to do that," I replied. "Not unless—"

"The spell is cast backwards," Peneira finished for me. "Yes. I know. It was your own accursed father who told me. Everything else must remain the same for the spell to work. The same mage. The same... people. It was a dare. He wanted me to see it was futile. *You need the child, too, and you will never touch her. I won't allow it.*"

I started to pull back. Her gnarled hands wrapped themselves around my wrist. Her wrinkled skin felt like death. "You were there," she hissed. "And so you have to be here *now* to see this through. We've been trying to capture you for years. The time your son was born was the closest we ever came."

"You didn't want me for politics."

She snorted. "Your politics don't interest me. It never has. No... we wanted *you*, Talyien Orenar, as the child who broke mine. We need you to undo what was done to my daughter."

"You tried to lure me out here. You used my son." I took a step back. The woman knew what I would do for my own child, too. "If you want my help, you need to bring him to me. No more words about how I just have to *wait*. You want your daughter back, old woman? I want my son. I want him here *now*."

"Grandmother—" Deng began.

"Stand down," Peneira said.

"If you tell her, she'll have no reason to help us."

"If you don't," I broke in, "I'll have less." I looked at Deng's eyes and saw what I feared from the very beginning. "You don't know where he is, do you? Because if you had him, you would have brought him out by now. You wouldn't risk my wrath if you could get my compliance an easier way."

Deng's face twisted into a grimace. I had them. But it brought no relief. I watched as the old woman finally let my wrist go. "We don't have the imp," Peneira said. "We never did."

"The finger—" I started, preparing myself to die fighting if they had somehow harmed my boy. That was as much as I allowed myself to think.

She pulled something out from her pockets and threw it in the air. It sparkled. I made a grab for it before opening my hands under the moonlight. It was my son's ring, fashioned after the royal seal of the Ikessars.

"Your boy is alive, as far as we know," Peneira said. "We heard there was trouble in Oren-yaro months ago and had sent men to scout it to wait for you. We got something better. Your boy, dragged out of Oka Shto in ropes by intruders. We tried to seize him. My men even managed to make off with him for a few paces, but we couldn't overpower his captors."

"I cut his finger off when I knew there was no way we could escape them," Deng continued. "All they wanted was the boy and were quite happy to let us go. Grandmother knew you would recognize your own son's finger. It would be enough, she said, to bring you all the way out here, and she was right."

"And now you'll help us," Peneira continued. "Or you won't be alive to save him. Deng isn't a surgeon."

"He fought quite hard," Deng added, baring his neck. There was a shadow of a scar there, a bite mark. "I left his hand a mess in return."

I breathed, trying to keep calm. *Later. Kill them later. You can't fight them now.*

"What you are asking is madness upon itself," Namra broke in. "If the mage isn't capable, it could leave those in the vicinity in the same state as Liosa. There is no guarantee anyone walks out of this alive, let alone Queen Talyien."

"And he *isn't*," Parrtha added, his voice shaking. "I can't do it. That was the last time I ever cast that spell. I swore I wouldn't again."

Deng stabbed him in the thigh.

Parrtha uttered a shriek and crumpled to his knees, blood pouring down his leg.

"Look at that," Deng crooned. "You think there's more where that came from?"

I lowered my sword. "We need to end this," I said. "Is that all you want? For me to help you with this ritual? You will be content with that?"

"I'm not a beast," the woman said. "And I am not your father. Give me my daughter back, and you can return to find your son."

"Beloved Queen, if the spell that did this to your mother was cast in the presence of those runes, then they need to be there again for this," Namra said. "You will have to return all the way to Oka Shto for this."

"There is no need for that," Peneira said. "Everything we need is in the Orenars' ancestral home. Isn't that right, Parrtha? These same spells are there?"

Parrtha swallowed, blood pooling under his heel. "Yes."

"That's why you attacked," I said.

Peneira smiled. "We had to get it ready for you."

I pointed at Parrtha. "Bandage his damn wound before we go. And I want a horse that doesn't doze with every step." I started to walk past her.

She laughed.

"What's so funny now?" I asked.

"I don't see my daughter in you at all. Not the slightest hint. She wielded power deftly, like a river that could carve rocks over time. You, on the other hand—you are Yeshin, through and through. You think power is like a hammer. If people don't yield, you'll break their knees."

"We all see whatever we want to see, old woman," I replied, echoing Rayyel's words. "But if that's true, then maybe you should tread with caution."

"I've wasted years doing that," she retorted. "I'm done with it." Her eyes gleamed as she stared at me. Only then did I recall she was a wolf herself, as wily an Oren-yaro as the rest of us. The thought filled me with dread.

I was among my kind.

Out of everything that had happened that day, it was the sight of them capturing Liosa that broke my heart at last. In the chaos, she didn't even recognize her own mother, who called for her with the wounded tones of the grieving while she ran from the men with the swords. Once they caught her, they bound her with ropes thicker than my thumb and she sat under the moonlight, staring into the distance while she uttered my name over and over as if it was the only word she knew. My mind had not yet accepted what my lips could say so freely, but I briefly wondered what sort of mother she had been in the days before the accident claimed her mind. She hadn't been that much younger than I was when I gave birth to my son.

"Beloved Queen," Namra whispered to me as we cantered up the road in the darkness. "I don't mean to sound conceited, but I did very well in my studies and I would *never* attempt what they want. I've got a fair grasp of the healing arts, too."

"We needed a ride to Burbatan, anyway."

"Burbatan calls to you like your father's voice from the fog," she said in a low voice.

"It's not like I'm ever really free, Namra—they only give me the illusion of freedom."

"I see," she said, in a tone that told me she disagreed but didn't want to argue. "What about your mother?"

"What about her?" I asked. "She can go back to the temple when this is all over."

"My queen, you'll have to forgive me if I don't believe you. That look in your eyes when the old woman said there was a chance...I didn't just imagine it."

"Maybe you didn't." I glanced away.

She sighed. "Even if this Parrtha fixes what he did wrong, Liosa still has to deal with the reality that she's been more or less absent the last twenty-something years. The shock alone might bring her back to the brink of madness. Perspective, my queen. She seems happy with her life, and risking *you* would be risking the entire nation."

"The life of one versus the life of many...yes. Khine and I discussed that in the past."

"It seems a simple enough choice, when you consider who you are."

"Who I am," I repeated, thinking of Anya's words. The doubt hung heavy in my voice.

She heard it, too. "My queen, when you play cards, sometimes you get the better hand. How you got there does not change what you hold. Guilt should not make you throw it all away, especially not when the stakes are this high."

"Khine has told me that, too."

She cleared her throat. "When you parted, was it to be the last?"

"If he's as smart as he claims to be, he would've taken the next ship out of these lands."

"You know he would never do that. He would've followed you to the end of the world. All you had to do was ask." She turned her head to the side. "Why didn't you?"

I hesitated. "You saw what Agos looked like after they killed him," I finally said.

That was not the answer she expected.

"Lives are not equal," I agreed, after another period of silence. "Having Khine beside me would make things easier. How often has he schemed us out of one mess or another over these last few months? But this isn't a game of *Hanza*. If I understood that from the very beginning, he wouldn't even be here—he'd be back in his home, trying to piece *his* life back together. Our lives are not equal simply because there is no single judge. And Khine's life, to me…" I watched the rising sun as I trailed off. I could say what I really meant in three words, except Yeshin's daughter didn't say those words.

"Of course." Namra gave an almost sad smile. "My lord didn't see this coming."

"Your lord didn't see many things," I said. "And maybe that's for the best."

We fell silent as we arrived at the edge of the forest. The town was built around a hill, enclosed by walls that spanned the height of five men. Even from where we were, I could see that the gates were closed.

"The idiots," Anya broke in. "That's a fortress."

"The term *war*lord isn't an affectation," I said. "The Orenar clan didn't rise to power overnight. Ask me how many have died on those walls."

Anya snorted. "Thousands, I'm sure."

"Tens of thousands," I said. It wasn't a thing to be proud of, and I wondered why I even bothered to correct her. We came around the bend of the road and fell silent. There were soldiers in the distance, outlaws armed with spears and swords. The number gave me pause.

Deng rode down to meet us. "Impressed?" he asked.

"The castle was guarded by a bunch of old men. I'll be more impressed if you can stand your ground when Ozo comes to liberate it."

"We'll be in and out," Deng said. "Ozo won't even have time to get here."

"What makes you think he's not on his way already?"

Deng glowered. "Then we'll have to do this fast, if it means having to run through all the peasants first." He snorted. "What's that look on your face for? You royals have done worse. Do you think we can afford to sit around with our fingers up our noses while you come to a resolution over how to rule this land? If I don't do this, *my* people will starve. These aren't just bandits. They're friends, family, cast-off members of the Nee clan that your father so conveniently stripped of what little wealth it had. You'd do the same thing in my place."

"Let me negotiate with them. Lord Ipeng will let us in if I ask him to. He still answers to me. He'll have to."

"While he sends a rider to Oren-yaro behind our backs...no, thank you. I know how you royals' minds work. Grandmother's whims aside, I want this town for myself. I mean, you're not just going to give it to me just because I asked." He placed two fingers inside his mouth and gave a sharp whistle.

From the distance, the whistle was returned, and men carrying long ladders emerged from the grove. They were followed by two rickety siege towers that creaked as they rolled along the road.

I glanced behind, to the clearing where a small camp had been set up, far enough to be out of sight of the battle when it happened. The hag was sitting next to Liosa, trying to calm her down. She hadn't stopped weeping since we left the temple.

"Tell me, Namra. What do you think I did wrong in my past life?"

She made a small sound in the back of her throat. "The Nameless Maker doesn't believe in past lives."

"Humour me."

She smiled. "Let me see if I know how this works. You were born to be queen, so probably nothing too awful. You were probably a righteous bandit like Anya here."

"I never claimed to be righteous," Anya snorted.

"Stole from the rich to give to the poor?"

"Why the hell would I give the poor something I worked hard for?"

"My apology for the mistake."

I dismounted from my horse and slowly stumbled towards the fire. Peneira looked up.

"You need to stop acting like I want to gouge your eyes out with my thumbs every time you see me," I said casually. "I was getting cold. It *is* winter, you know."

"Can you blame me?" she asked. Somehow, she had managed to convince Liosa to allow her to hold her hand.

"I am trying to work with you. You would think that I deserved less of your ire for it."

"You dare lecture me. A child like you."

"You really have been hiding in a hole the last three decades if you think I'm still a child." I took a deep breath. "Won't you consider abandoning this wretched task? You can take her to Dageis. How long do you really think you can hold this town against Lord General Ozo? He *will* come."

"He's too busy licking the Zarojo prince's boots as it is, just like he was too busy licking *your* father's when he was alive."

I nodded towards Liosa. "She's been through too much already. I think you know what you're getting yourselves into, but does she? Too much ill has been done to her already. Ozo won't care; he'll kill her just as easily as he'll kill the rest of you."

The old woman turned away and began caressing Liosa's hair. Liosa stiffened for a moment, but the action must've reminded her of who this was—if not her mother, at least the source of a familiar comfort. She leaned on Peneira's knee, allowing her to continue. I felt a rush of anger, followed by the weight of a grief I didn't think ever existed.

They attacked in the early hours of dawn.

We remained in camp, listening to the battle cries amidst the smell of smoke and blood. Liosa covered her ears, burying her face in her lap as she rocked back and forth. Peneira never left her side. "It'll be over soon, my love," she crooned, words I didn't think Liosa even heard.

This, I told myself, was why she looked at me with so much hate. My father's worst crime. Somehow, in the process of giving me my life, he had stolen theirs. I really couldn't blame Peneira. I was a walking reminder of what she had lost. If there was a way to bring Liosa's mind back without risk...

I heard a horn in the distance, three full blasts. Peneira adjusted the shawl around her neck and entrusted Liosa to one of the other women in the camp. "They've broken through," she said. "That didn't take long."

"Easy to take, hard to hold," I said, quoting a line from one of the books on military strategy Arro had made me read ten times over. I had thrown it on the floor on the eleventh. "That was why the Orenar clan left it when we built Oren-yaro."

"Don't lecture me on the Orenar clan. I was one of you, if you've forgotten." She walked past me as we went to the horses. My cooperation had earned me some freedom, at least—I was allowed to take the reins this time around. I followed Peneira's horse as we crossed the main road, which was strewn with so many bodies you could barely see the soil underneath. The town's gates were wide open.

"Lord Ipeng's soldiers have retreated to the manor," Noerro said.

"How many are left?" Peneira asked.

"A dozen, maybe," Noerro replied. "He knows he's done for."

"We'll all go together. Where's the mage?"

"Here, Grandmother," one of the bandits said, pushing Parrtha forward.

"I want my companions as well," I demanded.

Peneira frowned, but after a moment's hesitation, she called for them to be brought through.

The banners were being switched out on the towers as we took the urine-drenched steps leading to the hill. The town was in a sorry state, but nothing the residents hadn't prepared themselves for. An hour after takeover and beggars were already returning to the streets, holding up tin cups to the bandits.

A short bridge led away from the town. Peneira walked with the confidence of someone who had been there many times before—even as the bridge swung under our weight, wooden boards creaking, she strode blindly into the grey light. "This will frighten Liosa," I said as I followed behind her. "She might fall."

She paused for a moment, her jaw taut. "Your false concern isn't going to save you. One way or another, this *will* happen, even if it leaves you a drooling idiot. In fact, all the better if it does." Surprisingly enough, there wasn't a shred of malice in her tone—it was the voice of a woman already resigned to this. I had the sudden impression that even if you had told her the procedure would destroy us all, Liosa included, she would still carry through with it, just because she could. Just because it gave her a way to have the final say against my father—either she would undo what he had done, or hurt his daughter trying. Love and hate were edges of the same sword.

Light streamed through the trees and over the emerald-coloured lake as we came within sight of the house my father grew up in. It was nowhere near the size of Oka Shto—small even for a minor lord's estate. There were soldiers waiting at the gate, swords drawn. Behind them stood an old man in full warrior's outfit.

"Ipeng aren dar Yare," Peneira said, the venom dripping in her voice. "You've moved up in the world. Now you're keeping house for a dying clan."

"A dying clan?" Ipeng huffed. "Warlord Yeshin's fire doesn't die overnight." I saw his eyes as he spoke and the truth in them: They didn't love my father. They feared him. They feared *him*, and so their loyalty could never be mine. The daughter had the father's temperament, but none of his desire for blood.

Peneira laughed. "Empty threats." She looked around. Wistfulness replaced the expression on her face. "I was lady of this estate once."

Ipeng huffed over his moustache. "You gave that up when you ran away. Interesting, given we all know you only married Yeshin for his money and power. I suppose being a whore gets tiresome."

The smile on her face was cold. "Is this how you're going to get started on begging for your life? By insulting me?"

"As if I have any intention of begging," the old lord said. "Kill me now and be done with it."

Peneira nodded to her men, who rushed forward. I stepped to the side and watched in silence as ten Oren-yaro soldiers were charged by three or four times the number in bandits. By the time it was over, only Lord Ipeng remained standing.

"Throw him in the dungeons," Peneira said. "An honourable death would be too good for him."

Ipeng didn't reply, but the expression on his face made it clear what he thought of her. We strode through the gates as Peneira's men led him away. There, in the small courtyard with alcoves covered in trailing vines, the old woman paused. A shadow crossed her face, and her fingers began shaking so hard her cane rattled on the stone path.

"Too long," she exhaled. I was the only one within earshot, but I wasn't really sure she was talking to me. Her eyes were on the single terrace above the entrance, and I wondered if she could see something that I didn't. Memories. Ghosts of the past.

"You loved him," I said out loud.

"*Loved*," she repeated, like it was the most disgusting word in the world.

She spat. "He knew how to manipulate young women. I had no idea he was a self-serving, emotional fool—that his entire household quaked in fear of him. Arrogant. Conceited. A nightmare wrapped in golden foil. He ruined my life."

"Did you think you were marrying a pristine gentleman?" I asked.

"Choke on your amusement. You've hardly made the wisest choices yourself."

"I haven't allowed myself to be consumed with hatred as you have."

"Say that after you've watched your precious child abducted right in front of you, to be despoiled by a man old enough to be her grandfather," Peneira said in a low voice. "Say that after you learn that the girl whose existence you tried to keep from him, because he thought the woman he wed was a maiden, because you knew in the back of your mind he would take the life you had before him as an affront...is now broken and witless, incapable of remembering you or living a life for herself. So many years of love and care, so many years when I daren't even let a fly land on her, gone in the blink of an eye."

"They said she ran away from you. That he never really seized her as tribute the way I've been told he did."

"He might as well have. He turned her against me. I knew him well. It was his vengeance." She narrowed her eyes. "Are you really defending him?"

"I've never defended anything he did," I said in a low voice. "But if I knew about this from the beginning, I would've tried to help. Believe me, Peneira. I would've done everything."

"Everything?" She smiled. "Somehow, I doubt that." She made a sweeping gesture with one arm, bidding me to follow her into the house. The hall was empty—the servants must've fled as soon as the soldiers had decided to make their stance. I noted a solarium to the right before I strode into the main hall-way, where the floorboards had been polished to a bright sheen. To the left stood a large room, with sitting mats and houseplants arranged around a round table. I spotted the remains of a hastily abandoned meal of fried plantains. A dusty piano stood at the far corner of the room, half-covered with a red blanket.

The old woman went up the staircase, lit by orange sunlight broken by the wooden lattice of the old-fashioned windows. There were shelves with small fig-ures of Akaterru, potted plants, and necklaces of dried jasmine. Framed paint-ings hung above them as a sort of shrine. I found my father immediately—that same imposing figure, only younger; his was the smallest frame of the bunch.

My eyes wandered to the other paintings. An old, kind-faced man that I could only assume was my grandfather. Other young, lordly men, my father's brothers. Maybe it was because I had known him in life, but compared with them, my father's eyes seemed to burn the brightest. How an artist had managed to capture that light, I couldn't say, but I suppose it shouldn't have come as a surprise.

And there, on the wall directly across from Yeshin, I saw renderings of my brothers. Taraji, Senjo, Lang, and Shoen's images stared back at me as they never had in life. I lingered over the rendition of Taraji and swallowed. The brother I'd never known looked exactly as he had in my hallucination. The piano downstairs was his. I didn't even think to question it—some things you just know.

The old woman looked at me strangely. "How much did he tell you about your family?" she asked.

"Not much," I muttered. I turned to her. "You knew my brothers."

"I mourned when I heard what happened to the boys. Your father's carelessness..."

"I know. I know what killed them."

"I was married to the devil long enough," Peneira said. "His first wife died giving birth to Shoen. So yes. I watched them grow up. I cared for them, in my own way. They were good children. Taraji was a gallant young man—you'd have a hard time believing he was Yeshin's eldest. Generous to his friends, kind to his enemies. And Lang, that Lang...such a sweet boy. He loved dancing. He was convinced he would someday find the courage to convince your father to let him work at a theatre. My heart ached for his loss the most. They were good boys—nothing like Yeshin. But if you ask me, it's a good thing they died young. Look at what you've done in the three decades you've been alive." She turned to me, eyes hard. "If the rest of Yeshin's children had survived, the whole world would burn."

CHAPTER FIVE

TURNING THE PAGES

I was given a room with a mattress, where I attempted to gather a few hours' worth of sleep. The dreams came, as they always do; a muddle of images and memories, interspersed with everything I learned that day. Every single thread revolved around my father, the murderer, the sadist, the opportunist. An evil man, an unworthy man. A man I loved, all the same.

I woke up to realize Liosa had wandered into my room. From the light streaming through the windows, I figured it was late afternoon.

"What are you doing here?" I managed to croak out.

She didn't reply. But she held something out to me excitedly. A storybook. I pulled myself up against the wall and watched as she sat beside me and opened it to the first page. Her finger hovered over the words before she glanced back, looking at me expectantly.

I swallowed and began to read.

The words made no sense as my lips glided over them. I supposed it didn't matter. She wasn't listening to the actual story, just marvelling at the sound of it, at the rhythm, while her eyes skipped over the faded ink drawings on the pages. I fought not to become overwhelmed by the strangeness of it all. Reading to the woman who gave birth to me, who seemed more child-like than my own son had ever been... the tangle of emotions suddenly seemed more convoluted than my dreams.

I stopped at a blank page, which had been scribbled with the image of a dragon. The would-be artist had signed it with his name: *Shoen*, the youngest before me. Right at the very bottom was another word that made me laugh. *Father*, it said. The ink around the word was smudged, as if someone had dripped tears on the paper before wiping them away.

"Where did you find this?" I asked.

She gave me a puzzled look.

I held up the book. Recognition dawned on her face, and she pointed at the floor underneath my bed. One of the floorboards was loose. I got on my knees to take a closer look and found a box right below the floor, filled with all sorts of children's toys: dusty marbles, finger puppets, a wooden top. There were also more storybooks, and notebooks with bamboo covers, held together with string.

I dumped them on the floor between me and Liosa. She picked up one of the storybooks, her face full of delight. My attention, however, was drawn to the notebooks, my brother Shoen's journals. I flipped one open to a random page.

Father tells me I need to learn to be a man, that I have to put aside all childish things and join him in Oren-yaro. He says I need to train with the spear and sword, and be proficient in order to defend my brother Taraji when he becomes warlord. So I'm putting my things away. Captain Ozo is coming for me in two days...

The entry, too, had smudges. He had marked the date plainly at the top, making him twelve years old on the day he wrote it. I paused, remembering that he died in his twelfth year, probably not long after he wrote the entry. Knowing that the rest of the pages would be blank, I closed the journal and picked up another one.

This entry was dated at least a year earlier. Shoen was talking excitedly about Taraji's visit. Taraji, it seemed, took time fairly often from his duties to take Shoen fishing and to regale him with stories of his travels through the west, where he once met a young man from Akki on his way to Cairntown to seek his fortunes. I could tell from Shoen's tone that he worshipped Taraji, whereas he had a less-than-favourable opinion of the second eldest, Senjo, whom he described as "a turd stuck to the heel of Father's boot."

I must've laughed out loud, because Liosa suddenly looked up, her face bright.

"I'm sorry," I said, wiping a stray tear from my eye. "This trip has just been more than I bargained for. I knew nothing about all of you—not a damn thing. And yet here you are. You're all...real."

She must've thought I was offering to read again. She held the book out to me with such grace that I was startled. Gods, even without the use of her mental faculties, she made me feel awkward—me with all my muscle and bone and scars. Liosa still had so many years ahead of her. If she ever got her mind back...

Would she love Thanh the way I do? Could she still love me? My son and I were shaped by my father alone. The idea that a family was a web was not a concept I was familiar with. A part of me longed to find out what it would feel like to shed myself of the oppressive weight, to wrap myself in the assurance that the world was more than my father's creation. In Jin-Sayeng, family was everything, and yet my father and son were all I ever had.

"We were *his*, so he thought our lives were his to shape however way he wanted it," I said. "And it came at a cost. These things always come at a cost." I got up. "I suppose there's no sense in delaying this." She gave a soft sound of protest as I walked to the door. There was a single guard there, half dozing. I prodded his shoulder, startling him, and asked if he could fetch Namra and Parrtha.

It didn't take them long to arrive. They were followed by Noerro and Anya. "We need to get that spell ready," I greeted them.

"I haven't understated the risks, I hope," the priestess said.

"No, Namra. This is where you come in. *You* need to help Parrtha with the spell. You're the one who studied in Dageis. You'll be able to fill in his gaps of knowledge."

Namra's face turned white. "With all due respect, Beloved Queen, it's not that simple."

"Perhaps. We can only hope. The runes in my father's study—all they do is trigger a mechanism, yes? Arrows. Real arrows. I'm guessing you've got people refilling those if they ever run out." I glanced at Parrtha.

"Warlord Yeshin has many servants," Parrtha said. "I do not know them all—each of us only has a piece of the puzzle. But they're there."

"It's the shield spell that caused the damage in the first place. All that happened was that Parrtha didn't cast it right, so I think the presence of another *won't* affect the process at all. Namra—all you have to do is stay close and pre-emptively put up a spell from your end first. There's the simple part. This is something you're good at, you said."

Despite my words, she looked nervous. "I'm...competent enough," she replied.

"Competent enough to protect yourself, and the others?"

She nodded. "I'm just not sure it's something I want to toy with."

"Then I am begging you. Gods, Namra. Look at her. Tell me this isn't worth the trouble. She has a chance. Why would I deny her the chance to be well once more?"

She glanced at Liosa, who was tracing the dust on the windowpane while muttering softly to herself.

"One life," Namra managed. She shook her head without finishing the thought. "Inform your grandmother," she told Noerro. "We'll get started as soon as the moon rises."

The room imbued with spells in the estate was not in any sort of special chamber at all. Instead of one of the main bedrooms, Parrtha led us past the kitchens. Behind the massive stone stove, a spiral staircase led to a floor above. It was so narrow that only one person at a time would be able to fit through. I let the others go ahead and hung back, trying to convince Liosa to take the first step. The darkness frightened her.

"We've got books there," I said. "More storybooks. You'll love it." I mimed opening a page.

Her forehead creased.

"You'll be safe. I promise. I won't let anything happen to you." I felt my heart twist at my words. I was almost starting to believe it. She made one hesitant step, and then turned around to grab my hand. We made the climb slowly. As we reached the top floor, Namra gave me a look, as if understanding something that I didn't yet.

I frowned, trying to focus. We were in an attic, where various pieces of furniture were covered with white cloth and cobwebs. The dust was so thick I could feel it crawling into the crevices of my lungs.

"The spells are in the vault over there," Parrtha said. He made a line on the dusty floor with his finger. "Everyone who was not part of the spell the first time, walk to that far end. The rest, step over the line."

Everyone shuffled to do as he asked. He limped towards the other end, making a circle in the air with his fingers. Runes on the wall began to glow.

"Queen Talyien, please bring her forward."

I took Liosa's hand again. "Book?" she asked.

"Soon," I promised, hating myself for lying.

"Mistress Mage—" Parrtha began.

"I have a name," Namra said, a touch irritated, which was the closest I've ever seen her to angry.

"Please get ready. You ah—need to cast it a breath faster than I can."

"How long will your spell take?"

"Ten breaths."

"That's ridiculously long."

"I told you I wasn't very good. What mage would agree to work in Jin-Sayeng? They *decapitate* us out here."

"He's scared of decapitations and chooses to work for Warlord Yeshin," I sighed. "Great. I'm starting to question this man's capability."

"I told you," Namra smirked.

Liosa squeezed my hand. "Let's not waste another moment," I said. "Cast your spells now."

One moment. Two. I found myself turning to Liosa, my mother, and looking into her eyes, not a shred of recognition between us. Before I could think about it any further, the spells struck us and I felt that familiar sensation, that blackness engulfing me. I struggled to breathe.

I opened my eyes. I was sitting on a sofa in a foggy room. Liosa sat on another across from me, her hands folded on her lap. There was a puzzled look on her face.

"Are you all right?" I asked.

"Who are you?" she replied.

I opened my mouth. "You—" I began. "You're...*here*."

She pressed her lips together in a gesture that reminded me of Peneira. "I am, yes. What kind of a question is that?"

I wanted to laugh. I didn't. "Then it must've worked."

"What worked?"

"The spell. Parrtha's spell. He..." I looked around again, my eyes blurring for a moment. "But where are we? We should be back in that attic."

"You are not making any sense."

I cleared my throat. "What's the last thing you remember?"

"What an absurd question."

"Cooperate with me, Liosa. I don't want to spend an eternity in this...wherever the hell we are."

"If you insist on being so nosy," Liosa sniffed. "I was having an argument with my husband."

"I...see. What were you fighting about?"

She huffed. "Oh, I can't even recall now. My husband is an incredibly moody man. Every little thing sets him off...a picture frame at the wrong angle, mud tracks where they shouldn't be. I was threatening to march back home to my mother if he didn't mellow down even just a *little* bit, the cantankerous old git."

I nearly choked on my spit. "You told him what?"

"And of course he lost his temper and started throwing things, and I stomped out with the baby and..." Her face tightened. "I had a baby," she suddenly said, as if just recalling for the first time. "A little girl. Where is she?"

I stared at her, unable to reply.

My silence seemed to irritate her. "I just had her in my arms!" She sat up, glancing around the bleak whiteness of our surroundings. "Did you take her? You must have!"

"No."

"You shouldn't lie. Do you know who my husband is?"

"Warlord Yeshin."

"And that name doesn't make you quiver where you stand?" She gave me a smug smile. "No, you do know. I can see it in your eyes. You should be frightened! My husband is the most powerful man in all of Jin-Sayeng. You know he defeated the Ikessars, don't you? Oh, he was just pretending they have a truce—I admit I couldn't understand exactly why, but they said the child I was carrying would be queen if she was a girl and she was. You really haven't seen her?"

I shook my head.

"Help me find her. She's going to be queen someday, you know."

"What," I said slowly, "does that mean, exactly?"

"It means she's going to help us rule the world."

I tried hard to pretend the detachment in her voice didn't make my skin crawl. I got up, and she followed me into the fog. I couldn't tell if we were indoors or outdoors; it almost felt like we were in a void, that we could keep walking on and on and never hit the end of anything. No walls, no destination.

I turned to Liosa. She moved differently—a shadow of her mother, with a skip in her every step. I wonder if she noticed she had aged, and whether there was any wisdom in breaking the truth to her.

"I have to say," she blurted out. "If you are hiding something from me—"

I noticed shadows in the distance. "Over there," I said.

We started running. The shapes became more distinct, and I heard voices, but they sounded muffled, like they were coming from behind a door. We reached yet another expanse. The fog swirled around us, retreating momentarily to reveal an empty field before surrounding us once more.

"Where *is* Yeshin?" Liosa grumbled. "This must be his fault. He has been dabbling with—I don't know *what*, but he has all these strange people walking in and out of the castle at all times. I told him he needs to go to the temples to ask the gods to forgive his blasphemies and he just laughed at me, the absurd old man."

"I'm surprised he lets you talk like that."

"Oh, I am sure he does not hear half of what I say. He is hard of hearing already, though you will never get him to admit it."

"How...old is Warlord Yeshin, exactly?"

She wrinkled her nose. "He's in his sixties, I think. Seventies?"

"You don't even know."

She shrugged. "It doesn't matter."

"And you married him. Willingly."

Liosa made a sound in the back of her throat, the kind that told me she had heard the question before. "And why not?" she asked. "I am a grown woman. I can make my own choices."

"But you were—"

"A child? Who are you, my mother?"

"That's—"

"*You* do not seem to be deaf. What part did you miss about my husband? He rules Oren-yaro, the strongest province in Jin-Sayeng—an army of noble warriors at his beck and call, and loyal generals who will stop at nothing to protect him. The seers have prophesied that his blood will be the blood that will rule the land."

I stopped mid-step to turn to her. "Surely you know of his history."

"That he was married to my mother?" Liosa asked. "Insignificant details. It does not make him my father, so wipe that distaste from your face. My father is a meek, weak-willed man, and my mother would have done the family a huge favour if she had never returned to him. I would not have had to take matters into my own hands then. Oh, I have no doubt you are now judging me obscene, just like my own mother. I care very little about what people think. Marrying Yeshin has put me one step closer to becoming the most powerful woman in all the land, and I have *him* wrapped around my little finger, so what does that make me?"

"And your daughter..."

"A necessary inconvenience to seal the deal," she said, frowning now. "Most women will have to bear one sooner or later. I simply chose to make it so that my labour yields more than a mewling brat on my breast. How many women get the chance to be mother to a queen? My own mother should've understood what seizing an opportunity meant."

"You don't seem overly concerned about your child."

She snorted. "You must be blind. She will be queen someday—of course I am concerned. If something unpleasant has happened to the whelp, I suppose I just have to get down and make another. Yeshin is not too old, I hope, and there are plenty of nursemaids out there."

"You make marriage and children sound wooden."

She laughed. "Wooden. Listen to yourself! A woman your age should know better! Marriage is a strategic move, a thing that gives you a chance to position yourself better in the world, and nothing more."

"But love..."

I was starting to amuse her now. I could see it in her eyes. "Love," she repeated with glee. "Love is a complication. Tell me you do not believe in such a ridiculous notion. You must have a family yourself. You look old enough. Are you the kind of fool who married for love?"

I smiled in deference, not wanting to argue. "I have a son."

"And a husband, I hope?"

I gave a small nod.

"Do you love him?" Her eyes brightened when I hesitated; her youth was suddenly all too clear. This was not the same woman whose hand I was holding in the attic.

"Let me guess!" she continued, clapping. "You mourn the idea that marriage could bring so little solace. The world is not quite what they promised, is it? Why, you must love another! Just like my old mother! I should tell you how her decision to go back to *that* brought suffering to our lives. They said when she was married to Yeshin that we lived in a nice, big house, and she would send money and all manner of clothes and toys for me. Even my poor old father lived in luxury! But I remember nothing, of course. All I know is what happened after... the filthy hovels we hid in, the hunger, the fear of Yeshin hunting us down during the war! We would be dead if I had not seduced the old man. I am the only reason he left my family alone afterwards."

I turned away from her, gazing out at the fog.

"This new man of yours," she pressed on. "Is he at least a lord or something?"

"He doesn't have anything," I found myself replying.

She laughed. "And you, a royal! I can tell from the way you carry yourself. Well—I am sure you do not need me to tell you he is just using you. I may be young, but I am not blind to the way the world works. You would give yourself away for nothing?"

I walked a little faster.

"Tell me about him," she said, trying to catch up to me. Her curiosity seemed at odds with her demeanour.

"Let's just try to get out of here."

"Ah hah! Did I hit a sore spot?"

I closed my eyes for a moment. "There's not much to say. He is a good man from a good family, and he deserves better than me." My gaze settled on her, long enough to make her uncomfortable.

"Such a complication," she repeated.

"Like the child you've lost?" I asked. "No, don't say anything. I'm sure she's just leverage to keep you in this cushy position. Most powerful woman in all the land, you say." I walked past her, not wanting to see the look on her face. I didn't know which of the three was the worst: that my mother died giving birth to me, that she was a madwoman, or that she was as cold to the idea of motherhood as the iron railings of Oka Shto on a winter's day.

"That's a rotten thing to accuse me of," she said to my back.

Before I could answer, I heard the voices again. They were louder now, like my ear was suddenly pressed against that door. And they were screaming.

I tore into a dense blanket of fog and finally found what appeared to be a mirror imbued directly onto the ground. I recognized the attic and saw Namra standing in the corner. Anya was there, too. I called to them, tapping the mirror with my hands. They couldn't hear me.

Liosa appeared impassively beside me. "Interesting," she said. "My husband has a number of these things hidden in the castle. Are those your companions?"

"You don't remember them?" I asked.

"Why should I?"

I turned my attention back to the mirror. The screaming was coming from...

"No," I breathed as I saw what appeared to be Liosa's hunched figure in the far corner. I glanced at the woman beside me. Two of them. The Liosa that was with me didn't seem to recognize the one in the mirror.

"Just like that girl to go and get herself mixed up in every single issue in the bloody kingdom," I heard a voice call out. I saw the bulk of a man appear at the stairway, sword drawn. Lord General Ozo. He turned his head to one side, past where the mirror could see. "Ah," he said. "Hand that one over to me."

"Oren-yaro scum!" Noerro cried as he lunged at Ozo.

The general killed him with a single stroke that opened him up from the head to the hip. Blood sprayed Ozo's face.

As Noerro's battered body writhed in the corner, Ozo turned towards Anya. "This one is Yuebek's."

"Not anymore," Namra said.

"Since when?"

"Since she failed to—"

Ozo struck Anya without warning. She shrieked, managing to draw her sword. In the same instant, Namra cast a spell, which Ozo simply dodged. I found myself screaming, too, smashing the mirror with my fists as I called Ozo's name. It did nothing. I watched in horror as he turned on Anya a second time and slid his sword into her belly.

She spat blood, staring at him with wide eyes. "Fucking—" she started. He pulled the sword and stepped aside as her body slumped forward in a pool of blood.

"The queen won't like this," Namra gasped.

"The queen should know better than to trust turncoats," Ozo said.

"With all due respect, Lord Ozo, but aren't *you* involved with Prince Yuebek, too?"

Ozo ignored her as he looked at the Liosa that was in the attic with them. She was huddled in the furthest corner now, hands on her eyes. Ozo stared down at her, and for a moment, I thought he was going to kill her, too. Instead, he placed a hand on her quivering head in a gesture that was almost affectionate. Then he turned to something in the corner, to a figure I couldn't see. Liosa blocked my sight. But I could tell from the way Ozo's expression flickered that it was my body.

He turned to the mages. "Bring her back," he said. "Now."

"It's not that easy," Parrtha replied, quivering.

"You'd think so. What about you, priestess?" Ozo asked, turning back to Namra. "Don't tell me that fancy mage education was for nothing."

"We don't know what happened." Namra's voice was like steel, even through the fog. "She's reacted like this before, when I tried to create a portal—"

"I'm not interested in your excuses, mage! Have you forgotten whose coin was used to buy your way into Dageis? There's a reason the Orenar coffers are near-bankrupt!"

"My father never let me forget, Lord Ozo. But now is not the time."

"We're already running out of time! We could've done without you indulging her ridiculous whims. I should've known that old woman would meddle somehow."

"One doesn't simply tell the queen what to do, Ozo. Isn't that why we're here?"

Her voice faded, followed by the images.

"What did they mean?" I gasped as the mirror became a cold sheet of grey with nary a reflection. "Namra...gods, not Namra."

"I am not familiar with this Namra," Liosa said.

I turned to Liosa, who had an amused expression on her face. "And you—you were there."

"You are talking in gibberish," Liosa coolly replied. "I am *here*. Why would I be *there*?"

"Didn't you recognize yourself?"

"She won't understand a thing you say, Beloved Queen," a voice called out.

I froze.

Arro appeared like a gust of wind. Or at least, Arro as he had been when I was younger—still black-haired, with a wispy tuft of moustache and a fuzz of a beard you could see through.

"You nosy old man," Liosa snorted. "You must take perverse pleasure in following me around."

Arro's face turned red. "I must have told you a thousand times, my lady—if getting a rise out of me is what you want, you are wasting your time. As Warlord Yeshin's wife, you need to become more responsible. You are mistress of this household. You…"

"You see, *Magister* Arro thinks he is in charge of everyone," Liosa huffed. "A pity he could not marry his way into Jinsein royalty. I suppose being a Xiaran mongrel comes with its downsides."

Arro didn't even flinch from the insult. "I am perfectly happy with my wife, my lady. I at least know where my responsibilities lie. Do you know where yours is?"

Liosa flushed. "I was just looking for her."

"I warned my lord that a scatterbrained young woman would make for a poor mother. But our disagreements aside, the child—*your* child—should be our highest priority."

"All right, all right, I'll go look for her, you bastard," she said, breaking from the stiff, formal speech. She turned and walked away from us, disappearing into another swirl of fog. The air felt colder, with what appeared to be small shards of ice floating with the dust motes.

"Beloved Queen," Arro said, breaking the silence. "Why are you here? Do you not have a nation to rule?" It was almost as if he had forgotten all about Liosa.

"My mother…"

He frowned. "Don't fret about your mother. I know you must pine for the love you think she owes you, but she won't take you where you need to go."

My mouth went dry. These words…I must've asked him the exact same thing as a child. I had no recollection of it, but I remembered the response. I remembered that look on his face, that mixture of pity and something else. Regret? Affection?

He came up to touch me on the shoulder. "Leave the past to rot where it belongs," he said. "It is time for you to make new ground. Be the queen you could be. Show them what you are worth."

I was mistaken. He had said these things the night after my coronation, in the aftermath of Rayyel's departure. His expression was etched into the memory of my memories. I felt my heart clench.

"Arro…" I began.

I felt the ground begin to shake. I stepped away from my adviser's mournful face as the fog receded in a swirl of blue light. My skin began to crawl again, and then I felt something grab my arm—something colder and firmer than a human hand—pulling me into the abyss. The last thing I saw was Arro looking back with eyes that reflected my own, and I suddenly realized how much I missed him.

CHAPTER SIX

THE KEY

ᛏᚢᛗ

I heard the sound of hooves just as the scenery unfolded, the fog receding into wisps. The land was unfamiliar; mountains rose sharply ahead, reminiscent of the Sougen, but darker, more jagged.

It felt like I was awake, so for a moment, I was convinced someone had strapped me to a saddle. But then I saw hands that weren't mine tug at the reins, and I looked up to see two armoured figures up ahead. One had the height and bulk that could only be Ozo. Which meant the other was…

The horse I was riding snorted and stopped. A man in the middle of the road screamed at them to stop in a foreign language. When they didn't respond, he called for someone behind him. A robed woman approached us. She tested us with a language that sounded like Kag, and then she paused. "You can't go any further," she finally said in Jinan.

"And why not?" Yeshin's voice sounded younger. An old man already, but with none of the gravelly quality I associated with him. He glared at the woman with eyes of steel.

She stood her ground. "The land here is dangerous," she said.

"So I've been told," Yeshin replied. "We just came from Cairntown."

"You're warriors from Jin-Sayeng. What are you doing all the way west?"

"I'm the one asking questions," Yeshin said.

"You said *why not*," the woman replied with a smile. "And I answered."

"Your answer is insufficient." His voice had yet to rise, but already his eyes were blazing.

Beside him, Ozo had drawn his sword. "Don't play games with us, woman," he said. "Cairntown is in ruins. Kaggawa told us we would find the answer out here."

"You Jinseins don't believe in the *agan*," the woman said. She held her hands. Blue light hovered over her palms. "I think this is all the answer you need."

A bead of sweat appeared on Yeshin's forehead. "This is its doing," he said under his breath.

"My lord?" Ozo asked.

"Rysaran's dragon," he said with a snarl. "It did this. It destroyed the keep in Oren-yaro and killed my sons before Rysaran Ikessar rode it to Shirrokaru. After it burned down half of *his* own city, it flew all the way back to the Empire of Dageis. Their mages destroyed it in the wilderness here."

"You have that last part right," the woman broke in. "One of our mages was responsible. But it wasn't a real dragon. It was a construct, a creature of the *agan* made to be a weapon. Its destruction tore a rip in the fabric that separates the world you know from the spirit world. A small rip, but it's causing these disturbances—"

"A city lies in ruins and you call it a *disturbance?*" Yeshin snarled. "Why did you destroy it here? Why not in your own lands?"

"Thousands of lives would have been obliterated," the mage replied. "She did what she had to."

"So you put *ours* in jeopardy instead," Yeshin said.

"Kaggawa says this rip will get bigger," Ozo added. "That the stray magic has caused this land to become unstable. In time, it will spread to Jin-Sayeng. We have thousands of lives there, too."

The mage looked unfazed. "We're working on it."

We heard a scream in the distance. The horse under me fidgeted, dancing where it stood. Involuntarily, I tugged at the reins again.

A creature appeared from the woods, clad in tattered mages' robes. It jerked forward. "Help me," it gasped, its grey, clawed hand reaching for the woman. "Help—"

Yeshin stabbed it with his sword. The creature was so weak that it simply fell to the ground, jaw unhinged. Without missing a beat, Ozo drew his horse around and cleaved its head from its shoulders.

"*You're working on it,*" Yeshin repeated, sarcasm dripping from his voice. "This is how it was explained to me: Malevolent spirits have been using the rip to travel from their world to ours. They need hosts when they get here, or their consciousness will be swept away. When a host cedes to this corruption, they become a monster. How, exactly, are you working on it then?"

"Go home," the mage said. "We have it under control."

Yeshin burst into laughter.

My father's laugh was still ringing in my ears when I found myself sitting on a chair inside a tiny room lined with bookshelves from end to end. There was a single, circular window in the wall right above me, and a desk in front. My left arm was wrapped with a piece of bloody cloth—I could feel it sting with my movement.

Ozo stood beside me, arms crossed.

"The vision," I began. "You bastard. Was that you?"

"What vision?"

"You killed Anya, you son of a bitch."

"You mean Yuebek's worm. Just like you to get attached to every single filthy thing that crawls over to you." He spat.

"Where's Namra? And Liosa? Did you hurt them?"

"They're unharmed." There was an unamused expression on his face. "I ask you to do *one* thing…"

"You failed to mention the path to Burbatan was strewn with my grand-mother's bandits," I snapped. "She's wonderful, by the way. How *did* you all keep her away from me all these years?"

"You've met her. Wonderfully prickly old woman, isn't she? What other choice did we have?"

"These things would've all been very useful to know from the beginning, Ozo."

"No, they wouldn't have," Ozo said, crossing his arms. "They're gnats. We've been swatting them off you for years. What would the knowledge have done for you? Knowing you, you would seek them out in an attempt to foster relations. Look at how this all unfolded. Not a damn thing would have changed if you'd have found out years ago, and there's well over a hundred ways you could have screwed it up."

"Liosa—"

Ozo shook his head. "I know what you're going to say. I know it's a tragedy. But we can't live in the past."

"You all made me believe she died giving birth to me."

"The easiest lie. Your father forbade us to speak of her. Who were we to argue with him, girl? You know this better than anyone else." He ran a hand over his grey beard. "He cared for her in his own way. Grieved for her. She might as well have been dead."

"Cared—" I began.

He laughed. "Don't think I didn't tell him what it looked like. A man his age taking a girl like that to the marriage bed—the entire nation was gossiping as soon as he began courting! Guess how much he appreciated me voicing my opinions. And Liosa—*she* didn't care, either. She wanted this, and that was that! Your father didn't know what he was getting himself into. He didn't even think he'd live past the war, let alone sire another child. But deep down inside, he was still a man, and Liosa knew what she was doing." Ozo cast me a glance. "Those were not simple times."

"Neither are these," I breathed.

He growled under his breath. "Kaggawa...the betrothal was that Sume Kaggawa's idea. She doted on the boy Rayyel, I was told, and yet still she found a way to convince Ryia to...sacrifice him to us. Did Yeshin not have any daughters? Could a marriage not be arranged between Rayyel and one of ours? A tempting notion. Liosa was right there—Yeshin all but told me he would've been a fool not to take advantage. If she bore a boy, he would've tried to make another."

"So he lied to Yuebek's mother. He made it sound like Ryia's offer came after."

"He lied to everyone."

"Why here?" I asked. "What is so important about this place?"

Ozo turned towards the shelves. "I wanted to show you your father's research. I wanted to impart the gravity of the situation to that impulsive head of yours."

My eyes glanced at the books. You could fill a whole library with them. "My father was a warlord, not an Ikessar."

Ozo smirked. "I didn't know you were fond of those old labels."

"A gut response. You're right. Maybe I don't want to learn more about Yeshin. Maybe I've had enough of the past. The *agan* runes in Oka Shto. The cage used to transport Rysaran's dragon, the beast that destroyed Old Orenyaro, lies right underneath Oka Shto. Yeshin blaming the Ikessars for bringing it to Jin-Sayeng when he wanted it for himself, too. What's a Dragonlord without a dragon, after all? Liars, all of you." I walked over to a dusty bookcase and picked out a leather-bound tome at random.

"Be careful," Ozo warned.

I coughed against the cloud of dust as I pulled the book free. It was a collection of loose parchments, with faded ink in my father's handwriting. "This is about the *agan*," I said, after a moment. "Where would he get this information?"

"Thank your husband's uncle."

"Rysaran?"

"The prince's personal study in the Dragon Palace is filled with all sorts of obscure information he gathered during his travels. Your father became interested in this sort of thing long before your brothers' deaths. Prince Rysaran had asked us to investigate a caravan travelling through the border near Gaspar. There was a steel box, containing the dragon. You're right—we seized it for ourselves. But we couldn't have known what it was. The entire thing was covered in these strange runes that glowed when we touched them.

"I was young, then. Not even a general yet—nothing but an assistant to my uncle, who was lord general in those days. But I remember warning your father not to meddle with such things. Your father threatened to cut my tongue out if I kept talking. You can see how we got on." Ozo shook his head. "In those days, we suffered from famine, raids from Gasparians at the border, poor trade. Prince Rysaran was a monarch who only cared about his obsession—finding a dragon, convinced that this *one* thing could make all the difference for us. Warlord Yeshin thought that if we could take the dragon from him, then perhaps we could show the land exactly who should be in power. At least throw doubt on the Ikessars' capabilities."

"So you found mages to undo the spells."

Ozo snorted. "Not easily. I scoured Gaspar, not realizing *those* mages were bound to their god-king and that the mere act of asking if you could borrow them was a crime punishable by death. I barely escaped with my life. The Empire of Dageis? After Gaspar, I wasn't even going to try. And then I learned there were mages in Ziri-nar-Orxiaro. That's how we stumbled upon Parrtha and four of his companions. They were exiled from their academy, banished for the gods know what. I didn't want to know the details. We took them back to Oren-yaro, and they did it. They released the dragon from its cage. Except it wasn't really a dragon. It was a creature of death and destruction and it killed everyone including your brothers."

"How did you escape?"

"I wasn't there," Ozo said, shaking his head. "Or I'd be dead, too. I don't know how *your* father survived. But he wasn't the same for the longest time. Because the old keep was destroyed, he made his home here for a while. He started this research, gathering what he could. I believe Parrtha stole much of this from Rysaran's study over the years."

"So, my father was an aficionado of the forbidden arts," I said wryly. "I was starting to guess that." I gave him a look. "But that's not what we're here for. What else is there, Ozo?"

"Rysaran's dragon was destroyed just before the war broke out," Ozo continued. "Right in the mountains northwest of the Sougen."

"I know," I said.

"Did Kaggawa tell you that? The man truly fancies himself the hero of the west." He smiled wryly. "He was the one who tried to explain this to your father after the Shadows broke off from the Ikessars. Your father didn't believe it at first. He was too intent on winning the war. And we *were* close to winning. The Ikessars and their allies were weak, and without the Shadows' help, defeat was inevitable.

"But in the spring of that year, he and I went to visit Ojika Anyu. On the way back, he decided we should head to Kago—straight to the source of those disturbances, in the mountains north of Cairntown. There, we met the Dageian mages busy at work—the ones sent to fix what the first contingent couldn't. They explained they were trying to make repairs, even as they were clearly failing. The damage was allowing corrupted souls to walk among us, creating mad dragons and the gods know what else. In time, Jin-Sayeng will be overrun."

"My father always knew," I said. "And he didn't do a damn thing. Kaggawa was accusing us of putting our own interests first. He was right. All these arguments with the Ikessars, this pandering to the Zarojo..."

"We were in *the middle of a war*," Ozo snarled. "You've met Ryia. Does she look like the kind of woman who backs down just because you decide something else is more important? Don't accuse your father of not doing anything about it. He did. He sent letters to Zarojo. Made contact to seek aid. One of the mages introduced him to the Fourth Consort. We needed the War of the Wolves to be over, *fast*. We were bleeding everywhere—coin, food, soldiers. The Ikessars had withdrawn into the mountains and turned to sneak attacks. Some of the other warlords, the ones who initially refused to become involved in the conflict, were starting to think about riding up against us just to put an end to everything.

"So when the idea of a truce was brought up—the betrothal…your father seized the chance. It meant putting an end to the bloodshed, if temporarily. We needed the space. We needed to breathe, to plan our next step."

I returned the book to the shelf and made my way towards the window. The first rays of dawn were peeking over the mountain range. "The betrothal between me and Rayyel was to buy him time."

Ozo laughed. "Yes."

"Time to take over, to get power through his alliance with Yuebek."

"Time to fix the damages Rysaran's dragon caused."

"And how, pray, is this alliance with Yuebek going to do that?"

His lips quirked upward. "Have you forgotten, Beloved Queen, that Prince Yuebek is a mage?"

Bits and pieces of the last few months began to gather inside of my head. I could form a picture if I wanted to. I wasn't sure I did. I took a deep breath, pulling myself back into the chair. Finally, I glanced at Ozo's shadowed face. "Explain."

"Do I need to?"

My head was starting to hurt. "Just explain, damn you. We're here now."

"The mages in Kago were apprentices. No one, so far, had been able to spare a mage who could actually *do something* about it. But it could be fixed, if somebody with that kind of skill and power is willing to risk their life. The question is—who would do such a thing? Not for money. What else can your father offer that'll make someone care enough to try?"

"A whole kingdom."

Ozo crossed his arms, his scowl deepening. "A whole kingdom," he repeated. "One he couldn't just *give* away, not when it wasn't his in the first place. Not yet, at least. Not until you were on the throne. And even then, not if Prince Rayyel was crowned with you. We needed him out of the picture without starting another war."

The pieces expanded, turning months into years. In my mind's eye, I saw my coronation, the day I thought was my one chance to prove to everyone—my dead father included—what I was capable of. The same day I learned Rayyel had abandoned us. I tried to remember where Ozo had been then. I could only recall the chaos.

"Tell me," I said, "how the hell you had hoped to accomplish that."

"Chiha Baraji."

"Gods," I whispered. I wanted to scream it. "You played a part in that, too? My *father*? You said it was just Lushai! You…"

"Lushai didn't know we knew. We gave him hints; he seized them."

"You made it sound like he had done it to seize power. To have his own claim to the throne…"

"Impossible," Ozo said with a grimace. "A bastard sired by a bastard…no one would accept it. Lushai knew that."

"You went through all that trouble just to discredit my husband." I slammed my hands on the desk. "All these years—you put the blame on me all these years, when you knew very well what you were doing! And so? So she succeeded, with a healthy son as proof of her efforts. Well played, gentlemen. But did I spoil the surprise? Was I supposed to find out what Rayyel and Chiha were up to *before*, or *after*, my wedding?"

"After," Ozo said. "Your stubbornness was always a problem. It was supposed to be simple. Your brothers were obedient, compliant. Your father expected the same softness from you. But surprise of surprises—you turned out just like him. The only one of his children to take after him. Yeshin was convinced the gods sent you as punishment."

I laughed. "I'm sorry to have inconvenienced you."

"The whole ploy—all of it—was to give Prince Yuebek a chance to swoop in and save you," Ozo continued in a low voice. "If Rayyel had not left the day of your coronation, we would've walked in there with the bastard to declare him unfit for rule. We already had the boy in our custody. But he saved us the trouble. Only—his departure left you angry, irrational; we didn't know how to approach the idea of you remarrying, not with the way you treated every suitor that came your way. But then we caught wind of Lord Rayyel's desire to meet with you in Anzhao…"

"And the rest, as they say, is history." I tapped my fingers on the desk and fell silent, staring at the polished wood surface.

Ozo shuffled his feet. "Talyien. You have to make a decision."

I kept my mouth shut.

"Talyien," Ozo repeated, snarling. "You understand why we kept you in the dark. In the beginning, we thought we didn't have to. But your father realized we couldn't risk it. You would have rejected the plan outright, been convinced you knew better and could find another way. He found it hilarious, even as he warned us we would have to tweak the plan to stay ahead of you. I'm surprised we made it this far. I expected you to discover it years ago, and have all our heads for it.

"And Yuebek's reputation—it stank like a day-old corpse in midsummer. We knew not just his skill in the *agan*, but every controversy that surrounded him—his brother's death, the way he'd manipulated himself in his own father's court. We had to be careful. We needed him to think that your father genuinely wanted an alliance with him—that *you* wanted him. If you had fallen in love with him, all the better—we needed Lord Rayyel out of the picture and Prince Yuebek bound to us, bound to *you*, in marriage. Because the next step would be to grant him the Dragonthrone in exchange for saving Jin-Sayeng from this looming catastrophe. We need him to ride out to the Sougen and then north-west, to the mountains, to seal these holes once and for all." He stepped towards me. "Listen to me, Talyien. You need to marry Prince Yuebek. We need him trapped."

"And I'm the bait," I whispered. "My father...my father *made* me to be bait."

"It's not like that."

"He did," I said. "My position does not reflect the will of the heavens in any way, after all. Yeshin the Butcher made me just like he made that throne in Oka Shto, or that crown, or the chaos that's unfolding right in front of us. Queen Talyien is a commission of flesh and blood and bone." I took a deep breath. "You've seen Yuebek. How can you ask this from me? You'd let me whore myself out—"

"To save us all," Ozo replied. His eyes flashed.

"All of you brilliant minds who conjured the War of the Wolves, and this is the best you could come up with?"

"Even Dageis couldn't come up with a solution that didn't involve unleashing monsters into our midst. Look at our nation, girl, and tell me if you can come up with a better plan before it's too late. If you had just dropped everything after Rayyel abandoned you, if you had not insisted on holding on to your wretched love—"

"You bastards," I whispered. "You sons of bitches. My whole life was a lie. I am nothing but *bait*." The word felt like a dagger to my heart.

"Open that top drawer," Ozo said.

I really didn't want to entertain him any further, but I pushed against the chair and tugged the handle open. There were loose pieces of paper and a number of leather-bound journals. I picked one up.

"Read it." Ozo's voice sounded weary.

It was an account of our day-to-day life in Oka Shto, penned in Yeshin's hand. I didn't understand what Ozo was trying to show me. That my father was keeping records of everything that happened in my childhood? I flipped the page. More mundane details—descriptions of the dogs in the kennel, my studies for that day. What we ate, what I spoke to him about.

I flipped to the next page.

I expect her to unite the land, the text said. *It will be difficult, but I have made all the arrangements to ensure a smooth transition.*

"This is ridiculous," I said, pushing the journal away. "You expect me to change my mind just because my father thinks it's for the best?"

"Read some more."

"I will not."

"Talyien—"

"Fine," I snarled, flipping to another page. "More talk of grandeur. His legacy. His gift to the land. He—" I stopped, a sentence catching my eye. *The boy is not the smartest, but Ozo assures me that his devotion to her is pure. Apt, I suppose, that my general's son would be tasked with guarding my own daughter.*

"What the fuck is this, Ozo?"

He wiped sweat off his face. "I wanted you to understand that some of us have already made sacrifices for this cause. My son…"

"Your son," I repeated.

"Yes. Agos."

"Agos was *your* son."

"My greatest sacrifice," Ozo said. "I gave him up to your father so he could keep an eye on you. You were supposed to grow up together, so that you would trust him and tell him everything. So we would know exactly how to manipulate Rayyel, what steps to take so we could get both of you where we needed you. It worked well enough. Perhaps a little too well."

I remembered his presence at Agos's funeral, and the look in his eyes the day Agos died. How Hessa hated him. How Agos worshipped him like the father he never had, never knowing he was.

They had cloaked our lives with lies, and we were supposed to thank them for it.

I could barely recall a time when the fate of the nation seemed to rest solely upon my ability to keep a marriage intact. Now I could feel the fabric of my being dissolving right in front of me. Far from a blanket of lies, my father's rhetoric was actually a blindfold, one that allowed them to lead me straight into the slaughterhouse.

"Agos would've kept you safe from Yuebek," Ozo said, his voice shaking. "He never knew, but he was a key part in the plan—my eyes and ears beyond what you would've allowed me. Being one step ahead of you...wasn't easy. He gave us what we needed to guide you through. It wasn't treason—as lord general, my job was to keep you safe."

"You keep saying *we*," I murmured. "Who are *we*? My father is dead." I could feel my skin tingle at the words. Even a man like Yeshin couldn't possibly have created such an elaborate plan to be carried forth years after his death. It felt like something out of a dream.

"I told you there was a second pact," Ozo said. "The warlords wanted you ousted after Yeshin's death, and we couldn't have that—not with what we knew, and what we knew the rest of Jin-Sayeng wouldn't believe. You know who could believe it, though? Even though we deny the *agan* in this nation, it doesn't change the truth. Children with an affinity to it are born here every day."

"You blackmailed the nobility with those children," I said. "People like Ojika Anyu, with his son Eikaro..."

"*Blackmail* is too strong a word," Ozo replied. "I spoke to them. I reiterated your father's stance. Together, we can dream of a Jin-Sayeng grander than the one that came before it. We didn't blackmail them. True, we implied that disagreeing with us would result in...complications...but that was only for the good of everyone. We promised them safety and security for their children, whom we could send to Dageis to be schooled when the war was over. We promised them power."

"Who else was in on it? Warlord Ojika, Warlord Lushai, Warlord San..."

"Enough, Queen Talyien," Ozo said. "Do you want to sit here and count the stars? Or do you want to save Jin-Sayeng?"

"You're pretending you made these plans for the good of the nation when all you wanted was to win your fucking war," I said. "Tell me the truth, Ozo. Did you want Agos close to me so that after I'd been used by the madman, *we* could unite the land under Oren-yaro rule? You wanted power, too, didn't you? Everyone was getting a handout for complying with Yeshin's orders."

He looked startled.

"Oh, Ozo, you foolish old man. Your scheming killed Agos, just like my father's ambitions killed *his* sons, and now you want me in the funeral pyre with all of them. Who's next—Thanh? Did I spoil that as well? Was he supposed to be your blood so you could establish your own dynasty? And the fact that he is Rayyel's means what—that once this is over, you'll kill him to make sure the Ikessars never rule again?"

"You're letting your temper get ahead of you," Ozo growled. "I told you. It's not that simple anymore. You attacked Prince Yuebek in the empire. You *incurred* his wrath. We could've had him here without his army. He would have been alone, bending to our will, easily manipulated, *easy to kill* once we were done with him."

"How the hell was I supposed to react? I wanted to stab the man five minutes after meeting him. If anything, I was far too patient."

"You're the one trained in diplomacy, not me. But he was able to convince his father to allow him the use of his soldiers because of the insult you dealt him. Yuebek's Boon—a scourge the empire itself considered a threat. And how many more soldiers can he gather if we openly wage war? His father favours him. He may very well *have* to be our king. It's either that, or Jin-Sayeng as we know it is wiped out from within. You hold the key to our salvation, Talyien."

"My life. My life is the key. You want me to surrender myself to Yuebek."

"You keep calling yourself bait. You're more than that. You are *queen*, Talyien, with or without the man! And you'll be without him soon enough. We're going to kill him when it's all over."

"Ah, so in the meantime, I just play the willing whore?"

"You're the only one who can."

"Go to hell, Ozo," I said.

Someone knocked at the door. Ozo coughed. It opened, and Namra entered, head bowed.

"You," I whispered. "Just like the rest of them."

She bowed even lower. "I never lied to you, Beloved Queen. I only…omitted some details."

"You and everyone else," I whispered. I tightened my hands into fists. "I'll let you speak, and let the gods damn us both. Well, priestess? Explain your part in this before I decide to kill you, too."

Namra cleared her throat. "My parents fled Jin-Sayeng not long after your father's war began. In those days, Warlord Yeshin sought children like me— children born with a connection to the *agan*. I believe he started his investigations after the destruction of Old Oren-yaro. He was interested in why we existed in a land as dry as Jin-Sayeng."

"He was half mad with grief," Ozo grunted. "Don't hold it against him."

"Warlord Yeshin's agents were getting too close to my family," Namra continued. "My father wanted to leave, except…going to Dageis isn't cheap. We were of the craftsman caste, and though my father served the Ikessars as I once told you, it didn't pay much. The travelling expenses alone equalled what my father made in a year, in addition to lodging and food. My father…went to yours instead to beg for my life. To spare me."

"He would've liked that," I said, offhandedly.

Ozo snorted. "He wasn't the unreasonable man they believe him to be."

"Be that as it may," Namra said. "He not only let my father go, but gave him the coin both for our journey…and for my education in Eheldeth."

"The mage school in Dageis. Why would my father care about your well-being? He promised the same to these warlords' children, and yet he didn't go through the same expense for them."

She glanced at the study. "I'm guessing he wanted a mage that would be loyal to his cause, if not to him directly." She turned back to me. "My father told me that Yeshin only had one command: I was to return home once my studies were done to assist you. That was all, my queen. I wasn't told what the bigger picture was. I was convinced our plans up to this moment were sound. Now…" She turned to Ozo.

"This delicate operation requires mages," Ozo said. "Yuebek needs to learn the spells necessary to close the rift. Yeshin has amassed the knowledge for such spells. They are all in this room." He pointed at her. "It's your job to know what they are. It's your job to teach him."

Her face paled. "I—"

"*Mage child*," he said gruffly. "I signed the orders myself to send your mother the money for Eheldeth every year. She married some Dageian man to secure your citizenship, but the money was necessary to keep you there. We had been waiting for you for years. Why you decided to serve Rayyel Ikessar instead, I can't tell. You're as foolish as the queen. But you're here now. You're both here now. My job was to bring you all together, and then clean up when it's all done. The in-between? That's all you."

What now? I wanted to ask. But my tongue wouldn't work.

"If you had been open from the very beginning—" Namra began.

"With her?" Ozo asked, vaguely gesturing at me. "Is she listening now, after I've laid it all bare? Warlord Yeshin *knew* she would resist. He ordered me to get her to willingly fall in love with Yuebek. If I had to fool her, so be it! Sounded simple enough. I didn't know it would be like dragging a dead donkey. But I couldn't talk, not in court, not where the Ikessars' spies could be lurking about anywhere."

"We did have a lot of those," I said, thinking of Kora.

"We can't afford Yuebek finding out, and if that meant hurting your feelings, so be it."

I closed my eyes. "So why are you telling me now?"

"This study is safe," he breathed. "If you ignore the bandits trying to burn the whole place down. There's no way to do this cleanly anymore, Queen Talyien. We need you." He indicated the study, with all its books and knowledge, gathered painstakingly over the years. "I had hoped seeing how seriously your father took this problem was all it would take to convince you."

"Warlord Yeshin was aware of his daughter's temperament. He must've known we would be here at some point." Namra turned back to me. "Have you checked the room, Beloved Queen? Your father may have left you a note."

"Lord General Ozo," Parrtha called from the other side of the door. "The bandits have regrouped. They're in the courtyard now."

"For once in your life, Talyien, think about someone else other than yourself," Ozo snarled. He kicked the door open and stomped out.

I didn't even look at him. My attention was drawn to the painting of a bonytongue on the far side of the wall.

"Tali," Namra said, taking a deep breath. "I can understand if you won't—"

I ignored her and approached the painting. The paint had darkened to brown over the years, but it must've been black and orange once. I placed my hand on the frame. Nothing happened.

Cautiously, I pulled the painting from the wall and inspected the wood behind it. I expected markings, spell runes, anything of that sort. But other than the hook from where the frame hung, the wall was blank.

"Perhaps this was important enough for him that he took more precautions," Namra tried again.

"Perhaps," I replied. "Except this room was as much caution as he was willing to take. I'm assuming you needed my blood to open the door, you bastards." I waved my bandaged arm at her.

She gave an apologetic smile before wandering over to the desk.

"I already checked there," I said. "Maybe you're wrong. Why would he leave anything? My father isn't the sort of man to explain himself to anyone, let alone me. We've already proven that." I paused, glancing at the painting in my hand. A thought occurred to me. The painting was too crude, the sort of thing my father would've never paid money for. The artist's signature was scribbled in the bottom—it was my brother Senjo's name.

I peeled the bamboo from the back panel and pulled out a tattered piece of canvas. There were words on the other side. Crumpled, I couldn't see all of it immediately, and I held off for a few moments, wondering if I should even open it. Whatever words he had left for me . . . he could keep them. I didn't want to indulge the old man's whims anymore.

Yet I remained staring, my fingers pressed into the soft cloth with a foolish sort of reverence, and something else—the need for an explanation from a father that I always believed loved me in his own way, a longing forever damned because of what he was. Why look for love from a murderer? I unfolded the canvas.

Go to the Yu-yan dragon-tower. —Papa

I could hear his voice in my head, that forced gentleness, always mixed with the edge of the temper that lay beneath. Tears stung my eyes. Hot tears, tears of anger and bitterness and maybe a touch of hate. I didn't know if it was my father's handwriting or the abruptness of the message that did it. It could've been addressed to anyone else for all I knew, except for that last part, that old affection, what I used to call him when I was much younger and my whole world revolved around him. To use it knowing full well what he was truly asking from me . . . felt like the greatest betrayal of all. It wasn't just the world that thought of me as Yeshin's bitch pup. My father believed it, too.

I handed the letter to Namra and opened the door. I stepped into the shadows, feeling blood stick to the bottom of my boots. Anya's and Noerro's bodies were growing cold in the corner.

"Liosa," I started. "Where is she?"

"I—"

We heard screams in the distance.

I stepped away from the choking hold of that attic, and ran.

The sound of fighting exploded with the dawn. I exited through the kitchens, into a grove of bamboo where a path led straight to the servants' building. A narrow trail wound itself around the other end of the hill. I found myself at the shore of the lake, just in time to see Ozo faced with Peneira. She had my father's sword in one hand and her daughter's arm in the other.

Ozo's face was bleeding. "Your granddaughter comes to greet you," he said with an exaggerated bow. "I don't think you deserve the honour."

"This abomination is no granddaughter of mine," Peneira seethed. She turned to me. "The spell didn't work. Did you tell your mage to interfere?"

"She didn't," Namra said. "She wanted it to, Sang Peneira."

"You think I'd believe those lies?" Peneira laughed. "She's a hateful one, just like her father."

"I don't really care what you believe," I broke in. "But let Liosa go and you're free to walk out of here."

She stared at me in disbelief.

I stepped closer. "They say you married Yeshin for his name and his money. I wasn't there—I can't make that judgment. Perhaps your daughter did the same thing. Who can say for sure? Maybe you both loved him *and* the promise of the comfort he would bring to your lives." I took a deep breath. "What I do know is that it's over. You've made your choices and suffered for them. It's enough."

"Talyien—" Ozo began.

"It's enough," I repeated.

Ozo didn't look amused. "She's a snake. Let her slither off and she'll find a way to bite your ankle."

"He's right," Peneira hissed. "We can come back. Find better mages." She twisted Liosa's arm, pulling her further from us. Liosa whimpered.

"Your great-nephews are dead," Ozo pointed out. "Admit it, Peneira. You're old. You'll wither away before you can raise another army worthy of a challenge."

"It won't work, in any case," Namra added. "You need the queen for the spell, and she's blocked."

"Blocked," Peneira repeated in confusion.

"Something interferes with any spell cast on her," Namra said. "Possibly a result of the accident in the first place—I can't say for sure."

Her face tightened. "But—the ritual—it must have worked just a little." Namra drew back, and the panic on Peneira's face was suddenly palpable. "Tell me you know what went wrong. Tell me this was all worth something!"

"All I know is that it is impossible to re-create what happened in that room. I'm sorry. Liosa...cannot be healed. She will be like this until the day she dies."

Peneira uttered a gut-wrenching scream and lifted the sword. I was the closest to her and for a moment I thought she was going to attack me. Instead, she turned towards her daughter.

I rushed forward before she could bring the blade down on Liosa's shoulder. We both toppled to the ground, and I heard the creak of what sounded like bones breaking. I pushed myself off the old woman immediately. She lay curled in a ball, tears on her wrinkled face, still grasping my father's sword in her white knuckles. "Grandmother..." I began.

She didn't look at me. Didn't acknowledge the word. Still couldn't. To her, it sounded as empty as it made me feel. But she got up slowly and, with a precision that took me off guard, sliced her own throat with the sword. Her eyes never left the blade as it tumbled from her fingers.

I turned away. Liosa started crawling towards her mother's body with a low moan. I bent down to hold her before she could reach it. "It's all right now." I wrapped her in a tight embrace. "It's all right. She's just sleeping." I closed my own eyes, feeling tears creep into the corners.

I don't know if she understood anything, but the sound of my voice must've been soothing. She slowly relaxed. I could hear her heartbeat hammering away like a butterfly's wings, the first sound that must've welcomed me when I came into existence. "It's all right, my dear," I whispered. "You're safe. I won't let anything harm you." I stroked her hair as gently as I could, a mother to my own. Even if she could never love me, I could still care.

Off in the distance, Ozo undid his cloak and covered the old woman's body with a prayer on his lips. He returned to me, subdued. "I left the thinking to your father," he finally said, watching me with Liosa in my arms. "I got this far because I was at my happiest following orders. Tell me what city to conquer, whose head to lop off, and I'll do it. You accuse me of wanting the throne for myself. Why would I? Damn thing never brought you anything but trouble. Some people are born to follow; others were born to lead. Your father was... not ideal, but then who the hell cared enough to do something about all of this? He didn't have to. He could've taken the easier road."

He wiped the sweat off his face with the back of his hand. "What do I have to do to make you listen?" he continued. "Do you want me to go down to my knees? Beg you to save this land? You're the damn queen. Say the word and I'll do it."

"If you love it so much, you could save it yourself," I snapped.

"I would if I could. I've served Jin-Sayeng my whole life. I've killed for her, bled for her, gave her my only son. What have *you* done?" There was an expression on his face, one that—in the sunlight—was familiar. He *was* Agos's father. It stilled me to silence. The day of Agos's funeral came back to me. There had been no tears on Ozo's face, only resignation behind the shadow of grief—he had considered the possibility of losing his son to this cause long ago, had lived with the knowledge every day since Yeshin had told him what he must do. For Ozo to choose loyalty to my father over his child, to go as far as to love him only from the shadows, unacknowledged...

I slowly let Liosa go. "Look at this," I said, straightening up and watching her drift towards the edge of the water, mesmerized by the ripples from the wind. "Look at what my father's scheming has done to all of us. Look at what it did to *you*."

"Talyien—"

I went over to retrieve the sword from Peneira's corpse.

"One thing, Talyien," he whispered. "One little thing. One last sacrifice, to save many."

"One life," I replied. "Mine."

"It was never yours to begin with," he said with a crooked smile.

"How is that supposed to make me feel better?"

"It's not. It's supposed to make you understand that we are not the masters of our fate."

"I don't want to turn into him." I shoved Yeshin's sword into his hands. "My son is my only priority now."

Ozo's face darkened. "If you don't think you need him anymore, you're making a mistake."

"At least I made it myself."

He didn't try to stop me as I went down the path.

CHAPTER SEVEN
THE GATHERING CLOUDS

ⲒⲦⲰⲮ

The shadows of Burbatan latched on to my soul and refused to leave. Another fallacy of history books, this: the idea that who we are can be reduced to a few words. He was a hero. She was a villain. He was a good man. She was a whore. As if we don't, at the very least, change a little with every shift of the wind, molding ourselves to what was done to us. The Liosa who would use an infant to lord over both her mother and husband—was she the same Liosa who revelled in storybooks and held my hand with the resolution of someone who trusted that I could never hurt her?

You would think that everything I knew about my father up until that moment would be enough to console me. *Of course he used you. The man was a tyrant to all, but especially to his own family. You saw what he did to your grandmother and your mother. You've read your brother's journals. Yeshin saw you as meat to be sold to Yuebek. So what? You knew this before—why the rage now that you know why?* Because now I knew it wasn't from some misguided notion that he had found the better match. My father expected me to marry a monster. He had hoped for it since before I was born, yearned for a little girl child he could sell off. And when he got what he wanted, he molded me, trained me, orchestrated my entire world all so that his will would come to pass, never mind that it came at the expense of my happiness, of my whole life.

I suddenly wanted Yeshin alive again, if only so I could scream at him for what he had done and what he expected me to do. I wanted to laugh at his face, to tell him I'm rejecting all of it—his plans, his madness, his blood. I was done defending him, justifying his actions, pretending he was merely misunderstood and driven by circumstances to become the monster the land knew him to be. I wanted to tell him I hated him.

But anger at a dead man...was worthless. Nothing had changed. Rai still waited for me in the east; Inzali remained in possession of the papers we had signed and sealed, words enough to rescind our joint claim to the throne. But I couldn't very well go barging back there, to the Oren-yaro and the Zarojo who were waiting to possess me, body and soul—not without an army at my side. It was probably why Ozo was so confident in letting me go. On my own, they could always trap and overpower me. I couldn't go far without my own army, without guards. I prayed he was wrong in that.

I took the riverside road, intending to follow it all the way to the Sougen. Lord Huan had as much as assured me I had his loyalty. His assistance was my last hope. Not only would he be able to lend me soldiers, but his family had mages working on the dragon-tower and was probably more familiar with the problems in the Sougen than anyone else. They would have a solution better than my father's. The only question that remained was the price I was willing to pay. Years ago, Lord Huan had travelled to Oren-yaro to ask for my hand in marriage, a sure sign that he was as hungry for the throne as anyone else. He said it was my temperament that caused him to reconsider; I suspected his father, who was loyal to Yeshin's orders, would have ordered him to call off the courtship before it ever truly began. If I could convince Warlord Ojika, it might still be on the table. The thought filled me with unease, because it would mean I would have to ask Huan to set aside his wife—I, who had ruined far too many lives already. Where my father had embraced the reality that politics meant playing the villain, I still couldn't accept it. Perhaps the Anyus would agree to barter with other things—with lands, perhaps, or for a few seats in the council. This was the sort of thing Magister Arro was better at.

I could, at least, shed the title of *queen* when I didn't have people around to remind me. I didn't have much coin, save for what little Namra had given me from before Burbatan. I slept in inns without talking to anyone and paid little attention to news from the east. When they asked, I told them I was heading to the Sougen to see my son. It was true enough. By the second or third day, I noticed Zarojo soldiers asking for someone fitting my description, and I avoided the inns altogether. I left the main road and rode through the farmlands instead. It was countryside I knew well, which also made it easier to escape my would-be pursuers than back in the empire.

In Fuyyu, I learned that all the northern roads were barricaded and that none of the riverboats heading to the Sougen were allowed to leave. Kaggawa's army had conquered most of the towns along the region's borders, isolating Yu-yan from the rest of the nation.

"Has Dai Kaggawa laid siege to the city?" I asked one of the city guards.

"Not as far as I know," the guard replied. "But it won't be long now. Word has it that Warlord Ojika has called for most of his soldiers to retreat to Yu-yan. Kaggawa had a larger army than we anticipated. We don't even know where his soldiers are coming from."

"His family has a bit of fortune," one of the thwarted passengers replied. "Rice farmers. All they do is hoard their money, you know? Pity he's using it to hurt instead of help our nation."

"How's that any different from what the warlords do?" another piped up. "And that queen of ours—"

"Steady now," the guard said, tapping her spear on the ground. "We don't want trouble."

"I'm guessing they've seized control of the river."

"They have. We can't go north or east. Don't tell me you're still trying to get in."

"I've got family there," I said.

The guard shook her head. "Don't even dare. I've heard of travellers who go in and don't come back. Kaggawa's soldiers arrest them on the spot."

"No word from Shirrokaru on reinforcements?"

"Dragonlord Rayyel is still under arrest, the queen is missing *again*... it's safe to say the east is knee-deep in their own shit right now. We're the forgotten west. Always will be."

This, I thought to myself as I left the gates and ventured to the marketplace. *This is the kingdom Queen Talyien built. This is her legacy.*

I took no emotions from the words—I simply digested them as one who had read the details from a book. I wondered what that made me. A hypocrite, probably. No better than the thoughtless people who had birthed me into the world. Well, maybe I ought to share the blame. How was I supposed to learn when they were all I had to learn from?

I felt something on my arm and almost pulled away in irritation. And then I saw a boy staring up at me. I recognized him instantly. "Kisig," I said.

He smiled, Agos's eyes peering back at me. It reminded me of the dream

I had back in Bara and sent a spasm of grief into my heart. "Hello," he said, unaware of my trepidation.

"What are you doing here?" I managed.

"We live here." And then, as if just realizing something, his eyes brightened. "Mama will want to see you!"

"I'm not sure—" I began.

"We have a barn. I'll take care of your horse." Before I could protest, he grabbed the reins from me. I felt like a horse myself as I followed the boy down the street.

Sayu answered the gate as we arrived. I still couldn't get over her expression every time she laid eyes on me—there was always that glint of dismay, like one you'd get when the stray dog you've been feeding just won't go away. "Kisig... insisted," I said, by way of greeting.

"He would." She pressed her lips together, as if to stop herself from saying anything rude. She glanced at her son. A flicker of worry creased her brow. "Is that a horse?"

"She said I could take care of him." Without really waiting for his mother to agree, Kisig pulled my mount through the gate. He snuffed impatiently behind the boy, eager for treats.

Sayu cleared her throat. "It would be impolite for me not to offer tea, I suppose."

"It really wouldn't be. I shouldn't even be here."

She gave a small, impatient wave. "General Ozo sent me."

"When?"

"Back in Bara. He wasn't sure if you would ride north or south and begged me to keep an eye out for you here."

"Did he...say anything else?"

She looked at me with confusion.

I sighed. "I asked you to go home, Sayu."

She shrugged. "This *is* home. Before Agos took us to Oren-yaro...we spent a year here, when I was pregnant with Teo. Perhaps the happiest year of our life together. When Ozo asked me to go, I was going to say no—but then I realized I didn't mind." She spoke as if in a daze, and eventually gestured. I followed her into the building, up a narrow flight of stairs that creaked with our every step and through the first door. Her younger son was in the common room, playing with a ball. "Your brother has found himself a horse," she said. "How about you go to him, Teo? He's in the yard. Just don't get kicked."

"Horse!" Teo repeated. He scampered past us, back where they came from.

"Kisig is only...five, isn't he?" I asked as the door slammed behind the toddler.

"He doesn't act like it, I know," Sayu said. "He's had to grow up fast. Agos was never really home much."

And then, as if realizing she was hovering on the fringes of a difficult conversation, she excused herself to go out the back door and down another set of stairs. There was an outdoor stove in the yard where the boys were, as well as a pump. From the window, I watched her scold the children before turning to draw water into a bucket. Afterwards, I heard the crackle of fire and smelled the scent of smoke. Mundane, domestic things. I really didn't need to be there. But even as I told this to myself, I was loathe to move. It amused me to understand how lonely the last few weeks had been—so lonely that I was willing to face the woman whose own marriage I ruined if only so I didn't have to listen to myself for a while. My narrative had turned sour.

She returned with a steaming kettle. As she poured tea into clay cups, she said, "I frighten you, don't I? A queen like you. I'm a nobody."

"I don't think of it that way."

"Don't you?" She handed me the tea. I glanced at it. "Don't worry," she added. "I won't poison you."

"Thank you, I suppose."

"Small place like this...would be impossible to get rid of a body," she mumbled.

I smiled at her feeble attempt at humour—which I was all but ready to pretend it was—and took a quick sip. "I learned a number of things over the last few weeks," I said over the tea. "And if he hasn't told you yet, I think you ought to know. Agos was Lord Tasho's bastard and he has no heirs. No other children that I know of. When you return to Oren-yaro, I will make sure he takes care of you as he should've done all these years."

Sayu didn't reply immediately. She drank the tea, her small finger tapping the bottom. Eventually, she said, "If it's all the same to you, lady queen, I'd rather not."

"But—"

"I'm not sure I want my children in that life. You saw how it claimed their father. And then all the troubles we ran into the past few weeks..." She shook her head. "This here, it's uncomfortable, but it's ours. We don't have to answer to anyone. The children can go about their lives without the burdens Lord Tasho and the Jinsein royals will cast over them."

"He knows where you are. Once we're at peace, I'm sure he'll want them. The Tasho lands are some of the oldest in Oren-yaro. You will not want to deny your boys their heritage."

"I know," Sayu said in a low voice. "But for as long as I can, I want to keep them...mine. If it's only for a few more weeks, a few more months."

We heard laughter coming from the yard. Her firm face brightened for a moment.

"We were happy here," she said. "I just wanted to remember what that felt like." I pressed my fingers around the cup, feeling the heat seep into my weary joints as I listened to her. Eventually, she shook her head, as if she was almost ashamed for even voicing her deepest desires. "Your son—do you know where he is?"

"They've closed the road to the Sougen and I don't know how to get any closer. I know he is still with Kaggawa." I swallowed. "I pray he still is. It is all I can count on."

"I'm sorry I can't be of more help."

"It's not your responsibility."

"Well," Sayu replied with a small smile. "We're all responsible for each other, aren't we? I want to blame you for everything. But I knew what I was getting into. Knew he was Captain of the Guard—*yours*, and all the gossip that came with that. I knew he was running away from something. In time, he told me everything. I shouldn't have intruded. It's too late now."

"Do you regret it?" I asked.

"Sometimes, when I wake up to the boys crying from some dream or another and I turn to a cold, empty bed..." She rubbed at the stubborn tears that crept up her eyes. "But I think you know what I mean."

I nodded slowly, staring at my tea.

Sayu cleared her throat. "What else did you learn out there? If you don't mind telling me."

"I learned how despicable my father was."

"That's not news," she said with a half smile.

"No," I agreed. "Which makes it sound...contrived. Like the suffering of others didn't mean a damn thing until I learned that he ruined *my* life, too. He molded the perfect player for his inescapable game. And then they went and pretended it was all under my control, that I had the power. Be *everything*, Talyien.

Fulfill the promises made when they demanded you be queen. Unite this land of petulant sycophants and make no mistakes while you follow these rules . . . these old, broken rules. It was almost too much to ask from a single person."

"It is," she said.

"They knew from the very beginning. They made me so they could break me, so that the true hero could come and save the day. How do you fight what you are fated to fail? I don't know if I can overturn decades' worth of scheming—if I have any power beyond my father's name and whatever he had given me. But if I walk away, the land burns. I . . . I don't know what to do."

Sayu reached over to take the cup from me, returning to the table to refill it. The smell of steam filled the air. "Well," she finally said. "We both know you're not going to walk away. Knowing my husband, he would've already asked you to. A practical man, for all his faults. The fact that you're here means you refused. That fact that he's dead means there was a disagreement there somewhere."

I made a soft sound of assent, not wanting to dredge up the details. She didn't need to know them.

"Were you carrying my husband's child?" Sayu suddenly asked.

I didn't answer.

She looked almost embarrassed to have been the one to bring it up, but I saw her swiftly try to recover. "Castle gossip," she said at last. "They said you were very ill the week he was killed. You discreetly called for a healer. A midwife."

"Evidently not discreet enough." I cleared my throat. "It was . . . a precaution."

"A necessary one?"

I gave a thin smile. "Does it matter?"

"I suppose not." I heard rustling and saw her walking towards me with a letter she had retrieved from somewhere in the cupboards. Still almost hesitating, like one word from me could crumple her, she handed it to me. "He sent that not long before . . . his death."

I stared at the ink seeping through the parchment before unfolding it. It was a small note, penned hastily. There were inky thumbprints on the corners.

Sayu,

With luck, by the time you get this, we'll be long gone.
*   I won't ask you to forgive me. I know what I'm doing is rotten. I wouldn't know how to explain. Can't explain it to myself. Knew since I was a boy that*

what I wanted can't be. Shouldn't have done this to you, I know. I told you I couldn't make any promises. Told you I was fucked. Well, I can't blame you. You've a good heart. I took advantage of your kindness. Don't think I wasn't happy. I was. But she needs me.

Can't do poetry, so I'll say this. Tell my mother everything. She'll help care for the boys. And me? Forget about me. Never speak my name again. Find someone else. You deserve better.

Agos

I read it twice before I returned it to her. She folded the accursed letter carefully and returned it to its hiding place. They were painful words, but they were his last words to her. It looked like she was still deciding if she wanted to throw them away. Just like she probably hadn't decided whether she was going to kill me.

"I suppose he wouldn't have had the same suspicions as you," she managed. "Else he would've said so."

"His opinion wouldn't have made a difference," I said. "The midwife took care of everything." I tried not to think of the blood on the sheets. There had been so much of it.

Her lips quirked at the corners. "Are you sure about that?"

"The people who birthed me into the world have done worse," I said. "I can't be like them. The child—had there been a child—would be doomed simply for being mine. My son has it hard enough already. Why have another share the burden? She couldn't have existed."

"She?"

"I . . . I dreamed about her once." I swallowed. "I'm sorry, Sayu. I would have loved her like the sun loves the sky, but it is better this way. I will not bring another like me into the world."

"You yearn for love, but cannot bring yourself to take it."

I looked at her in confusion.

Sayu scratched the side of her cup with a fingernail. "Agos . . ." she started, giving a sad smile. "He told me once that for a time, he was convinced you saw him as a way to get out of your world. If you didn't love him then, you could learn to love him in time, a far cry from everything else you've been forced to love all your life. He didn't look like it, but he was a romantic. A foolish, romantic man."

She drifted back to the kitchen. "Akaterru, but then I was, too. I believed what we created could change the truth, could change the things he felt about you, the pattern of your lives. Love is complicated." I glanced up, startled at how she mirrored Liosa's words. "Life is complicated. And yet this is all we get. Brief glimpses of happiness. Joy, once in a while. Agos had that with you. And maybe with me, too. And I have my sons. I keep them alive. They're strong and healthy. Even if Ozo never comes for them, I'm confident I will find the means to apprentice them to a trade somewhere. I don't know what they teach you royals, but my mother once told me that to ask for more than what is given to us is presumptuous."

I took a deep breath. "Sayu—I am sorry about Agos."

"So you've said."

"I didn't know you existed. I thought he…"

"Was yours to use as you pleased, knowing you would discard him at the first opportunity?"

The words stung, but she wasn't incorrect. I nodded.

"Well," she grumbled, as if surprised I didn't try to argue. "I assume it is a common fallacy for someone in your position. Don't apologize again. It's unbecoming from a queen. We are where we are. Don't think I don't appreciate what it means for an Oren-yaro to come to my house with her tail between her legs."

"You're allowed to crow about it forever."

She gave a small shrug. But eventually, she grew thoughtful again. Her eyes drifted to the window. "Maybe it hurts, but you do what you have to, for all that you know you are damned anyway. You were wrong and now you are going to make it right. It won't absolve you—I'm not sure I can ever forgive you, if I will be completely honest. But at least you can work towards peace of mind for yourself. At least you can make his death mean something."

Outside, the boys began laughing again.

"I mean, what else is there?" Sayu asked. "You still have to face the hours between now and the day you die. You might as well fill them with something of worth." She gave an expression that was as close to a smile as I was ever going to get from her—a resigned acceptance of my presence, which I suspected came from years of practice—and left me to gather firewood.

Later that evening, I watched her prepare our meal in silence. I thought about how there was something blessed in women like her. They were, in my mind, a deliberate attempt by the gods to keep the world afloat even as it falls into pieces.

True courage didn't resemble my mad rushes of faith. True courage looked like this, in the unfazed way this woman made a place for me at her dinner table as if I was an unexpected guest rather than someone who had torn her family apart. In the silent way she looked at her children, the sorrow slipping at the sound of their laughter. In spite of the exhaustion crawling between the lines on her young face, she moved with the ease of someone who knew she could bear the burden another day. After she put the children to bed, I watched her lay out parchment, ink, and quills on the kitchen table and begin to copy from a worn-out manuscript. Only then did I remember that she worked as a scribe.

"Your handwriting is significantly better than mine," I said, after observing her for a few moments.

She pulled her sleeve up, lifting the quill before replying. "I would guess that you're the sort of person who needs to remember she is holding a pen and not a sword."

"Is it that obvious?"

"Agos was the same way," she said, her face expressionless. "Your fathers trained you well, I give them that." She carefully wiped the nib on a sponge before dabbing it in the ink again. "The key is to go slowly." She made a careful stroke. Her script looked so elegant it could go on banners. Beside hers, my own would be chicken scratch.

"What are you working on?"

"An account in history. A small memoir on the merchants' war in Reshiro Ikessar's time."

"A classic. The Seven Shadows were heroes to every child in those days."

"This one seeks to paint the merchants in a bad light. The name Kaggawa, after all, is involved—Dai Kaggawa's grandfather. Their family is involved with nearly every uprising from the common class in the last century. The author believes it will sell quite a bit in these troubled times." She gave a soft sigh.

"Making history must be the family trade."

"Same with you?"

"I'm really not sure what you mean." I cleared my throat and gestured at the paper in front of her. "Do you ever wonder how much power you hold when you have that pen in your hand? Warlords have been felled by controversies from such books."

"I don't think beyond what I do," Sayu commented. "I am paid to copy books, nothing more."

"The things they say about me…" I started.

"Have you read any?"

"I try not to. It's probably not good for my health." I shrugged. "But it is inevitable what they will say after this. What I am. What I've done. What I *should* have done. And the worst part is that most of it will be true."

"There is the truth," Sayu said. "And then the truth." She held the pen towards me. "They'll write their truths. Go and write yours."

"I don't know what that will do."

"It'll keep you out of my hair, for one thing. You talk too much."

I gave her a pained smile and took the pen. A drop of ink fell on my toe.

"Write it all down—the madness that brought you here, and what you did to break free. So at least if you are bound to fail, the world will know exactly how. Fail freely, then, and leave the judgment for the gods."

CHAPTER EIGHT

THE SOUGEN
DELIBERATION

ᜊᜓᜆᜒᜆ

A nd so, in the presence of that one woman who had more reason to hate me than the rest of them put together, I wrote my truth as I remembered it.

It was as if the act of holding pen to paper was a floodgate. The words poured out in waves, dredging up old memories, things I've tried to leave behind, thoughts better left unsaid. I recorded everything I could, knowing that another's words wouldn't have the same weight. A skilled writer might be able to portray this story right down to each significant event, painting every detail with the sort of elegance and wit that would make critics clap their hands and cry with glee. A great writer would know exactly how to fill in the blanks, to lead their wayward reader down a path strewn with dazzling sunlight and the insight of the ages. But no one else would know how to peel back the layers—to lay it all out exactly as I have felt in the hopes that you might be silent long enough to understand. Be still for a moment, and listen. These words are my heartbeat. If this is all I have, then I have to make this right.

The days turned into weeks. I wrote while waiting the rest of the winter out in that cramped, two-room flat, wrote while I tried to find a way past the road barricades. I wrote between reports of Jin-Sayeng's apathy towards my rule, of yet another Dragonlord who disappears when it's convenient, of Kaggawa continuing to bring mercenaries into the region while the warlord of Yu-yan remained sheltered inside his city, refusing to send aid to his own people, choosing instead to watch his opponent build an army without batting an eye. I wrote even when I knew the Zarojo soldiers were in the city looking for me and it was only the grace of Sayu, who had her neighbours convinced I was her cousin and assistant, keeping me safe. I wrote through the fear of what Yuebek would do the longer I eluded him. I wrote while my son's finger rotted away in my pack, deliberately forgotten, because to face the truth that he could be dead or dying and there was nothing I could do would shatter me.

The flow of words brought comfort, and an escape.

But it wasn't all terrible. The monotonous life with Agos's family was peace I hadn't felt since the time I spent with the Lamangs well over a year ago. I woke to the sound of crowing roosters each day, and forced myself through the cold morning to feed the horse and take him for a brisk run before the rest of the city woke up. We wandered the beaches and watched the waves roll in—swathes of dark-grey water lapping over darker-grey sand. On stormy days, they towered higher than houses, crashing against each other before breaking apart on the jagged rocks in an explosion of foam. I would head to town for news from the plains, and then return around noon to assist Sayu in what little ways I could. Although I was useless with most of the household chores, Sayu figured she could leave Teo with me while she ran errands. She seemed happy enough that he wasn't dirty or drowned by the time she got back.

The rest of the time we spent in silence, bent over our writing—her hands clean, mine completely covered in ink. For hours, we would listen to nothing but the sound of scratching on paper while Teo and Kisig laughed and argued outside. In the late afternoon, right before sunset, Sayu's landlord—a chatty old woman with the sort of wrinkles that came from smiling too much—would come by with a basket of food: ground pork and carrots wrapped in egg roll wrappers, rice cakes with cheese, or deep-fried plantains covered in shredded coconut.

I slept in the common room, curled up in a wool blanket near the window. To the naked eye, I was nothing but a homeless peasant relying on the charity of others.

It was odd to recall a life that used to be so much more than filling one's days with work and sustenance. That I could now find comfort wedged in the corner of a wall and a cold, stone floor, or numbly take orders from a woman younger than me. *Change Teo's clothes, Tali. Kisig ran out again, find him for me.* Who was the queen of Jin-Sayeng? Lately, she seemed like a stranger. One time Errena, the landlord, came by complaining about the price of rice, which had climbed since the Sougen had been cut off from the rest of the world. As the kids helped her pick out small pebbles from the substandard bushel she was forced to buy, I listened to her talk about news from the east, of Prince Rayyel's imprisonment and the raging debates in the council concerning the foreign prince, of the jokes about the queen following Dragonlord Rysaran's legacy. "He was rarely seen at court, you see," she said. "Why did we expect the next Dragonlord to do better?" They sounded like stories from a faraway land. After Errena was finished, she glanced down at the papers spread all over the floor and the kitchen table, and asked, "What's this you're both working on, then?"

"History," I found myself replying.

"Learning from the past *is* important," Errena said with a slight shake of her head. "But today? *Today* we're alive."

Spring came with vehemence—steady drops of rain that didn't quite resemble the torrential monsoon, but which made every day wet and dreary. I thought about Thanh and if the snow was melting up at the Sougen. I imagined the mountains up north would still be covered in a layer of ice. I had yet to hear news of him, which I chose to believe was a good thing. If the boy was dead, they would talk. I wondered what the last year had done to his perception of the world. He had his father's habits, and perhaps a little bit of his temperament, too. On most days, Thanh shifted between mild interest in current events and deep retrospection on the mundane. He once spent an entire summer ruminating on the differences between brushes and quills.

"Would the style of writing not affect the thoughts of these scholars?" I remember him asking me one hot afternoon, a particularly rare, quiet one that wasn't interrupted by meetings with angry delegates and impatient emissaries. "The Zarojo favour brushes since their language and scripts allow for shorter writing, but Jinsein language is richer, isn't it? Or maybe it's just because we like to go on and on—"

"...and on," I finished for him, wiping a streak of ink from his face. "You're seven years old, Thanh. Let's go fly kites."

I paused from the memory to Sayu clearing her throat. I lifted the quill away from the parchment before I could dribble more ink on it and turned to her. "You're thinking of your son," she said.

I looked up.

She glanced at the window. "You go into a trance whenever the boys are out," she explained. "You hear them laugh, and your mind wanders."

"The roads to the Sougen are still closed. I wonder...how he is doing. How long I can trust the same chains that damned us both." I bowed to her. "I'm sure you must be tired of feeding me."

Sayu cracked a smile. "I am. You eat like a construction worker." She glanced over at my work. "But at least you've improved your handwriting. Small miracles."

"Thank you."

"Given how you started, it's nothing to brag about." She handed me a wet towel.

"I *am* going to be out of your hair soon, Sayu," I said as I wiped my hands. "I know I've taken advantage of your hospitality."

"Well—" She gave a small shrug. "You've kept the children entertained plenty."

"Still..."

We fell silent. I returned the towel to the basin.

"We both have to face what's waiting for us out there someday," Sayu said at length. "Me, for my sons. You, for yours." She gestured at my manuscripts. "I'll bind these myself. No sense letting you ruin them after you've worked so hard. If you do want to be useful, I need more ink and parchment. Could you go to Anong Joset's and pick up a crate of each?"

I got up without complaint and left to do as she'd asked.

Allowing trade from the Kag over the last half century or so had resulted in Fuyyu hosting a variety of shops and establishments that looked like nothing in the riverlands. With only an aging mayor to oversee things, Fuyyu became a hub for Kag construction, favouring heavy wood columns, plain rooflines, and clean facades, marked only with bamboo panelling—the only Jinsein feature of many of the buildings.

The shop Sayu sent me to was an older establishment, built right at the cusp of the war. The windows were unwashed, covered by tattered curtains. An old man was inspecting them with a look of quiet contemplation. He was neither Jinsein nor Kag, as I've come to know Kags. His skin was dark—darker than Khine's or someone from the islands, a stark contrast with his white hair and beard.

"Staring at them won't wipe them clean, you know," I said.

The old man gave a sigh that sounded like it rattled his bones. "I don't even know why I bother. Joset never gets anything done right."

"Are you the owner?"

His eyebrows quirked up. "Some days I'm the boss, some days I'm the unwanted visitor." He spoke Jinan with an odd lilt—not uncommon for someone who had picked up the language later in life. "Joset went for lunch, so I suppose today I'm the help, too." He gave a grand gesture, inviting me into the shop.

He went straight to the counter as I stepped in. A tall, much younger man with yellow hair greeted us. "You're Miss Sayu's guest, aren't you?" he asked cheerfully. He was Kag, but his Jinan was fluent. "I'm Geor. I delivered her packages to your place at the start of winter. How is she doing? I asked her to let Joset know if she needed anything, anything at all, and—"

"I remember you," I said. "You cut your hair."

He rubbed the fuzz with a grin. "I've been on the road. Fleas, you know. Are you running errands for her? Tell her she works too hard."

"Her client wants twenty copies of his book by the end of the season. She's convinced she *isn't* working hard enough."

"A woman that talented could find better work."

"I wouldn't know. I've got her list here." I handed him the piece of paper.

"The boss will take care of that for you," Geor said.

The old man rolled his eyes. "With employees like you..."

"You know I can't read Jinan, boss."

"Invest some of the money I pay you for an education." The old man leaned over the counter to look at the note. "I think we have these. Pull up some of the new shipment, Geor. A bit of activity would be good for your circulation. And your gut."

Geor grumbled as he placed the broom against the wall and limped towards a pile of crates on the corner. I noticed one of his legs was covered in bandages.

"Rough journey?" I asked.

"You have no idea. It's war up in the Sougen. Barely got out with my life, too." He pointed at a splotchy bruise on his chin.

"But the roads are closed."

"Not really a problem for wily merchants," Geor said with a grin. "The river tunnels..."

The old man cleared his throat.

"What I really meant—"

"Ah," I said, placing a finger on my lips. "I understand."

"If the soldiers catch us, there'll be hell to pay," Geor whispered. "We're not supposed to be bringing goods in there. But they've got the best beetles for red—"

"Should I have you drawn and quartered, Geor? Or pickled in a jar?" his boss wondered aloud.

Geor laughed. "You've got to love the boss's humour."

"I really don't think he's joking," I said. I glanced back at the old man. "Were you with him?"

"Gods, no," the old man said. "Travelling here is difficult already. All the cold air isn't good for my bones."

"No desire to see your nephew, boss?"

The old man grimaced. "I wouldn't call him that. Pisspot troublemaker. Should've cut his arms off when I had the chance. Are you going to open that crate or do I have to hire someone who talks less?"

"You can hire the neighbour's girl if you can stop staring at her bottom long enough for her to get work done," Geor said with a grin. He cut the twine around the crate with a knife and stepped aside to pry it open.

The shop owner approached us with the list and began pulling out the proper items. "You know a way into the Sougen," I said as I watched him work.

He smiled at me. "The less you know, my lady, the better."

I glanced at Geor. "And *you* had a run-in with the soldiers. Kaggawa's, or Anyu's?"

"Ah, you don't have to worry about me," Geor said, crossing his arms. "It was an accident. No need to tell Sayu, either. I don't want her worrying."

"What prompted it?"

"Looking at them the wrong way."

"Kaggawa's, then," I said.

The old man snorted. "Kaggawa's men are uncouth louts from the west. Mercenaries who are in this line of work because they're good for nothing else. What did you expect?"

"I heard Kaggawa's family is well-connected," I said. "Money for a whole army."

"If that boy thinks he can take over a whole country with a gang of no-better-than-thieves, he's got a harsh lesson to learn," the old man snorted. "I wouldn't be surprised if he's used up whatever he has on this ridiculous tirade."

"They'll have a better chance of securing the region if he hires better sol-diers," Geor broke in. "His men wanted to confiscate our goods. Said the roads were closed, which meant I was doing something illegal, whatever *that* meant. But they had another prisoner there who pointed out that there was no legality when they themselves were breaking the law, and...well, he said other things that confused the soldiers long enough for us to make an escape."

"Fraternizing with prisoners. That's what I pay this useless slob for." The old man returned to the counter to prepare Sayu's package.

"This wasn't just a prisoner, boss. He spoke Jinan with an accent. Quite the smooth-talker, too."

"Like me?" his boss asked.

Geor pointed at him. "Like the exact opposite of you."

"This man," I began. "Was he Zarojo?"

"Hell if I know," Geor said. "I can't tell you people apart. Unfortunately, he got me out of that mess only to lead me straight into another one. The sol-diers decided they didn't like getting tricked and sent a whole troop after us. I was injured during the attack. Spent the rest of the winter recovering in Kag-gawa's main encampment. Rat bastards let me out at the start of the season. Dai Kaggawa himself ordered my release, apparently. Thought he was try-ing to make amends, show the region he isn't just some warlord hell-bent on taking over for his own good. Good luck with that—he's getting off on the wrong foot."

"Must be getting too big for his breeches, thinking he's winning his little war," the old man commented. "They'll be in for a surprise once the Dragon-throne decides to put an end to things."

"That won't happen any time soon," I said.

"You've little faith in the system."

"I'm surprised *you* do."

He grinned. "Girl, I've survived enough wars to know it works out in the end. For merchants like me, anyway. Always remember, it's vultures who out-live them all."

"What happened to your friend?" I asked Geor. "The one who tried to help?"

"He wanted to speak with Kaggawa himself. Said he knew him, said he treated his daughter's leg the last time he was there. Last I saw of the poor bas-tard. The soldiers weren't happy. Whatever they did to him, I hope it was fast."

My mind must've blanked for a space of time, because the shop owner was suddenly beside me, his face a mask of concern. I took Sayu's package from the counter and handed him his coin. "Thank you," I managed without getting tongue-tied. I walked out of the store, the contents of the box jingling.

Khine. The man in Geor's story... it had to be Khine. Why did I assume he would run back to the empire as soon as he was free from me? There was nothing in the Sougen for him, and so he could have only gone there to rescue Thanh.

My thoughts throbbed like an aching tooth. I made a wrong turn and found myself in a narrow street that smelled of urine and excrement. A dog ran past me, barking.

I started to retrace my steps and paused when I saw the shadow of a woman in the distance. Her rags were almost falling off her emaciated frame and her eyes were swollen shut. But she must've heard me, because she banged her cane on the wall and held out an empty cup, asking for alms.

I took a coin from my pocket. Two steps towards her, I stopped as a white flash overwhelmed our surroundings. The now-familiar prickle of the *agan* drifted over my body, and I realized the rift's effects had finally arrived all the way south. I dropped the coin.

When the light disappeared, the woman's face changed. Sharp fangs filled her mouth and veins crawled down her face, turning her skin the colour of granite.

Without a sword to protect me, I shielded myself with the package as she lunged. Her claws sank into the wood. She flung the box aside before rearing to tear my right arm clean off its socket.

She fell before I could even blink.

The old man from the shop stood over the withered body, bloodied sword in hand. "So," he grumbled. "It's happening all the way here, too." He turned to me, as if just remembering I was there. "This region has been growing unstable over the past few decades, and it's only getting worse." He flicked the blood off his sword—a wave-patterned blade only slightly longer than his arm—before sheathing it.

"You know about all of this." I couldn't take my eyes off the corpse. Half of it was crumbling into dust, but enough was left behind that you could see what the woman looked like in life.

He uttered a sigh that verged between exasperated and amused. "I'm a merchant. It's my business to know. I'm certain a few cities will soon be eradicated from the maps—filled with nothing but monsters and corpses. Cairntown is already gone, and Ni'in will be next."

"I've been to Ni'in," I replied.

"It's despicable, isn't it?" He pushed the body aside, almost gently. He removed the cloak from around his shoulders to cover it before he retrieved Sayu's package from the ground. "Despicable that such places can fall into disarray, and worse when others take advantage of the downtrodden."

"People like you?"

"Like me," he admitted freely. "Cheap prices, and war and desperate souls who will pay anything for necessities... you'd be a fool merchant not to snap at the opportunity. But still, I was talking about the corrupted souls seeking hosts. You must understand—it is difficult for another soul to take over a body. They need permission from the host. It's a fool's transaction, a pact of the damned. So only the damned and the desperate would think to make it."

"The more destitute a region, the more likely these corrupted souls will find a way to convince a host to accept a rider."

"A *rider*. You have an interesting choice of words here in Jin-Sayeng. But you have it right. It's like a disease that only spreads when the weather is warm and humid."

"There are no supplies headed for the Sougen. With famine on the horizon..."

The smile faded from his face. "Famine. Always a great wartime tool, but maybe not the wisest to use in this region at this moment in time. The famine would create a horde of these things in the Sougen, deep inside the very city the warlord is trying to hold. That foolish boy, indeed." The old man sighed. "I'll walk you back. Where do you live?"

"I can manage it."

"Not trusting me is smart. On the other hand, you know the smell of blood draws them out, don't you? There'll be others."

With a slight frown, I bade him to follow me to the right street.

"That's strange," he said, when I pointed out the building. He shook his head at my confused look. "Nothing. It's just funny how fate has a habit of bringing us back. These streets are dirtier than I remember."

"How long ago was that?"

"Too long. I was a young man then. I've been around since." He nodded towards the street. "There's another."

The creature was drinking from behind a thick clump of tangled roots hanging over a gutter. Its back arched, the veins showing beneath its nearly translucent skin, which covered a brittle-looking skeleton. This one was so far gone I couldn't even tell it had once been human. Black hair, grey skin, a thing you couldn't even call animal. A shapeless bag of bones would have been more accurate.

The old man drew his sword and held the handle out to me. "If you will do the honour, my lady? I'm afraid my back is starting to hurt."

"You just don't want to get your shoes dirty."

He glanced down at his boots, which were meticulously shined. "Among other things."

I took the sword from him and approached the creature. It turned at the sound of my footsteps. I lifted the blade, bracing myself for an attack.

It looked at me with a face that was both human and beast. "Help me," it gasped.

I stopped, sword in mid-air.

"Please," it said, holding one clawed hand out. "It hurts."

"It's not the first time one of you has tried tricks on me," I replied. "I'm afraid this is it for you."

It looked confused. "Please," it said again. "Rip it out."

"Rip what out?"

"My heart," it croaked.

"You want to die?"

It nodded, a movement so forced that it looked like it was being jerked up and down with strings. "It hurts so much," it said, its voice so low now that it sounded like the hissing from a kettle. "I tried to fight. I'm still fighting. But it was too strong. It took over."

"If you can still talk, then it hasn't taken over. Can't you convince it to let you remain in control?"

"And then what?" it gasped. "So I can stay like this forever?"

I had no answer. It stood up, allowing the afternoon sun to shine directly on its ragged clothes, most of which were covered in blood. From this angle, I could see the skin stretched over its rib cage and its sunken stomach. Every breath it took seemed to accentuate its gauntness.

"I killed them all," it continued. "My family—my parents, my husband. My...my children." Tears ran down its face, past the patches of fur. "It made me kill them. It wanted me to eat them, too, but I said no. And I ran. But it was too late."

"You haven't fed since," I said, pointing at its body. "You've beaten it."

"What did I beat? The people I love are gone." It flexed its claws, the tips of which were covered in sludge. "Kill me," it whispered.

I took no revelry, no joy, as I slid the sword into its heart. It welcomed it, bony fingers wrapping itself around the blade so tightly that the blood ran like rivers down its arms. As it dropped to the ground with a satisfied sigh, the face began to change, grey wrinkled skin smoothing away to reveal a woman so much younger than me. "The gods have left us," she whispered. Her last words were so garbled you could've taken it as her final hissing breath. The body that remained was nothing more than a skeleton, wrapped in a thin layer of clay.

I heard a child's cry. "Tali?" Kisig called, his voice shrill.

I looked down. My hands were covered in the woman's blood. The iron scent filled my nostrils, so sharp it made me feel as if a dagger had been jammed from my nose to my skull.

"Kisig—" I began.

He shrieked and darted for the gate.

I dropped the shopkeeper's sword and turned to chase after him. I found him in the main hall, wedged in the corner of the staircase where people kept their shoes. I opened my mouth to explain what happened, what the creature was and why I had to kill it, but the terror in his eyes was answer enough for me. There was no outrunning these shadows.

It was time to wake up.

CHAPTER NINE

THE RIVER CAVERNS

ᴠ ᴛ ᴠ ᴐ

I knew about the network of underground rivers in the Sougen even before
our misadventures last fall, but I didn't really understand to what extent they
infiltrated the region until Geor mentioned them. Several main tributaries have
been mapped, but my understanding was it was an unreliable means of travel,
especially with the wide Yu-yan River running right through the plains anyway.

"Can't imagine why," I told my horse as I stared at the entrance of that first
cavern, a few hours' ride from the western road. Large stalactites and vines
fringed the mouth of the cave. The water was cerulean green, so clear in parts
that I could see the fish darting in and out of the mangroves. The surface
remained calm, with only a slight gurgle coming from within. I wondered how
deep it was further up the caverns. I needed to find one that wasn't completely
underwater, sections that could be crossed by horse or on foot.

Hooves sounded from the path up ahead. Shadows danced behind the soft
glow of twilight as two riders appeared between the trees.

"Nothing to see here," I called to the figures.

"We thought we'd find you here," the shop owner from Fuyyu replied, leaning over his horse.

"You've upset Sang Sayu," Geor added. "She told us you've been trying to get
to the Sougen for weeks. Something about your family—but she didn't want to
say more than that. Boss had to give her a few months' worth of ink and parchment to cheer her up."

"Had to. You make me sound like a miser," the old man grumbled.

"You aren't?"

"As one of the most generous souls this side of the continent, I am honestly insulted, Geor." He removed a sword from his saddlebag. "A pity someone who clearly knows which end of this to swing would run around without a blade. It's nothing much, but it should serve you for a time."

He threw the sword, which landed by my feet. It was a Jinsein grass-cutter with a wooden hilt, as plain an implement as anything else. I picked it up and tucked it into my belt. "Thank you. You didn't have to."

Geor dismounted. "We're here for another thing, of course. The boss insists I go up there to help you."

"Insists," the old man said with a sigh.

"What's in it for you?" I asked.

"The man I mentioned, the one who saved me," Geor continued. "He's a friend of yours, isn't he? I saw how upset you were over the news."

I didn't reply and led them back to the small camp where I'd been staying the past two nights. The fire was still blazing.

The shopkeeper heaved himself off his mount, limping towards the promise of warmth. It was surprisingly chilly, despite the clear sky. "We'll need to build a raft," Geor said, showing me the long staves he had brought. "The water in the main cavern isn't as strong as you think. We can paddle upriver."

"Are you sure you remember the turns?" the old man asked.

"I marked it," Geor said. "I didn't know *where* we were going to end up. For all I knew, those soldiers had sent us on our way to a slow death. I stacked rocks every time we stopped," he explained to me. "Bit of an old trick I learned back home. If we're lucky, they'll still be there. If we're not—"

A sound resembling a wolf howl tore through the distance. I glanced at the old man, who returned my smile. Geor nervously pulled out an amulet from under his shirt. It looked like a tree, a symbol of the Kag god Yohak. He clutched it in both hands and pressed his lips over it.

"You may be right about the war making this worse," the old man said, pushing a stick into the fire. "Gods. It never ends, does it? A war today, because a long time ago, someone tried to stop another. My dear, if you only knew what your sacrifice would bring…" He glanced at the sky thoughtfully, his eyes full of sorrow.

My dear. The fondness in his voice as he spoke told me he knew more than he was letting on. "Did you know the mage that destroyed Rysaran's dragon?" I ventured.

He paused before nodding, as if the acknowledgment brought him much pain. "It should have been me," he said, at length. "I could have tried."

"You're a mage."

"A poor one," he admitted. "I wasn't trained. Didn't want to be. Perhaps I would have failed. I'd like to think I wouldn't have, and she would still be here."

"If we can stop the war…" I began. "If we can fix the rift…"

"That'll be the day," Geor commented. He made his way to the edge of the forest with his axe.

"Solve one problem and another will take its place," the old man said. "I know I sound cynical. But you don't think people have tried to fix this over the years? How many times has the Empire of Dageis sent mages?" He gave another sigh. "Maybe I'm just angry that our sacrifices amount to nothing in the end. Do you know what truly happened to your old King Rysaran's dragon?"

"It was destroyed over the mountains to the north," I said.

"Ah," he said, giving a small, mirthless chuckle. "My heart. You've pierced an arrow through my heart without even knowing it. *It was destroyed.* How simple it is to break down something significant to such few words, to erase the person behind the deed. We may give up everything for a cause, but what if the cause rings empty? Is it worth it? Not all of us can be heroes."

I stared at the fire, thinking about Ozo's words. *One last sacrifice…*

"But if we're not all heroes," I managed, "then who is? Who makes that first step?"

"Some people believe you are born to it." He shook his head. "I think that's hogwash. I think it's all in the narrative you choose to tell yourself. The mage who took it upon herself to bring an end to Rysaran's dragon was all but convinced it was her life's work to make a difference. She felt too many sacrifices had been made for her sake and that she, the sole survivor, owed it to them to bear the responsibility. But she forgot everything else along the way. I sometimes wonder if she was happier this way, or if her own happiness was even part of the equation. It kills me to think she never got to make that choice. And now…" He gestured at the sky, at the blue-touched blackness, and what we both knew lay beyond it.

"You're boring her with your old-man prattle," Geor broke in, pausing to wipe the sweat off his brow.

"My old-man prattle keeps you paid, so keep chopping," the old merchant said.

"What if…" I began. "What if that narrative is all you have? Perhaps she couldn't conceive a world where her happiness meant anything."

The old man gave me a curious look. "All I know is that it is too easy to let yourself be dragged into everyone else's idea of important. Look at what that kind of reasoning could get you to. You forget the things that truly matter: the people you love, the people who love you. You may even end up starting a war." He rubbed his hands together and got up. "I should return to the road before it gets too dark. I've no desire to sleep in the woods."

"Boss would rather be in a nice feather bed with some nice bosoms." Geor grinned.

"Unless it's the bed that has bosoms, just the first would do," the old man said. "My back won't like the other one."

"Nothing that some potent herbs and deep meditation won't cure, boss. And we all know you won't let that stop you anyway."

"Yet for someone who talks like you do, you've gone out of your way to help a stranger," I said. "I don't even know your name."

He gestured towards me. "Nor I yours. What value is there in names? Sometimes they're a burden, mud in a glass of water. They fade in time. But what we do changes us, or so I've been told, and maybe the little things can still change the world. Mmm. Well. It's probably just sentimentality. I *am* old."

"Take my horse. You should be able to sell him for a good price."

"I'll never get over how full of hope you young ones are," he smirked. "I appreciate the gesture. I may bring him back to the scribe and the boys. The little one was quite upset about his disappearance."

"Will you be all right travelling back to Fuyyu on your own?"

He brushed it off with a snort. "Nothing an old man like me hasn't done a thousand times before." He went up to the horses, pulling out the saddlebags and throwing them on the ground. "There should be enough provisions to last you both through the trip. Geor—I'll be headed west by the time you get back. Try not to bankrupt the store."

"Never in one place are you, boss?" Geor smiled. "Don't worry. Joset keeps things running."

"Astounding optimism. I was actually thinking of firing him." With one last wave, the old man swung onto the saddle and led the horses away from the forest. As soon as he was gone, I got up to fetch firewood from Geor's scraps. Green wood was wet wood; it sputtered in the hot blaze, but it kept the campfire alive. No more sounds came from the forest, and I was able to doze for a few minutes as the first rays of dawn appeared on the horizon. I woke to Geor's whistling and saw the small raft he had made, a rickety-looking thing made from logs tied together. It was barely large enough for two people.

"It'll work," he said, noting my concerned expression. "Water should be gentle enough. No snowmelt yet, and it hasn't rained the past few days."

I threw my boots onto the raft and waded into the freezing water with him to push the raft deeper upriver. A few steps into the sand and then we clambered in, half shivering, oars in hand. The raft rocked slightly under our weight.

We began paddling, the raft drifting from side to side. Even with the relatively still waters, it was a struggle to travel upriver. We reached the mouth of the cave, where the river narrowed and the current became more turbulent. "Hold tight," Geor called. He leaped towards the bank, rope in hand. The other end was tied to the raft. Muscles straining, he pulled the raft past the worst of the rapids. I jumped after him a moment later.

We made progress this way, walking as far in as the cave would let us. When the water calmed, we returned to the raft. Bursts of sunlight broke through the cavern in sections. I felt like we were in a temple made of rock and shadows.

"So," Geor began. "What's worth going all the way out here for?"

"I should ask you the same thing," I immediately countered, forcing my attention on keeping the raft from splintering on the rocks ahead.

"I've made friends with some of the soldiers during my captivity. I'm bringing gifts. Pipeweed, dried poppy…"

"The truth emerges. You're a smuggler. Did your boss approve?"

"It's his idea, really," he said cheerfully. "Dai's soldiers pay well, and they've got their vices like everyone else."

"So you can go in and out of Dai Kaggawa's camp without a problem."

He nodded. "Why?" he asked. "Do you mean to go with me all the way in there?"

I gazed at the splotches of light that guided us through the darkness and didn't answer. I was afraid of what I would sound like if I did—of the tremble in my own voice, of the weakness of my heart's truest desires. I needed to be making my way to Yu-yan without getting distracted with frivolities. *Those frivolities are your son, Tali. Your son, and Khine.*

We found the first of the rock cairns Geor had left. The caverns widened here, giving way to calmer water even as the river split into several tributaries. We went as far as we could until we were exhausted, stopping on flat spots to eat and rest. Two days later, we broke into open ground. I saw the emerald-green grass looming over us as we left the raft and climbed up the bank. "There'll be a trail," Geor pointed out.

There were several running through the thick grass. I paused, hearing the crunch of heavy boots. A group of soldiers appeared from one of the trails. I counted three. They were clad in plain leather armour, Kag-fashion, swords so long they touched the ground.

"You there!" a soldier called. "Who are you?"

I glanced at Geor, who held his hands out to show he wasn't armed. "We're simple merchants."

"Merchants don't just pass through the Sougen," the soldier replied.

"We were sent by Captain Boros. He'll know if you talk to him. Tell him it's the Kag from over the winter. He'll know."

"Captain Boros was executed a few days ago for insubordination. Who did you say you were?"

I attacked.

He wasn't expecting me. I didn't think they even noticed I had a sword. One clean stroke across his neck took him down, the blade cracking his clavicle before severing the vein. Amidst the spray of the hissing blood, the remaining two lunged at me with remarkable speed. Holding my left hand out to protect my face, I bent my legs and dragged the sword along the ground like a wolf stalking her prey. As soon as they got within striking distance, I turned in a half circle, the blade hooking upwards as I swung. I caught one on the leg, ripping flesh down to the bone. I jammed it as deep as I could before kicking him off. He dropped to the ground.

But there wasn't time to go for the kill. They were better than I gave them credit for; I was hoping they wouldn't be familiar with my attack pattern, forgetting that they had spent the whole winter fighting Yu-yan soldiers. As I spun to recover my footing, his friend got between him and my blade and I stumbled back, trying to deflect blows from a sword bearing down on me like an axe.

The remaining soldier suddenly fell, bleeding from the back of his head. Geor appeared behind him, holding a small log that he must've wrenched loose from the raft. With renewed effort, I struck the soldier's knuckles, flaying off a strip of flesh from his fingers. He lowered his sword, his hands now drenched in blood. The tip of mine came up to his throat.

He lifted his hands. "Enough! I yield! Who are you people?"

I poked his chin. Blood dripped down his neck. It was impressive he could still keep calm. "What happened to Captain Boros's soldiers?"

"They were reassigned," the man gasped.

"Tell us where and I'll let you go."

"I don't know about everyone. A few of them are guarding the southern gate."

I pricked him again.

"I'm not lying!" the man exclaimed.

"You better not think about calling for help. Think of how bad it'll be for you when you tell them a woman and a merchant killed the rest of your men."

"You won't see hide or hair of me, I swear."

I waved my sword at him. "Go."

He nearly stumbled over his companions in his haste to get away from me. I found the second soldier still bleeding on the ground. I must've severed an artery. Piss and shit were already leaking down his backside. I put him out of his misery as quickly as I could before I turned to Geor.

"Maybe I should be asking the same question they did," Geor said, hesitating. "Who are *you*?"

"Let's not make this more complicated than it has to be," I replied. I wiped the blade against the scabbard to get rid of the blood before sheathing my sword. "The southern gate, Geor."

I saw him silently weigh out the advantages and disadvantages of fleeing. Eventually, he gave a small nod. We dragged the bodies into the grass, grabbed the rest of our things, and made our way up the trail where the soldiers had been.

Belatedly, I realized my hands weren't shaking. They always used to after a fight like this. I didn't think it meant I had conquered my fears. They were still there, roosting like dragons. The thought of why that was made me so ill that I pushed it deeper into the recesses of my mind, into the cracks I hoped my father hadn't reached.

A soldier called to us from the gate as we appeared on the road. Geor strode ahead, a grin replacing the trepidation on his face. "Larson!" he called, followed by something in the Kag language that I couldn't make out.

The soldier said something in response. I saw his figure clamber down from the tower.

I took a moment to take a good look at the encampment. Sturdy palisades made of hewn timber went as far as my eye could see—Dai's army had the numbers to give any warlord pause. No wonder the Anyus were struggling to contain his rebellion. We were deep in the plains and I couldn't get a glimpse of the river anywhere. I did spot mountains in the distance, which meant we were somewhere in the western edge of Yu-yan.

"New assistant?" another soldier asked.

"I wanted to see what opportunities are out here," I answered for myself. "The old man doesn't pay enough." Lies came so easily to me.

The soldiers laughed. One leered at me, breathing through his mouth. "Have you got any special skills?"

"I can gut a boar from its balls to its throat," I replied with a grin.

They laughed, slapping the offending soldier's back as they let us through. I took a deep breath, my heart hammering so loud I could *feel* it. *My son is somewhere here.* I glanced at the tents and pavilions, spread out in neat rows on each side of the path, in the hopes of catching a glimpse of him. And Khine…

I followed Geor into one of the bigger tents off to the far end of the fences. A man in a dirty apron greeted us, and I caught sight of Geor's packet of contraband exchanging hands.

"How's it been out here?" Geor asked.

The man thumbed his nose. "The same old. Men dying, men trying not to die. And of course, there's the killing." He laughed at his poor attempt at a joke. His Jinan had the tinge I was starting to associate with those who grew up in the region around Ni'in—a fluency that still sounded like a different language altogether. He used words I understood but wouldn't use myself.

"Don't know where we would be without our new camp surgeon," a soldier broke in. "Stroke of luck, too, since we lost the last one and General Dai didn't have a backup. Hard to feel confident about your general when he neglects the little things."

The soldier called Larson, who'd met us at the gate, came up to us. "Are you talking about Lamang?" he asked. "General fished him out from prison, too. Tells you about the state of affairs. We were promised easy pickings. He promised the warlord in this province is weak and that his soldiers would cave within a week. It's been months now, and they give us shit if we raid the farms for supplies. This war has gone on too long and we're not getting paid enough for it."

He continued talking about other things, about the chaos in the fields and the weakening resolve of Dai's mercenaries, but I stopped listening. I suddenly felt like I could breathe again. At some point, Geor broke off from us. He looked almost relieved to be rid of me.

"Will Doctor Lamang be looking for assistants?" I asked, once Larson paused for breath.

"He already has one," he said. "She was in the infirmary tent the last time I checked."

"Maybe they could use another. You said yourself. This war is chaos."

"I'll take you there now if you want."

I found myself following him through the camp. I kept my head down, assuming the demeanour of a placid peasant as we strode past soldiers going through their daily exercises. Keeping my silence was easier these days than it used to be.

We went through another gate, past the stables, and reached a large pavilion. My throat tightened. Larson spoke to the guards and they gestured to me with a wave. I ducked under the tent flap and was greeted by rows of cots, most of which were filled with injured soldiers in various stages of recuperation. The smell of sweat and blood, with a hint of pus, filled my senses. My heartbeat was now threatening to drown out my thoughts; I scanned the area for Khine, but he wasn't there. My eyes settled on the woman changing the dressing on a soldier's leg. Rayyel's sister.

Karia regarded me with silence as I approached her. She looked puzzled, but her mouth remained closed. "I'm looking for Doctor Lamang," I said. "Perhaps he has a job for me here." I gave her a knowing look, hoping she wouldn't raise the alarm. If she was working for Kaggawa...

She turned to the soldiers behind me. "The doctor's gone to get more herbs," she replied, her detached tone mirroring mine. She wiped her hands on a towel. "I could use the help. Thank you, Officer."

Larson saluted before stepping back outside, leaving us alone. She handed me a roll of bandages and returned to work.

We really didn't talk for the next few hours. I kept myself busy by making small talk with the soldiers. The fresh wave of injuries came from a recent attack by Huan Anyu on one of their smaller camps by the river. They had managed to regroup and attack his flank.

"Unfortunate that the slimy dog escaped!" one of the men fumed. The others nodded in agreement. They seemed to hate Huan the most. He was a foolhardy battle commander, given to pushing his men in situations that would've deterred others. And his soldiers loved him, which meant they fought like cornered lions. Two or three were needed to take down one of his.

But they all seemed confident in their numbers. Another fresh thousand were expected to come via riverboat, which explained why Dai had seized control of the western roads. The river was the surest route for him to replenish his army. The only thing left for them to do was lay siege to Yu-yan, and they were getting ready for that. "It's going to be bloodier than these little skirmishes," the soldier told me. "But think of the rewards. General Dai promised ample riches to those who hold their own."

It was late evening and the lamps were burning low by the time we finished bandaging everyone. But before we could start cleaning up, I heard the clink of heavy footsteps outside. A small woman on crutches limped in.

I immediately turned to the shadows to hide myself. Dai Kaggawa's daughter would recognize me immediately. She had been welcoming and honest with me the last time we spoke, but that was before a dragon had torn her leg off her body and dropped her from a tower. I did feel a shadow of relief that the young woman was still alive.

"Is the new salve working?" Karia asked as the woman settled into an empty cot.

"It's itching less," Lahei said. "But the wound still hurts."

Karia unwrapped the bandage around her stump. "It smells clean."

"I shouldn't be complaining. I know people who've died from smaller bites."

"The doctor says bodies react differently to dragon spit," Karia said. "Yours is healing, it's just slow. He still has trouble with his, too."

"His arm?"

"He says he can't move it as well as he used to. Says his stitching has become sloppier."

Lahei gave a thin smile. "I'm sure these men wouldn't know the difference. Our last camp surgeon worked on pigs down at Fuyyu. Anything the man touched looked worse going out of his tent than in."

"Lamang takes pride in his work."

"I don't disagree. He saved my life." She shook her head. "It's a shame he's still clearly the queen's man. My father let him stay on, but we all know he's really here for her son."

"She would worry for his safety."

"There's nothing to fear," Lahei insisted. "My father knows what he's doing. Prince Thanh isn't a hostage. He's a guest. We'd never let anything happen to him. Once we win Yu-yan and have the Anyus' heads on a string, my father intends to gift the city to him. A wedding present."

"The poor child is just a puppet. At his age, he cannot possibly consent to his own marriage."

"We're all puppets," Lahei said, her eyes fixed on the ground. "Pieces being moved on a board. My father has been speaking with Prince Thanh and thinks the boy understands, better than his parents."

"He's just a boy," Karia said. "What would he know?"

"As Queen Talyien was once just an infant. Soon, he'll grow up, and the power of the blood running through his veins can't be understated. My father knows this better than anyone else."

I stopped myself from throwing the table aside in my horror. Dai couldn't get to us, so he was trying to get to my son. An impressionable boy, still so young. It would be easy to twist his mind. I knew I had to get him out of there.

"Even if he's a prince, he's a child like any other," Karia continued. I didn't know how she could keep calm.

"And we understand that. We take good care of him, don't we? If we weren't at war, I'd go down to the city to get him a new book or two. He's cleaned out whatever we have here in the fort."

Karia didn't answer and began to put salve on Lahei's leg.

"Father says we're in a good position to besiege Yu-yan soon. I hate that I can't be there. I'm useless. All I can do is trip on things. My father doesn't say it, but I think he'll start training my sister Faorra to take over some of my responsibilities. Faorra. All she's ever cared for are pretty dresses and dolls! If the damn stump would stop hurting at least I could try to ride a horse. And the ship...I miss my ship. I hope Father hasn't sold it for scrap material to pay for his war. He won't tell me where it is."

Karia retrieved a fresh set of bandages. "The doctor told me that perhaps if you rested more, you'll heal faster."

Lahei frowned. "He's just saying that to irritate me. Where is he, anyway?"

"Up in his hut. He went to get herbs. He won't be back for a few days—he has to prepare them first."

"Probably sending a message to the queen." She sighed. "It's strange. Father warns me not to trust anyone. But then he also tells me drinking cold water will make me sick and I drink it anyway. Lamang's heart's in the right place...he just hasn't put up the proper walls around it. Love makes fools of us all."

"Family has always been enough for me."

"I'm sorry if they're affected by all of this," Lahei said. "War is awful for the common folk, but it's always an opportunity for those of the right mind. I know how that sounds. But change cannot happen without some kind of upheaval. We've tried our best to limit the impact on the people, but predictably, not everyone is cooperating, which makes things harder than they should be. If we could just all agree on who the enemy is, things would be easier."

"To be young again, and so full of hope," Karia said, patting her arm. "Good night, mistress. It's late and we have more work to do."

Lahei glanced in my direction. I stepped further away, pretending to inspect one of the sleeping soldiers. I picked up a towel to dab the sheen of dirty sweat from the man's arm. He groaned, the stale stench of his breath mingling with the earthy tang of the herbal drink that knocked him out. "You've got new help?"

"Don't worry, mistress—I'll ask the doctor to pay her out of his own pocket."

"We don't pay him enough for that, but you people know what's best for you," Lahei said. "Good evening, Sang Karia."

As soon as she and her soldiers were gone, I sidled up to Karia. "I need to see my son," I whispered.

"Not tonight," Karia whispered back.

"But—"

"You'll alert them," she said, closing a jar of salve to put away. She began to arrange the remaining bottles on the table. "I don't even know why you're here. I thought you sent Lamang to take care of things."

"I didn't."

She motioned and drew me away outside the tent, near the edge of the palisade. The night wind was crisp on our skin, and I could see stars above us.

"Thanh is in the officers' lodge in the middle of the camp," she said. "It's well-guarded. Two levels. He's at the top floor."

"A building that size would've taken a few months to build. Kaggawa must have been planning this war for years," I mused.

Karia didn't even look surprised. "He would have, to have secured the services of so many mercenaries."

"His attempts at trying to make *me* see the light to avoid war were false," I sighed. "I figured nobody is that reasonable. You've seen my son with your own eyes?"

She nodded. "He's doing well. Healthy. Doesn't know who I am—I thought it best to keep it that way. He looks like Rai—his eyes anyway, when Rai was a boy. Acts like him, too. Maybe with a touch more humour. I don't know why he ever doubted him."

"I'm surprised you care."

She gave me a look. "Your boy is family," she said, with a conviction that took me by surprise. "I would've visited if I had the chance. But Princess Ryia forbade contact with you. After my brother sent me to Bara to care for Anino, I couldn't show my face in court anymore, either."

"You hid the boy from your lady."

Her expression darkened. "The clan failed my brother. They offered him up to your father just for the chance for things to stay the way they were, for them to keep what power they could. He wasn't an Ikessar. Is that a surprising thing to hear? He wasn't—they could've found someone better. Rysaran's father had brothers. They had sons. But that would've required deliberation and talks and they wanted to use someone that had no true value—Rayyel, a bastard and a mere soldier's son. A mere soldier that Rayyel's mother never even loved. They made him the Ikessar heir thinking he wouldn't last long, not with an Orenar on the throne. Look at him now. Have the Ikessars done a damn thing to help him?

"Anino was a child. A baby of two at the time. My brother begged me to keep him safe. To keep him away from his family, and from you. You must know—he only found out after he left Oren-yaro on the eve of your coronation. He made a vow of silence soon after."

"You're still afraid of me for Anino's sake, aren't you?" I asked.

She stared back, her jaw tight. She didn't need to answer—I could see it in her eyes.

CHAPTER TEN

THE WAR CAMP

ㄒㅈ℗

We spent the following day patching up the freshly wounded and making rounds through the camp for simple tasks. The soldiers, for their part, were friendly. They were starved for women, and I learned this was in part because Dai had chased out the brothel that tried to set up shop outside the fort. He wanted to conquer Yu-yan, wanted the men to understand that the luxuries they desired were inside the city and that if they wanted to partake of them, they had to win the war first. A risky strategy—one could just as easily end up with disgruntled soldiers as victory.

I used it to my advantage. A kind word here, a stray look there...and by the next morning I was allowed through the inner gates where the officers' lodge stood on top of a low hill, surrounded by a number of smaller pavilions. The smell of smoke and freshly baked bread filled the air.

The tents were for the lower-ranking officers, some of whom had been injured in the last battle and needed help with their dressings. Despite the bruises, sword cuts, and broken bones, they were still in high spirits. Warlord Ojika's refusal to send more than a handful of soldiers to control Kaggawa's growing army had resulted in a morale boost favouring the merchant. Their attendant directed me to a table, where the first soldier who approached must have forgotten where he was. A tall man with more hair on his chest than his head, he leered a little too close, his breath smelling of drink, and I could tell he would have made a grab for my chest if I didn't stop him. I pinned his injured arm to the table before his hand could wander and then gave him the consideration of pretending like nothing had happened.

"When do you think you'll start the siege?" I asked, dropping enough salve on his wound to sting.

The soldier grimaced. He looked like he wanted to start trouble and would have if not for the friendliness in my tone and the fact that his companions were chatting as if nothing was amiss. He eventually slumped into his seat. "Within weeks, if we're lucky," he said. "Look at these boys. They're all itching to hack Jin heads off!" He laughed, not seeming to care that he was talking to one or that he was insulting us in our own language. It wasn't the first time I heard the slur thrown around the camp. I pretended not to hear it. You got used to pretending not to hear insults to get things done, even words you once would have slain for.

"You should learn how to fight better."

He sneered. There was brown and white stubble all over his face. He looked like he shaved himself with an axe. "Silly girl. What do you know of war?"

I tightened the bandage so hard he yelped. "I know you're not very good at it." His wound was a long, jagged thing on his back, right underneath the left arm. Either he was caught unaware by an opponent or he was running from them. Something told me he wouldn't admit to the truth, even if he was court-martialled.

"You should've seen the other guy."

"If you don't use that hand too much, you'll probably heal faster. Try to control yourself." I turned to the other soldiers. "Next!"

"Not interested in helping me with it?" the soldier asked, hanging around the edge of the table.

"No thank you," I said, pretending not to look at him. "Maybe one of your soldier friends could help." It was difficult to maintain a cheerful tone while deflecting a man's advances, and I knew he would have acted differently if we had been alone—or if we were in a camp with very different rules. He reluctantly extracted himself when the next soldier arrived. This one, thankfully, was less interested. As far as he was concerned, I was invisible.

After I had changed more bandages than I cared to remember, I took my leave, and the attendant led me out of the tent. I stammered a quick excuse about being able to find my way back on my own. The attendant seemed happy to be relieved of the burden. As soon as the door flap closed behind me, I turned the other way, towards the lodge. Red flags hung below the windows, marked with a sigil unknown to me: a yellow stalk of rice in front of a white sun. I gazed at the upper floor, wondering where my son was.

I didn't realize I was walking straight up the path until a guard came to block me with his halberd. "You're going the wrong way," he said.

"I wanted to make sure I've seen everyone," I said. "Doctor Lamang is very specific about patient care, and I don't want to have to walk all the way back here."

"It's good exercise," the guard quipped.

I frowned.

"We'll send them over to you later."

I suddenly looked up. "Is that coughing?"

"I didn't—"

"No. From inside. Look, there's a window open. If someone's coughing up there, I should check on them. The last thing you want is an epidemic wrecking the whole camp. Have you heard of Rat Pox? One day it's coughing, the next your whole body's covered in boils." I said it with such gravity that the guards glanced at each other with worry.

"We really can't let you," the guard said with some reluctance.

"You know we're attacking Yu-yan soon, don't you? Sickness is the last thing you want."

"Let her in," his companion grumbled. "It's a damn woman. How much harm can she do?"

"Mistress Kaggawa's inside," the first guard replied. "We'll get in trouble."

"Lahei!" I said brightly. "I'll explain everything to her."

The guards stared at each other for a heartbeat. "Be quick," one finally said, leading me up the steps. "If you're caught stealing anything, camp rules state we're to cut off your hands. General Dai's pretty adamant about that one."

There was a giant table right in the middle of the main hall, atop which were woven baskets filled with boiled sweet potatoes, apples, and wrapped loaves of bread. I could also smell baking bread coming from the kitchens. I turned to the stairwell, where I could see shadows dancing along the wall. I heard voices and lowered my head as three men walked by.

They barely looked at me. I couldn't understand what they were discussing—all three were Kag—and they left the way I came from. I swallowed, waiting. When no one else appeared, I strode up the stairs, heart pounding. It felt like a lifetime had come between me and my son, and nothing was going to stop me from seeing him. I would sooner die.

I reached another open space, where stools were stacked along the southern wall. Kaggawa's war room had a stark simplicity that would put most warlords to shame. There was a large table of sand in the middle, marked with figures and a model of a city. Based on the layout of the clay soldiers on the sand, Dai's strategy for overtaking Yu-yan was based on brute force. He didn't need much more. He had cut off Yu-yan's supplies the whole winter through, and with no help from the Dragonthrone, Yu-yan was doomed. All he needed was to break the gates down and then walk in.

Whispers began inside my head. I tore my attention from it, trying to remind myself what I was here for, and turned for the chambers. At the nearest door, I paused, thinking I could hear a child's voice inside. Laughter.

All caution disappeared. I placed my hand on the knob.

Someone came up to push my hand away. I turned and my eyes met Khine's. For a moment, I simply stood there, unsure if I was just imagining everything. Something in him had changed. He had grown a beard, a patchy thing that covered his chin and the sides of his face, but it wasn't just that. There was a note of self-assurance on him, as if the months had chipped away the unassuming man I had last seen.

My astonishment faded. To see him alive, to see him safe after so many months...

Even now, I still can't put it into words. Poetry confuses me. We could try to capture our feelings on paper and it could still ring empty, bells tolling in an abyss. I could say I loved someone and you would tell me it wouldn't be sufficient, that the only way you would listen is if I found ways to describe the feeling with subtlety and eloquence, maybe compare it to the contents of a leather-bound book or an azure sky. Love, you want me to say, is like the sound of trumpets heralding the arrival of some benevolent god-king of old, or the pearlescent cabochons on the breasts of the bronzed goddess in the temples. Big words, pretty words that pretend they mean something, as if throwing a bottle of perfume into a puddle would give it enough depth to drown in.

Maybe you would rather I don't talk about it at all. There are more important things, and plenty of people—my own parents included—survive without it. Poetry may have us believe otherwise, but we don't need love to breathe.

I pushed my feelings back, reminding myself where they needed to be. I was no longer that young girl who would hang on to Rayyel's every word in the hopes that he would offer me a sliver of affection. I tried not to feel the spasm of disappointment when Khine said nothing by way of greeting. Instead, he placed a finger on his lips and motioned for me to step around the corner. When I was safely behind the wall, he opened the door.

"Doctor, you're back." I recognized Lahei's voice.

"Khine!" My son's. I closed my eyes, my heart hammering against my chest.

"It's broad daylight," Khine said. "You're both hiding here like baby rats and your skin isn't looking much better. Lahei—you won't get around much if you don't practice with those crutches. Do you want your other leg to fall off?"

"It hurts, Lamang."

"It's supposed to."

"Not the physical pain. But to know that I'll never run again, or fight…"

Khine made a sound in the back of his throat. "Well, and what do you want me to do about it? I can't make your leg grow back."

"I can still *feel* it," Lahei grumbled. "That's the worst part."

"The sooner you accept the loss, the better."

"General Dai says he means to kill the dragon responsible for this," Thanh said. His voice filled me with ache, the kind that springs from absence. I mistakenly thought I would be numb to it by now. "He told me he'll make sure to clean Jin-Sayeng of all its ills. He says Mother was distracted all these years, but he'll do his best to support her."

I closed my eyes. *Is this what you're doing, Dai? Painting yourself as the saviour, telling my boy these lies.* He never wanted Thanh dead—it stands to reason he would try to mold a king after his own desires instead.

Khine made a dismissive noise. "Worries for another day. Someone said you've been coughing. Let me look at your tongue."

There was a moment of silence.

"Hmm. I may have to come back later. At least you've still got both legs. What's *your* excuse for not going outside? Forget baby rats. You're as pale as the moon's behind."

"Someone has to keep Lahei company."

"I won't argue with you, but for your health you need to do more than just hide indoors. Let's change those bandages, Lahei." A pause. "Looks like the salve's doing its work. It's—"

There was a loud scream, followed by a flurry of apologies from Khine.

"My clumsy fingers—just keep your eyes closed, Lahei. It's just bitterbark and mint. The sting will go away soon." He reappeared around the corner and beckoned for me to step forward.

I entered the room. Lahei had her hands on her head, eyes screwed shut. Khine was holding Thanh close, whispering something in his ear.

Subdued, Thanh barrelled into my arms in silence. I held him there, as if the hollow between the shadows of my body could protect him from the chaos I had made of our lives. Once, that cocoon was all it took. Would that I could turn back time to such simplicity. We exchanged no words, not a single sound—I couldn't even weep freely. All too soon, Khine placed a hand on my arm, and I pulled away from my boy, the second time in a year that I had parted from him after only a few heartbeats. If you don't understand how painful that moment was, then I won't waste your time trying to explain. We don't need love to breathe, but without it we would wither soon enough, like trees bereft of sunlight.

If I cannot write poetry, I can at least tell the truth.

I kept one step behind Khine on the way to the infirmary tents. Months apart made him feel like a stranger. Months apart, after saying goodbye the way I did.

"Khine..." I began.

"Not here," he whispered in Zirano.

We entered the tent in silence. Karia looked up and then turned away just as quickly. Close. We were too close. I should've never come here. I forced my feelings down and watched as Khine approached Karia, asking her to stabilize one of the soldiers, a man who looked like he had run straight into the wrong end of a spear. He reached over for a pot of salve.

"Doctor," I said. "Let me do it."

He still wouldn't meet my eyes, but I saw him nod towards the patient. I opened the lid and smeared a handful on the wound. It resembled a black crater that oozed yellow liquid along the edges, the sort of wound that Khine would leave unbandaged for a few days to give it space to breathe. The man screamed when I dabbed the salve over his skin, straining as Karia held him tight.

"Well, that's good," Khine told him once he was done howling long enough to catch his breath.

"What the hell do you mean?" the man gasped, tears in his eyes.

"Means your nerves still work and you've got a healthy set of lungs." He prodded the leg. "Does it sting?"

"Of course it does!"

"We'll see how it is tonight. Maybe I don't have to get my saw out."

"You've got a poor sense of humour, Doctor."

"I like motivating my patients to prove me wrong." He patted the man's leg, eliciting another howl. "I think we can bandage it now," he told me, eyes not meeting mine. "Loosely."

"I hear we may have a case of Rat Pox in camp," the man said as I worked on his leg. "Tell me you have it under control, Doctor."

"I've been back for an hour," Khine replied. "Give me more time."

"I don't think we *have* time. One of the guards was telling everyone about it. They said it started in the officers' area and now it's spreading."

"An hour, spirits help me," Khine repeated, glancing back at me. I wasn't sure if he was amused or irritated.

The camp saved the serious cases for Khine, and we spent the next few hours stitching raw flesh, cutting off rotten bits, flushing out grime and pus and grit. Hours of mending what I could break in mere seconds with a sword—an irony I tried not to sit with. Healing is harder than causing harm. I mostly took orders from Karia—Khine was clearly avoiding me. Perhaps he, too, had thought he would never see me again. Perhaps the lies we tell ourselves are so flimsy they make the fates laugh.

It was late evening by the time we were done. All but a handful of soldiers had returned to their tents—the ones that remained were drunk on herbs in the far corner. I wiped my forehead, realized I was mixing my own sweat with someone else's blood. I found a towel and cleaned my hands as best as I could. Even with that, I could still smell the iron inside my nose. I gazed at the sleeping soldiers. They were Kag, not my own people, but I wondered if the scene here was mirrored somewhere inside Yu-yan's gates. So many dead, and dying, while I was *distracted*. Dai was right.

Khine took a moment to slump onto a stool. "You look like you need a good meal," Karia said, passing by with an armful of linens.

"We still have this false plague to deal with," he grumbled. "The last thing I want is the general scrutinizing our work."

She gave a small smile. "Lahei says they're well aware you're only here for the prince."

He gave a lopsided grin.

"It doesn't concern you? They said they're watching you closely."

Khine ran his hands over his face. "Dai needs a surgeon, and his options out here are few and far between," he said, at length. "We've spoken about this.

He's confident in his guards, and he doesn't take me seriously. Once he's conquered Yu-yan, *then* perhaps I will no longer be useful."

"We have to move before then," Karia whispered. "It will be harder to get Thanh out once he's inside the city."

Khine got up, motioning to me. "It's time to make our rounds. Pox victims need prompt treatment."

"I'm glad to see you safe," I whispered as we left the tent. "I wasn't sure what happened after Onni."

"I promised I would find him, with or without you."

His words made my insides knot.

He took a deep breath. "I'm afraid to ask what you did to get in here," he continued.

"I only killed two soldiers."

"Ah. *Only.*"

"I'm here now," I said. "You don't have to stay any longer. If Dai knows you've betrayed him—"

"Weren't you listening? He already knows. He doesn't care."

"Only because he doesn't know *I'm* here."

"Of all the times you've told me to let you do things alone," he pointed out, "when has it ever succeeded?"

"Khine..."

"Let me do this for you first," he said. "We can talk about other things later."

We fell silent as we presented ourselves to the gate guards. "Better take care of that Rat Pox, Doctor," one said. "Everyone's panicking." They directed us to the lodge, where the guards let us walk through without even a second glance.

On the second floor, Khine went to peek into Lahei's room. "Sleeping," he whispered. He closed the door and pulled a stool in front of it. Then, drawing me aside, he led me to the far end of the corridor, where he knocked twice.

"Is that you, Khine?" Thanh whispered. He opened the door a crack. "Mother," he croaked.

I took his left hand without saying anything. The flesh where his ring finger had been was raw and pink, though the scar looked cleaner than I expected. I closed the rest of his fingers over the stump and pressed his fist against my heart.

"You knew," Khine said.

"They gave me the finger back in Onni," I whispered. "I thought they had him in the north."

"That's why you left me." His voice had a thoughtful note to it now.

"I didn't want to say why. I couldn't. What right did I have to ask for more, with this life and what it demands for the people in it?" I showed him Thanh's hand. "He will never grow it back. He can never hold a sword as effectively, or—"

"It's fine, Mother," Thanh broke in. "I don't even remember it hurting that much. And I don't care about fighting."

"Are they treating you well?" I asked, struggling to contain myself.

"They're kind," Thanh said. He furrowed his brow. "But I'm bored."

"Bored but alive," I agreed. I cupped his face with my hands. "You've lost weight."

"You have, too, Mother. You look different." His face suddenly grew serious, and he pulled away from me, his hands dropping to his sides. "They said that Father means to kill me. Is it true?"

I shook my head. "No." *Not anymore.*

"But—"

"The nation is in chaos. Everyone is waging war against everyone and nothing will be as it was, but . . . we love you, child. That has never changed."

I don't know if he believed me, or if he understood exactly what I was trying to say. He looked different, too. Older. His skin had browned under the sun, and even his shoulders were a touch wider than I remembered. And there was a spark in his eyes, one that went beyond his years. I glanced at the mat, where he had placed a book he had been reading. *Memoirs from the Beginning of the Wolves' War.* My heart dropped.

My son was too young for this, too young to know the shadows that danced around us. I tried to place the image of him against the memory of his birth. How could this be the same infant that once fit so easily in my arms? I wouldn't even know where to begin to explain to him the tangled webs I had discovered in Burbatan. Do I follow my father's footsteps and keep them from him? Or do I tell him now and erase the last traces of his childhood?

I chose the coward's way out. "We're going to get you out of here soon. They're holding your father prisoner in the east. I'm going to our allies to get help for him. But you—you have to leave the kingdom."

The disappointment in his eyes was suddenly palpable.

"What do you mean leave?" Thanh asked. "You want me to abandon Jin-Sayeng?"

I studied his face. Why did my boy sound like he considered it a betrayal?

"To keep you safe."

"But this is *our* home," he said, incredulously.

I took a deep breath.

"Mother," he continued, "I can't just leave everyone behind. You're queen. I'm the crown prince. There was war when Grandfather was alive and now there's war out there again. People are suffering. They need us."

"I know, Thanh. I know. But *you* don't have to be here." I glanced at Khine. "He'll take care of you."

"But he—" he started. "He's just the camp surgeon. Mother, I'm needed here, because Jin-Sayeng is still in chaos. Dai says—"

It was as I feared. "Kaggawa has been feeding you nonsense."

He looked flustered. "It's not nonsense. He says that those of us who care about the nation should do something about it. And he's right. He..."

"My love," I said. "Don't you think it was Rysaran the Uncrowned's cares for the nation that set a mad dragon loose through our cities? Or that it was these same cares that drove his sister Ryia, or your grandfather Yeshin, to assassinations and blackmail and mass murder? I'm aware of Kaggawa's ideologies. He's masked them well, but deep down, it's the same. We start out believing we are chosen, but that isn't right at all. We choose ourselves, and in the process it inflates us, twists our minds, makes us think we are exalted above the rest and thus beyond reproach. We—"

"Tali," Khine warned. My voice was starting to rise, and Thanh's face had turned sheet white. There was terror in his eyes.

I took a deep breath. "I am queen and you are crown prince," I whispered. "It doesn't make us gods."

Thanh glanced down, his eyes skipping past the book on the floor.

"We can't stay here the whole night," Khine broke in, taking Thanh's wrist. "I believe your mother may have told them you have Rat Pox. I need to pretend you're under treatment. Cough."

Thanh managed a small one.

"Now spit into this bowl."

"Khine..."

"Spit."

I gazed at them both, Thanh's words echoing inside my head. My son was nearly nine; I could argue that he didn't really know what he was talking about.

But something about them made me consider the scene in front of me. Trying to grasp moments is as futile as reaching for the wind. I know that much, at least. When Khine's examination was over and it was time for us to return outside, I held Thanh and whispered an apology into his hair, so light I didn't think he even heard it. If there ever came a time that he learned the horrors I would rather remained in the darkness, I hoped he would at least remember this moment. *Remember, Thanh. I have so little else to give, but remember my love and let it shield you from the rest.*

CHAPTER ELEVEN

THE END OF THE ROAD

The lanterns were all out by the time we arrived at the infirmary tents. Khine made his way to the pump around the back to fill a bucket with water. I took a seat on a pile of sandbags, gazing up at the starless sky and thinking back to the conversation I just had with my son. My boy—somewhere along the way, my boy had grown up. Before I left, he was still easily distractible, still just as concerned about his toys as the nonsense in his books. How could a little over a year have done this?

The thoughts churned, like restless dogs trying to sleep.

Khine paused over the pump handle. "Back there…you said you wanted *him* to leave Jin-Sayeng."

"You did say you wanted me to let you do this, and he cannot stay here—not when the whole nation is like this."

He looked conflicted. I could tell he was trying not to lose his temper. "His freedom signals yours. Without your son's safety on the line, why do you have to stay here?"

"I can't just walk away, Khine."

"Because you're your father's daughter?"

I stared at him, wondering how often I'd said such words for him to be able to throw them back at me so easily. "Yes," I conceded. "And not for what you think. My father has done too much. I can't just close my eyes and pretend it has nothing to do with me."

"Does it?" he asked, exasperated. "You're not him."

I pressed my knuckles on my knees. "I know," I said.

He was quiet for a moment, before grumbling, "Yes. Well. Your nation has made it clear you have many faults, but choosing the easy way out has never been one of them."

"Are you complimenting me, sir?"

"Maybe." He gave me a grin before looking away.

"My son," I said, growing serious. "He's not the infant at my breast. Hasn't been for many years. He really... doesn't need me anymore."

"I can assure you, Tali—that is the furthest thing from the truth." He paused, gazing at the bucket at his feet. He must've been thinking about his own mother.

"I know," I said. "In a perfect world, I would agree with you. But it isn't a perfect world. All I have now is the hope that Lord Huan would give me an army, that his alliance could forge others for me for when I ride back to Oren-yaro. I need people loyal to me, not my elders."

"He's at war with Kaggawa."

"I've noticed."

"And you believe you can rally everyone under you and Rai, even after you've rescinded your claim to the throne?"

"It won't stop other wars from breaking out in every corner of Jin-Sayeng. It will be like the War of the Wolves all over again—every region forced to pick a side, with everyone secretly trying to plant their rump on the throne. Like throwing a hunk of meat into a pack of starving dogs. It will be nothing but chaos. Peace will be a long time coming." I gave a grim smile. "You're wrong about me. I *would* choose the easy way out if I knew what it was. If there was one. But there isn't."

Khine returned to work at the pump. Water sloshed into the bucket, spilling down the sides. He noticed too late and swore under his breath. He straightened his back and turned to me again. "Do you remember Kyo-orashi, the day before we all went into the arena with the dragon? Agos thought he was going to die there. I was to stay back and let him deal with the beast to save you. He asked me to tell you what he felt. Said if he could pluck each and every one of the stars from the sky for you, he would. He believed you shouldn't waste another moment of your life with that prick Rayyel, because you deserve better." Khine swallowed. "I undermined his plan."

"It was a lousy plan," I said. "The one you replaced it with wasn't any better."

"I don't disagree. I wasn't thinking." He paused, scratching the back of his head. "I told you I could be selfish."

"You...didn't stop me when I chose him over you." Would I have gone to him instead, if he had? It was a question that had haunted me since. The other way around, Agos might still be alive, and Khine the one dead.

"You weren't mine to stop. For all I knew, you loved him, too." He cleared his throat. "But it's Jin-Sayeng that matters most to you. Listen to yourself telling me about overturning a system that has kept this nation running for hundreds of years, simply because it's the only way you can make it work. It's madness, but you'll do it anyway, or die trying. Neither of us should've expected less from the woman we loved. It's why we loved you, after all. At least why I do." He sighed. "I will take you to Yu-yan. I don't want to, but I will."

"Thank you, Khine," I managed, trying hard to ignore what his words made me feel.

"I need to make more salve, anyway," he said, in that voice that could mean anything.

We left while it was still dark. Karia accompanied us all the way to the gate. I observed her interactions with Khine quietly, and felt my stomach stir. I pinpointed it as revulsion over my feelings. I didn't own the man. What he did with his time was none of my business. Still, I couldn't help but notice how touchingly tender he was with her, a stark reminder of how he had been when we first met. Nor did he limit these interactions with her. On the way out, Khine clasped one of the guards on the back. "If she needs any help..."

"Of course, Doctor," the guard said, returning the gesture. "We're all fond of Karia here." The man flashed her a grin, one which she didn't return. Rayyel's sister, through and through. If I didn't believe it before, I did now.

We went up the road, Khine's box of empty herb pots jingling on his back.

"How did you manage to make Dai give you this much freedom?" I asked, in an effort to chase away the awkward silence. "The last time we saw each other, he wanted to kill you."

"He—or the soul he shares his body with, at least—is an intelligent man. I don't know for sure what sort of discourse they had about me, but I think they decided it was better to have me on their side. It helped that their surgeon had gone missing."

"Missing," I repeated.

He gave a wry smile.

"Don't tell me the man is under the Yu-yan River somewhere."

"Heavens, no. I just gave him enough coin to run off to Fuyyu. He didn't like having to treat foreigners, especially ones hired to attack his own country-men. He had an apprentice and I paid that one off, too."

"And where, pray, did a man like you get all that money?"

"Karia is related to one of the old rice lords in the area, someone opposed to Dai's war," he said. "He provided all the funds."

"Anino is with him, I assume."

"Maybe."

"Khine—"

"I know. You haven't got a hair on your head that could hurt that child, or any child. It's the people around you I worry about."

"They do give you that impression," I said. "I can only guess what they'll do to my son."

"If it's assassins you're worried about, don't be. There's a few of us who are watching him. Karia. Larson, whom I believe you're acquainted with. A num-ber of the other soldiers."

"Do they know he's the prince?"

"No. Dai wants it kept a secret from most of the soldiers. I've let it slip he's the son of a rice lord that Dai is holding hostage, and that if the boy is alive by the end of summer, there's a reward waiting for them. A tangible reward, one they don't have to die for...higher in value for people like that. Dai doesn't know it, but we've not left Thanh unguarded since I arrived. If not for Karia, you wouldn't even have gotten close to him."

I must've been staring at him too hard, because he suddenly looked away, a hand on the back of his head. I turned to counting my steps in the blue-grey darkness and heard him take a deep breath.

"So," Khine said. "You were going to tell me about what had happened after we last saw each other. I recall you giving me a taste of my own medicine."

"How does it feel?"

"Awful. And uncalled for."

"I'm not sure you'll like the outcome, in any case. Anya's dead."

He grunted. "I told her to go home. She wouldn't listen. That damn woman. Did you do it?"

"Ozo."

"Jiro...Jiro won't take this well." He swallowed. "What else happened out there?"

"I met my mother."

His eyes flashed. "I thought she died giving birth to you."

"I thought so, too." I turned the memories in my head, hating even speaking them out loud. Hearing all of it shamed me. "But it was worse. The spells in my father's study had addled her brain. He *had* been conspiring with mages this whole time. With mages, and his lords and bannermen, none of whom were ever loyal to *me*. My father died, but he remained in charge. And they made it all happen. Everything. Chiha. Anino. *Agos*. Agos was Ozo's bastard son and they placed him beside me solely to be my confidant."

"Agos is Ozo's bastard," he repeated, blinking. "I *thought* Ozo seemed familiar."

"They wanted to tear my marriage apart, damn the consequences, and they made sure they gave us everything we needed to make it look like we were doing it ourselves. They gave us enough rope to hang ourselves with."

Khine frowned. "A dead man...creating a plan to be carried out after his death, one that hinges on *your* actions..." He trailed off in disbelief, and he didn't even know the half of it.

"I was a mark," I said with a smile. "A mark who didn't always do what was expected. But Yeshin had supporters who are all still very much alive, all brilliant minds who are waiting for their moment under the sun. They worked together to anticipate my next move, whatever that may have been. Agos and Chiha alone created the scandals necessary to push us whichever way they desired. If Thanh had been Agos's, Ozo would've probably whisked him away as soon as the trial's results were announced. Let Ryia's retaliation be the reason to declare war on the Ikessars. If Thanh had been there and everything played out as it should, I'm convinced Ozo would've gifted Yuebek with my son's head."

Khine looked almost impressed. He of all people knew the feeling of a con being carried to fruition, all the little things that had to go just right. Hard enough for a man to pull off, let alone a dead man. I wasn't sure how I felt about him admiring my father's handiwork.

"My father's instructions to all of us ensured a skeleton of sorts," I continued. "A backbone, to keep us all running in the same direction."

"And this whole time, your father relied on your obedience to his will?"

"He relied on it, but he knew, even early on, that I would grow up to be just as stubborn as he was. I'm told it plagued him for his last few years."

"But he expected it," Khine said.

"Yes. Is that so hard to believe?"

"From what I've heard of your father? It is. My understanding is that he was suspicious, given to declaring everyone but himself incompetent. Knowing what he knew about you, why would he create plans spanning decades that would rely on *your* obedience? Something's not right."

We continued to walk. I tried hard to focus on the explosion of birdsong around us, the feel of the cool morning breeze, and not the growing dread inside of me. I didn't want to talk about what my father truly wanted. Even admitting it to myself stung.

"What was she like?" Khine asked, breaking the silence. "Your mother."

"A woman caught in an updraft." I turned away, my attention drifting towards the column of black smoke rising in the distance. There was sufficient sunlight for me to see two trails of it.

Khine swore under his breath. Without a word, he bolted down the road. I watched Khine disappear down the hill for a few conflicted moments. After what felt like a hundred knives running through my chest, I hurtled after him.

The smoke was coming from two overturned wagons, sacks of rice spilling into the ditches. Whatever animals had been pulling the wagon—horses or oxen, I couldn't tell—were gone, the harness lines cut. Khine stood in the middle of several corpses, facing down two Kag soldiers. Both were older men, with white stubble equally covering their balding heads and faces. Their skin was red, suntanned.

"Go back to your herbs, Doctor," the Kag said, his Jinan scraping like sandpaper. "Nothing to see here."

His companion sniggered. "Unless you're planning to report us?"

"General Dai was adamant the commoners be left alone," Khine said. "It's one of his few rules."

The first soldier gave an exaggerated bow. "These aren't just commoners. These were spies."

I came up behind the furthest one. He didn't hear me, didn't notice I was there. His attention was on Khine, his jaw muscles tense. One hand hovered over his sword.

"What proof do you have?" Khine asked.

"Don't need proof," the other soldier said. "They're carrying rice. Only the enemy eats rice."

"Bland, disgusting Jin food," his companion agreed.

"The villages are starving," Khine said. "Some of the rice lords would've sent relief."

"Like I said, aiding the enemy," the soldier said with a smug grin.

"It sounds to me like you consider everyone the enemy." Khine's voice was barely a whisper.

"But that's true, isn't it?" the soldier asked. "If you're not with us, you're clearly against us. And when you all look alike—"

I slid my grass-cutter across his throat, cutting his voice box before he could finish his sentence. As his body dropped to the ground, I turned to the other one, who came barrelling towards me with his heavy sword. Heavy sword, heavy armour, and all he saw was a woman who got lucky. I tripped him with my foot and we both came crashing down the ditch, into the muddy field. I stabbed him in the neck before he could recover.

I kicked the bleeding body away and crawled out of the ditch. Flies were already starting to gather over it. Both kills had lasted less than a minute.

"You weren't going to talk your way out of that one," I said, before Khine could say anything.

He looked at the dead soldiers. "I know."

"I don't like doing that," I continued.

"I know that, too."

"I'm not my father, Khine."

He looked away, and I felt my senses blur as we returned to the dusty road. I felt that stone wall come between us again.

"Lofty dreams," Khine finally said, as if answering an unasked question.

"I'm sorry?"

"Belfang's words. He was right, you know. There was a time I looked down on people like him, people who were... resigned to their lot in life. People who had no desire to make something better for themselves and the world around them. But what did that do for me? I couldn't even make my own dreams come true. And then you showed up, and I—"

Thunder rumbled overhead. Grey clouds were beginning to gather and I could feel the wind growing colder. I shivered, my skin prickling.

His mouth quirked into a smile. "At least it's not dragons."

"We should go before we're proven wrong," I said. My heart was racing, and I wasn't sure anymore if it was the fear of lightning or my nearness to Khine that was doing it. I showed up, and then what? *I am content as I am*, he had told me in Oka Shto, except he wasn't. It should've been clear to me from the beginning that Khine Lamang was a man who was forever at odds with himself. In him was ambition, tempered by reality. What did he really see in me?

The road turned into a small field, wedged between several low hills. We climbed up a path that bordered a wide stream, entering a copse of maple and elm trees. There were still patches of compact snow on the ground here, a signal that we were further north than I thought we were. "I'm surprised rice grows out here at all," Khine said. "You're probably going to say it's got something to do with the dragons."

"Of course it's the dragons," I replied. "It's too cold out here otherwise, but they've changed the soil somehow. How far are we from Yu-yan?"

"A couple of hours on the river should take you straight to it. It's not far." *Now* the lightning flashed. I clenched my fists and closed my eyes as the first shower of rain arrived—what seemed like rain. It sounded like falling pebbles. We sought shelter under a tree further up the path as the hail poured down around us, covering the ground with patchy white layers. I tucked my hands under my arms, shivering from the sudden blast of cold air, and glanced at him, at his face. With the beard, he looked more sombre than the cheerful man I met in Shang Azi. We all had our masks. It was only that his had never been so clear before.

"I failed my last year's exams on purpose because I was angry with my teacher," Khine said, out of nowhere.

I stared back at him patiently, waiting. Listening.

"And I was angry at Jia. She was carrying my child. She went to him without my knowledge and had it . . . taken care of before I even knew it existed." He swallowed. "I was angry and I didn't think that she was young and frightened, and that her father would've beaten her if he found out. I thought she understood that I would've taken care of her. I thought she did what she did because she didn't really love me. And Tashi Reng Hzi—after all his talks about the value of life—couldn't even let me know? He said it was her choice, that my decision wouldn't have made a damn difference, but all I heard were the words of a hypocrite. I made it about me when it wasn't. So I failed the exam in vengeance."

His voice had cracked. He was staring at his own hands.

"Khine..."

"It sounds so ridiculous now," he continued. "Like a joke you tell about someone else. It's in the past. We all make mistakes. I was young, too. And stupid. So stupid." The hatred hissed through his teeth. "But you see the result of one little mistake? Do you see what I did? If I had passed that exam, my mother might've been safe in Anzhao City before Yuebek got his hands on the villagers. She'd still be alive. My family...wouldn't be scattered across two continents. My sister—my sister is involved in *your* messy politics."

"I can ask Rayyel to let her go, if you want."

"And he'd listen, no doubt," he snapped. And then, realizing he'd raised his voice, he turned quickly away. "It's—that's not it. But don't you see? You have the power to do these things—I don't. People like you run the world. I hate it, but I understand it. And I don't know if I followed you all this way because of that. I've been seeking penance all this time. Is that what I see when I look at you? A chance to redeem myself? I don't know if..." He moved as if to reach for me.

The hail stopped. He pulled away, hands balled into fists, and stepped out onto the path. We reached the hut, ice crunching under our soles. There were herbs hanging from ropes strung between trees. The sudden turn of weather had sent about half to the ground.

Khine began to swear as he bent over to pick up the wilted leaves. I came up to help him.

"All I know is I'm here." He wiped a hand over his knee. "Helping your son, but also helping a man who by all rights is your enemy, helping his people because...that was always when it was simplest for me. When I help others. A direction in my otherwise pointless life. Because I've let my own selfishness and arrogance ruin the lives of the people I'm supposed to protect. Now I've been a thief and a con artist for so long I don't even know if I can be anything else."

"That's not true," I whispered.

"It is," he insisted. "I've created my own prison, Tali, and I can't let you be the key to get me out of it. You have power. I don't. What if Belfang was right? What if I'm like the rest of them, just waiting to take advantage of a good opportunity? I've seen what this world does to you. I've given you enough grief over it. But you can't help what you are and I can't change what you represent so perhaps what I need...what we both need...is for me to see you from another perspective. Perhaps then I could let you go. That would be a start, wouldn't it?"

I felt a twinge of pain, but not an unexpected one.

He dropped the leaf he was holding, shaking his head. "These are ruined. I'm going to have to go get more." Without waiting for my reply, he walked straight into the forest.

CHAPTER TWELVE

THE DANCE OF
THE LIVING

ᛏᚢᛗ

An entire winter of habitation had left the hut in a state of disarray. Even if I hadn't known Khine was living there, I might've guessed it. There was a mortar and pestle on the single table, and more bundles of dried herbs hanging from the ceiling. Empty jars that needed to be washed, clay pots that smelled like rancid spices. Two thick books on the windowsill—manuals written in Zirano. Gifts from Dai, no doubt. Or Myar? I couldn't tell how much of Dai's actions were his and how much were those of the soul who resided in him. Perhaps there was a reason we didn't accept such things in Jin-Sayeng. Souls, the *agan*, fabrics and streams...it was easier to just name things you could see.

I glanced at the floor. A single blanket lay next to the firepit. It looked slept in, with no sign of a pillow or anything more comfortable. A single woolen blanket, to ward off the cold. Something about that stood out. He had been here for months. Why did I think there would be a mat at least, or two?

The mess started to grate at me. In an effort to quiet my nerves, I picked up a broom from the corner and swept the floor. When there was still no sign of Khine, I went to fetch firewood from the shed and stacked it on the firepit in a square, one log on top of the other. Kindling in the middle, tinder at the base. I struck flint with a dagger and it caught on fire almost immediately.

I found an iron pot and filled it from the rain barrel outside. The water was cold, swimming in ice pellets. I took a quick drink before placing it on the fire. With two handfuls of rice, it was full; I stirred with a ladle, trying not to think about earlier. The spilled rice, the dead men, the flies that whizzed around the bloated bodies. The soldiers, dead by my hand. Realities of a war of which I was the center. Khine saw it clearly. Thinking about the words he had uttered was painful, but I needed to learn to accept them.

I heard a rustling sound from outside. I got up to open the door, expecting Khine. Instead, horses appeared, carrying Yu-yan soldiers. Warlord Ojika's banner, with the brace of yoked oxen, flew over their heads.

"You said this was Kaggawa's doctor's hut," one called, striking a man. A peasant, dressed in farmer's clothes, stumbled forward. His face was covered in bruises.

"It is," the man insisted. "I've helped him myself a few times. His assistant stayed at the village whenever they went here. I don't know who this is. Please. I'm telling the truth."

"Miss," the soldier said, turning to me. "Where is he?"

"I have no idea what you're talking about," I said calmly. "What's with all the screaming? Do you want to rouse the neighbourhood?"

The soldier laughed, dismounting from his horse. "No neighbourhood for hours, miss," he said, tipping his head forward. "We're ridding the land of pests. Are you one of those pests?"

"Does Lord Huan know you've been harassing villagers?"

He laughed again. "Helping the enemy is treason."

I tried not to shudder at how his words reflected Dai's mercenaries. "You cowards have retreated behind city walls," I said. "How do you expect people to survive? Kaggawa pays well and treats his men fairly. Can you say the same for your warlord?"

The soldier reached for my wrist, yanking me closer to him. He drew a dagger.

"Lord Huan," I repeated. "If he learns of this, you know what he'll do."

"Captain—" one of the soldiers called out.

The captain's face tightened. "If I kill you when I'm done, Lord Huan won't know a damn thing."

I smiled. "You think I'm alone?"

"Search the area," the captain said, gesturing at his soldiers. "I'll show this woman exactly how she's supposed to regard her betters."

"They were right about you, then," I hissed. "Warlord Ojika forced himself into this land. No wonder you're faced with rebellion. You think it ends with me? Your royals are embroiled in a pissing match in the east, the Sougen is in chaos...and you're worried about putting some woman in her place? Put your priorities in order!"

"It's clear, Captain," a soldier broke in. "But there's tracks leading away from here."

"Find him. And take care of her."

"I should remind you, Captain," I said, "that Lord Huan detests mindless killing. Surely you've heard of what he did to the soldier who disobeyed his orders several years back. The cage. The ants. The man screamed for days, I heard."

I saw the doubt flit across his face. "How do you know this?"

"Everyone knows it."

"No, they don't," he said, yanking me so hard I could feel the blood pounding through my wrist.

I looked up. "All right," I conceded. "Perhaps they *don't*. But I do. What else can I tell you? Ah. Lord Huan once punished a man for forgetting to put his belt on properly. The knot, he said, was inside out. He made the man run barefoot around the barracks in the middle of summer, hard enough that he died a day later. Lord Huan felt awful about it, but he knows that all it takes is a reputation for tolerance, and..."

"Captain," the soldier said behind him. "She's right. I've heard Lord Huan say such things."

"I know," the captain hissed. "But this is classified information."

"She must be a mistress of his," the soldier whispered. "We can't take the chances, Captain. We'll all be punished if—"

The captain gave a roar, dropping my wrist and shoving the soldier aside. "We've got to ride back to the village," he snapped. "No proof, no inquiry. Quickly!"

They mounted their horses and thundered back down the path. I approached the peasant, who remained kneeling on the ground. I touched his head. It was bleeding.

"Come," I said. "I'll fix you up."

"Thank you," the man gasped. "They killed my friends. They're all the same...murderers, all of them." He wiped tears from his eyes, leaning against me as he staggered towards the hut. I left him on the deck and returned with bandages.

"I'm taking a ship to the Kag," he continued as I wrapped his wounds. "There's nothing left for Jin-Sayeng. The people who are supposed to be taking care of us...aren't. You were right about Kaggawa. He *is* fair. And committing treason. What kind of a damn nation is this, where a traitor offers better than our queen?"

"It'll be over soon," I said.

"I like your optimism, but I don't believe it will," the man said. "It's just starting. It'll get worse before it gets better."

He left it at that. I finished bandaging the rest of his wounds, apologizing for the lack of salve. He shrugged it off. "Give my regards to the doctor," he said. "And if you're wise, you'll get out while you still can."

"I don't think those soldiers will be back," I told him.

"That's not what I meant," he said as he waved goodbye.

The rice was burning. I returned inside to remove it from the fire, but I didn't eat anything—I didn't really have the appetite. Instead, I slept, dreaming the dreams of the damned.

I woke up to darkness and the sound of crickets. The fire had died and a black sky hovered where the sun had been. I was still alone. The rice remained where I left it, a cold, hard lump inside the pot.

Wrapping the blanket around my shoulders, I put my boots on, hoping the moon would give enough light. I should've looked for Khine earlier. What if the soldiers had found him along the way? If he had encountered a wild animal, or fallen into the river, or...

I opened the door. Khine was asleep on the porch with his back to the wall. He looked both troubled and at peace—as if, having wandered the woods the whole afternoon, he had decided that the threshold was where he would rather be. I knew, because I felt the same way. How many times had we tried to say goodbye to each other over the last year? How many times had it failed?

You still have to face the hours between now and the day you die.

Maybe it was the silence and the cold, and the pressing shadows around us, so deep it felt like there was no one else on earth. Maybe the relief swept everything else away but that one thing, that fragile, unsustainable thing, a blade of grass on parched earth. I wrapped my heart around it, begging it not to leave, to stay another day. Tomorrow—anything could happen tomorrow. But today? This night? *Oh, gods, let me have just this night.*

I walked up to drape the blanket over him. His eyes opened. Without a word, I slipped beside him, pressing my lips against his. Despite everything he had said earlier, his fingers trailed over my cheeks as he returned the kiss, slow and lingering. I didn't really know what I was doing—my whole body was shaking, but that didn't seem to stop me. I wanted to taste him with a fervour I had never known in my life.

"I'm frightened," Khine said when we stopped for breath.

"I am, too," I told him.

"If I don't have you, I could never lose you."

"I know." I grazed his chin with my teeth before whispering into his ear. "But my love, I think it's too late."

"We could always...stop." But even as he said that, he traced a line across my cheekbone, refusing to meet my eyes.

"Khine..."

"Don't."

"You are the only thing I have ever wanted that has nothing to do with this damn life."

He gazed back, disbelieving. Unwilling to understand. Whatever he saw in me, it was not a woman who would love him back.

"I can go," I continued. "If that's what you really want. I just thought you should know. I can go if—"

"No," Khine breathed. "Please, Tali. I can't bear that, not anymore." He pulled me down to him for another kiss. Still hesitant, still restrained, like I was something fragile he could break. I noticed him fumbling with my collar and loosened my robes to help him. For a man who seemed so sure of everything else—of his cons, of the care for his patients, of his witty remarks—he seemed terribly uncertain about how to touch a woman. Or perhaps he just didn't want to presume. I tested it by taking his hand, placing it where it needed to be as I coaxed him to follow my lead, and had my answer. The cold air stung, but his fingers were warm. His eyes never left me, as if he was watching my reaction, listening to the sound of my breath quicken. It didn't take long. I sought his mouth as my body trembled over his, and felt his own, surprised gasp.

I settled into his lap, untying the knot in his hair. Unbound, the black strands didn't go past his shoulders, but the added shadow gave his expression a gravity that made me shiver. His fingers slipped down my bare back. I shrugged the shirt off his shoulders before I kissed his neck, allowing my teeth to graze his jaw. He responded to my attention, his breathing growing sharp. "Out here?" he asked. "Aren't you scared of monsters?"

"Not when I'm with you."

The answer shocked him into silence. I could feel his heart racing under my fingertips as I touched the faintest traces of the hair on his chest, could feel him swallow as I undid his belt, freeing the rest of him. There was no room for doubt anymore. Love as duty, love as distraction...I knew these things well. Love for itself was new, unexpected. Did he know what I meant with the things I said? That I understood the danger in this lay not in who I was or what was about to come, but what the past had done to us, how we had once nearly drowned in love and somehow sworn we never would again?

Broken promises. The stubborn never learn. I lowered myself onto him, falling into his arms as he filled me. We both wanted deeper, wanted that water over our heads, the sensation of losing yourself in another even if it came at a cost. We knew, we both knew, and it no longer mattered. Nothing else in the world mattered. We moved together, breathless against each other's mouths in a sensation that went beyond pleasure—a far-reaching darkness where I could no longer tell where he ended and I began. Heat and belonging, in a shot of darkness; I bit his shoulder to stop myself from screaming his name.

He had no such reservations. "Tali," he gasped, kept gasping. As if we had melted into each other, leaving behind nothing but whispers, echoes of the broken in a world where nothing could ever be enough.

"Damn you," Khine whispered, long after we were done, wrapped up in that single blanket on the floor next to the fire. "I always knew you wanted to kill me. I just wasn't sure how." He laced his fingers through mine, watching the shadows dance over our skin.

I didn't answer at once. My thoughts were very far away.

"Do we head to Yu-yan in the morning?"

It wasn't what he was really asking. I pressed my head on his chest, breathing in the salt-sweat of his scent. "Maybe another day," I whispered. "We could use some sleep. And food. And your herbs won't pickle themselves or whatever it is you to do them."

He turned my hand over, pressing the fingers of his other hand over my wrist, where bruises were starting to show. A frown flitted over his lips. "Did I hurt you?"

I smiled.

"I can't be sure," he coughed.

I placed his hand over my cheek. "That was the soldiers from earlier. But I made sure they won't be back. Even if they do, I'll take care of it." I allowed my fingers to drift over his beard, his face. Even flushed from lovemaking, I still couldn't get over the feel of him.

He smiled at my touch. "And how are you planning to do that?"

"Maybe I'll dig a moat, put up some spikes...you wouldn't happen to have some crocodiles handy?"

"I saw some up in the river in Oren-yaro. I decided to leave them alone. I've had enough of things with sharp teeth."

"I suppose I'll have to fight them, since you're entirely useless with a sword."

"As you are with a broom."

"Ingrate. In case you haven't noticed, I swept your hut for you."

"I did notice. Did you realize you're supposed to dust *out*, and not *in*? Corners aren't for gathering dust heaps."

I smiled, tracing my fingers over the scar on his shoulder. The skin was puckered where the wound had healed, a lighter pink against his tanned skin. I didn't look much better. "Yours and mine match," I said, trying to drown out the memory of him getting those scars in the first place.

"They can put us on the same shelf." He brushed the hair from my face and took another ragged breath. "Gods, Tali. I'm dreaming. I just know it."

"I see. Are these sort of dreams, perchance, a frequent occurrence?"

He smirked. "More often than I'll ever admit."

"And here I was thinking you're the sort of man better suited for sainthood."

"Not all men are like your husband, Tali."

"That's a low blow, Lamang. And you certainly seemed to have done a commendable job pretending *you* were."

"Now you flatter me. You yourself have mentioned I've been slipping. And I admit...if that beast back in the Ruby Grove hadn't interrupted us..."

"This would have happened sooner?" I laughed. "You're such an optimist."

"Not an optimist. Just a fool. I'm still almost sure I'm going to wake up in a puddle of my own drool in the morning."

"That might not be entirely inaccurate."

"And I must've already committed a number of crimes I could get executed for."

I knew he was still jesting, but I found the tears stinging my eyes as I shook my head. "No, Khine," I said, my voice growing serious. "I won't let that happen. Ever."

He pulled me into his arms, and I felt him press his lips on the top of my head, a faint reflection of that night we spent back in Anzhao, the night in the shed. There was safety in his embrace. Acceptance. I fell into the kind of sleep that wrapped you in warmth and pulled you deep into solace, the sort that made you feel like you never wanted to wake up again.

But I did wake, to the sound of frying garlic, which Khine was cooking in a pan with rice and some eggs he must've grabbed from the village while I slept. I watched him go through those now-familiar motions, trying to burn every moment into my mind—how he paused to remove an eggshell from the bowl, or stared thoughtfully through the window as he stirred with the ladle. How he would look up once in a while to gaze at me in silence, his expression fire to light my veins.

A day, I told him. I wanted it to be two. Three. A lifetime. After years of lies and treachery, of believing one thing and realizing it was nothing but a story I told myself, I knew that to fall into this again was the greatest mistake. I remembered what Nor once said during our trip through the Sougen with Dai, a brief remark when the subject of Rayyel came up. "You give too much. You should have held back. We all need to hold back if we are to survive this unforgiving life." After everything Ozo had told me, I knew now that it was a sentiment they all shared back in Oren-yaro.

But it didn't feel like a mistake. It felt like the one right decision I'd made in my life. Crossing the chasm didn't seem to throw a wedge into what we were before. Things remained as they were, as effortless, with one difference: Where there was once fleeting touches and brief embraces, he now reached for my hand often. He would draw me to him and kiss me hard enough that it was clear he, too, wanted time to stop.

We gathered herbs, made salve, picked mushrooms to eat with our rice and strips of dried buffalo meat. He showed me how to grind dried herbs and how to sweep properly, which somehow resulted with us on the floor in a tangle of dust and shredded leaves. "You *are* hopeless," he chuckled, wiping dirt off my face. I grabbed his shirt with both hands.

"Never forget me," I whispered.

He laughed, misunderstanding. "And if I say no, you'll strangle me, I'm guessing."

"No, I mean—" I pulled him down to me.

He saw the expression on my face and grew sombre.

"Just say it," I said. "It doesn't have to be true."

He took my hands in his and kissed them. "Never, Tali," he swore.

I closed my eyes, wishing I could promise the same thing, knowing I couldn't. Knowing the dance of the living means we breathe in the air until it is all gone and we fall on the wayside and the world learns to dance without us. What would it have looked like if I spent the last eight years like this? To know happiness so unreal, my days would've been spent worrying over losing it someday? Looking at it that way, I supposed eight years would look a lot like twenty. All I had was the one day, and it was almost over.

We could own nothing and still have everything.

CHAPTER THIRTEEN

THE USURPER'S DOMAIN

ᒣᛉᎣᎧ

A s much as I wanted to linger in the hours of that second night, morning came with abandon. We left the hut just as the dawn swept the sky with traces of red and orange. We took a trail that wound around the hill. A few hours later, we reached the edge of the river, where a boat was docked next to a tree.

"You surprise me, Lamang," I said.

"You're saying that *just* now?"

"Someone has to put you in your place."

"I *am* in my place." He gave me a knowing look.

I pretended to sniff. "Barefoot in mud?"

"You don't look much better yourself." He clambered into the boat after me, handing me an oar. "But this suits you."

"Maybe." I gazed up at the sky, closing my eyes as the wind blew past us. It was tinged with the scent of pine, and leaves drenched in rainwater from last night. I felt Khine begin to row. Taking a deep breath, I dropped the oar into the water to do the same.

"Have you heard from your siblings?"

He frowned. "Changing the subject already."

"Give me this, Khine," I said. "Please."

"Inzali has written about Rai—"

"Not her," I grumbled. "Nothing to do with that life. Tell me about your family. Did Cho get back to Anzhao safely? How is Thao doing?"

"I don't know, Tali," Khine said truthfully. "It's been war, remember? I wouldn't even know how to get in touch with them if I knew where to find them."

"When you've freed Thanh, take him with you and go home, to your family."

I heard him draw a quick breath.

"What would I do there?" he asked, after a moment of silence. "Without Lo Bahn or Jiro Kaz's support..."

"They're thieves, Khine."

"As I am."

"You know you're worth more than that."

He laughed.

I placed the oar on my lap and turned around. "Look at you now. You're working as a surgeon, not a thief."

"But I *am* still a thief," he said. "The surgeon act is a ruse. Your son is the chest of gold."

"You told me you were helping those people because they needed it. A direction. You care for your patients, Khine. There will be something for you outside of this world. There has to be."

"You seem to have forgotten that I'm useless outside of war. Gaspar is hostile to foreigners, Dageis has their own physicians' guild..."

"Go home," I said. "Retake that exam. Finish your last year. Funds won't be a problem—I'm sure we can do something about that. You—"

"Stop, Tali," he replied. "I don't want to talk about this."

I took a deep breath. "I know you hate handouts. This isn't a handout. But I want you to show my son that there is a life outside of this. That he can be... more... than what he thought he was destined for."

"You sound like someone who's given up," he said.

"I haven't," I replied. "But let's be honest, Khine. I am tearing apart everything that has kept me alive all this time. If the Anyus agree to assist me, I will need to return to Oren-yaro. Perhaps the very action of showing up at the gates with an army will make them panic. Perhaps they will execute Rai before I get the chance to speak. Every attempt at diplomacy comes with the chance of causing chaos. It would fill me with despair, except..." I smiled. "If I know you're with my son, that you're both safe, that *you* are rebuilding your life again..." I trailed off, noticing the shadow on his brow. A part of me wondered if I hadn't tried hard enough to show him we didn't have a future together. And then, halt-ingly, *What if I'm not trying hard enough to make sure there is?*

I turned back to rowing. The boat continued to drift downriver. By mid-afternoon, we passed by the Yu-yan ridge. I spotted the Anyus' dragon-tower and felt my skin crawl. *Go*, my father had commanded. And despite everything, despite my insistence that I wanted nothing to do with him ever again, here I was.

"I've been trying to warn Lord Huan about the people turning into crea-tures," Khine said, breaking the silence.

"War and famine will only make things worse."

He grimaced. "Dai plans to besiege Yu-yan soon. I hope we can get Lord Huan to understand what this means. He doesn't want to listen. He thinks they're chil-dren's stories, that I've spent too much time listening to Kaggawa's folk tales."

We were so close to the city, it became hard to ignore the rift in the sky. I pointed. "And has he seen that? Have you experienced the flashes of *agan* out here?"

"He's seen it, and yet his eyes glaze over it as if he *can't*. He tells me I just need a good, long rest. Those flashes of light? He laughs and calls them thunder-storms." He glanced at the sky, as if expecting another; but apart from the rift, it remained achingly blue.

"Then he knows. Huan isn't the sort of person who denies something out of cowardice. He would have been ordered to keep silent."

"I suspected his father had something to do with it."

"Warlord Ojika was one of the men my father blackmailed into carrying out his wishes."

"So what makes you think he will agree to support you? If he's on Ozo and Yuebek's side, he could just send you back to Oren-yaro, all tied up like a pig for slaughter."

"Because there is nothing left to blackmail him with," I said. "I, on the other hand, know more about his son Eikaro than my father did. I have no plans to threaten Warlord Ojika—Eikaro is gone, if not dead, and I won't use him that way. I simply want to lay out Warlord Ojika's options and show him that being on my side is better than being against it."

We reached the shore and left the boat attached to broken pilings, remnants of Old Yu-yan. Before the Anyus' arrival, it had been an open city, spilling out along the riverbank and beyond. Now it lay behind walls, a fortress that could rival any of the other warlords' out to the east. A necessity, I was told last time, because of the dragons, but...

You would think that impending disaster was all it took to unite people. That we could learn to set aside our differences, and seizing power was less important than making sure there was a land to fight over by the end of it all. But I had seen enough after five years of rule not to be surprised. People would rather set fire to their own house than swallow their pride, and watch as the flames take them with it.

Khine led me to what appeared to be the gates to the guardsmen's barracks.

"Closer," he whispered, dropping his hand to my waist. Even after everything we had shared, I felt my cheeks flush.

"Is that Lamang?" a guard whistled from the tower. "Who's that with you?"

"A friend," Khine said, allowing the implication to settle in.

The guard laughed. "*You?*"

"Even a hermit gets lonely."

"She'll have to stay out there," the guard said. "You're the only one Lord Huan has cleared."

"Can't you make an exception?" Khine asked. "Come now, she's been dying to see the city. What can one woman do?"

"If she's a spy for Kaggawa..."

"I have news about Kaggawa's movements," Khine said. "Spy or not, she won't be able to do a damn thing. And I've been meaning to stay a few days here." He gave a smug grin. "I have to keep my bed warm *somehow*."

"You rascal. You should've told me. We've got whores in the city."

"I trained to be a physician. That's not something I'd recommend to *anyone* who wants to keep their parts intact."

The guard laughed. "I always did say you were a joker."

"It's really not so much a joke as a health warning."

The guard laughed and disappeared around the corner.

"I apologize for this," Khine said in a low voice.

I pressed his hand into mine, squeezing. "It's not the worst act I've played."

"I can only imagine what you had to go through with Lo Bahn."

"He's still angry about it. Like it's my fault he can't hold his liquor." I pressed even closer to Khine as the guard appeared, my hand on his chest.

"The officers will let it slide for now," the guard said. "But if there's any trouble..."

"I won't cause trouble," I crooned, in a tone low enough to make the guard flash me a grin.

We were allowed to step through the gates, which opened up to a dark, dirty alley. Khine took me by the hand, leading me past the marketplace. Down another dizzying turn, and then we found ourselves in front of a small tavern, guarded by an old woman with one eye.

"Name?" she hissed.

"We go through this every time, Sang Iga," Khine groaned.

She pursed her lips together. "You're going to have to speak up, I'm a little hard of hearing."

"Khine."

"Kayin?"

"*Khine*. Lamang."

"You're speaking gibberish."

He gave an irritated smile. She blinked at him before turning to me. "And this—one of the new girls? You'll have to go through the back, missy. Although—aren't you too old?"

"She's not terribly old..." Khine began. I jabbed him.

"Oh, just go on, then," she finally said with a sigh. "You'll talk the ears out of me and I just don't have time for that." She clacked her tongue and waved at us with a cane.

"You've been making friends," I said as we strode through the narrow doors and into an even narrower hallway.

"I've been exploring my options," he whispered. "I didn't know where to turn to if ever Thanh needed help, and Huan seemed honest in the brief time I've known him. He thinks I'm his spy in Kaggawa's camp, which keeps him happy about my presence. Sang Iga, and others...are his trusted servants. He's been gathering people."

"For what?"

"You'll see." We reached a common room, one so small that I could only count six tables. A few faded paintings decorated the dilapidated walls.

A group on one table erupted with raucous laughter. One of the heads turned as we approached them, and I saw Lord Huan's face turn bright.

Khine pressed a finger on his lips as Huan got up to meet us. "Meet one of my new assistants," Khine said.

"A pleasure, my lady," Lord Huan said, taking my hand. He was visibly struggling against the need to show me the proper respect.

"A little less obvious," Khine hissed in Zirano.

Huan scratched his cheek. "Where'd you...uh, get this one, Lamang? Her, uh, behind looks...promising."

"Why are you two so bad at this today?" I whispered under my breath.

"Lord Huan is always bad at this," Khine grumbled.

"What's that?" one of the soldiers from the table called out. "Is that Lamang with a woman? We were starting to wonder." He leered at me with unsteady eyes, and I wasn't sure if he was trying to size me up or just trying to focus.

"That's too bad," another chimed in. "One of the girls has been asking for you. Said she was going to bring a friend if you're interested."

"Tell her I appreciate the thought," Khine said. I glared at him, and he wrinkled his nose. "But I'm quite preoccupied at the moment." His eyes never left me as he spoke.

"Gentlemen, as lovely as this has been, the good doctor and I need to chat alone," Huan interrupted. He clapped his hands. The soldiers got up, swaying slightly as they marched past us. After they strode through the doors, the old woman, Iga, came in to bar it.

"My apologies for their rudeness, Beloved Queen. They were drunk."

"You're making excuses," Iga snorted as she returned, one hand on her hip. "Those men need more discipline, Lord Huan. I'd have smacked their skulls with a bamboo stick."

"It's war, Sang," Huan replied. "Too much discipline will sow dissent."

"And here I thought you run a tight ship," I said.

"Tight enough where it counts. My queen, I suppose Lamang here has updated you on your son's situation?"

I nodded.

Huan grimaced. "We will assist any way we can, of course—anything to deal a blow to Kaggawa's ego. He thinks having the prince in his possession can make *him* king. What I'd give to wipe the smug look off his face. He claims he's going ahead with Prince Thanh's betrothal to his daughter as soon as he lays claim to the city."

"You and your little war. You're like children playing games." Iga turned to me now, a scowl on her face. "I *thought* it was the queen. I recognize the look."

"What look?" I asked.

"Yeshin's," Iga snorted. "I'm Oren-yaro, child. I served at your castle for a while before your father sent me here. It's about time you showed your face. I thought the west would be in smithereens before you ever graced us with your presence."

I paused to let her words sink in. I wasn't going to bother correcting her that I was here months ago, when I came as a hostage, not a queen. Now I was. Even with every intention of burning my father's claim to the ground, I was here to save Jin-Sayeng, as her queen should have been doing all these years.

I bowed, accepting her admonition. "I know I've neglected my duties out here..." I began.

She shook her head. "That's not what I meant. I was chief builder at Oka Shto. I know how your castle was built—exactly how." She gave me a knowing look "I had my opinions about it. When I told your father, he sent me here to work on the Yu-yan dragon-tower instead."

She got up and shuffled towards the kitchen. She returned carrying an armful of scrolls. Huan's face was twisted into a scowl, but he said nothing as she unrolled them. They were blueprints—plans for the base of an elaborate dragon-tower.

"You told me this tower was recently built," I said, glancing at Huan. "But these plans were dated from when Warlord Yeshin was alive."

"The foundation was started years ago," Iga said. "I had my opinions about *that*, too, but by then my husband was dead and my own children's lives were on the line. I'd learned my lesson, and I kept my mouth shut."

"Are they back in Oren-yaro?"

She nodded, and now I understood the hatred brimming in her eyes. "I've got grandchildren now, too. I haven't heard from them since this war broke out. I hope you haven't lopped off their heads."

"Why didn't you go back home?"

She shrugged. "After they were done with me, I was told to keep quiet and wait here for you."

"I was here before," I said. "Why didn't you come to me then?"

"It wasn't time."

"This is ridiculous," Huan broke in. "If I had known you were just like my father, I—"

"You would have what?" Iga snapped. "Sent me home? Retired the poor, senile grandmother?" There was no questioning she was Oren-yaro now, even with her accent masked from the years she spent in Yu-yan. Some things you could never erase.

"Let's not start this, Sang," Lord Huan said as he pulled out a chair for me before he stepped away. He returned with two sealed envelopes. I recognized the wax seals immediately—they were the letters Rayyel and I had written before his arrest.

"Namra must have sent you those," I said. "Did she tell you everything else? About our plans to use our downfall to rally those sympathetic to us?"

He nodded. "I agree there is a chance it could work. It's brilliant, really. Many of the warlords hate you already, but if you paint both of you as victims, they'll transfer their grievances to the ones they see in power: the Oren-yaro, the Zarojo, and maybe even the Ikessars."

"All you're doing," Iga said with a snort, "is slathering her with raw meat before throwing her to the dogs."

Huan ignored her. "We could send these now if you want. I have trusted riders who can make their way through those roads."

"I was hoping to bring them east myself," I said. "With enough reinforcements to support me. The enemies who pretend to be my allies won't like what I'm about to do."

"Namra warned me this might be the case." He crossed his arms. "I will need time, Beloved Queen. Until we can take care of Kaggawa, I need every soldier behind these walls. He's relentless."

"And marching towards you as we speak," Khine broke in. He was carrying a tray of cups full of blood-red tea, which he placed on the table before taking a seat.

"I know. We've seen his movements," Huan said. He picked up a cup and sipped, contemplating. "Soon. There'll be a siege soon. Gods. Officially, we're not doing anything about it. My father thinks Kaggawa is bluffing, that his soldiers will see our walls, piss their pants, and leave. He orders attacks on them that seem ill-advised—small raids on his camps here and there that do nothing but irritate, like gnats. It's as if he's intent on wasting our time." He gave a nervous laugh. "So I've been going behind my father's back. None of my attacks on Kaggawa were sanctioned by him. If I had died out there, he would've declared me an errant child, and appointed a cousin or something as his heir."

"Is this what these secret meetings are all about?"

"*Someone* has to ensure the safety of the Yu-yan people," Huan said with a smile. "I've been carrying out preparations to defend us from the impending siege, too. Many of the officers are of the same mind as I am, and were only too happy to finally do *something*."

"Perhaps if your father sees Kaggawa's army for himself..."

"My father is more concerned about capturing the dragon," Huan mumbled.

"What dragon?"

He gave me a look. "You know the one. The dragon that killed my brother."

I glanced at Khine before turning back to him. "That dragon, Lord Huan—"

"I hate the bloody thing, too," he said, his fingers tightening around his cup.
"The bastard took my brother away. But we've wasted too many soldiers trying
to capture it. Our soldiers as dragon fodder, when we're at war! I've agreed to
humour my father about it for now. I want the beast destroyed so he can focus
on our real problem. So he can help *me* rule his bloody lands."

"Lord Huan," I said. "Eikaro isn't dead."

He smiled. "I appreciate your attempt at levity, Beloved Queen, but..."

"Eikaro is inside that dragon."

He paused for a moment. "Did you put anything in this tea, Lamang?"
Huan asked, turning to Khine.

Khine cleared his throat. "She's serious."

"You're the one who told us he was dead," Huan said to me.

"He asked me to say that."

"While inside the dragon." His voice was growing cold.

"Lord Huan, I know this is hard to believe—"

He got up. "Queen Talyien, I know the last few months must've been difficult
for you. I can only imagine what you have been going through. Agos's death, the
trial, your son in Kaggawa's hands...believe me. I understand your struggles.
But to tell me my brother is inside this *beast* like this is some sort of fairy tale..."

We heard panicked knocking from the door.

Iga got up and walked towards the window, where she parted the curtains.
As she peered out, the air flashed white, and I felt something I hadn't in the last
few times I'd seen this happen—a sort of burning sensation that enveloped my
entire body, filling my nostrils with the scent of charred corpses.

"The troubles of this land..." Iga began. "How well do you know them?"

"Too well," I said.

The knocking came again, followed by what sounded like snuffling between
the cracks of the door. I saw a shadow outside the window.

There is a story my father used to tell me about a boy who loved to read. "You
can read all the books on that shelf," his master told him, "except for that golden

book at the end." The boy asked why he couldn't, and his master wouldn't tell him. So one day when his master was off to town, the boy took a ladder so he could reach the shelf, and went straight for the forbidden book.

The book taught him magic. Suddenly he could turn into whatever animal he chose—a falcon, a swan, a goat. As soon as he mastered these tricks, he ran straight to his father. "I've found it!" he told the old man. "I've found the answer to our troubles!" And he turned into a stallion, the most magnificent his father had ever seen, with flowing locks of white hair and a coat that shone like diamonds. "Take me to the market," he instructed the old man, "and find the highest bidder. Once you have the money, remove the ribbon around my leg. I will turn into a boy again and come back home to you."

My father must've known other stories, but he would tell me only the one. I remember curling up next to him as he went over the familiar words in his clear, honeyed tone, staring at the wall as I imagined the story come to life. The details changed; sometimes the boy turned into a prized bull first. Sometimes he was a white donkey. But it always ended the same way—the boy's master would buy him the third time they tried the trick, and the father, stricken with fear, would fail to pull the ribbon. The boy would remain an animal until he found a princess to remove the ribbon for him. There would be a tense battle between him and the old magician, and then he and the princess lived happily ever after.

I once asked if the boy returned to his father like he promised. "He's a prince now," Yeshin would say, drawing his brows close together. "Isn't that what matters?" It wasn't the sort of thing storybooks cared about, and Yeshin didn't, either. But after he kissed me good night, I would lie awake thinking about how sad it was if the boy didn't. What was a kingdom compared with a father's love?

The sound of Huan's shallow breathing brought me back to the present. He must have seen the flash, too, and heard the unhuman movements outside the door. But it wasn't confusion etched on his face. I realized that in another time and place, I would've held the same expression. What was happening out there was too much to consider, too much to accept when you knew it was your job to fix it.

"You children think you can change the tide as easily as a fish can change directions," Iga said, folding her hands over the table. Her voice rang through the silence, and the shadows behind her seemed to grow taller, as if *she* was queen in that room, not I. "That all it takes are good intentions and the desire to do what is right. But none of you have been paying attention."

"If our fathers had not kept us in the dark, things wouldn't have gotten this far," I said.

She laughed. "You speak like your elders weren't where you are now, scratching their heads, screaming into the void in the hopes that the gods would save their children from what's about to come." She pointed at Huan. "Your father is an idiot, but not the sort you make him out to be. War tactics? Strategies? He knows them like the back of his hand; he wouldn't have been able to take Yu-yan for himself otherwise. He was the one who ordered the first attacks on Kaggawa. Kaggawa made the threats, but he has been making those threats for decades. Tell me what finally moved his hand, little Huan. Tell me!"

"The arrival of the Zarojo prince," Huan mumbled.

"The arrival of Prince Yuebek," Iga repeated. She laughed. "You don't see what's happening here? How Warlord Ojika's attacks were designed to *lengthen* his war with Kaggawa? He gives them victories here and there, to whet their appetites and increase their confidence. Every few days, Kaggawa thinks he is winning his war, and so he orders more mercenaries with his family money. But of course, you thought you knew better, didn't you, little Huan? You started attacking without authorization. I've kept track of everything..."

His hand dropped to his sword. "You would dare betray me, old woman? You—!"

"I've been keeping track of your attacks," she continued calmly. "There is no betrayal in observing things, is there?"

"You had my full confidence. I thought—"

"You thought wrong," she said. "Your ill-advised attacks wounded Kaggawa's army more than they should have. Of course he'll be mounting a siege soon—he's desperate, and throwing all of this on one last attempt to subdue your father. It won't happen, if you have your way. Your soldiers will crush his mercenaries at the gates, *which is how you will doom us all.*"

Huan swallowed. "My father," he finally said, "is a traitor, and so are you." Tears pricked his eyes.

"Let's not throw such careless words around, Lord Huan," I broke in. "You knew your brother was a mage, and you kept that from me. We need to gather our forces. Our problems are out there."

"It's easier to close your eyes and pretend it has nothing to do with you," Iga said.

Something heavy thudded on the rooftop.

"Unfortunately," she continued, "that's not the way the world works."

"I think we have to go now," Khine broke in.

"This war…" Huan began.

I thought Iga would hit him across the head. "This war is not all there is!" she hissed. "This war is a sham, just like her marriage, just like her last five years as queen! And if you pay close attention, maybe you'll survive the end of it!"

She had barely closed her mouth when the window closest to the table shattered. A bloody snout reached into the room, sinking its teeth into Khine's shoulder.

He struck it in the face with the hilt of his sword the exact moment I stabbed it between the eyes. I grabbed it by the neck and hurled it into the room. It lay facedown, covering the floor with blood in its death throes. It looked like a rabid wolf, all black fur and claws and teeth. A trail of saliva dripped from its open jaws. Like many of the others I'd met before, there wasn't a trace of human on it, even as its body began to disintegrate.

I turned to Khine. "Just a scratch," he said, placing a hand over his wound. He glanced at Huan. "Whether you like it or not, Lord Huan, this scourge is upon us. Supply lines have been cut since the start of the season, and you're almost out of food. Do you know what a siege will do to your city?"

A howl from the other window answered his question.

"We can't stay," I said. I turned a table onto its side and pushed it against the glass, blocking it.

From the other side of the room, Khine was unlatching the broken window. He jumped into the adjoining alley. "It's clear from here," he called.

"Move, Huan!" I shoved the stricken lord through the window after Khine. I turned around to help Iga up. We found ourselves in a tight street.

"The soldiers—where are my soldiers?" Huan gasped. "They were supposed to be outside. They—"

A decapitated head, still inside its helmet, dropped on the ground beside us. I looked up and saw another creature standing on its haunches at the edge of the roof. There were few markers it had once been human—its elongated mouth twisted into an inhuman grin, revealing yellow fangs that glinted in the moonlight. Matted hair streamed like waterfalls along its shoulders, and grey flesh poked out of the tattered remains of its shirt. It was too preoccupied with its meal to attack. Against the darkening sky, it looked like a grotesque statue.

"Keep walking," I said. There was no room to swing my sword, anyway.

Another howl in the distance sent my skin crawling. There were more of them out there.

Iga led us down the alleys and deeper into the city. A shadow near the footbridge startled me, but it remained a crippled beggar with stumps in place of legs, holding out a bowl. The sky flashed white; after it disappeared, the man still sat there, his arm rattling. He pressed his lips together, smacking his toothless gums.

"Not everyone makes the trade," Khine whispered.

"Then how do we know who to fight?" I found myself saying out loud.

No one replied at first. Eventually, Iga cleared her throat, taking hold of my arm with cold, wrinkled fingers. "I know nothing about the *agan* or the effects of this rift," she said. "They told us the people will soon become as mad as the dragons, and nothing else. I'm just a builder. I can only show you what I was ordered to."

Around us, the wind grew colder.

The dragon-tower called to us like a beacon. Iga ushered us past the rusted gate and down the stone steps to the basement, which she unlocked with a key she kept around her neck. As soon as we stepped inside, I felt the sensation of having entered a tomb—a wet, musky scent permeated the walls. I turned to Iga, trying to discern her against the blackness of our surroundings.

"How many of you did my father leave behind?" I asked. "Guardians of his secrets. Servants. Pawns. The man's bones are ground up in a jar and yet here you all are, still following his orders."

"Your father knew how people's minds worked," she said. "And he was willing to do what others can't even fathom. He had influence, he had power, and he used that to get what he wanted. Does it matter if the man is living or dead? It is the *living* carrying out his will. If I wilfully disobey, which of my children's heads will grace my doorstep the very next day? Like you, we don't know how many he's coerced, how many servants he's left behind. We don't know, and we don't have the power to change anything, so we obey."

"You obey, when you can still fight."

"And what would fighting do? Add more bodies to the top of the pile? My pride isn't worth adding to my dead, Queen Talyien. My pride won't make stiff lungs breathe again. When you can't fight, you lower your head and you do what needs to be done, even when it's against your will, because you know you are just one person and yearning alone cannot change the world. But you're here now. I can wash my hands clean of this guilt, at least." She opened another door and stepped aside, beckoning for me to enter first.

The next room was an expanse—strange for a chamber well beneath the tower. The walls were circular. There was a well in the center, which went from the floor to the ceiling. I remembered that I had seen a dragon-fire well at the first level of the tower when I was there. This must be the same one. There were grates set against the stone. I could hear wind whistling through the hollows, which brought with it a surge of discomfort. The smell of death was now unmistakable.

I glanced at the wall and noticed glowing runes. They were similar to the ones I had seen before—in Burbatan, in Oka Shto. I noticed Iga keeping her distance while gesturing for the others to do the same.

"Do your blueprints say that? Avoid at all costs unless you're Talyien Orenar."

"The exact words," she said with a hint of a smile.

Not knowing if she was joking or not, I approached the runes. They glowed.

"Tali…" Khine warned.

I allowed my hand to hover over the runes before giving a quick smile. "Namra told me back in Oka Shto that she doesn't believe my father would knowingly hurt me."

"You knew him best," Iga replied.

I touched the runes. I was expecting another explosion. Arrows. Fire. At least an earthquake or two. Nothing of that sort happened. The grates simply popped open.

"That's not so bad…" I began.

Small skulls rolled out of the holes.

I felt my senses darken as I turned to Iga for an explanation.

"I was told these were children that showed a hint of the *agan*, gathered across the land," Iga said. "Your father's mages wanted them in particular. They drained these children of their blood to soak the very foundation of the tower. The Zarojo mages seemed to think it was necessary for certain spells to…take hold."

Huan's face was sheet white. "My father couldn't have agreed to this."

"It's not a matter of agreeing or not," Iga said. "I didn't, either. But your brother would've been one of these children if your father had said no." She placed a hand on his shoulder. "We didn't believe Warlord Yeshin at first. The man had seen too much in his life. The loss of his children, the war...had he been any other man, they would've put an arrow through his skull. But he wasn't just any man. He was a warlord of a royal clan, with thousands of soldiers at his beck and call and loyal generals, in spite of everything. I did my job with anger."

"Your anger didn't do a damn thing for these children," Khine said.

She snorted. "Of course it didn't. I never claimed to be a saint. It didn't do a damn thing, either, when the mad dragons came along and I realized there was truth in a madman's words. All I could do was stay—stay and fulfill my duties like an Oren-yaro should. I've kept my post for twenty-seven years."

"Gods," I said, finding my voice at last. "The castle in Oka Shto...did he do this there, too? Did he kill children there?"

She looked at me. "Is that really a question you need an answer to, Queen Talyien? You can't change the past. The future, on the other hand, is all yours."

CHAPTER FOURTEEN

BLOOD OF THE BROTHER

ᜊᜓᜁᜓᜉᜒᜈ

This is beyond ridiculous," Huan broke in, his face flushed. "I need to speak with my father." He walked out of the chamber, slamming the door behind him.

I moved to follow. "Leave him be," Iga said. "Royals and their pride. I'll go find his guards. The ones that still have their heads attached." She left me and Khine alone.

I turned my attention back to the well. One of the grates was larger than the other. I peered into it and saw an alcove, carved right into the walls. At the bottom was a stone disk, about the size of my palm, engraved with runes around the edges. It glowed when I drew near, so I placed my hand right on top.

A trapdoor floor appeared, the edges glowing blue. I drew close, tugging at the handle to open it. Another glow against the blackness revealed stairs, but not much else—the light wouldn't reach all the way.

"Want to take bets on what's waiting for me down there?" I asked.

"Not particularly," Khine said. "Maybe...maybe you shouldn't go."

"Mmm," I replied.

"Tali..."

"I want to see," I said.

He placed his hand around my wrist, his eyes begging me not to.

"He would never hurt me," I managed to mumble. Without waiting for Khine's reply, I forged blindly into the darkness.

The shadows, I noticed, did strange things with every step I took. It was as if there was a bubble, an invisible shield that kept the light in, and everything else out. A strange, prickly sensation clung to my skin, and the damp air was getting thicker. I wiped my nose as I reached the middle of a chamber. I couldn't see the walls, but I could guess at the immensity of it from the echoes my footsteps made.

A source of light illuminated the room with a greyish glow, like twilight during a storm. I looked up. I *should* have taken that wager, because I would've won. There was another mirror, just like the one in Oka Shto. It was gazing out at another tower, one I didn't recognize. The surroundings, however, indicated it was deeper into the mountains. I could see the jagged rocks of the peaks, still covered in snow, and talus slopes streaming down into the ragged valleys.

"You're killing me here, Tali," Khine called. "Tell me you're all right."

"I'm alive," I called back.

"What's down there?"

"More questions." I stared back at the mirror, wondering what I was missing. My father had planned *everything*. There had to be a reason for all of these. *Go to the Yu-yan dragon-tower.* No explanation, no apologies. He knew I would come.

I walked to the other end of the room, hoping to hit a dead end. Perhaps the fewer strands there were to puzzle over, the happier I was going to be. Instead, there was a door. I pulled it open and found myself in a study that was smaller than the one in Burbatan. But instead of shelves of books and other things, all I saw was a single desk with a letter on top.

"Is this a treasure hunt, Father?" I said out loud. "When do I get my present?" The darkness hummed from the sound of my voice.

I felt the prickling sensation travelling through my hands as I looked at runes on the door. I picked up the letter. Time had turned the paper frail, and I was almost afraid it would crumble as soon as I touched it. I unfolded it. It was too dark to read the words, but the ink glowed a little, even in the darkness. As soon as I touched them, my senses exploded and I crumpled to my knees.

I woke up in bed, my joints aching with every breath. Somehow, I felt like I should be panicking, but I wasn't. I felt oddly at peace—confident, even. A warrior at her prime.

Too much at peace. I jolted up with a start, wondering where my guards were. They should've been there in the room, standing by the doorway. I beheld the crumpled bodies on the floor before turning to the lone figure sitting by the windowsill. The moonlight shone, revealing a woman's face.

She looked...unremarkable. A woman whose face you could see in every market corner of the world, or on any random street you could cross. But she was familiar enough, and she gazed at me with the confidence of someone who knew she'd caught her prey at last. I stared at her and laughed.

"So," I heard my voice say. It wasn't a woman's voice, but a man's, croaking and in need of a glass of hot ginger tea. "You win, after all. They told me not to underestimate Ryia, but it was always you I needed to fear, wasn't it? You were always the wily one. So unassuming, so harmless...until you're not."

I slowly got out of bed, my knees shaking. She could kill me with a poison dart at any moment, the way I could tell she did with the guards, but she wasn't going to do that. This was the sort of woman who needed to look her enemy in the eyes before she killed him. Years ago, I could've used that. Years ago, when I was a young man and the world still made sense.

I slowly began to pull myself away from my—no, from *my father's*—thoughts. It frightened me that it took me so long to realize that. Was it that easy for me to slip into his skin? Even as I struggled to jump out of the body, the thoughts were too familiar, and all too quickly, I found myself lost in the current once more.

I turned back to the woman and drew a long sigh. I wasn't going to kill her. I decided that a long time ago, when I first met her through the haze of my grief for my sons' death. She'd been a nobody then, one of the sycophants at Rysaran Ikessar's heels, the way her father had been with *his* father before him. That connection glorified her in Ryia Ikessar's eyes and she quickly became her right hand, even with the famed Magister Ichi rok Sagar at her side.

She smiled. *Don't lick your lips, woman,* I thought. *If I reach my sword, I may not be able to help myself.* Except I didn't sleep with my sword anymore—it brought me bad dreams, and good sleep, for a man my age, was about all I wanted these days. "I heard you got married again," she said. "Congratulations. I should've sent a gift. Where is your wife?"

"In the room across the hall," I said easily, knowing it didn't matter. If she wanted to hurt Liosa, she would've done it already, and this woman—from what I knew of her—wouldn't have it in her to kill an innocent. "My snoring bothers her, and her frequent visits to the chamber pot bother *me*."

"Then a double congratulations is in order."

"Don't play coy with me, Kaggawa."

"I am not, my lord. She must be pregnant."

"With a man my age?" I laughed. "Let's not bandy words about. You detest me, Kaggawa—I can see it in your eyes. You'd kill me if you could. Since I'm not dead yet, I'm assuming you need me alive. Spit it out, then. What does Ryia want?"

"I don't work for Ryia Ikessar anymore," Kaggawa replied.

"I always thought your family was loyal to the Ikessars. What's the matter, girl? They didn't pay enough?"

She turned away from the question. "You were in the Sougen a few months ago," she said instead. "I believe you spoke with my nephew Dai."

"He wants me to remove Ojika Anyu from Yu-yan," I said. "He was rude and demanding. I think I'll do the exact opposite. I think I'll *grant* Yu-yan to the usurpers when I'm done."

"This isn't a joke, Warlord Yeshin. You know what's happening out there. You've seen it yourself, so I've heard."

I crossed the room, towards the chair where my sword lay. My gaze lingered on it for a moment before I chose to grab the blanket draped behind it instead. Wrapping it around my shoulders, I turned back to the woman. "Not Ryia, then," I said in a low voice. "What do *you* want, Mistress Kaggawa?"

"What we all do," she replied. "Peace in Jin-Sayeng. We've been at war too long, with no end in sight."

"You're only saying that because I'm winning," I sneered.

"You win battles, Warlord Yeshin," Kaggawa said. "But you won't win the war. Every victory of yours costs you an ally. The more reasons you give them to fear you, the more the others will defect to Ryia's side. This will all be for nothing, after all."

"If you're convinced she'll win, then let her win," I said, dismissing her with a wave. "Let her win, Kaggawa! What are you disturbing an old man's rest for?" I leered at her, though I knew I wouldn't be able to frighten her with my yelling. She was one of the few people I knew who could face me like that. I respected her for it.

"Because you owe Jin-Sayeng," she replied in an even voice. "We called it Rysaran's dragon, but really, we should've christened it Yeshin's dragon instead. You were the one who seized it from the Ikessars because you wanted that power for yourself. To be the first Jinsein royal dragonrider, after so many years…"

"I know full well what I did," I said. "What will you do next? Throw my dead children at me?"

"You killed them."

"I killed them," I agreed.

There was a flicker of surprise in her face.

"I'm old," I conceded. "And I believe my time is up. Sometimes a man has to admit a few things before he dies. I watched the creature I set loose upon the world rip my sons apart. All my hopes and dreams, gone in an instant. Taraji. Senjo. Lang. Shoen. I say their names with my prayers every night, hoping the gods granted them rest, at least. Hoping that their father's sins didn't doom them for eternity." I slowly sat at the edge of the bed, staring at my hands.

She approached me, arms crossed, that look of defiance on her face. She didn't just hate me—she was disgusted by me. It meant something that she would even step so close. "It may not be too late, my lord."

"What?" I asked with a laugh. "Because you think my wife may be with child? It may not even be mine."

"You can fix this," she said.

"Me?"

"Your fascination with the *agan* didn't sprout overnight. I should've known when you alone survived the razing of Oren-yaro with nothing but a little bit of madness to show for it. You're a mage, Warlord Yeshin."

I stared at her before I began laughing. "Now you've moved to conspiracy." But even as I said this, I felt my fingers tingle, and I saw the water-like glow lifting from her body. I shook my head, forcing my eyes to focus. It used to be easier to ignore.

"My daughter is a mage, too, my lord. I know the signs. I denied them for a long time." Her face tightened. "You hold a faint connection to the *agan*, and perhaps more than just faint. This is enough."

"For what?"

"For you to fix the rift yourself."

"Kaggawa, I've always liked you more than I did your mistress, but now I'm starting to think that was a mistake. If you're so daft you think I can do what dozens of *trained* Dageian mages have been unable to, then this conversation is over. I can't stand idiots." I moved to grab my sword, willing the *agan* stream to wrap around the hilt. It flew from the chair straight into my waiting hand.

She wasn't lying about her daughter; there wasn't a flicker of surprise on her face. She accepted the reality of mages as one who lived with them. "Party tricks," she said easily.

"I am capable of nothing more," I replied.

"The mages cannot fix the rift all the way from the ground, and airships cannot fly through those skies," Kaggawa said. "*You* can."

"How?"

"Rysaran's sacrifice has done one good thing for us. They might be mad, but the dragons *have* returned," she said. "Tame one. Ride it to the sky. Close the rift. Then *maybe* the gods will forgive you."

A shiver ran through my withered body. For one long, painful moment, I imagined it exactly as she said it. For an Oren-yaro to close those rifts and save Jin-Sayeng on the back of a dragon...the words alone had the makings of a legend.

But then I tried to lift my sword, and my arm shook so much I had to put it down again. I flashed Kaggawa a regretful smile. "Even if I had the skills necessary for such an endeavour—even if I knew how to *tame* the damn things without losing my head—you forget that I am an old man. I can barely fight anymore."

"That's unfortunate," she said in a voice that said she didn't believe me. "So you would rather sit here and rot, then. Very well. When the Ikessars are dragging you to your execution, remember you had the chance to win the throne and you refused it."

"What the hell do you mean?"

"What I am offering, Warlord Yeshin, is a truce. You may have a child in your wife's belly. It could be a daughter. If you don't, find another—a niece, a great-niece, we don't care, so long as this girl is your heir. Ryia has a son. Together, they can rule Jin-Sayeng, and this war will be over at last. You and Ryia both win. Promise to lay down your arms in exchange for a betrothal, and I promise you, I can get Ryia to do the same. She wants peace as much as anyone else."

"Not I," I told her.

"You," she agreed, "can secure the throne for your bloodline with this arrangement. You can play the hero while you're at it. Remember, you've tainted the Oren-yaro name more than your predecessors ever did. This will undo the damage and assure the history books will forever speak favourably of your people. What more can you ask for, Warlord Yeshin?"

"You'd entrust me with that?" I asked. "I, a man you despise with your every breath?"

"We all have to make sacrifices." She returned to the window and pointed at my men. "Your guards will be awake soon, and you can pretend this never happened. But if you change your mind, send word. You know where to find me." She started to climb back down the rooftop below.

"Sume," I said.

She paused.

"Do you truly think my wife is with child?"

"Perhaps you should ask her yourself, my lord."

"I can't do this again," I said. "I can't." I thought about my dead sons and knew I would hate the next infant I held in my arms.

"I cannot even begin to imagine your sorrow, Lord Yeshin," Sume replied, looking for all the world like she meant it. "But regret alone won't absolve you." With that, she disappeared into the night. I laughed at her foolishness just before my thoughts dissolved and became my own again.

When I woke up, I found myself staring at the mirror, at the shadow of a dragon passing by. It dropped to the tower, its snout right where the window was. It roared—a sound I couldn't hear but *see*, flames licking over its mouth. It gazed out at something in the distance.

It felt odd to be looking at a dragon that wasn't aware of me. This was smaller, a female from the shape of her head and the long frills along the side of her neck. Her scales were dull, pale, the colour of dirty snow, with dots of blue on her forehead. Scars marked most of her breast, and part of her face looked as if it had once been ripped apart by another dragon. I couldn't decide if she was ugly or beautiful. Both, I think. Gracefully, she spread her wings and roared a second time.

Another dragon arrived to answer her call. This one was black and long-limbed, with red splashes on the scales of its pointed muzzle. I was expecting it to attack the first dragon, but instead it butted its head against the female. The black-and-red dragon dwarfed the white as they pressed their necks together in a gesture that was oddly tender. They must've been a mating pair, which seemed odd considering what I had seen from the creatures so far.

Something about the image tightened the grief around my heart. I sat up, staring at the letter in my hands as I tried to shake myself loose from the memory I had just witnessed. There were runes along the edges of the paper, which

I hadn't seen before. Did my father get a mage to put a spell on it? Did he do it himself? I wafted between my feelings, over the disbelief that my father had an affinity for the *agan* and that he would want me to find out this way—with the revelation that I really was nothing but a tool for him. He didn't want to raise another child. His life was over when I came into the picture.

And yet in the scant light of that room, I caught a glimpse of the first few words in his letter. *My Dearest Daughter . . .*

The ground began to shake.

I regained my composure and dashed up the stairs. "There must be a dragon on the platform above us," Khine said as I re-entered the chamber. "Are you all right? What took you so long?"

I flashed the letter at him before stuffing it inside my shirt. The roar above started a second time. It was beyond deafening.

We strode out of the basement. At the base, right outside the steps, I saw a dark shadow. I shielded my eyes from the sun as I stared up. A familiar black wing grazed the sky. I blinked, recognizing Eikaro.

In the distance, I heard horns.

"It's Eikaro," I said. "Do you see the shape of the crest? He must have travelled back to familiar surroundings after Kyo-orashi."

"Are you sure?" he asked. He looked nervous.

"What do you mean?"

"I suspected as much, but I didn't know how to break it to him," he said. "That's the same dragon they've been chasing for months. Huan wants vengeance. Those horns—they're going after him again. He's eluded them so far, but—"

"We can't let them kill him. We need to get to the platform."

"There's a lift for taking construction supplies up the ridge."

We started for the path towards the cliffs.

Another roar split the horizon. Heart pounding, we found the lift at the bottom—a rickety wooden structure held up by ropes as thick as my arms. Khine slammed his wrist into the winch, which immediately began to unwind, taking us up to the ridge.

"Watch yourself," he warned as the lift began to sway.

I grabbed the railing to support myself and spotted the dragon's tail just as it made a sweep at the top of the tower. "Eikaro!" I tried to call out, but I was too far away. The rush of the wind swallowed my voice. I spotted soldiers advancing with spears and poleaxes.

We reached the first platform. I leaped up the rocky slope, my feet scrambling across the wet soil. The ground shook with every roar the dragon made.

I recognized Huan's helmet from the walls. He was making his way to the top of the tower.

"One of them will kill the other."

"What else we can do?" Khine asked. "By the time you get up there, it will be too late."

I scanned the perimeter. Soldiers were streaming in from both sides of the wall, heading for the tower. *Eikaro, what by all the gods are you doing?* He knew what they did to dragons here. To land on the tower itself and then stay there...

Madness. That was my only explanation. The dragons here were mad, untameable, and all because of the corrupted soul that served as the *rider*. That was what Dai Kaggawa had called it once. But Eikaro's soul was alone inside the beast. I had *seen* the corrupted thing switch into his human body before it plummeted to its death. Could it have left a part of it inside of him?

I caught sight of a horn laid out near the wall ramparts and sped up towards the bridge. The last of the soldiers had slipped into the tower, but I didn't know if more would come. I passed the tower, heading straight for the horn.

Two short blasts, one long blast—the signal for an impending attack from the enemy's army; Huan used to think that military protocol made for fine conversation when out drinking with women. As soon as the last trumpet blared through the wind, I was gone.

Khine met me at the bridge. I turned around, hoping the soldiers would be thrown into panic. The result was even better; the horn blasts startled the dragon to flight. We went to take cover in the bushes just as his enormous shadow swept past us.

"He almost killed us in Kyo-orashi," I said, watching the silent dragon disappear into the sky. "Something is going on with him." I heard horses. Huan rode past us towards the ridge, along with several soldiers. He was followed by Warlord Ojika, who was flanked by two people in robes.

As soon as the last hoofbeats faded into the distance, I returned to the path. Khine drew his sword. "I'm not looking forward to facing that thing again if I can help it."

"That thing has a name," I said.

"If he's forgotten it, there's not much we can do. He'll kill his father and brother or they'll kill him."

"They want to tame him. Those two looked like mages. Lord Huan told me the last time I was here that they've been trying to tame dragons by using the mages to pull the corrupted souls out of their bodies, but the process has failed each time because the hosts are killed by the riders. Maybe they know there is one soul left inside this dragon—maybe that's why they want him so badly."

"Or maybe they don't know, and their process will kill him anyway. Why is Ojika Anyu so obsessed with taming dragons in the first place? I understand the symbolism that riding a dragon has to your nation, but they're in the middle of a war *he* started."

"My father would have ordered him to."

"But why?"

I paused. "I believe my father had been dabbling with the *agan*," I finally said. "And I believe the original plan was for him to use a dragon to ride to the skies and close that rift himself."

"But he's dead."

I turned away, wondering. My father had pretended to agree with what Sume Kaggawa had proposed before he switched plans at the last moment. Did she know he didn't want to die out here? Was the plan to draw Yuebek to Jin-Sayeng hers, too? I didn't even know if she was still alive; Dai Kaggawa seemed unaware that his aunt had spoken to Yeshin, and my father had all but made it look like he wasn't doing anything about the west for years. It was like trying to make out an image drenched in mud. I focused on leading us into the woods. The horses had crashed into the bushes without care, leaving a trail of broken twigs and crushed leaves. Further on, we encountered a layer of packed snow.

"Did Eikaro look thin to you?" I asked.

"I was a little preoccupied with trying to keep away from those snapping jaws the last time we met," Khine said with a grimace.

"He looked thin. He wasn't sure if the dragon's body would even accept his soul." I gazed up at the sky, where the first stars of the night were starting to shine through the clouds. I thought I heard another roar—one that sounded frail, and exhausted. I shivered. "Perhaps it's already consumed him."

In all the years since I had first met them, the Anyu brothers were inseparable. They looked alike at first glance, but it was easy to forget they were twins once you got to know them better. Eikaro was soft-spoken, thoughtful, and always a step behind his brother. A *spare*, he had called himself once, and the recollection of the last few years made it difficult to deny that he had been raised as such. He didn't seem to have a single thought that wasn't an echo of his brother's.

Huan was louder, brash, unquestionably the heir. He was good-natured when it suited him, but he overlooked his brother as elder brothers tended to, never mind he was only older by a few minutes. I had no inkling that the past few months would weigh as heavily on his mind as they had. An error on my part—in my mind, Eikaro was still alive. In Huan's, he was dead. Against that backdrop, my revelation held no weight. One way or another, this dragon took his brother away from him.

"He's tried to be strong these past few weeks," I said. "He had to be. It's the way we were raised. To uphold your duties first before personal interests. But we're not made of steel, no matter how much we want to believe it. The cracks will show, eventually."

"As I see it, the fault lies with their father," Khine said. "Why do you think Huan didn't arrest me when he saw me working for Dai? He's had it with his father."

"Is that how he found you?"

"I encountered his patrol while accompanying some of Dai's soldiers. I was grateful he decided not to stick his sword into me before asking questions."

"I hope he grants his brother the same courtesy." I glanced around the wilderness. I wasn't keen on the idea of tramping about further without a clear guide. The frenzied rush from earlier was replaced by a cold, impending sense of doom. I felt Khine's hand on my shoulder. Wordlessly, I turned to him, dropping my head against the crook of his neck and allowing myself to breathe in his scent. I felt him smooth the hair from my face.

The dragon roared in the distance.

"We never catch a break," Khine said with a slight grin. "I can see fire." He pointed in the distance.

"Good enough for me," I replied.

The snow reflected what little light there was, which helped us pick our way along the trail. I noticed that the roaring had grown soft, even as we got closer. I could also detect the sound of conversation, without a trace of the panicked screaming from earlier.

We came upon a low hill, fringed with trees, a few of which had already been set ablaze. Khine pointed at the rocks, and we started climbing in an effort to avoid the main trail. Moss and heather cushioned our knees as we gained ground. I parted the brush as we neared the ledge and was greeted by a quick blast, a gasp of air.

The dragon was bound. Loops of chain around his limbs stretched his body between the trees, preventing him from taking more than two steps at a time. His shoulder bled freely around a broken spear, wedged between his scales. *Eikaro*, I mouthed, hoping to catch a glimpse of his thoughts.

The dragon gurgled helplessly, beating wings into the air. A soldier approached and he snapped as he tried to take flight. The trees bent with his effort, but he didn't seem strong enough to break them.

"Leave it there," Warlord Ojika's voice called. "It'll tire itself out eventually."

"Must it be *this* dragon, Father?" Huan said, appearing beside him. There was a look of distaste on his face.

"We haven't come close to capturing one of this size before," Ojika said. "The others we've tried the procedure on were too weak."

"This dragon...and my brother..."

"This dragon is the first untainted one we've seen in decades. If we tame it, then at least your brother's death wouldn't have been in vain. Are you going to pout this whole time, Huan?"

"No, sir."

"Because you're not a child anymore. Stop acting like one. Whatever misgivings you have—deal with it." He placed a hand on Huan's shoulder. The other patted his cheek. "I'll ride the bloody thing, and maybe we'll be able to turn this war around because clearly *your* efforts haven't been enough. Is that clear?"

"Sir," Huan grumbled.

"I didn't hear you."

"Yes, my lord."

Ojika and the soldier walked off, leaving Huan alone. He was staring at the dragon, his face shadowed. I noticed his whole shoulder was drenched in blood, though he wasn't holding it in a way that made me think he was injured. It must have been the dragon's, or another man's. He unstrapped his cloak, letting it drop to the ground. He took another step towards the dragon.

The dragon lunged at him, teeth snapping.

"It can't be you," Huan wheezed.

The dragon opened his jaws. No flame blast—there wasn't enough air for that. The fire simply curled around his fangs, climbing over his bloody snout.

"My brother was my right hand," Huan continued in a low voice. "My shield. In all my life, I have never considered I would someday rule this region without him. And you took that away from me, you son of a bitch. From *us*. From his daughter, who will now never know her father."

The dragon roared.

"Lord Huan!" I called.

His face clenched, and his eyes darted towards the darkness. "My queen," he said, his expression softening. He walked towards the edge of the cliff.

"You need to believe me," I said.

"It's too much," Huan replied. "How could my brother be *inside* that thing?"

"After what you saw down there today, why would you even question it? He was a mage. He did it to preserve his life."

"My queen..."

"He was too injured. He believed there was no way he would've been able to make it off the ridge alive. So he switched with the dragon. A spell of some sort. I saw it with my own eyes."

Huan gazed back at me, realizing I was serious. He swallowed. "You spoke with him, you said. Why can't I hear him myself?"

"Something about our souls touching during the first switch," I said. "I was right beside him when he did it. But now—I can't hear him now, either. Lord Huan...I think your brother may be in trouble."

Huan looked like a man at the verge of madness.

"If you love your brother as you say you do..." Khine began.

Huan's face tightened. "It is not a matter of love, Lamang. What Iga told us down there. The blood of innocents...on top of this..." He turned to me, his jaw quivering. "Your father has done too much to this land, Beloved Queen. We need to put an end to it all."

"We *are* doing that," I said. "But killing this dragon won't bring your brother as he was back."

He didn't reply.

"Lord Huan," Khine said. "You're exhausted. The dragon isn't going anywhere. Perhaps you should rest. When does your father plan to carry out the procedure?"

"This dawn," Huan managed to croak out. "Most of the soldiers are heading back to the city. You should, too."

"I'm not leaving him alone with you like this," I said.

"I appreciate it, Beloved Queen. Believe me." Huan turned away and climbed back to the top of the hill. I saw the dragon lunge at him a second time, but he reeled away, refusing even to meet his eyes. I think he was afraid he would see Eikaro's familiar gaze in them.

After Huan had disappeared, I approached the dragon. He swung his head towards me, his swollen tongue flicking past his fangs. From this close, he was a sorry sight—blood dripped with his every motion, and his scales were dull and chipped. "My friend," I said, holding my hands out. "Eikaro…"

The dragon didn't attack, but he didn't answer, either. I saw him droop his head.

"Eikaro, you need to let me know if you're still there." I took another step. "Let me help you."

Eikaro suddenly swept his tail around, barrelling towards me. The chains rattled with the motion.

He stopped a hair's breadth away, so close he could easily grab me with his teeth if he wanted to. His tail stopped, too, bent in the soil like a coiled whip, a snake about to pounce. Carefully, I placed my hand on his nose, feeling the hot blood pulsing under my skin.

He gave a low groan.

I reached for the spear on his shoulder. His eyes snapped open, but he kept his claws to the ground and his teeth away from me as I attempted to pull it out. It wouldn't budge.

"I'm sorry," I whispered. I walked back to Khine, who looked pale. "Is there any way you can treat his wounds?"

He glanced at the dragon. "Tali, I'm not sure I want to get close to him ever again. I don't even like it when *you* do. You still can't talk to him?"

I shook my head.

"But the fact that he didn't try to tear you apart…" He swallowed, giving a nervous laugh.

"He isn't mad, Khine," I said. "It's the corrupted soul that causes the madness, and I know there isn't one inside of him. Look at him. There's light in his eyes."

Khine glanced at the dragon. He didn't look like he believed me.

"I've seen the mad dragons. They look nothing like these. If he's mad, none of us would've survived the arena at Kyo-orashi. But we did. He left as soon as he found an opening. We fight him, so he fights back, just like any wild animal. Look." I turned back to Eikaro, holding my hand out again. I heard Khine swear as the dragon lumbered closer.

Eikaro nudged me with his muzzle, a gurgle running through him. His scales quivered. I stroked the side of his face before leaning over to press my head against his. He closed his eyes.

"Gods," Khine breathed.

The silence inside my head was deafening. Had we lost our connection somehow? Was Eikaro still trying to talk, and I simply couldn't hear? The dragon now gazed back, yellow eyes gleaming, and I suddenly felt as if he was begging for something. A thought occurred to me.

"Are you trapped in there?" I asked.

He looked confused.

"Eikaro, hear me out. Why can't you speak? Did something happen? Are you still in there?"

Slowly, as if he was focusing all his energies into the one, small act, he nodded. Such a human movement looked odd on a wild beast.

"Tali," Khine broke in. "The soldiers."

"I'll be back," I promised the dragon. As we dropped to the ledge, I heard him croon after me, a long, lonely sound. It made the hair on my arms stand on end.

CHAPTER FIFTEEN

THE DRAGONRIDERS OF JIN-SAYENG

ᰍ ᰓ ᰝ ᰘ

We found shelter in a small cave not too far away. Khine swiped fire from one of the blazing trees and we spent the rest of the night busying ourselves with the campfire. There wasn't much else we could do in the dark. Khine insisted he would keep watch, that he was used to staying up and I could sleep until there was enough light to move around again, but I couldn't really fall asleep. My thoughts circled around what we had discovered in the dragon-tower earlier that day. I could still hear the sound of the small skulls rolling along the floor, couldn't get the image of my father beating Eikaro out of my head. *Beat him bloody against the wall* were Eikaro's words. Why did I dismiss it as a mere quirk of Yeshin's? I was so used to his ruthlessness that Eikaro's story seemed like a passing thought.

Not that his own father was any better. *This is the beat of the land, didn't you know, Talyien aren dar Orenar? Dragonlord, Bitch Queen—you would know this better than anyone.* I reached for my father's letter, pressing my thumb against the thin paper, yellowed with time. I felt the desire to burn it in the fire then and there.

I opened it instead.

My Dearest Daughter,

You always were stubborn. It was both my greatest joy and my greatest sorrow. You don't bow easily—I know, because I wouldn't. I suppose I carry much of the blame for this, but that is all in the past.

I showed you my memory of Sume Kaggawa's proposal because it is a momentous occasion in history: the moment that assured Oren-yaro victory once and for all. We won then, my child. It will take years for it to come to fruition, but Jin-Sayeng will finally belong to us, all because a woman thought she could twist my grief for her own. Penance cannot give your brothers back to us. Penance cannot raise the dead.

By now, I'll be dead, and if everyone did their jobs as they were supposed to, the tensions in the west should have reached a tipping point. Dai Kaggawa should be at war with Ojika Anyu. Such men, who wear their hearts on their sleeves, are always so useful. Haven't I warned you against such carelessness all your life? Dai Kaggawa wants power, Ojika Anyu wants power, and this war they are waging to control the Sougen is everything.

And by now, you should be married to Prince Yuebek. You now hold the key to everything. Implore him to ride west to subdue the war and win the love of the people. Defeat Kaggawa and have him executed—the brat never did know his place. Speak with Ojika Anyu. I have doubts about the man's competence, but surely by now he would know how to tame the dragons. I've supplied him with more than enough mages and time.

Listen carefully, Talyien...

I read the rest. The unease turned cold on my fingertips, turned to anger, and then something that went beyond—a sinking feeling of devastation, one I wanted to fight against from the bottom of my heart. My father, the egotistical madman, had wanted nothing but absolute dominance over the land. He had pretended to be concerned for its sake, but here was proof that power was all that mattered to him. The worst part was that he had succeeded so far.

No—the worst part was that I was surprised. I could question my father's love for me, but for the longest time his love for Jin-Sayeng was a certainty as real as the sky. Now, I held the proof that I was wrong about that, too.

"Is that the letter you found in the dragon-tower?" Khine asked, arriving with an armload of firewood. He frowned. "Can I read it?"

"You can't read Jinan."

"That's an unbelievably rude thing to say. I can learn."

"You're not going to learn Jinan by going through my father's letters, Lamang." I tried to keep my voice light.

He placed the firewood on the ground and slumped down next to me. "You look troubled."

I turned the letter in my hands. There was nothing else in it. Nothing else that mattered, in any case.

"What aren't you telling me, Tali?" Khine asked.

I stared at the crackling fire. Eventually, I took his hand. I looked at our fingers intertwined so I didn't have to look at his face. "My father couldn't close the rift himself, so he decided to ally with Prince Yuebek, who is a known mage. The man could do what he couldn't."

"What—he couldn't, or wouldn't?"

I stared at the letter. "My father was very old."

"So he didn't have much life left in him. Was he afraid? Why didn't he just end this when he could have? Did he expect to live forever?"

"He wanted power," I said. "Just as Yuebek does. The man will be risking his own life, and so you needed to give him a reason to come out here in the first place. And what does he want, beyond anything else?"

"You?"

I smiled. "My dear, you're reaching. It's not me he really wants."

He squeezed my hand and pressed it over his lips. "I'm biased, I suppose."

"He wants his own kingdom, which he will never get in the empire, not even if he assassinates his own brothers. Jin-Sayeng is the easier prey. But if he takes the whole nation by force, he'll be dealing with rebellions until the end of his days. My father arranged all of this knowing I would somehow find myself here, after everything."

"Your father is dead, Tali. What he thought shouldn't matter anymore. Surely another mage can do what Yuebek can. That *is* what you came out here to find out, isn't it?"

I hesitated, glancing at the letter.

He held his hand out. After a moment's hesitation, I let him have it. "If only you can see what you look like when you hold on to their words as if you don't matter. Will you let go, Tali? Can you live without that burden?"

I continued to stare at the letter until my eyes began to burn. "I don't think I have a choice," I said at last.

"Then..." Without waiting for my reply, he turned to the fire and dropped my father's letter into it.

I lunged forward to try to salvage it from the flames, but it was too late. I watched the fire consume the letter, soot curling up around the ink. *Listen carefully, Talyien...*

My insides felt numb as I watched my father's words turn to ash.

I heard voices in the shadows and reached over to grab my sword. The grasscutter felt light in my hands, a farming tool not really meant for fighting. I'd been lucky the last few times, but how long until my luck ran out? As I wrapped my fingers around the wooden hilt, I felt my joints creak, remnants from the vision my father had forced into my mind. I wasn't as old as he was, but somehow, I felt just as exhausted.

"If they are loyal to Huan, you may not have to fight," Khine said in a low voice.

"I don't think like that, Khine."

"I know. But let me talk to them. These people are just trying to survive the night. Not everyone is an enemy, Tali."

I was suddenly conscious of how tense I was, and I saw that he could see that, too. Even out of my cage, I was still a wolf. Just like my father, who couldn't simply accept the collar and chains that would ensure the land's salvation, who always had to have the upper hand. A wily wolf, until the end. Always a wolf. Always...

My throat tightened as I watched Khine step out into the open, calling for the soldiers. I stood at the ready, still expecting an attack, expecting to have to hack our way out of there the way I had done too many times before.

They approached him, lowering their own swords. The familiarity with which they regarded him brought to mind my own lack of diplomacy. My father raised me to be a politician, to always be on guard, to layer my every demand with a promise of what would happen if it wasn't met. But that sort of thing only worked when you had an army at your back, ready to lend weight to your empty words. Significance could be bought. The kind of queen I wanted to be had to learn to stop fighting.

Khine gestured to me, and I sheathed the sword and walked towards the soldiers, who bowed before stepping aside, revealing the two mages that had accompanied Warlord Ojika from the city. One was a tall man, the other a short, squat woman, both rendered soft and plump after years of rich Jinsein food.

They bowed low, in Zarojo-fashion, eyes on the ground, and named themselves Zuha and Direh, from some province in the empire I'd never heard of.

"Beloved Queen," Direh said, her voice quivering. "Lord Huan said you were here. You've graced us with your presence at last."

"Your father offered us a home when no one would," Zuha added. "Safety. Security. Everything we could've ever asked for, and more besides—he gave us a purpose, something to *live* for. Do you know what it feels like to be thrown out into the world, knowing people like you can be killed, exploited, without the right channels?" He held his hands out. "May I?"

I conceded. He took my hands in his, pressing both of them against his cracked lips. I felt ill at the thought of people giving me reverence out of the memory of my father.

"Is this why you've stayed all these years?" I asked.

"We've nowhere else to go," Direh replied. "Dageis seems such a strange, hostile land...the rules they hold over their mages are not the same as the ones back in Ziri-nar-Orxiaro. Too rigid, too...intrusive. And their customs are strange. Jin-Sayeng is...familiar. Rustic and provincial at times, but we prefer it that way."

"You mean to say that you have free rein to practice whatever foul spells you've got up your sleeves," I said mirthlessly.

Direh flushed. "That's not—"

I waved her explanation away. "The skeletons in the tower. You must've sold my father on the idea."

"Damaged children," Direh said. "They wouldn't have lived past their fifth year, if even."

I narrowed my eyes. "Is that the lie you tell yourselves?"

"It's the truth, Queen Talyien," Zuha broke in. "Not all who have a connection to the *agan* are as you see us. Many...are born not whole. Deformed, disabled, weak. Broken."

"That doesn't mean they didn't deserve to live."

Direh shook her head. "Some of these children couldn't even speak. They would have been a burden to their families."

"Did their families tell you that? Did you ask the children themselves? How would you have known? You didn't give them a chance. You killed them instead of showing them mercy!"

"Your father did," Direh said. "Insisted on doing it himself."

I had an image of my father striking Eikaro against the wall—of Eikaro grappling with those strong arms, thinking there was no escape, trying to pry him off anyway. The same arms that had held me up with such fierceness...

"Beloved Queen, they couldn't contain their abilities," Zuha finished for her. He sounded calmer, as if what they had done was a fact of life, like the turn of the weather. "What Warlord Yeshin did for them *was* the mercy. And at least their deaths were not in vain."

"You do not have systems in place to control the flow of *agan* in Jin-Sayeng," Direh added. "You used to, because of your dragons."

Almost as if he heard us, we heard Eikaro bellow in the distance.

Zuha held out his hand. "The children's blood—provided amplification for the spells we imbued in the dragon-tower. And Oka Shto, as you may know by now. Have you noticed the mirrors?"

"Hard not to." I struggled to contain my rage. If I had my way, I would burn it all down where I stood. But nothing I did could bring those children back.

"There's another dragon-tower out in the mountains," he said. "Right under the sky where Rysaran's dragon was destroyed years before your father's war. An older one that remains intact."

"I don't understand," I said. "We don't ride dragons anymore. Why do we need dragon-towers?"

"They're connected to the *agan*, and to each other, or they were in the old days. All the old cities had dragon-towers, each connected to the others, forming a backbone to Jin-Sayeng that was its greatest source of strength."

"I know that much," I said. "They captured excess dragon-fire, for when it built up inside the dragons, which we used for homes in the city." I paused. "Was this part of my father's plan? To establish Oren-yaro as the center once he found the secret to taming the dragons?"

"*Once* he found it?" Zuha asked, glancing at Direh. He gave a small smile. "No, my queen. You have it all wrong. He knew how to tame the dragons from the beginning. That's why we needed the dragon-towers."

I stared at her. My father said he was leaving it up to Ojika to discover the secret in the first place. *No, Tali. Remember how his mind works. He trusted few, and certainly not the ambitious. He knew how, but that wouldn't have been enough.* Warlord Ojika was a *test*.

Direh glanced at the fire we'd built and gestured towards it. "If you'll sit with us, Beloved Queen, we will explain the secret of Jin-Sayeng's dragonriders and why you've lost it all these hundreds of years."

———

Here is one funny thing that should be painfully obvious to most. History books lie.

History books lie because people lie, and those of us who find ourselves with the power to do so will bend the truth in order to make it fit the trajectory of our lives. The trajectory we believe we are destined for, that we deserve.

Somewhere along the line, someone—I am not going to say an Ikessar, but it was very likely so—decided that riding dragons had lost all meaning. The Ikessars rose to power because they rode dragons first, but with nearly every warlord and his bannermen in possession of dragons, their influence had grown stale. Little by little, over the years, dragonriding became a thing to vilify. Not directly, of course. This was still a land that worshipped dragons, and changing people's minds couldn't happen overnight.

But suddenly, a warlord with more than his fair share of dragons was too ambitious, too aggressive, and needed to be knocked down. Suddenly the Dragon-throne was demanding tributes from the provinces—their best hatchlings, which were then sacrificed in the waters of Lake Watu. Suddenly the Ikessars had brought in a new religion, a Nameless Maker no one in the nation had heard of before.

The mages were the next to go.

"You always had mages," Zuha said. "You didn't use the word. But they were members of your community—they maintained the dragon-towers, and the *agan* flow, and all the little tasks necessary to keep dragons in the first place. And they were needed for the nobles to ride dragons. Because you don't ride the dragons so much as you *become them*."

I suddenly remembered what Eikaro had done; how effortlessly he had traded his mangled body for the dragon's. Did these mages train him? Someone who was both mage and dragonrider—no wonder he found a way. I didn't want to trust these mages, but I had seen firsthand what Eikaro went through, and it all added up. I rubbed my temples for a moment before gazing at the mages through the fire. "So the Ikessars committed sabotage to retain power," I said. "They caused us to lose this knowledge over time. They made *us* forget. But they always knew?"

"The knowledge was hidden in their vaults for centuries. Your father was the first to find them in years."

"Tell me the details."

They explained. Dragons were large, intelligent, and prone to aggression, snapping their handlers' necks whenever they chose. But the Ikessars' ancestors, up in the mountains, somehow stumbled on the secret that certain people could tap into a dragon and share a body with it momentarily. That gave the impression that dragons were being ridden, when in truth the *rider* became the dragon, or at least was sharing the dragon's space. More skilled riders could even switch, as Eikaro had done, and gain full autonomy over the dragon's body; you just had to do it with a more placid dragon that you could trust would stay on the saddle without gnawing your own arms off. In most cases, both rider and dragon were inside of the dragon's body.

This left the rider's body without a soul. To keep it alive, and to offer a clear pathway back for the rider's soul, the riders were tattooed with spell runes—masked as elaborate tattoos that covered their arms and bodies, the pattern of which many Jinseins still wear today. The dragon-towers were built to further help with the transfers—each was built with spell runes that allowed riders to switch without a mage's help.

"So all you need are spell runes, or a mage, to ride a dragon?" I asked.

"No," Direh said. "Only Jin-Sayeng royals can ride them."

"What makes us so different?" I asked.

"The Ikessars stumbled onto the secret when they married women mages," she said. "It seems almost like sheer accident that this particular trait happened, because it's not exactly the same thing that connects a mage to the *agan*. Is it a mutation of the *agan* itself? An attunement made possible by the close proximity of dragons in those days? We know the basics are similar. Skill in the *agan* is traditionally passed down through the motherline—your mother or your father's mother. And so even *agan*-blind royals are capable of dragonriding—or more precisely, controlled soul-switching. Only those who carry the trait are capable—they've tried with others, even mages that don't carry the blood. Somehow, the very act of transferring kills them."

"The other clans followed the practice," Zuha interjected. "Which gave the royals the impression of power over time. It made the land believe the royals are *blessed*."

"Son of a bitch," Khine exclaimed. I gave him a look, and he closed his mouth.

"Didn't you ever wonder why your *motherline* is more important?" Zuha asked. "Why the council still recognized Lord Rayyel as his mother's heir, even when his father is a commoner?"

My own mother had come from Nee, once a royal clan. I stared at the flames, trying to piece together my own thoughts, trying to contrast them against what I had learned of my nation and what I was learning now.

"When the Ikessars began to dismantle the system they created, anything involving the *agan*, and mages, became blasphemy," Direh continued. "Suddenly, it wasn't such a good thing to have a child with the gift for the *agan*; suddenly, they were throwing such children to the sea. Suddenly, the dragons were becoming harder to ride, and even harder to capture, and no one seemed to remember why. The towers crumbled in time, and the dragons themselves started to disappear."

"Until Rysaran's dragon," I broke in.

Direh nodded. "It wasn't even a real dragon. That creature was nearly pure *agan*. An abomination, but it was like bringing water to a parched land. For all the destruction it caused, it also tipped Jin-Sayeng back to balance, calling your dragons back home."

The sky flashed. My skin felt as if it was burning, a far cry from the mere prickling it had felt so far. I wondered if it was because we were so near the rift, or because it was getting worse. "Some home," I said, when we could talk again. "Now it's breaking at the seams, and despite all this knowledge you've yet to tame an actual dragon."

"We were hoping it would work with this one," Zuha said. "It's taken longer than we had hoped, longer than Warlord Yeshin could've ever expected. All our experiments in the past have been failures. *Mad* dragons were not part of the equation, and the flow of *agan* in this area has simply become more unstable over the years. But this one doesn't seem to be mad."

"That's because Lord Eikaro is inside of it," I said.

The mages looked concerned.

"He switched successfully months ago, losing his own body in the attempt," I continued. "Did you teach him how to do that? He's the reason Warlord Yeshin entrusted you to Warlord Ojika, after all."

Direh's face flickered. "We did—in theory. But that's impossible. That dragon is too vicious."

"All I know is he's still in there," I said. "But it's like he's losing himself."

"The, ah…switch is dangerous in that sense," Zuha broke in. "You're not supposed to ride a dragon for very long. If it is as you say, then Lord Eikaro is forgetting what it's like to be a human. His thoughts are inside a dragon's brain, after all. If this works, then, it will be good—he may find reprieve in becoming a person once again."

"As his *father*," I replied.

"That makes it easier to connect them."

"He'll be wearing his father's skin."

They stared back at me, as if wondering what was so awful about that. I didn't know how to explain what I'd felt in the few moments Yeshin had thrown me into his memories. It was hard enough trying to shed your father's shadow all your life. To *become* him, even briefly…

"I need you to promise me Lord Eikaro will not come to any harm," I said.

They gave each other a wary glance. "Promise? No. We cannot promise anything, my queen," Zuha said. "The *agan* is unpredictable. Mastery of it is an art, no matter what the Dageians try to make you believe. We don't know the details—all we have are theories. We're blind painters, drawing mountains we've never seen."

A horn blasted in the distance.

"That's the signal," Direh said. "Please excuse us, Beloved Queen." They stepped away from the fire and back towards the hill. The soldiers saluted us before turning to follow them.

I turned to Khine. "Have you still got your sword, Lamang?"

He clinked it as an answer.

"You remember how to use it?"

"Are we fighting dragons again?" He looked concerned.

"With any luck, no," I said. "But if their ritual works, that'll be Warlord Ojika inside a dragon, and I'm not sure I like the sound of that at all."

CHAPTER SIXTEEN

THE MIRROR

ᛏᛁᛗ

Dawn lit the snow-covered hills like they were on fire, and for a moment I was convinced the dragon's flames had caused it. But the burning trees from last night were ashes on the ground, and there were no new ones ablaze. In the background, the scar above the mountains seemed faint against the grey clouds—an unremarkable strip, even as it brimmed with enough power to consume the world.

I heard a soft growl as we climbed up the trees and breathed a sigh of relief at the sight of Eikaro's hunched shadow in the distance. Ojika stood nearby, having shed his heavy armour; he was bareheaded, clad only in leathers and a small sword. His breath fogged around his mouth like smoke. You would have thought he had turned into a dragon already.

"It looks tired," Ojika said, observing the beast with a hint of amusement. "Will it even fly? Or will it go rolling down the hill like a dead log? Perhaps you were right about finding another."

"We're already here, Father," Huan replied. "I apologize for my harsh words last night." He, too, looked worn out, as if a whole night of fighting his father was as arduous as the hours his brother had spent fighting chains.

"You were always weak, Huan," Ojika laughed. "How do you expect to rule after I'm gone? Without a backbone, you'll have nothing to hold up that empty head of yours. You don't have your brother to do your thinking for you anymore. Learn to speak up."

"Yes, Father." He wouldn't meet his eyes.

Ojika turned to the mages. "You see what I have to deal with here? An obedient son, but not a lick of fire in him. No wonder you haven't been able to put an end to Kaggawa. You know, sometimes I *envy* Yeshin for his bitch pup. A pain, that woman, but imagine what a daughter like that could've been with the right guidance." He nodded. "Let's not dawdle."

"Be careful, Father," Huan called after him.

Ojika ignored him as he walked up to the exhausted dragon.

"They haven't told him," Khine whispered.

"Look at the man. You think he'd listen? An obedient son, he calls Huan, but Huan's just lost all energy to refuse him."

The chains rattled as the soldiers unclasped the locks. I saw Ojika huffing on top of the dragon, sweat rolling down the folds of skin on his neck and face. "Now, my lord!" Zuha cried, and I didn't see what they were doing, but I felt the prickling sensation on my skin.

The dragon took to the sky, chains dangling mid-air. I could barely see Ojika's figure between his wings. I watched the dragon soar like a bird, and for a moment stopped caring about the spell or if it worked. To see him free again, free to stretch his wings and dip into the clouds, was one of the most beautiful things I have witnessed in my life. I emerged from the clearing to join Huan, who acknowledged me with a small nod. "I know it's a stretch," he said, "but right now, I feel as if we can regain all of Jin-Sayeng's lost glories."

"If he's trying to claim the title of Jin-Sayeng's first dragonrider since Rysaran the Uncrowned," I said, "he's too late. Your brother has already claimed the title. But the months he's spent as a dragon have taken all of his senses. He needs to become human again, and they think if your father switches with him, this will give him that chance again."

His face flickered. He did believe me; it was only that the possibility I could be wrong was too painful to consider.

"Zuha!" Direh suddenly called out. She was bent over runes on the ground, her hands glowing. "It's not—"

"I know!" Zuha replied. "I'm trying!"

"Are you trying hard enough?"

"What's happening?" Huan broke in.

"I believe Warlord Ojika's soul isn't travelling to the channel. The dragon is rejecting him."

We heard a scream as the dragon dove. I noticed the movement of an animal trying to break free, like a horse attempting to dislodge its rider. Before I could even call Eikaro's name, he made a sweeping circle and the fat lump sitting astride him fell to the side, plummeting to the ground.

Huan dropped to his knees, his face white with the knowledge that either his brother or his father was dead. I squeezed his shoulder before racing down the hill to follow the soldiers. The dragon was making another sweep in the distance, legs curling under his body as he shot a full blast of flame through the clouds.

Ojika's body had been swallowed by the woods and was nowhere in sight. "The warlord?" I asked Zuha as he came running past me. "Or the son?"

"I don't know," Zuha said, his voice cracking.

"What the hell happened back there?"

"I don't know," he repeated.

"You said you were masters of the art," I hissed.

"I said no such thing," Zuha muttered. He looked at me, his eyes wide with fear. "But this wasn't a complex spell. You said Lord Eikaro did it, and he was as untrained as they came."

"Did the warlord's body reject the spell, Zuha?" Direh asked, appearing beside us.

"I don't know," Zuha said a third time, his eyes watering. His lips, too, were quivering, and I detected fear that went beyond a failed ritual and Lord Huan's wrath.

"I'm going into the forest," I said. "Stay with Huan, Khine. He might do something dangerous."

"And *you're* not going to?"

"Please. I'm always careful." I unsheathed my sword and strode into the forest. I followed the smoke rising from the burning branches and came across a trail of blood right at the edge of the wood. The branches must've broken the warlord's fall—I could see splintered wood and scattered leaves everywhere.

I followed the blood towards a low, flat building that contained crates and what looked like sacks of sand and rocks for the road they'd been building. Ojika was wedged between two wooden crates, as if attempting to keep his body from falling apart. One arm was ripped, and I thought I could see bone jutting out of his shoulder.

"Bitch Queen," he hissed through bloody teeth as I approached.

"Warlord Ojika, I presume."

His nostrils flared. "Are you a hallucination? Or have you come to gloat?"

I glanced at his injuries. "You have more to worry about than what I think."

"Gloat, then," he said, waving red fingers at me. "You killed Lushai, now you come for me. I knew we weren't careful enough. Obeying Yeshin, keeping you at bay. Not as easy as it sounds. You're a dangerous bitch. What the hell were we supposed to do? He wanted us to keep you in the dark."

"I don't know what you're saying, my lord. You seem to have done this all yourself."

"Spell should've worked," he wheezed. "It didn't, and you're here. Go on, then. Add to your list."

"I didn't come here to kill you."

"Didn't you?" He took a laboured breath. "Fucking Yeshin. Should've slammed my door on him the day he came."

"Greed makes fools of us all."

He laughed, sending red specks flying through the air. "He gave me legitimacy. The price you pay when you stick your nose into the royals' business. If not for him, the others would've torn us apart within the year." He wiped his mouth and stared at the blood, as if he couldn't quite believe it was there. "Well. I tried to keep my end of the bargain. Tame the fucking dragons. It sounded like an honour." He spat.

"I read my father's letter," I said. "He told me he needed the war here to draw Yuebek out."

Ojika tried to move his neck, realized he couldn't, and gave another smile. More blood continued to spurt out of his mouth with every breath. "Keeping a war going with a meddlesome son is... hard."

"What I don't understand is why take all that trouble?" I asked. "Why not get one of the other mages to do it?"

"None of those mages can ride a dragon," Ojika said. "They're Zarojo scum. You need Jinsein royalty."

"Then send them up with a rider."

Ojika shook his head, a smile tugging the corners of his berry-red mouth, as if he would have found my suggestions amusing if he wasn't on the verge of death. "A mage can protect themselves. A rider can't. That rift will kill an unprotected rider before the mage can reach it."

"You know this? You've *tried*?"

"This is the first dragon we've gotten close to taming," Ojika said. "And look at me." He snorted. "An honour. A nightmare. I got the hardest job. If I had a daughter..." But he trailed off as he attempted to wipe the bubbling blood from his mouth. "Yeshin wanted Yuebek up there. It wasn't my place to question it."

"He could've done it himself."

"Yes. I should've told my lord, the man Jin-Sayeng calls the Butcher, *he* should risk his life. Feel free to tell him, child, whatever good it will do for us now. Maybe the dead will rise from the ashes."

"He knew we need someone who is both a mage and a dragonrider. He could have at least tried. He was the only one who..." I paused, gazing at the smile that continued to graze the dying man's face.

"Apart from my lord, there are a few others who fit that description," Ojika said. "My son Eikaro. But closing a rift... is hard. Requires skill. Power. Proper training. Lord Yeshin thought my son's connection to the *agan* was... too weak. All I could do to convince him not to throw him with the others."

I thought about the skulls in the dragon-tower and heard them again, the hollowed sound of them rolling through the chamber.

"Warlord San's daughter," Ojika continued. "But San... is an arrogant asshole. Wouldn't give her up. Lord Yeshin threatened to expose her to Jin-Sayeng, but San held firm. *I'll obey you in everything but that*, the bastard said. *He* had the easiest job. All he had to do was not interfere." He coughed again, and waved his shaking fingers at my face. "None of them were right, anyway. Outside of Jin-Sayeng, no one would call them mages—they're untrained, unskilled. Royals in *name* only. We used to use the name *aron dar* to denote those whose motherlines are tainted with common blood, but even that has fallen out of favour, if your husband is any indication.

"This leaves one. Son of an *aren dar* Jeinza. Of a Lady... Maharay. That was her name. Was? I don't know if she's alive." He coughed. "She left Jin-Sayeng in Reshiro's time. Married an emperor. Fourth Consort, they called her."

"The Fourth Consort..." I began. "Yuebek's mother." *No*, I thought. No. That pustule of a human being—if you could even call him that—couldn't be Jinsein. I was counting on his foreign blood to discredit everything my father had offered him, but if he had the correct motherline, he could sway the people to his cause.

"You don't believe me?" Ojika asked, staring at my face. He made a haphazard wave. "Go back to the castle. Find the records. I've done what I can, pup. It's all on you. Try to spare my family. Huan's dumb enough to kneel. Save my legacy, just like I saved your father's. It's the least you can do after all this."

He lunged. I sidestepped, but he was only going for my sword hand. Pulling my arm up, he pressed the blade against his throat. I stared into his eyes. I thought about my son and my father, and then I thought about my father's letter burning in the fire last night. My own eyes watered.

I slit his throat cleanly, then stabbed him through the stomach and up the heart to make it quick. His expression bordered between pain and gratefulness. The broken body slumped to the ground. Blood spurted from his fat neck, congealing between the creases.

A dark shadow crossed the sky just as I left the forest. The dragon was above me, trying to rip the chains off his limbs. He managed to dislodge the one on his wrist. As the chains dropped from the sky, he made a gliding turn, his wings like a canvas laid over the clouds.

I stood my ground, prepared to defend myself with a mere grass-cutter blade. The dragon missed me entirely. He crashed to the ground, his snout digging into the mud.

"*My queen.*" A faint sound, as thin as a stray thought, flitted by.

"You're still there," I said.

The dragon narrowed his eyes and snarled. But he didn't try to take my head off, either.

"If you stay inside that body, we'll lose you," I said, holding out my hands as I approached him. "Why didn't you accept him? He was your father."

He touched my palm with his nose before turning his head, his eyes settling on someone behind me. Huan appeared, a thin line over his brow. "I know what he wants," Huan croaked out.

Eikaro curled his neck. His mouth opened.

"You rejected our father for this, brother?" Huan asked. "I suppose I know what you'll say next. That he'll be the ruin of us all. But he was our father." He shook his head and turned to the mages. "You know what to do."

"But Lord Huan—" Direh began.

"It's *Warlord* Huan now," he said, baring his teeth. "Weak, Father called me. Let's see if it's true." He gestured at Zuha. "The spell."

Zuha swallowed. "Very well, my lord. Step forward."

Huan held his arms out. The dragon rushed forward to meet him, and for a brief moment I had a recollection of how we had been in the arena in Kyo-orashi, how he had attacked us like a wild beast, pounding rock into dust and snapping at us with razor-sharp teeth. I was almost afraid he would savage Huan on the spot.

Instead, they embraced each other.

The dragon's large head draped over Huan's shoulder, pulling them together as the *agan*-blue glow surrounded the air. Huan's own arms reached around the dragon's neck. "I'm sorry, brother," I heard Huan whisper. All the anger was gone from his voice. "I would have come sooner if I had known. But it's over. It's over. I'm here now."

Silence surrounded us, broken only by the whispering of the wind.

A moment passed. "Lord Huan?" I asked.

The dragon grunted.

The man stepped away from him, looking at his hands with a smirk on his face. "I never imagined I would...that I would ever find myself..." His voice was a touch higher. Softer.

"Welcome back, Lord Eikaro," I said.

He grabbed my hand and dropped to his knee. "My queen. From our time on the ridge and all the way in Kyo-orashi—even when I tried to hurt you, you never gave up on me. What did I ever do to deserve it?"

I pulled him up. "You're a friend, Eikaro. Isn't that enough?"

He gave me the briefest of smiles. It felt odd not to even think of him as Huan; it was Eikaro's mannerisms that set him apart from his brother, and they were all coming back, as if he had never left. He turned to the dragon, who was staring at his surroundings, as if not quite sure what to make of his new body.

Khine approached us now. "The spear..." he said, pointing at the dragon's injuries.

"He won't hurt you," I said.

"*Not much*," I heard Huan reply.

Khine, sensing the exchange, gave me a nervous glance.

"He agrees," I said.

The dragon spread his wings as Khine approached. With Zuha's help, he managed to pull the spear out. "Let it bleed," Khine said, examining the wound. "It's a clean cut. It'll heal soon."

"You should try flying, Huan," Eikaro said.

"*Shall I end this war, then?*" Huan's voice was clear, and just as distinct in my head as Eikaro's dragon-voice had been.

"We're ending all of it," I said. "Kaggawa is here because we've done nothing about the rift. Let's turn his hero's charge into a tyrant's slaughter." I turned to the mages. "You were looking for a dragonrider this whole time. It's not what you expected, but now you have him. Both of you can ride Warlord Huan to close the rift."

They stared at me, as if I'd just asked them to grow an extra head.

"Beloved Queen..." they began. "This isn't how it's supposed to go. Your father—"

"Is dead," I said. "I don't care what he wanted. My father was a treacherous bastard who wasted his last years looking for more power when he could have taken care of this immediately. I'm not him. Do this, and you will both be rewarded. Don't, and..."

I saw Huan's wings unfurl. His mouth was half open.

I stopped him.

"Don't," I continued, "and you are both free to go. I cannot force you to do something you won't—I will not ask you to die for *my* land." I got to my knees and bowed until my head touched the ground. "But you know more than anyone here how important this is. You are our only hope. Please."

Direh stepped over to take my hand. "We told you this is our home now, too," she said, pulling me up. She turned to Zuha. "We will do as you ask."

Zuha hesitated for a moment before nodding. "Will he know where to go?" he asked, looking with trepidation at the dragon. "Is he..."

"He remains your lord," I said. "You may not hear him, but he is as he was when he stood here before you."

Huan shook himself before bending down to offer them a clear path to mount him. "*Kaggawa will lay siege soon,*" he said as the mages clambered to his back. "*Talk to my general about it. Even if we close the rift now, we still have to contend with the attack.*"

"We'll hit him from both sides. Be safe, my lord," I said. Huan dropped his head once before taking to the sky.

"*You'll want to see your daughter, too,*" he called to us, just as he disappeared between the hills.

"A daughter?" I asked, glancing at Eikaro. "Did Tori give birth already?"

"Just over the winter," Khine said, wiping blood from his hands.

Eikaro seemed dumbfounded by the idea. "I'd never thought I'd get the chance to see them ever again." He gazed back at Khine. "I thought I'd lost myself. In Kyo-orashi—that was you, wasn't it?"

Khine rubbed his shoulder, as if the very act of reminding him about those events made it hurt.

"I have to apologize about that," Eikaro continued. He glanced at me. "I wasn't myself. They starved and beat me before they threw me in there. I almost didn't recognize the queen, either."

"Kyo-orashi is a long way from here. What were you doing out there in the first place?"

"I wanted to keep an eye on you, and the only way to do that was to scour the roads. Warlord San's scouts were looking for dragons, and I wasn't careful." He was still staring at the sky. "And now I'm worried about them."

"I'd love to see what's happening out there, but as we are, we can only wait and see," I said. "Let's go back to the city."

He sighed. "If I can remember how to walk."

I held out my arm for him. A moment, and then he took it, leaning against me as we made our way down the path. We didn't look back, nor did we talk about his father's death. Some things were better left unsaid.

"You're going to have to pretend you're your brother," I said as soon as we saw the tower looming before us, the mountains receding as the silhouette of Yu-yan grew closer. "Your father tried to tame a dragon and was thrown to his death. That's all we need them to know."

There were soldiers waiting for us up ahead. Eikaro straightened himself as best as he could, and I suppose to the untrained eye he could pass for Huan well enough. "Warlord Ojika is dead," he said, striding forward. "The others are with his body up at the ridge. Send men to fetch it before the dragons come."

The soldiers didn't even question it. They saluted, heads bowed. "Yes, Warlord," they all said. They scattered immediately.

Eikaro wiped his forehead. "This may sound strange, but I've never done this before," he whispered nervously. "You'd think we would've played that old trick on people at least once in our lives. But to take Huan's place, even for a prank, seemed like sacrilege. And now..." He glanced at the sky.

We returned to the castle through the most discreet path possible. A woman, several months' heavy with child, came running to us.

"Huan!" Grana exclaimed. "I heard what happened with Father. Are you—"

"I'm sorry." Eikaro drew away from her offered kiss with discomfort. "I can't lie to her. My queen…?"

Grana turned sharply, noticing me for the first time. "Beloved Queen? But why—"

"Not out here, please," Eikaro continued.

She dropped his hands, recognition flitting over her face. Anyone who knew them both well would know the difference immediately. But her lips wouldn't acknowledge what she knew stood right in front of her.

"It's me," Eikaro said. "My brother and I—we switched."

She remained silent.

"I wasn't dead," he stammered. "I've been inside a dragon the last few months. I—"

I held a hand out, gesturing at all of them to keep quiet.

We walked to a chamber, one I figured must've been Warlord Ojika's personal meeting room. I saw Eikaro's eyes wander over to his father's things—to the ceremonial armour, strapped to a dummy in the far corner. He looked ill.

Grana's face had turned sheet white. "Where is he, Eikaro?" she finally asked. "What did you do to my husband?"

"Huan is safe," Eikaro replied. "We've switched, and we can always switch again. He's flying north right now, but he'll be back soon." He rubbed his nose. "May I see my wife, please?"

She looked like she wanted to argue. But after a moment, she gave a soft sigh and stepped through the door.

We didn't speak while waiting for her. Eikaro rubbed his arms repeatedly, as if he was cold, and he kept glancing around the room with the unease of a caged animal. He wandered back to his father's armour, his lower jaw quivering.

"I didn't want to reject him." He glanced at me. "But the dragon's rage felt like my own. No—it *was* my own. The things that used to restrain me, his command, his words…I was a dragon! What need did I have for them anymore? And he barged in like…like I was nothing. Like he still owned me, the way he acted when I was still a child. My brother's spare, his shield, whatever my father decided I was. Now he wanted me to be his dragon, his *pet*. He didn't even recognize me. He screamed at me to step aside. I called for him. *Father*, I said. And he laughed." He flared his nostrils, as if trying to blow away a puff of smoke that wasn't there.

Grana returned, her twin sister, Tori, right behind her. There was an infant in her arms. "You're lying," she told her sister, her eyes on Eikaro. "He's wearing Huan's robes. Grana, what a rotten trick to play. I shouldn't have come—"

Eikaro rushed forward to hold both her and the infant, tears rolling down his face. Tori's own lip quivered. He whispered something in her ear, and then suddenly she, too, started sobbing. He pulled her and the infant into his arms, and I had the distinct impression that even if you tried to break them apart, you wouldn't be able to. A wave of wistfulness overtook me. It was like looking into a mirror that showed you what you most truly desired: a snapshot of something that could never be. I turned away quickly before the unease could show on my face.

Someone knocked. I went to open the door and came face-to-face with my cousin Nor.

CHAPTER SEVENTEEN

THE SIEGE

M y first-ever meeting with Nor happened during the uproar over my husband's disappearance six years ago.

I had been pacing in the great hall, arguing with Arro about how I was
handling the entire situation. He was telling me to calm down—that I needed
to show the nation my strength, which included remaining coherent enough not
to start threatening every single royal who *seemed* like they supported Rayyel's
behaviour. I must've told him the most convenient places to stuff his advice in.

And then Ozo arrived, bearing news of my new Captain of the Guard. "Nor
aron dar Orenar," he introduced, right before I could begin shouting at Arro
again. I managed to hold my tongue and turned to face the tall, straight woman
standing like a pillar behind him.

"Excellent," I drawled. "Now they'll really think I have something to hide."

"That ship sailed the moment you sent Agos away without so much as a
word of warning to me," Ozo replied. His voice was the same way a river looked
at the widest part—calm and measured at first glance, but narrow it down and
watch as the current turns to raging fury. I knew I needed to tread carefully.

But I was young, and all General Ozo had ever seemed to me in those days
was an old man trying to grasp at the last threads of the power he shared with
my father. Had I thought to win the influence of the region's bannermen for
myself in those days, he might've had a harder time masterminding the events
that would bring me face-to-face with Prince Yuebek. Of course, my personal
problems took precedence. "I was trying to protect Agos," I said.

Ozo's eyes flashed. "From what?"

"From scandal."

"Sending him away *proved* whatever scandal you're referring to. If he had stayed, we could've smoothed it over."

"And if he had stayed perhaps he'd be dead by now. You know how the Ikessars work!"

"Not in all the years I've been alive has an Ikessar assassin been able to make its way to the palace," Ozo said. "For them to risk political upheaval to take care of a mere *guardsman*..."

Looking back at it now, it must've rankled Ozo to call his son that, and nothing more. His greatest sacrifice, he'd said.

"It's done," I had said, lifting a hand to silence him. "I've made a decision."

"Look at you," Ozo said. "They crown you queen and suddenly..."

I got up from my throne, my hand dropping to the hilt of my sword. Whether he thought of me as a spoiled child or a true threat, the movement made him turn away. "Captain Nor," he said, changing the conversation as quickly as if we'd just been discussing the weather, "is a second cousin of yours. Her mother's sister rules one of the holdings in the foothills."

"We welcome you to our humble abode, Captain Nor," Arro said with a bow. "I've heard much of your work with the city guard. I am pleased to know the queen will be in safe hands."

She stepped forward to take my hand, pressing it against her forehead. I had her pegged as someone who never missed a day of training. She didn't say anything then, didn't greet me, didn't offer any pleasantries. A rock cut from the earth itself.

Now, years later, she remained just as silent.

"General Nor," Grana said.

"General," I repeated. "You've moved up."

"The previous general met an untimely...end...during that first attack on Kaggawa's estate," Grana replied with a smile. "General Nor proved herself quite valiantly in the battle, and she told us you no longer needed her services, so...here we are."

I gazed at my cousin with a smile. Here we were, indeed. I knew it wasn't her fault, but a part of me wanted to blame her for what had happened since. Would Nor have been able to detect Kaggawa's men trailing us, or smell Agos's treachery from a mile away? If she had, would he still be alive?

It was the kind of conjecture that could ruin a person just because of how easy it is to lay it all on a straw man. She was my sworn guard—most would've expected her to die for me. I certainly did. And yet Agos made just as much of a mistake, choosing his own interests over mine. Power may make us think otherwise, but we don't hold people's minds and we don't hold their hearts. An irony that must've kept my father awake all those years—that we would be given these responsibilities and expectations, bestowed the blessings of the gods in front of thousands, and yet faced with a thing as simple as human desire we act like children screaming at broken toys. Move, we tell them. *Move.* Can't you see? It's all for your own good. I'm...

No better, I know. Especially not after the last few days. As I stood there, wondering what else I would say to her, she walked straight across the room to salute Eikaro. "My lord," she said. "Kaggawa's men are at the gates. The siege has begun."

Nor led us to the battlements, to the top of the southwestern defense tower. I held my breath. There were so many soldiers camped in the distance that the sea of green that the Sougen was known for had become a sea of black, and the red and yellow of Kaggawa's flag. Off in the distance, I spotted logs piled high next to flat wooden pads.

"Bases for trebuchets," Khine commented, noticing my gaze.

"How long can you hold?" I asked Nor.

She stared down, unblinking. "Hard to say," she finally admitted. "We've got a few weeks' worth of supplies left. With the gods' blessings, it won't have to come to that. Warlord Huan had tasked me with gathering forces for a counter-assault. All we need is to brace ourselves for the first wave. Later tonight, we'll meet them at their own camp and cripple them any way we can."

"Do you have the numbers for an attack like that?"

She looked uncomfortable.

"Father was...counting on the dragon to turn the tide," Grana broke in. "That's what he told me."

I noted the lie immediately. Warlord Ojika would have kept the truth from her.

Nor shook her head. "With all due respect, Lady Grana, I told Warlord Ojika it was lunacy. His untimely death proves just that. We know nothing about these creatures, not anymore."

I stared at the army down below, remembering my father's letter. He had asked Warlord Ojika to draw the war out in order to increase Kaggawa's confidence, because he needed it to be a big enough threat to give Yuebek an excuse to travel here with his army and quell it. It had worked so far, perhaps too well. Kaggawa had used up all his resources to transport his mercenaries to the plains, and now I couldn't imagine a way to get rid of them. Was there merit to Warlord Ojika's lie? I imagined he could burn a path to break apart Kaggawa's soldiers, where the Yu-yan defenders could pick them off from the wall, but that would leave *him* open for their arrows, too. I didn't know how many arrows a dragon could hold against, but I could imagine enough would kill one. And that sort of brazen display wouldn't do anything. Make a dent on this army, and they would still come. Kaggawa still had my boy. Only stabilizing the region would make him see reason. Only closing the rift could get him to stop. I glanced at the sky, hoping Huan's task was as simple as it seemed. *If it was just like closing a door, maybe.*

I kept my thoughts at bay as Nor continued to take us through the city defenses. She was in her element—screaming at the soldiers and the city guards, directing them to where they needed to be. It made me wonder why the Oren-yaro decided she would spend the last five years as my guard captain. Did the Oren-yaro find me so unstable they would waste a woman of her talents on me? "Is it wise to attack now?" I asked again. "Most people would wait until the enemy is worn out from hunger."

"Warlord Huan is convinced their confidence can be shattered easily. They're mercenaries; if they know we won't go down easily, it will affect their morale. Isn't that so, my lord?" She glanced at Eikaro, who glanced down.

Suspicion flitted over her features. "Warlord Huan," she repeated.

"I…"

She turned back to me. "Something's wrong," she finally said. "What did you do to him?"

"Nothing," I said.

She glanced at the soldiers around us before crossing her arms. "Tali," she finally said. "I've known you long enough to know what *nothing* means, coming from you. Be straight with me."

Before I could answer, we heard a roar from the sky. The dragon's dark shadow blocked the sun as he glided into the city.

"Blessed Akaterru," Nor muttered under her breath. "Get the archers here, now! That beast is going to burn us all!"

"Stand down, General," I said. "You were looking for Warlord Huan, and he's returned."

"The queen is right," Eikaro said. "My father's death was not in vain. We have a dragon on our side."

Black smoke blew like tendrils in the distance.

"I don't think we do," Nor said, just as the first screams sounded from the western district.

We dashed down into the city, through the chaos of soldiers attempting to shoot the dragon down. Even before I reached the street, I knew something was wrong; Huan wasn't attacking the city. He was flying in circles, as if struggling with something himself. An archer from the battlements made it up to the roof below and sent an arrow flying towards his head.

The arrow grazed the side of his muzzle. Huan threw his horns back before he came crashing right into the tower. "*Direh fell,*" Huan called into my thoughts. "*You can't send a person up there. This one—*"

A creature leaped off his back, a gnarled, twisted beast that wore Zuha's robes. Its fingers had turned into claws. It sniffed the air before it made a running leap.

Nor lifted her sword before it could get close and swung with the surety of someone who had done this sort of thing since birth. The full weight of her sword struck the mage's shoulder—blood sprayed as the blade sank in, tearing out a hunk of flesh to reveal the bone underneath. The injury didn't seem to faze it. It dropped to the ground like an animal, the arm uselessly hanging beside its rib cage, before it made another mad dash, jaws snapping, aiming for her legs. There was no room for her sword to swing at that angle, but she kicked its snout as it came close with such force it threw its head back. In that instant, she readied her blade and cleaved its head from its body. The head rolled a few feet away, jaws snapping as it left a black trail along the ground. The headless body toppled on its side, leaking more black fluid. It smelled vile, like a corpse that had been left too long to percolate in its own juices.

I darted for Huan, who was struggling to stand. Blood dripped from the wound on his chest. "What happened?" I asked.

"*We couldn't get close,*" Huan said. "*The* agan *is too strong out there, and the mages' shield failed. Something struck us. I crashed against a cliff and Direh fell to her death. Zuha held on, but by the time we reached the edge of the mountains he wasn't talking anymore. He turned into that thing. I flew back this way hoping I could get rid of him on the plains, but he was too much."*

"They said even the Dageian mages weren't immune to the corrupted souls," Eikaro said. "The rift must be making it difficult to keep up defenses."

"We're running out of mages," I said. "Do you have others up your sleeve, my lord?"

Almost as if it heard me, there came a gurgling sound from Zuha's headless body, which had bloated to twice its size. *"Step back!"* Huan roared, lunging, his bent body contorting so he could cover us with his wings. The body burst, like a tick squeezed too hard. Spiders crawled from the black sludge left behind.

The air started flashing, as if lightning continued to strike. The world began to spin; I heard screaming from every direction, punctuated by Huan's roars as he tore into an unknown enemy I couldn't see. I fell to my knees as the chaos mounted, blood on my hands. The iron scent crawled up my nostrils, making it hard to breathe. I reached for my sword, the damn grass-cutter, and struggled to draw it.

Well, Talyien? My own thoughts held my father's voice. Even now, after everything, I couldn't get rid of them. *What do you do now? How can you be queen if all you're good for is chasing your own tail?*

I drew the sword just as a beast appeared through the flashes. It was in soldier's armour, which told me this wasn't someone who'd made the trade willingly. Somehow, Zuha's body had brought with it a taint, something making it possible for the corrupted souls to invade people without their permission. It was a dizzying thought. Who was turning, then? Who was the enemy?

I slew the soldier, intricately aware that the only answer to my question was *ourselves.* We were killing ourselves to survive. I kept my back to Huan, who was still snapping. "Where's Eikaro?" I called.

"Right here, Beloved Queen," he said, before another flash. He stumbled; I caught him right as a creature appeared between us. It reared, claws swiping empty air. I struck it on the rib cage, one slice downward. It pounced, saliva spraying in the air. I stumbled back and found myself fending its teeth from my throat with the short blade. Huan picked it up from behind, his massive fangs crushing its body. Guts leaked through the punctured flesh, and its organs burst like grapes. Jowls dripping with blood, Huan sent it flying through the air.

"That body is causing this," I said. "Is there any way you can contain the *agan*, or whatever this is? Seal it."

Eikaro looked worried. But all he said was, "Get me there."

"You heard him, Lord Huan," I called.

Huan charged ahead, a massive battering ram of scale and horn and teeth. In the same breath, I met an incoming beast with a strike across the chest. The edge of the blade sank into bone almost immediately; I pulled out and watched as the body spun to the ground, jaws snapping. I could see Zuha's writhing corpse not far ahead. Even half desiccated, it wasn't hard to miss—the entire thing glowed blue between bursts of black clouds.

The air crackled as Eikaro approached it.

"I don't know what to do," he gasped.

"You call us *agan*-blind," I said as I fended off another incoming creature. "So *you* must see something we don't."

"I see the tendrils connecting something in the body to the main *agan* stream," Eikaro said. "They look like glowing threads."

"And they say *agan* flows freely behind the fabric," I said, sinking my sword through yet another belly. My arm was starting to tire from hacking, and my sword to dull from the assaults. "A fabric separating us from the spirit world. Do *you* see it?"

"No," he replied.

Huan roared behind us as he grabbed two creatures, ripping both apart in the air at once.

"So, this fabric isn't visible to anyone, but damages to it could be. We can see the tear from the sky. There must be something like that inside the body."

He grew quiet. I turned my attention to fighting, hoping I was correct. Maybe we could only see the one in the sky because it was so big. How *do* you fight an enemy you don't see? And if you do see it, how do you know how to defeat it? There was no certainty in our actions; we were grappling blindly in the wind, making a mess out of things we had long forgotten, magic we had turned our backs on. *Three mages, two mages, one. Do you give up, Talyien? Or would you sacrifice your land because you are too stubborn to bend? Why did you think it took me years to plan this? What made you think you could find an easier answer in months?*

"I see it!" Eikaro suddenly called. "I see the hole!"

"Shut it," I said.

"How?"

I wanted to yell at him. I wasn't a mage—I knew less than he did. But then I glanced at the battlements and caught sight of Khine scanning the streets for me. "Like a surgeon," I suddenly said. "You can control the flow of *agan*, Eikaro. Sew it shut!"

I wasn't sure if he understood, but I saw him hold the body down with his foot as he bent over it. Huan blew a quick breath beside me, his wings half curled.

The flashes stopped and I could suddenly see our surroundings again. Eikaro toppled backwards, landing on the cobblestone. He was shivering. I pulled him up. The monsters were still coming, slinking from the alleys and the streets. The ones who had already turned weren't turning back.

We found Nor yelling at the top of her lungs from the bottom of a guard-house. There was a flash of relief on her face as she saw me before she ushered us through. As soon as we ran past her, she slammed the door shut. Bodies smashed against the wood behind us, followed by the scratching of sharp claws.

"Gods, I thought I'd lost you," Khine breathed, reaching out to pull me in his arms. There was blood on his shirt, as if his wound from yesterday had reopened. I stiffened, oddly conscious of the people around us even though everyone was too busy reinforcing the door to pay any notice.

Give up. The voice was becoming impossible to silence. *You have no mages left to use and your only dragon is bleeding with every step. This man, and all the others—they will die soon if you do nothing.*

"Are you all right, Tali?" he whispered in my ear.

I didn't answer as I pulled away. Ignoring the screaming and the snarling from the streets, I climbed up the ladder to the battlements. I looked over the wall, where I noticed siege towers rising in front of my eyes.

"The gods have abandoned us," Grana whispered below. "Attacks on the outside, and from within...how are we supposed to win this war?"

"And we haven't closed the rift, either," Eikaro said. "If we did, we could parley."

"Could you do it?" I asked.

He looked at me in panic.

"If you switch back with Huan—"

"You saw me back there," he said. "Queen Talyien, if the rift is twice the size of that hole, I wouldn't know how to deal with it. That trick we pulled probably won't work. And it's bigger—much bigger. Warlord Yeshin always suspected I didn't have the power to pull it off, and he's right. I'm useless. I can't do it, I'm—"

"If we catch them by surprise, we might have the upper hand," Nor said. "Isn't it clear? We have to defeat Kaggawa first."

"No," I said.

They stared at me like I'd gone mad.

"We can't win this war," I said. "Not as we are. Look outside—that didn't happen overnight. That happened because Warlord Ojika *let* it—because he gave Kaggawa time to build an army while his own people starved. You won't get rid of it overnight, either. To attack now would be to court certain death. *Don't.*"

Nor grabbed me by the arm. She pulled me back down to the guardhouse, and for a moment, I thought she would hit me. "This isn't the time for this. You're breaking morale."

"This isn't about morale. It's the truth."

"The truth!" she spat. "Some queen you are. There is a time for truths and now isn't it. If you acted more like a queen, I would've never left your service. But you never did. You were always a little girl, sulking that she didn't get her way, and now we all have to pay the price!"

I pretended that her words didn't sting. "I could've had you beheaded for what you did," I replied, standing as tall as I could so I could look her in the eye. "I didn't."

"Do you expect accolades for your thoughtfulness? Of course you could've had me beheaded. A better queen wouldn't have thought twice. I'm alive. A walking, breathing proof of your inability to lead."

"Nor—"

"But Agos," she continued. "The one loyal to you. Him, you get killed. You are trying to act like a queen, like your word is law, but it's over, Talyien. Look outside those walls. Look beyond. This isn't Warlord Ojika's fault, nor is it Dai Kaggawa's. No law exists in these lands anymore—you've doomed us to a fate worse than death. We have to fight! What else can we do? Hide while we starve to death?"

The snarling outside the door continued.

"Queen Talyien," Eikaro broke in. "We could also surrender and seek Kaggawa's assistance in ridding the city of these... things. Our wives' mother is on

Meiokara. If we can make our way to the islands, maybe we can ask them for help, too."

"We can't surrender," Nor snapped. "Kaggawa has no reason to spare *or* listen to us. He certainly won't spare your family—your father has goaded him for far too long. Open those doors and his mercenaries will slaughter us before we could blink. *Queen Talyien*, make a decision, one that won't kill us all."

I listened to my own heartbeat, reflecting the war drums around us.

Listen carefully, Talyien...

I stepped back to the guardhouse. The soldiers were trying to hold the door closed.

"Back down," I ordered. I grasped my sword with one hand, readying myself. They looked at me in confusion.

"There is no sense arguing while we're in the middle of a fight," I said. "And we can only fight from here on. Let them in."

The soldiers stepped aside. The door fell in almost immediately. Monsters streamed through the narrow opening, two at a time. It was easy enough to hack them to pieces.

Defining moments do not exist. Arro told me that once. If you wait for answers to reveal themselves, you'll be standing with empty hands for the rest of time. Deities do not descend from the heavens to part the clouds and shoot sunbeams over what must be done. They do not sing songs to guide you, nor send prophets to gather the lost. Those who think otherwise are usually mad.

We fought for our lives that night without hoping for an escape, killing the corrupted—those who dared reveal themselves—as they came. By midnight, their bodies were piled high along the streets, desiccated grey forms that looked like they had been left for weeks under the sun. We barely had time to breathe when the first wave of flaming logs and boulders smashed against the ramparts, taking down the top of at least one tower. The Yu-yan soldiers met the attack with a flurry of arrows, and we waited in silence until the trebuchets stopped.

There were more bodies by dawn, arrow-riddled on the field before us. We surveyed the carnage from the battlements over lunch—two pieces of unleavened bread, the standard ration for the entire day. I felt my stomach tighten as

I watched Kaggawa's men attempt to fetch their dead in the distance. Some of the Yu-yan soldiers tried to shoot at them for sport. Nor watched all of this from the battlements, her silence speaking volumes.

"We may have to hold, anyway," she finally said, drawing a deep sigh.

I was sitting with my back against the wall, resting my sword hand on my knee. I laughed. "Warlord Yeshin," I said, when I could catch my breath. "I want to rip apart everything about me that reeks of him and burn it to pieces. But how much would that leave behind?"

"Nothing, if I know how procreation works," she said flatly.

I sniffed. "Ever the humourless bitch."

She scowled. But after a moment, she slumped down beside me with the back of her head against the wall. "What do you want to do now?" she asked.

"Defeat Kaggawa, free my son, close that rift, and get rid of Yuebek somehow." I closed my eyes briefly, and then opened them again. My mind was still filled with the images of the dead and dying.

"Let me reiterate. What do you want that's *possible*?" She pointed at the field. "Escape now, with Kaggawa at our door, will be difficult. If I send guards with you, they'll see you and shoot you down before you do anything useful."

"I can sneak out alone."

"And then you're going to travel back to Oren-yaro alone, too, I suppose? Like you've always done? No. I'm not your captain anymore, but someone has to do the job." She tapped her fingers on her knee. "If you can escape along the river, I can have Lord Huan send word to his scouts. They'll accompany you all the way back." I noticed her avoiding saying the word *home*. Maybe the thought was as painful for her as it was for me.

"They can meet us at Khine's hut," I said. "I believe Lord Huan knows where it is."

"Lord Eikaro's idea of imploring Meiokara for help sounds tempting."

"Meiokara is all the way in the islands," I replied. "And if I recall correctly, they don't easily get involved with the fighting on the mainland."

"They might if their daughters are involved."

"They won't fight for me," I said. "I haven't earned it."

Nor grunted.

"You could say I'm wrong, you know."

"But you're not."

"I know." I sighed. "I came all the way here because I thought I could find people who would dedicate themselves to my cause. That people would see me for myself, not my father, and that would be enough. And yet look what happened. I can't even ask *you* to do anything without questioning me, and I don't blame you. I'd have done more if I was in your place. Stuck a sword through my gut and twisted it. Good intentions are worthless on their own. Who was it who said that? Iga did. Ryia, too."

She flexed her fingers. "So you've finally met her."

"She's even more humourless than you are, if you can believe that."

"I can."

"I think they're right," I said. "Everything I own, all the power I thought I had, everything was given to me by the most treacherous soul in this nation. You don't erase that overnight. I can close my eyes and pretend I don't sit on a throne of skulls, but I cannot change the truth of what I am and what brought me to this world. I want to. I want to save Jin-Sayeng. I want to see sunlight in these lands again, I want to see the fields covered with ripe, golden grains instead of bodies and blood, to hear birdsong instead of warhorns. I want to see our people laughing in celebration, not cowering behind walls. I want to be queen, to rule with mercy and kindness, to bring peace and prosperity because it's about time we had those things, isn't it? It's about time our people don't sit in fear of losing everything they owned. Jin-Sayeng deserves it. It deserves every bit of happiness the gods can bestow."

"It's never about what we want," Nor said.

"I know." I took a deep breath. "I am Yeshin's daughter, whether I deny it or not, and my father has hurt Jin-Sayeng too much. Nothing will ever change that." Realizing my fate was sealed with those words, I got up, sheathing my sword, and made my way down the guard tower.

Nor followed silently.

We went back to the castle, to the libraries.

"Do you know why I joined Yu-yan?" she asked as I searched through the shelves. "It's because I saw everything happening out here and the fear became too much to bear. I have a daughter to think about, too. But all I can do about it is fight. I can fight until someone comes down here to tell me they've found a better way."

"There is no better way," I said. "Only *a* way, and I don't even know if I want to acknowledge it." I found the crate of scrolls I was looking for and yanked it out of the shelf. You could find bloodline papers in just about any royal's library—nobles were obsessed with them. I placed it on the ground and pulled the scrolls out, laying them on the floor. I eventually found Maharay aren dar Jeinza's name. There were inky thumbprints on the edges, as if someone else had opened the book right on that same page. Her line ended there, marked with an *X*, which signalled a departure from the royal bloodline. It meant she married a commoner, or decided to leave Jin-Sayeng. She could have gone to the empire. She could have given birth to Yuebek. Mage, monster, with the blood of dragonriders running through his veins.

I stared at the name so long my eyesight blurred.

Did I have other options? Every moment of indecision brought my land closer to ruin. Every day I spent in search of answers, people died. I didn't have an army to defeat Kaggawa with. I had one dragon too weak to close the rift and two mages who couldn't turn into dragons. That left my father's solution. His horrifying, unthinkable solution. A skilled mage who could also ride dragons. Yuebek, only Yuebek. I could almost hear his voice now, as slimy as his hand around my neck. My skin crawled.

You got this far. Aren't you tired of running, Talyien? Your life, in exchange for everyone else's? It's not too great a sacrifice. Perhaps it is time you learn to submit. Sooner or later, the road was meant to end.

My thoughts drifted to the rest of my father's letter. Khine had burned it in the fire, but those words would die with me.

Listen carefully, Talyien…

Maybe you already know this by now, but Yuebek is a cruel man and we are playing with fire. His mother himself warned me. Let me paint you a picture: Yuebek killed his brother when he was but a child. Choked him, gouged his own eyes out with his thumbs, and then watched as he burned to death. Time has not mellowed him. He has instigated all manner of strange deaths for his rivals, and is said to have been found in bed with the corpse of one of the nobles' daughters. When asked of this incident, he merely laughed it off, saying he had killed her for pleasure. They never could prove the murder, or if she was already dead when he defiled her.

His father, the emperor, indulges him. It is not obvious to the naked eye these days, but Yuebek has been his favourite son since childhood. That is the only reason he is still alive, that his crimes have been swept under the rug. He would be crown prince if the entire imperial court wasn't against it.

But the rest of the empire is repulsed by him. They actively hamper Yuebek's political attempts, and threaten to bring him to court if the emperor does not do anything about him. His exile into the west was his father's faint attempt to protect him. It has not tempered his ambition one bit.

The Fourth Consort is adamant that I understand what I am getting into. She is frightened of her own son. She loves him, but he is unstable. His powers make him doubly dangerous. I wasn't even sure I believed the stories until I met him myself. Everything amuses him. Worse still...I'm convinced he's afraid of nothing, the sort of man who'll cut himself, if only to see your reaction...

I know I am asking for too much. But believe me, if there had been another way, I would have taken it. If I had not been too old, if I had all this knowledge when my joints could still hold my bones, I would have done it myself. But this is all that's left. It is your decision, in the end. You can have him killed to save what's left of your pride and doom Jin-Sayeng in the process. Or you can accept the truth and be the daughter I always knew you would be. My heart, my dearest love, you are our only hope.

Sometimes the answer is clear. It's simply that we don't want to listen. We don't want to know our stories are not written by a loving hand, or that they may never get the ending we believe we deserve. We don't want anyone to tell us our efforts may go unrewarded, our sacrifices unrecognized, and whatever we're given—whatever little we're given—may be all there ever could be. The light at the end of the tunnel does not exist for everyone.

"I need you to hold the siege for me," I said at last. "I need a reason for Yuebek to come here."

She kept her jaw firm. I think she wanted to denounce me all over again. Instead, she gave a resigned nod and left me with the rest of my thoughts, ringing as loud as funeral bells in the night.

CHAPTER EIGHTEEN

WHAT CANNOT BE KILLED

ᛏᚢᛰ

Khine and I returned to the boat and rowed our way upriver, beating against the lazy currents. In the quiet aftermath of a battle, you wouldn't think we were at war. Birds chirped, insects buzzed, flowers quivered in the sunlight. The wind whispered the way it would've on a quiet morning in a land untouched by war. I wanted to stop rowing, to let the boat float by itself and take us wherever the river willed. I was so tired of fighting. I had done it all my life.

"Khine," I said. "I'm going south by myself."

A deep breath. "I knew you were going to say that."

"You can't come with me. You don't want Dai to think you've turned against him. And my son—"

"Karia's with him," he said. "She'd die for him, you know."

"Still…"

Silence followed, interspersed by the slap of water against the oars.

"Khine," I said. "I think you know what I have to do."

He remained silent.

We drifted through the water, sunlight trailing behind us. I pulled the letters from my robe, the ones Rayyel and I wrote. After a brief hesitation, I tore them. The pieces drifted into the water. Khine looked on, the grief plain on his face.

"Rai has to take the fall," I whispered. "I have to marry Yuebek. It's the only way to save this land."

He didn't answer. The words sounded like death.

I turned to the sky, forcing the tears not to leak through my eyes. The irony...that I would embrace this only after I had finally found him. A breath of air, before the hangman's noose. All there ever could be.

We drifted from the river down to a small tributary, where the boat hit the sandy shore of the bank. I waded in, water up to my knees. Khine grabbed my arm. Pulled me towards him. Kissed me with the anguish of a man who has seen enough and understood.

He understood, which somehow made it all the more damned.

What would the history books say of Khine Lamang? I could imagine that if word of this affair ever got out—as these things tend to—they would drag his name through the mud. Or worse, reduce him to nothing more than the queen's lover, one of many. A con artist, a thief who might've been a physician—the same way Rayyel will always be the king that never was, or I the queen that couldn't be. As if we are defined only by our failures.

No wonder, then, the desperate scrambling to make our mark in time. Behind us, an army was poised to strike at Yu-yan because one man was convinced *he* was the fated hero. The same fallacy that drove my father to commit the massacres that would define him...that drove Yuebek, mage, forgotten son, to do whatever it took to catch his Esteemed Father's attention, if it meant bringing war to a land that wasn't his...

Such grandeur, such delusion, when life could be dragged down to these moments. Hands touching, fingers entwined, rough lips over smooth skin, the rush of the river around us as loud as the blood coursing through our veins. I didn't know if he was telling me not to go through with it, or if he was trying to make me forget, or if he was trying to make himself forget.

"Khine," I whispered, light-headed, loath to make it stop. But despite the heat stirred by the act, I was starting to shiver.

He shook his head, that silence again. But we tied up the boat and made our way back to the hut, where the air overflowed with the scent of dried herbs. Stripped of our wet clothes, we picked up where we left off. Now his lips were on me again, and I was arching against his fingers and his mouth, begging him to stop, knowing I didn't want him to, knowing he knew *that*, too, that I was forever a liar in his presence. Desire and desperation, pleasure and pain. Nothing is ever simple.

"Tali," Khine whispered when we were done, his heartbeat on my bare chest. "I can't let you. I would rather die." He was on the verge of tears.

"It's not your decision," I whispered.

"Even a man like your father would have his oversights. And if there's one person who can find them—"

I caressed his cheek with the back of my fingers. "You've already done more than you could ever know."

His face hardened. "How could you give up so easily?"

"I have nothing else, Khine," I whispered. "Especially not *time*. I think my father knew that. That's why it had to get this far. Remember when you asked why he would do this, when he knew I would be too stubborn to accept my fate? He must've known, too, that in the end I wouldn't have a choice. Or perhaps he would've been happy if I *did* find an alternative. But I didn't."

"He doesn't have to win."

"This is beyond that, now," I said. "It's not about winning or losing, or bowing down to Yeshin, in the end. It's about saving Jin-Sayeng. It's about doing the right thing even when the right thing hurts." But my own words filled me with sadness, echoing with anger that had sapped me of all my energy. Perhaps I was just being the coward I had always been. Perhaps I was just giving in to what was easiest. Could I say these words with Yuebek in front of me? Would I shove a knife into Khine's heart before running into those rotten arms? I would rather die, too.

It was better, then, that it looked like Khine didn't hear me at all. "I can't..." he repeated, his words an echo of what loss had done to him. What impending loss was doing to him now. I wondered what it meant that I did not share the grief. Nothing in all my life had prepared me for this, for *him*. My breath of air, to be lost too soon...

Yet what would I have changed, knowing it would lead me to this? If the end of the road meant I would find myself right here, I would do it all over again. I would live through every painful detail, every mistake, every hurt. He was worth it. I think that was why, against his disquiet, I was oddly at peace. Khine had known joy in its purest, the kind that came before the brush of sorrow. A mother and father who loved him, a brother and sisters who shared his plight, a lover whose only crime against him was youth—who seemed to have loved him just as fiercely as he had her. Of course he would want to hold on.

My own approach to love had been dull, duty-bound. Where Khine was grasping, wanting to keep it all, I had already resigned myself to looking back at him from memory. To becoming a memory for him, in return. What semblance of courage I held lay in my ability to put the people I love behind an impenetrable wall. I did it all those years with my father and Rayyel. A gift, if you think about it—how the same skill I used to survive made the unbearable feel like a passing thing. I should thank them.

He soon fell into a troubled sleep, his face darkened by lines I couldn't smooth away if I tried. I knew his mind was sifting through the details, convinced he could outrace my father and his plans. I wouldn't put it past him. But he couldn't know what I didn't tell him. My father understood what Yuebek was and told me because he also understood what *I* was. I, stubborn, unyielding queen of Jin-Sayeng, had once obeyed out of duty and could do it again. Khine didn't need that burden. I am many things, but I am not heartless.

I didn't sleep myself. A part of me wandered down the aisle of wishful thinking. It was difficult not to engage in indulgence when the maddening hours persisted on drifting by. If somehow we could be together, how long would it last? Would he grow bored of me? Would I tire of him? I dreamed of such things with Rayyel before, and maybe even Agos, in passing, but my knowledge of such partnerships was limited. To love someone for so long you can no longer remember life when you didn't love them, to know passion that continued even after the fires had burned low... how could such a perfect thing exist in an imperfect world? I knew better now than to believe another fairy tale.

Somehow, even my musing passed, leaving behind a longing for something I just had, and maybe more. I tried to wake him—softly at first, and then in more urgent ways he couldn't ignore. We made love blearily, him half awake, gazing at me as if out of a dream, as if he couldn't believe I was real. I felt the same, though it would be cruel to say such words now. Let him think it ended here, let him think I couldn't love him. He tasted like wine, a potency that stung. I fell asleep in his arms and time slipped through my fingers like water poured from a jug.

Dawn came, and then the knock on the door, the death knell. I left Khine naked on the pallet, wrapped myself in the blanket, and got up to answer it.

Huan's eyes widened, and then he quickly turned, his cheeks red. Huan, not Eikaro; he was armoured, with his helmet on. Eikaro would've made every effort not to tromp around in heavy plate if he could help it.

"Warlord Huan," I said.

He coughed. "We've come to take you to the outpost."

"The second switch was successful?"

"It was," he replied, clearing his throat. "Even without the mages to help him. I wonder what a formal education in the *agan* would've done for him. Maybe we'll never know."

"I hope there was sufficient time for him to recover from being in the dragon's body too long."

"An hour or two would've worked, he said," Huan replied, scratching his cheek with a finger. "As it was, we only switched a few hours ago. I wanted to give him at least until last night so he could spend some time with his wife."

That made me pause. "That was...generous of you."

Huan gave a soft smile. "Generous of *my* wife, you mean. Another woman would've found it obscene. She simply told me not to bother telling her anything, especially if it turns out that I recall...details."

"We need less sorrow in the world, Lord Huan. I'm glad to hear your wives are understanding."

He nodded towards the hut. "And him? Is he as understanding?"

I gave a wry smile. "We never really get the answers we want, do we?" I glanced at the horses he had brought with him. "I'll meet you outside in a moment."

Huan bowed and drew away.

I closed the door behind me and returned to Khine. I draped the blanket over his body, not wanting to wake him. I got dressed, gave him one last kiss, and then I strode out into the grey light to meet my fate.

ACT THREE

THE ROPE AND THE BREAKDOWN

CHAPTER ONE

THE MAD PRINCE'S COURT, REPRISED

ᴉᵀⱳⱴ

Huan rode with me to the first outpost, where he entrusted me to soldiers that would take me the rest of the way. As if I needed another reminder of the urgency of my task, a messenger arrived, informing us that Kaggawa had renewed his assault.

"With any luck, he's diverted his soldiers from the villages to pad up his charge," Huan said. "Maybe I can send patrols to gather food while he's occupied."

"If you do that, the villagers won't have food," I said.

He grimaced. "Then you need to be quick. Every second counts. Return to us before we all die." He cracked a smile. "But I think you already know that."

We reached Fuyyu and the main road, the one that ran all the way east, to the riverlands along the banks of the River Agos. In Osahindo, we boarded a riverboat, which sailed north with the wind against the currents. Not long afterwards, I saw Oren-yaro on the horizon, embracing the sun under the mountain's ever-protective shadow. Oren-yaro, with its ruins and misshapen dragon-towers, slowly crumbling into the river every year. My father's city, my home, my brothers' tomb, cradle of every sorrow that shaped my life. I began the process of hardening my heart.

Easier said than done. I would spend hours going over the logic of it with my father's precision, reminding myself *why* I needed to do this, what we would lose if I didn't. And by the end, I would almost understand, except I would wake up the next morning and begin the process all over again. After everything that had happened, the thought of offering my hand up to Yuebek was vile. Imagining the words I would tell him—how I understood now how I had wronged him, insulted him, that he had been so generous, so compassionate, in his own actions after what my husband Rayyel had done—made me want to vomit. And then afterwards? To entertain his cold touch and perfumed corpse-stench, to have to lie in bed and let him sate himself on me so that he would later be pliable to what we would ask from him. To love him, so I could ask him to die for my nation, and he wouldn't bat an eye…

I told myself I couldn't falter now. My son was still trapped in the Sougen, the price I paid for my father's schemes. Did he know his damn plans would harm his own blood? No, he couldn't have; he was dead, dead, dead, not even a damn corpse anymore, nothing but ashes and dust I could be rid of once I returned to Oren-yaro and flushed him down the river. How could he have so much power? How could a person so vile and corrupt be kept alive in the memories of others? How could his ideals remain?

I couldn't even bear thinking about failure. My throne, my life—they were meaningless in the face of those thousands of lives that would perish if I failed. Thousands more, on top of the thousands my father had already taken from the land. But every breath I took was a struggle not to turn back. All I had to do was think of Khine and I would reach the precipice of what little courage I had. There is only so much you can steel yourself for. The contrast of what I left behind to what awaited would drive anyone mad.

I hated my father now more than ever. I thought he raised me not to be just some lump of flesh placed on a seat to appease the nation, nor a mere vessel for childbirth, but as someone who could carry all the things I've been told gave a woman substance. Duties and expectations, woven into the fabric of everything I thought I was to be: wife, mother, daughter. Queen. Except the truth was a bowl of sand in the dark, given in place of rice. Chew and swallow, Talyien—don't you dare spit a grain out! My father had hardened me for nothing but slaughter. Everything I had been taught, everything I've felt in his presence and beyond, my very *being* was the true cage. My every step had been determined, anticipated, manipulated, all so we could use that putrid exhalation from hell for our own purposes. My true prince. My nightmare.

I met Lord General Ozo in a tavern in Oren-yaro, after I'd sent word ahead. He arrived with Namra.

"The fact that you're here now, and not running around like a squealing pig…" Ozo began.

"Yes," I snapped at him. "I get it."

"I'm glad to see you well, Beloved Queen," Namra said, bowing. "I've worried for you since Burbatan."

"I'm still alive, at least," I said. "Is...Liosa...?"

"Your lady mother is well," she replied. "I oversaw her return to the temple myself. She was happy to be back home."

"I'm not a monster," Ozo grumbled.

"I would've guessed otherwise," I said.

He pressed his lips together as he gestured at the table. I took a seat and grudgingly accepted a cup of sugarcane wine, though I had no appetite for the dishes of jellied chicken feet or fried tofu in sweet chili sauce. The sight of Zarojo food only reminded me of what awaited in the castle.

I took a long drink. "First things first," I said after swallowing. "How sure are we of Yuebek's lineage?"

Ozo snapped his fingers. A servant approached with several scrolls, which he offered to me with a bow. I swallowed more wine before I took them. Unrolling the paper proved harder than I thought—they were thin and flimsy, weathered from improper storage.

They were various documents detailing Lady Maharay's departure from Jin-Sayeng. They were insidious; her clan had tried to hide it in an attempt to deflect political scrutiny. Any sort of power grab from one of the major clans would be sure to raise hackles, and they wanted to curry Zarojo goodwill in secret. Some reports mentioned she was simply visiting a summer home in the southern empire, where they said the beaches were as white as marble. But the story was there, if you read between the lines.

The last few reports detailed the arrival of the Fourth Consort and her subsequent acceptance into the Esteemed Emperor Yunan Tsaito's harem. By then, her name and titles had been erased. It was as if Lady Maharay of Jin-Sayeng had ceased to exist. I didn't know if the Jeinza clan expected that; clearly, their move had not done much more than establish additional trade routes for the city of Sutan, which carried its Zarojo influence with pride.

I stared at the documents after I was done reading, before draining my cup. "Namra," I finally said. "We tried to send the last two mages in Yu-yan to the rift. It didn't work. They died before they could touch it. Huan said their shields broke. How do we make sure the same doesn't happen to Yuebek?"

"He is powerful," Namra replied. "You've seen it with your own eyes. His work in Phurywa—the blood magic...surely you remember."

"I do, and every day I wish I could forget."

"Perhaps to the untrained eye, all skill in the *agan* looks the same," Namra said. "It isn't. I could have told you those mages wouldn't be able to do it. *I* wouldn't. That sky is extremely unstable, and only the strongest mages could withstand its effects. I've been going through your father's research. The rift could obliterate everything within the vicinity. And yet attempts to close it haven't worked, because you have to be right next to it. Dageian mages tried to do it from the ground, and you've seen what happened there. If anything, they made it worse."

"So what you're saying is that it's simply because Yuebek is powerful enough to shield himself when he gets up there. He's the only one you know who should even attempt such a thing."

She bowed again. "I can't even fathom the depths of the man's power, but I feel it every time he's near. I can't imagine how he's accomplished half the things he's done. The man defied death, Queen Talyien. You *killed* him already, and yet he's still here."

"The bastard will definitely survive that sky, then," I said. Even saying it made me want to stomp off. "But would he know how to close the rift, once he gets there?"

Namra placed a scroll on the table. I stared at the confusing mass of runes and symbols. "It's the design for the spell," she said. "It's the same spell the Dageian mages tried to use on the rift in the beginning. Your father paid for my education because he wanted me to help you. I'm modifying the spell for a rift that size. Yuebek doesn't have to do a thing but fly up there."

"It will close by itself, as long as he takes the spell to the sky?"

She grimaced. "It needs power. The spell will draw from him first."

"Will *that* kill him?"

Her face darkened. "I know it will kill most mages, but Yuebek?"

"We'll kill him anyway," Ozo broke in. "It doesn't matter."

"I'm not sure that will work," Namra said.

I could hear the fear in her voice. *I don't know if he can die.* But surely no one could be immortal? No one could be that powerful. "I was still really hoping someone else could do it." I sighed. "Not that it matters, I guess. Our last attempt injured our only dragon, and *you* can't turn into one. Come on, blurt it out, Ozo. You're *agan*-touched, too, aren't you?"

"You wish," Ozo snorted.

"There were other things in the study," Namra said. "Your father mapped out everything his mages and builders did. It's quite impressive. Once the spell draws power from the holder, it will use it to create separate connections to the *agan* stream, which will close the hole. I'm not sure if I can explain it very well to you..."

"You don't have to," I said. "I think I know. Eikaro did something on a smaller scale. Like stitching a wound."

"You—you have that right." She looked a little relieved that I understood that much. "That's just the beginning, too. Once the rift is closed, it will create more surges of *agan* that cannot just be allowed to spark freely through the air—that will only create more holes. The new dragon-towers are designed to capture the energy and spread it through the land slowly, straight through the old dragon-towers. They're all connected."

"This won't hurt the people in the city?" I asked.

"For a few days, you might see furnaces in the older buildings—the ones still connected to the dragon-tower infrastructure—light up. Jin-Sayeng used to run on this power, Beloved Queen—I don't believe we have anything to worry about there. However..."

"There's always a catch," I said, frowning.

She gave me a sympathetic smile. "The problem is that Prince Yuebek is a trained, educated mage. Explain all of this to him, and he *will* see that closing the rift *may* kill him. He'll know it's a trap. You cannot just tell him to do it— he will know we're trying to get rid of him, and the gods know how the man will react to such an affront. He needs to come to this conclusion himself. He needs to see how closing it will be beneficial for *him*."

Ozo tapped the table with a closed fist. "Which is why Warlord Yeshin wanted someone who not only had the skill to do it, but could be convinced of the plausibility of earning the people's support as Dragonlord because he has the proper royal bloodline." He balled up his other fist. "The classic *two truths* to a single story."

"Does Yuebek know his mother is Jinsein?"

"We were hoping you could tell him that. You need to convince him to put his head on the chopping block."

I laughed. "And I'm supposed to have the charm and wit to do this. I'm supposed to make Yuebek bend to my feminine wiles."

"I can hardly blame your father for making that mistake," Ozo huffed.

"Your brothers had all that charm and wit, and so did your grandmother and your mother. If he saw you as you are now, he'd be horrified."

"Thank the gods for that."

"You should curse them for it," Ozo said. He gave a dismissive wave in Namra's direction. "The priestess's fears aside, we need Yuebek dead, regardless. And ideally it would be *after* you have every right to what he owns so his army doesn't turn on us while they're on our soil."

"So many *ifs*, Ozo," I replied. "And you didn't even bring me enough wine, damn you."

"Think about what you get in return if it all works out," Ozo said. "Think about wiping that smug grin off Ryia's face when she realizes the people are celebrating in *your* name." He heaved his barrel chest. "Yuebek is waiting for you in Oka Shto. We've told him you simply needed time to think it over—the past few months have been overwhelming for someone in your position, but you're close to making a decision. As a show of understanding and goodwill, Prince Yuebek has chosen to stay his hand."

"How generous of him," I said in a low voice. "What would he have done otherwise? Taken the whole nation by force? He doesn't have the numbers."

"That's not what I meant," Ozo bristled. "Your husband—"

I felt dread run through me. "What has he done to Rayyel?" I asked.

Ozo got up. "Come home, and see," he said.

Pretend you owned a dollhouse. A wonderful piece of craftsmanship with doors that open and close, windows with real stained glass, walls stained and oiled to a polished sheen. The furniture is exquisite, life-like, every corner carved lovingly by a master toymaker. And your father gave you this dollhouse before he died, and you were convinced that despite everything, despite that last, turgid letter he left you, you could turn it upside down and another letter would come flying out, one that contained just a few words. Three or four, it didn't matter—words that weren't just instructions, that were enough to somehow make it all right again even if a part of you knew it was too late for that. Words enough to soothe the pain.

Imagine walking into your room to find that dollhouse burning in the fireplace.

That was exactly what I felt when I returned to my castle and saw the Zarojo had taken over. For every one Oren-yaro guard, I counted five of Yuebek's. The Oren-yaro banners were gone, replaced by Yuebek's own standard: a white dragon set against a dark-blue sea, swallowing the yellow moon. It took me aback. The whole motif was new, something he must have had designed recently. But more than that—the moon-swallowing dragon was a Jin-Sayeng legend. It was a statement. He was making an impression in the worst way possible—by taking what was ours and claiming it for himself.

I turned away from it to gaze at the other affront. The trees in the courtyard, the tall, stately maples, had been cut. The rounded stumps were still in the ground, a reminder of what used to be there. "They wanted room for the soldiers," Ozo explained when he saw the horror in my eyes. "They said the barracks are too far away."

"We never had room up here in the first place," I said.

"What would you have me do?" Ozo shot back. "Yuebek doesn't trust us. He wants his army close. I believe the man doesn't even sleep, not since he's stepped foot inside the castle." He dropped his voice. "It's up to you, now. Ease his mind. Let the prince believe the story we've fed him. Seal the deal, Queen Talyien."

"Gods," I breathed. "I hate you all. Maybe you the most."

He gave a mirthless chuckle. "Don't you think I hate myself, too? For doing this to you? For what I did to my own son?"

"Please. You're a sadistic bastard."

He shrugged. "I never said I wasn't."

"I've heard of the things you did during my father's war. People feared and hated him, but you? You repulsed them. Hessa loathed you. I've always wondered why—I shudder to think what you did to her to put Agos in her belly."

"Believe what you want, my queen."

"Hell, I'm still convinced the only reason you never really seized power when you could was because you couldn't be bothered. They respect you, but not half as well as they respected my father. You'd have your hands full with rebellions you wouldn't know how to crush."

"Save that tiresome prattle for your new prince," Ozo said through gritted teeth. "He's all you have to worry about." We reached the front doors, where two of Yuebek's guards stood, halberds crossed.

"The queen has returned," Ozo announced. "Your prince is expecting her."

They remained unmoving, hard eyes scrutinizing me.

"Step aside," I ordered.

The guards didn't even look like they heard me.

I heard Ozo suck in his breath.

My hand dropped to my sword. "If you don't step aside—" I began.

"Beloved Queen!" a familiar voice called out from the end of the courtyard.

I turned to the newcomer. "Lo Bahn," I greeted. "What games are you playing now?"

"No games, Queen Talyien," Lo Bahn exclaimed. He gave a sweeping bow. "No games at all. But maybe we should be asking the same question of you."

"What the hell do you mean?"

"You played a rotten trick on me back in Bara," Lo Bahn replied, smirking. "Not the first either, if I recall correctly. You'll have to forgive us for casting doubt on your intentions now."

"*I* played a trick on you?" I asked. "Weren't *you* conspiring with Warlord Lushai?"

He looked away. "I don't know what the hell you mean."

"Ah hah!" I exclaimed. "Can't even keep your own interests under a lid, can you? I'll let you get away with it. It's nothing to me. Lord General Ozo must've told you. The last few months—"

"Were an affront to your poor, delicate sensibilities? Were you experiencing fainting spells the whole winter through? You poor, weak woman, having to deal with such brutes when you were promised gentlemen." He snorted. "We know you better than that, Queen Talyien."

I smiled in return. "Is that what you told Prince Yuebek?"

Lo Bahn gave a dismissive gesture. "Believe it or not, my opinions are meaningless as rat turds to His Esteemed Highness. I did try to warn him—suggested that we should all just go home, that it's pointless trying to wrest your kingdom away from *you*. But he would have none of it. He suggested, in return, that maybe I'd be better served as a headless figure in Shang Azi, and my cock and balls bronzed and donated to the whorehouses for pleasuring their more particular clientele." He gave a crude laugh, and only then did I notice that he couldn't really stand straight. He was limping on one leg.

"He had you punished for my escape," I said.

"I'm no stranger to torture," Lo Bahn reminded me, showing me his nail-less fingers. Injuries he had incurred back in Shang Azi, courtesy of Governor Qun while under the pretence of looking for me. I've never laid a hand on him, but he would forever carry the mark of my name on his body. "But you can't say I didn't try, Queen Talyien."

"Why do you try at all? You're risking your life here."

"I was a dead man the moment I met you. I'm not sure which I would rather face—his wrath, or *yours*." He nodded towards the castle. "He knows you're here. We've known you were here the moment you landed on the river this morning. A trip from the south, I wagered. From the Sougen?"

I took a deep breath. There was no point in lying. "Yes. I went to see my son, Lord Han."

"Ah," he replied. "I figured. This Kaggawa has him?"

"He's a prisoner there. I managed to sneak into his camp to see him, but…" I swallowed, trying to keep my voice light, trying to channel that *charm* and *wit* I'm supposed to have. "Prince Yuebek is the only way I can save my son. Kaggawa wants him to marry his daughter so *he* can take over Jin-Sayeng. A commoner…"

"What's wrong with commoners?"

I frowned. "There is nothing wrong with commoners, but it is absurd to use my son as a prop for political power. I can't have it. Prince Yuebek, at least, will understand my position better."

Lo Bahn looked at me, squinting. Thinking. I'd fooled him once before, and he must have sworn to himself he would never allow it again. I suddenly understood exactly why Yuebek wanted *him* under his employ, for all that he was not the sort of man the nobility would be caught dead with. Lo Bahn knew too much. He knew me. He knew the people I cared for. That was his one task—to see through me and warn Yuebek of impending treachery. Perhaps Lo Bahn himself was convinced it was all for my own good, too.

Turn the gem, Talyien. Turn it. Your enemies are your friends. Your friends are your enemies. Nothing is constant, nothing is safe. Suddenly this whole ruse was harder than it should've been. I had done this, too; made it more complicated than my father ever intended. If I'd submitted from the very beginning, Yuebek wouldn't have been on guard. But the plan needed me to yield only in some ways and remain clad in iron in others. Only Yeshin the Butcher would have dared.

"Qun mentioned your unnatural fondness for your whelp," Lo Bahn conceded. "I've heard it's chaos down there."

"Kaggawa is seizing power," I said. "He's laid siege to Yu-yan. My son is in his war camp. I need the west stabilized if I can hope to rally support from the others. You don't know how it works out here, Lord Han. This isn't Shang Azi. This is a nation of warlords who will hole up in their castles and let the rest burn to the ground if it saves them the trouble."

"I know that much, woman," Lo Bahn snorted. He stepped to one side, leaning heavily on his good leg. Veins on his neck strained from the effort. "He wants me to show you something first."

I felt a bead of sweat on my forehead. I didn't even have the courage to wipe it off.

"You could've stopped this if you'd been there," Lo Bahn continued. "Remember that, before you blame me." With a sweep of his hand, he led me down to the sloping path that came around the courtyard. There were no dungeons in Oka Shto. The barracks were at the base of the mountain, closer to the city and a more convenient spot for prisoners. Lo Bahn led me to the kennels.

I couldn't hear anything as we approached the path leading to the building. Normally, the dogs would've created a ruckus by now. My hands grew cold, the chill climbing up my spine. "Lo Bahn," I said, gritting my teeth. "What did Yuebek do to my dogs?"

Lo Bahn pressed his arms to his side. "You don't see them?" he asked, turning his head to the bare trees that fringed the mountainside, past the ledge. It was spring—the leaves should've grown back by now. My gut turned.

My dogs were dead, bound to the tree branches. I didn't want to count to see if he got them all, didn't stop to look at their faces, didn't stop to go over the details of what was done to them. Bile stirred in my throat and I turned all my attention to forcing it down, to burning away the image in my memory.

"The gods help you if you did this, Lo Bahn," I said in a low voice.

He glanced at my hand, which was toying with the handle of my sword. He gave a quick smile. "You'd kill me if I said yes, I suppose."

"I will gut you like a fucking pig and decorate those trees with your innards."

"I told you I have no power against that man," Lo Bahn said. He craned his head away from me, as if the venom in my threats had unsettled him. "As it stands, I didn't have to do a damn thing. Me, as I am? He did it all himself. Didn't even want the soldiers to help."

"He must be covered in bites."

Lo Bahn laughed. "There's some truth in that." He nodded towards the kennel. "He left you one dog."

"Of course he did," I said under my breath.

He unlocked the kennel door, and we entered. The smell of the unwashed floor, of urine and liquid dog feces, stung my nostrils. I held my breath as I turned to the lone figure at the end of the row. My husband sat there, hands on his knees, his bedraggled hair covering half his face. It was wet. There was a bucket above him, one that leaked water a drop at a time. Rayyel was collared and chained in such a way that he couldn't avoid it even if he wanted to.

"You kill my dogs and torture my husband..." I started.

"What did you expect, Queen Talyien? Tea and egg pie while they wait for you to come to your senses? Bah! Even *you* should know better."

I stepped around the cage. Rayyel hadn't moved to acknowledge our arrival, though I knew he was awake. I could hear his rhythmic breathing, could see his fingers clasping his sullied robes.

"Rai," I whispered. "I'm here now, Rai."

He didn't respond.

I glanced at the dripping water. How long had they been doing this to him? Each drop was supposed to land on the same spot on his head—what seemed like a mere annoyance at the first glance would be unbearable after a few hours. It was one of my father's favourite tortures. Forcing the anger at bay, I ripped out a piece of my sleeve and reached into the cage.

"You shouldn't do that," Lo Bahn warned me.

"Fuck off," I said, draping the cloth over Rayyel's head. It absorbed the drop of water. "Rai," I repeated, pressing my hand over his face. His skin was clammy, cold.

I heard him draw a quick breath. His eyes finally opened, his long eyelashes caked with dirt and grime. He didn't speak.

Lo Bahn clicked his tongue. "I've seen men rendered senseless in an hour with that. He's been here for weeks. They fill that bucket at least twice a day."

"They chose the worst method to break an Ikessar with," I said in a low voice. I glanced at Lo Bahn. "I wouldn't mention that to Yuebek if you know what's good for you."

Lo Bahn snorted. "Like I'd risk telling him he was wrong about something. He's in a mood, in case it isn't obvious. Your disappearance last winter gave him more trouble than he could chew."

"What do you mean?"

He nodded towards Rai. "That one's mother. She and Yuebek nearly killed each other."

"That would've saved us some trouble," I grumbled.

"It's why he's here in the first place," Lo Bahn said. "His mother spat on the prince before humiliating him in front of the council. Didn't know you royals could be as vile as the meanest bitch in Shang Azi. He seized Prince Rayyel in response and rode out here. She didn't have the soldiers to oppose him, but she swore she would return."

"Where is she now?"

"Slunk back into the mountains." Lo Bahn gave a nervous giggle. "How fast can she gather an army? Sounds to me like the bitch's got clout in your little nation. Ong warned the prince not to take her lightly. The prince had him beaten for his insolence."

"Even my father couldn't kill that persistence." I turned, hearing Rai take a deep breath.

"My queen," he croaked out, as if having just woken from deep slumber. "You've returned. You . . ." He trailed off, looking at me with bloodshot eyes full of uncertainty. He must've thought he was talking to a phantom.

"He can't treat you like this," I said. "I'll get you out of here, Rai."

"Don't make promises you can't keep," Lo Bahn commented. "Hope can be the most painful thing in the world."

CHAPTER TWO

THE COURTSHIP

ᘔᓄᑕᔨᑕ

I could've told Lo Bahn he was wasting his words. I knew that already, as well as I knew the memories I swore to lock behind me forever. But I had no intention of making *this* promise empty. I returned to be queen, not simply to pander to Yuebek's desires. If he wanted to be Dragonlord, he needed to treat the nobility with care, Rayyel included. If nothing else, my husband deserved a clean death.

I squeezed his arm, which had grown remarkably thin since I last saw him, and pulled away. But I didn't ask Lo Bahn to take me to Yuebek immediately. First, I grabbed the shovel from the kennels and went back to the grove of trees where Yuebek had killed my dogs. Lo Bahn watched silently as I cut each of them down, bonds and all. My heart was all the way up to my throat and it was difficult not to recoil from the scent of rot and old urine, but I forced myself through the motions.

Eight dogs in all, each as stiff as a board. Only eight. Some were missing, but I didn't stop to think about what else might've happened to them. Three of the bodies I didn't recognize—they were young, born after I left for Anzhao. The way their bones jutted out, the lack of muscle along their hindquarters, and the clumps of hard feces matted on their fur told me they hadn't seen much of the outside of their cages, if at all.

The things that fall to the wayside when we focus on the unattainable. Life could exist, even thrive, in the fringes of what we consider important. I should've paid more attention. I buried them in death with the reverence I never gave them in life, knowing I was going to have to make a habit of this. To hold the grotesque close, awash in memories of everything I loved. My mouth tasted faintly of grave dirt when I was done. I wiped it with the back of my arm, sweat pouring down my face. The sun was high in the sky, sending a clear light that made the shadows from the now-bare tree branches dance.

Lo Bahn cleared his throat. He hadn't uttered a word the whole time I was shoveling dirt. Apt, I suppose, that we had made a habit of burying the dead since Shang Azi. I should've asked him to join me, but it was something I needed to do myself. My life, my dogs. Their deaths were on me. I took a deep breath, unshed tears stinging my eyes.

"You should probably wash up," he said. There was a hint of concern in his tone. "You can't present yourself to him like that."

I glanced at him, holding the shovel like it was a sword. The temptation to strike Lo Bahn and bury him with my dogs, then go down to the castle to do the same to Yuebek, was strong. But I didn't want to taint the sanctity of their graves. People like us—we belonged in a garbage heap. Instead, I turned away. Just as I came down the path, I heard a whimper.

I sucked in my breath as Blackie emerged from the bushes, limping. I dropped to my knees. He grabbed my sleeve with the front of his teeth and buried his nose in the fold of my arm, breathing in deeply, as if asking where I'd been, what was wrong, why did it take me so long, he thought he had lost me forever. I ran my fingers through his dry coat. His shoulders were laced with crusted wounds, his claws were filed down to the quick, and his fangs were broken. But despite his injuries, the joy exuding out of him was pure; his tail beat against his gaunt hindquarters with as much vigour as it had when he was a young pup. Whatever I had done to him and his kin, whatever useless thing I was chasing out there only to end up bringing this foul beast back with me... none of it mattered. I was home; all was forgiven.

My tears leaked out. He licked them before they could run down my cheeks. I wanted to sob into his fur, but held myself. I couldn't let myself be undone by a dog before I'd begun.

"That one," Lo Bahn said, clearing his throat. "I didn't think he'd come back. Take him away before the prince sees him. He broke those fangs on the prince and kept coming. Prince Yuebek won't forget that easily."

"Good dog." I scratched his face. "You got him, didn't you? You crazy bastard."

He whined at my voice, beating his tail against my leg as if my praise was music to his ears.

I started down the hill, whistling. He rushed to follow me. But he was so weak that he toppled two steps in, so I braced myself and picked him up from the ground, lifting him over my shoulders. Blackie was a big dog, and the last time I carried him was well before his adolescence. Even just placing his paws on my knees was enough for me to think he could crush them. The fact that I easily could carry him spoke much of the neglect he had suffered the past few months. He pressed his paw on my arm as we came down the path. What was I doing? He could walk. If I just gave him another moment, maybe two, he'd prove it. As if realizing he wouldn't be able to change my mind, he turned to licking my ear.

Yuebek's soldiers were waiting as I emerged into the courtyard. I could see them glance at each other with uncertainty, wondering if they should alert their master. I almost wanted them to. Let him come out. Let him defend his actions. Let me wring my hands around that pristine neck, too polished to be *real*…

I focused on breathing, ignoring the oily scent of dog hair under my nostrils and the strain in my arms. I caught Ozo's eye as I walked past him. He stood aside, as if he understood what I was doing. Every heavy step I took filled me with courage.

I carried Blackie all the way down to the barracks. An Oren-yaro officer appeared to see what the commotion was all about. I handed the dog over, and ordered him to take care of Blackie with the sort of voice I used to tell people I was going to chop their heads off. He looked at the dog's injuries with horror on his face and didn't even try to argue. We all knew what was at stake, but we couldn't forget our humanity in the process. For what else were we fighting for?

As I returned to Oka Shto, I heard Blackie call after me with a low moan, a howl that struck my bones. It sounded like he was saying goodbye.

Ingging and Yayei took over from Lo Bahn. Both handmaidens were quiet, subdued, and clearly frightened out of their wits. Ingging slipped pouring water into the bath, while Yayei brought the wrong kind of soap at least twice. They refused to meet my eyes. I noticed bruises on Yayei and didn't want to ask who laid a hand on her. Yuebek, Yuebek's soldiers, why did it matter? Ozo must've told them the same things he'd told me. Bear it. This is bigger than all of us. We are, each of us, a sacrifice for the greater good. *A wolf of Oren-yaro suffers in silence.*

So, they said nothing as they went through the motions of transforming me from a bedraggled woman into a queen yet again. They cleaned dirt and blood from my fingernails, trimmed my hair, scrubbed my skin smooth with pumice and oil. I sat at the edge of the bath with my feet in the water with only a heavy piece of cloth draped around my shoulders and wondered why I should even bother. Even without a mirror, I could see the pale lines running over my sun-darkened skin. My hands alone had more scars than most people had on their bodies.

I gave a grim smile. My father wasn't infallible. Even without the scars, I was already too old. You use fresh meat to bait beasts, not gristly meat—I held no trace of the young, desirable beauty he must've dreamed of when my mother gave birth to a girl child. I didn't think Yeshin ever considered that I would be a match for Ozo in my prime. If not for the power I represented, I was sure Yuebek wouldn't even bother. It worked in my favour that he really didn't want *me*. He wanted what my hand in marriage could do for him. *We're beyond your scheming, Father. All of that disappeared the moment you died. I am nothing like what you wanted, and yet here I still stand. Maybe the gods have not given up on me after all.*

Or so I tried to convince myself, working to gather courage over the thought of facing him without the barbed words I'd used to shield myself in the past. But it was hard not to remember that first night I spent in Zorheng City, how Yuebek had pawed at the door I had the foresight to block. Rape to subdue, rape to terrify...if things never went much further than that, I think I could manage. I've been told you can harden yourself to such things. Close your eyes, count in your head, maybe think of a song. Anything to pretend you're not there. I wasn't a virgin. I'd been with men. There was no longer anything mysterious or terrifying about the act.

But if he wanted *more*...

I covered my mouth with my hand, trying not to vomit into the bath my maids had worked so hard to fill.

"Beloved Queen," Ingging whispered over my shoulder. "Your dress is ready."

"Forgive me, Ingging."

She looked at me, confused.

"I met Liosa."

"You shouldn't have," Ingging replied. "That's all in the past. None of that was your fault."

"Isn't it?" I asked. "I came from that damn union. I don't know what's worse—the girl who wanted so badly to be mother to a queen, or the old man who knew better than to indulge her because it would be the sweetest vengeance of all."

"My queen..."

I wiped my mouth. "I need you to find the best herbalist in the city. Whatever that monster does, I will *not* carry his child in my womb. I'd sooner kill myself."

She pressed the back of her fingers against my cheek and bowed, withdrawing.

"Beloved Queen," Yayei broke in. "Is this necessary?"

I sucked in my breath before slowly nodding.

"But—"

"Your Lord Rayyel," I said, changing the subject. "Who takes care of him?"

"Prince Yuebek's soldiers," she replied. "But they won't let us near him. They don't even like us talking about it. One time, Ingging yelled at one after he went back to fill that infernal bucket a *third* time during the day when they'd been ordered to do it only twice, just to see what would happen, and he..." She swallowed and looked away.

"Is that all they've done?"

"They beat him when they first arrived," Yayei breathed. "Tied him to one of the trees out front. Stripped him down, lashed him until he bled. Prince Yuebek was waiting for him to cry out. He said he would stop if Prince Rayyel would just cry out."

"He didn't, of course. The stubborn fool."

"They tried to starve him," Yayei continued. "But the Ikessars do that to themselves for fun..." She almost laughed, and stopped herself just in time.

"It's true." I shook my head. "When did they put him in the kennel?"

"When the starving didn't work, Prince Yuebek threatened to have him torn apart by your dogs. He...I'm sorry, Beloved Queen, but he ordered us to starve them, too. One of the guards later told me all Prince Yuebek wanted was for Prince Rayyel to acknowledge him as his superior. He wanted Prince Rayyel to kiss his feet. When he still wouldn't do that, they poured kitchen grease all over him and then dragged him down to the kennels in rags. Prince Yuebek opened the cages himself. He was laughing like a madman, taunting them. Taunting your husband. The dogs were snarling.

"They rushed out as soon as the cages were open. We thought they would tear everything in their path apart. But Beloved Queen, your dogs didn't hurt Prince Rayyel. They crowded around him, licking him, tails wagging. Even after weeks of starvation…"

"He's my husband," I said in a low voice. "They're my dogs. Blackie would remember him. Yuebek is an idiot."

"Yuebek was furious his plan didn't work. He came stomping for Prince Rayyel and we thought he would kill him then, but your dogs turned around and went after Yuebek like hellhounds. They were out for blood. The old one, Blackie—he tried to go for his throat. I thought for a moment that he *did* rip it out."

I stared at the water. "He didn't, though. It wouldn't have been more than a scratch to Yuebek."

"It was strange," Yayei said. "He tore the dogs from him as they attacked before trying to get away. He toppled down the steps…and he fell."

I tried to conjure the image in my head. It was difficult. Even thinking I'd killed him that first time couldn't convince me the man could ever fall.

"I was sure he was dead," Yayei continued. "He was *bleeding*. He started calling for one of his men—Ong, I believe the name was. But no one came. And then he grabbed the foot of a soldier and then…"

She swallowed.

"What happened, Yayei?"

"I'm not sure, Beloved Queen," she said, shaking her head. "He got up again and there were no wounds on him. The soldier, though, was convulsing on the ground. I think he died. They made us go away after that, but I'm sure he died."

My senses darkened. "Yuebek is…" I couldn't finish it. My mind turned to another image: of my dogs charging him, drawing blood, almost succeeding. Almost. A foolish courage, but it was courage, still. Was I capable of the same? I didn't return here with my tail between my legs. But I thought about what we needed to happen after he had closed the rift. We needed him to die. How were we supposed to kill him? I had *stabbed* him in the heart, watched with my own eyes as the fear of death flushed over his porcelain face. Yet here I was, getting myself ready for him, dreading every passing moment.

"Lord Ozo says we have to embrace our new lord." Yayei swallowed. "It can't be true, can it? He's really not going to stay here forever? Even your father wasn't—"

I got up, stepping away from the bath. "The dress, Yayei," I reminded her in a curt tone.

Her cheeks flushed. She bowed, rushing to get it ready.

Even your father wasn't like this. It wouldn't have been the first time the castle was forced to entertain the whims of a foul-tempered master.

But the comparison made my skin crawl. I thought about this as I made my way from the back door and then down to the great hall. Judging from his letter to me, my father's distaste over Yuebek came with enough respect in return—enough for him to remain cautious.

Yeshin knew he needed Yuebek—needed his abilities as a mage, and the power and influence even a younger son of an emperor can hold. But I had the impression that my father really didn't think much of Yuebek until he met him himself. Until that first visit to Zorheng, Yuebek was a story, the sort you tell little girls to make them grow up prim and proper so that they'd never be given to such a man. My father seemed to have thought it the easiest thing in the world to manipulate him into accomplishing what we needed him to do. Only after they had spoken in person did Yeshin understand exactly how delicate the operation needed to be. For the gods to bestow such a vile person with wit and untold power was beyond comprehension. The letter told me that Yeshin barely got out of Zorheng alive.

Listen carefully, Talyien…

He didn't go over the details. Rayyel would've written me a novel about every single thing, from the time of the day to what he ate every morning, but my father only told me enough to warn me. Yuebek was a gracious and generous host in the beginning. He welcomed Father to Zorheng with open arms, begging him not to bow—no, we were sister cities now, Oren-yaro and Zorheng, pledged together long ago. Just during my father's war, in fact. His poor mother—now so ill, and kept locked away in the capital of Kyan Jang for her own health—had told him of how Warlord Yeshin first made correspondence with her. The highest of honours, that such a powerful warlord would bestow attention on such poor, humble servants of the Empire of Ziri-nar-Orxiaro…

My father sensed anger in Yuebek's words and sought to find the source of it. Yuebek was not pleased that my father had set him aside in the first place, let alone that a mere bastard was allowed to *sully* me. My father reminded him that I was too young, only ten years old. Yuebek interjected, claimed he wanted to marry me immediately. My father had to lecture him about how our government worked—that the agreement was that my marriage to Rayyel would allow both of us to rule together. Otherwise...

Yuebek grew increasingly impatient. Furthermore, he seemed obsessed with my virginity, which my father deflected as best as he could. He offered to have Rayyel killed; my father rejected it. Enraged, Yuebek had him seized.

Yeshin didn't say what happened afterwards. If what Yuebek had done to Rai was any indication, I assumed he was tortured. Somehow, Yeshin managed to convince Yuebek of his hatred for the Ikessars—perhaps not the most difficult thing in the world—and that he was genuine in his desire for an alliance. *I would rather bed with Zarojo mongrels than Ikessar snakes.* It made me shudder to recognize that I was the currency that exchanged hands during this delegation.

My thoughts died as I entered the great hall and beheld Yuebek sitting on my throne, a bored look on his face. In all the times I had seen him before, he wore an expression of sheer delight and amusement. Now he regarded me as one might regard a piece of dirt. There was no one else in the hall, and yet Yuebek and the disgusted look on his face was presence enough to fill a thousand seats.

"I offered you my heart," Yuebek said, "and you shat on it."

I approached him, each footstep echoing through the empty hall. "My lord—"

Yuebek laughed. "Spare me the pleasantries. I know what you really think of me." He turned to me, eyes sharp. His face remained immaculate, with not a single sign of the dogs' attack on him. It was almost as if he was made of wax and his mages had simply... molded him back to the way he was. Except now I knew better than to believe that. I had not seen other mages the whole time I was at court. I glanced at the veins running along his neck, a thin web of blue that contrasted with his white skin. I wondered what was healing him. Something kept him alive when by all rights he should be dead.

I was so close I could smell the rotting-mothball scent of him. I placed my hand on the throne's armrest.

Yuebek turned to me and scowled.

"I have been a terrible queen," I said, the words stinging as I spoke them. "I see that now, my lord. I escaped you because I didn't want to accept the truth—that I've been weak, a woman beating my head against an oaken door. My influence is a drop of water in a barrel of wine. My own soldiers won't even *listen* to me. They continue to follow my father's will."

"And now I'm supposed to believe you've seen the error in your ways and have come slinking back to me?" he spat out. He laughed. "You've all but made it clear that I disgust you, Queen Talyien."

I gritted my teeth. "It wasn't disgust, my lord. But a woman in my position— well. To understand that I need a man to save me after all, when I've been convinced I didn't need anyone's help...is an uncomfortable position to be in." I tried to touch his arm, but couldn't bear to, and ended up curling my fingers on the throne. Breathing the same air he did was too abhorrent already.

He leered at me. "And you expect me to believe that? Did you think I was born yesterday, Queen Talyien?"

"I think you are an intelligent man," I said. "Intelligent enough to know, too, that your movement is hampered without my support. I hear you've been playing warlord."

He turned his head with a snort. "Playing. Of course! What else do you do here? You've no arts, no *culture*...everything you have out here is a poor mimicry of the Empire's might and history. I tried to attend one of your tiresome plays. Talentless actors, a nonsensical plot, music that grated my ears...how have you people survived all these years? No wonder you turn to war to amuse yourselves. It's pathetic."

I grabbed my anger by the throat, forcing it back. "There are other theatres, of course."

"I went to the one your general recommended."

"I'm convinced General Ozo has never stepped foot inside a theatre. But I believe it doesn't make a difference. You're not here to discover Jin-Sayeng's cultural authenticity. You're here to become Dragonlord."

He turned to me, a thin line of disgust on his face. "That title," he said with a sneer. "I'll admit—the very sound of it excited me once. Better than a mere husband to the daughter of some backwater governor. But maybe I don't want this after all. When I was a boy, my father promised me an empire where the sun will never set, an army that can trample continents. *This?* Your war-torn nation is nothing but a collection of squabbling nobility and mindless peasants."

"Did you start thinking this before or after Princess Ryia unmanned you?"

He lifted his hand to strike me. I saw the movement and could have avoided the blow if I wanted to. Instead, I let it land on my cheek, on my mouth, hard enough to cut. Blood dripped from my lip.

"Your people—" he snarled. "Your people know *nothing* about how to treat true royalty. Look at you. You claim to be deferring to me, but you have yet to kneel. Do you think you are better than me, my queen, I with the army that could crush yours? I, the *real* emperor's son, compared with you, a mere warlord's daughter? What right do you have to look at me like I am less than you are?"

I bristled. My knees felt locked at the joints.

"Kneel, Queen Talyien," he commanded. "Now!"

I could feel the shadows pressing against me as I finally dropped to the ground, my hands and forehead on the cold wooden floor of my own throne room.

CHAPTER THREE

PRENUPTIALS

ᜁ ᜆᜒᜀ ᜑ

Yuebek began to laugh.

It was nothing to me. I convinced myself it was nothing to me. Pride wouldn't save us. Pride wouldn't save my son. I heard him stand up and fought against the instinct to defend myself. If he decided to rape me in the great hall, no one could stop him, me included.

Eyes shut, I also fought back the onslaught of memories I wanted to reach into for comfort. *You are already dead*, I told myself, burying all desire to be back in the Sougen, to be back in Khine's arms. *Dead as the corpses of the last war, as dead as the ones piling up now. Dead the moment your father decided to sacrifice you for the greater good. The dead don't feel anything, Talyien. So feel nothing.*

The ground quaked as the doors swung open. Soldiers stomped in, their armour clinking. "Prince Yuebek," General Ozo said. "Queen Talyien."

I rose to my feet as he bowed to each of us in turn. Yuebek looked irritated.

"A messenger has just arrived. Princess Ryia is at our borders. She brought... friends."

"Whose army?" I asked.

"Ikessar supporters from the north, I've been told. Darusu has also stirred. Warlord Hhanda aren dar Hoen has allied himself with the princess and has lent her his full force."

I cleared my throat. "She's managed to repair relations with the Hoen clan?"

"Momentarily, so it seems," Ozo said, bristling.

"To have been a fly on the wall during those negotiations."

"Crush them," Yuebek said, returning to the throne. He slumped down the seat. "All this is squabbling between ants."

Ozo licked his lips. "I would rather we speak with them first. The queen has returned; she can formalize her accusations concerning Lord Rayyel."

"He's confessed," Yuebek snapped. "What need is there for that?"

"The need to have an intact army at the end of it all if your plan is to seize control," Ozo said. "If the entire nation bands against us, we're done for. This would've all been for nothing."

"This prattling bores me," Yuebek replied.

"There's also the issue with the Oren-yaro bannermen..."

"I thought you had them under control," I said.

Ozo ran a hand over his forehead. "Your disappearance has led a number of your foothill lords to...question...what is happening." He was deliberately softening the words. *Question* probably meant they were on the verge of stabbing each other. "You need to unite them under your rule once again."

"And how, pray, am I supposed to do that? Considering you've done everything within your power to weaken the influence of *that* rule?"

He snarled. It was somewhat amusing to see him hold himself back.

I turned to Yuebek. "General Ozo is right. We need a formal trial. That'll stay Princess Ryia's hand. The Ikessars do everything according to law. Or at least, that's what they want people to think, something even your presence in this land won't change. If you want to unite Oren-yaro's lords..." I swallowed. "The best way to do it would be with a wedding."

His eyes danced towards me. I wasn't sure if he looked amused or even more irritated. His eyebrows were raised, but his mouth was turned into a scowl. "So," he said. "You really *are* that desperate, aren't you?"

I didn't disagree. A stranger was sitting on Oren-yaro's throne, and here we were: Yeshin's daughter and his right-hand general both cowed, heads lowered, eyes not really settling on one thing. I heard Ozo take a deep breath. "What are your wishes, Beloved Queen?"

"Announce the trial," I said. "For that, you need to begin treating Lord Rayyel as befitting his position."

"I've treated him exactly as befits his position," Yuebek snapped. "Better, in fact. Bastards like that have no business pretending to be someone of importance. I told his mother as much. Rallying an army simply because I spoke the truth—you people are hopeless."

"What you're doing to him—what you may have already *done* to him— won't serve our cause," I replied. "Show the people you are capable of respect. Put Rayyel in a proper prison, at least. There's one in the barracks."

"That's too far away."

"Lord General Ozo will see to it that he doesn't escape."

Yuebek gave me a scrutinizing look. "Do you still love him?"

"I don't see what that question has to do with—"

"Do you still love him?" Yuebek repeated.

"No," I replied easily. "Of course not."

"Then why do you care what I do to him?"

"Our politics demand it," I said.

"*You* demand it. General Ozo doesn't give a damn. Isn't that right, Lord General?"

Ozo inclined his head to the side, as if he agreed but didn't seem to want to open his mouth to do it. Was it because he was afraid how I would react? I struggled to remember a time when I trumpeted both my rage and my love for Rayyel from one end of the land to the next.

"You will let him go," I said, struggling to maintain my composure. "Lord Ozo, rally the lords. We will speak with them during the engagement party."

"Presumptuous bitch. I haven't even decided if I still want to marry you," Yuebek said.

"You have," I replied. "You're still sitting on that throne."

"It's a comfortable seat, but not as comfortable as my lap."

I stared at him. Even Ozo looked startled.

Yuebek began to laugh again, a sound that sent shivers up my spine. And then, without another word, he lurched out of the throne and glided past the doors, calling for his guards.

"You push him too much," Ozo told me as we were left alone in the great hall.

"You want him to believe I've grudgingly accepted him," I said. "Not that I'm pretending. A castrated dog still bites."

"That's what you think you are?"

"No, that's what *you* are," I hissed under my breath. I turned back to the throne. After a moment's hesitation, I placed myself on the seat. It was cold, as if no one else had just been on it.

"Yeshin's child," Ozo said, shaking his head. I couldn't tell if it was an insult or praise.

"That's what you want to see, isn't it?" I asked. "Or are you just going to complain again, Ozo? If you wanted me to be demure, there's hundreds of other royal daughters you could've dangled in front of his nose."

"You're the queen. You're all we have."

"How pathetic." I turned away from him in distaste. "Your grand-children…" I began.

"They're nothing until this is all over," Ozo grumbled. "Safest place for them to be. If they're nobody, they can't be used against us."

"Is that why you never told your son he was yours?"

Ozo's face tightened. I found myself glancing at the scarred floor, where Agos's sword had gone through while trying to pursue Rayyel. Hard to remember it was just this winter past. Time had lost all meaning. When you are holding yourself against an unforeseen future, everything becomes distorted. I glanced through the broken windows of my castle, counting what stars I could see, and for a moment imagined that things had not changed much at all.

I remembered holding court here. How there was always an Ikessar representative or two making sure I was adhering to their laws (the land's laws, they called it), in addition to Magister Arro and the rest of my own advisers. I did nothing that wasn't recorded several times over, and argued and deliberated upon in the coming weeks, never mind if I did it on a whim. Offer assistance to a peasant woman who just lost her husband and they'll tell you that we don't have the resources to do it for everyone else—if one family must starve to stop the riots of a thousand others, then so be it. Threaten to kill a warmonger and they'll whisper repercussions in your ear.

A bird screeched outside. The doors opened and Yuebek walked in, dragging a chain. Rayyel was attached to the other end.

I didn't move.

Yuebek shoved Rayyel forward. He was so weak that he toppled over easily.

"Do you care if I kill him?" Yuebek sneered.

"You've been threatening that for months," I said. I pretended to stifle a yawn. "If it'll make this all go away, then by all means, bury the bastard. But I'm not your problem here. The Ikessar army at our borders is your problem. I don't care what you think about this man—he's still *their* heir. The uncrowned Dragonlord, as far as the rest of the land is concerned."

Yuebek gazed at me, a smile on his lips. How well could he read expressions? I still cared about Rai's well-being, but the desperation was gone. Even he had to see that.

He pressed his foot against Rai's back, pinning him to the ground. "He doesn't seem to feel pain," Yuebek said, cocking his head to the side like a curious dog. "Is he man, or stone?" He kicked the crumpled figure. Not a single sound erupted from Rai. His eyes were staring at the floor. It was as if he had disappeared completely inside of himself.

"I've been married to him for years," I said, looking at Rai's hollowed face. "Stone is an appropriate description. What's the point of trying to break him, Esteemed Prince? The gods know I've tried to do it our whole marriage through. There's nothing inside of him worth finding."

"A woman scorned—" Yuebek began.

"So I was," I said. "All the more reason for you to believe I'm willing to dissolve this marriage now. I gave this man everything I was asked for, and more. Too much more. We all marry for convenience, for alliances, because our parents were audacious enough to plan out our lives before we ever got a say. But you all know this was more. I loved this man."

A surprise, then. He wasn't made of stone—not entirely. I saw Rayyel's face twitch before his eyes slowly turned to me.

"I loved him," I repeated, staring back at him, knowing I wasn't acting this time. I wasn't lying. "From since I was a girl, too young to understand what I felt. He irritated me at first—my father's upbringing had ensured I held no fondness for the Ikessars. But because I thought my destiny lay with him, I made myself fall in love with him. Or maybe I did. The line between my father's orders and my own feelings blurred over the years.

"I know one thing. Wisely or unwisely, I know I gave it all. You think you gave your heart, Esteemed Prince? That is nothing to what I offered this man. I was his to cherish or ruin, and he chose to ruin. Why would you think there was anything left? Now that I don't have to be with him—now that I have a way out—why would you imagine that I, my father's daughter, wouldn't choose to take it?"

"A magnificent speech," Yuebek said with a smirk. "You do seem overly fond of them." He kicked Rayyel a second time, fishing for my reaction. When he got nothing, he made a wide circle around the prostrate body. "If I kill him now, will you still marry me?"

"I'd marry you, but I wouldn't be very happy about the complications his death will bring," I said lightly, tapping my fingers along the throne. "Do you want to be Dragonlord, Esteemed Prince? Or are you just a sadist?"

"A sadist. I like that. No one's ever called me that before. Not to my face."

"I find that hard to believe."

"Will you marry me with his blood on my robes, Beloved Queen? Kiss me with *that* between us?"

Bile stirred in my throat. Without waiting for my reply, Yuebek turned around and clicked his fingers.

His soldiers stepped forward and I readied myself. If he was going to kill Rai, I couldn't very well stop him now. *Does the end justify the means?* I looked back into Rai's eyes and realized he was still staring at me. Despite my resolution to see this farce through, my hands went to my sword. I couldn't help myself. I could suddenly see something that wasn't clear before. They were Thanh's eyes—the very same colour, a soft shade of brown.

I got up. But before I could do anything, the soldiers drew closer, dragging another figure behind them. Inging.

Yuebek grabbed her arm, yanking her up. "This one was caught sneaking back here," he said. "I believe *you* know exactly where she came from. An herbalist, I'm told. Why so much secrecy, Queen Talyien? Were you planning on having trysts with your husband?"

"That's absurd."

"And yet you say you don't want him anymore. It's *me* you want now."

I swallowed. "Of course, Esteemed Prince."

"Even if I do this?" He laughed, his hand reaching for her throat. My eyes widened as I saw his other hand rip her dress.

She screamed. I tore down the dais to stop him. Ozo twisted me around, making me face the throne, his big arms holding me still, blocking me from what was happening behind us.

"You will not do a damn thing," he said in a low voice. "Did you think my son was the last casualty?"

"He should be!" I tried to strike him. Any doubts I might've had that he was truly Agos's father disappeared; even for his age, the man was just as strong. He didn't budge even as I shrieked and struggled and bit him so hard I drew blood. Behind me, Ingging's cries bounced off the walls, as if each had a life of its own.

I will not describe what happened in that throne room. I don't think I have to. War has enough horrors to sate the most ravenous appetites, and the sum of Ingging's life did not revolve around those moments. I will not revisit her pain to give weight and colour to my words, or sensationalize another person's suffering to make a point. I didn't write this to entertain you, and Ingging deserved better. I will say this: In those few, horrific minutes, I suddenly understood that monsters like Yuebek aren't born. *We make them.*

We make them when we hand power over to another. When we pull the blankets up to cover our eyes and pretend the world isn't ours to change. When we take the gifts handed to us without questioning where they came from, how they were taken, who suffered to give us what we pretend is our due. We were all to blame for what happened there. And though nothing can change that this is the way the world works, I can at least allow myself to carry the weight. To do nothing is also a choice. We did nothing until it was too late and all we had left was a madman's solution, sitting in the palms of another madman. The sins of the world lie in too many sparkling hands, washed clean of the blood they've shed. Even writing this is a sin. The stories we tell you, the stories we tell ourselves—they twist things, make the tangible insignificant, remove barriers between truth and fiction until nothing sounds real and everything is a lie.

And so those who grow mad with power learn they can do these things because no matter how we say we abhor them, a part of us will allow them to happen if it means holding on to those little comforts that make *our* lives worth living. Monsters know what they are. I am not much different. My desire to tell the truth comes at a price: the disregard of the ones who suffered the most while I spend pages upon pages immortalizing creatures like Yuebek and Yeshin. Such is the way of the world.

So let me tell you what I later learned about Ingging instead.

She was born a servant in one of the Nee estates over in the foothills. As children, she and Liosa used to tear after each other through the rice terraces, knee-deep in mud. They loved to wake up early to get tofu with caramel from town, and visiting the temple during winter—less so to worship Akaterru than for the steamed purple rice cakes they sold on the temple steps. She was often scolded for encouraging Liosa's foolhardiness; later, as they grew older, she tried to become a voice of reason, which Liosa often scoffed at.

After Liosa left Oka Shto, Ingging married a potter from the city and bore him four children: Gurtal, Liaong, Landing, and Talyeng. The last one was a daughter, half my age and born the same day I was. She loved that it was a link she could share with her old friend, was convinced it meant the gods understood us in some way. That there was a pattern to our suffering, our fates written in the stars. I don't know if I shared the sentiment, but I appreciated the thought all the same. She raised her children well, from what I could tell. They were polite even while hearing news of their mother's death, though I was sure they wouldn't be if they knew the details. On the way out of the small house she had managed to scrounge up from the meagre pay we gave the castle staff—her husband having died a long time ago—Talyeng accompanied me to the gate.

"Did she suffer?" she asked. Her voice was still a child's voice, high and chirpy.

"No," I lied. "It was as if she died in her sleep."

And then I prayed that she might never learn the truth.

Not even my darkest nightmares could say what else Yuebek might have done after he killed Ingging. Rayyel was still on the floor, and I think his intention was to rip him apart, or worse. Whatever was done to Ingging could very well happen to him, too. I steeled myself. But a guard arrived, bearing news that an Ikessar emissary was at the gates. Ozo released me and turned to Yuebek. "He needs to be cleaned up *fast*," Ozo said, pointing at Rai. "You can't let the Ikessars see this. If they attack now, we're done for."

Yuebek reeled back. He looked exhausted. "Very well," he said. He glanced at me with eyes filled with hate. "You win this round, my queen. Take care of your dear husband for now. He won't be for very long."

I wanted to rush to Rayyel's side. I hesitated, and gestured at the Oren-yaro guards. They picked him up, dragging him from the great hall. I turned back to see Lo Bahn slinking in. Yuebek pushed him aside, yelling.

Not wanting to see the rest of it, I followed the guards instead. They took Rayyel to the guest chambers. Yayei appeared at the door, white-faced, shaking. "Water and towels, Yayei," I told her.

"Beloved Queen…"

"Yayei," I said. "Please. You can't think about it. We have to keep busy. Don't let her death be in vain."

Her teeth rattled as she drew away.

I pulled off Rayyel's filthy robes and cringed as I saw how thin he was. I could count every rib on his body. I found a pair of scissors and began to trim his beard. The motions kept my thoughts at bay.

His eyes finally focused on me. "What are you doing?" he asked.

"Saving us," I replied.

"You were supposed to be gathering forces, not be back here."

"Don't know if you've been paying attention, Rayyel, but your mother's already done that," I said.

He pushed my hand away. "You could have waited. Let her thin out his soldiers first."

"In my city, using my people as fodder? I am nowhere near as heartless as you all think." I snipped around his moustache, smoothing it with my fingers. "I don't believe she has near the number of soldiers to hurt Yuebek, either. You know what he is."

"You do, too," he said in a low voice. "Why are you making him believe you're going to marry him?"

"Because I intend to."

"Why, by all the gods—"

"Rai," I said. "Listen to me, for *once.*"

He opened his mouth, but no words came out. If I had attempted to talk to him like this during the early days of our marriage, it would've been an argument long into the night. But something had changed between us. Without my feelings for him hanging in the balance, the rest of the fire had gone out.

Yayei returned with the basin and towel, and clean clothes for him. She bowed and withdrew a second time.

I returned to trimming Rai's beard. "There is no point gathering an army. We cannot save Jin-Sayeng by defeating her enemies because her enemies were brought here for a reason. If you keep your mouth shut long enough, I'll explain everything to you."

Rai swallowed. "I do listen." Trembling, he reached up to place his hand on my arm. His fingers were cold. "I heard everything you said out there, too."

I didn't reply. Once his beard looked presentable, I placed the scissors on the windowsill and turned to grab the basin and water. Wringing soapy water from the towel, I began to wash his face slowly, mechanically, while I whispered Yeshin's plans into his ear. I told him everything, because Rayyel ran on reason, and the man who could keep his silence about his doubts about our son for five years could keep quiet a little longer. He listened without a flicker of emotion, ever the stone wall; it was the first time I found comfort in it.

When I was done, he took a deep breath, his throat bobbing. "Since you're still alive," I said in a low voice, "then you can help us bring a sense of order to these things. Yuebek hasn't broken you, has he?"

Rai shook his head. "His methods of torture were... laughable. I counted the drops until I knew how many were in each bucket. I simply... anticipated it after that. Focused on the counting. I can now tell you how many approximate drops there are in a bucket that size."

I dipped the towel back into the basin and turned to his back. The once unblemished skin was now covered in dark, brittle scabs and scars. "I saw our son," I said as I washed it.

"Is he well?"

"He's in Kaggawa's camp. Dai at least... cares for him. He is fed, guarded. Healthy. But..." I paused, remembering Thanh's words back at the camp. "Rai, I think he's poisoning our son's mind."

Rai frowned. "Kaggawa intends to wield our own son like a dagger against our throats."

"Perhaps we have nothing to worry about until he's finished with his war with the Anyus," I said. "In any case, I feel at ease knowing there's a whole army between him and Yuebek. Believe me, Rai, it is the only reason I can sleep these days."

"And the boy... have you spoken?" Somehow, mentioning Thanh seemed to invigorate him.

I nodded. "He's bored. Spends the whole day reading. When I saw him, he had that infernal book by Sagar."

"It is an excellent book."

"I beg to disagree, Rai."

His face twitched.

I gave a soft smile. "Lamang is... keeping an eye on him."

"Lamang," he repeated. His eyes brightened. "Inzali's brother."

"Yes. He's working in Kaggawa's camp. And your sister. Karia."

"I see."

"You could say more than that, Rai. *By the way, dear wife, did I forget to mention I had a sister?* All these family reunions..."

"They hid that from me, too," he said. "Karia had been a maidservant in the Citadel when I was growing up. I knew her, but not who she was. When I learned of Anino, I asked her to keep an eye on him. I didn't know who else to trust. Only then did I find out she was my father's daughter."

"Worms underneath the wound," I reflected.

"Knowing what we know now, it is difficult to disagree with your father about keeping you in the dark."

"Don't say that, Rai."

"I don't mean it that way. But you can see why he came to the conclusions he did. Cleansing fire might be the only hope this land has."

"And us, the logs to stoke it. Yes. That's the sort of twisted thinking that got us to where we are now. I've *just* decided not to kill you—don't let me hear this from you again or I might change my mind." I sighed, finally pulling away from him. He looked clean now, which wasn't saying much. You can't wash away the shadow of starvation and torture overnight.

Rai reached for a clean shirt. He couldn't seem to bend his elbow, so I helped him put it on. He looked embarrassed to be so weak. "Speaking of Lamang," he said as I tied his belt, and I thought for a moment he was going to ask about *that* and turned my head away. "Inzali managed to escape from Bara during my arrest. I believe she went to your bannermen."

"Which explains their discontent," I said. "Well, time for her to undo what she did. We need to be united. We need the full force of the Oren-yaro to march with the Zarojo towards the Sougen. Which is going to be tricky with your mother roaring for blood out there. You understand why I need you now, Rai? Your powers of diplomacy…"

"You finally admit I have them," he said.

I glanced at him.

"A joke," he explained.

"Yes, I figured."

"You know, because—"

"Yes, Rai. I got that."

He frowned. "But you didn't laugh."

"Rai—"

He cracked a smile.

"You do enjoy getting a rise out of me, don't you?" I asked.

"More than you realize," he confessed.

We fell silent, listening to the crackling of the fireplace, to the wind roaring outside. After a moment, he took my hand. I squeezed back, knowing he understood the gravity of what was about to come, the burden we all needed to share.

I cleared my throat. "I will formally accuse you. You'll acknowledge everything, which means there's not much else the council can do. I won't lie. They may agree it is in the land's best interests to execute you. And if Yuebek decides to hasten the process...I can't stop him."

"Fair enough," he replied, as simply as if I'd asked him to take a walk in the garden with me. "And then you'll marry him, that thing out there? After what he's just done?"

I closed my eyes, trying to shut out the memories of the last hour, and took a deep breath. "Yes," I said, holding back both tears and vomit. "Yes, I will."

CHAPTER FOUR

THE WEDDING

ᛏᛁᛖ

The wedding of Talyien aren dar Orenar to Prince Yuebek Tsaito, the Emperor Yunan Tsaito's Fifth Son, might have been the most sombre wedding Jin-Sayeng had ever seen. From the way the lords and ladies greeted us, eyes settling on anywhere *but* the two robed figures in their midst, to the way the musicians seemed to choose the slowest, saddest songs, it was indistinguishable from a funeral.

Not that Yuebek himself noticed. He chalked it up to Jinsein tastes, criticizing the celebration—which we held in the city square, underneath the silhouette of the crumbling dragon-towers. An apt image. I tried to focus my attention on them each time Yuebek reached for my waist, laughing at the dancers. "When I'm Dragonlord, I'll make sure you people learn what *real* culture looks like!" he jeered, breath stinking like the back of a slaughterhouse.

The patron of the wedding was Akaterru, the River God. A petition had been made to have at least priestesses of Omionoru and Immiresh present, as if somehow the more deities they could offer prayers to, the less damned the wedding would be. Both parties refused. If Oren-yaro was going to make a fool of itself, it could do so alone.

The ceremony went on for the better part of noon—long prayers uttered in the Oren-yaro tongue, so ancient I could barely understand the words. It was nearly a relief when the priests came to give their blessings and to wrap us together in beads, signifying the start of our union. Nearly. I tried not to smell Yuebek's corpse-stench as they pushed us next to each other. The crowd watched in silence, unamused but unable to tear their eyes away from the spectacle. One of the priests held up his hand, anointing both of our foreheads with water.

My groom reached forward to kiss me.

I pulled away almost as soon as our lips touched, my eyes on the grey towers. *If I don't do this, the land will burn*, I told myself. But it was a struggle not to recall that day with Khine in the Sougen—the way his eyes crinkled when he smiled, the way his laughter seemed to burn inside his chest before it burst out.

"You look hungry," Khine had said that morning, noticing me staring at him. "Come and have breakfast, my dear."

"Will you let me cook for you next time?" I asked, coming up to him.

The laughter, then. "Oh," he said, pretending to grow serious. "You're not joking."

"You do this for me so often and I want to return the favour." I settled beside him as he handed me the bowl of rice and eggs. "I did try to cook once, if you recall. Back in your house in Shang Azi."

"Can't say I'll ever forget it. All that smoke..." He pretended to think. "You're right, though. I do feed you too often. Maybe I should stop altogether."

"So that we starve to death?"

"I don't mind starving beside you."

"Your sisters are right. You *are* an idiot."

"Have you ever heard me contest it?"

I laughed in return. He smiled, as if he could see something that he didn't want to tell me—a secret he wanted to keep to himself. I stared back at him, wanting to know what it was, wanting to be lost in his eyes forever.

The footsteps came, jolting me from the memory. People arrived to hang coins from the beads, held together with red thread. Lords and ladies from all across the foothills and the riverlands, and then Yuebek's officers. Radi Ong was nowhere to be seen, and neither was Jiro Kaz. All the better, probably; I was sure he knew what had happened to his wife and that I was at fault. Another soul to hate me, to add to the crowd. The fact that I had set Prince Rayyel aside and was marrying this foreigner was enough to make the commoners hiss from the sidelines. When Yuebek led me down the street, which had been covered with green, gold-threaded hemp cloth for the occasion, I could hear them cursing my name in the alleys. "Bitch Queen! Traitor! A new man to fuck, when there's war on our doorstep!" The guards came to chase the onlookers deeper into the shadows.

I kept my chin up, my jaw steady. We returned to the square for the feast: roasted pork, grilled over hot flames, roasted duck, stewed squid swimming in black ink. Fresh river fish, stuffed with onions and tomatoes, fried noodles with tough native chicken and whole quail eggs, and java rice flavoured with lemongrass. Yuebek would occasionally pull me towards him to try to feed me with his hands. I had no appetite for anything, and deflecting Yuebek was like trying to entertain a child you didn't want to be around. I could feel my bannermen's eyes on me, could see the ladies turn to their husbands to whisper their observations into their men's ears. With Lushai nothing but ashes back in Toriue Castle, the only two people there who really knew what was happening were Ozo and I. The secrecy my father had bound him to meant that after everything, and with Inzali Lamang's unwanted help, Ozo's influence was slipping.

You could tell from the *gifts* that were brought midway through the meal. They weren't presents so much as they were subtle insults. A wall-eyed stallion the Lady Daya proclaimed was the best of some nonexistent breed; a dozen emaciated fighting roosters; an entire trunk with copies of Sagar's poetry, when it was well-known he was a controversial figure the Oren-yaro would've loved to burn alive. Little things that someone like Yuebek wouldn't have picked up on, but we all knew what they were saying.

If I wasn't going to stop this madness, I was going to be mocked forever for it.

After the last gifts were bundled away, Yuebek got up, holding a cup of wine towards me. "To my queen," he said with flourish. "I bring you my own offering. I think you will be quite pleased with this one."

I felt the blood drain from my face. Rayyel was my first thought. Rayyel—whom I had not seen since that evening when he went out to confront the Ikessar emissary. They had left Oka Shto together. Later, Rai made his confessions from the Ikessar temple down at the city, and the head priestess herself arrived with documents dissolving our marriage. I was told that she had been waiting the last few months and didn't need much more than Rai's word. As he had admitted to abandoning his responsibilities, he wouldn't need a trial, either—the priestess herself had taken him into custody. If the Ikessars wanted him, they would have to promise to try him themselves.

Two of Yuebek's servants arrived with a box, the perfect size to contain a head. Lo Bahn strode over to pick it up with a look of distaste. He limped to where we were seated and held it up with a flourish.

The guests had grown silent. I stared at the box, frozen to my chair.

"Open it," Yuebek said, grinning.

I didn't move.

The mirth disappeared from Yuebek's face. "Open it!" he ordered, grabbing my wrist.

I yanked my hand away from him. "I bestow the honour of unwrapping on you, dear husband," I said in a flat tone.

Yuebek frowned, but I wasn't going to give him the satisfaction of bending to his demands. Resisting him was dangerous, but giving in was too suspicious, and with the game I was playing, I knew what line I needed to straddle.

He seemed to decide I wasn't merely testing him. At the very least, it looked like he didn't want to be embarrassed—amazing, given everything that had transpired so far. He got up, giving his guests a small grin before he walked towards Lo Bahn. He pulled the silk covering away. The rotting corpse-stench was now unmistakable. Yuebek picked up the box and turned it upside down, allowing the head to roll down the street.

I heard Ozo cry out.

I was trying not to stare at the head directly. Now I glanced across the table and saw that it belonged to a bald man with a long beard, no one I knew. But Ozo did. "You killed the emissary!" he roared.

Yuebek laughed. "I did! I changed my mind. These people have insulted my queen—someone has to pay."

"The Ikessars—"

"Let them come," Yuebek said. "I have the queen's love. What more do I need?"

"You—" Ozo's face was red. "He was staying at their temple. Those are sacred grounds!"

"Not sacred to me." Yuebek shrugged.

"You raided the Kibouri temple," Ozo stated. He glanced at his men. "When?"

"About an hour ago," Lo Bahn broke in. "Around the time your priests blessed Prince Yuebek and Queen Talyien's union. Damn priestesses put up quite a fight, I can tell you!" He bowed towards me awkwardly. "There's another present, of course, one I'm sure the queen will appreciate more. It's what the prince sent us out there for in the first place."

He clapped his hands.

Two guards arrived, escorting Rayyel. He was groomed, clean, unchained. Alive.

I felt like weeping. We traded glances for a moment before I turned to Yue-bek, who laughed at my expression. "I knew it!" he said. "I knew you would appreciate it! Deep inside, you still care about the idiot, don't you? Well, I can forgive it. I can forgive your woman's sensibilities. He's free now. Free to walk away from here if he wants to. Why does it matter to me? You're *mine*."

"You fool," Ozo whispered in Jinan. "This careless display has hastened our deaths. This…"

"The lone wolf still has to carry his tail," I replied, quoting an Oren-yaro saying as I looked back at the man I would never call my husband again. Rai stood there in silence, his posture straight, unyielding. The farce couldn't have asked for better players.

The silence was broken by the sound of Yuebek clapping his hands. "Such a dark mood!" he proclaimed. He took his sword and swung towards Rayyel. I bolted up in spite of myself, but before I could act, the tip of Yuebek's sword stopped inches away from Rai's neck.

"Dancing," Yuebek said, his eyes lighting up.

"You want to dance with Rai?" I managed, my knees growing weak. "Be my guest."

He turned to me with a grin. "Your humour is lovely, dearest wife. No. You and him. A parting gift to your waiting lords and ladies! This whole thing, after all, is history, is it not?"

I heard Ozo turn his head and cough in discomfort.

Without a word, I walked towards where Rayyel stood. I knew only one dance; he must have been thinking of the same one, because he held both hands out, marking the beginning of it.

Someone startled the musicians into playing.

I approached Rayyel, taking his hands in mine, cold fingers touching. We drifted together, and then let go, twirling where we stood. It felt like yesterday that we were practicing the steps—I could still hear Arro tapping the window-sill to the beat with his fan, clicking his tongue every time I made a mistake.

"You're as wooden as a fence post," Arro said. "This is going to be your wedding dance, Princess, not a sparring competition. Try to pay attention."

"He's not much better," I fumed, pointing at Rayyel.

"Never mind him, Princess. All eyes will be on *you*."

"It's not fair!"

"Of course it's not fair. You'll be the one in a pretty dress."

"Then let him wear it!"

Arro chuckled. Rai, of course, looked far from amused. "If the princess will not take her duties seriously—"

"Choke on your tongue, Rayyel," I snapped. "Before I make you swallow it."

"Magister Arro," he said, turning away from me. "Since the princess cannot be bothered to learn a skill every other daughter of Jin-Sayeng is expected to know, might I suggest a replacement? No one will know the difference."

"Oh, they will," Arro grumbled, scratching his cheek.

"Because they're expecting a wolf pup in a dress," Rai sighed. "You're right." Arro held his tongue.

"I hate you," I told the boy I loved. I guess he believed me. A mistake, one of many.

How the last ten years had turned us into different people, I couldn't tell. All I knew was that the Rayyel in front of me was not the stiff-necked prince he once was. I was no longer that arrogant little girl. We danced with our eyes on each other, remembering every step as if the years hadn't gone by in a flash. Never as husband and wife had we been in such harmony—for a moment, I caught a glimpse of the marriage I always wanted. Maybe he did, too. It felt bittersweet. Like saying thank you and goodbye, all in one breath.

It ended, the music fading with the past. With a measure of reluctance, he let my hands go. "The queen is generous," he said simply, before turning to Yuebek with a bow. "As is her new lord. I am grateful for my life, though it was not necessary. My death, for my sins, would be well-deserved."

He bowed a second time before walking away from the square. My hands were cold as I watched him walk past the guards and disappear into the next street. I was still expecting Yuebek to change his mind and cut Rai down from behind. Even when I could no longer see him, I found it hard to feel relieved.

It was in the middle of it all that Warlord Nijo—Lushai's son, whose sister, I noticed, was absent despite being invited—finally got up. He was a rotund man, tall, with a beard that looked more like patchy moss on his face. He had worn a conflicted scowl since the start of the ceremony, one that deepened with every hour. "Is no one going to say anything?" he asked.

"Return to your seat, boy," Ozo snapped.

Nijo turned to him. "Your stint as a warlord has ended, Ozo," he snarled in return. "What makes you think you still have the right to continue to drag us by the nose? My father may have yielded to you for some reason, but I am not him. Unfortunately for us, he's no longer around. Is murder no longer a crime in this godsforsaken land?" He turned to me.

"Warlord Lushai attacked first," I said, walking back to my spot at the table to take a sip from my wine. "It was not murder. I have a witness."

"Where is this witness?" Nijo thundered.

"I'll vouch for it myself," Ozo replied. "Lushai was brash and had no love for the queen. Or do I have to remind everyone about your own family's ambitions? The secrets *you've* hidden? Perhaps you want us to dig through your family history a little further—we've plenty enough reason to now. This doesn't bode well for your rule, Warlord."

Nijo finally sat down, grumbling under his breath. But another lord got up. I recognized Ipeng.

"I am not trying to be confrontational," Ipeng said, his voice shaking—with anger or age, I couldn't tell. "The gods know I am not that sort of man. But Warlord Nijo brings up a good point. Just because Ozo sanctioned this marriage..."

"*I* did not sanction it, Lord Ipeng," Ozo said. "Warlord Yeshin did."

Ipeng nodded. "And I understand his memory is important, but my lords and ladies—Warlord Yeshin is sixteen years dead. Queen Talyien may still rule the land, but that means her relations are our concerns, as well."

"You own me, you mean," I said simply. "You think I should have asked for your permissions first, as if all of you were my grandmother."

Ipeng refused to take the bait.

"Did that attack on Burbatan rattle your skull?" Ozo asked.

"You control well over half our army, Lord General," Ipeng said. "But not all of it."

"You'd threaten war in your own region," Ozo remarked. "How many men do *you* have, Lord Ipeng? Last I remember, the Nee bandits all but obliterated your soldiers. Without me, you would have lost Burbatan, your whole family included."

"Enough," I broke in. "Your old men's prattling is turning this into the worst wedding of the century."

"Isn't it, already?" Ipeng asked. His eyebrows knotted. "Tell me, Beloved

Queen, why it was so necessary to turn to foreigners for help? We've been at the empire's teat for far too long in our history, and we were doing well at keeping away from them the last century or so. Should not Jin-Sayeng's troubles remain her own?"

"Because we've done such a remarkable job ourselves this whole time," I replied, dryly.

Yuebek got up, draining an entire cup of rice wine in one go. "I've heard all the Jin jabbering I've wanted to for the whole day," he said, shooting his translator a dirty glance. He was holding his sword loosely in one hand. "It's clear you don't like me. Which is wonderful, because I don't like any of you!" He laughed at his own joke, jumping at the lord closest to him, which made the man nearly drop his own cup in shock. Yuebek placed his foot on the table and ran his naked blade along the panicked man's shoulder.

"I've heard you Jinseins prefer to negotiate with blades rather than talk," Yuebek continued. "A most marvellous arrangement, really! I wish we still did such things back in the Empire. I'd have been emperor in a year!" He pulled his sword away and without warning, flung it towards Ipeng from across the table. The sword struck Ipeng's head with such force that it flew off, landing with a spray of blood next to the roasted duck.

The guests backed away from their seats. Some drew their swords.

Yuebek smiled, and his own blade carefully flew back into his hand. Ipeng's headless body toppled over.

"Sorcery!" Nijo gasped.

"What if it is?" Yuebek asked brightly. "Isn't it time you monkeys embraced what you've denied all these years?"

Nijo pointed at him. "My father may have entertained you, but this is the last straw. I'll have none of it." He gazed back at the others. "You wolves of Oren-yaro—you would let this man continue to insult us? Where's your Jinsein pride?" He turned to me, eyes blazing. "You. I suppose there's no point asking where yours is, you whore."

Yuebek's guards raised their halberds. I gestured for them to stop before they could strike him. They stood aside as I left my table.

"Dear wife," Yuebek intoned. "Let me gift you with another head." Only Yuebek could make such words sound almost sincere. He looked like a hound slavering for the hunt.

"Marrying the queen doesn't make *you* Dragonlord," Nijo hissed.

"You weren't invited here to stir trouble, Warlord Nijo," I broke in.

"Tell that to your new husband. First, the Ikessar emissary, and now your own bannermen!"

"Lord Ipeng overstepped his bounds," I said easily. "As have you. An insult to the Dragonlord is punishable by death. Have your brains all been so addled the past few months that you've forgotten you still had one?"

Nijo's mouth opened and closed, like a fish yanked from the water. "That's—"

"I'll be gracious," I said, holding my hand out. Ozo appeared with a bow, pressing my father's sword into my palm. I stared at it for a moment, feeling the urge to reject it like I did back in Burbatan. Instead, I allowed my fingers to wrap itself around the hilt. "We'll settle it with combat."

Nijo laughed. "You! I'd kill you!"

"Isn't that what you want?"

He started to shake his head, before drawing his sword. "Don't say I didn't warn you, *Beloved Queen*."

I bent down to rip the lower part of my wedding gown, leaving my legs free, and attacked.

Nijo's confidence was a fool's confidence. I knew the way he fought, from way back when we were young. No strength, no finesse. His footwork was shoddy, and he struck like someone who had never been in a real fight before, who didn't know the panic of having your life flash before your very eyes. It wasn't unlikely. Many warlords' sons and daughters were kept cloistered behind a teeming mass of guards and servants. Even Ozo didn't seem worried.

A deafening silence fell on the crowd. All eyes turned to me—all wondering, I suppose, if I *had* gone as mad as this man I'd married. As mad as my father. A wedding and a show, with the Ikessars breathing down our necks? She must've. I could hear the *scritching* in my head as I imagined the scribes writing it all down, interpreting events to their hearts' content. *Ruined by scandal, both hers and his, Queen Talyien finally discarded her husband for a more powerful man* . . .

And then: two possibilities. Jin-Sayeng is saved, or Jin-Sayeng burns.

I didn't know which of the two I was driving towards as I battered at Nijo's sword, a touch faster than he could ever be. It was nothing but sparring practice. I didn't even know if I intended to kill him or not. I held no love for the man. Growing up, he treated me with the sort of politeness that barely masked his contempt. But I didn't really want him dead. I didn't even want *his* father dead.

Still, I knew already that what I wanted mattered less now than it ever did. The world might never forget this moment. They would record only the sorts of things that people want to hear, and then they would embellish it, twist it into something foul and unrecognizable. They would state the obvious: that I did this to preserve my honour and my new husband's, that I wanted to prove I wasn't a whore queen, bending over for a madman just for power.

As if I hadn't gone far beyond caring about such things. It was better that they know nothing else. My memories of the Sougen could stay there. I couldn't expect more, I couldn't hope for more, and so why should it bother me what they thought about what I needed to do? I heard Yuebek laughing just as I struck Nijo across the chest, so deep it all but ensured his defeat. I could take his head with a second blow.

Instead, I held back, pulling away from him.

"We are fighting amongst ourselves at the cusp of war," I said. "*That* is all this Jinsein pride has ever done for us. That is all it's ever done. I have a proposition. Whoever thinks they know how to turn this around may take the title of Warlord of Oren-yaro from me. You have my blessings. I can't guarantee the rest of the nation will agree, but that's nothing we all don't deal with. It's not going to get better from here on out, either."

A grumble of discontent rose among the crowd. Nobody wanted to take me up on the offer, that much was clear. Easy enough to say what another was doing wrong; harder to know exactly how to make it right. I noticed my left arm was drenched in blood—Nijo wasn't completely incompetent.

I turned back to Yuebek, who was clapping his hands in glee. Just as he opened his mouth, an arrow lodged itself through his neck.

Yuebek coughed, blood spraying. For a moment, I felt a rush of relief, followed by horror. And then Yuebek's eyes turned towards me. His blood-streaked mouth turned up at the corners as he craned his head to the side and pulled the arrow out. He slowly walked back towards our table. As if nothing was amiss, he unstoppered a jug of wine, poured himself another cup, and drank. Wine and black liquid oozed from both sides of his neck.

Another arrow came flying. It shattered before it could touch him.

Chaos erupted around us.

I found myself back-to-back with Nijo as a swarm of soldiers in plain black armour streamed through the square. They moved effortlessly, rushing straight for the bannermen, most of whom didn't have the foresight to bring their swords. A dozen bodies were on the ground before I could blink.

"Watch your side!" Nijo barked as two soldiers rushed us.

Horror turned to fear. We were both injured, and I didn't think the soldiers meant to capture me alive. I attacked blindly, the blood from my arm pooling around my fingers. One soldier sidestepped and lifted his arm to strike.

The tip of a halberd appeared in his belly. Blood spurted from his gut as Ozo kicked him aside, making a sweep that all but shattered the second attacker's knees. "Behind me," Ozo snarled. I didn't even stop to think, just dragged Nijo by the collar to where Oren-yaro soldiers were making a formation behind Ozo, giving us a clear path away from the bloodbath.

In the midst of all of that, I heard a roar that sounded like waves striking a cliff during a storm. Any doubts I ever had of my father's claims about Yuebek's power were immediately laid to rest. He had taken one of his own soldiers aside, his lips around the man's mouth. Blood gushed out of the man's nostrils and eye sockets as Yuebek drained him of—something. *Agan*, I guessed, from the bright glow of Yuebek's eyes. He eventually dropped the soldier like a discarded husk—the man was dead, hard black veins protruding from his neck.

Only then did Yuebek turn to the attacking soldiers around him and obliterate them with a sweep of his hands. Blood and bone and entrails splattered on the ground, covering the gold-threaded cloth and flower petals. The latter were jasmine, but for some reason, the air seemed to hold the thicker fragrance of frangipani—funeral flowers, the smell of death.

I didn't see the rest of the carnage. Ozo insisted I return to the castle immediately, and I didn't have the desire to stay, anyway—not after what I had just witnessed. Only after we returned to the great hall did Nijo break his silence. "Your new husband—" he began, turning to me.

I wondered what it was in my eyes that made him stop mid-sentence. "I can see," I said in a low voice. "I am not an idiot, Warlord Nijo."

He gave a hissing breath. "I can't decide what you are either, for what it's worth."

"I'm still your queen. I know that much."

Nijo walked down to the end of the hall, hands on his head. "Queen," he repeated, staring at the throne. He shook his head at the word.

"We've been through this before," Ozo said, striding through the door behind us. "Those were Darusu soldiers behind us. She was right about one thing back there. We can continue to bicker amongst ourselves and all but hand our lands and our titles over to the enemy. Or we can learn to swallow our pride."

"And you think that'll be enough to turn the tides?" Nijo asked.

"There are no guarantees," I replied.

"My bannermen have been at my throat," Nijo grumbled. "After Father's death, getting them under control has been a nightmare. What will they say if I support you? If I support *this*?"

"Tell them what you saw out here," I said.

"You won't even have to," Ozo added. "The entire region will be gossiping by the time the night is out. I suggest you ride back home now, boy. Don't even clean yourself up. Let them see you as you are. Let them understand *exactly* what they're dealing with."

After a moment's hesitation, Nijo slunk away. He had barely disappeared around the hall when the doors opened and Yuebek entered like a high-stepping horse. His robes were steeped in blood, but he looked about as fresh as someone who had just walked out of a bathhouse—not a single bead of sweat or dirt marred his face.

"A most wonderful wedding!" Yuebek exclaimed, holding his hands out. He was holding a decapitated head, which he flung haphazardly to the ground as he strode through the great hall. "A dance, a duel, an assassination...what wonders await our wedding night?" He reached for me like a cat scooping a mouse into its jaws.

I pulled away from his searching lips. "Forget the wedding night. We're at war."

"Boring details," Yuebek laughed. "How do you want me to crush them, my queen?"

"We don't need to crush them," I said. "We need to show the land that they're the ones overstepping their bounds. We may still have a chance if we reach Yu-yan quickly, before word of what you did at the Kibouri temple gets out."

Ozo sniffed. "We could just as easily say we ransacked the temple after they attacked us. Those assassins were Warlord Hhanda's." He waved the bloody cloth in his hands, a piece of garment ripped from one of the assassins. It contained a crest: a golden eagle flying against a mountain horizon. Just like the Ikessar banner, it was black. The Hoen lands were east of the same mountain range the Ikessars traditionally held as their territory. They had conflicts over the years, and the Hoen clan was well-known to support rebels that openly defied the Ikessar regime. For them to knowingly attack the queen in support of an *Ikessar* meant the world truly was on fire.

"They must've been here days ago, waiting, watching. They were very thorough," Ozo continued.

"Not thorough enough." I glanced at Yuebek's neck. There was only a faint line where the arrow had gone through. Soon, even the scar would disappear, just like with my dogs' attack.

Yuebek, ignoring our conversation, clapped his hands, calling for more wine. I wondered if it would drain into his clothes.

"We have to show the people that we haven't forgotten them," I said. "My lord prince, your path to the Dragonthrone is clear. We need to *ignore* the Ikessars and subdue the Sougen. This will ensure support from the rest. Our only true opposition are the Ikessars, and they have all but dug a hole for themselves with today's attack. I won't be surprised if even Darusu abandons them."

Yuebek looked up just as a servant handed him his wine. "Mundane details," he repeated. "That witch declares war on me, and you'd have me fight another?"

"War isn't about demolishing everything in your path."

"My first argument with my wife!" Yuebek laughed. "You've got barrels more fire than the old one, I'll give you that! Speaking of which, where by all the spirits is Ong? Ong!"

"Esteemed Prince," Radi Ong said, appearing from behind the shadows. I wondered how long he had been hiding there. He dropped to the ground, kissing Yuebek's feet.

"You missed my wedding, Ong. Don't tell me you're still holding grudges about your daughter!"

"I never—"

"A jest!" Yuebek slapped the old man's back. "Do you think I don't praise you enough, Ong? Just tell me if I don't. You keep my army fed and watered, which is more useful than anything that daughter of yours ever did. Well, I'm about to make you even busier! My queen tells me we have a war to fight. Make arrangements."

Ong bowed again before scrambling for the courtyard. General Ozo saluted and turned to follow him.

"Are you happy?" Yuebek asked, turning to me.

"We march tomorrow," I said. "We can't afford to miss this opportunity. After an attack like this, it's a statement the nation can't deny."

"Tomorrow," he agreed. "But tonight…!" His eyes danced wildly as he ran his hand across my neck, leaving behind a streak of blood on my skin.

CHAPTER FIVE

THE SACRIFICE

꠸ᦢ

There were just enough casualties from the attack to drive the point home. On top of Ipeng, I lost three other bannermen, whose heirs immediately pledged themselves to our cause. The threat of civil war was long gone. It was upon us whether we liked it or not, and indecision and arguments would only ensure victory for our opponents. I was wrong about a wedding proving to be the factor that united us; it was bloodshed, after all. Bloodshed, ever and always. The land may switch hands, but people's hearts remained the same. My father had known that from the beginning. "Do you think people are content with words?" he once told me. "Do you think talking pretty is all it takes to change minds?"

"The Ikessars do it all the time," I remember replying.

He laughed. "And the people love them, no doubt about that. But it is one thing to *praise* empty words and another thing to get up and do something about it. The Ikessars have ruled us for centuries, and yet even they couldn't provide the sort of leadership that would allow us to progress beyond the darkness of this age. Change cannot happen without sacrifice, Talyien. Never forget this. *Never.*"

The afternoon had come and gone. Servants swept the streets and carted off the rest of the remains before they could begin to rot, bringing all manner of foul birds and animals to the city. Double guards were on patrol throughout, all the way up to Old Oren-yaro, where it was believed the assassins had hidden themselves. The old keep where my father had lost his sons, the untouched graveyard—nobody had thought to look there. It all needed to be burned now, a symbolic show of solidarity. The Ikessars wronged us yet again.

But look, instead of *answering* them, we are marching west to subdue the real threat, as Dragonlords should. We know where our priorities lie. Do the rest of them?

We play with lives when words alone cannot suffice.

My wound was washed and treated, and then I changed into a clean dress and returned to what remained of my guests, now gathered in the castle's great room. In a bizarre display of the royals' priorities, the celebration continued— the feasting and wine, followed by entertainment, provided by the few servants who weren't preoccupied with preparing pyres for the dead. Lo Bahn's dancers in their bright silks and paper fans lit up the great hall, a stark contrast with the bloody gutters in the city below. "Tomorrow, we can mourn properly," we told ourselves. "Tomorrow, we march for war." We repeated this over and over again until even I started to believe it.

I retired early, the exhaustion creeping up from inside my bones. I remembered making the same excuse the night I married Rayyel. Yet where back then I trembled at the thought of facing the man I loved—who had wronged me, and who I had wronged—now it was something horrid, sinister, and gut wrenching. *Sacrifice.*

But I went through the motions. Bathed, scrubbed the last splotches of blood from my fingernails, changed into my sleeping gown. Yayei helped me, tears in the corners of her eyes. When I finally got up to return to my chambers, she took my hands in hers, pressing them together before bringing them up to her lips. She didn't say anything—couldn't, I think, find the words that would add a spray of sunlight to what was about to happen. On the way back to the castle, I thought of the prisoners I executed in my years as queen and envied them.

"The Esteemed Prince has gone ahead of you," one of the servants told me as I came up the stairs. "He ordered us to tell you to join him as soon as you're able."

She disappeared around the corner. I stood where I was, forcing myself to calm down. I heard footsteps and saw Rai appear from the shadows.

"What are you doing here?" I hissed. "He gave you a way out. You should've taken it and run!"

"Run where?" he asked.

"Anywhere but the lion's den, you idiot."

He gazed into my eyes. I felt a twinge of emotion. Had he always looked at me that way? "The kingdom is burning," he eventually said. "There is nowhere to run to. I belong where I'm needed." He swallowed. "Besides, the time for running is over. I won't do it again."

I turned away. "You can assist where your life isn't in danger."

"We still have sympathizers in the castle. It's not my safety I'm concerned about. We can't risk you in there with him. Every minute you spend with him and him alone isn't safe. If this inane plan is to even work, you need to be alive."

"He won't kill me," I said.

"He killed his first wife."

I swallowed. "I admired Zhu—I really did. And I still wish I could've found a way to save her. But Yuebek's a fool if he thinks I am anywhere near as malleable. If he tries anything—"

"He raped and killed your handmaiden in the great hall. How many more women must die before you take this seriously?"

I stared at the ground. "He won't—"

"Talyien," he said with a sigh. "Your courage borders on carelessness. You know this has ever been my conflict with you."

I resisted the urge to respond with my own sigh, because it was the sort of thing we could do all night if we were inclined to. "And here I was hoping the lectures would stop after our marriage ended."

"Your other handmaiden expressed her concerns. She says she's seen Yuebek talking to himself in the halls. Talking about you betraying him. Talking about strangling you once you do. Not *if*, Talyien. He's certain you will."

I closed my eyes.

"You can't possibly pull off an act convincing enough for him," Rai continued.

"You don't know that—" I began, before closing my mouth. He probably did know, if the last few months had been any indication.

"Your skill with a blade doesn't make you a convincing liar, Beloved Queen," Rai said. "Not when you are required to look the other person in the eye and pretend you love them." He glanced away. "If you...if you lie with him tonight, he will see through the act. You've seen the man. He will use any excuse. Perhaps he will not kill you, but if he kills you, what then? We can't save Jin-Sayeng if you're dead, Tali. We can't take that chance."

"So what the hell do you want me to do?" I hissed. "Do you want to trade places with me? I'm pretty sure he'll notice the difference, and believe me, Rai, you are absolutely no good at seduction."

"This is not negotiable," he said. "If the man kills you, this would have all been for nothing." He turned his head. I glanced down and caught sight of a woman. Chiha. She was dressed in the exact same robes as I was.

His plan dawned on me. He really *did* want me to trade places.

"Rai, you..."

His jaw tightened.

"This is vile!" I hissed. "I think I can almost forgive half of the things you've done, but this? This is beyond despicable!"

"I'm aware," Rai repeated, a hint of irritation in his voice. "Do you think I like half the things I'm forced to do?"

"Forced? Who in hell *forces* you to do these things? Show me so I can scream at them!"

"My duties. My responsibilities. And—"

"That stick up your ass, I get it." I turned to Chiha. "And you, you damn woman—you'll entertain this man's foolish notions?"

Chiha bowed.

"You don't have to do this," I snapped. "I've never liked you, Chiha. I still don't. But if you think for one moment I'm just going to step aside and let this happen, you must be out of your mind."

"If he kills me tonight," Chiha said easily, "the servants will come and fetch my body. And you will carry on in the morning as if nothing happened, as if it was all just a trick of the mind. As if anyone could kill Talyien Orenar! By then you will be marching for the Sougen, to carry out whatever foolish thing your father planned. The same foolish thing my father died for."

"Why would you do this?"

She gave a wry smile. "Not for you, if you must know. I hold no love for you."

"Obviously."

"And in your position, I wouldn't have spared your son. I wouldn't have given it a second thought." She pulled her arms from underneath her robes, gracefully showing her smooth, unblemished arms. "Talyien Orenar, you are not the only person who cares about this land. You are not Jin-Sayeng's only daughter, nor the only one willing to sacrifice herself to see it withstand the coming days. Let me do my part. You still have yours to worry about."

I opened my mouth to argue, but she pulled away from me to give Rai one last glance before walking down the hall to my chambers. I, coward that I was, let her.

Rai led me down to Thanh's room, which he opened with a key. I wondered which of the servants had lent it to him. Yayei, probably. "You'd allow this," I said, as soon as he closed the door. "I always knew you could be a heartless son of a bitch, but Rai—you *loved* that woman."

He stared at me in surprise.

"You did. Don't even deny it. I know this much about you: You wouldn't have made a gods-damn bastard if you didn't. Was it her idea or yours?"

"Hers," he conceded. "I am as powerless to stop her as I am if *you* had made a decision."

"I don't know if that makes it better or worse. This is obscene. It's..."

"Necessary," Rai said. He walked over to the bed and sat on the edge of the mattress, his face completely blank except for a small line on his forehead.

"How do you do that?" I asked.

He looked at me, the line growing deeper.

"Dismissing the people you care for so easily, for the greater good. It's..." I stopped, remembering Agos. Remembering the night in Kyo-orashi, the sacrifices I felt I had to make for the sake of the people I cared for. Hurting others while foolishly thinking we were only hurting ourselves could only take you so far. Life wasn't a bubble, duty not black and white. Our mistakes had run their course. He left Chiha for me because he thought it was the right thing to do. He tried to love me the same way I tried to love him. And now we were here, all of us bearing scars in some way, all of us still attempting to hold the pieces together in spite of that.

"Our parents would be so proud," I whispered, shaking my head. "At the end of the day, we're no different." I sat down beside him, turning to gaze at my son's bookshelves. The servants had arranged and dusted them as usual, but I noticed a few open books on the desk—not the same ones my son had been reading the night Kaggawa had taken him from the castle. "Did you spend the whole afternoon here?" I asked.

Rai shrugged, rising to pick up the books and return them to the shelves. His movements remained clear, methodical. "After what you told me, I was curious what else the boy has been preoccupied with. For a child his age, his interests seem...odd."

"Don't say that."

"Politics? Economics? Agriculture? At his age?"

"He...was trying to impress you."

Rai's eyes flashed.

"For when you returned," I continued. "He loved to ask about you. What interested you, what you used to do during the day."

"And you told him I spent my days reading these things?"

"Didn't you?"

He must've really thought he didn't. I watched him stare at the bookshelf with a grave expression. "Some of these are mine," he managed.

"I used to let him rummage through your things and take what he wanted," I said. "I would've burned them all otherwise. I suppose, in your absence, that they sufficed."

Rai swallowed. "I don't...think I've ever told you this before...but you've raised our son well. The stories I hear from the servants. He sounds...like a wonderful boy. My mother may never recognize it, but she and I will have to disagree on that one, too." He glanced back at me. "I don't think going down the road your father took is the answer, but leniency cannot serve this land, either. We may want to have nothing more than the cares of ordinary people, but we aren't, Talyien."

"My father said the exact same things, Rai. You see? Not that different at all."

"I'm not happy about what you have to face, nor what Chiha has to do tonight for our cause."

"Your feelings on the matter won't lessen her burden," I said bitterly. I sighed. "Will it even work?"

"What do you mean?"

"In the dark, can she...pass for me?"

Realizing what I was asking, his cheeks turned red. "I'm not talking about this," he said bluntly.

"Well, you're the only person in the world who can compare," I pointed out.

"It's been too many years," he murmured.

"You're not really answering my question."

"He's had a lot of wine."

I narrowed my eyes. "I see. You don't know. Of course you wouldn't."

"Talyien—"

"I'm just curious. You both seemed fairly confident about this."

"We couldn't risk your life!"

"Yes, so you've said. So *are* we the same in bed?"

"No!" His ears were red now, too, and he turned away, grumbling to himself. "I don't know if this makes a difference anymore, but from the moment I married you, I swore the past wouldn't get in the way."

"It did, anyway," I said, growing sombre. "Pity we learn such things too late."

He glanced back at me, taking a deep breath. "A tragedy."

I turned away from his gaze in discomfort.

To my relief, he broke it to walk to the window. He flipped the shutters open. "We need to consider what happens once Yuebek accomplishes his task," he said. "Will he still be alive after? I believe so, and General Ozo agrees with me. Furthermore, his army will likely still be intact. His generals. Even with Oren-yaro, Yu-yan, and Bara together, you will not have enough to crush them. And my mother will be at your heels. Yeshin should have considered what it would mean for your child. Thanh is still crown prince."

"Not after this."

"Why not?" Rai asked.

I looked at him, flustered. "Because—"

"He has the blood of Jin-Sayeng's royal lords in his veins. Ikessar, but more important, *Orenar*. He was raised to be king. This doesn't go away overnight." He considered my silence and frowned. "He isn't—he isn't just yours, Talyien."

"*Now* you want him?"

"He was promised to the nation."

"As we were. Look how well that turned out for us."

He chewed on his lip. "I am not dismissing your concerns, Beloved Queen, but these things are in his blood. You can't deny it. You love him as a mother loves her child and I can never fault you for that, but you must consider this nation is the boy's inheritance. As it was ours. The balance of everything..."

"He's just a boy," I murmured, not wanting to dig deeper. Thanh was *my* son. I didn't want to think about things beyond that.

"It is important we find a way to set things right for the future. For his sake," Rai said. He paused. "And yours. I...I cannot imagine tomorrow without you, Tali." And then, as if hating himself for saying such words, he turned his head away.

We fell silent, the night stretching into eternity around us. Rai shuffled his feet, returning the rest of Thanh's books to the shelves almost reverently. I lay back against my son's bed, my eyes on the ceiling as I counted the passing seconds. I didn't realize when I fell asleep.

I woke to the sound of knocking. The door opened and Chiha stepped inside. Alive. I automatically searched her face for bruises and didn't know what to think when I saw none. Her neck was free of handprints, all the way down to her perfect breasts. I wondered how she explained the lack of scars. Yuebek must have been very drunk.

"Did you hear the warhorns?" she asked, before I could say anything.

I glanced at the window. It was dawn—grey and cold, a hint of rain on the horizon.

"It's time," Rai said, getting up from the chair. "Go, Beloved Queen. We will be right behind you." He looked like he had aged ten years.

Chiha's arm blocked the door before I could follow him. "I've carried my hatred for you since I was a girl and I knew what you were going to take from me," she said.

I looked into her eyes. "I know that now," I managed.

"I'm not sure what I'd do without it," she continued. "I know you are as much of a player in all of this as the rest of us, but every time I see you—every time I hear your name..." She shook her head. "Damn you both, and your duties with you." But she kept her chin high. The woman was prouder than I could ever be, and my own failings had forced her to cover for me.

"Keep it," I said. "A little hate goes a long way."

She smirked. "I suppose it's comforting to know I still don't have to like you."

"I echo the sentiments, Chiha."

She gave me a bow, so gracious that for a moment, you would've thought it was sincere.

Warhorns. Wardrums.

The sound of a city wide awake, perhaps for the first time in over twenty-seven years.

It all felt like a page from the history books, come to life. My heart was hammering with the beat of the drums as I followed Ozo down the vast yards in the barracks. Soldiers saluted in unison as we passed, more than I had ever seen in one place before.

We entered the commander's tent. The Oren-yaro army officers were gathered around a table and bowed as I walked through. A young girl dashed towards me with a cup of wine, and I waved her off as I took a seat beside Ozo, who was marking the map with stone figures.

"There won't be much time for deliberation," Ozo said, tapping the map with his finger. "The faster we subjugate Kaggawa and liberate Yu-yan, the clearer our statement. If they catch us on the road, they can always say we rode against *them*."

"Attacking them on the road, a stone's throw from Oren-yaro?" one of the generals broke in. "Who'd believe them?"

"We know the Ikessars can twist anything," Ozo snarled.

"If we're lucky, the Ikessars will attack Oren-yaro behind us," I said.

Ozo gave a bark of surprise—Lord General Ozo in his polished ceremonial armour, a set that must've been gathering dust in his quarters since the end of my father's war. It was a wonder he still fit in it.

"To hear you say that..." he began.

"Are you implying I like the idea of sacrificing my own city to make a point?" I said.

He smiled. "Isn't that what you're doing?"

"Captain Lakas is manning the city defenses," I continued. "I have no doubt he'll do a remarkable job. Isn't that right, Captain?"

Lakas bowed. "The queen's confidence fills me with joy," he said in a voice that suggested anything but.

"A true Oren-yaro. Are you aware that on the other side, Nor Orenar is commanding the Yu-yan soldiers?"

"Yes, Beloved Queen. I've received reports."

"Then you know that if the Ikessars *do* attack, keeping them at bay will likely help us succeed in saving your wife."

"I will not fail our people," he said, seemingly oblivious to what I just said. I wondered if he and Nor were on good terms, or if he found her defecting to the Yu-yan army a betrayal of Oren-yaro pride. It happened often enough with the other royals. But for an Oren-yaro to do such a thing...

"We can goad them into attacking the city, too," Ozo said. "Let them think we have fewer soldiers garrisoned here than we really do. Surprise their waves.

The Ikessars never attack as one force, you understand. They're cowards at heart. Never felled a city in all of history, at least not without another army's support."

"They have the Darusu army," I pointed out.

"Like the Hoen clan would ever willingly die for an Ikessar," Ozo sneered.

A guard appeared. "Lord Han Lo Bahn comes with a message from the queen's husband. Shall I let him in?"

"Why not?" I asked, glancing at my officers. "Have we anything to hide?"

Ozo snorted. Laughed. War was his natural environment, and he looked like he was having the time of his life.

The guard pulled the tent flap apart to let Lo Bahn inside. He glanced at the officers with a sniff.

"A message, eh?" Ozo broke in. "He should come out himself. Would be good for his skin."

Lo Bahn gave the grimmest nod. "Perhaps you can tell him that."

"What does he want?" I asked.

Lo Bahn approached the table, crossing his arms into his sleeve. He looked at the map for a moment before nodding. "Over here. This is Yu-yan, correct?" He made a swirl, following the southern road. "Yet this road follows the river, leading us away from it."

"It's the only road," I said.

He snorted. "You just came from the Sougen. Your journey took weeks."

"So?"

"Prince Yuebek is convinced it would be faster if we went southwest, bypassing the road in favour of the wilderness."

"Most of our rice fields are west of here," Ozo bristled. "We'd be trampling an entire season's worth of harvest."

"Bah! A season alone? Does it matter?" Lo Bahn asked. "I've been told you have more rice up in the hills."

"The western rice fields account for a good third of our harvest," Ozo said.

"I don't even know why you're complaining. There's an army behind us. The sooner we get this done, the better."

"There's mountains and wilderness after the rice fields," I added. "Though— the valleys..."

"The valleys are passable by horse," Ozo said. "But there's no roads. Navigation alone will be a nightmare. It might take as much time as going on the road."

"We've been told the other warlords have their hackles up," Lo Bahn countered. "We'll be passing through at least one territory on our way to the Sougen, maybe two. How many wars must we fight before we get to the battle we need?"

"Warlord San and Lady Esh won't interfere," Ozo said.

"You can't be that sure. Let *us* worry about the wilderness. Our soldiers are well-equipped to travel through such conditions. You forget a good portion of the empire is wild wasteland."

"Queen Talyien." Ozo turned to me.

I hesitated. Ozo, reading into my expression, shook his head. "A season's worth of harvest, Queen Talyien. A third of our rice crop. The people will starve."

"They will anyway," I said in a low voice. "Even if the Ikessars choose not to attack Oren-yaro, they'll certainly burn the fields behind us. They've done it before. The faster we get to Yu-yan, the faster we can declare them traitors." I turned back to Lo Bahn. "Tell my lord husband that we agree to his proposal. We will ride west."

Lo Bahn gave a smug grin.

"War, and then famine." Ozo shook his head again.

I swallowed. "No change without sacrifice."

"You learn fast, Yeshin's child," he said in a grave voice, as if he didn't know whether to be proud or scared.

CHAPTER SIX

BEYOND THE
SETTING SUN

ᚠᚢᛗ

With a sweep of my hand, I killed my first wave of innocents, fulfilling my part as Yeshin's daughter.

I didn't have to cut them down myself. But I might as well have when those thousands of horses trampled the rice fields, destroying crops halfway through their cycle. What sustenance remained in the unripened grain and broken stalks, drowned in mud and horse shit? Trade with the Empire of Ziri-nar-Orxiaro was still closed, and would remain so indefinitely if our plan was to work. Flour and barley from the Kag were limited. Gasparian rice was expensive. Would there be enough coin in the Dragonthrone's coffers to buy our people food after we were done? I didn't even have access to those while we were at war with the Ikessars, and just feeding the soldiers was sufficient to make a dent in the Oren-yaro treasury.

And then, the inevitable. Somewhere out there, some poor farmer will run out of options and sell his land piece by piece to feed a pregnant wife and a dozen children. Private land, taxed way too high and all but worthless to investors—one of the lords, whoever gets to him first, will likely take it off his hands for dirt cheap. Paltry money to buy a few sacks of rice, which will dwindle as the days go on, because adding water to gruel cannot really make it go further and a dozen grumbling bellies do not stay full for very long. Until one day he has nothing left but the land on which his hut stands, and his wife dies labouring to twins, and he has no coin to buy milk so one of the infants starves to death and he himself dies of a broken heart...

These things happen. They happen while we royals throw accusations and argue and kill each other for the most banal reasons. But knowing these things didn't change what I needed to do. Seeing the stricken faces peering from their huts as we galloped by made the burden heavier, but I couldn't stop now. We were in too deep. Storms don't end when you wail to the heavens; you can only weather them. If you are lucky, you get to rebuild. But first you must stand your ground.

I saw very little of Yuebek during that first leg of the journey, which may have partly been because of my insistence at sticking close to my own army. He detested the smell of horses, and I encouraged him to stay in his carriage for his own comfort. I reasoned that I needed to keep an eye on my bannermen, that they were arguing, and that until I was sure I could disappear without them killing each other, I couldn't very well take the time to even share a meal with him, let alone his tent.

Yuebek seemed oddly compliant, almost bored, with my excuses. I voiced it out to Lord General Ozo on the third day. He laughed it off. "He's not made for this," Ozo said. "All of this—the travelling, the wilderness, it's out of his element. He can't caper around like a monkey in court out here, and he's no good at dealing with soldiers, either. Especially not *ours*. Consider it a breath of fresh air, Beloved Queen. He'll be himself soon enough."

Ozo's words, meant to reassure me, only made me more concerned. Yuebek's silence was unexpected. When we finally left the rice fields behind, entering the low-lying valleys that separated the outer reaches of Oren-yaro from the Sougen, I saw neither hide nor hair of my new husband. Here, the winds whipped us like sails, and though most of the snow had melted into the bubbling creeks and streams, it soon became so cold I needed another layer of clothing.

We reached the first village three days into the valley. Provisions were running low, and I got the impression that the Zarojo soldiers intended to ransack the settlement for what little they could milk from their larders. I rode ahead in time to see Radi Ong and Lo Bahn attempting to negotiate with the village elder. "Anong!" I called, interrupting them. The elder turned to me, and I could see the look of relief on his face at hearing someone speak in Jinan.

"Young woman," the elder said, unaware of who I was. He reached for me with shaking hands. "I'm trying to tell these men—we don't have *enough* for you all. What good will gold do for us? You can't eat gold! The entire Sougen is under Kaggawa's iron fist. We haven't seen merchant caravans since the start of the season. He promises to send provisions once this war is over, but when will that happen? We'll be dead soon."

"We will camp near the creek, Anong, and these gentlemen will ensure the water isn't fouled. Isn't that right?" I said the last part in Zirano and glanced at them both. Ong turned his head, while Lo Bahn crossed his arms.

"I'm guessing you're making more promises," Lo Bahn snorted. "I warned you about that. How much further is it to this Yu-yan?"

I glanced at the horizon. "Once you catch a glimpse of the river, it'll be another day or two of riding. It won't be far, now."

"A day or two. Or three," Lo Bahn sniffed. "The men are tired. Hungry. They're going to start eating their shoes soon."

"It was your idea to cut through the mountains," I said. "There would've been plenty of chances to resupply along the main road."

"You agreed to it," he bristled.

"We're not in Shang Azi anymore, Lord Han. Shake these villagers upside down as much as you want—if they've got nothing, then there's nothing." I dismounted from my horse and waved at the elder. "Can you give our officers lodging for the night? We'll be grateful even for just a warm bed and clean sheets. We'll send the soldiers foraging to keep them out of your hair."

The elder pulled away to confer with the other villagers, who were gathered around the gates. I stepped forward, close enough to touch the bamboo fencing. I saw heads shaking, which slowly changed to nods as the conversations deepened. Better not to resist the invaders. Have they not heard of the queen's new husband, the Zarojo prince? Were these not Zarojo? They eventually fell silent when they saw me staring at them.

"Queen Talyien," the elder said. It wasn't a question. There was a tremble in his voice. "I was almost sure you weren't real. A figment of history so rarely seen in court, like Dragonlord Rysaran before you. Jin-Sayeng has had her fair share of absent kings and lost queens, hasn't she?"

"I'm here now," I replied. "We're putting an end to the troubles that plague us all."

"Is that really what you came out here to do?" the elder asked, sliding his fingers through the gate and blocking it with his frail body, as if he was afraid I was going to tear it down. "You have no idea what troubles we've been having. Why should you suddenly care?"

"I'm your queen."

"That means nothing to us."

"Anong," I said. "I know it doesn't. But this time I am trying to do right by you all."

My words took him aback. His eyes watered. "You all say that," he said. "Well, what can we do? *What can we do?* You can kill me where you stand. You could do that and still live out the rest of your days without worry. You're here now, but it may very well be too late." And then, having said that, he pushed the gate open, the withered bamboo rattling against the ground. He grudgingly stepped to one side. The rest of the villagers, taking his cue, followed him. *Don't hurt us*, their faces said. *You've done enough.*

It is never like in the stories, after all. The weary conqueror isn't always greeted by weeping children and dancing maidens. I returned to the army in silence, and was led to where Yuebek's personal guard were stationed. The carriage doors were flung open. Yuebek was staring across the rocky streambed, arms tucked into his sleeves.

He took a deep breath as he heard me come up behind him. "I'm concerned about our marriage, my lovely wife."

"Yu-yan isn't far from here," I said. "We need to discuss the impending attack. The villagers are letting us stay for the night—if you keep your men under control, then we'll have no—"

"You're changing the subject," Yuebek snapped. "You really did just marry me for my power, didn't you?"

"I thought we were both aware of that," I said.

He pressed his lips together. "That's not what you told me during our wedding night."

"I—"

There was a flash of anger in his eyes as he walked past me. "Never mind," he said. "You've avoided me these past few days. You still detest me—that much is clear. You're just like Zhu."

"Your last wife," I said. "The one you murdered."

It was like he couldn't hear me. "She was everything a wife needed to be," he said with a half snarl. "Kind. Subservient. Perfect in every single way except *I was nothing to her.* A child to pacify, except not *hers*, no. Someone else's brat—an irritating gnat! Do you know what that feels like, Beloved Queen? To be nothing to someone? I thought you did. I thought you would understand after everything that pisspot bastard put you through. I shouldn't be surprised. You're all the same!"

The rocks began to shake as he screamed—a few rose from the ground. I tried not to pay attention to them and wondered if Yuebek even noticed. How much, exactly, was he in control of his own abilities? Could he turn me into dust where I stood?

All I knew was that he was throwing a tantrum exactly like the child he didn't want people treating him as. My own son would've never been allowed to act like this. It took all of my patience not to throw my hands up in disgust and walk away. I didn't know how he would react to that, but I could guess that it wouldn't end well. I remembered my father's warning—how he himself had dealt with Yuebek's temperament when he was in Zorheng City. A firm touch. A delicate touch. The gods had thrown me into a battlefield.

I swallowed my trepidation. "My prince," I said, curling my hands into fists. "It's been a long march. You're tired, exhausted." I didn't want to get close to him at all, but I forced myself to put a hand on his arm.

He looked at me like I had stuck a dagger into him, eyes filled with disdain. I wondered, for perhaps the first time, why the man claimed to want my love. Why, when it looked like he wanted to break me in half? What did he think I could give him? It felt like neither my body nor my kingdom would satisfy him. It felt like he wanted to tear into my very being and use my soul to fix whatever parts of him the world had broken. I wanted to tell him it was a fool's gamble; no one could do that for anyone.

"I will ask the elder to lend you the best house in the village. We will speak when you've had the chance to breathe."

"This *best house* will be a hovel in the middle of this barren land," he said.

"My prince—" I closed my eyes. If Chiha had done worse, I could do this. Carefully, I cupped his face with my hand, a distortion of the affection I had shown to the one man I have ever allowed myself to love freely. Because what I really wanted was to seize his neck with my fingers and wring the breath out of him.

I thought of Khine and that laughter that could set my heart at ease. It must've shown on my face, because I saw Yuebek recoil with a measure of distrust, as if wondering if the sentiment was genuine. It was frightening to see the longing in his eyes. I dropped my hand, fighting back the revulsion that crawled along my skin at the thought that I could muster so much as an ounce of pity for such a man.

"I'll humour you," Yuebek finally said. "We'll talk war."

"You must be patient, Esteemed Prince. A kingdom is not won in a day, and neither is a woman. You know my heart has been broken. It will take time to mend."

I heard him mutter something under his breath. He didn't believe me. I might as well be offering promises to the wind. But he allowed me to lead him to the village, where Lo Bahn and Ong were already busy making arrangements for his comfort. I noticed that none of the villagers were around to greet the Zarojo prince. I expected the youngsters to at least be curious, but their elders must've told them to keep away. A servant appeared with refreshments—wine and tea while we waited for whatever they could scrounge for the stewpot.

I didn't drink. I listened to Ozo explain his scouts' latest reports. Kaggawa's siege was still ongoing; Yu-yan had bravely withstood the first few attacks. There was talk of a dragon providing distraction during the latest, most brutal assault, which allowed the Yu-yan soldiers to deal a blow decisive enough to halt Kaggawa's movements for the moment. It was the perfect time to strike. They didn't know we were coming.

But Ozo didn't want us to attack in one wave. We didn't know what Kaggawa had in store. His last assault used war buffalo, imported from Gaspar. How he loaded them onto ships and brought them halfway around the continent was anyone's guess; the creatures were useless as transportation, but a charging warhorse was sure to get crushed by those massive horns. A prudent commander wouldn't be so careless.

What then, asked one of Yuebek's generals—a young man clearly appointed to the position because of his noble blood—would a prudent commander do? He said it in a sardonic tone, full of barbs.

Ozo spent well over an hour lecturing them on who *he* was and the battles he had won for my father over the years. By then the sun was setting, Yuebek was yawning, and the watery beef, plantain, and cabbage stew had all been consumed. Ozo finally revealed that he wanted Yuebek's army to split into four divisions, to be paired up with a number of Oren-yaro soldiers. We were to attack each of Kaggawa's supporting camps, the ones not actively involved in the siege. The strategy was simple: hamstring the foolish merchant who dared play king.

As Yuebek's men began a discussion amongst themselves, Ozo gestured to me. I got up and followed him. He took me outside the fences, to the edge of the forest.

"Thanh is in one of those camps," I said. "What will Kaggawa's men do to him if you put pressure on them?"

"I am sending people to extract him first," Ozo murmured under his breath. "Yuebek's becoming suspicious already. What if he catches wind of this?"

"Our hands are tied, Queen Talyien," he said. "Either way, Kaggawa will feel our wrath."

"Extracting Thanh . . . is too delicate of an operation to trust to a handful of soldiers."

"We're not just doing it with soldiers," Ozo said, leading me into a thicket. By now it was so dark that I could barely see a step ahead of me. He whistled twice.

Three hooded figures appeared. I heard Rayyel's voice, followed by Inzali and Namra. I greeted them with a nod.

"Mistress Lamang, you've been busy," I told Inzali.

"I have," she said, a hint of a familiar amusement on her face.

"Your brother has his ruses, and you have yours. How many years have you spent studying military strategy?"

"One gets bored teaching rich children, and it's amazing the sort of collections their parents have. All those books, gathering dust on shelves."

"So of course you had to read them all."

She gave a small bow. "It would be a shame not to."

"I've been told such a thing can be dangerous," I said with a grin. "Explain what you've been doing."

"It's not so much a ruse as it's been manipulating events to your favour," Inzali said, glancing at Rai. "We knew that Prince Yuebek wasn't going to be diplomatic with Princess Ryia and decided to use that to make sure your bannermen were *well*-aware of what he is."

"I was going to say you made things a little inconvenient for me."

Inzali laughed, a sound that was rare for her. "I concede that I might've. But it is important to know how much support you have. You do not want your lords and ladies turning on you in the middle of this battle."

"And will they?" I asked.

"Your people, Queen Talyien, seem overly fond of the sentiment of *wait and see*. So as long as they think you are winning, their support and respect is guaranteed."

I sighed. "I guess that's better than nothing. I'd take more offense if you weren't a Lamang."

Her eyes twinkled. "Is that right?"

"I meant—"

She patted her robe. "I have a letter from my brother."

I felt my insides knot. "That sounds...risky."

"I hardly think you've got anyone from Lay Weng Shio skulking about. He writes to me in our native tongue. You know he's careful." She gave me a look that could've meant anything.

"When did this letter arrive?"

"A few days before your army left Oren-yaro. I believe his plans to remove Thanh from Kaggawa's camp can be complemented with Lord General Ozo's plans. I will try to contact him again to see if he can hasten things from his end. With any luck, Prince Thanh will soon be with us."

"It's time I do something for my son," Rai said in a low voice. "I haven't... been a good father. I told you I would try." He gestured at the women behind him. "And should I ever stray, these two will see to it that no harm comes to him, even at the cost of my life."

"You have our word, Beloved Queen," Namra said, bowing a second time.

"Enough talk," Ozo broke in. "I think it's time we return to your lord husband, Queen Talyien."

"I wish you wouldn't say that," I said.

"It's a habit we all need to get used to if he's getting as suspicious as I think he is," Ozo snorted. "We're running out of time. Hopefully with the war to preoccupy him you'll be able to continue dancing around this damn marriage of yours."

"Is that smoke?" Inzali suddenly asked.

I turned towards the village. Black smoke. I was about to mention the campfires when I noticed one of the rooftops was ablaze.

"I told them to keep away from those villagers!" I walked back to the village, drawing my sword with Ozo at my heels. Halfway down the path, a soldier came running towards us, screaming at the top of his lungs. He dropped several paces away in a pool of blood.

The beast tearing itself into his spine looked up and grinned.

———◆———

Facing the beasts one-on-one always had the sensation of chasing after a nightmare. There was still a sense of escape, that all you had to do was walk around the edges and you would wake up. It made it easier to manage your fear—to hold it just within arm's reach, like a towel you could use to dab the sweat off your face. It remained just as unreal back in the city, with seasoned soldiers around me—you could at least pretend there was a way out.

But to see a horde of them streaming through the walls in a remote village in the dead of the night—ah. This was what it felt like to have the nightmare come after *you*. Now you're drowning in fear, in terror, and there is nowhere to run. Screaming soldiers blocked every possible exit. I turned to Ozo, who had his sword in one hand and his dagger in the other.

"Close to thirty years since I last saw one of these things," Ozo snarled. "Thirty years and they still haunt my nightmares. Just my damn luck they've spread this far, and an entire village at that. Stick to me, girl, if you know what's good for you."

"This girl has killed one or two of these before, Ozo. Maybe more."

"Is that right? You look like you've pissed your pants."

"I was going to say the same thing about you, but I didn't out of respect. I assumed it was incontinence."

He laughed as a creature came bearing down on us. Its sparse, splotchy hair gleamed—I felt my stomach lurch when I realized the sheen was from the clump of maggots crawling on the surface of its grey skin. Ozo kicked it to the side and smashed it from behind with his sword. The creature uttered a guttural howl as its gaunt, beastly form was torn in half, its rib cage cracked open like a nut pressed too hard. Even with its insides spilling on the ground, it continued snapping its jaws, looking vaguely like a slaughtered wild boar with fangs instead of teeth. I stabbed it in the throat and turned to cut the next in line.

Fighting beside Ozo was almost like fighting beside Agos. Almost, but not quite. For a man of his age, Ozo was faster, and he used his sword like a hammer, sending chunks of flesh and bone flying into the air. If a creature came too close, he would strike with his dagger, gnashing his teeth through the blood spray like a dog shaking a rat. The old wolf had plenty of piss and vinegar to spare.

I tried to keep up, for my part. We reached the gates and he laughed again. "You handle a sword like your father, girl."

"I appreciate the compliment, but—"

"It's not a compliment. For all that the history books speak of him as a warrior, he was better with his books." He wiped his face and removed his cloak.

Panting, he gazed up the house where we had left Yuebek and his officers. An entire section of wall was torn out. It was a wonder that it was still standing.

Yuebek stood in the middle of the debris, eyes glowing. There were five creatures tearing chunks out of him.

He turned to me. "Wife!" I didn't know how he could still speak when I was sure I spotted one of the things nibbling at his voice box. "I thought you left me!" He raised his arms, grabbing one of the creatures from the back of its head. It split open, like a watermelon struck with an axe. Without missing a beat, he turned to the others, killing each of them that way, before turning to embrace the next wave.

It was as if I forgot about the swarm surrounding us. The only thing I needed to fear was right in front of me. I wrapped my hands around the hilt of my sword, wondering if his powers were truly limitless. They couldn't be. He nearly died during my attack on him back in Anzhao City—it took him months to recover from that. Why did it seem endless now?

I noticed a body curled up below the hut, underneath the bamboo rafters. Ong's brightly coloured robes were dredged in dirt.

Against better judgment, I darted for him.

He was still alive. Skin still warm, though it was pale, rapidly growing cold. I shook him. He opened his eyes. "Zhu?" he asked.

"Not yet, Ong," I said.

He gave a chuckle that sent blood dribbling down his chin. "Soon, then. Well. Gods know I've plenty to answer for. To her, especially. I didn't think this would happen. A prince, for my child! What father wouldn't be flattered?"

"What is he, Ong?"

"You know what he is," Ong replied. "What more do you need?"

"Can he even die?"

"We all die," he said with a smirk.

I tapped his face. "Ong. Stay with me."

He gripped the ground with his fingers. "His experiments...as a young man. Forbidden necromancy. An army. But you ruined it. No choice. Used soldiers instead. Using them..."

"You're not making sense, Ong. He stabbed you. What for?"

"Soldiers. Too far away," he whispered. "Needed something here. I was the closest. Never thought much of me. Just in the way. Always in the way. Just like Zhu..."

I think he was trying to apologize, but the words came out as an exhale. He slipped away, his breathing slowing to stillness. I squeezed his hand and stayed with him until I couldn't see his chest rise anymore. I wondered if Zhu's ghost came for him, if redemption could be found beyond the cares that drive our waking moments. Nothing could change the fact that her own father might as well have pushed her into the grave himself. If Yeshin came striding towards me with arms wide open, would I still run into them?

I couldn't see the answer on Ong's face, of course. The dead do not speak. We leave behind fragments of our intentions, and nothing more.

By the time I returned to the street, it was over. Shapes piled on top of each other, bodies melting away with the shadows as night fell. Yuebek stepped towards me, torch in hand. His hair was loose, streaming down his face like rain. For the first time since I met him, he looked like a real person, covered in dirt and blood and sweat. "You've been hiding this from me," he said.

"How did you want me to explain?" I asked. "Welcome to our new house, my love, and by the way, the roof is leaking?"

He lifted his arm, poised to strike me the same way he had before we were wed. But this time, he stopped himself. Snarling under his breath, he caressed the side of my face with the back of his fingers, leaving a trail of blood on my cheek. The movement was so out of the ordinary that it stunned me into stillness.

"So your precious little nation is broken," Yuebek said. There was no ounce of disbelief or surprise in his eyes. "And now I know why you came begging for *me*. You want me to fix this! Is that right, my queen? Tell me!"

I closed my eyes. "My lord," I said. "Please save my land."

"Beg for it," he said, his eyes turning to steel, "like you begged me during our wedding night."

I felt myself grow dizzy. He watched my expression, watched me hesitate, unable to form the words, not knowing what he was really looking for. I sank to my knees. "Please, my lord," I managed, the words catching at my throat. I felt like vomiting them out. I pressed my head into the dirt, soil under my fingernails and nostrils.

He grabbed me by the hair, his cold hands digging into my scalp, even as I wanted nothing more than to lunge and stick a blade into his heart.

But as I held my breath, he eventually turned away, arms spread out. Laughter billowed out of his lungs, and for a moment I thought he actually had trouble breathing. "My queen didn't want just my army. She didn't want just a husband, either!" he exclaimed. "She wanted a hero! A hero to save her!" Still laughing, he strode away from the village to rejoin the rest of his soldiers. I felt my skin crawl. I had underestimated how out of touch the man was with the world around him.

We were back on our horses by dawn, riding southwest at full speed. No longer did Yuebek cloister himself inside his litter. He rode his horse at the head of his army, sword in hand and hair unbound, every bit convinced of this new role he was playing. When we emerged from the valley, nothing I said could now stop them from tearing into the first village we saw and burning it to the ground. They were all sport, as far as the Zarojo were concerned. A tainted people, marked for the Esteemed Prince's conquest. And I couldn't do a damn thing to stop it.

I watched with Ozo from a distance, hearing the cries grow louder. I was straining my ears, trying to determine if they changed. I couldn't tell. A dying human's screams could be remarkably animal-like. "For all we know, it's too late for the rest of the Sougen..." I began.

Ozo shook his head, adjusting himself in the saddle. "Don't start thinking like that. You'll falter if you do. Too many battles are lost before the first soldier lifts his sword. You have to rush in, believing you can win."

"They pick the poorest people to latch on, these corrupted souls," I said.

Ozo cleared his throat. "I know very little about these things. Hard to pay attention to half of what's going on when your father is involved. But I remember the mages explaining that these souls cannot just *barge* in. One needs to be invited, to be allowed in even for just a moment."

"And someone vulnerable and desperate would be more likely to make the trade." I shrugged. "Or they're tricked, somehow. But that's harder, I suppose. Maybe the things promise to make a host better, stronger, smarter. And by the time they realize what's at stake, it's too late. If we make people aware, could we stave off the corruption? At least until we fix things?"

"People don't listen. Queen that you are—you should've known that by now."

"If their lives are at stake..."

He laughed. "They'll think you're mad. They already think it. Your name is buried in scandal, you married *that*..."

"How about Rayyel?"

"His name is ruined, too. He made that choice when he accused you *falsely.*" He clicked his tongue. "Your father didn't turn into the feared Warlord Yeshin overnight. He was always a hard man, yes. Your brothers would fall over each other trying to please him. I remember Taraji—"

"I didn't know you knew him."

"We grew up together. We were friends."

"But you're old."

Ozo bristled. "Time has a way of doing that to you."

I stared at him, at his creased face and bulging belly.

He sniffed. "I *am* old. And your brother would be, too, if he had lived. Probably be half my size, I can admit that much. But then if he was alive, *you* wouldn't be. He was the complete opposite of your father: levelheaded, diplomatic, charming. Almost an Ikessar, if you think about it. The perfect heir." He glanced at me, and I thought I saw him wrinkle his nose.

"You do have a way of making me feel confident about myself," I grumbled.

He laughed. "If it makes you feel better, your father would've still favoured you. Taraji wasn't as hot-blooded as he wanted him to be. The arguments they had…he couldn't see why Taraji wanted to learn about the world when he could be applying himself to learning to rule the region. Your father breathed down his neck, so he did what any reasonable Orenar would do—he escaped whenever Yeshin's back was turned. And wherever he went, I'd be right there beside him."

"That sounds familiar."

"We always knew about your antics. I did, anyway. I chose to turn a blind eye. I understood, more than you know." He sniffed. "Taraji and I—we were like you and Agos."

"Like us," I said. "You mean—"

"Like I said," Ozo continued, a faraway look in his eyes. Eventually, he cleared his throat. "When I saw how attached my son was getting to you, I was frightened for him. That sort of loyalty to your liege—that *love*—it's a damned road. You can't love the hand that feeds you. It goes nowhere. But at least he died for you. Brains like an ox, but the other way around is worse. My prince died. Unaided, defenseless, alone, and I couldn't do a damn thing for him. He was… only your age." The shadows on his face looked weary, as if as far as he was concerned, the wrong people had lived too long.

"I'm sorry," I found myself saying, despite the fact that Ozo was talking about my brother.

He gave the faintest smile underneath his scruffy grey beard. "Warlord Yeshin fell apart when he heard the news. If you had seen him then, he looked just like any mad old man. The whole city was in mourning and no one else wanted to take care of him. He'd apologize to me after I fed him and tell me he wasn't worth the trouble. He was ready to follow his sons. He would ask every day why I didn't just return to my father's holdings and leave him to rot. I didn't tell him it was my way of mourning, too. If I wasn't busy taking care of the old man, I would have followed my prince to hell itself. Close your mouth, girl. A fly could get in."

I glanced back at the burning village on the horizon. The screams were fading. The attack had lasted less than an hour.

"They forced his hand," Ozo continued. "Dragonlord Rysaran tricked him into bringing that dragon to his keep. He knew what it *really* was—not a true dragon, but a creature of the *agan*. And instead of denying it, they put all the blame on my lord. Anything Warlord Yeshin did—his attempts to get into the council, the laws he would pass in his own region—was met with insults and threats. He couldn't get them to listen. So he turned to force. All he wanted was to make his sons' death count for something in this world."

"Does that justify the slaughter?" I asked.

"He was very old," Ozo said. "And very tired of the world."

"I know," I replied. I had felt it in the memory. "He was not prepared to be a father again, but he was never one to squander an opportunity when it presented itself. And suddenly, there I was."

He laughed, and I turned back to the sound of my father's world, too entrenched into it to back away now. The screaming, the sound of blade on flesh, the smell of smoke and blood and urine...I hardened myself to it. Hundreds to save thousands, and the worst was yet to come. Not for these villagers, at least. For them, it was over quickly.

Like gathering clouds, Yeshin's shadow descended upon the land.

CHAPTER SEVEN

THE NOOSE

ꓱꓕꚰꓴ

Three days. Three more villages. Yuebek looked like a man in his prime, unscarred, untouched. A demon from the fires of hell, or a great, terrible god; people couldn't decide.

I spun between pretending to praise him, feigning that none of it bothered me, and hating myself for allowing it all to continue. Each time I could see Ozo watching me, his eyes flickering. *Patience*, his expression told me. He knew me too well, knew I was resisting every step of the way. But I couldn't drown out the screams. I heard them in my sleep, so I stopped sleeping. I drifted through the hours like a ghost. Patience? I was the epitome of patience, a cracked thing holding together at just the right places because my father was smart enough to know exactly where to break me. If Yuebek wasn't human, then I couldn't be, either. No human could possibly face so much blood and death without going insane.

"They were already doomed," Ozo told me as we carved our way into the fourth village, stinking of blood and sweat himself. He struck a hapless villager where he stood, the body spinning like a top before falling facedown into a pigsty. "Doomed by the carelessness of the past. They're all starving. They'll turn by the end of the week if they haven't already. We need to see this through, Tali. If we do not bear our part, if we abandon it now, then we are no better than the ones that came before."

"You sound almost wise, Ozo," I said. "Too bad I hate you."

He laughed. "I bear no love for you, either, yet here we are, united in resentment. Your father would be proud."

We rode further into the village, breathing in smoke and ash.

Ozo gestured at a passing soldier. "Ride to the prince and tell him to proceed to the river to begin the fording. We don't want to waste his time."

"Akaterru forbid," I grumbled as the soldier saluted and rode up the road.

"We're not far," Ozo said. "This is all play. The real work begins with Kaggawa's army. Has that sword seen blood today?"

"I—"

"Go kill that woman over there."

"Is that really necessary, Ozo? We can help her escape."

He spat. "Where will she run? If you do not kill her, I will do it myself. Choose."

I stared at the ground.

He scowled, the lines deepening on his face. "Will you lose your nerve at the end, Beloved Queen? Strengthen your will now before it's too late. Whether your sword bleeds her, or that soldier behind me does, it's all the same. Remember what I said. This is *all* on us. Don't you ever pretend you can close your eyes and pass the burden to another. Kill her, or I will. Choose, Talyien."

I dismounted and drew my sword, approaching the woman by the creek. She dropped the laundry she was carrying and held her hands out.

"Mercy—" she began.

I attacked quickly, thinking about how she wasn't going to survive the night if I didn't; how Yuebek's soldiers would probably rape her to death or she would die somewhere in the wastelands anyway. Reasoning to myself, justifying my actions, hearing my own lies, just like the other cowards. But I listened to Ozo—I didn't close my eyes. I watched her bleed out until the creek turned red and my body felt weightless. Only when I was sure she was dead did I tuck the sword back into my belt. I turned to meet Ozo.

A horn blasted, a warning call from deep within the village.

"Ride back, back!" Ozo snarled. I threw myself up onto my horse and kicked it down the path. We had barely left the bend when I saw that first soldier, dressed in Ikessar black and silver, come bearing down on us.

Ozo blocked him from reaching me, crushing him with his halberd. "How did the bastards—"

More appeared. Too many. They must've been hiding in the huts. I saw Ryia at the head of the group and laughed.

"Ah," I said. "I should've known."

"What the hell are you blabbing about?" Ozo hissed in the Oren-yaro tongue.

"Drop your weapon, Ozo. She's got us. She knew we would ride out here. She's been waiting for us."

"Which I could have told her wasn't smart." He turned to her. "You realize you don't have the numbers," Ozo commented, switching to the Jinan lingua franca.

Ryia approached us. "I don't need the numbers. All I need is what's right in front of me."

"I'm worthless," I said. "It's the foreign prince you really want, and you have no idea what he is, do you?"

"We were hoping you could tell us," Ryia replied. "Explain what the hell you just let into our land."

"He's come to save us," I said. "He will liberate Yu-yan first, and then—"

"Don't feed me that same bullshit propaganda, pup. I was playing this game long before you were born." Her face darkened, and she pointed at the horizon. "If you've been counting on this man to turn the tide for you, I have bad news. Your new lord seems to have abandoned you. Our men spotted him crossing the river, even after we rode behind."

I glanced at Ozo, who didn't respond. Evidently, it was news to him, too.

The guards came to relieve us of our weapons. I could hear Ozo swearing, but he was a war veteran and understood defeat. If he had been younger, we would all be dead. He threw his sword into the bushes, far enough to make it inconvenient for the soldier who came to fetch it, and spat on the ground.

"Such a poor sport, Ozo," Ryia exclaimed. She stepped close and placed her fingers on both sides of Ozo's grizzled face, a gesture that was almost intimate. They had been at war so long it had become a sort of dance. "Time has not been kind to you. You used to be handsome."

"Save your breath," Ozo snarled.

"You're a hound, too well-trained," Ryia said, pulling away with a smile. Without the court watching, the vitriol dripped freely from her tone. "A fat, neutered hound. I told you you were wasted at Yeshin's side. What did you need to serve him for, anyway? You were Taraji's, and if revenge for him was what you wanted then you were on the wrong side. But then I suppose a thirty-year *I told you so* loses its potency. You're loyal, Ozo, I give you that, but a loyal dead man is a dead man all the same."

"Just kill this dead man already," Ozo replied. "You damn witch. You're licking your lips in front of prey. It's embarrassing."

"To have an Oren-yaro school *me* about embarrassment..." She smiled. "Take him away. I'll decide if I want him decapitated by dawn."

"Ryia—" I began.

She glanced at me. "No respect? But I guess that's to be expected. You never were the sort, and now that I'm no longer your mother-in-law..."

I took her hand. She held it away from me for a moment, but she finally conceded, stiffly letting me touch the top of her fingers to my forehead.

"Princess Ryia," I said, attempting to lower my voice to the appropriate level of deference. "Perhaps if we had a moment to talk—"

"Talyien," Ozo growled. "*Pup!*"

"Talk?" Ryia asked, pulling her hand away. "Whatever for?"

"We have the same goal," I said. "We both want to see this land truly united, and not just in name. Can we not be at odds for once?"

"The time for that is long past," she replied, her jaw tightened. "We could have had peace if your father had simply let my brother Rysaran rule without defying him. Or if he had allowed my sisters to live after my brother's mistakes. Do you think I never gave him a chance to surrender? I gave him plenty. I wanted the bloodshed to end. The whole war through, all Yeshin had to do was lay down arms and I would *forgive* him for his crimes. Stubborn, your father. And you? Do you think, for one moment, that I'd ever believe you'd willingly bow to me? You're just as stubborn."

"Princess, I am not. You are grandmother to my child. You—"

"Ah," she said, her eyes growing dangerously dark. "I'm surprised he's still alive."

"He is of your blood, Princess—we've already proven that. For the sake of family..."

"Is he, really?"

"You were there at the trial. You saw what happened."

"I meant *alive*." Her eyes flashed. "I heard Kaggawa wants him to marry his daughter so he can start his own dynasty. If the boy is alive, he won't be yours for much longer. But perhaps it won't come to that. I heard your new husband knows where he is. Maybe that's why he was in a hurry to leave you behind."

I felt my blood grow cold.

"Princess!" someone called in the distance. "A moment! Warlord Hhanda's men are here!"

"Take them away," Ryia ordered. With our hands bound, the soldiers forced us down a narrow crevice in the cliffs to the north, along a path beside a trick-ling stream.

"If my son were here…" I heard Ozo murmur under his breath. He had reverted to the Oren-yaro tongue, which would sound incomprehensible to our Ikessar guards.

"Now isn't the time," I retorted.

"When, then?" he bristled. "The witch accused me of being wasted on Yeshin, but she had no idea what waste truly means. It was my son who was wasted on you. I could've recognized him as my heir. He might've been back in my castle, learning how to rule the Tasho clan as was his right."

"That was on you, Ozo," I said. "Not me."

"Maybe. My damn loyalty to your clan has ruined everything I hold dear."

"You still have your grandsons. Give them what you failed to give Agos."

He glanced at the sky, his creased face squinting at the light. "It's too late," he said, before turning around to attack.

I crashed against the rock, Ozo's weight bearing down on me. But his hands missed my head. The guards moved to pull him from me and he turned to steal a sword from the closest one.

I kicked the guard furthest to my right just as Ozo made short work of the two around him. A struggle followed, which somehow left us with three bodies and Ozo's ropes on the ground. He brandished his stolen sword at the rest of Ryia's soldiers before reaching back to quickly cut me loose.

"Oldest trick in the book," Ozo snorted.

"I think you hit my kidney."

"You've got two. Piss blood for a bit and deal with it."

He charged the other soldiers. I came up to fight at his flank, drenched in blood from his butchering before I could even sink my blade into an opponent.

I saw more soldiers streaming down the path from the village.

"Run," Ozo said.

"The hell I will, I'm not leaving your old-man ass behind."

"You—" He grabbed my arm, yanking me up to his face. "If you're going to be stubborn, use it for good. We can't both die here. Did you hear the witch? Yuebek cannot find the prince first. If he's already looking for him, it's bad news. The bastard is already suspicious of us. We can't control him if he's got the upper hand." He struck me against the chest with a fist, hard enough to make me stagger back. "I sent General Mangkang to meet Khine Lamang and take the boy from him. Rayyel knows the meeting place. You'll probably want to ensure he's safe before you return to Yuebek."

I hesitated. "I can't," I said. "General..."

"What?" he asked. "Are you scared you can't do this alone?"

I stared at him for a heartbeat.

He laughed. "You don't have a choice, do you, child?" He turned and pushed me aside. "I'll greet Agos for you," he snarled before thundering down the path to meet the soldiers.

I didn't want to watch him die. I turned and ran.

The trees spun above my head as I found myself deeper into the wilderness. When I couldn't hear the fighting behind me, I turned and saw a crack along the cliff to my left, where roots jutted out, forming steps. I took off my belt, restrapped my father's sword to my back, and made a running leap. I grabbed the closest root. Rocks scraped my wrists as I managed to make my way behind a tree just as the first soldier rushed below.

I breathed as slowly as I could as I watched four more follow him. They were arguing about where I had gone, swords in the air. I didn't want to move in fear of giving away my position and began to watch even my own breathing.

They disappeared further down the crevice. As soon as the last footsteps faded, I pulled myself further up the cliff. Just as I reached a flat ledge, I heard movement in the bushes in front of me and moved to unstrap my sword. I couldn't draw it fast enough; the sword clattered behind me, and I turned to flee instead. But then I saw Rai appear, looking like he'd been running, too.

"Nameless Maker," he breathed. "Tali, I thought she got you. We were riding north when I saw her army from the ridge, and I turned back."

"We have to save Ozo."

"It's too late," he said. "I saw them cut him down."

I swallowed. I'd wanted Ozo dead enough times in the past few months, but the thought of losing him now seemed unbearable.

"Ozo's dead," Rai repeated, guessing what I was thinking. "We will mourn him later."

I tried to focus my thoughts. "Did Yuebek really ride north?"

He nodded.

"Ryia couldn't have spooked him. He saw her intercept me and decided to leave me behind. He knows, Rai."

"He must have sent scouts ahead to look for Thanh himself," Rai said. "He had months to do it."

"More than that. I think he knows something's up. That I've been trying to lead him here for more than what I've let on." I picked up my sword and returned it to my waist. "Thanh. We have to get Thanh out first. Ozo said he sent men to assist Khine. He said you know the meeting place?"

Rai nodded and led me to the horses in silence. We rode away from the woods and up the road, leading towards the mountains. Not long after, a cloud of dust appeared on the horizon. Inzali came riding towards us, her usually placid face twisted in panic. I realized what it was even before she could open her mouth.

"It's Khine, isn't it?" I asked. The sound of my own voice felt like an iron shackle around my throat.

She nodded.

CHAPTER EIGHT

THE CONFIDENCE MAN

ʋȝɔ̂ɾɪ̈ɾ

Over the past few weeks, I dreamed of Khine with a maddening frequency. Sometimes, I couldn't tell if my mind was simply running through the memories with what little sleep I could catch, distorting them until I couldn't even remember what was real and what was not.

In a recurring one, I sat there picking herbs with Khine, listening to him explain how his cons work.

"There's stages to it," he said, turning over the leaf in his hand to smooth away the dirt. "You need to identify the mark and then know what you can about him. Why him, and not someone easier? What stands out about him that you can use to your advantage? His habits, his quirks—but also his temperament, whether he's easy to anger or quick to forgive. Everyone is a little bit different, and you need to understand what makes your mark special.

"Because once you set things into motion, you've got to take advantage of whatever wiggle room you've got. Things *won't* go your way. They never do. You need to be able to adjust to the circumstances, and you can't do that without knowledge of your mark. You need to know how his mind works—what he wants and *why* he wants it. When you're roping him towards you—convincing him how going along with the plan is in his best interests—you can't do it against his will. If he's fighting you, you're not conning him, you're bullying him, and a bullied mark *will* fight back."

"I didn't realize there was so much to it."

Khine gave me a wry smile. "You think I stayed in Shang Azi for no reason?"

"I thought the reason was you couldn't afford anything better."

He laughed. "It's safer to hide out there. I've conned businessmen with connections out in the other districts, but the authorities won't touch Shang Azi with a ten-foot pole."

"So are you saying you've conned me, and I still don't know it?"

He coughed. "That's not—"

I came up to brush dirt from his face. "So...tell me more. You don't want the mark fighting back."

"No," he said. "You want them...compliant. They'll be suspicious, of course. It's human nature to be suspicious. Which is why *knowing* what drives them is important. You form a story around the mark, you see, and you *want* them to start believing this story themselves. Because there may come a time when everything breaks down and the mark sees the con for what it is, but you want it to be too late by then. You want him to believe everything you promised him...you want him to want it so much that the sun rises and falls with it and he knows he cannot live until it becomes reality. You want him to put the noose on himself, and thank you for it."

Khine gazed at me as he said the last part. *Not a memory*, I told myself. *A dream. It was all just a dream.*

It had to be.

Inzali explained everything on the way back. She had met up with Karia at the hut, who told her Khine's plan of pretending that Thanh was deathly ill—too ill for the confines of a camp. He needed to visit the hot springs, which weren't far from the hut. He was to be accompanied by Dai's men. Ozo's men were supposed to descend on them and extract the boy in a brief battle. In no time, we would have custody of Thanh, and we could watch Yuebek crush Kaggawa's army at Yu-yan's gates without fear of repercussion.

But the hours came and went, and Khine didn't show up. Neither did Ozo's men.

I knew the hot springs she meant. Khine had shown me the hot springs the morning after we spent our first night together—a surprise, he'd called it, his face beaming, still so convinced he could peel off the cracks of my shell and find something underneath. Khine saw the good in everything, even in someone like me.

My ears buzzed. We met Karia and I didn't even stop to observe whatever tepid reunion she had reserved for her brother. I went straight up the path to the hot springs, to the small cave where Khine was supposed to have handed my son over to Ozo's men that afternoon. It was dark now, and the cave was empty.

I heard footsteps behind me and I looked up, heart pounding. But it was just Rai. "You need to rest." He stepped towards me and then stopped, still hesitating.

A smile flitted on my lips. I wasn't sure what to make of Rai becoming more thoughtful these days. "Tell me, Rai," I croaked out. "Do you admire your mother?"

"I respect her," Rai replied, after a moment of contemplation. "I disagree with many things she has done over the years, but she has been an effective leader of our clan nonetheless. The Ikessars do not have a region they can rule on their own, much like the Sougen rice lords, but—"

"History lesson aside," I said. "Do you not sometimes wish you were born a rice farmer instead of a prince?"

He lifted his eyebrows. "Because their cares are easier? It's never that simple, Tali. Politics is much like farming. We don't know if our actions, our words, our laws, will truly yield results, but something must be done. Pests, an early frost, a hurricane…these things can render a crop useless. Yet a farmer who plants nothing today won't reap a single thing tomorrow."

"I think I've found the answer to how you can act like nothing bothers you."

"It all bothers me," he said with a wave of his hand. "But life, you understand, cannot be contained inside a bubble. Chaos is inevitable. Cyclic. The important part is to not allow yourself to be so swept up by everything that you turn into one of those self-serving idiots we're surrounded by. When all is said and done, order can be restored, even for just a little while."

"In exchange for a few lives, in the meantime."

Rai frowned. "The truth may not always be saccharine. In fact, it very rarely is. The sooner you accept it, the easier it is to protect yourself."

"I sometimes wonder if your bluntness is a blessing or a curse."

"You've never liked it," he agreed. "I've accepted that, too. A long time ago."

"Teach me how to do that."

"There's nothing to it," Rai said. "It depends on how you were raised to view the world. An Ikessar is taught that nothing is ours. We are servants of the Nameless Maker. We—"

"I've heard that somewhere before. *Swords first. Servants first.*" I gave a grim smile. "We come from the same tired words, made by the same tired people who didn't understand that life is not a game. Do you not see why I don't want this for our son?"

"What life would you have for him?" Rai asked. "This is all we know."

"It is a big world, Rai. He's a smart child. There are many things he could yet be, given the chance. A librarian. A scribe. A cartographer. Honest jobs where he has a chance to be *happy*."

For a moment, he looked horrified, like I had just suggested our son become a thief or a beggar. Strange, given he was all but ready to sacrifice Thanh's life to save him from Princess Ryia's wrath. But then he sighed, his shoulders shaking. "I just want him safe," he murmured.

Before I could reply, I heard the crunch of leaves outside the cave. We stepped into the shadows.

Kaggawa's mercenaries appeared at the entrance. "If they're not here, he's fucked us over," a voice called. "If he's fucked us over, I'm going to kill that son of a bitch." I recognized Larson, the guardsman.

"He wasn't trying to fuck us over," one of his companions said. "Those were Zarojo soldiers on the road. They're the enemy. I hear they're marching to Yu-yan to help with the defenses."

"He could've followed us. The wily rat turned his horse the other way. Didn't even hesitate."

They arrived at the pool. Larson swept his torch over the water, his face a mask of fury. "There's no one here. The treacherous rat!"

"We don't know that, Officer. Maybe they're just late."

"Late? Unlikely. We were going to sell the boy to the highest bidder. Did you know who he really was?"

The soldier shook his head.

"The fucking crown prince of Jin-Sayeng," Larson said with a snarl. "That's why Kaggawa's been keeping a close watch on him this whole time. Lamang gave us this information so we would help him get the boy out of camp. If I see Lamang I'm going to wring his sorry little neck."

"We have to get back to camp."

"No, we don't. The Zarojo were headed that way. Are you out of your mind?" He pushed his companion back through the entrance, their shadows skipping over the cave. Eventually, their footsteps receded.

"Khine does that," I said. "He was a con artist in Shang Azi. He was playing them against each other."

"Why *didn't* he follow them?" Rai asked. "He could have taken the boy here."

"Do you see Ozo's crew anywhere? They were supposed to be here to get rid of Kaggawa's soldiers. Something must have happened on the road. Something must have happened to them."

Rai frowned. "Yuebek's men—perhaps they've found something."

"We can trust Khine," I said. "Something happened and Khine took Thanh elsewhere because it wasn't safe to take him here."

"Can you hear yourself, Talyien?" Rai asked. "A con artist. I don't care how much faith you have in this man or why, but you have to face the truth. There's a chance he's sold our son to someone else."

I shook my head and stumbled from the cave, my heart hammering against my ears. I went straight for the horses, flinging myself into the saddle in the dark. "You're going to break your neck out there," Rai thundered behind me.

"I'm heading to Dai's camp to find out what happened," I said. "Don't try to stop me."

He grabbed the reins. "I know that's pointless. I'm riding with you."

"Then don't slow me down." I yanked the reins back, and dug my heels into my mount, tearing into the darkness.

We rode past the village and then down to the main road, where the rice fields stretched out before us, dark stalks swaying with the soft breeze. I swung north, Rai's horse barely keeping up with mine. My mind was skipping through what little I knew. Zarojo soldiers…what would they be doing here? Even if they had managed to build the pontoons fast enough, they would still just be crossing the river. It was impossible for Yuebek's men to have launched an attack unless they were already here in the first place. Just like Rai said, Yuebek must have sent scouts in advance, long before we rode down here.

Down I rode, my mind dredging up worse possibilities. It was like falling down a cliff with nothing to hold on to, but you knew you needed to grab something anyway, because you didn't want to find out what was waiting for you at the bottom. My horse's breath rose in clouds; as the road wound downhill, I pulled at the reins to slow her down.

Something crashed out of the bushes. A figure, a shadow. It was too dark for me to see much else, but it came for the saddle, fingers outstretched, uttering a low, guttural moan. I saw its teeth flash—before it could grab my leg, I stabbed it in the neck with my sword.

"Talyien!" Rai roared.

I pulled back as his own horse galloped close. He had a lantern in his hand. The light revealed a man in rags, a common villager, now a crumpled corpse on the road. In the dark, I'd been convinced it was possessed by a corrupt soul, but I couldn't tell anymore. I reeled away, gasping in horror. "I didn't see—" I began. "I didn't..."

I heard a cry. There was a girl crawling out of the ditch. "Father," she called. She looked about ten or twelve.

My senses reeled. I watched as she approached the body, oblivious to the both of us on horseback. She was barefoot, and her clothes were torn at the back, half burnt. On second inspection, the dead man, too, had burn wounds on his hands and legs, so bad you could see the tendons peeking through the black flesh.

"This chaos needs to end," Rai said.

The girl was cradling the body. She still hadn't acknowledged us, almost as if she was just waiting for us to kill her. "I'm sorry," I croaked out. The girl didn't hear. Pretended not to. I removed the coin purse from my belt and threw it at her direction. It landed near her father's bloody fingers. I didn't know what good it would do her in a land that was burning to the ground. She must've thought the same thing, or else she just didn't care anymore—she barely glanced at the purse. Instead, she continued to murmur over her dead father, crooning as if to a child, her forehead pressed over his damp white hair.

I couldn't look at her again. I turned my horse around and continued cantering down the hill. The smoke led me all the way to Dai's camp.

It was slaughter right from the gates. Zarojo soldiers battered themselves against Kaggawa's mercenaries, making short work of the ill-equipped men. The gates were flung wide open, revealing tents on fire.

I remembered the soldiers we had treated there, many of whom were so wounded they would be out of commission for months. Everything we had done was pointless. Those men wouldn't be able to defend themselves. And the man I just killed—what was he? A mere servant probably, someone trying to make ends meet, even if it meant working for the same people bringing the destruction around them. I clambered down from the horse and tried to swallow, but my throat had gone dry.

Rai placed a hand on my shoulder before wordlessly drawing me into his arms. I stood there, stunned. He quickly pulled away. "We'll go around," he said. "Find another way in."

"I thought you would say it's too risky."

"It is," he murmured, and left it at that.

We left the horses in the woods and approached the back gates. By now the clouds of smoke all but covered the black sky, making it difficult to breathe without coughing. I could see mercenaries fleeing one by one, some with hardly a speck of blood on them. Easily routed, these mercenaries; Dai should've known better than to put his trust in them. As we came up the garden near the officers' lodge, I caught sight of a handful of Jinsein guards armed with grass-cutters.

"Halt!" they called.

"We're looking for Lamang," Rai said. "Have you seen him?"

"The surgeon? The bastard who let the Zarojo in?" They drew their swords and advanced towards us.

Rai didn't move. "Two questions for a question, soldier," he said. "We're not here to fight."

Something in his voice must've been enough for them. "You're Jinsein," one finally said. "I think you are. Those fucking foreigners..."

"Blood will tell. Blood will always tell," the other added. "Lamang is a turncoat. He came riding in here tonight. He was friends with the gate guards. They left their posts and by the time we realized what was happening the Zarojo were here."

"That was after he left with the boy?" I broke in.

"He and Officer Larson took the boy somewhere for his health. There's been an outbreak. He returned without either of them."

"He's not here," Rai said, drawing me aside.

"A clue, perhaps, of where they'd gone..."

"Talyien."

I turned to him, my eyes focusing. "Khine once told me that there's a point in a con when things don't go according to plan, and you have to make it up along the way." I swallowed. "I know what I sound like," I managed.

"You find it hard to believe people will betray you."

"Perhaps," I said. "I did that with you. They couldn't see why I held on. I had every reason to have you killed and instead...I waited, like a fool. Chased after you, like a fool. Because in the world we live in, you are either a fool or a monster. Look what happened on the way here. I'm turning into the kind of person who sees shadows everywhere she looks, enemies pouncing on her every which way. Our world demands that we turn into monsters. What if our illusions are all we have, Rai?"

The sound of fighting drew closer. I turned and saw that the Zarojo had broken through the inner gates. I didn't bother to run. The first man through was familiar—the tall, bearded figure of Jiro Kaz. He spotted me at the same instance. "Queen Talyien!" he cried, voice booming. "You're supposed to be back with the prince. What are you doing, still running around like you don't have a nation to rule?"

"I should ask you the same thing. I thought you were with Yuebek's army."

"Prince Yuebek's orders," he said. "He sent me ahead to go look for your son."

"I figured. But my boy isn't here."

"I know *that*," he said, laughing. There was something in his voice.

"You know something," I said.

"I know you're not acting like a very loving wife right now," Jiro pointed out. "You've disappointed Prince Yuebek, Queen Talyien, more than you'll ever know. You're supposed to be by his side. Maybe he's right. You're hiding something from him."

"What the hell are you saying, Kaz?"

"You," he said, "are a liar." He pointed at me. "You have no intention of ruling by the prince's side and he knows it. He knows you've tricked him, and I do believe he intends to lay it out on your boy when he gets the chance."

"You son of a bitch. You know where he is."

"I do," Jiro said with a smile. "But first, tell me, Queen Talyien, how *did* my wife die?"

He came at me with his spear so fast I didn't have time to dodge. But his intent wasn't to kill. He simply struck the wall behind me, leaving the spear lodged in there. Still grinning, he wiped the sweat off his face.

"You and your wife…" I whispered. "You walked into something well beyond your capabilities."

"That may be," Jiro said. "We're all just looking out for ourselves, in the end. Me. You. Lamang." He smiled. "Your son," he continued with a bow, "will be delivered to the prince's hands soon enough."

"What the hell do you mean by that?"

"Is that a note of surprise?" He clapped his hands together. "That's right.

They said you were close. *Too* close. But you did say so yourself. Lamang is one of us. He's always been one of us. Did you expect a tiger to change his stripes? The man conned his own lover's father. You didn't know that, either, I suppose." He licked his lips. "Poor baker. Coffers cleaned out, and there wasn't much in the first place. Why else did you think he moved to Kyan Jang? You never thought to ask—maybe you didn't care. Maybe you thought he would change. Ask him when you see him. Ask him why he still carries that guilt around like it was the whole world."

You want them to put the noose on themselves, and thank you for it.

There was a movement from the top of the steps, so fast it looked like a blur. Out of nowhere, Lahei threw herself at Jiro. She drew a sword, spinning low and managing to graze him along the belly. It was as if she had forgotten she was injured; the crutch remained firmly embedded under one arm like it was part of her. Watching them fight, I almost forgot, too. Jiro lumbered after her like a blinded buffalo, huffing and swearing.

She spun again, sweat pouring down her face. Lacking the power to strike him with one blow, she was whittling him down, tearing at him with small wounds where she could. He tried to grab her crutch and she rewarded him by jamming it up his windpipe.

He staggered back just as her men arrived. They took over, driving him back to his own soldiers.

"Tali," she said, whirling around to meet me.

"Tell me you know where my son is, Lahei."

"If Lamang didn't bring him to you..." she started.

"You knew? And you didn't warn your father?"

"I did the opposite. I looked the other way." She wiped the sweat from her forehead. "I was the one who told my father we could trust Lamang. His decision to wage war on behalf of the commoners is misguided. We don't win Jin-Sayeng over by force. Especially not with a foreign army! He *knows* this. But his arrogance got the better of him. If I was stronger, I would've tried to put a stop to it." She glanced at the fighting in the distance. "Well, it's over now. I don't think my father will ever forgive me. If he survives the night. But I think he's going to die soon. I think we all are." There was sorrow in her voice, as if she had already started grieving.

"You don't have to die with him."

"Most of your soldiers are gone," Rai broke in. "This camp *will* fall, whether you want it or not. The Zarojo are unforgiving. Defeat these ones, and it won't matter. More are riding to the plains as we speak."

Lahei gave a nervous smile. "I knew that. It seems difficult to act when it's all laid bare like that. Defeat was not...on the table."

I gently placed my hand around her wrist.

She glanced down and smiled. "You know we're not enemies."

"I've never considered you an enemy," I murmured. "Go, Lahei. It's not too late for you."

She hesitated. The terror in her eyes at the thought of abandoning her father and defying his orders was so clear that I felt a tremble of it within myself. But she was stronger than I was. She broke it easily. "Until we meet again, Beloved Queen," she said. She took my hand in hers and bowed before she limped down the path. Her men came up to protect her from the Zarojo.

A dark shadow crossed the sky, blocking the moonlight.

I managed to look up and shield my eyes just as a shot of fire hurtled down towards the fighting, burning Zarojo and mercenaries alike. "Eikaro!" I called to the dragon as it settled on the roof of the lodge.

"*Huan*," the dragon corrected me with a roar. He stretched his wings across the sky before he glided down, smashing into the soldiers, tearing them limb from limb. Almost before I could blink, it was over, and we were two lone figures standing in a sea of fire.

The black dragon gracefully landed beside us. Rayyel looked terrified, but he didn't move. I had warned him about the brothers before, and somewhere in the back of his mind he must have remembered. Maybe I was wrong about him. Maybe I was the one who didn't know how to listen.

"*Why are you here?*" Huan asked. He shifted his head towards Rayyel, steam rising from his nostrils.

"We were looking for my son," I replied.

"*I'm sorry, my queen, but you can't worry about him now. You're needed there. Prince Yuebek is slaughtering everyone in his path, ally and enemy alike. He'll kill everyone before he steps foot inside the city.*"

I turned to Rai. "He's still attacking Kaggawa's forces," I said. "Why is he still doing it? If he knows I've tricked him, he wouldn't dare."

"Who knows how that man thinks," Rai said.

"I have to go there."

He didn't argue. Too many lives had been lost to get us here. If I faltered now, would it all have been in vain?

I stepped on Huan's proffered leg and hoisted myself on his back. There was a look on Rai's face that I, as always, couldn't read. "You are the first true Dragonlord in centuries, do you realize that?" he asked.

"Some Dragonlord," I murmured. "Does it sting that it's not an Ikessar?"

Rayyel shook his head. "No, my queen," he said, bowing as we took to the sky.

CHAPTER NINE

THE SIEGE, REPRISED

ᜩᜒᜉᜒ

Huan wasn't lying when he said *slaughter*.
We reached the fringes of the battlefield. As soon as we passed the trees, a wave of arrows came flying for the dragon. Huan roared, shifting to the side. An arrow pinned itself into the scale between his shoulders, right below my knee. I directed him behind a hill, where he managed an abrupt landing, huffing smoke and steam into the air.

I kicked myself off him just as three Kag soldiers came for us. Huan snapped his jaws, taking two down mid-stride. I struck the third man across the elbow, and then again, the heavy blade tearing chunks out of the cheap armour. Before I could finish him, Huan swept his tail low into the ground, sending the soldier toppling forward; he stepped on him and snapped his head off.

"*I'll cut through the lines*," he roared.

"The risk to you—"

He ignored me and went barrelling around the field, crashing into a group of soldiers. I kept myself behind his shadow, taking down stragglers in my path. Battlerage, bloodlust, desperation—call it what you will. I felt like a dragon myself, tearing hunks of flesh off bone before turning for the next. In a fair battle I might've only felled a handful before exhausting myself, but there was nothing fair about what was unfolding in front of us. Not anymore. I lost count of how many died at my blade, sinking to their knees while screaming for their mothers. I couldn't even breathe anymore—it seemed as if nothing but blood and piss and excrement went down my lungs.

We were creatures of death, us warlords of Jin-Sayeng.

Arrows blotted out the sun as we tore through the field. Huan shielded me with his wing as a well-timed volley landed on the Kag soldiers in the distance, pinning about half to the ground. The rest scattered, so frightened they barely offered a second glance at the hulking dragon nearby. I let the stragglers run past us, killing those who lay writhing on the ground. *Don't you ever pretend you can look away.*

We reached a low embankment. I heard Huan roar and turned. Before I could take two steps, a shadow crossed the sky. A large net flew from the cliff, trapping him mid-flight. The weights tangled around his feet and he stumbled forward, wings crashing into the boulders ahead.

Huan reared as he attempted to bite through the net. Mercenaries appeared behind the trees, rushing to bind the ropes around his feet before he could get up. Huan thrashed with one wing, knocking a man aside. Two quickly rushed forward to replace him, throwing hooked chains that looped around the dragon's mouth. He went down in a cloud of dust as more mercenaries piled on top of him. "We've caught the dragon!"

"*Leave me, Queen Talyien,*" Huan roared.

"You heard him," Dai said. He appeared on horseback, his armour dented in several places. The heat and exhaustion was plain on his face, but he regarded the dragon with an expression that bordered on amusement. "What have you royals done?" he asked. "You're playing with powers beyond your understanding."

"This power is Jin-Sayeng's oldest secret," I said. "Let him go."

"That's one of the Anyus, isn't it?" He tapped his head. "One of the sons. I can hear him, too."

"*An abomination has no right...*" Huan began.

Dai threw his head back and laughed. "You call me that, and yet look at you!"

"*One body. One soul.*"

"A pot calling the kettle black," I broke in. "You can argue about the details later. Kaggawa, if you truly care about this land like you say you do, you will withdraw now. The Zarojo are here."

"A paltry force," Dai said.

"They outnumber you."

"It doesn't matter. I've got my soldiers intercepting that foreign prince of yours. Cut the head off the snake and the body will follow."

"You can't possibly think you can kill him."

He crossed the field towards us and pointed at Huan. "Dragons," he said, "are creatures of the *agan*. Their bodies and souls are open doorways. People have to accept a corrupted presence—the barriers of those blind to the *agan* make it difficult for them to invade. Dragons don't get that choice."

"We don't have time for your lectures, old man."

He gave a small grin. "Old. I guess I *am*. It feels odd, having lived so long to be called that."

"You're not... you're the other one, aren't you? Myar."

"Dai detests warfare," the man admitted. "He would rather wait it out." He placed his hand close to Huan's nose. Huan snapped at him and he pulled away with a grin.

"Let us work together," I said. "You and Dai. Your talents are wasted when we're against each other."

"You must've asked Ryia Ikessar the same thing. I hear her army is behind us as we speak."

"I did. She refused. Will you see the sense she didn't?"

He gave a soft sigh. "The Ikessars are weak. If we break through the siege this morning, we'll be able to mount defenses against them without too much trouble. And I have every intention of doing just that. We—"

"Are you listening to yourself? That city is crawling with those creatures!"

"We know. Your General Nor is impressive. How she's been able to defend the city from both within and without will be the talk for centuries. But even the strongest pillar will fall, if you chip at it long enough. And she's chipped. They've been throwing corrupted bodies into the river since last week, and many are in armour."

"*He laughs at our sorrows,*" Huan sneered. "*This man pretends to be righteous, but he's just like the others.*"

"Your sorrows are mine, too," Myar said. "I've been in Jin-Sayeng too long."

I shook my head. "You can't possibly understand."

"Perhaps not. But I am willing to do what none of you are."

"Why do you think I'm heading back to Yu-yan now? We've found a way to stop this plague and this war."

He looked amused. "No, you haven't."

"Prince Yuebek—"

"Let me stop you right there, Queen Talyien," he said. "Whatever you think you've found, you have absolutely no guarantee it will work. Don't you think

I've heard rumours of Warlord Yeshin and his obsession with *agan*-addled children? Of what your fathers have been up to? *His* father? Look at him." He nodded towards Huan. "Listen to me, children. Everything is an excuse to seize power. Everything. Words are easy to shape and intention is hard to see."

"You're doing the same thing."

"I am, at least, not lying about it. I showed you what you were up against. Made the effort to bring you out here so you could see with your own eyes and understand. And what do you do? You *cling* to your old ways. You marry a foreigner in an attempt to seize control, a known *madman*—"

"That's not what's happening here."

"War is in your blood. It's in all your blood."

"Says the man with an army at the city gates."

"We are here to liberate the people."

"And how, pray, are you going to do that?" I asked.

"Dragons are creatures of the *agan*," he repeated with the patience of a tutor. "They hold the key to ending this madness. But first we need a blank slate. We cannot do anything in this chaos. The corrupt must be taken care of. And since we don't know who is or who isn't—"

"You're going to kill everyone."

He wiped his face with the back of his hand. "Something must be done."

"Gods in heaven, you can't be serious!"

"I am," he said. "The time for flimsy decisions is long gone. Someone has to take up the burden of change."

"They're right," I murmured. "You either die a hero, or…"

He smiled. "So you said yourself. I've lived long enough. *Old.*" He laughed and turned back to the dragon. "Come, Anyu. Your sacrifice will be heralded by the gods. Be proud."

Huan flamed as he approached. In the same instant, the sky darkened, turning everything pitch black. I felt the now-familiar sensation of *agan* in the air and knew something was happening. The rift? Yuebek? Did it matter?

If we didn't kill each other here, the rest would kill us anyway.

I dashed for the last thing I saw—the dragon's bright snout, snapping through the net. I reached him just in time. In the darkness, I managed to grab hold of the webbing, which was made of thin wire. Too strong for the dragon to break easily, but so light I could lift it over his head. I untangled the weights from his feet.

That was all he needed. As soon as his legs were free, he wedged himself through the opening, nearly knocking me back with a wing in his attempt to extract himself from the net.

"It's escaping!" a mercenary screamed. Huan silenced him with a quick crunch. And then he arched his neck and lit the brush on fire.

The branches were wet, so they didn't burst into flames immediately. The embers burned low, the red crawling against the darkness like veins. But it gave enough light for me to tear off the rest of the net from Huan's body.

Myar reached us before he could take flight, his sword sinking into Huan's leg. The dragon turned to strike him.

"Don't!" I screamed.

Huan balked. "*What? Why?*"

"Wake up. Myar, Kaggawa, whoever you are. It's not too late. We can still work together."

"*It is too late, my queen,*" Huan roared. "*He said so himself. He, too, is just using this opportunity to seize power.*"

"He doesn't know he can't do that anymore," I said. "My son. He's not in your custody. Your camp has fallen."

Myar's face flickered. "Our daughter?"

"She's safe. But you don't have my son—you can't use him. And this siege? My father wanted this civil war to happen to bring Prince Yuebek out here. You were used, just like the rest of us. Win this one and it will be for nothing. You think I don't know the insanity of what we intend to do? That we are going to rely on that man to make this go away? I've barely slept in weeks because I *know* this is a fool's errand. But we have nothing else, Lord Merchant! We have absolutely *nothing* else!"

He drew back, hesitating.

Huan's temper flared. He struck the man with his wing, sending him flying across the field. Myar—*Dai*—roared back. I recognized the sudden change in his expression. The warrior, not the scholar. He drew his sword and charged. I watched helplessly as they circled each other, my screams lost in the wind.

Around us, men continued to die.

Is this what you wanted, Yeshin? All of this? Needless death, needless destruction . . .

But no. He would have never believed it to be needless. Cleansing fire, Rai had said. They all believed it. The land was too far gone, there were too many edges to be filed off, and all we had to go on was despair. I didn't know if my son was still alive, or would be by the end of the day.

Trumpets sounded in the distance.

The light returned, seeping through the clouds like blood. I thought for a moment the air had settled at last. But then the screams changed, rising to a timbre that reached into my spine.

Dai struck a blow across Huan's chest. As the dragon staggered back, Dai swept an arm across the ridge below. "Do you see that?" he called. "Look down below, Queen Talyien!"

I narrowed my eyes. Dai's army was cut between the city walls, with the Zarojo and Oren-yaro at his flank. And there, off where the sun was rising, men fell around a single, shining figure, like toy soldiers struck with a broom. Huan had it right—he no longer discerned between friend or foe. He walked through their midst, feeding on everyone in his path the way he did back in that first village. Every soul that fell made the air pulse black and blue, leaving his own body dripping with black fluid, like he'd been drenched in a vat of oil. His presence alone swallowed the morning light.

Dai began to laugh. "You think you can make that save us all?"

I had no words for him.

Huan suddenly swept behind me, pushing me with his snout. "*You have to stop him,*" he said. I turned around and clambered up his back.

"You coward!" Dai called as we took to the sky.

No archers went for us this time. Huan glided down past another throng of soldiers, blasting fire and sending them running for cover. More than enough mercenaries fled. A dragon, on top of the carnage, was too much for most.

"My lord!" I screamed at the top of my lungs. In the distance, Yuebek turned, his head jerking with the movement. The sight of the dragon didn't seem to faze him.

"My queen," he said, his robes drenched in my people's blood.

"It's over, my lord. We're winning the battle. We must've already won. We—"

He charged the dragon.

Huan was airborne when Yuebek reached him, which may have saved his life. Yuebek's sword slid through his shoulder like a hot knife through butter, right above where his heart would be. He shot a blast of flame. The tendrils curled around Yuebek before dying.

"Dragons," he spat. "What else were you hiding from me, my whore queen? What other lies have you tried to feed me all these weeks?"

"My lord, if you would just listen—"

He pulled the sword and turned to strike at me. I lifted my sword, blocking the blow and then the next. It felt like holding back an avalanche. My arms began to crumble under the strain, my fingers trembling amidst the blood.

"Your mother was Jinsein," I gasped. "Do you not desire to become a Dragonlord, Yuebek?"

He stopped, his eyes watery as he stared at me, as if he had never imagined I would dare utter such words. "My mother?" he snapped. "*This* is why Warlord Yeshin came for *me*?"

"You must've known where she came from."

"My father had everything about her erased! How did you—no, of course. You'd keep records here, too. The Dragon Palace. Your archives! They'll be the first to burn when I ascend the throne."

"Her blood will allow you to ride dragons, my lord," I said. "Only those descended from Jinsein royalty through the motherline can ride them."

Yuebek didn't even acknowledge my words. He walked past Huan's snapping jaws, pushing him back with another unseen blast. Back to the throng he went, still babbling to himself. Back to the slaughter. It was as if I had simply ceased to exist.

By the time I dismounted from Huan within sight of the city, the dead were piled in the fields and crows circled the skies.

Several other events happened that dawn, most of which I learned from Huan secondhand. Jiro's attack caught Kaggawa's main camp off guard, which sent the soldiers on the field into a panic. What was left of Dai Kaggawa's army was surrounded before noon.

We had expected him to surrender. He didn't.

I liked that about Dai. For all that he was an ambitious maniac like the rest, he had guts, at least. He split his army in half—one part to deal with the threat behind him, the other to continue with the siege. A risky maneuver, but they were desperate, and his men fought all the harder for it.

But Yu-yan was desperate, too. Weeks under siege had left it battered, bruised, and starving. Things that could break morale in many cases, but turn water into fire in others. And in any case, my orders to the Anyus had meant that they still had the numbers—they did the bare minimum to protect Yu-yan from Kaggawa's assault, spending most of their time trying to protect their people from the attacks inside. So when that final charge came, they gave it their all. The rest immediately dropped their weapons in surrender. It was astounding to see weeks of preparation be reduced to a few key minutes. *Years*, if you counted everything my father had done.

The Zarojo army marched through the gates to the crowd's deafening roar. But they weren't cheering for the foreigners. "Dragonlord!" the people were calling. "Dragonqueen!" The chant shook the city to its very foundations, the cry of a people who could not—*would not*—bow even at the edge of desperation. You say this pride cannot feed us, but perhaps we understand that at the worst of times, it is all we may ever have. It is pride that can sustain us another hour, pride that can see us through where others break.

On any other day, I might've taken heart from it. But after the last few days, I could only feel exhaustion, could only feel my senses darken with every step I took. I couldn't remember how I managed to make it through the gates without getting crushed between the soldiers. I slipped and fell to my knees in the next alley. Fighting for grip in the mud, I felt someone grab my arm and hoist me up. "My queen. Everyone's been looking for you," Eikaro said. "Your husband—"

"Don't call him that," I snapped.

"Prince Yuebek," he corrected himself with a thin smile, "is waiting for you in the keep."

I would die a happy woman if I never saw him again. "First I need sleep, my lord."

Eikaro didn't argue. He found me a bed in the barracks—probably an officer's, hurriedly vacated on his orders—where I allowed myself a few hours of blessed darkness. Not that it did much good. In my dreams I was running again, screaming for my son, screaming for Khine while dragon wings hummed in the background. I woke up to the sensation of grief, as if someone had died during the night and I was swimming in the aftermath. Not wanting to dwell on it a moment longer, I stumbled out of the room.

The soldiers allowed me to take food from their mess hall, where the excitement of the recent victory was palpable. There were smiles on the hollowed faces, laughter. The cook was ladling out gruel in generous portions. "No rations tonight!" he told me with a grin. "We've got supplies raided from Kag-gawa's camps!"

The same camps where others were dying or already dead. A celebration on one side, a wake on the other. I couldn't share the revelry, not when I could still hear the dead's screaming every time I closed my eyes. I supposed it was easier to be a soldier in this regard. Every battle could be the last, and so victories seem to last forever. I knew better. The world wasn't built by well-intentioned souls. The right answers exist only in the dreams of the delusional.

I took my bowl to a quiet corner and managed to get a few bites in before I heard movement beside me. I looked up. General Nor's face was a steel mask.

I placed my spoon down. "I'm in trouble, aren't I?"

"We need to talk," she said.

I ate a bit more before eventually sliding off the bench to follow her. She took me up the stairs to a guarded hallway, and then into a private room with fur-covered stools arranged around a large desk. Eikaro sat near the window, staring at the wooden figures on a map marking the location of Kaggawa's army from last night. Nor stalked over to it and carefully removed each one, replacing it with two other figures.

"The Oren-yaro and the Zarojo," she explained, crossing her arms.

"Go on."

"I'm told the Zarojo outnumber us. But that's not important. What's impor-tant is that Yuebek's army is currently divided. He only has a thousand men in the city—Yu-yan doesn't have enough resources to sustain them and they've been dispersed, per the late General Ozo's orders, to Kaggawa's war camps. What he wanted was for the Oren-yaro to begin attacking them once your part is under way." She scowled. "You're supposed to take Prince Yuebek to the ridge, if I understand correctly."

"That's not even half of it," I continued. "General Ozo's death leaves us a dilemma. He was supposed to help me find a way to be alone with Yuebek up there. We need him to use his powers to fix the rift in those mountains and hopefully put an end to all of this, Yuebek himself included."

"I saw what he did to Kaggawa's army," Nor replied. "I couldn't believe it. I still can't. Tell me it's a dream. What is he, Talyien?"

"An abomination," Eikaro answered for me. "My brother and I were flying near the ramparts when he first appeared. You told me he's dealt with blood magic, Beloved Queen? Then it stands to reason he's been using it on himself. He's linking with his own soldiers, using their blood as his own personal sustenance. I wouldn't be surprised if it has turned his own into pure *agan*. He's a walking tomb, filled with the dead."

"That explains why he is nearly invincible around his soldiers," I said. It seemed oddly wasteful to me. Yuebek used villagers' blood to give life to dummies—couldn't he have done the same thing here instead? *Perhaps that was the plan. Perhaps he wanted the dummies* and *his army here, and you ruined it, just like you ruined everyone else's plans.* I would have been pleased with myself if I had any humour left. "If he has hundreds of soldiers in the city..." I slumped into my seat.

"Yu-yan's soldiers aren't in the best shape, either," Nor said, after a few moments of silence. "The surviving number less than a thousand, and more than half are wounded. We're prisoners here."

"A familiar feeling. We're chained to our duties, but surrendering isn't an option."

"Cowards will disagree, my queen," Rai broke in as he walked into the room. He looked just as exhausted as I felt, his clothes streaked with dirt. He was followed by Namra. "Surrender is always an option. The battle is over for now, and I believe there is nothing more you can do. Yuebek is a lost cause. He no longer trusts you."

I gave him a thin smile. "So you want me to run away, just like you did."

He strode up to the window and tugged at the curtains, allowing light to stream onto the table. "You were not raised to be prudent," he said. "But sometimes the battle is lost, and there is nothing more we can do but pull back and plan again."

"Did you look outside, Rai? Prudence will not serve us anymore." It hurt, thinking that. Forcing courage, knowing you had lost nearly every weapon at your disposal but that you must live to fight another day... We were close. We were so close. Were our attempts nothing more than flailing at the wind?

I stared out the window, my mind racing. Everyone was looking at me. I took a deep breath and picked up a chalice from the table.

"Get me some wine," I told Nor.

"Drinking at this hour—" Rai began.

I shot him a look. "Wine," I repeated.

Nor, realizing what I was doing, gave a small nod. She strode out of the room and returned with a jug of coconut liquor, which she poured into the cup. I bared my right arm.

"We have nothing but ourselves. Rai is right. We can still run. But then who would clean up the mess? Do we do what our fathers did and leave it to our children? Enjoy the rest of our lives and let *them* deal with it? I can't. I can't just sit back and repeat the mistakes they've made. I don't know what we're supposed to do now, but I know I have to do something."

I pulled the grass-cutter from my belt and sliced my arm. Blood ran down my elbow, dripping into the wine.

"This ends with us," I said. I picked up the chalice and held it out for Namra.

"My queen, I am not a royal," she whispered.

"We are Jinsein," I said evenly. "Royal or commoner—we're the same. Maybe our elders didn't understand that, but we're not them. Even when they snatch the hopes from our very mouths, they cannot take this away."

She swallowed before accepting both the cup and the blade with a bow. She drew blood from her wrist and gave it to Nor beside her, who followed suit before passing them to Eikaro.

"I bleed for both me and my brother," he said as he sank the blade into his flesh. "And for those who cannot be here. We are children of Jin-Sayeng. We will fight for her." He turned to hold the chalice and blade out to Rai.

Rai paused before taking each of them. "This ends with us," he repeated, before cutting himself. He lifted the chalice and took a drink. He passed it back to me. I touched the rim of the cup to my lips and swallowed. The acrid taste of the blood and wine lit my veins on fire.

"Gods have mercy," Eikaro breathed. "We may lose our lives, and everything with it."

"It is calmest in the eye of the storm," Nor said, solemn as a priestess.

CHAPTER TEN

THE VICTORY FEAST

ᴛᴵᴹ

I spent several hours getting ready, knowing there was no point in hurrying. I even took time to write. Yuebek could wait; the farce had to go on. Servants came to clean me up and dress me in royal robes, marking me as queen. Queen of a dying land. Nor came up to fetch me, and together, we marched like prisoners being led to the executioners' block.

"Stand firm, General," I said as I left her to go up the steps on my own.

She thumped her chest with her fist and bowed.

The victory feast was held in the Anyu keep's great hall, one that felt dizzyingly out of place with the carnage that still marked the fields outside the city. There stood all the royals of Yu-yan—pathetically sparse, since the Anyus had wrestled their way into land that belonged to the common people—and not even looking like they had dressed hurriedly in their expensive clothing after that last, sleepless night. Warlord Huan Anyu cut a magnificent sight in his ceremonial armour. Lady Grana and Lady Tori stood on each side of him, their heads held high. Their retinue were scattered in the hall, chatting amiably amongst themselves, cups of wine in their hands. It all looked just like any other celebration except for one little thing: the expression of sheer fright on their faces.

It was a mockery that managed to surpass the wedding. Many of these people must've thought they were going to die the night before. Food stores had been running so low that some of the poorer districts had turned to eating rats; the cats and dogs were left for the royals. So the turning point of victory must've felt like ashes in the mouths of those who could see who delivered it. Nobody cares about the person behind the hand that reaches for a drowning man. It is only afterwards...afterwards...

Yuebek was standing in the warlord's spot. He looked bored, restless, a far cry from his usual jeering self. His eyes fell on me as soon as my arrival was announced, and never left the whole time I walked towards him.

"You," he said under his breath. He lifted one hand, snapping his fingers. Music began to play.

"Why are you angry?" I laughed as I beheld his sulking.

"The witch at our flank, the *dragon*..."

"We're at war, Yuebek. A war *you* helped start, if I'm not mistaken. No one told you to attack those priests."

"You see how my wife dredges up past mistakes?" Yuebek asked, glancing at the silent crowd. "But then, I shouldn't be surprised. Given *your* reputation, I should've known you would do something like this to me. After everything I've risked for you—all the things I was willing to overlook...!" Spittle gathered at the corners of his lips as he spoke, and his eyes were blazing.

"I don't understand, my lord," I said, trying to keep my voice steady. "Have I not proven my loyalty after all this time?"

"Proven? My lady, you've proven *nothing*. On our wedding night, I thought I finally had your heart at last—that my new wife was going to give me every-thing I ever wanted, everything I have been looking for my whole life. Instead, you betray me." He leered at me, holding his fingers up. "Three times. Three times, you betrayed me! Bring them in!" he roared.

The doors opened. Yuebek's guards strode in, dragging a child and a woman behind them. It was Anino and Chiha, both bound with thick ropes.

Chiha and I looked at each other in silence. Her head was held high, proud. With a painted face and in royal robes, she looked every bit the queen that I never could be.

"My men found this one hiding with one of your rice lords while they were looking for your son," Yuebek said. "A Jin-Sayeng royal, with some brat! The wrong brat, but I thought she looked familiar."

Yuebek walked up to her. Chiha turned to him, defiant. He stroked her chin. "It was definitely you," he said, a wistful look on his face. "My sweet, beautiful dream. I should've known it was too good to be true."

She spat at him.

His eyes blazed, but he smiled. "What I don't understand, my wife," he contin-ued, turning to me, "is why you would even dare such a trick. It's not as if you had any purity to preserve. Were you afraid you couldn't please me? Is that what it was?"

I gave a thin smile, refusing to answer.

Yuebek snorted. "Such wonderful women you have here. So much pride and strength. A pity they're such deceitful creatures. Deceitful as my mother." He clenched his fists. "You know what's coming, Beloved Queen. Should I kill the boy first? Or the mother? One will have to watch the other die. Both sound so delightful!"

"Mercy is—" I began.

"Please, Talyien," Chiha spoke up. "Look at the man. He relishes pain. I don't know about you, but I won't give him the satisfaction of begging for our lives."

"Smart," Yuebek said. "Maybe I'll keep you around."

She gave a thin smile. "Not a chance in hell after that night with you. I expected more from an Esteemed Prince. What a disappointment." She pulled out a knife she had hidden inside her robe. "Don't look, my love," she ordered.

Her son shut his eyes as she stabbed herself in the gut.

She didn't die immediately. Chiha lingered long enough for me to reach her side, to grab my hand with her blood-drenched one. She squeezed it with a strength that took me aback. Not an ounce of fear, or regret—I was the one shaking, not her. She pulled me close so she could whisper in my ear.

Only then did she lose her grip on life. Blood on the floor, on my robes, the smell spinning inside my senses along with her words. I laid her down gently. I couldn't even remember a time when I was the one who wanted her dead. Old memories, old wounds. I felt nothing but grief.

"Take the boy and lock him up," Yuebek said. "Bring the next prisoner."

His soldiers saluted. I turned and saw them dragging the bound figure of Dai Kaggawa through the doors just as they removed Anino and Chiha's body from our presence.

Yuebek strode past me to yank Dai to his feet. He looked into Dai's eyes for a moment before pushing him away. "Your second betrayal. You told me this man was a threat. Told me the whole nation would see this liberation as a sign of power, as something to be grateful for. Yet his army fell apart at the mere sight of mine. This worthless commoner could've never taken this city." Yuebek drew his sword.

"My lord—!"

Yuebek stopped, turning to me. "You're going to beg for *his* life?" he asked.

"Talking sense isn't begging," I said. "There's been enough death already, and this one won't do a damn thing. His army's gone. He's of no value dead. Even mopping the floor would be too much trouble."

Grana cleared her throat and whispered something to Huan. "Queen Talyien…" Huan broke in. I could see his face twitching, as if he was avoiding looking directly at Yuebek out of fear of being recognized as the dragon. "We would like to take custody of him. He's a traitor. A public execution in the future would do a world of good in stabilizing this region. Maybe the rice lords will think twice about crossing us again."

"Just kill me already," Dai finally said. "All this talk is loathsome."

"I'm claiming the prisoner for myself," I replied. "You've yet to send me a wedding gift anyway, Warlord Huan."

Huan smiled. "Well, we were going to send you that horse you liked from your time with us on the ridge…"

"I can take two presents." I walked over to where Dai was kneeling and placed a hand on his shoulder. "You consider him a traitor, but then, so was Warlord Ojika when he decided to take over this region. My father forgave him."

"If you're suggesting we simply let him go—"

"No. I want him locked up for the time being. I'll decide what to do with him later."

"Are you looking to make an example of me, *Beloved Queen*?" Dai asked. "You will win few friends in this region if you do. The Jin-Sayeng you know and the true Jin-Sayeng are not the same. Already they speak of your decision to marry this…thing…with disbelief. What are you doing, Talyien Orenar? Do you even know yourself?"

I turned away from him.

"I see," Dai said, rising to his feet. "I'm not even worth a conversation now that you're surrounded by your royal friends. And yet when you had no one—"

"You were there. I know," I replied, not looking at him. "And I thank you every day for that, Kaggawa, believe it or not. But we all know you did it for your own gain. I cannot be grateful when my son was nothing but a pawn to your own power play."

"You're a fool," Dai gasped. "All of you are fools."

"Take him away," I said. I glanced at Yuebek, daring him to contradict me.

Huan gestured at his soldiers, who returned to grab Dai by both shoulders. "The land will burn," Dai roared as they dragged him off.

As soon as the doors closed, Yuebek began to laugh.

I felt my arms tingle as he strode towards me. "Is there something you're not telling me, Queen Talyien?"

"I'm not sure what you mean," I said. "It's been a long day, my lord. Perhaps—"

Yuebek inclined his head towards the doors. "What that man was saying... I've picked up enough of your infernal language after studying your father's writing. *The land will burn*, he said. Tell me, why is that, my lovely?" He grabbed my chin, his fingers digging into my skin.

I turned my head. "He's a madman, lusting for power. Who's to say what he really means?"

"Perhaps my other guest might have more answers," Yuebek said, his eyes wide with merriment. The change in his mood was tangible. "He claims every single one of your treacheries boil down to one. He says that you need me to put an end not to this petty civil war, but to an instability in the *agan* fabric in the mountains. That I am the only mage powerful enough to carry such a spell. This marriage, your father's maneuvering, all of it—just because you knew no one with the necessary skill could be so foolish to risk their life."

I swallowed, my eyes burning.

"You were to lead me here," Yuebek continued. "Your soldiers were to quietly dispose of mine while we make a little trip to the mountains, just you and me and a handful of your men. Assassinations in the dark, probably this very night." He clapped and held out his hand.

A soldier rushed forward, carrying a bag that dripped blood to the floor.

"Murdering guests!" Yuebek continued. "To think a queen would stoop to such lows! But no matter. No matter, my dear. I've taken care of it, I've ironed out your treachery. Every single Oren-yaro soldier in the city has been put to death. It's too late for them now."

I barely heard him. I stared at the bag, nauseated.

"Oh," Yuebek continued, noticing my silence. "Are you afraid I've done something terrible like you thought I did the last time? Show her," he ordered the soldier.

The soldier bowed and upended the bag. A head casually rolled out, still wearing the wolf's helmet of the Tasho clan. I guessed it was General Mangkang.

"I mean, why would I let you miss this?" he sneered, clapping his hands.

The doors opened a third time, and Khine strode in like he owned the room.

I felt my heart leap to my throat, felt it tighten. The rope, now. There was no point resisting. I would dangle soon enough.

I thought I could be calm. Had tried to tell myself to accept the inevitable, that gnawing over that restlessness wasn't going to do anything. If he had betrayed me, what good would anger do? And here he was. Here he was, and I couldn't even make myself hate him. How could I? Rai abandoned me with our son for five years and I held on to that love until I choked on it.

I couldn't wrap my thoughts around what I was feeling with this one. *Raw* couldn't even begin to explain it. I felt beaten. Exhausted. Empty. What was it that Chiha had told me earlier?

"I have the easier job," she'd said. "You? Your silver plate is shit-stained. I may have hated you, Talyien Orenar, but believe me, I never envied you."

Khine took a deep breath. "I *am* sorry, for what it's worth." His voice was raspy. "But you should know better than to trust a thief and a con artist. I'm Shang Azi scum. I've told you often enough, Queen Talyien."

Less than you've told me other things. It hurt what the sound of his voice still did to me.

There was another figure behind him. Before I could take another breath, Khine pushed Thanh forward. Thanh shrugged away from him and scampered down the hall.

"Does this all sound right to you, my queen?" Yuebek continued as I grabbed my son. He laughed. "Does it sound right that you claim to love me, that you claim to need a *hero*...when all you really wanted was a mage! A mage, with Jinsein blood! I just happen to fit, and you vultures swooped in without a second thought. Isn't that right? You lied to me, my queen! Used me! I, who came to you from the goodness of my heart!"

The mimicry of my own feelings, coming from this man, made me feel ill. I held on to Thanh, my arms around him. I couldn't stop him from hearing everything, but if Yuebek decided to pull a sword on us, I was hoping I could block the blade with my body.

But Yuebek wasn't even looking at me. "And yet—" he snapped, turning around with a sweep of his arm. "I was a fool. You denounced the bastard too easily. Of course you did! I was looking at the wrong man! What love could you have given me when you've been seeking warmth elsewhere?"

My mouth felt dry. I gazed up at Khine, who gave a small smile. I was reading him now, trying to untangle the knots, as if I could find a different answer than what stood in front of me. As if I never learned.

"He wanted to know everything," Khine said. "So I told him."

"Everything," I repeated.

"Everything." He smiled. "Your new husband deserved to know, Beloved Queen. He deserved to know how you've used other men before, all to get something out of us. You used our love for you to bleed us dry. You let Agos take the fall for your disastrous marriage to Lord Rayyel and he paid dearly for it. You used me to save your son, even if it meant putting my head on the chopping block. Both of us, blinded by our desire . . . we let you have your way. I told him the truth—it isn't your fault and he shouldn't blame you so much for what you can't give. The Bitch Queen of Jin-Sayeng is simply . . . incapable of love."

Khine's words tore a hole through my heart. *You're lying*, I thought, looking at him. *You're lying again. You're such a good liar. I've never met anyone better.*

But then again, he could have been lying to *me*.

Yuebek began to laugh again before I could make up my mind. The whole show amused him to no end. "Is she hopeless, then?" he demanded. "Is the woman beyond redemption?"

"*Redemption* isn't the word you're looking for, my prince," Khine said, his eyes skipping past me now to gaze at Yuebek. It looked like they had an understanding—a quick, sneering joke between men, made at a woman's expense. The sort of joke that stripped us of our value, made us nothing more than lumps of meat appraised on a butcher's block. "You have her back against the wall. You have her son—she knows she can't resist you or worse will fall on the boy. Do with her what you will. You can still have everything you ever wanted."

The grin on Yuebek's face told me they'd had this talk before. I felt ill. *You're lying*, I repeated to myself. *How can you do this so well? You need to teach me someday.* I needed him back—the man who couldn't say such things, whose kindness could shine a light that would throw the shadows far to the walls. I needed him so much I could barely breathe.

"What was the price?" I asked. "What did he offer you in return?"

"Something irresistible," Yuebek answered for him.

Soldiers appeared from the side, this time with an old man in thick grey robes. A single jewel on a chain hung around his neck. "Tashi Reng Hzi," Khine greeted, bowing.

The man gave a thin smile. "You'd still use the honorific. What do you think that would do?"

"Nothing," Khine replied. "You know that's not what matters to me."

"Oh?" the old man said. "You didn't go through all of this just so I can restore your title? One word from me and the guild will let you retake that test. One word from me and they'll sign you *without* it. Isn't that what the prince offered you?"

"He did. He also mentioned one other thing," Khine said. "My child, Tashi Reng. He said my child survived."

I realized, at that moment, that this was real.

I thought I still knew Khine, despite everything. I knew what drove him—ideals, his own personal honour. But love, mostly love. His family, his friends, his patients. And I think he did love me—I still wanted to believe that—only that couldn't eclipse what had been there before. The shadow of his separation with Jia still haunted him. If the child he thought he'd lost was alive after all—if there was a chance of repairing what he once had—then I knew, without a shadow of a doubt, that it was over. Had I been in his place, I might've done the same thing.

Yuebek returned to hover over me and my son like some twisted, protective shadow. "I am a generous man," he said. "This peasant came clean to me, and so he will get his just reward. I *should* kill him for defiling you. I should have his innards draped over the courtyard for all to see! But I won't. I can do better than that. Denounce her, peasant!"

"She is nothing to me," Khine said, in a voice as cold as winter ice.

"What was that? I couldn't hear you."

"Queen Talyien is nothing to me," he repeated, turning to the crowd. "I made a mistake. I won't repeat it."

"You see?" Yuebek asked, grinning. "Look at this weak fool! These people know nothing, my dearest. Only someone like me can understand someone like you. Only *I* can ever truly love you, Talyien. The faster you accept that, the easier it will be for us. No—I won't make him into a martyr. I won't make you pine for his sorry hide. Instead, he will get his child, a position with the physicians' guild, riches beyond his wildest dreams—everything a man like him could ever want!—so that you will remember how *empty* his promises were every time you think of him." He nodded, and Khine walked off to follow Tashi Reng Hzi. He never looked at me again.

Yuebek placed his cold hands on my shoulders. "I can be generous to you, too," he said in a low voice. "You know this. I kept your pathetic Rayyel alive, didn't I? I listened to your every demand." His fingers tightened so hard his nails dug through the fabric of my robe, into my skin. "I was going to kill you tonight," he hissed. "I planned to murder you right here and burn the fields along the way back to my father's palace. I am not wanted there, either, but at least *I know*!" His eyes danced. "But he's right. Why waste this opportunity? Why let a wretched woman like you *ruin* my life? I came all this way, and now I have you at last. Not the way I would have wanted it—but I *have* you. To think—if you had only been truthful in the first place, none of this would have been necessary!" He turned to the crowd, still laughing. "I'll do it! She may hate me, my queen, but I'll save your damn nation, whatever it takes! It's mine now too, isn't it? Mine to save! Mine to destroy! All mine!"

And then, as if to prove his point, he kissed me with a mouth that tasted like death.

CHAPTER ELEVEN

THE RECKONING

In the whirlwind that followed, Nor's harsh words became my guiding light. *It is calmest in the eye of the storm.*

I waded through my emotions, boxing them in every possible corner. Anger. Hurt. Unease. Disgust. Each of these didn't serve me, so off they went.

But erasing yourself is easier said than done. We did not will ourselves into existence; we cannot will ourselves out. I made a mark on the world before I even drew my first breath. I understood there was no escape. I was right where I needed to be, the last piece left in this unbeatable game of *Hanza*. I needed to believe Khine's words: Queen Talyien is *nothing*. A name, a puppet, a simulacrum of a human being. Those with lives less shackled than my own can judge all they want. What do they know, they who have never walked in my shoes? Critics, spectators with wagging tongues. You scream at me for allowing my emotions to cloud my decisions, for not seeing two steps ahead at all times. Tell me—what would you have done in my place? I assume, whatever it is, that you believe it would be exemplary. That you could create peace and harmony with one or two words, or bring order and justice with one strike of your sword. The wisdom of the sages, from the mouths of those who know everything.

I assume you also think fairy tales are real.

This is all I know: I played my part. I was playing it still. I—coward, villain, murderer, bitch, whatever other cruel name you can unearth for me—had every reason to walk away, and I didn't.

After the feast, a messenger came, bearing news of the Ikessars' impending arrival. Princess Ryia had reconvened with Warlord Hhanda's forces and they were marching towards us, several thousand strong.

Yuebek laughed in response and called for horses, claiming he didn't want to delay the inevitable. "The sooner we get this done, the sooner I can get rid of these other pests," he said, his face twisted into a maniacal grin. Nobody argued. But dread filled me to the bones when Yuebek turned to the stable hand and exclaimed, "Bring a pony for the boy!"

"He's not coming with us," I said.

Yuebek nearly spat in his laughter. "If you think you're going to pull the wool over my eyes again, my queen, you're sorely mistaken. You and me and the boy—we're the only ones going up there."

"Esteemed Prince," Huan began, his lips curled in distaste as if we were back on that battlefield and he was convinced he could tear Yuebek apart with one bite. "There are dragons there."

"I know there are," Yuebek said, giving me a look.

"Then let me come, along with a few of my men. Your soldiers wouldn't be equipped to handle them, but mine have faced the creatures many times already. We know what we're doing."

Yuebek smiled. "You'd like that, wouldn't you, lordling?"

Huan's face darkened. "My lord, I—"

"You're her dog. That's as clear as day. You Jinsein scum really think I'm that much of a fool. And my own? Who knows if she's sunk her claws into *them* as well. We've been on the road this whole time. We all *know* my dear wife's reputation. She must've slept with every single one of them while my back was turned. No—we will go. Alone." His eyes turned to me. "The boy ensures your good behaviour. One wrong move and I will snap his little head clean off his body. Leave the dragons to me."

"It is dangerous up there," I said. "A man or two, perhaps—"

"We will not have guards," Yuebek spat. "You may have your sword. I'm being generous, *my queen.*"

I tightened my jaw and kept my silence as a servant appeared with my father's sword. She bowed, allowing me to take it and push the scabbard through my belt. "I need a knife, too," I said. "A grass-cutter blade. You can never be too sure."

Yuebek flashed an angry stare at the crowd.

Someone coughed. A grass-cutter was a peasant's sword, but somehow, eventually, one was procured.

"You test me," Yuebek said.

"You knew I would," I retorted.

He turned to his horse, just as I felt my son's hand in mine. "It'll be all right, Mother," Thanh whispered. "I'm not afraid."

You should be, I thought in anguish. I didn't say it. I touched his smooth face, wondering why he looked so much older than the last time I had seen him. It had only been a few weeks. My son was growing up too fast. After all the things the gods had done to me, they could've at least given my son a few years of joyful ignorance. They could've given him time.

I held back against the thoughts and kept silent as I allowed him to mount the proffered pony, awkwardly placing himself in the saddle—all bones and angles, a mirror image of his father in everything but looks. Subdued, I turned to my own horse. Huan was true to his word—it was the mare who had served me well on the ridge last time, the one Khine's brother had ridden back to Yu-yan in safety. Recognizing me, she butted my shoulder before turning to my pockets in the hopes of finding a treat. I whispered apologies to her ruddy nose.

We rode up the tower, past the bridge, and into the ridge. I kept as close as possible to my son, straining my ears for the sound of dragons. Huan assured me they would be busy this time of the year; it was mating season, which meant they were preoccupied with each other.

A mage met us at the end of the road, the last remaining of my father's.

"It's dangerous from here on out," Parrtha said. He looked none the worse for wear since Burbatan, though despite his brave words, you could see the fear dancing in his eyes.

"We all know *that*," I grumbled.

"We are hoping the Esteemed Prince will help us walk through undetected," he added. "A shield spell that only he can hold up..."

"Testing me already, are we?" Yuebek snorted. "You people are so pathetic it hurts. I won't humour you. Let the bastards come if they want." Without waiting to see what Parrtha had to say, he pushed his horse forward.

"You heard the man," I said, digging my heels into my mount.

Thanh smiled. "Mages everywhere," he observed. "It's like we're *not* in Jin-Sayeng."

"Hush your mouth," I grumbled.

He laughed. My son really wasn't the sort of child who took his mother seriously, and I felt myself latch on to that. I would've never laughed at my own father. *With* him, yes. At him? The very thought still shook me to my core. He would've taken it as an insult. What was the value in a child who didn't listen?

Of course, I never once agreed with that diatribe. My son had been free to question me since the day he was born. I watched him ride a little ahead, torn between telling him to stay with me and continuing to marvel how he could be so...carefree. I thought back to the day of his birth, to how the sight of him in my arms made everything I had just endured seem like butterfly kisses.

The living are built for pain.

We continued through the dry riverbank until we passed beyond familiar land, where we found ourselves fully entrenched in the wilderness, layers of mountains on every side. Behind the waning orange light, they looked like shadowed fortresses. Off in the distance, I heard a dragon call, but none appeared in sight. I didn't know if I was supposed to be relieved or not. A dragon unseen was still a dragon.

"You can see the dragon-tower from here," Parrtha said, a tremble in his voice.

I squinted. It looked like a needle at first, but it began to take shape as we drew closer—a small tower, three times taller than it was thick.

We dismounted at the base, tying the horses near some trees. I took Thanh by the hand, resisting the urge to talk about the architecture. I wanted to point out how it mimicked the dragon-towers in Sutan—the rings around every window, the stained glass, the dark stone. Yuebek watched us from a corner, eyes unblinking.

"This thing is ancient," I said, turning to the mage.

Parrtha nodded. "The dragon-tower marks the border where the damage to the *agan* fabric in the region begins," he said. "You can see it, too, if you try hard enough."

I glanced at the sky. There were faint purple streaks in the air, touched with grey, like scabs on a wound. The stars in the background looked distorted. Even if I knew nothing about the *agan*, I could tell something was very, very wrong.

"And it goes all the way to the north of the Kago region, you say?" I asked.

Parrtha frowned. "It is quite a span. You can see why ordinary mages have their work cut out for them. If Dageis cared to send their best, perhaps we wouldn't have this problem."

"They knew about it."

"When did such a powerful empire ever care for a nation as small as ours? Your father tried to make contact with the Dageian hegemony several times, always to no avail. He was dismissed right at the gate—there was absolutely no chance for his letters to reach the proper channels."

"Simply because we're from Jin-Sayeng?"

"What is Jin-Sayeng to the outside world but a nation of ignorant, squabbling monkeys?"

I turned to him, bristling.

He held up his hands. "I am simply saying what the rest of the world thinks."

"For someone who accepted Jinsein hospitality, you don't seem to find it very impressive."

"The land itself is impressive. The people, not so much. Your people are stubborn, Queen Talyien. They refuse progress. Your internal politics take precedence over more serious matters—you would rather bicker, and then indulge yourselves forgetting there was anything to bicker over in the first place. And so things like this happen." Parrtha glanced at Yuebek, who was stalking towards us now, hands at his side. "Esteemed Prince. Would you like to hear our plans now? I have the spell scroll with me, but first, we will guide you through the process of riding a dragon."

"I might as well," Yuebek said, glancing at me. "It's what my queen wants from me, isn't it? *All* she wants from me? I do so much for her, and yet still she looks at me with hate in her eyes."

I moved away in discomfort. Thanh, I noticed, was watching me carefully, hands on his lap.

"Is there anything I can do for you, Mother?" he asked.

I forced a smile. "What makes you think I need anything at all?"

"You look sad." He pressed his hands on my cheeks, looking into my eyes the way he used to when he was younger and he wanted to make sure I heard every word he said. "You shouldn't be. I told you. It'll be all right. Things will work out. You'll see." His voice, I noticed, was deepening. He wouldn't be a man for a few years yet, but he wasn't a little boy anymore.

"Thanh," I whispered. "What if I told you the world is bigger than what we see here?"

"I know it is," he said.

"There are airships and cities twice the size of Shirrokaru, with towers full of people—towers that aren't crumbling like ours. There are ships that can go through islands of ice and snow..."

"Icebergs, I think they're called."

"You've read about them in books."

He nodded solemnly.

"And they exist *outside* of those books, too."

He didn't understand how much saying that made me sad. How much it gnawed at me to think of the life he'd led, cloistered behind a castle, his every move watched and recorded by a nation that held no compassion for him. He didn't know. "Did you see an airship?" he asked, his eyes twinkling.

"I did, back in the Zarojo empire."

"That must've been amazing! Did you get to ride it, too?"

"No."

"It'll make me dizzy. It would probably make *you* dizzy. You complain when we ride on river-ships."

"No worse than riding a dragon."

His eyes looked like they would pop out of his head. "You rode a dragon? *You?*"

"I *am* Dragonlord, you know," I huffed.

"You are," he conceded. "You don't tell people that often enough."

"Is that what you think?"

He nodded. "In the books, all the Dragonlords just did what they wanted. You never do that. You never just tell people to... to leave you alone."

"Why do you think that is, Thanh?"

"It's because you care too much, I think."

"And do you think that makes me a weak ruler?"

He shook his head. "It's the others who need to learn that a ruler can't be everything. Our lives, the future, it's all... it's all of us responsible for it, isn't it, Mother? Not just the Dragonlord?"

"Perhaps. Who can say? We can only work with what we have, and people are blind."

"It isn't fair."

"The world doesn't work that way." I smoothed the hair from his face. "You may think we were dealt a bad hand, but it is far from the truth. There are people dead or dying behind us who have no idea why things are the way they are. Many are born into suffering, and accept it as a fact. Answers don't fill bellies, Thanh. Principles, theories, politics... don't really feed people, though we can pretend all day that they will. Rulers need to be able to balance both cares, and those of us with the power to do something at all... must do our part."

Thanh's expression told me he was trying to think through what I'd just said.

"But for what it's worth," I continued, "you are the best thing that ever happened to me. I love you, my dear. I love you so much."

He reached over for an embrace. I stared up at the sky as I held him, praying to the gods—all of them, deaf though they might be. Praying they hadn't given him to me as another cruel joke. Because for a woman like me—after everything that I was and everything I had done—to bear such a child seemed almost like a crime against nature.

I heard Yuebek give a cry and set Thanh aside to return to them. "A spell of that magnitude, and so far away—" Yuebek was saying, gesturing at the rip. "I suppose you expect me to sprout wings next."

"We do," I broke in.

His face twisted. "What the hell are you saying?"

"You want to be Dragonlord, don't you? Well—we are bequeathing to you the lost secret of the Jin-Sayeng dragonriders. We never tamed dragons, Prince Yuebek. Our souls *rode* their bodies. And the ability to do this effortlessly is stamped on the Jinsein royal bloodline. Did your Esteemed Father know this when he seized your mother as tribute years after Dragonlord Reshiro broke ties with the Empire?"

The words made his face turn red, and he dismissed me with a snarl. "Blood or no, I'll have it done," he snapped. "Show me the dragon."

Parrtha pointed to an outcrop of rocks near the tower. "The Yu-yan soldiers prepared everything before we arrived. The trap is set, Esteemed Prince. With any luck, it won't be long before—"

An air-splitting roar sounded in the distance.

"I guess we're doing this tonight," I said. I turned to Yuebek with a smile. "It's time to show the land your worth, dear husband."

I fingered the grass-cutter hidden inside my robe as Yuebek approached the large dragon, which stared back at him in trepidation. Two creatures, sizing each other up. I knew who was the bigger monster.

"There's a corrupted soul inside that thing," I said. "It doesn't like it if you try to get rid of it. It would rather kill its host." I wondered what Yuebek thought of my honesty, or if he was past caring now.

"I've spoken with Lord Eikaro, and he told me these things like the idea of *trading*," Parrtha broke in. "They were human once. They'd rather be human again. And so if the Esteemed Prince isn't opposed..."

"You want this creature to inhabit my body," Yuebek said.

"My lord, we think that with your power, it isn't a problem."

"Of course it won't be a problem," Yuebek snapped. "I'm not a child. Get started before I lose my patience."

"I'll have to chain you," Parrtha said. "It will keep the creature contained for when we switch you back."

Yuebek didn't seem to hear, or care, and held his hands out without hesitation. Parrtha strapped manacles around Yuebek's wrists, one for each. He looped the chains through them and began attaching them to the two nearest trees.

"Do you see what I'm doing for you, my queen?" he asked as Parrtha began to work on the runes. "Prove my worth, you say. Look at me when I'm talking to you. Look!"

He was laughing now, the moonlight shining over his form. Black hair streamed down his shoulders, contrasting against his pale skin. I wondered if he would even seem any different with the corrupted soul inside of his body. Yuebek's very being...was tainted enough as it was. I glanced at the dragon, similarly chained at the far end of the grove.

It was larger than Eikaro, covered from head to toe in black scales, touched with red. I recognized the dragon I had seen from the mirror before, the one overlooking this dragon-tower. The rocks around its feet glowed red, remnants of its struggle mere moments ago. Now it had run out of breath. It stared at us with yellow eyes, teeth gnashing. Only a curdle of flame was left on its lips.

"Do it!" Yuebek cried, all but embracing the dragon.

Parrtha drew on the *agan*, starting his spell. I felt the ground begin to shake. I pushed Thanh behind me just as the dragon's chains shattered into thousands of tiny pieces, like sparkling ashes. It filled the air with blue shards.

Yuebek's body howled, rattling the chains like a wild animal. In that same instant, the dragon lifted its wings, turned to Parrtha, and hopped after him, snapping at his legs. There was nothing human about its movement. Parrtha found his exit blocked by a boulder.

The dragon smashed right into the shield spell, sending blue sparks flying. Once, twice, and then again. The shield spell broke. The dragon grinned, grabbed Parrtha by the legs, and snapped both limbs clean off before he flung him to the sky. In one breath, I lost another mage, and the spell scroll necessary for Yuebek to close the rift in the first place.

But I didn't have time for grief or surprise. I crashed into the nearest bushes, Thanh's hand in mine, heading straight for the trees. I could hear the dragon stomping behind me.

"What's the matter, my queen? Do you not love my new form? Was this not what you wanted?"

His voice was like an echo in the wind. I could *hear* him, not simply get a glimpse of his thoughts in my head like with Eikaro. The horror on Thanh's face confirmed it. We reached the first row of trees, a dark wall against a darker night, just as he slammed behind us. The trees creaked, snapping. I barely missed a branch from taking my head off. "Keep running," I told Thanh. "Don't look back. Whatever you do, don't look back!"

CHAPTER TWELVE

THE CHRONICLES OF
THE BITCH QUEEN

ᴛᴜᴍ

M oonlight streamed between the trees.

The ground crumbled under our feet, untouched forest ground, sinking up to our ankles with every step. I could no longer hear the dragon behind us, which did nothing to set my heart at ease.

Thanh began to wheeze.

I slowed down, turning to him. "Are you all right?"

"Just…breathing…" he gasped.

I placed my hand on his back, rubbing it in a circular motion. The wind rushed through the branches above, shaking the leaves. Spring air, a touch of damp instead of frost. But cold, still—cold enough to worry me. I glanced at my son, who eventually straightened up, wiping his mouth with the back of his hand. "Why is it attacking us?" he asked.

I didn't answer.

"I thought they said he'd be fully in control. We need him to carry a spell, don't we? They said—"

"It's too late. The scroll is gone."

"But—"

"Please, Thanh. Please be quiet."

I glanced at our surroundings. A shroud of clouds drifted over what little of the sky I could see.

"Mother—"

I reached for his hand, not sure if I was trying to give him comfort or trying to find it for myself. How was I supposed to explain to Thanh that nothing was guaranteed? It was difficult to accept that my son's future was as uncertain as mine. I was here at the heels of my father's own guesswork. I couldn't give my own son more.

I breathed, trying to focus. I could still see between the gaps of the trees. *Do we go deeper into the forest, towards whatever other foul things lurk in that wilderness? Or do we risk going back to the field, leaving us open for another attack?*

I knew I couldn't fight a dragon of that size. Ozo meant for there to be an entire contingent of guards with me to take care of Yuebek once we were done. The entire affair was a shot in the dark already. If I was going to salvage it, I needed a better plan. And to come up with a better plan, we needed to survive.

I tightened my grip on my son's hand, feeling my own cold sweat on his skin. "We'll go deeper into the forest," I said, gazing at the foreboding darkness. My stomach curdled. It could be a decision that would lead to our deaths. Every step could be death—a ravine, a wild animal's den, even a stray rock that would make us slip and crack our skulls. But staying meant the same thing. What if the dragon caught up to us? What if it got colder?

We walked slowly. I could hear nothing beyond the pounding of my heart and our steady footsteps. Trying to calm myself while I could hear my son shuffling beside me was the worst feeling in the world. The number of things that could go wrong was limitless. I would die first before I would let any harm befall my son, but then what? How would he get himself out? The last time we were out here, only half of us returned alive, and we didn't even go this far into the wilderness. Back then, there were soldiers and enough weapons to take down a dragon or two. Now everything we carried from Yu-yan—tents, food, water—was left in the field with the horses. All I had was a sword and a rusty grass-cutter *and my son.*

As if he could read my thoughts, my son glanced up. "I'm hungry," he said. It wasn't a complaint, but the thin sound added to the burden.

I squeezed his hand. "We'll find something to eat soon."

"You mean...from the woods?"

"Why not? I've done it before."

"Like an *animal?*"

"Thanh, sometimes I can't tell if you're purposely trying to irritate me when you act like your father."

"I don't even know what that means."

I tapped his nose. "There, right there."

He paused for a moment, taking a deep breath. "Father has really left us, hasn't he?"

"Oh, Thanh, no. I was with him before I went to Yu-yan. Of course he couldn't be seen in the city. Prince Yuebek would've killed him."

"Because Prince Yuebek is your new husband."

"Thanh..."

He pulled away briefly. "I know why you married him, Mother, even if the rumours say otherwise."

"Don't listen to the rumours."

He shook his head. "It was Father's fault. Khine says I shouldn't blame him, but—"

To hear Khine's name on my son's lips, uttered with such affection, stung. "It's just you and me now, Thanh. We have to accept that."

You and I, we are enough.

The sudden memory of my father's words stilled me into silence. My worst fear was staring me in the face. I had turned into him. My choices, my decisions, led my son to that moment in time, and now we had no one else. We were alone.

I thought I caught a glimpse of a star peeking through the clouds.

Tali, I thought I heard my father say. *Do you understand now? Why you are my sword beyond the grave?*

Thanh fidgeted. "Khine says—"

"Forget Khine," I said.

I must've sounded harsher than I intended. He cringed.

"I'm sorry, Thanh. I'm just worried." I placed my hand on his shoulder to keep him close. Darkness settled in, covering us completely.

The wind whistled above us. At least, what I thought was the wind.

"Oh, Talyien..." The sound scraped at my skin.

I grabbed Thanh. "Cover your ears."

"But—"

"Don't argue with me, my love, please. Cover your ears *now*."

He lifted his hands, pressing them on each side of his face, slick with cold sweat.

"Talyien, why are you hiding, dear wife? Are you scared of me? But you shouldn't be! Remember what you told me that night? You promised...you promised..."

I couldn't tell where he was—if he was hovering above, or hidden in the clearing to the right. I knew the spaces between the trees were too narrow for his body to fit in, but he could try to stick his head in while we passed. His voice faded again, and I thought I heard the sound of wings beating the air.

"Is he gone?"

"Do you want a story, Thanh?"

"No."

"I'll tell you one, anyway."

"Mother—"

"Once upon a time, there was a boy who loved to read. And he loved to read so much that he found a job with a man who owned a lot of books. The man told him, 'Feel free to take any book from the shelves in here. Except that one, in the corner—you can read all the books here except that one...'"

I don't remember what version I told Thanh. Most likely my own, cobbled together from faded memories, with none of the flourishes my father loved to add. At home, I always read to Thanh straight from books, and we would embellish them together, sometimes making our own endings ourselves. This time, out here in these woods, he didn't try to interrupt me. He listened quietly, even when I stumbled over the words or repeated phrases I wasn't sure of.

By the time it was over, there were tears running down my face, and I was suddenly grateful for the blackness. I didn't want to have to explain why I was crying. I didn't think I could. How was I supposed to begin untangling what I felt about my father? I couldn't even explain it when I was young, when he was alive and right in front of me. Spinning between fierce love and hatred, until every fond memory came with the fear of having it all snatched away and you learned to be content with so, so very little. And now I was too old—the memories had been distorted with time. My father's treachery, strewn over the canvas of my own mistakes. I was at an impasse, at the edge of an abyss I wasn't sure I wanted to cross.

My son and I continued to walk in the dark. When we got too tired, I slumped down beside a tree and gathered him in my arms, where I listened to his breathing as he slept. I had done the same thing the night after the bandits attacked, and all those long, lonely nights after his father left. Keeping up a face, pretending nothing could harm us, scraping what little courage I had for his sake...was second nature.

Somehow, like all those other nights, we survived.

Daylight came with a shock of frosty air and fog, cresting above the treetops—orange on white with a hint of green. I got Thanh to suck dewdrops from moss before we began to walk again, briskly shaking ourselves in an effort to drive the cold away. Up ahead, the trees were beginning to thin, and we found ourselves at the edge of a lake, still half frozen. The hills around it were covered in a layer of snow.

"I think we've gone too far," Thanh breathed, the fog gathering around his mouth. "Are we lost, Mother?"

I glanced up at the sky. "We can't be. I think those mountains in the distance were the same ones from last night. I saw them from the clearing."

"We walked a long time."

"And we may have to walk even longer. Maybe we'll try to find something to eat here first."

"Khine told me that you can cut a hole in the ice, and if you hide just right, you can spear a fish as it pokes its nose out."

I sighed. "I don't have a spear."

"We can make one. There's some branches over there." He pointed at a pile of driftwood that had gathered along one side of the shore, barely peeking out of the snow. Tucking my hands into my sleeves, I glanced around before deciding to humour him.

It was quiet. Eerily so. I heard a bird calling in the distance, and recalled Huan's Captain of the Guard telling me that dragons made similar sounds, too. How active were they in the morning? Did it matter? The damn things were mad—who knew if they even followed the rhythms of nature anymore? I turned back to Thanh, who had found the perfect stick. It was his height, thick enough to lean on. He held it out for me. I unstrapped the dagger so I could begin whittling a point for it.

The ground rumbled.

"*There you are!*" The dragon appeared around the hill, slithering over the bank where we had emerged. Panicking, I realized there was no other way back into the forest.

"*The boy has your love. We'll take care of him first. We'll kill the boy first!*"

"Run, Thanh!" I screamed. I didn't even have to. He was already scrambling along the bank, trying not to slip with every step. I followed him, feeling the hot breath of the dragon at our heels as Yuebek lunged.

He missed, crashing into the trees near the driftwood. But he recovered fast.

"There's nowhere to go, Mother!" Thanh called.

I turned, realizing the sandy shore had given way to thick boulders, too tall to scramble over. We were trapped.

I reached him, grabbed his hand, and darted for the frozen lake.

The ice cracked with my first step. I managed to pull my boot back up and found a solid portion, one that held my weight better. "Over there, now," I told Thanh. "Follow the patches of snow."

"Mother—"

"I'll be right behind you."

There was terror on his face, but he nodded and plunged ahead. I watched him scrabbling forward, growing smaller in the distance. I wanted to hold him, to keep him nearby, but my weight and his together would be too much. The ice was too thin.

Behind me, the dragon roared and began to beat his wings.

I took two steps into the ice, struggling to keep upright.

The fog began to close in. I lost sight of Thanh.

"*Oh, Talyien,*" Yuebek crooned. "*Is this how you want to play it? You want me to hurt you slowly? I can do that. I can tear you limb from limb and leave you alive, leave you alive . . .*"

He began to hum, a sound that sent shivers up my spine.

I caught the shadow of a wingtip above me and managed to duck just in time as he dove for me. I felt the snap of teeth over my shoulder.

My other foot broke through the ice. There was no escape.

As he came for me a second time, I drew my sword and struck him across the nose.

He howled, crashing into the ice. Half of his body fell. He snapped again, grabbing my leg and lifting me up into the air. I thought I felt a tooth go through my calf and rip the ligaments down to my ankle. I felt my senses slip, as if all the blood had drained from my skull. I felt if he didn't let go, either I would pass out or my skeleton would jump through my eye sockets. I struggled to keep myself steady and stabbed him in the gums with the smaller grass-cutter.

He dropped me into the water.

After that first, icy shock, I managed to grab the frozen edge of the ice sheet.

My fingers were raw, sending sharp spasms up my arm like they'd been jabbed with nails. Shivering, I heaved myself over solid ground, grass-cutter in one hand, sword in the other. My leg was covered in rapidly freezing blood. It felt like glass shards. Everything felt like glass shards. I almost couldn't wait for the cold to blot out everything.

Yuebek struck me with his tail before I could recover.

I slid a foot along the ice and rolled to my right. I pressed my elbows into a patch of snow and forced myself to stand. The leg he had bitten was pouring blood, ripped skin quivering against the freezing wind—the sight of the mangled flesh alone made me nauseous. Better if I didn't think about it. Better if I focused on my breathing even though I couldn't tell how I still could. I was shivering and my weapons were becoming too slippery. But the dragon was having just as much difficulty. He was still half in the water, struggling to get out. Icicles hung from his wings, thick enough to weigh him down.

The next time he shot out of the water to strike at me, I tried to go for his eye. The sword slid past his brow, catching at his cheekbone. I slipped under the momentum. My father's sword was too heavy.

In the distance, I heard Thanh scream. I caught a glimpse of him through the fog. The dragon's weight shook the sheet of ice, cracking it from all across the lake. I could hear the crackling, followed by a *snap*, a singular sound in the dead air, so loud it felt like the whole world revolved around it. I waited for everything to sink.

Somehow, the ice remained floating. "Thanh!" I called.

Silence. I felt dread crawl up my spine. Had he gone through?

"Thanh!" My voice felt weak. I wanted it to be louder, loud enough to pierce the heavens with. Loud enough for the gods to hear.

The dragon charged once more, his fangs nicking the sword, which I could barely lift now in my exhaustion. My arm shook. My teeth chattered. This wasn't a battle I could win. I wasn't even sure it was a battle I could survive.

"Mother!" The shriek threatened to stop my heart. The fog had closed in again. I had no way of knowing if he was safe or not. My son could be dying. My son could be dead. What was the point if my son was dead?

I glanced down at my father's sword, at the hilt that was becoming sticky with my own blood. As another red streak crested down the aged wood, I realized it wasn't carved like a sea serpent after all. It was a bonytongue, with bulging eyes and a mouth that could fit all my father's lies. I didn't even know why I was still holding on to it. Without a second thought, I dropped it over the edge. As it slid into the murky depths of the icy water, I wrapped both hands around the grass-cutter and stabbed Yuebek's eye just as he lunged again. Behind me, I caught another break in the bank, and I thought if I could just reach it in time, perhaps...

He reared. The ice snapped, and we both plunged into the lake.

The water engulfed me. The sun looked like a pale disk behind the shimmering depths, so small I could wrap my fingers around the light. I felt a moment of peace and wanted to stare at it while I sank. But then my body resisted, my lungs screaming tight in my chest, begging for sustenance. I found myself swimming to the surface. Sunlight danced between my eyelashes as I took that first gulp of air.

I made it to the shore just as the dragon bore down on me.

"*My queen!*" he screamed, his eyes completely black. "*You promised I was yours! Don't you want to be mine again? Don't you? We can be together forever!*"

He grabbed my arm and threw me again, like a dog with a bone. He wasn't going to kill me without toying with me first. I could hardly see straight from the pain and cold combined, and didn't react as he clambered out on the bank, jaws open wide. His tongue pulsated.

The temptation to let it end there was strong. But the thought of my boy kept me hanging, and my body hadn't given up yet. I struck Yuebek across the neck, the rusty blade cutting through scales and into the flesh. The dragon roared as blood sprayed across my face. Everything turned black.

I opened my eyes to the crackling of fire.

Startled, I lunged upright. I felt a hand on my shoulder. "Easy, Queen Talyien," Namra said. "Easy. You're with friends."

I blinked. "Was it all a dream?"

"Unfortunately not," another voice said. Rayyel. He peered down at me, arms crossed. "The beast Yuebek is still out there. We barely got you out in time."

"Thanh," I managed, though my senses were still hazy. "Did you see Thanh? He was running ahead. He—"

"I'm here, Mother," I heard Thanh squeak. He was suddenly near my feet.

"Oh, gods," I breathed, pulling him to me. His robes were dirty and wet. He must've fallen through the ice several times, too—his elbows and cheeks were scratched. It was a wonder he was still whole.

"I ran," Thanh said. "Like you told me to." He squirmed a little, and I let him go. He glanced at Rai. "And then Father was there, and the priestess. I thought they were ghosts at first. I'm glad I didn't run the other way."

"You hear that, Rai?" I asked, coughing. "Your own son thinks you're a ghost. Tells you a lot, doesn't it?"

"I don't even know how you can joke at a time like this," Rai said with a frown.

"Making fun of you amuses me. And anyway, I can't feel my leg."

"It's ah...I did what I could," Namra broke in. Her hair was wet, which meant she must've been the one to wade into the lake after me. "But I'm not a healer."

"Could've fooled me last time."

"That was only with Lamang's help," Namra said. "I sealed the bleeding with fire. That's about all I can do."

"Is there anyone else here?" I asked.

"Just me and Prince Rayyel," Namra replied. "We left the night before you did. Sang Iga helped us sneak past the gates to the ridge. We brought assassins, but we separated right before the lake."

"Why did you bring assassins?"

"For Yuebek, you know. For after."

"I hate to break it to you, Namra, but there is no *after*," I said. "Yuebek killed Parrtha before he could even hand him the spell. Now he's a dragon, as deranged as the rest."

She gave a soft sigh. "I had that feeling when we saw the dragon raging in the sky. It's why we had to get here as fast as we could."

"What do you mean *here*?"

"We're at the last dragon-tower," Namra said, looking up.

I gazed at our surroundings. We were on the floor of a narrow chamber, one with a ceiling that seemed to go all the way to the sky. It didn't look much like a tower at all—more like a termite mound. The walls were smooth, as if they were made out of clay, fashioned from a potter's wheel.

She took a deep breath and continued speaking. "Your father wanted me to find this fourth dragon-tower. It's ancient, and I believe not connected to the one your father built in Yu-yan."

"What's so important about it?"

"I'm not sure myself," she said. "His letters indicated I should lead you here if the inevitable occurred. With this." She pressed a scroll into my hands. It was a copy of the spell Yuebek was supposed to cast. She'd made two. My father had ordered her to make two.

"I knew it." I shifted a little to the side, staring at the dancing shadows from the fire. "We need someone else up there. A second dragon."

Her face flickered. "He never explicitly mentioned that. Perhaps he simply means that you have to find a way to bypass the man's madness."

"What other way is there to bypass a madman?" I asked. "That's my father for you, Namra. He never tells you more than what you need to know." I took a deep breath. "When my father met Yuebek, he had been hoping the prince would do these things for us willingly in exchange for becoming Dragonlord, and my king. But what he saw... troubled him. He was afraid Yuebek, for all his body's strength and power, possessed too frail of a mind. So in his panic, he left me one last letter, one that seemed to go against the grain of his grand plans. He told me it frightened him that he was at the end of his life and *Yuebek* was all we had. He said nothing else—he merely implored me to remember my duties, as if I needed the reminder. I thought he was begging. But my father detested begging. Now that we're here, I understand."

"My queen..." she started, still confused.

I turned to meet her eyes. "My father loved puzzles, and he thought himself so conniving, so intelligent, that no one could possibly follow his schemes. None, perhaps, but me. He left no final instructions because he knew I wouldn't need them. I'm not that smart, Namra—I just know him very well. A second dragon has to go up there, and only someone with royal blood can do it. And that rift is very strong. Outside of Yuebek, I'm sure it will kill everyone else. Whoever we choose... won't be coming back."

There were a few moments of blessed silence. I gazed at the ceiling, at the mossy fissures of the old stone and the cracks on the surface. Eventually, I said, "Is there a safe place you can take Thanh to, Namra? Rai and I need to speak."

"We're deep in the forest," Namra replied. "No dragon can land outside. Come and help me find sticks for the fire, Thanh."

He got up without arguing and followed her, disappearing through a door on the far side of the chamber.

Rai sighed. "Your dragon… Warlord Huan's brother… he might be the best candidate. Skill in the *agan* is connected to the soul, not the body. You said he was a mage? Or very nearly one? He might be able to conjure a shield to protect himself during the process."

"Or he might not, and die anyway," I said. "He's untrained, not like Namra, and that dragon's body is too injured from the battle at Yu-yan. In any case, I will not ask that from him. He has a daughter. They just got him back. This is our problem to solve. We're supposed to be the Dragonlords."

He looked startled. "We."

"Don't make me repeat myself."

"But all these years, you've never—"

"I know," I said. "I've had a change of heart. Truth be told, I think you would've made a fine ruler, if only you… you know, stayed."

He flushed.

"As it is, it's not like I've set a high bar myself," I grunted.

"You signed a policy on river waste that I thought was commendable."

"Arro did that."

"And the fishing schedule—"

"Arro."

"How about—"

"Pay attention, Rai. Arro did everything for me." I closed my eyes and sighed. "Gods, if only he was here."

"I'll do it," Rai managed, after a brief silence. "Your father would have planned that out from the beginning. For *me* to make this sacrifice."

"Maybe. Perhaps he was hoping I would follow his footsteps and be just as deceitful as he was. That I would keep you around, just so I could fool *you*, too." I took a deep breath. "But I don't think so."

"Don't try to humour me."

"I'm not. If things went exactly as he wanted them, you'd be dead by now."

His face flickered. "I see."

"That's why he wrote that letter. I know him. I know what it sounds like when he is asking me to do something important to him. He doesn't need to remind me of my duties, but he knew how to twist his words to make me obey."

"You don't need to obey him anymore. You're too injured."

"That's exactly why it has to be me. Between the two of us, you're the one better equipped to get Thanh out of here. I'd just slow us down, and I'll bleed enough to send every dragon from here to Gaspar into a feeding frenzy."

Rai chewed over this, his jaw hard. Logic. It was ever his forte.

"Talyien," he finally said. "I understand what you're saying. But I feel as if it would be cowardly of me to agree to it."

"Cowardly?" I asked. "When was that ever a problem for an Ikessar?"

"Dishonourable, then. Unbecoming of a prince, of someone who was supposed to have ruled beside you." He swallowed. "Unfair. You alone cannot carry the burden of this land."

"You're starting to understand." I beckoned to him, pulling the blanket away to show him my leg. He cringed at the sight of the mangled flesh. "How far do you think I can walk on that? We barely escaped back there, and my body was whole, then. And anyway..." I stared at the fire, listening to it crackle, wondering if it was normal not to really feel the heat emanating from it. Everything felt so cold. "Anyway, I think I'm dying already."

"You're not," he said, incredulously.

"I've lost a lot of blood. Namra's procedure didn't work very well." I placed my hand on the dirt, lifting up a handful. It was wet, a slurry of black and red. Even such a simple movement made me dizzy.

"If I ride back and find Lamang, he'll know what to do," Rai stammered. "He's saved me once. He'll save you."

I smiled. "Remember, Rai. He sold us to Yuebek. He'll be long gone."

"If I ride fast—"

"Rai," I said. "What are you doing?"

His nostrils flared. "I can't just let you... die. I can't. How am I supposed to listen to you talk like this?"

"And you call me emotional?"

"This is different!" he snapped. "You have a son. He needs his mother. He—"

I placed my hand on his wrist.

"You ask me for the most ridiculous things, do you know?" He ran his hands through his hair.

"Thanh will be fine. He's old enough. He's smart, he's brave, and he's been loved all his life. Some of us have done all right with less. He survived you being away all these years, didn't he? Survived you wanting him dead, even."

"That's nowhere near—"

"And now you're here for him. My dear," I whispered, "he has everything he needs."

He shook his head, trembling. "Tali—please. What do I know about raising children? He doesn't even know me."

"That's not really my fault, now," I chided lightly.

"This is not the time for jokes."

"He's angry with you. But anger can go away. I've proven that much. Rai…" I touched his face. "We can still salvage the one good thing that came from all of this. Maybe there is no escape. Maybe the land will burn anyway. Promise me one thing: No matter what happens, Thanh *lives*."

I dropped my hand to hold his. He looked down, his face twisted in a way I had never seen it before. His eyes were wet. I felt slightly vindicated. He wasn't a stone wall after all.

"I'm just sorry Chiha went ahead," I said. "You could have married her."

"By the gods, Tali, this isn't the time."

"I'm joking."

"You're dying. You shouldn't be."

"You're just saying that because you don't want us catching up. I regret not getting the chance to do it in life." My lips twitched as I laced my blood-soaked fingers through his own, clean ones. "You should do right by Anino, at least. The boy has been through enough already. What I'm trying to say is that it's all in the past. I've forgiven you, Rai. Maybe you need me to spell it out first." I took a deep, ragged breath. "It's funny, isn't it? How the things we used to hold on to fervently could one day be swept away, just like that. It was nothing, after all. There are more important things. This—here now, what's about to happen—it'll pass, too. Even the worst pain is only temporary. I've learned that much."

"Stubborn fool," he grumbled.

"Like you?" I gave a soft smile. "My father wanted this. He wanted it to be me from the very beginning, to ensure he won't be a footnote in history. To ensure he would remake it instead. His legacy is Jin-Sayeng's salvation. In the end, we all lose, and Yeshin…Yeshin wins, after all." I swallowed, thinking of the sword in the bottom of that lake.

"You are the bravest woman I know."

"High praise, coming from you." I shook my head. "But no. I'm not. If I was brave…there are a thousand things I would have done differently if I wasn't so afraid. I'm just...very tired of running. There's only a little bit of fight left in me, Rai, and I don't even know if it's enough. But it's all we've got. Let's not waste it."

He took my hand, heedless of the blood, and pressed it against his lips.

I closed my eyes.

———————

Namra went to find a dragon to trap while I tried to keep the worst of the exhaustion, the pain, away. Through the haze, I saw Thanh settle beside his father, who had been staring at the wall in silence. I didn't hear what he said at first, but Rai's face flickered. Carefully, he lifted his hand and placed it on Thanh's cheek. Thanh hesitated before turning to wrap his arms around Rai's neck.

"We are still family, Father," my boy whispered. Damning words in so many cases. Redemption, in others. Seeing them together after all these years put me at ease. It was as if a great weight had been lifted off my shoulders.

Later, Rai tried to feed me a broth made of dried mushrooms and meat. I dribbled soup everywhere and swallowing hurt, so I stopped after a few spoonfuls. I told him about Sayu then, and the journals I left with her, as well as the ones I kept locked in the hidden throne room in Oka Shto. Our lives, penned forever in ink. I warned Rai they wouldn't be very flattering; he didn't seem to mind. He even pulled out a blank parchment from his pack, which I suppose shouldn't have surprised me. I was too weak to do anything but narrate the ending—from after the battle of Yu-yan to these last few hours in the wilderness. For the next few days, I drifted between talk and sleep, my mind floating between memories. Rai wrote in silence.

We don't always get to choose, but we can do so much with so little.

Sayu told me I needed to write all of this down to tell the land the truth. What did I want them to know, they who will distort my name in time: the Butcher's Daughter, the Foreigner's Whore, Bitch Queen? Perhaps not much more than that I was human. I hold the power to lie and paint myself a hero, like others before me, but I would rather not. Life is oddly simple, for all that we try to take more than we deserve, and even a queen cannot change the rules. That I made it this far, all things considered, might hold meaning for another one day.

Or maybe it won't. Likely this will all be lost—as impermanent as the hand that penned the ink, even if we want to believe something in this world has to outlast us. But I didn't write this to justify my actions. There is only so much our minds can grasp. We must step forward or we sink like rocks. Pretending our struggles amount to something brings its share of comfort. All stories begin somewhere. All stories end. And Tali, you've reached the end. May what's left absolve the sins that brought you this far. Be content—even as you are, you are luckier than most.

So I spend my last energy on these words, and I look at the man I spent so many years loving and hating with the same breath. I call my son, and hold him tight enough so he would forever remember that I didn't really want to let go. Namra arrives to tell us the dragon is here and that it is time. It is time.

What lies beyond is no longer my story to tell.

INTERLUDE

THE SEND AND THE TOUCH

ᴣᛏ〇ᵞ

Namra arrives to tell us the dragon is here.

I push myself up, my legs shaking, while Rai offers his arm so I can lean on him. Blood pools under my feet with every step, and I wonder if I have any left to spare. At the door, I turn around to look at Thanh one last time. "Stay here," I say. "Stay where it's safe." There are other things I want to tell him, but this will have to suffice.

"Yes, Mother." He stands tall as he speaks, looking me in the eye. I have never told him he looks like my father. The ears, the lips, even the shape of his eyes, if not the colour. He probably doesn't need to know. The sooner this is all over, the better for him. I do allow myself a moment to wonder what sort of man he will grow up to be. A good one, I tell myself. I can at least believe such a thing is still possible in this world.

We walk around the base of the tower, which is half covered in mossy rocks. If the tower where Yuebek's switch happened is old, this one is even older—the architecture is ancient, the sort I must've seen in the older cities. I can't really remember. It is hard to remember much when your senses have thickened to a point where you feel like you're swimming in black water. Like the other tower, this one is pointed at the top like a needle. The platform where dragons land is absent.

I'm not sure why we even call it a dragon-tower. An affectation, living here. Our lives used to revolve around dragons. And now the land's continued existence suddenly depends on them again. It is apt, in a way, the sort of thing you can write poetry about. I guess it is too late for me to learn.

We are, I notice, at the bottom of a canyon, as Namra must've mentioned earlier. Or was it yesterday? Three days ago? Everything is a haze. I hear a rumble, halfway between a roar and a chirp.

Namra has trapped the dragon further down the canyon, in a narrow crevice on which she has managed to cause a landslide of rocks. It is the pale female dragon, the mate of the male Yuebek is riding. She looks disoriented, and her leg is slightly bent from injury. It amuses me that mine looks worse.

"This one isn't mad," I say.

Namra nods. "They're not all mad. It is rare to find one like this."

"Yet its mate was. The one Yuebek has."

"It makes it easier for us, I suppose. I wasn't looking forward to seeing one of those things inside your body."

"This is wrong. What we're about to do is wrong."

"It is not too late to turn back," Rai breaks in.

I admonish him with a shake of my head. "This must be done. But it doesn't mean I need to be heartless about it." I reach out to touch the dragon's nose. It croons, blinking at me. Has it seen people before? It is strange to see a dragon so unaggressive. But then again, we used to live beside these things. Surely not all were vicious.

"She's beautiful," Namra says. "How she's survived all these years around the others who are more or less...monsters...is a marvel."

Another apt metaphor. "A sign of hope, at least," I say. I pause for a moment, bracing myself at a spark of blackness in my vision. And then I touch the dragon again, scratching her cheek. "Lend me your strength, my friend."

"Are you ready, my queen?" Namra asks as she finishes strapping the scroll to the dragon's leg.

I close my eyes and take a deep breath. "I'm ready."

"Remember: The scroll needs to touch the tower when Yuebek is near," Namra says. "It will activate with his presence and use him as a source of power as it closes the rift."

I nod. Every movement feels like my last. I want it to end.

"My queen," Rai says. "It's been an honour."

"Don't cry, Rai," I tell him. "It doesn't suit you."

Namra begins her spell. The dragon and I stare into each other's eyes. The pain finally drifts away.

The dragon doesn't want to leave. She lets me stay. The others walk with two souls inside of them; why not her?

I start to ask her what happens to my body if there is no soul inside of it. Won't it die? *But it's dying already.* Another moment, and suddenly I do not care. Namra is breaking the rock that has our wing trapped with a spell, her face sweating from the effort. She is tired. We are all tired.

The dragon tells me she wants to be with her mate.

The rock breaks. It is all we need. We roar and take to the sky.

She tells me, as we drift above the clouds, that her mate will not come to her. It has a new friend, one that refuses to listen to him as the other has. A corrupt soul, even more corrupted than before, blackness seeping from within.

An irony. That the other thing trapped inside Yuebek's body is more harmless than his own, true self.

Her mate, she tells me, is still inside. She knows it.

We spin around the hill. Our leg hurts, but not as much as mine did earlier when...when...

I do not recall anymore. Why did I think I had another injury? I throw a lick of flame on an oncoming breeze, watching with satisfaction as it curls around our mouth. The fire feels good along our throat and inside our lungs. Even the smoke that climbs out of our nostrils is comforting, like a warm blanket on a cold night. I still remember blankets. The dragon does not, but the image makes her smile.

We see another shape in the distance.

Danger, she tells me. It is not her mate. But I recognize the shape of the other dragon. I tell her it is a friend. She doesn't believe me. We fly towards him anyway, wings beating against the air.

"*Beloved Queen,*" Eikaro calls, his eyes wide open. "*What have you done?*"

"*What must be done,*" I tell him back, relishing at how effortless it seems to talk without really talking. Do we remember a time when it feels so difficult to get words out? She wonders if being human is really as complicated as I make it sound. Yes, I tell her. Yes. But it shouldn't be. We should have done this a long time ago.

"*I saw him flying above the eastern wind,*" Eikaro says. "*I was following him. I don't know what went wrong. Wasn't he supposed to cast a spell? Why is he trying to kill you all?"*

I feed him everything from the last few hours. Eikaro, I think, is more human than we are. There is no dragon soul within him. He swears.

"I have the spell with me," I explain, showing our leg. *"I just need to lead him to the right spot. Namra told me where."*

"A boundary, cast between those two dragon-towers?"

"You've been paying attention to your tutors. Well done, my lord!"

We hear a call from the distance and see a dark shadow drifting between the mountain peaks below us.

"He is looking for you," Eikaro says.

"Then I suppose I should go to him, shouldn't I?"

"My queen..."

We forge ahead. I can feel my dragon's excitement at the sight of her mate. Steady, I tell her. Steady. But she worries for him, and I cannot fault her for that. We think of love as this thing we need to do without, as if the ability to live without it is strength, something to aspire to. To not need anyone, to not care for others, to have a heart like an empty vessel filled with nothing except one's faith in one's self... seems like the loneliest thing in the world. I find nothing admirable about it.

The black-and-red dragon spots us before we reach the mountain. It lunges, faster and bigger, frightening my dragon. She calls for her mate, reaching for him. The *other* thing inside him, she tells me, the one before Yuebek, lets him take over sometimes.

Now it is as if he has disappeared. She can sense him, but it is all Yuebek on the surface. All madness. All—

"You relentless bitch!" Yuebek calls, realizing what I am.

I don't answer. I have no desire to trade words with him anymore. We stop mid-air, turn our wings. Our tail whips the air.

Yuebek's teeth snap towards us, missing our shoulder by a whisker. We kick away, spinning towards the dragon-towers in the distance. They don't seem that far apart. Do I remember spending a whole night running from one to the other? My son was with me, I think. My son. I cannot remember what he looks like. I only remember that I love him.

My dragon tells me her sons are all grown, and her daughters, too. The last clutch flew off months ago. She was hoping to have more, soon. There are some growing in her belly.

I tell her how sorry I am.

We are close to the first tower when Yuebek smashes into us. We struggle to keep ourselves in the air, wings flapping, teeth snapping back. I realize he has torn the scroll off our leg. How was it even supposed to work? I know the...the woman...priestess, I think...I don't remember her name. But I know she told me how. I don't remember.

It is now floating to the ground. We cannot chase after it. We are busy trying to shove the black-and-red dragon away from our neck.

The black dragon appears, snatching the scroll with his teeth as he flies beneath us.

"*Queen Talyien,*" he calls.

Who?

"*Queen Talyien!*"

My dragon thinks he means me. I don't understand her. How could I be a queen? I'm a dragon. Titles are a human thing, and so are names. Dragons have no need to hide behind empty words and masks and charades. We are as we are.

The black dragon sweeps past us again, trying to draw the black-and-red dragon's attention towards him. But the black-and-red dragon ignores him, as if he is nothing more than an irritating gnat. We manage to sink our teeth into the black-and-red dragon's leg and he throws us towards the tower with more strength than we anticipated. Our wings flap helplessly as we try to regain control of ourselves.

We smash into the tower. A slight shock courses through our body. My dragon tells me, once more, that she cannot reach her mate. She thinks something terrible has happened to him. She is grieving.

We push against the tower walls just as the black-and-red dragon draws close. We make for the forest.

The black dragon appears next to us. "*You need to touch the scroll to the top of the tower while he's close,*" he tells us.

"*What do you mean?*"

"*Namra should have told you. Don't you remember?*"

I don't. I am only filled with concern over my dragon's mate. Over our mate. What happened to him? He left, even after he promised he wouldn't. But he loved us. I know he did. He had to leave. It wasn't his fault.

My dragon tells me I am confused. Her mate never left her. He was taken from her. I must be thinking about my own.

But…

The black dragon thrusts the scroll into our mouth. We take it, unwillingly. My dragon tells me it must be important, even if we don't understand anymore. *"Take it to the tower,"* the black dragon repeats. *"I'd do it myself if I can get him to follow me, but…"*

The black-and-red dragon reaches us and grabs the black dragon by the wing, tearing through the membrane.

We shriek, attacking the black-and-red dragon's face. The black dragon manages to break free and falls backwards. We watch him crash to the ground, rolling along the bushes.

"The tower, Queen Talyien!" the black dragon calls.

Although we do not know who Queen Talyien is anymore, we fly towards the tower with the scroll in our mouth and the black-and-red dragon right behind us.

We drape the scroll on the tower.

Lightning flashes across the sky.

The black-and-red dragon's body is glowing as it reaches us. We fly away into a swirl of blue and purple light.

My dragon calls for her mate in vain.

The glow on the black-and-red dragon's body is becoming stronger.

I don't know how long we fly. We feel weightless when the black-and-red dragon eventually catches up to us. There is nothing around us but grey clouds and blue sky. Our teeth latch onto his neck as his bite down into ours.

My dragon finally touches her mate's mind. It is over, he tells us. He has completely lost control. My dragon doesn't mind so much. She is with him at last.

Yuebek doesn't agree. His fury engulfs us as our bodies entwine. We plunge down, down into clouds, and then into the sea.

You gaze at me with that faint smile on your lips, the one you think people don't see, as if you are perpetually amused by everything.

I shouldn't be surprised. Your father warned me about you. He told me I would have my hands full. A challenge, he called it. Wasn't I up for it? Wasn't it tiring playing games in Zorheng? Sculpting such a foul, horrible city to my heart's desires, mages at my disposal, servants at my beck and call. A man of my talents could do better, go further. Why waste my time pandering to peasants? They can't even keep their stink down... they ruin everything, always whining, pretending they know what they're talking about when they don't. Pretending like their opinions matter. Like *they* matter. But then you throw coin their way, promises, lies, and they're running like dogs after a scrap of meat.

I would respect them more if they had a lick of integrity.

That Ong, scraping his head on the ground if I so much as scream at him, at least stands firm in his beliefs. At least tries! Still a coward, but at least he knows.

The rest of them don't even realize the hypocrisy. The bastards do as they please and then blame you when it doesn't suit them. Ask for their understanding, and they can't see beyond their own stinking feet. *I wouldn't do that! Why would you? How could you?* Ask for an iota of contribution, and they spit at your face. Ask them for patience, and they throw rocks at you.

So of course I did what I wanted, too. Why not? Do I look like a martyr? I'm just joining the pantomime.

And then they called me a tyrant for it. For using them! But I didn't run around threatening everyone with my sword. I was generous. I was kind. I gave them what they wanted.

That's why Zorheng grew the way it did.

Of course, no one saw it that way. They called it a disgusting, wretched thing. I agree. I completely agree! I would burn the squalor down to the ground if I could. But it was all I had to work with. My Esteemed Father shoved me into that stinking hovel, expecting me to turn it into a paradise. Wanted me to turn fistfuls of shit into gold. Make Zorheng into a city to be proud of, he said, and then maybe the court will see your talents. Maybe the court will understand you. Maybe the court will be less afraid!

Me! Why would they be afraid of *me*?

Because I could see things they couldn't?

Because of my mother?

Why should *that* frighten them? Isn't my muddied blood the very reason they wanted my father to send me away? The reason I could never be emperor?

No, it's not just the peasants. They're all despicable. You would think those who know better would act better. But they don't. They hem and haw over the most useless things, drag themselves down into these ridiculous arguments instead of trying to work together. I hated them all, too. Why not? They hated me.

Maybe I treated them like ants. If they had the power I did, they'd do the same thing! Except for one thing. One little thing. *I always gave them a chance.*

Did they see it that way? Of course not, the impudent fools! They see my Esteemed Father throwing blessings my way, and they protest. *Why him and not us? What is he but a freak? A freak who worked hard to gain his father's trust and attention, but a freak nonetheless?*

They think everything was handed to me on a silver plate. As if they didn't know my father. As if he showered his sons with gifts for the sake of it, instead of demanding they live up to the name. His eldest is a drunkard and a dimwit—born first, but do they not understand he isn't crown prince for a reason? The second, a lustful buffoon who thinks of nothing beyond where to stick his cock into, boys and women alike. And their empress hag of a mother thinks my Esteemed Father favoured me for nothing? I was the perfect son! I excelled at my lessons, I took his advice, I obeyed even when I didn't want to. What did *her* sons ever do that wasn't about satisfying themselves? She thinks it was my mother's seduction that did it, that she had manipulated my father's preferences, not even realizing that my own elder brother was a rat that no one will ever speak of again... not unless I let them. Fifth Son? You would think I was the only son! But of course, I couldn't be emperor anyway, so why would they care?

Rats, all of them. Blind, wretched rats.

And *you*, I thought you would understand. Your father all but convinced me you would!

He told me about you, about your sham betrothal, and a prince that had yet to grace your presence. Told me they were terrified of you, a mere girl, because of who you are, what you are, what you represent. It's a glorious thing, isn't it? To be born on such a pedestal? To not have a say over how people see you and treat you, and when you lash out it's still your fault, still your responsibility, what sort of monster are you for not taking their abuse with open arms?

You see? You know exactly what I mean! All you ever wanted was a chance, all you ever wanted was to love *them*. And what you did in all those years after everything they did to you—wasn't that enough to see they weren't worthy? You should've learned. Beating your heart against those walls wouldn't have done a thing. Why should it? The world is deaf and cruel. It always will be! We could've done it, we could've looked down on them in disdain together. We could've ascended as gods, spitting down on those worthless mortals who can't cobble two thoughts together. Our legacies could've surpassed our fathers'. They would've been so proud! Think of the honour I would've brought the Esteemed Emperor. Think of the honour you could've given yours. Forget Yeshin the Butcher—they would think him enlightened, a genius, a figure for your descendants to worship for all of time. Didn't you want that? To clear your father's name once and for all?

Instead, you joined them!

You hated me. And the more I showed you my generosity, the more you despised me. Your lies, your deceit, I allowed them because I thought you would finally accept me.

And what you're doing now...

You think they'll know? You think they'll care?

You think this sacrifice will mean *anything*?

I wanted to believe it was you that night! Silky hair draped over my chest, soft skin by the moonlight, warm lips... it had to be a trick. I could've killed her then, and you for the insolence. But I let it happen. I wanted to believe the lie. Don't we all?

But come, wife. At least in death, we can be together at last!

Lake Enji swirls, surrounding the gigantic bodies in salt water, swallowing them whole.

ACT FOUR

THE BLOW-OFF

CHAPTER ONE

THE YU-YAN RUSE

ʋɜ̂ɾɪ̈ɾ

The first deaths happened innocuously enough, or so he was told. Barred inns and brothels, knives plunged into sleeping bodies. Bloody, but quick. It wouldn't have been possible without the city folk's cooperation.

Still, Khine was glad he hadn't been around for that first wave. He had participated in his own share of killing while breaking into the city walls, and it took all of his energy not to spend half an hour vomiting into the gutters afterwards. And he'd *killed* before. How did Tali do this so easily? Learning how to fight and learning how to deal with the aftermath were completely different things, and he was ill-prepared for exactly how much. Perhaps she could tell him someday.

If she forgives you.

He tried not to mull over that. He knew it would break him, thinking about things he couldn't control. And the last thing he needed right now was to break.

"Lamang!" a voice barked from the end of the street.

Khine darted towards the sound. Huan Anyu pulled off his helmet, sweat running down the sides of his face. "They're concentrated in the western district," Huan said. "Bastards aren't going down without a fight. And they can fight all right—takes two or three of my bloody soldiers to stick one."

"How many left?"

"Let's just say there's plenty left to concern me." He chuckled nervously. "My wife wants to know if you've got more mercenaries under your skirt. I think she's convinced if she shakes me hard enough, more will fall out of my ears."

"Those were all I was able to woo from Kaggawa," Khine said, frowning. "How many Zarojo soldiers did you catch unaware?"

"Three hundred at most. Maybe less. Hard to do a head count when you're trying to keep yours. You heard anything from General Nor?"

"She's got her hands full, last I heard, but at least the remaining Oren-yaro seem to be following her."

Huan swore. "Hands full. And here I was hoping for relief. The Oren-yaro are trained soldiers."

"Aren't yours?"

"Unless we're fighting dragons, I'm not ashamed to say they're better than mine."

"They're not invincible. Nor's trying to whittle Yuebek's soldiers down one by one. Pulled out a division to assist one of the other camps, hoping for a faster victory. The others retreated with soldiers at their heels to buy the rest of them some time." Khine saw Huan's brow furrow, and sighed. "Look, find me some stones maybe so I can show you—"

"I'm starting to hate the words *war* and *battles* and *strategies*," Huan said. "You've a better head for it than I do, Lamang. I'll take your word for it."

He laughed. "It's one thing to talk about it on paper. I still have to get used to the rest."

"*Have* to?" Huan asked.

"Well…this is her life, isn't it?"

"And she hates it even more than I do," Huan said. "You ought to know."

Khine didn't need to be reminded of that. Chewing his lip, he glanced at the mountains in the distance, wondering why it all seemed eerily quiet past the chaos of the streets. What her father wanted was a shot in the dark, and it wasn't even a flaming arrow at that. *Please*, he started to think, before stopping himself. Would prayers even help? He was almost sure he'd stopped believing in gods since his mother's death. He'd stopped believing in hope, at least. Finally, after all these years…

A horn blasted from the city walls.

Huan swore again. "My soldiers are worn out. With our luck, this'll be the shortest-lived rebellion in history."

"Give me an hour," Khine said.

"I don't know if I have an hour," Huan replied. "But go, with the gods' blessings."

He flashed him a grin before heading deeper into the shadows.

Please be safe. Please…

They had trained him not to live on hope back in the academy. Doctors, they said, need to try everything first. Hope creates doubt, slows your reflexes. Sometimes a patient's survival can hinge on a split-second decision. You have to believe that everything that can go wrong will go wrong and then you make yourself find the answers anyway. Some of his peers from back in the day turned to hardening their hearts, making sure nothing slipped past. When you don't care for a patient, you don't panic. To many, the people on their operating tables became nothing more than slabs of meat to prod and poke at their will. Success wasn't about prolonging someone's life, but solving the unsolvable.

Khine... always did the complete opposite.

He made sure he committed every patient's name to memory. Almost within the first hour or so of meeting them, he knew about their lives—what they planned to do tomorrow, or the name of their childhood dog. Hopes and dreams. They weren't always pleasant, but Khine *tried* his best to see things their way. And he tried his best to save them because he cared for them, because their deaths would be a blow to *him*, too, and he didn't like that. He didn't like losing people. He always knew he would've suffered as a doctor as a result of it. Tashi Reng Hzi warned him often, and his siblings echoed those sentiments every chance they got. Perhaps it was a good thing he never went far.

He saw a group of Zarojo soldiers at the far end of the street and ducked into a narrow alley to avoid them. The alley looped around the fringes of the city, right next to the walls. As he turned into another corner, a figure in black clambered down from a rooftop. From the height and shape, he guessed a woman.

She tugged at the mask around her mouth. "Are you a soldier?"

"No," he said, seeing the glint of a dagger in her hand.

She smiled in a way that made it clear she knew he was aware, and he had the unsettling feeling that she didn't care one way or another.

"Kaggawa's in the castle," he said, realizing she was waiting for another answer.

"I see," she replied.

"Are you an Ikessar, come to assassinate him?" He wasn't sure, but her accent didn't sound right from a Sougen native.

She said nothing. She was still watching him, observing him through thick lashes. She eventually straightened herself. "No. I've come to talk."

"I'm sure he'd like that," Khine replied, keeping an eye on her dagger. He wasn't sure he knew how to avoid getting skewered if she decided to use it. "I...

I need to go." He took a step back and then, uncharacteristically, decided he would take his chances with fleeing. Perhaps she wouldn't think he was worth the trouble.

"Mongrel," she called, just as he reached the end of the street.

He turned, cursing himself as he did so. Getting killed would be inconvenient. But then she could probably outrun him if she wanted to. He smiled, hoping it would hide his nervousness. "You know me," he commented.

"My people have been watching you since Oka Shto."

"Princess Ryia."

"You're a quick one."

"I have my moments." He glanced at the rooftops. "In retrospect, running wouldn't have done a fucking thing, anyway. You've got people waiting for me up there, don't you?"

She laughed. Men appeared, and Khine caught sight of their drawn bows. He counted about ten strung arrows—ten arrows that would easily make their mark if he made the wrong move. He thought of Agos and tried not to be frightened. Easier said than done.

"Tell me what you want," he said.

"We want to know where she is."

"She's gone," Khine said. "That's all you need to know. Hell, that's all *I* know."

"They said you betrayed her, but you're still here."

He said nothing.

"Probably to take the Zarojo off guard. It must've worked. They said she went to the mountains with him alone. To kill him there? Clever," she continued. "But not clever enough. I could have you gutted and beheaded where you stand before you could blink. How do you think she'll take that?"

"I honestly don't know."

"You're lying again."

"For once, Princess, I'm not. I'm sure I'm dead to her. And she…" He swallowed.

Ryia's eyes flashed. "What did she do up there, Lamang?"

"I don't know."

"There was a massive storm the night before the battle broke out. People thought they heard dragons swallowing the sky."

Khine smiled. "You people hear dragons everywhere."

"She hasn't returned, and yet you're here."

He stood there, weighing out his options. If Tali was here, she would've certainly advocated running straight into Ryia in the hopes of breaking her nose. He didn't always agree with her decisions, but there were times he had to grudgingly admit they worked. They sometimes worked, so she kept doing them. Her recklessness was oddly comforting.

He wiped sweat off his jaw. He wasn't as foolhardy, not even close. Everything in Khine's mind had to be weighed perfectly, every possible outcome mapped out, every decision touched on at least three times, if not more. Remote possibilities birthing more possibilities, so that you always had a way out—*always*. You needed that, living the life he did. He was quick because he had to be. You needed to be either quick or lucky to survive the fringes of society, and luck was intractable.

Of course, running straight into her messes is as foolhardy as they come. The fact that he was still alive either meant he *had* a bit of luck or that the gods were very sadistic. He'd never bet on anything he hadn't rigged himself first, but if he *was* as much of a betting man as the people he tricked, he knew exactly where to hedge them.

"Come and work for me," Ryia said, breaking the uneasy silence. "My army is waiting to sweep away the winners of this battle. It's been over thirty years of fighting—I'm ready to take this land for myself. You and your sister would make useful allies...fine generals, even. I've heard reports of her work, and you—I'm willing to guess *you're* responsible for all of this."

"You're mistaken," he replied.

"You're lying again. I don't think you've fully considered what I'm offering. A general in my army is no small thing. Take over a city for me and I may reward its governance to you. Destroy a warlord and his forces and I may even grant you a whole province."

"That sounds lovely."

"You don't believe me. It is more plausible than whatever that prince offered you."

"I do believe you," he said, straightening himself. "I believe you need the right people at your side if you're to finally claim the throne for yourself, and of course you need to find ways to reward them if they, unfortunately, don't die during your campaign. But indulge my curiosity. Why didn't you succeed the last time? You had the blood for it. You're certainly no fool nor lacking in the necessary viciousness. From my understanding, you had great advisers, too. Kaggawa's aunt—"

Her face tightened at the words.

"—and Ichi rok Sagar, whose qualifications rivalled Queen Talyien's Arro rok Ginta."

"Ghosts of the past," Ryia said. "That I was my brother Rysaran's rightful heir wasn't enough in those days. We were following the Zarojo ways too much—the Empire of Ziri-nar-Orxiaro, where women couldn't rule. If there was one thing Warlord Yeshin did right, it was to restore Jin-Sayeng to how it used to be, before we allowed the empire's influence to taint us. My son's wayward ways helped. They had no choice but to let the bitch rule alone all these years."

"Her rule tamed the fires. Because of her, now *you* can be queen without the rest of the land blinking an eye," Khine agreed. "All that's left is for you to subdue them."

"I'm impressed. If you can understand these things, then you can understand why accepting my offer is the best thing you can do for yourself. If you can convince your sister to abandon my son and become *mine*, she will get just as much." Ryia sniffed. "I mean, what other options do the two of you have? You're not what you seem, Lamang. I'm not convinced you'll be content just sitting, watching the world go by. And I am not as cruel as they say I am. I do what I must as a harbinger of change."

"Heavy words," he said.

"They are."

"And exactly what they thought *she* was."

"That whelp?" She laughed. "I won't deny that I sound like a bitter woman past her prime. But you've been by her side this whole time. Some say you're even lovers. You would at least know the challenges she faced. So I will tell you why she failed and why I will succeed. I *want* this." She held her hands out, showing him the dagger. "But maybe you're as foolish as my son. Maybe you'd rather die."

He swallowed. "I'd rather not, actually."

"Then be wise, Lamang. Consider the possibilities."

For one moment, and maybe longer, he did.

Khine saw his dreams being handed to him on a silver plate, saw a twist in the narrative he had hated for so very long. *A general could move armies, save lives.* He remembered telling Tali something like that once. If he had that power, he could bring peace to the land of the only two women he had ever loved. He could make the lives of those he'd lost matter. He could make his own failures count. It was a dizzying thought. A tempting thought.

But for someone who had scrapped for every little thing his whole life, admitting defeat wasn't easy. He didn't like that Ryia knew she could dangle this over him like a piece of meat, that she knew he was liable to snatch at it like any starving dog. Royals had their pride. He didn't know what someone like him had—not pride, certainly, if he could lie and steal just to get by. But it made him angry. It made him angry to know another person had that power over him.

It also made him angry to understand how much he wanted this.

"You're loyal to the bitch," she said. The anger faded. She had that right, too. It was a truth that made him feel at peace.

Knowing it was probably going to end in his death, he shrugged and waited for the inevitable.

Khine thought he heard them loose the arrows and tried to think of what he would tell his mother about how he got himself killed. He couldn't remember half the wisdom she had imparted on him over the years. He had been, at a time, more insufferable than his brother Cho. It was part of the reason he had kept himself in Anzhao City and refused to even so much as visit his mother, even when he knew she was waiting for him. He had wanted his homecoming to be a time of celebration and joy—that he would come home with everything he once said he was capable of, power and wealth enough to take his family away from that sordid life.

Instead, Mei had seen him at his lowest point. He had yelled at his own mother that night in Phurywa, when she had learned he was no longer going to be a doctor. He had told her she could do better than believe in him. "You have other children!" he cried. "Why don't you look to *them*? Thao is working hard, Inzali's even smarter than I am, and Cho—that boy! Cho doesn't even *try*! He needs a guiding hand!" He was the one who had walked out on her, fuming, thinking he would apologize once he had calmed down. His last image of Mei was of her looking through the shutters, her eyes red. He should've gone back to wipe the tears from her face. He had many regrets in his life, but that was the greatest of them all. One moment. One moment he could never take back.

Her sacrifice had confused him, made him ill. *Now I've gone and made it all insignificant. And for what?* he imagined he would say. *I've already hurt her. It's not like she was there to see. I could've denounced her and no one would have to know. A trick, like all the others. That's who I am. A liar. A cheat.*

Only he was starting to realize he didn't have the stomach for such things as he once thought. That last betrayal, seeing how she looked when he had uttered those words in front of the mad prince and his court—he had been having nightmares about it the past few days. He couldn't do it again. Even if you did nothing right, you could remain true to yourself. She'd taught him that much.

He heard the wind blowing and looked up to empty rooftops. Ryia had sheathed her dagger.

"You'd be dead if you had said yes," she said. "I can't abide disloyalty. Go. Find her, if that's what you'd rather do. It'll be for nothing. She's done for, and so is that son of hers. You'll be back. I may still reconsider." Ryia turned around and stepped away, leaving Khine to feel like he could start breathing again.

Legs shaking, he found the street he had been looking for and came around the back alley. There were two doors. He kicked one down. It led to a storeroom. He turned to the other one, expecting it to be locked. It wasn't.

He walked in. Lo Bahn and Jiro were alone, sitting around a table wedged tight in the corner of the room.

"Gentlemen," he greeted, trying not to show how shaken he still was.

"I told you he was a rat," Lo Bahn sniffed. He didn't even try to get up. Instead, he poured himself a cup of wine and downed it in one go.

"No hard feelings, Lo Bahn," Khine said. "You know me."

"I *do* know you," Lo Bahn snorted. "I never once fucking believed you'd bail on the bitch. You? Pah. But I didn't give a damn. This was doomed from the start. It's all the same to me. Kaz, now. He *really* thought you had a change of heart."

Khine turned to Jiro. "Don't tell me you're holding it against me?"

"The bitch got my wife killed," Jiro said in a low voice.

"Come on, Kaz. *You and your wife* got Anya killed. No one said you had to come here."

"The prince's shiny gold said they had to," Lo Bahn interjected. "Not like you got blackmailed into it like I did. Bah! Greed'll do you in. It always does. Don't I know it." He drank again. His nose was so swollen, it looked like a plum.

"She tried to save Anya, for what it's worth," Khine said. "But if it makes you feel better, you can fight me in her memory."

Jiro laughed. "Fuck, Lamang, were you washed in holy water after birth? I'm not going to kill another thief just for Anya."

"Don't be too quick to judge him. He's probably seen how much wine *you've* drunk. Look at him. Damn boy's confident he can beat you."

"You're over-praising me, Lo Bahn," Khine said.

"I know you too well," Lo Bahn snorted. "You're the smuggest son of a bitch ever to crawl out of Shang Azi's loins, and hanging around the bitch has turned your head inside out. You're playing general now, too, aren't you? I heard what they were saying out in the streets. You took off with some of Kaggawa's mercenaries and then led them back here. And now maybe you'll actually win the city back."

"Maybe," Khine said. "I won't lie. It's an uphill climb. Yuebek's soldiers are good fighters, and they'll be even better when they get their heads together. The element of surprise doesn't last very long."

"I *really* don't care," Lo Bahn grumbled. He glanced at Jiro, irritated. "And you won't either, Kaz, if you know what's good for you. Sit your ass down. With any luck they'll forget about us and we can go home."

Jiro slumped back into his seat with a frown.

Khine shuffled forward, taking an empty chair. He gestured at the wine. Grumbling, Lo Bahn pushed it over to him. "Seeing as you gentlemen have already given up on life," Khine said, pouring half a cup, "I've got a proposition."

"That's touching," Lo Bahn sniffed. "You haven't forgotten about us, after all."

"Why did you think I would forget my best friends?"

"Around the time you started playing Jinsein hero to impress the bitch," Lo Bahn said. He lifted an eyebrow. "Tell me it was worth it, at least."

"What was?"

"You're useless."

"Not always," Khine said, taking a sip. "Look. From where you're both standing, Jin-Sayeng considers you enemies. And our bond of friendship doesn't mean a damn thing to these people just because *I* say it exists. On the other hand, if you work *with* me, I can convince them you've just been unwilling victims in this whole charade."

"You want us to betray Yuebek," Jiro replied. "Forget about it. Have you *seen* that man?"

"Have you?" Khine asked. "I meant, lately. It's been a few days, now."

"Three," Jiro said, holding his fingers up. "Not enough to convince me he's not coming back."

"If this rebellion fails, you're still Jin-Sayeng enemies in Jinsein soil," Khine said. "This invasion is not as easy as it looks. There's at least another army camped in the western wilderness, waiting. Who knows what *they'll* do once they realize what's happening out here?"

"I'll bite," Lo Bahn said. "I'm tired of playing servant to a man-child. What do you want us to do?"

"Convince Yuebek's officers to lay down arms."

"They'll murder us," Jiro said.

"Well, some might want to," Khine conceded. "But surely you know which ones are more amenable to reason. We just need to give the Jinseins an edge. They'll be grateful for it."

Lo Bahn took another drink. "You're not seriously considering this?" Jiro asked.

"In case it isn't obvious, we're fucked, the both of us," Lo Bahn said. "And we didn't even have half the fun Lamang here had."

"I'm really not telling you anything, Lo Bahn."

"Which is telling enough. Fuck off, Lamang."

"So yes? You'll do it?"

Jiro sighed. "I suppose it can't be any worse than sitting here waiting for our deaths."

"It won't be," Khine said. "I promise. Warlord Huan is a decent fellow, and I'm not just saying that."

"The last time you convinced me someone was a decent fellow was—oh, right. I ended up losing my entire fortune," Lo Bahn grumbled.

"Correction. It was a woman. Women are always more complicated."

"I hate you."

"I want you both to get back home," Khine said. "Alive. We've lost too many already."

"I know." Lo Bahn tried to pour more wine, and then threw the bottle when he realized it was empty. It didn't even shatter—it just bounced off the wall. "Well, that's that. Let's go get our heads chopped off, Kaz. Better than sitting around here staring into each other's eyes without a damn thing to drink between us." He got to his feet, swaying slightly, and started for the door.

Jiro got up to follow him.

"Tell me, Lamang," Lo Bahn said at the door. "Did you kill Reng Hzi?"

"No," Khine replied. "He's safe with one of the rice lords."

"I figured Yuebek had his arm twisted, too—I just couldn't guess *how* until you mentioned a child. So your brat survived after all?"

Khine paused for a moment. It was not a conversation he liked having, and it had become habit to check himself for that old pain, the one he had tried to drown in a rush of bad decisions for so many years. "A lie," he said at last. "Yuebek believed it because...well. He *had* mentioned a child. Tashi Reng Hzi's grandson, Jia's child. She married Tashi Reng's son."

"That fuzzy-lipped worm practicing in Kyan Jang?" Lo Bahn asked. "She married *that* one?"

"Not a bad vengeance, considering what you did to her father," Jiro considered.

"Ah, the baker," Lo Bahn said. "Khine had nothing to do with that. It was one of my captains. Fucking idiot took advantage after he heard of Khine's troubles. Had him executed for it, but I didn't think...ah, fuck. I guess we did that. I'm sorry, kid."

"Not a kid anymore," Khine said with a smile. "Good tidings, Lo Bahn, and until we meet again."

"I'm not really looking forward to that, but the gods seem intent at throwing you at me like some cruel joke."

"I hope this makes us even. My debts..."

Lo Bahn laughed. "Not a chance in hell."

They left him alone to finish his wine.

———◆———

The effects of Lo Bahn and Jiro's undertaking became clearer once Khine found himself at the bridge leading away from the dragon-tower. "That's a good third of them fighting *for* instead of *against* us," Huan said as he handed the horse's reins to Khine.

"You don't look very happy."

"More bad news," Huan said. "The Ikessars have moved."

"We've expected that," Khine replied, thinking of Ryia. He didn't know if he should warn Huan. Better to keep quiet and have them focus on the battle at hand for now. Khine wasn't convinced Huan had the temperament to deal with a problem two steps ahead of him, and he could always send a message later.

"And Bara, and Kyo-orashi, and Kai…" Grana added, shaking her head.

"They're all fighting for them, too?"

"No," Grana replied. "We don't know. No one's made proclamations or anything. Tori thinks they're all fighting…against everyone, *including* the Ikessars. This has been too much. Nearly every province except Meiokara and Sutan is joining in. She thinks they're taking advantage of the fact that both Oren-yaro's army and the Ikessars' influence have been severely weakened, and I'm inclined to agree with her. It looks like there's going to be more bloodshed by the time this is over."

"You need to leave, then," Khine said. "Take your family and run."

"I can't do that," Huan replied. "My brother's still out there and I won't leave him again. There's no room for dragons in Meiokara."

"The children, Warlord Huan—"

"I know." Huan glanced at his wife. "I was hoping to strike a deal with Kaggawa. He's still got connections, and he cares for the Sougen as much as we do. I am not my father, and he knows that."

"Will you consider giving him the seat if he asks for it?"

Huan bristled. "Warlord Dai? Doesn't exactly roll off the tongue. I don't know, Khine."

"A steep price, but you may have to pay it if you don't have a choice. Whatever you decide, don't show him all your cards at once."

"I won't," Huan said. "I'm not entirely sure he wants to be warlord anyway. Something about royals and commoners and the dividing line. If he works with us, I'll entertain him. The bigger concern is what you're going to find out there." He nodded towards the mountains. "My brother hasn't shown himself, and I'm beyond worried."

"You and me both."

"We *need* a Dragonlord," Huan said. "More than ever. We need a symbol to unite this land. It's not ready to function without it. If you can bring even just one of them back…"

"My dear," Grana broke in.

Huan took a deep breath. "I know. I didn't mean it to sound like that. But gods. I always knew this wouldn't be easy—I just didn't think it would be *this* hard. I just want our family safe."

"We all want that," Grana said. "Promise me that if things don't get better, you'll let me take us back to my father's home. It won't be cowardice, and they won't attack Meiokara—none of them have the fleet to launch an assault across the sea."

"There's always that." He glanced back at Khine. "Will you be all right on your own? I can send soldiers."

"You need every single one," Khine said, heaving himself into the saddle.

"I do, don't I?" Huan laughed. He saluted. Khine kicked his heels into the horse and tore down the road.

Staying calm was now becoming more difficult, a feeling more dreadful than anything he had ever felt with his patients. What was he doing? It was like pounding on the chest of a dead man, hoping to bring him back to life. Everyone was about ready to give them up for lost. No one would think the worst of him if he did. Inzali had called him an idiot for his stubbornness.

"I'm fond of them, too," she'd said back at Nor's main camp, the one that used to belong to Dai the eve before they turned against Yuebek's ilk. "But that was a doomed undertaking, and we all knew it. We've both secured the trust of these people, and if things improve, we're looking at a good position for ourselves at their court. Why risk your life?"

"I think you need to go home."

She looked reluctant. "I want them all to come back safe, but that's not how the world works. It's not like a litter of puppies. What we want and what we get don't come from the same basket. You're older than me—you should know that."

"What has Mother's death turned you into?"

"You need to ask yourself that, Khine. I just want her death to mean something. Slaving away for gambling lords in the slums won't make that happen. You can do so much if you don't piss your life away. You *know* what you're going to find out there. You *know* what it's going to do to you. Give it up. There's nothing we can do anymore, and we've tried everything. When this is over, we can mourn them properly..."

He threw his hands up. "Gods, Inzali, I can't do that! I'm not going to mourn what isn't dead!"

His words were now coming back to haunt him. *What if she is? Please, gods...*

He was ready to start talking to the gods again. His mother's loss had almost been too much to take, and he knew he wouldn't be able to go through that another time. *Even if she hates me forever. I know what I did to her. I know it was a step too far. It had to be done, but...*

Had to be done. Tough words to swallow. But they had been running out of time. The Zarojo they encountered on the road had been carrying General Mangkang's head around. Ozo's men, dead before Khine could hand the boy over to them. Where was he supposed to take him? Yuebek was at least one step ahead of them. It was all the soldiers could talk about. The prince *knew* something foul was afoot, that his wife's refusal to fully entrench herself in their marriage was a clear sign she was keeping something from him. For all that the man pretended to be a dimwit, he wasn't. Yeshin had done his best. All his precautions implied he knew how clear that demented mind could be. Pulling a con from beyond the grave would be a feat in itself already; to try to do it with a man as intelligent as Yuebek was more daring than Khine could've ever imagined. He would've been impressed if he had the time. As it was, if he didn't find a way to warn Tali, or do something—*anything*—everything she had suffered for would be for nothing.

It wasn't even Khine's idea. It was Thanh's. "We can't run away forever," the boy said after they escaped the soldiers. "What if we gave ourselves up?"

"Your mother will kill me, Thanh."

"No, she won't."

"We're talking about your mother, right? The Bitch Queen of Jin-Sayeng? *That* woman."

"I just have the one."

"Oh, good, because I thought you got confused for a moment there. *She will kill me.*"

"You said she's trying to trick them. But they know they're being tricked. What's the point in hiding? It'll only make them angrier. The last time Mother and I tried to trick the Ikessars into giving me a day free from my lessons, they knew, and they—"

His words lit a fire in his mind. "Gods," Khine said, grabbing the boy by the shoulder and turning him around. "You brilliant child. You have your mother's mind!"

"I do?"

"I hope you can act better than your father."

"I don't understand."

"That's a *no*, then. But you can keep silent, at least. What if we pretend the Zarojo are these Ikessar guardians of yours, and we're trying to fool them."

Thanh's eyes brightened.

"There. You're right. They're onto us, and it's only a matter of time before they turn this whole thing upside down, right on your mother's head. But if we give them what they want—what they *think* they want—they'll be too distracted patting themselves on the back. They'll let their guard down. It'll give us a chance to think of something new."

That *something new*, of course, was a lot harder to find than he first figured. With Thanh in the shadows behind him, he decided to pay the Zarojo camp a visit in the hopes that a plan would reveal itself. It did, in the form of Jiro Kaz. Khine learned they were going to attack Dai's camp that night and offered to make it easy for them. He knew people on the inside. They could just open the gates and let them walk in uncontested.

A sensible solution, and Jiro trusted him enough to ride ahead to carry this through. He warned the mercenaries of the impending attack and embellished the number of Zarojo soldiers to triple what they really had. Most immediately split, including the injured. And because some of the mercenaries made their way to the other camps to tell their friends, there was very little resistance elsewhere.

One nail in. The next came the next day. Khine went straight to the river just as the rest of the Zarojo finished crossing, where he convinced Lo Bahn to take him to Yuebek. The man almost didn't want to entertain him. He grovelled, said he knew things the prince *had* to know, and then showed them the boy as a show of trust. He was granted an audience. And in speaking with Yuebek, he realized exactly how deep of a hole they were all in.

His gut was correct. The man had guessed Yeshin's plans after seeing the tear in the sky. It filled him with a cloud of resentment and suspicion. Tali's disappearance, followed by Ryia Ikessar's attack on his forces, only deepened his doubts. He meant to kill her the next time he saw her. He was going to make her confess, and then he was going to kill her.

Before Khine began to reconsider, Yuebek changed his mind again.

No. He wasn't going to make it easy for her. He was going to pretend to go along until he conquered the city. And then he was going to let his soldiers take turns raping her before doing it himself. He could kill her then, right in front of her whole court. Spit on her stained body. He didn't even really want her kingdom.

Khine saw red. Had to hold himself steady. Had to. Had to. He repeated this to himself over and over again before he stood up and admitted that she, too, had fooled him. They were lovers before she ran off to get married, picking up right after the last one. Agos, him, Yuebek—she was using them all. Yuebek had every right to be angry. But didn't he know her reputation? Didn't he know she could turn his own men against him, too? She had that power, and men were weak.

There was a better way to put her in her place, if Yuebek was smart. *Give her what she wanted*—but on his own terms. Why waste all his efforts? Why demand what she couldn't give? Nothing stopped him from taking what he wanted. He could still be king, even with a wife that hated him. He could take his time, break her over the years, make her regret ever standing up to him. Marriages and dynasties had been built on less.

Yuebek almost agreed with him. Almost. Looked at him then, dubious, his own mind poisoning him every which way. He was just like the rest of them, all those merchants and gamblers Khine had fooled over the years—already on the edge of that gap that stood between where he was and what he wanted. All he needed was a push.

"The boy," Khine said. "Bring the boy with you. He's the key to her obedience. Don't hurt him, but always make her think you will, and she is yours. She's not as strong as she makes herself seem. Her past husband, the boy… weaknesses she should have cut off long ago. She will bend. Maybe not easily, but she will bend."

He hated the words falling out of his lips. Hated how he had to smile at Yuebek, waiting for him to see things from the stilted perspective he offered. *What kind of a man knows exactly how to hurt someone he loves? How can you ever look at her again? If she buries you for this, let her. It will be exactly what you deserve.*

"I will take my men—" Yuebek began.

He interrupted with a wave of his hand. "My lord, your men will only complicate things," he said. Inzali's letter had told him they suspected Yuebek drew on his men for sustenance. Not just any men, but his soldiers, specifically. She said Namra suspected rune tattoos had been forced on the soldiers during the trip across the empire. Illegal blood magic, like he did to the elders, like he did to Mei. Yuebek committed sacrilege as easily as a man batting his eyes.

Khine wanted to tear him apart with his bare hands, but even if he had the means to do that, even if they didn't need Yuebek up on that rift, he wouldn't be able to. To kill Yuebek, he had to be on his own, unable to leech off anyone's strength. "Do you think she would rest for a moment if she knows your soldiers are around? I've told you what she's capable of. Are they castrated, Esteemed Prince, that they can resist her wiles? She can use them the way she used us. No. You and her—you need to be alone so she can't turn your guards against you. She won't try anything if her son is there. What power can she have over you with the boy as extra weight? They'll have nowhere to run in that wilderness. Go with them alone. Relish the moments. Conquer her nation, and then conquer her. It will be worth it, my lord, believe me. I've had but a glimpse of it. You could own it all your life."

With those words, Khine held the noose in his hand. He watched as Yuebek considered his words, watched as he danced over the possibility that it was still all a trick and he was a lamb being led to slaughter. But he wanted it too much. He hated and wanted her all at once, he wanted her kingdom, he wanted the power that came with having the Bitch Queen on a leash. He wanted to lord it over the woman who dared defy him so greatly he would die for it.

Too blinded by his rage to see the holes in Khine's logic, Prince Yuebek stuck his head in.

Khine saw that first dragon-tower under a clear blue sky. Half of it was crumbling, and it seemed almost impossible that it was still standing after all that damage. Nearby, chained to two trees, was Yuebek, half naked, covered in dirt, foam around his mouth.

Khine approached the tattered figure.

Yuebek turned to him. "You!" he snarled. "It's you! Shang Azi scum—unchain me!"

"What happened here?" Khine asked.

"I've done it!" Yuebek howled. "She didn't even think I could, but I did. I did it, and then I came back. What did they think I was? That I could jump into a dragon's body without making a connection back for myself? That I wouldn't tear their assassins in half while I had the power to soar the skies? Did they think any of this would kill me? Idiots, all of them. Idiots!"

"Where is she?"

"*She* is blind to the *agan*!" Yuebek exclaimed. "Lying, snivelling bitch. She thought she had me. But where is she now? Dead in the bottom of the sea. And me? I'm still here. My poor wife, we can always say she tried her best. Maybe I'll stay after all! I'll be Dragonlord of her nation! What are you doing? Don't you know who I am? I'm the Esteemed Emperor's Fifth Son, the Esteemed Emperor's most beloved son! If you kill me, you'll never become a physician again!"

Khine stabbed him in the heart with a dagger.

Ah, he thought, watching as blood burst from Yuebek's mouth and his body slumped against the chains with one final shudder. *So that's how.*

It did get easier, after all.

CHAPTER TWO

THE MEMORY CHAIN

ʊ ȝ ʊ ɔ

The horses watched him warily as he rode down to the edge of the forest. Khine caught sight of Tali's scarf stuffed haphazardly into a saddlebag. He knew it because he had given it to her. *Lent* it, actually, during their journey through the Ruby Grove; he had covered her mouth with it and somehow never got it back. He didn't know she'd had it this whole time.

He made himself take the scarf out. Her scent was all over it, strong enough that it felt as if she was right beside him. Suddenly, the courage that had taken him all the way out here dissipated. She was real, not just some figment of his imagination. More real than Jia had been all those years he had wandered through her neighbourhood after she left, searching for her ghost or whatever it was he thought could make him feel better about the things he'd done. He thought he caught a glimpse of that when he first saw Tali that day, on that same street in Shang Azi where he'd screamed those last words at Jia and swore to himself he would never love again.

Funny how that worked.

Tali—that unpredictable, infuriating, unrelenting woman—had accused him of seeking that shadow, had shown him exactly how foolish she thought he was being. To die for love was easy. And she had been right. He *had* been running away. He hadn't known how to separate her from what he thought he still felt about Jia, or what she signified, what a person like her was against the dirt and muck of his world. But the night she left him for Agos, he had stayed awake and forced himself through what he knew was happening down that hall, through the anger and jealousy and rage to find something unexpected. To die for love was easy, but to live for it? To forgive, to understand, and love anyway...

It was a gift. The one thing he needed to pull himself out of the haze of near-death, both inside and out. She didn't know that the Khine who loved Jia would've never spoken to her again. She didn't have to. It already unsettled him that she accepted what he was without question. She could have her pick of princes—of kings and generals and other better, more accomplished men. He was just a thief, a quack. A liar. She knew what he was, knew better than to trust him, but she did.

He heard what sounded like gusts of wind, one after another, and turned to see Eikaro descending on the clearing. He looked—well, dragons didn't have much in the way of facial expressions, but Khine pretended he looked sad. Thinking about it was a good distraction; he was already on the verge of tears.

He went up to him, hesitating before he tentatively tapped the dragon on the nose. "Lord Eikaro," Khine said. "What do I do now?"

The dragon huffed, glancing towards the horizon before draping one wing to the side.

"You want me to ride you?" Khine asked.

Eikaro didn't move. Khine drifted to his side and noticed that his wing was wounded and stuck oddly together. He lifted his hand to touch the ragged flesh.

"I'm not sure you should take my weight, friend. You need to heal."

Eikaro nudged him with his tail, sending him toppling forward towards his shoulder. "Fine," Khine said, clambering up. "But don't blame me if you start flying crookedly. Not that a fraud would know a damn thing."

The dragon made a sound that could've been laughter before taking to the air.

They left the horses behind and made their way past the forest, and then a lake, the edges of which were wrapped in chunks of ice. Off in the distance, Khine spotted another dragon-tower and a campfire.

Eikaro made a wide circle around the tower before dropping down.

Khine walked to the campfire, which had been built right at the entrance to the tower. There was a man standing outside. He drew his sword as Khine approached.

"Rai," Khine said. "It's me."

"I know. I saw."

He held his hands up. "I'm a friend."

"You will have to forgive me if I don't agree."

"What happened down there was—"

"Another trick?" Rai asked, glancing at Eikaro, who was limping up towards them, wings curled partway. "I don't know what to believe anymore."

"You can ask Thanh. It's civil war now, Rai. All the other provinces are marching towards Yu-yan. The Zarojo are losing, but they need you down there. Both of you." He held his breath.

"She..." Rai began. He lowered his sword. "Come and see for yourself." He stepped to the side of the entrance, beckoning.

Khine stepped through the threshold and saw Thanh and the priestess bent over Tali's unmoving body.

Hope. Forget hope, Tashi Reng Hzi used to say. *It's like prayer. It's all well and good when you've got nothing else, but for the moment, pretend that there is something, and that something is* you. *You're the gate and death is on the other side. Stand firm.*

He dropped down to her side, reaching for her hand. It was very cold.

"What happened?" he asked, turning to Namra.

"She fought a dragon," Namra said.

"Tell me something new," he croaked out, trying to make light of things.

"I couldn't stop the bleeding in time." Namra pulled the blanket away from the pale body, showing the swollen flesh around her leg. Khine had seen the worst a battlefield had to offer, but he still found himself recoiling from the sight of it. How could she look so frail? Even when she had fallen into the feather-stone, she had been solid, the sort of woman who wouldn't—*couldn't*—go down without a fight. He had relied on it all this time, leeching off her strength because he knew his couldn't be enough. He would have died back in Phurywa without her.

Now...now she looked like she belonged in a grave.

"I don't know if it's worth the trouble," Namra said.

"She's still breathing."

"She's gone through so much, Khine. Perhaps...perhaps we should just let her rest."

"How could you say that? *She's still breathing.*"

Namra placed a hand on Tali's chest. "And she shouldn't be. She rode a dragon, and we think it died when they sealed the rift. You saw it outside? The clear sky? The tainted glow is gone. It worked."

"This is all nonsense to me."

Namra's face tightened. "She's still breathing. No soul went into this body; by all rights, it should've died when she jumped into the dragon. It didn't. But if she's here, why hasn't she woken?"

"Bullshit," Khine gasped. He looked down into her face—another thing Tashi Hzi used to warn them against. *You're trying to save them, not crawl into their skins. You can't start conceptualizing their pain. If you break before you can do anything, then you can't help them at all.*

But this was different. He loved this woman with a madness he couldn't explain. If saving her meant reaching into his own chest to rip his heart out, he would do it without a second thought. "Tali," he whispered, watching for a reaction, a sign that she could hear him.

"We tried that already," Namra said.

"Tali, it's me. Please. Wake up."

"Lamang," Rai broke in. "Enough of this. You're upsetting the boy."

Khine turned to Thanh, who had yet to say a word the whole time. He was trying very hard to keep still.

"Let's deal with the wound first," Khine said. He didn't wait to see if they agreed. Rai didn't try to stop him as he asked for a dagger to cut off the infected flesh. Namra hadn't done a bad job of it at all—just not as thorough as a trained physician would've. And Khine wasn't a physician, but he knew what he was doing. Most days he was convinced of it, anyway.

After he managed to recauterize and bandage the wound, he went to wash his hands in the lake, tears stinging his eyes.

He must've stayed there longer than he intended. The moon was starting to rise in the distance, a full brightness on the dark-blue sky, when he heard footsteps behind him. Rai cleared his throat. "Thanh explained everything." He paused, taking a full breath. "I appreciate what you've done for my family. You didn't have to."

"I wanted to," Khine said.

"So that part of it... that you were lovers..." Rai looked almost embarrassed to have brought it up.

Khine nodded, unsure of how else to respond. It didn't even occur to him to deny it.

"I thought there was more truth than lie to that." He looked pensive, not angry. Different from the man who had stomped off for the better part of a decade in his haste to correct what he thought was a grievous sin. Now he was standing here, his own hands as drenched in her blood, his face hollowed by what could have only been a sleepless last few days as he cared for her dying body. Khine wondered what she had told him. She would have found a way to make it hurt, because of course she would. But somehow, she had made him listen at last. He wished he knew exactly how.

"I'm..." Khine began. "I'm not sorry, if that's what you're asking." *Loving her was the easiest thing in the world. I am sorry you didn't feel the same way, because it would have saved her a lot of pain.* Maybe she would have been happier if Rai, from the very beginning, had fought for her the way she was willing to fight for him. But then again, if he had, Khine wouldn't have the memory of her in his own arms. Sometimes love could be selfish.

"At least you're not asking for a duel like the last one."

"I think we're well past such things."

He nodded. "That's fair. I...I didn't know what...what I was throwing away. I thought once everything was over, I could...she would let me fix it. And I had every intention to fix it. But..."

Khine cracked a smile. "She told me you thought you were protecting them. I understand. She did, too."

"But it wasn't enough to keep her." Rai looked down, eyes red. "I lost her."

"We have no say on what people feel about the things we do, even if we think we're in the right." Khine swallowed. "Look at us. She'd laugh if she saw us crying over her."

"She already did that. Laughed at me."

"She enjoys pulling your leg, Rai. Hell, she'll run off with it if you let her." He paused, his chest tightening around the words. Was that a mistake? Did it all belong in the past, now? She didn't give up easily; he couldn't, either. Tashi Reng was the most intelligent man he had ever met, but there was one thing he didn't quite understand. Hope might be a bitter drink, but we'd all drain the bottle given half the chance.

He turned his gaze to the tower and noticed the top of it was glowing blue.

Oh, Tali, he thought. *Not yet, my love.*

He started running, a confused Rai at his heels.

"Namra," he said, startling her. "Something's keeping her here."

"What are you saying?"

"Dead dragon-towers don't glow. They didn't in the cities. But outside, just now... have you noticed? It wasn't clear in the daylight, but it looks like a torch up there."

Namra rushed out to look while Khine checked Tali's pulse. A glint in her hair caught his attention, and he placed his fingers on her head. He felt a bump on her scalp. Gently, he parted the roots of her hair.

"She's got something tattooed on her scalp," he said when Namra returned. Cradling Tali's neck, he motioned for her to see.

Namra's face flickered at the sight of the black ink, embedded on her scalp between her ears and above the nape of her neck. It glowed slightly. "That's a spell rune," she said.

"Did you know about this?" he asked, turning to Rai.

"I've never seen it in my life," Rai said. "But then again, we weren't... as intimate as..."

"I don't think *she* was aware of it, either," Khine said, to save him from further embarrassment. "But it's clear who put it there. I found it hard to believe from the beginning that a father would so willingly sacrifice his child."

Shame flooded Rai's face. "It... happens."

"It does," Khine agreed. "But a man as controlling as Yeshin wouldn't have just stopped with her death. He found a way to keep her safe. The dragon-tower. I think she's in the dragon-tower."

"A connection," Namra breathed. "If her soul was torn out of the dragon after the rift was closed, then this dragon-tower could've captured it. It's not connected to the others, so that would protect her from the rush of energy coming out of Yuebek. That's—that's why Yeshin wanted me to find this place. That spell rune is tying her body to the dragon-tower, to offer a clear path for her soul to return. But... why doesn't she?"

"I'll find out. Send me to her," Khine said.

"What?" Namra asked.

"My soul. You can send me to where she is."

"That's like asking me to chop your head off and then put it back on."

Khine shook his head. "If this dragon-tower is keeping her, then if you send me along the same channel, maybe—"

"You can send me instead," Rai said.

"No," Khine replied. "You're needed here, Rai. I'm not. We don't even know if it'll work. If it kills me, I don't mind."

"I... need your blood," Namra said.

Khine bared his arm.

A bright light surrounded him. Khine found himself walking on all fours. There was a pond on the road, and he paused to look down on it. A dog was staring back at him—a mangy-looking one with ears that flopped both ways and whiskers that made it look like he had been sniffing through the gutters of Shang Azi.

Things are not very stable once you're out of your body. I think the tower cuts a small hole through the fabric, which means you'll find yourself in a closed chamber on the other side. Your body's not attuned to your soul having a strong connection to the agan, *so you might not look like yourself. Neither will she.*

But a dog?

He decided not to let it worry him and began to run up the road. He found himself darting through a dirty alley, past sewage canals large enough to swim in. Everything faded around him after a while; he didn't know exactly where he was going, but something was drawing him in a certain direction, calling him like a master whistling to her hound.

He reached the gates of what he recognized as Oka Shto. The sound of battle was rising in the air. He managed to dash past fighting soldiers without anyone noticing him, but closer to the doors leading to the great hall, in the courtyard, he found himself stopping. There was a man in the midst of it all, an old man, a blood-drenched warrior.

Not far from him was a woman cradling a child.

"What did you think this little rebellion would do, woman?" the old man hissed. "There's nowhere to go! Would you kill her to get to me?"

"Papa!" the child called. She couldn't have been more than three years old, maybe four—Khine hadn't been around enough children to know for sure.

The old man ignored her, his eyes focused on the woman. "You belong in the fires of hell, Yeshin," she replied, cold fury to his rage. Her arms were keeping the child from dashing towards him.

Yeshin approached, sword in hand.

The woman picked the child up and began to run.

"There's nowhere to go!" Yeshin repeated, laughing. He stalked after them.

Khine found himself dashing after all three, down the dusty halls of Oka Shto. With all feet on the ground, the shadows of the alcoves looked even more imposing. Somehow, he found himself overtaking Yeshin; he was now at the woman's heels as she led the child up the stairs, up onto a familiar floor. Yeshin was right—the woman didn't know where else to run. She was looking around in terror.

Halfway down the hall, she seemed to come to a decision. Khine followed them all the way into Yeshin's study. The woman placed the child on the ground and made her touch the wall, unlocking the hidden chamber. Spells disabled, she picked her up again and went down the steps, two at a time.

They reached the throne room.

"This is completely pointless, Mara," Yeshin's voice thundered behind them. "Lord General Ozo is taking care of that mess outside as we speak. Didn't imagine the old woman still had fire in her, but that's Peneira for you. Did she promise she would take care of the child? You realize that was all a lie, don't you?"

"When my husband finds out about everything—"

"Ah, so you haven't told him yet," Yeshin said.

"You're a fool if you think he won't discover what you have planned for the child. You are a cruel man, Yeshin. Arro will see you for what you are."

"Maybe he will, maybe he won't," Yeshin replied easily. "By the time he's back from the empire this will all have been swept under the rug. And you? He'll think you left him for a rich Kag merchant. He'll never want to speak your name again."

"You—"

He stepped forward, sliding his sword into the woman's belly. She opened her mouth, gasping, and turned as if to shield the child one last time. But Yeshin plucked the girl from her arms and pushed her body away. She fell towards the throne, her blood pooling around the base.

"There," Yeshin said, patting the girl's head. "Did she scare you?" He turned to the staircase. A man and a woman were climbing down the steps.

"Is it over?" one asked in a heavy Zarojo accent.

"The bitch actually thought she would succeed," Yeshin snorted. "Nothing to it. Come. Let's finish what we started." He turned to the child. "Close your eyes, my dear. Be brave for me. This will be over soon."

She did. The others advanced, hands glowing blue.

The fog drifted in, covering everything. When it receded, Khine was no longer in the throne room. He was back outside, at the top of a hill. There was an estate in the distance—a giant mansion that seemed even larger now that he was closer to the ground. He trotted up the stairs, and then found himself in front of doors. Giant doors for a giant mansion, with knobs that seemed hopelessly out of reach.

He scratched at the surface and barked.

The doors opened, swinging inward.

He walked in. The doors closed as soon as he was out of the way.

He found himself in a rectangular great hall, one with several doors on each side. In the middle were several sofas facing each other. Behind that was a foreign-looking table, one that Khine had never seen before. He went up to it, sniffing at the polished edges. There was a single stool in front of it. He placed his paws on the table and then jumped back when he heard a loud noise, almost—but nowhere near—like melodious cymbals.

The white things on the table made the noise every time he pressed them. It was a musical instrument of some sort.

He turned away from it. There was a fish tank near the wall, with a sleepy-looking bonytongue inside. It was surrounded by the bobbing bodies of smaller fish. He wondered why *it* was still alive, considering the toxic water, and then remembered that technically *he* wasn't, either. Namra said that across the *agan* fabric, nothing was. Everything functioned as they had in life, but it wasn't quite the same.

He sniffed, recognizing a scent coming from the room behind the tank.

Tali.

Scratching at the door of this one did nothing, but the knob was at just the right height for his mouth. After a few tries, he managed to turn it.

The room was empty except for a little girl sitting on the floor next to the bed with her arms wrapped around her knees. He recognized her immediately.

Tali, he said, going up to her. He nudged her arm with his nose. *It's me, Tali. It's Khine. I promised I wouldn't leave you, didn't I? I'm sorry if you thought I did. I'm sorry about the things I said. It was the best I could do. We had nothing else, and he was burning in hate. On his own, against you, he never had a chance. I knew you could take care of him yourself and you did. You did it, Tali. Now it's time to come home.*

She didn't respond.

I'm sorry, Tali. I was wrong to say those things. I was wrong to put it all on you.

Whining, he flipped her arm out of the way so he could wedge the front half of his body onto her lap.

Her eyes opened, and her fingers slid through the shock of fur around his neck, as if out of habit. He realized why he had taken this form. A common mongrel, a stray dog. It was one she still trusted, among everything else.

"Khine," she finally said, looking into his eyes. Her voice was very soft, as child-like as her appearance.

Her recognition of him, even in this form, made him so happy his tail began to wag. *You can get up. Old Iga all but screamed at me to bring you back, and your son's waiting, even Rai... Rai never left your side, Tali. Everyone's waiting. Come back to us.*

"I'm..." She swallowed. "I don't think I want to."

Why not?

"I don't think I can do it anymore."

He whined. *That's not true. You're strong, Tali. You've always been strong.*

"And he used it, didn't he? My father. The rest of them. They made me strong so they didn't have to be."

Tali...

She pressed her face against his. Tears leaked into his fur like rivulets of rain. He kissed them away.

We'll stay here, he said, *if that's what you want.*

"No, Khine. You can't do that. Your family..."

Don't worry about them. I'm where I belong. Here, with you.

She pulled him closer to her, wrapping him in her arms.

He could've stayed there forever if she had wanted him to, and for a time it felt that way. But eventually, she lifted her head. "Did Namra tell you why this place exists?"

We saw the dragon-tower glowing and guessed the truth. Your father made arrangements for your safety.

"More than that. I think my father made this all himself."

He sensed the weight behind her words and kept silent, though he had the urge to pant a little. She was silent for a few moments, too, combing through his ears, pinching the fur between her fingers before smoothing it flat.

"I should've known from the start," she said at last, her voice barely a whisper. "This is the same chamber I told you about, the one I found myself in when I was in Yuebek's dungeon. I've been here several times since. I believe I get dragged in every time I'm around a strong current of *agan*."

This isn't Yuebek's doing?

"No. That bonytongue in the tank—that was my father's. The piano...I saw that thing in Burbatan, in my father's old home. My brother used to play it, they said. I never made the association until now." She absently stroked the side of his cheeks. "Yuebek, I think, tried to drug me back then, and then tried to get his mages to do something to me. Something to make me more...pliable to his desires. It didn't work. I must've fallen unconscious."

But your story...the assassin who stalked you...you killed her, you said. And Yuebek had used her to make you believe Rai sent her.

"I think all of that was true," she said. "I think Yuebek *did* take me somewhere so that all of that could happen once I woke up. I was seeing this place *and* that other place. Half in and half out. I'll show you."

She scratched his chin, bidding him to follow her. He trotted beside her as she walked to the next room.

"Yuebek's chamber was empty," she said. "I remember everything that happened, but I think the entire time I was just sitting in that empty chamber while my real self wandered *this* place. I thought Yuebek left me these cryptic messages to get me to forget Rayyel." She sat down on a sofa, gesturing at a *Hanza* set on the table in front of it.

Khine sniffed the edges.

"Do you play *Hanza*, Khine?"

Not very well.

"That's surprising. I figured you were an expert. All those tricks..."

Lo Bahn tried to teach me before. I find it too stiff. Finite options. I like marks that move by themselves. Saves you so much work.

"Maybe you're just saying that because you're bad at it."

That, too.

She nodded towards the pieces. "Every time I find myself here, the pieces are always in the same spot. An unwinnable game, unless you sacrifice the king."

Apt.

"Blunt and subtle at the same time. Too subtle for Yuebek, though. He wanted to be my king; my father would have me rule alone." She got up and this time moved towards a door, which opened into a library. There were books everywhere, but one particular one caught his eye.

"That one, too," Tali said, noticing his gaze. "Can you read it?"

No. It's in Jinan.

"You'd think I would've noticed that. I can read Zirano, but your letters make me dizzy."

You were disoriented.

"I'll recite it to you. Once, there was a soldier whose king was on his deathbed.

"The soldier was utterly devoted to his king and swore he would remain by his side until the very end.

"He stood guard at the door. He no longer had a sword, so when wild dogs came, he fended them off with his fists. But there were too many, and they ate his knuckles.

"When the crows came, he beat them with his stumps and his elbows. But there were too many, and they made off with his nose.

"When the vultures came, he smashed them with his head. But there were too many, and they pecked out his eyes.

"When the king's enemies came, he had nothing. He charged at the voices, but they only laughed and walked past him and they killed the king.

"What is the moral of the story? The moral of the story is that you can suffer in silence and the world will not care." She swallowed. "He was warning me."

That's bullshit. It's all bullshit, Tali. Look. He nudged her knee with his nose.

"He designed this place to protect me after that final spell. Because he always knew I would sacrifice myself; that I would do what no one else would. And then what?" Her voice sounded bitter. "Congratulations, Father, your plan worked after all...let's ignore that it came at the expense of my whole life."

It's over. You don't have to listen to him anymore.

She shook her head and closed the book, her thumb scratching a line over the cover. "It's not that simple."

Then help me understand.

"It's all over and he's still not here," Tali said with a gasp. "Why isn't he here, Khine?"

She said it simply, nothing more than a child seeking a parent's hand. He had no answer. What she desired...was a simple thing. Everyone had it. Patients close to death had whispered it in his ear. To know the world you were born into made sense, that you were wanted, that it was all designed to fit perfectly together and there was a reason for every hurt and injustice and suffering. But it didn't work that way. Life didn't work that way. The mess was all you got.

Look at us, he wanted to tell her. *If everything came out just right, we wouldn't have this.*

But it felt presumptuous to say so—to assume she wasn't allowed to grieve the man who was still her father, no matter what he was in life. He watched her drift to the door in the corner of the library. Her hand lingered at the knob before she turned it. It was locked.

"He was down in the dungeons here that first time," Tali said. "So I can't tell if the cells belong here, or in Yuebek's realm. I don't know. I don't want to think about it. I just know that this whole place... *reeks* of him. Everywhere I look, I see the details only he would've known to put. Messages to me, things that meant something to him. Only he's not here."

How do you know that?

"I tried to look, and..."

Let's look harder.

She didn't argue, allowing him to lead the way. He pushed the door back to the great hall. The main doors were still closed, but he took her down to a room that was lined with fish tanks wall-to-wall. Monstrous fish peered at them from behind the glass, razor-sharp teeth glinting with blood. There was a door at the very end of the hall.

She hesitated at the entrance.

"I don't want to go down there."

You are looking for him, aren't you? Why didn't you check down here?

"I don't want to, Khine." The fear was clear in her voice now. She had been lying to herself. She *knew* what waited at the other end.

He walked back to her, nudging her hand under his head. *I'm here. We'll do it together.*

Her fingers gripped his fur. She took a deep breath before nodding. They strode down the hall, the monstrous fish watching them with every step. She opened the door.

The next room was filled with small skulls, just like the ones in the basement of the dragon-tower in Yu-yan. There was a throne in the middle of the pile. An old man sat on it, staring at them from behind strands of greasy white hair.

"Father," Tali said.

The old man lifted his head. "Come to me, child," he said.

Tali didn't move.

Yeshin placed his hands on his knees and laughed. "You're finally here. Which means it worked. It's all fixed. Now you need to go back down there and claim your rightful place."

She stared at him in disbelief before slowly shaking her head. "No."

"Don't test me, daughter. You've come this far! We've made it. We—"

This isn't really your father, is it, Tali?

She shook her head, her brow furrowed in confusion.

"The Ikessars won't know what hit them," Yeshin said, still rambling. "You want to know what's wrong with Jin-Sayeng? The people don't know who to obey. Their families? Their clans? Or is it their warlords? Shouldn't it be the Dragonlord whose words eclipse all? A strong hand—it's what the nation always needed. The people grow bold, otherwise. Which, if they were the sort of people who understood their responsibilities and what *sacrifice* meant, wouldn't be the worst thing in the world. But in Jin-Sayeng, we need strength! We need strength, or the people will falter!

"Except they won't listen that way, either. The Ikessars get by because the *romantic* is more palatable than the *practical*. So here: They have their hero, their champion. Go back there and take what's rightfully yours, Talyien. You've earned it!"

"No," she repeated.

His eyes flashed. "You'd defy me? You? After all these years, child, you still—" He reached forward, as if to strike her.

She cringed.

Suddenly, he wasn't there anymore. He was pacing along the edges of the room. "So much sacrifice," he said. "All these children, these people who died for you, for us…"

Tali, Khine murmured. *You don't have to listen to this.*

"I do," she whispered back. "I have to understand everything."

You already understand. What more is there to learn?

"He's right about all the people who died. About everything. I—"

Tali. This isn't your father.

She stared at him in disbelief.

He glanced at the figure. *It's a ghost. A figment of the past. In here, only you and I are real.*

She shook her head, refusing to listen.

We still have our bodies keeping us suspended in here. Yeshin? Yeshin is dead.

"Listen to the boy," Yeshin suddenly said, pointing at us. "He's right. I wanted a place to contain all my memories, everything I cared for."

This is all a stamp, an imprint of when he made this place, his memories working with yours.

"The ghosts of Taraji, and my mother..." she began.

"Everything, Talyien," Yeshin replied.

"You lied to me all my life."

Yeshin returned to the throne, his bones creaking. "What if I did?" he asked. "It was all for the good of our people. Now the Oren-yaro will rule Jin-Sayeng, all thanks to me. All thanks to you." He nodded towards her.

"Did you even love me at all, Father?"

He stared back at her, eyes hard.

This time, his twisted face grew soft. "Ah, child," he said. "Is this what this is all about?" He smiled. "Do you remember the story I used to tell you?"

"I do. You only had the one."

"Only because it was the only one you ever asked for." He held his arms out. "Come, child. Forgive an old man his eccentricities. You know I never meant to hurt you."

Don't listen to him, Tali.

Tears streamed down her face. He was confused at first, until he realized that the answer was startlingly simple. She loved her father. It was forever the conflict of her life—that she knew exactly what they were, these people she cared for, and it never stopped her from giving what she'd been looking for herself. What they couldn't give, in return. It was what drew him to her from the very beginning—all that love, given without ever a care or thought about what it did to her. She loved, even when it ruined her.

He grabbed her by the hand, pulling her away from the room. She didn't resist, though he could tell her feet dragged a little. The ghost allowed them to leave.

Instead of the hallway with the tanks, they found themselves in a courtyard, reminiscent of the one in Oka Shto.

Tali.

She wasn't responding. He nudged her again.

"Tali."

His hackles rose at the familiar voice, which was slightly higher-pitched than he was used to. There was a boy standing at the edge of the path—tall, lanky, the beginnings of fuzz on his lip.

"Agos," Tali said, looking at him with what seemed like both longing and grief.

Not real, he reminded her.

"I know," she whispered, placing a hand on Khine's head. But she approached the boy, who rubbed his cheek with a sheepish grin. "Hello, Agos," she continued out loud.

"Hello," he replied.

"You...look well."

"After what happened to me, you mean."

She furrowed her brow.

"Your memories and your father's, remember? Hey..." he said, cocking his head to the side. "Don't worry about it. I'm fine. Better than fine. We all die. It's what we leave behind that matters." He glanced in the distance, and Khine followed his gaze to see other forms. Three young men and another boy, all resembling Tali in some way. Her brothers, perhaps. Ozo. A woman he recognized from the castle, Ingging. And then, a little closer to them than all the others—an older man with grey hair and a white beard, whose appearance seemed to catch Tali off guard.

He gestured at Tali, who hesitated.

"Go on," Agos said.

She swallowed and started walking. Khine whined, bounding after her.

The man was sitting under a frangipani tree. The fragrance of fallen flowers made Khine's nose itch. He watched as the man picked one up and tucked it into Tali's ear.

"The flower of death," he said with a smile. "And yet I can almost forget that, looking at you. Some people may find it ghastly, but it's fitting. You have to understand the world that came before you were born. The thousands dead. The isolation your father insisted on for you."

"Did you know about it, Arro?" she asked. "Did you know what they were doing?"

He looked startled before breaking into a smile. "That has been bothering you awhile, hasn't it?"

"Answer me, Arro."

Instead of replying, he smiled again, looking off into the distance. A woman approached them.

"Mara," Arro said, holding out his hand. The woman came to take it. "My wife," he continued, turning to Tali. "You don't remember her?"

Tali shook her head.

"She was friends with your mother. With Ingging. After your mother went mad and your father sent her away, we...all of us...took care of you."

"Arro the most of all," the woman said. "We couldn't have children of our own."

Tali looked at the woman with disbelief. "I do know you," she finally murmured. "In my father's throne room. I saw you there."

"Your father killed me in that room after I discovered his plans," the woman replied.

"He couldn't have been that careless."

"No," Mara said. "He wasn't. But what I learned was enough." She glanced around. "To do all of this, he needed to burn a spell into your mind. I caught his mages during that first attempt. Arro wasn't in Oka Shto, but I stole you away and sent a message to Peneira to get us out. It didn't...work. He killed me, and they did what they did to you. The procedure must have erased your memories of me."

Tali looked down, tears in her eyes. "And you, Arro?" she repeated, voice so clearly a child's.

"I didn't know a damn thing."

She didn't reply.

Arro laughed. "I'm dead, child. Ozo had me killed in Anzhao. That was never an accident. Because if I knew, none of this would have ever happened. I would have never let them touch you."

He placed his hands on Tali's shoulders. "I know what you are really asking. You want to know if there is a way to wash out all the pain and bitterness, if he could've loved you better if you had done better, or if he would've loved you even if you were worthless to his grand plans. You want to lift this shroud of pain and suffering and find the life you always wanted, the happiness you dreamed of, the family you deserve. But it can't be like that. It will never be like that. He was... what he was. I can say he loved you in his own way, but I know that is worthless in the face of everything he has done. Still, you don't have to let it define you. He is dead and you are still alive. You don't have to carry that burden forever. There are others in this world. Have you forgotten that *I* loved you, child?"

He pulled her close, allowing her to sob in his arms. Khine, realizing he was treading on private grounds, turned away.

They returned to the room, where Tali watched her father from the doorway—a child again, frightened of getting yelled at. But eventually, she balled her hands into fists and came up to him, her chin held high. She kept her jaw tight. He could tell she was awash in fear, but even that didn't stop her from facing the object of her terror head-on. That was courage, wasn't it? To stand your ground when it was easier to walk away.

"Arro's poisoned you," Yeshin snarled. "He was always trying to turn you against me. Him and that wife of his..." He spat to the side before straightening his back, revealing a crown on his knees. It was a small, golden thing, etched with figures of wolves.

Tali gazed at the crown and swallowed. "I'm..."

No, Khine warned. *You're not sorry. Not anymore, Tali.*

The old man, seemingly noticing her hesitation, pulled his head up sharply. "You speak of love, but what need do you have for it now? You have everything. You're queen, and now queen without question. You've saved the land. If they doubt you again, all you need is to remind them and the rest will rally behind your banner. Do you not see that all I did, I did for you?" He held the crown out.

"I do," she managed, looking away from it and into his eyes. "But it won't happen, Father. I won't take that throne."

"Don't be foolish. This little tantrum will subside."

"I did my part. You're right about that. Others did, too. Arro, Agos, Ingging, Ozo, Chiha... everyone who gave their lives for this cause. We all did what you couldn't—what you *wouldn't*, because in the end you cared more about power than fulfilling your promises to the people who believed in you. Now it's over. Ryia can have it all if she wants."

Yeshin's face was red with rage. "Ridiculous child. You'd undo everything I worked for?"

"I would rather die than sit on the throne again."

"You—!" He sat up, grabbing the crown. With one careless motion, he flung it against the wall, where it smashed into a thousand pieces.

In the silence that followed, Khine thought he could hear the spectre breathing. Sunlight danced over the shards on the floor, dazzling in their brilliance. A single red gem rolled down the aisle. It shone the most, casting streaks on the two figures. Yeshin's form was shadowless.

Tali glanced at the ground, at her father's feet, before looking back up. Resolve filled her expression. She stepped over the throne to embrace her father. Surprise flitted through Yeshin's face.

"I love you, Father," she whispered. "But now I have to say goodbye."

She turned to Khine. "Kill him." He heard it around him, a clear thought that pervaded the air. He didn't hesitate. He lunged, crushing the ghost's neck between his teeth. Yeshin screeched and gurgled and toppled to the side.

Tali pushed the body away and turned to him, covered in her father's blood. "And now me," she said.

He stared into her eyes once before doing as she asked. It took him all but a moment to rip out her throat. Unlike the old man, she never uttered a sound.

It was dawn, and warhorns were blasting so loud across the horizon that they could hear them even from the mountain. Rai stood at the edge of the lake, staring at the melting ice with half-lidded eyes. His robes fluttered with the breeze.

"How old are you, Lamang?" he asked as Khine came up the hill to join him.

"That's an odd question," Khine said, scratching the back of his neck.

"I'd just like an answer."

"Twenty-six by the end of summer."

Rai's nostrils flared. "I didn't realize you were that young."

"Thank...you?"

"I'm thirty-one, and I still feel hopelessly ill-suited for...for what's out there," Rai said. He sighed. "Then again, she was even younger, and she managed to keep it together for five years."

"Blessed hindsight," Khine agreed, not really wanting to broach the subject further.

"You're a responsible man, Lamang. Fairly respectable, too, from what I gather."

"I feel like you missed out on my numerous crimes, but I'll bite. Where are you going with this?"

"My son," Rai said, glancing at the dragon-tower. "I don't want him here. They will descend on him like vultures, my own mother included. She will kill him. If I stand in her way, she will kill *me*. And if there was one thing Tali made me promise, it was to make sure Thanh lives."

"So you want me to watch over him."

Rai nodded. "For now. This land...it needs to be stabilized if it will ever be safe for his rule. It may take a long time, but I don't know who else to trust. Namra, perhaps—but I need her with me. She's the only one who can explain all this *agan* business so that they can understand what happened here."

"Maybe they don't have to," Khine said. He shrugged. "It's not like they'll listen. Let her...rest in peace, Rai."

"I suppose. Still...it seems wrong for her to have done all of this and not at least let them know that their queen never abandoned them."

"I know. But it doesn't matter. She didn't do it to be remembered. She did it to be forgotten."

Rai took a deep breath. "The boy prefers you, if that makes you feel any better. He thinks Namra is too...stuffy. I can only imagine what he thinks of me."

"I wouldn't ask."

Rai frowned.

"Give him a few years," Khine continued. "He has no memories of you beyond all of this. But what you did out here for him and his mother will be a start. Give him a reason to remember you as his father, and not the man who abandoned him. You have more than enough time."

Rai gave a thin smile. "I will hold myself forever grateful to you for this, Lamang."

"Khine," he corrected. "You've got another Lamang to worry about. Inzali will be waiting for you. Tell her not to fuck it up for me."

Rai grimaced for a moment before nodding.

Eikaro appeared on the horizon, gliding lopsidedly towards them.

"Keep him away from them," Rai said. "Keep him safe."

"With my life."

They gripped their forearms in a handshake just as the dragon landed nearby, roaring into the sunlight.

"Where will we go?" Thanh asked when they returned to get their things ready.

Khine paused to stare at the boy. He didn't know much about children, and to realize he was now this one's guardian filled him with a momentary pang of terror. This boy, who like his mother carried war at his heels—could Khine really protect him? He could remember his own arrogance, the careless words he would throw at others while he wrestled with the emptiness of his own life. Now, gazing back at him with his mother's eyes, the boy was a responsibility greater than he ever imagined, and he had to live up to it somehow. But this child was everything to the woman he loved, and quite abruptly, the terror was replaced with warmth.

"I don't know," Khine admitted. He paused for a moment before reaching into his pocket. He pulled out a small wooden figure of a *rok haize*, threaded through a thin rope. He handed it to the boy. "Here. Your mother would want you to have it."

Thanh held it in his palm, his eyes taking in the intricate craftsmanship with the same intense observation his mother did with everything. She had claimed the boy took after his father, but Khine wasn't sure he believed that. The boy was hers, through and through.

"Where did she get it?" Thanh finally asked.

"In Shang Azi," Khine replied. "In this little shop by the fountain. That's where I first met your mother."

"Did you steal it?"

"Did I steal—of course not! Stealing is very, very wrong, Thanh. Never do it."

The boy narrowed his eyes. "I'm not so sure you'll be a good role model."

He rubbed the back of his head sheepishly. "I'm not sure, either. I guess it's about time I learn."

Thanh suddenly looked thoughtful. "Shang Azi is in the empire, isn't it?"

"Yes."

"It sounds like . . . it's so very far away."

"It is. Don't be scared."

"I'm not. I'm excited. Do they have airships there?"

"There's plenty of things in the empire to see, Thanh."

"I want to see airships."

Khine ruffled the boy's hair, choking back the sudden rush of tears at the sound of longing in his voice. He forced a grin. "Airships it is."

EPILOGUE

Long trails of foam crawled up the golden sand with every crash of the waves, drawing back in layered white sheets like the edge of a wedding gown. The tide sometimes swelled so high that for the first few months, she was almost sure they would wake up underwater. But Khine had assured her the sea wouldn't reach that far. Their little hut, and everything precious inside of it, was quite safe.

He had needed to do that more times than she was comfortable with. He told her it was normal, that she used to be worse. That she had slept for so long they didn't think she would ever wake again. During their trip out of Jin-Sayeng, she seemed incapable of speech or thought, responding only to direct commands.

She couldn't remember, but after seeing how upset he became recounting those days, she decided not to ask any further. There was much she couldn't remember—giant, black gaps and shadows where memories ought to be. At first, Khine had been afraid she didn't know him at all—they were on a ship and she had woken in the middle of the night screaming, and when he appeared she asked where her husband was. They were the first words she had uttered in months.

"Rayyel?" Khine asked, crestfallen.

She wasn't sure why, but she knew it was a mistake the moment she had said it. "No," she said, reaching for him, hands cupping his face on each side before slowly pulling him over her. "No, no, my love." And she coaxed him to share the blanket with her, for warmth and comfort, and didn't admit that it took another few hours for her to remember his name. She knew *him*, if not the details—knew his scent, the feel of his fingers, his lips. In that sea of uncertainty, something about him felt right. The rest could wait.

It all began to make more sense when they reached the other shore, the city with the airships. Here, she began to get flashes of memory—nightmares, really, at random times during the day. She tried not to show her panic; it worried both Khine and Thanh, and she was sure they knew from the way she would squeeze one hand or the other. Some days it felt like a shadow breathing down her neck, one that could easily enter her lungs and strangle the breath out of her if she let it. Fending it off took all her strength.

She didn't know how much time had passed. Long enough that the boy's head was nearly up to her shoulder now, and there was dark fuzz on his upper lip that in another year or two might turn into hair. Sometimes it felt as if she had fallen asleep while he was a baby, that she had missed out on all those years of his childhood. Another thing Khine had to remind her wasn't true. She had been with her son all this time.

She didn't have the heart to explain to him it wasn't the same. Even trying to put the right words together was a struggle, and most days she lapsed between frustration and anger, wondering if it had anything to do with the fog in her head or the brief flashes of terror that would come out of nowhere. Sometimes she would get the sensation of drowning and it was all she could do to keep herself together, to make it look as if nothing was amiss.

But Khine thought she was improving, and she tried to believe him. Anyway, it made him happy to see her making small steps forward, even if it was just to take a walk around the beach on her own or be left alone so he and Thanh could run errands. She didn't like being left alone, but she no longer stopped them the way she did when they'd first arrived. Somehow, the darkness was becoming manageable. Small steps. She wondered what Khine really thought, watching her leaning on her cane, unable even to walk without losing breath. A part of her was afraid he would lose interest in her scarred, fragile body soon. She tried not to dwell on it most days.

The sea, at least, was soothing. She settled on a rock, both hands on top of her cane, and took a deep breath, salt air seeping into her senses. In moments like these, she could almost convince herself she could pass off as normal. That she wouldn't see things lurking in every corner or spend hours after waking up in the middle of the night, staring at the ceiling, breathless in fear of something she couldn't even name. That she could be strong again the way they said she once was—that sure-footed fighter, the warrior-queen. Almost. Any movement brought her back to reality—to the pain of being crippled, helpless as a child.

"Tali, look at this!"

She opened her eyes to see Khine striding up to her, a fish in one hand. It had deep-red scales, and its cheeks bulged, as if it had stuffed itself with too much food.

"First catch of the season," he said. "The fishermen are pretty pleased. Think they'll reconsider settling here. The elders will have something to do, at least— they promised there'll be more than enough work mending nets and boats. Let me find a pot for this bastard. What do you think, should we stuff it with some onions and tomatoes?"

"You know best," she replied.

"Or we could roast it over some hot coals..." He strode into the hut.

She gathered her breath and tried to get up to follow him. A sharp pain flared up her leg, and she decided to sit a moment longer. "Where's my son?" she asked.

"He's off with his friends somewhere."

She was surprised about that. It must've been clear in her silence, because Khine came back out, wiping his hands on a towel. "The fishermen's sons seem to have taken a shine to him. You should come down and visit with me. He's safe, if that's what you're wondering. Everyone assures me they're good boys."

"Friends," she repeated, shaking her head. "He's never had friends before. Just like when I was growing up."

"Well, *you* have friends now, too. We can pay Lo Bahn a visit. You'd give him a heart attack. It'll be amusing."

She looked at his hands. He was carrying a letter.

He glanced down at the wet envelope. "Fresh from An Mozhi. I can hide it with the others, if you'd like."

She took another deep breath. "I think...maybe I'm ready for you to read it to me now."

His face brightened. He wrapped the towel around his neck and slumped down next to her, thumbing his finger over the wax. She placed a hand on his shoulder before caressing his hair wistfully, relishing how it wouldn't stay in one place.

"Here," Khine said, flicking the letter open. "'Dear Tali'—oh. It's the first one he addressed to you." He glanced up at her. "Should I keep reading?"

"Please do."

"'Tali,'" Khine repeated, trying to deepen his voice to sound like Rai, which made her smile because he still couldn't erase the husky brushes of his own natural tone.

I hope you are well. I have been updated on your health, and that of the boy, and I am glad you have found a safe haven.

Jin-Sayeng is… not as it was. We may have solved a few problems, but it is worse than it has ever been. Without Yuebek's guidance, every Zarojo soldier has either fled or been slaughtered by our combined forces. But now every warlord has proclaimed themselves kings and queens of their own domains. Oren-yaro is under Lady General Nor's rule, acting as regent for a warlord-not-yet-named. They cannot decide if they should put forward the Tasho heir, Kisig, or Nor's own daughter, Suya. Lady Nor has the proper bloodline, and without you she could petition to have their name changed to aren dar, but support for the Orenar clan is weak. I do not know how long before they unseat her. If she is wise, she will make preparations to protect herself and her family, but I have little clue what she is planning. I have sent her a letter and have yet to receive a reply.

Dai Kaggawa remains a prisoner of Yu-yan, and we have not heard from his daughter. Warlord Huan promises to keep me informed and remains an ally to our cause. I, for my part, retain Shirrokaru, which is in shambles. The handful of councillors who support me may change their minds very soon. I now sleep with a dagger under my pillow and Namra outside my door. In any case, none of this matters much. There is too much squabbling within the region, and no one questions my mother's claim to the title of Dragonlord. She is, as far as we are all concerned, the new queen of Jin-Sayeng.

I will not weigh you down with the details. These things are no longer your concern. If it gladdens your heart, there have been fewer troubles with the corrupted creatures. We believe the ones that remain made the trade before the rift was closed, and so far it seems we have it under control. The attacks on the Sougen by the dragons seem to have waned—it has been a full few months since we've last seen one. There is a sense of peace for now, in a way that peace can be achieved when there are too many enemies but people still need to get fed. It will not last.

That said, while I am sure not everyone believes that you are truly dead, as both Namra and I insist, the farce serves its purpose. The land wants to believe it. It suits everyone's ambitions; in the same way, recovering Thanh would not further anyone's stance. Take what comfort you can from it, and do not let it trouble you. Stay where you are, wherever that may be. Stay safe.

Ever Yours,
Rai aron dar Hio

Tali blinked. "He's taken his father's name. He's truly broken ties with his mother. And he's—as an *aron dar*, he shouldn't even be ruling a region, should he?"

"All your rules have gone to hell," Khine said. "As it is, I believe he is ruling as regent, for your son's sake. Thanh *aren dar Orenar*. He intends to have Thanh's name changed in the records should...you ever want to return."

"An Orenar, ruling Shirrokaru? Gone to hell, indeed." She swallowed. "I could tell him it's a fool's task. I have no desire to ever return to that life. Queen Talyien *is* dead, and so is her son. There is no Talyien and Thanh anymore, only Tali and Tahan now. My father's reign ends with me." But even as she said that, she could feel the cold breeze prickle her skin. *A wolf must remain a wolf.* There were things she couldn't quite shake off, no matter how she pretended she could.

She gazed back at Khine. The gentle look on his face always took her aback. Kindness, after years of bitterness and rage...still seemed too much to believe. "How long will you remain nursemaid to me?" she asked.

"For as long as it takes," he replied easily.

"I've already been more trouble than I'm worth."

"Don't say that," he said. "I need this more than you can imagine." She realized he meant it. These were the same shores where his mother had died. Helping others had ever been his guiding light. They all had their prisons; you coped, however you could.

"Maybe I do want to go down to the village now." She took his hand. She wasn't sure if she really believed the words, but he looked so pleased hearing them that she felt she owed it to herself to try.

They strolled down the beach slowly. Every step felt like pins and needles. She forced herself to concentrate, to focus on Khine's presence instead. It was a lesson she vowed she would always remember. Life was more than pain.

"In time, you'll be able to walk without a cane again," Khine said. "Which I may not be too happy with. I'm starting to enjoy having you as a patient."

She smiled. "You've been enjoying it *too* much."

"I won't deny it."

"You realize if I'm a patient that you'd have lost your standing with the guild by now."

"Only if you complain. Do you, er...have a reason to complain?"

"Let me think." She pretended to pause. "So far? No."

"Then I'm glad I'm not a doctor." Khine placed a hand on her waist and spun her around so he could kiss her. His fingers lingered on her face. "You..." he said. "Have I told you how beautiful you are?"

"No—" she began, before giving a soft smile. "Not often enough."

"I'll rectify that immediately. You are. From the moment I met you, I..."

"I don't remember how we met."

That shadow crossed his face, and she suddenly regretted opening her mouth. "What I meant to say," she quickly added, "is that maybe you need to get your eyes checked. I am a ghost compared with that woman."

"If anything," Khine said in a low voice, "you're more beautiful now, scars and all."

She flushed.

They heard laughter in the distance. She recognized her son's voice and pulled away from Khine to spot the boy shrieking as he scampered past one of the bridges. Scrawny limbs just like his father, hair as long as his shoulders now, bronzed from spending too much time under the sun. Her heart fluttered. "I have to tell him to be more careful. I—"

"He'll be all right, Tali," Khine said. "Those bridges are strong. We used to fly over them when we were kids."

"And how long ago was that?"

"Not *that* long, from your perspective."

"You're terrible."

He grinned as they climbed the steps leading up to the first row of houses. "There you are, Khine," a woman called out. She saw Tali and looked startled. "You're here."

"Thao," Tali said, bowing.

She coloured. "You shouldn't bow to me. You're—"

"A nobody," Tali said.

Thao gave a knowing smile. "So you say. How do you feel?"

"Like I've been trampled by a dozen water buffalo. Which is an improvement from twenty."

"Your humour has returned, at least," Thao laughed.

Tali glanced at the fish laid out on mats along the pier. There was even a bucket of squid and an octopus. Fishermen and villagers hovered over them, chatting away.

"We're separating which fish are going to be dried out and which ones will be given to the elders for dinner," Thao continued, noticing her gaze. "The fishermen are eager to stay. These are rich waters, so long as you brave the waves."

"Does your concern have anything to do with that swarthy fellow with the sideburns, the one you've been way too friendly with the past few weeks?" Khine asked, narrowing his eyes.

Thao sighed. "It's a bit too late for you to do the concerned-big-brother act."

"Tell him I can't afford a dowry."

"If I need a dowry, I'll ask Inzali. *You're* useless." She turned back to Tali. "Your room in the old mayor's house will be ready soon. I don't even know what he was thinking, moving you into that shack. You could catch a cold. Some doctor he would've made."

"Tali likes the sound of the waves," Khine countered.

"She won't like it during hurricane season," Thao snapped. "And anyway, Qu—Tali. You're welcome to help us out here any time you'd like. I know Khine has been saying you should move around more and it must be tiresome to have no one but him for company. I'm not sure how you can stand it."

"You know, even if I could afford a dowry, you're not getting one," Khine sniffed.

"If you don't mind…" Tali began.

"We won't," Thao said, smiling. "And I'll gossip about my brother as much as you want. You'll want to know all the things he fell into as a little boy, or the time he used to talk to rocks."

"I miss Inzali," Khine said. "The mean one."

"You're just saying that because she's an entire ocean away," Thao huffed.

Tali turned her head just as the sound of laughter drew closer. Tahan was running across the street in the distance. He was followed by two other red-cheeked boys.

Somehow, she found herself drifting towards him, just far enough that she could see him careening around the shore.

"Maybe he can do this," Tali said as Khine came up to join her.

"So can you," he whispered.

She turned to look at him. "But I don't want to presume. I'm not my father, Khine. I don't know what awaits us. How long until we wake to assassins, or zealots ready to bring our heads to the highest bidder? How long will this peace last? Are we destined to be fugitives forever?"

"They think you're dead," Khine reminded her. "They think *he* might be, too. These fears may never come to pass."

"It's naive to believe so."

Her boy darted down the causeway to join them. "Mother!" he exclaimed. "You're here!"

"You seem to be enjoying yourself with your friends," she said, running a hand through his damp hair.

"They said there's a library in An Mozhi. They've never gone in, but I'd like to. Do you think Khine can take me someday, Mother? I'm getting better at Zirano. If we can open up trade with the empire someday—"

"Tahan!" the boys called.

He turned to the sound of his new name as if he had been born to it. Grinning, he dashed back down where he came from, already so different from what little she could recall of the boy he had been. Different, and yet the same. As if the process of breaking chains was just the beginning, and you can only let go when you turn around and let it all back in.

"Let it be, Tali," Khine said, noting her silence. "Tomorrow's worries."

"What will he be tomorrow?"

"I don't know. Happy?" He cleared his throat. "I know I'm just a dog of Shang Azi, but I can see that much. He *is* happy, Tali. Maybe he can be all his life."

She saw the truth in his words as she watched her son disappear in the distance. And then she turned to him, to this man who dared love her even now that she had nothing left to give. A smile flitted across her face. "We'll be dogs together," she murmured, lacing her fingers through Khine's. "Let's go home, my dear." In his presence, her fears were weightless.

He kissed her softly before brushing a stray strand of hair from her face with his thumb. "Mmm, and I doubt the boy will be back until dark. Maybe there's time—"

"For you to show me how to cook that fish?"

He flashed her that roguish grin, the one she must have loved since she first met him. She would have. "I...had other things in mind."

"I'm going to file that complaint now."

"How about I cook and you just watch? You might burn the hut down."

"I could practice my handwriting. I seem to recall that work can be found as a scribe, and I would like to find a way to write back to Rai. Queen Talyien is dead, but surely there are other things I can do for Jin-Sayeng. I won't subsist on your charity forever, Khine."

"It isn't charity," he said, growing serious. "But I know."

She took a deep breath. "And then maybe I'll open that package and start putting my journals together."

"If you think you're up for it. Don't force yourself."

"I'll remember it all sooner or later," she said. "I'd rather it be sooner. I will not allow myself to remain an invalid. The past *will not* dictate what I am today, or what I will be tomorrow. For as long as I have breath in me..."

She wasn't her father. She was more. She had survived darkness, lived with it still. That had to count for something. To her son, she could be everything Yeshin never was.

They strode back in silence, hand in hand, the sea beating softly on the shore behind them.

AFTERWORD

Dear Reader,

When I first finished the whole trilogy, I had no idea that this series would ever get this far. When I wrote the ending, I didn't know that Talyien would ever find her people—readers who would not just flip through the pages of her story but would grow to love her, too. To see so many laugh and cry and scream as they go along for the ride has been nothing short of amazing. We tell stories to reach into the void—not just to entertain, but to offer perspective, to comfort, maybe even find a place to belong. There is power in that, I think. Magic. It never ceases to amaze me.

I write for so many reasons, but many times to ease loneliness, to make sense of a broken world that often dares to ask too much from us. I started this series on a whim; that this world and characters have become a refuge, a place for others to share their own stories and bare their hearts, fills me with a deep sense of gratitude.

So understand, truly, how much this means to me. Thank you for sitting next to the fire and listening to this storyteller. I am honoured to have shared this journey with you.

Sincerely,

K Hithoro

ACKNOWLEDGMENTS

They say it takes a village to raise a child, and I think the same could be said of books. A whole team helped get this series out into the world. The care, dedication, integrity, and passion that went into every stage of the process blows my mind away. It is one thing to work in a business selling books and another to believe in the power of stories. To the Orbit/Hachette team, for those on the frontlines and behind the scenes: Tim Holman, Alex Lencicki, Ellen Wright, Paola Crespo, Angela Man, Nazia Khatun, Nadia Saward, Bryn A. McDonald, Maya Frank-Levine, Laura Jorstad, Isa G. Jacinto, Lauren Panepinto, Laura Fitzgerald, Dominique Delmas, James Long, and everyone else whose work and support made this possible...I wrote a story, and you amplified my voice. Thank you for that.

My gratitude also goes out especially to Simon Goinard and Catherine Ho, both of whose work made Queen Talyien spring to life. Simon's impeccable art captured her essence, and the power and emotion in Catherine's voice truly made the audiobook a remarkable experience. You are both artists at the top of your game, and I remain in awe of your breathtaking talent and skill.

To the myriad of bloggers, reviewers, readers, and fellow writers and colleagues who make this community so wonderful...you're all fantastic. Thank you for all you do.

And finally...I want to thank the first few readers of this last and, to me, the most meaningful installment of the Chronicles of the Bitch Queen. It's scary to write something so terribly raw and straight from your heart, offer it up to people, and hope they don't tear it apart. They did so much more than that...They got it. This is a once-in-a-lifetime book, and I'm so glad I could share it with you first:

To Hannah Bowman...you've been like a midwife to me birthing this series out to the traditionally published world, telling me to breathe, letting me squeeze your hand (sometimes really, really tight). Thank you. To know you have my back in this strange and wonderful career means everything.

To Hillary Sames, your editorial notes provided such fantastic insights. The best feedback doesn't just tell you what you could improve on, but also talks about what works, and seeing your notes on what made you laugh or cry just about made writing this book worth it. I'm so, so grateful for your support.

To Bradley Englert, you have been Queen Talyien's champion from the very beginning, and you have no idea how truly honoured I am to have worked with you on this series from start to finish. I love that you tell me to slow down and indulge in characters, emotions, relationships, and atmosphere even when we're fixing action or pacing; I loved realizing you valued the same things in stories as I did. I can vividly recount every instance your feedback or suggestions pushed me to make the story fly. Your editorial guidance has kicked my craft up a notch, and I will carry everything I learned here for the rest of my life. Thank you for breaking a pattern I thought I had figured out. Thank you for taking a chance on me.

And lastly, to Mikhail Villoso, who for twenty years and counting never once said, "You can't"...here we are. We were two young fools who somehow made their dreams come true, and I'm still eager for more. You know this already, but I love you.

extras

orbit

meet the author

Photo Credit: Mikhail Villoso

K. S. VILLOSO began writing while growing up in the slums of Manila amongst tales of bloodthirsty ghouls, ethereal spirits, and mysteries under the shadows of the banyan trees—a world where fantasy meets the soiled reality of everyday. She immigrated to Canada in her teens and was briefly distracted working with civil and municipal infrastructure. When she isn't writing, she is off dragging her husband, dogs, kids, and anyone insane enough to say "Sure, let's go hiking—what could go wrong?" through the Canadian wilderness. She lives in Anmore, BC.

Find out more about K. S. Villoso and other Orbit authors by registering for the free monthly newsletter at orbitbooks.net.

if you enjoyed
THE DRAGON OF JIN-SAYENG

look out for

THE JASMINE THRONE

Book One of The Burning Kingdoms

by

Tasha Suri

Tasha Suri's The Jasmine Throne *begins the powerful Burning Kingdoms trilogy, in which two women—a long-imprisoned princess and a maidservant in possession of forbidden magic—come together to rewrite the fate of an empire.*

Exiled by her despotic brother when he claimed their father's kingdom, Malini spends her days trapped in the Hirana: an ancient, cliffside temple that was once the source of the magical deathless waters, but is now little more than a decaying ruin.

A servant in the regent's household, Priya makes the treacherous climb to the Hirana every night to clean Malini's chambers. She is happy to play the role of a drudge so long as it keeps anyone from discovering her ties to the temple and the dark secret of her past.

But when Malini bears witness to Priya's true nature, their destinies become irrevocably tangled. One is a vengeful princess seeking to steal a throne. The other is a powerful priestess seeking to find her family. Together, they will set an empire ablaze.

PROLOGUE

In the court of the imperial mahal, the pyre was being built.

The fragrance of the gardens drifted in through the high windows—sweet roses, and even sweeter imperial needle-flower, pale and fragile, growing in such thick profusion that it poured in through the lattice, its white petals unfurled against the sandstone walls. The priests flung petals on the pyre, murmuring prayers as the servants carried in wood and arranged it carefully, applying camphor and ghee, scattering drops of perfumed oil.

On his throne, Emperor Chandra murmured along with his priests. In his hands, he held a string of prayer stones, each an acorn seeded with the name of a mother of flame: Divyanshi, Ahamara, Nanvishi, Suhana, Meenakshi. As he recited, his courtiers—the kings of Parijatdvipa's city-states, their princely sons, their bravest warriors—recited along with him. Only the king of Alor and his brood of nameless sons were notably, pointedly, silent.

Emperor Chandra's sister was brought into the court.

Her ladies-in-waiting stood on either side of her. To her left, a nameless princess of Alor, commonly referred to only as Alori; to her right, a high-blooded lady, Narina, daughter of a notable mathematician from Srugna and a highborn Parijati mother. The ladies-in-waiting wore red, bloody and bridal. In their hair, they wore crowns of kindling, bound with thread to mimic stars. As they entered the room, the watching men bowed, pressing their faces to the floor, their palms flat on the marble. The women had been dressed with reverence, marked with blessed water, prayed over for a day and a night until dawn had touched the sky. They were as holy as women could be.

Chandra did not bow his head. He watched his sister.

She wore no crown. Her hair was loose—tangled, trailing across her shoulders. He had sent maids to prepare her, but she had denied them all, gnashing her teeth and weeping. He had sent her a sari of crimson, embroidered in the finest Dwarali gold, scented with needle-flower and perfume. She had refused it, choosing instead to wear palest mourning white. He had ordered the cooks to lace her food with opium, but she had refused to eat. She had not been blessed. She stood in the court, her head unadorned and her hair wild, like a living curse.

His sister was a fool and a petulant child. They would not be here, he reminded himself, if she had not proven herself thoroughly unwomanly. If she had not tried to ruin it all.

The head priest kissed the nameless princess upon the forehead. He did the same to Lady Narina. When he reached for Chandra's sister, she flinched, turning her cheek.

The priest stepped back. His gaze—and his voice—was tranquil.

"You may rise," he said. "Rise, and become mothers of flame."

His sister took her ladies' hands. She clasped them tight. They stood, the three of them, for a long moment, simply holding one another. Then his sister released them.

The ladies walked to the pyre and rose to its zenith. They kneeled.

His sister remained where she was. She stood with her head raised. A breeze blew needle-flower into her hair—white upon deepest black.

"Princess Malini," said the head priest. "You may rise."

She shook her head wordlessly.

Rise, Chandra thought. *I have been more merciful than you deserve, and we both know it.*

Rise, sister.

"It is your choice," the priest said. "We will not compel you. Will you forsake immortality, or will you rise?"

The offer was a straightforward one. But she did not move. She shook her head once more. She was weeping, silently, her face otherwise devoid of feeling.

The priest nodded.

"Then we begin," he said.

Chandra stood. The prayer stones clinked as he released them.

Of course it had come to this.

He stepped down from his throne. He crossed the court, before a sea of bowing men. He took his sister by the shoulders, ever so gentle.

"Do not be afraid," he told her. "You are proving your purity. You are saving your name. Your honor. Now. *Rise*."

One of the priests had lit a torch. The scent of burning and camphor filled the court. The priests began to sing, a low song that filled the air, swelled within it. They would not wait for his sister.

But there was still time. The pyre had not yet been lit.

As his sister shook her head once more, he grasped her by the skull, raising her face up.

He did not hold her tight. He did not harm her. He was not a monster.

"Remember," he said, voice low, nearly drowned out by the sonorous song, "that you have brought this upon yourself. Remember that you have betrayed your family and denied your name. If you do not rise... sister, remember that you have chosen to ruin yourself, and I have done all in my power to help you. Remember that."

The priest touched his torch to the pyre. The wood, slowly, began to burn.

Firelight reflected in her eyes. She looked at him with a face like a mirror: blank of feeling, reflecting nothing back at him but their shared dark eyes and serious brows. Their shared blood and shared bone.

"My brother," she said. "I will not forget."

1

PRIYA

Someone important must have been killed in the night.

Priya was sure of it the minute she heard the thud of hooves on the road behind her. She stepped to the roadside as a group of guards clad in Parijati white and gold raced past her on their horses, their sabers clinking against their embossed belts. She drew her pallu over her face—partly because they would expect such a gesture of respect from a common woman, and partly to avoid the risk that one of them would recognize her—and watched them through the gap between her fingers and the cloth.

When they were out of sight, she didn't run. But she did start walking very, very fast. The sky was already transforming from milky gray to the pearly blue of dawn, and she still had a long way to go.

The Old Bazaar was on the outskirts of the city. It was far enough from the regent's mahal that Priya had a vague hope it wouldn't have been shut yet. And today, she was lucky. As she arrived, breathless, sweat dampening the back of her blouse, she could see that the streets were still seething with people: parents tugging along small children; traders carrying large sacks of flour or rice on their heads; gaunt beggars, skirting the edges of the market with their alms bowls in hand; and women like Priya, plain ordinary women in even plainer saris, stubbornly shoving their way through the crowd in search of stalls with fresh vegetables and reasonable prices.

If anything, there seemed to be even *more* people at the bazaar than usual—and there was a distinct sour note of panic in the air. News of the patrols had clearly passed from household to household with its usual speed.

People were afraid.

Three months ago, an important Parijati merchant had been murdered in his bed, his throat slit, his body dumped in front of the temple of the mothers of flame just before the dawn prayers. For an entire two weeks after that, the regent's men had patrolled the streets on foot and on horseback, beating or arresting Ahiranyi suspected of rebellious activity and destroying any market stalls that had tried to remain open in defiance of the regent's strict orders.

The Parijatdvipan merchants had refused to supply Hiranaprastha with rice and grain in the weeks that followed. Ahiranyi had starved.

Now it looked as though it was happening again. It was natural for people to remember and fear; remember, and scramble to buy what supplies they could before the markets were forcibly closed once more.

Priya wondered who had been murdered this time, listening for any names as she dove into the mass of people, toward the green banner on staves in the distance that marked the apothecary's stall. She passed tables groaning under stacks of vegetables and sweet fruit, bolts of silky cloth and gracefully carved idols of the yaksa for family shrines, vats of golden oil and ghee. Even in the faint early-morning light, the market was vibrant with color and noise.

The press of people grew more painful.

She was nearly to the stall, caught in a sea of heaving, sweating bodies, when a man behind her cursed and pushed her out of the way. He shoved her hard with his full body weight, his palm heavy on her arm, unbalancing her entirely. Three people around her were knocked back. In the sudden release of pressure, she tumbled down onto the ground, feet skidding in the wet soil.

The bazaar was open to the air, and the dirt had been churned into a froth by feet and carts and the night's monsoon rainfall. She felt the wetness seep in through her sari, from hem to thigh, soaking through draped cotton to the petticoat underneath. The man who had shoved her stumbled into her; if she hadn't snatched her calf swiftly back, the pressure of his boot on her leg would have been agonizing. He glanced down at her—blank, dismissive, a faint sneer to his mouth—and looked away again.

Her mind went quiet.

In the silence, a single voice whispered, *You could make him regret that.*

There were gaps in Priya's childhood memories, spaces big enough to stick a fist through. But whenever pain was inflicted on her—the humiliation of a blow, a man's careless shove, a fellow servant's cruel laughter—she felt the knowledge of how to cause equal suffering unfurl in her mind. Ghostly whispers, in her brother's patient voice.

This is how you pinch a nerve hard enough to break a handhold. This is how you snap a bone. This is how you gouge an eye. Watch carefully, Priya. Just like this.

This is how you stab someone through the heart.

She carried a knife at her waist. It was a very good knife, practical, with a plain sheath and hilt, and she kept its edge finely honed for kitchen work. With nothing but her little knife and a careful slide of her finger and thumb, she could leave the insides of anything—vegetables, unskinned meat, fruits newly harvested from the regent's orchard—swiftly bared, the outer rind a smooth, coiled husk in her palm.

She looked back up at the man and carefully let the thought of her knife drift away. She unclenched her trembling fingers.

You're lucky, she thought, *that I am not what I was raised to be.*

The crowd behind her and in front of her was growing thicker. Priya couldn't even see the green banner of the apothecary's stall any longer. She rocked back on the balls of her feet, then rose swiftly. Without looking at the man again, she angled herself and slipped between two strangers in front of her, putting her small stature to good use and shoving her way to the front of the throng. A judicious application of her elbows and knees and some wriggling finally brought her near enough to the stall to see the apothecary's face, puckered with sweat and irritation.

The stall was a mess, vials turned on their sides, clay pots upended. The apothecary was packing away his wares as fast as he could. Behind her, around her, she could hear the rumbling noise of the crowd grow more tense.

"Please," she said loudly. "Uncle, *please.* If you've got any beads of sacred wood to spare, I'll buy them from you."

A stranger to her left snorted audibly. "You think he's got any left? Brother, if you do, I'll pay double whatever she offers."

"My grandmother's sick," a girl shouted, three people deep behind them. "So if you could help me out, uncle—"

Priya felt the wood of the stall begin to peel beneath the hard pressure of her nails.

"Please," she said, her voice pitched low to cut across the din.

But the apothecary's attention was raised toward the back of the crowd. Priya didn't have to turn her own head to know he'd caught sight of the white-and-gold uniforms of the regent's men, finally here to close the bazaar.

"I'm closed up," he shouted out. "There's nothing more for any of you. Get lost!" He slammed his hand down, then shoved the last of his wares away with a shake of his head.

The crowd began to disperse slowly. A few people stayed, still pleading for the apothecary's aid, but Priya didn't join them. She knew she would get nothing here.

She turned and threaded her way back out of the crowd, stopping only to buy a small bag of kachoris from a tired-eyed vendor. Her sodden petticoat stuck heavily to her legs. She plucked the cloth, pulling it from her thighs, and strode in the opposite direction of the soldiers.